79 PARK AVENUE

was the address of a most unusual model agency....

To keep up appearances, the management occasionally sent a girl out on a legitimate job.

But the real business came in over the private phone. The customers paid well—as much as a thousand dollars a night. And why not? You could call up for a girl at any hour—and the service was the best in town.

79 PARK AVENUE
was originally published by Alfred A. Knopf, Inc.

79 PARK AVENUE

●●●●●●●●●●●●●●●●●

HAROLD
ROBBINS

 A POCKET BOOK EDITION published by
Simon & Schuster of Canada, Ltd. ● Richmond Hill, Ontario, Canada
Registered User of the Trademark

79 PARK AVENUE

Alfred A. Knopf edition published July, 1955

A *Pocket Book* edition

1st printing .... May, 1956
39th printing .... August, 1969

Standard Book Number: 671-78020-4.

AND *they began to go out one by one, beginning with the eldest, till Jesus was left alone with the woman, still standing in full view. Then Jesus looked up and asked her, Woman, where are thy accusers? Has no one condemned thee? No one, Lord, she said. And Jesus said to her, I will not condemn thee either.*

THE GOSPEL According to St. John, CHAPTER 8

CONTENTS

The State vs. *Maryann Flood*

I PULLED the car into the parking-lot across the street from Criminal Courts. Before I had a chance to cut the engine, the attendant was holding the door for me. I eased out slowly, picking up my briefcase from the seat beside me. I had never rated this kind of service before.

"Nice day, Mr. Keyes," he said, falling into step with me as I walked toward the exit.

I looked up at the sky. It was—if you liked gray December days. I nodded. "Yes, Jerry."

I stopped and looked at him. There was a grin on his face. He didn't have to tell me that he already knew. I could see it. That was why I rated today.

"Thanks," I said and cut across the street to the court-house. It had been only twenty minutes since I myself found out. Eight miles and twenty minutes ago, in a hospital room in the Harkness Pavilion. Yet they knew it down here already.

The Old Man's face had been gray with pain against his

pillow. I was standing at the foot of his bed. "You're gonna have to take it, Mike," he whispered.

I shook my head. "No, John. I can't."

"Why?" His whisper had an almost eerie quality.

"You know why," I answered. I hesitated a moment. "Give it to one of the others. You have enough assistants. Why pick on me?"

His whisper exploded into a sharp sound. "Because they're all political hacks, that's why. You're the only one I can trust, you're the only one I hired for myself. All the others were shoved down my throat, and you know it!"

I didn't answer even though I knew he wasn't speaking the truth. Ever since Tom Dewey had been D.A., the office had been free of political persuasion. The only thing political about the office was John DeWitt Jackson's ambitions.

His eyes were fixed on mine. I couldn't turn away from them now. "Remember when you first came to me? You were a cop then, and the soles of your shoes were almost an inch thick. You had your law diploma in your hand. You even called yourself by your fancy real name, Millard Keyes. There were marbles in your mouth when you asked me for a job. I asked you: 'Why my office?' Do you remember your answer?"

I remembered, all right. That was the only time I didn't use the name people called me by, Mike. I didn't speak.

"I'll tell you what you said." He raised his head on the pillow. "You said, 'I'm a cop, Mr. Jackson, and there's only one side to the law for me.'"

"I gave you the job because I believed what you told me." His head sank back against the pillow wearily and his voice returned to a whisper again. "Now you want to run out on me."

"I'm not running out on you, John," I said quickly. "I

just can't take this case. It's not fair to me, and I'm afraid I wouldn't be fair to you. I told you that when it first started."

"I wasn't worried about you then and I'm not worried now," he whispered vehemently. He turned his face away for a second. "Damn this appendix! Why couldn't it keep another few weeks?"

In spite of myself, I smiled. The Old Man didn't miss a trick. He pulled out all the stops. "You know what the doctor said. This was one time he couldn't freeze it for you," I answered with a proper show of sympathy.

He nodded sorrowfully. "That's doctors for you. On the eve of the most important trial of my career."

I knew what he meant. A few months from now the boys would be sitting down in the back rooms all over the state. By the time they got around to opening the windows to air out the smoke and whisky fumes, the next Governor would have been picked out.

The Old Man had timed it very cleverly. Not so early they would forget, not so late they would have decided. But now he was scared. What would serve for him would serve for the others. And he didn't want to take any chances.

He looked down the bed at me. His eyes filled with an inexpressible sorrow. "Mike," he whispered, "you've never been like the others. You've been almost—well, almost like a son to me. You were my one hope, the only thing in the whole damn office that I was proud of. You were my boy.

"I'm not a young man any more. I've made my plans, and if they miss, I accept it. It's God's will." He shrugged his shoulders almost imperceptibly in the white cotton hospital nightshirt. He was silent a moment; then his voice grew

hard. "But I don't want any slimy, son-of-a-bitchin' oppor-
tunists climbing up my ladder!"

We stared at each other silently for a few moments, and
then he spoke again. "Go into court for me, Mike," he
pleaded. "You got a free hand. You're the boss. You can do
anything you like. You can even ask the court to dismiss the
charge on the grounds that we haven't been able to make a
case. You can make a monkey out of me if you like. I don't
care. Just don't let any of the others climb on my body."

I took a deep breath. I was licked and I knew it. I didn't
believe he meant a word of what he had said, but it made no
difference. He was mean and crafty and gave away ice in
the winter, but there were tears in my eyes and I loved every
lying bone in his body.

He knew it, too, for he began to smile. "You'll do it,
Mike?"

I nodded. "Yes, John."

He reached under the pillow and pulled out some type-
written notes. "About the jurors," he said, his voice stronger
now. "Look out for number three—"

I interrupted him. "I know about the jurors. I've been
reading the minutes." I headed for the door. I opened it and
looked back at him. "Besides, you promised me a free hand
—remember?"

The reporters hit me almost before I set foot on the
courthouse steps. I smiled grimly to myself as I tried to push
my way through them. The Old Man must have been on the
phone the minute I left the room.

"We hear you're taking over for the D.A., Mr. Keyes.
Is that true?"

He wouldn't have gotten an answer even if I had been so
minded. I hated people who made it sound like *keys*. The
name was Keyes, rhyming with *eyes*. I kept walking.

They followed me with a barrage of questions.

I stopped on the steps and held up my hands. "Give me a break, fellers," I pleaded. "You know I just came back from my vacation this morning."

"Is it true that the D.A. sent you a telegram before he went into the hospital the day before yesterday? That the adjournment was only to give you time to return?"

I pushed my way through the revolving doors, turned right, and headed past the press room for the elevators. A couple of flashbulbs exploded, sending crazy purple spots flashing across my eyes. At the elevator door I turned and faced them.

"We'll have a statement for you at the noon recess, gentlemen. From then on I'll try to answer every question I can. All I want now is a few minutes alone before I have to be in court."

I ducked through the door, and the operator shut it in their faces. I got out on the seventh floor and went to my office at the end of the hall.

Joel Rader was waiting there for me. He came toward me, his hand outstretched. "Good luck, Mike."

I took his hand. "Thanks, Joel," I said. "I'll need it." Joel was one of the men the Old Man meant. He was bright, tough, and ambitious, just a few years older than I.

"How's the Old Man?" he asked.

"You know him," I said, grinning. "Bitchin'." I walked toward my desk.

"Man, you should've heard him the other day when the doctor gave him the sad news," he said, following me. "Practically tore the doctor's head off."

"I can imagine," I said, tossing my hat and coat on the small wooden bench opposite my desk. I sat down and looked up at him. "I didn't mean to cut in on your deal, Joel," I said.

He smiled insincerely. "You're not cutting in, Mike," he answered quickly. "After all, you worked with the Old Man on the investigation. I understand."

I understood, too. He was clearing himself in advance in case anything went wrong. That didn't mean he wouldn't have wanted it for himself. He was headline-happy, but he wasn't taking any chances. "Is Alec around?" I asked. Alec Carter was the other attorney who assisted the Old Man in court with Joel.

"You know Alec." Joel deadpanned. "But he left the Old Man's notes on your desk for you."

I knew Alec. He had nervous kidneys and spent most of his time in the can before going into court. He was all right once he was in the courtroom. I looked down at the desk. The neatly typed notes were in front of me.

I turned back to Joel. He beat me to the punch. He was five years my senior in the office and wasn't going to give me a chance to dismiss him.

"I'll be in my office if you need anything, Mike," he said.

"Thanks, Joel," I answered, watching the door close behind him. I fished a pack of butts out of my pocket and lit one before I looked down at the papers on my desk.

The indictment was right on the top of the pile. I picked it up and stared at it. I turned my chair so that the light from the window behind me would fall directly on the paper. The heavy black type flashed up at me.

People of the State of New York against

Maryann Flood, Defendant

I could feel a sudden pain clutching at my heart. This was it. Everything that had gone before was like nothing. Now I have to live with it. I closed my eyes. I shouldn't have let the Old Man con me into it. The roots went too deep.

I took a deep breath and tried to clear the pain from my chest. I wondered if I would ever be free of her. I remembered the first time I had seen her. It seemed a thousand years ago. But it wasn't that far back. It was the summer of 1935.

Remember what it was like that season of anxiety? Men out of work, the summer heat resting heavily on their already overburdened shoulders. My father was like the others. Two years of being a house superintendent had made a prematurely aged man of him.

I had a job of a sort. At the corner newsstands at 86th Street and Lexington Avenue. Saturday nights and Sunday mornings. Putting the multiple-sectioned papers together. I came on at nine o'clock at night and worked through until ten-thirty in the morning. I was sixteen then and Mother insisted I shouldn't miss Mass. So I made the eleven o'clock Mass at St. Augustine's on my way home.

This Sunday had been no different. I got into church at the last minute, crept into an almost deserted rear pew, and promptly fell asleep. Almost before I had shut my eyes, I felt a nudge in my side.

Automatically I moved in to allow the newcomers to enter the pew. Again the nudge. This time I opened my eyes. It took almost a minute before what I saw registered. Then I drew in my breath and let them pass.

I gave the older woman no more than a glance. The faded gray-blond hair and weary face didn't interest me. She passed me muttering something under her breath which

I took for an apology. It was the girl, her daughter, who hit me where I lived.

The ash-blond Polack hair that fell like shimmering gold around her face, the wild wide mouth slashed sensually with scarlet, the slightly parted lips and white teeth just showing beneath their shadows. The thin, almost classical nose with nostrils that flared suddenly below highly set cheekbones, the brown penciled line that delineated her eyes.

Her eyes were a book in themselves. They were wide-set and lazy brown, flecked with hell's own green around the edge of the irises. They were warm and bright and intelligent and hinted at a passion I was yet to understand. They touched you and drew you, yet chased you in a subtle manner. I tried to look beneath their surface, but couldn't get through the invisible guard. There was something about brown eyes I could never fathom. You couldn't look into them and read them the way you could blue eyes.

She looked away from me as she passed in front of me, and a million tiny electric shocks ran through my body. Her mother, who was twice her size, had passed without touching me. But not she.

"Excuse me," she whispered, a hidden laughter in her voice.

I stammered an unintelligible answer that was lost in a rustle of clothing as the congregation knelt in their pews. I looked at her as I got down on my knees.

She was already kneeling, her hands folded demurely on the rail before her, her eyes down. Beyond her, her mother rested her head heavily on her clasped hands, praying indistinctly in some foreign tongue. My eyes came back to the girl.

Her body swelled against the light summer cotton dress. A warm muskiness came from her, and I could see the faint patch of perspiration spreading slowly on the dress under her arm.

I closed my eyes and tried to concentrate on my prayer. A few seconds passed and I began to feel better. It wasn't so bad if I kept my eyes shut. I felt the girl shift slightly next to me. Her thigh pressed lightly against mine.

I opened my eyes and looked at her. She seemed to be unaware of the pressure, her eyes shut in prayer. I moved slightly away from her and held my breath. Her eyes still shut, she moved with me. I was at the edge of the pew now and could move no farther without falling into the aisle.

I stayed there as best I could and tried to concentrate on God's Word. But it was no use. The devil was at my side.

At last the prayer was over and the congregation got achingly to their feet. It was not until then that I dared open my eyes and look at her.

She didn't look at me; her eyes were focused carefully forward. I started to step out of the pew, but she was already passing me. I stepped back in the pew, and she stopped and stepped back with me.

I was startled, but she smiled politely and let her mother cross in front of her. She leaned back against me as her mother passed out into the aisle. Then she slowly turned completely around.

I stared into her eyes. There was a teasing laughter in them that I had never seen in any eyes before. A wild, dangerous fire that crept into my soul. Her lips parted in a smile and suddenly I heard words from her, though I could swear her lips never moved. "Havin' a ball, Mike?" she breathed.

It wasn't until a moment later when she had been lost in the crowds of people pushing up the aisle that I realized she knew my name.

Slowly I moved up the aisle, wondering who she was. Maybe it would have been a better life if I had never found out.

I drew the blinds down on memory. The papers were still in my hand. They still had to be read. In another forty minutes I would be in court. Slowly, in order to concentrate, I began to read the indictment word by word.

We entered the courtroom through the side door. A hush fell over the crowd of people as we made our way to our seats at the table to the right of the court. I didn't raise my eyes to look at the spectators. I didn't want them to see the anger I felt at their insatiable curiosity.

I sat down in a chair, my back to them, and began to spread my papers out on the table. I could feel the tension growing inside me. In a way, a trial was like a prize fight. I wet my lips slightly and hoped the knot in my stomach would loosen.

For the sake of hearing my own voice, I spoke to Joel. "What time is it?"

He glanced at the big clock on the wall. "Almost ten."

"Good." It wouldn't be long before the court would convene. I stole a glance at the defendant's table. It was still vacant.

Joel caught my glance. "Vito always stalls to the last minute. Gives him a chance to make an impressive entrance."

I nodded. Vito knew his business. He was one of the most successful criminal lawyers in New York. A tall, good-looking man with a shock of gray hair framing piercing blue eyes. He lost very few cases. He worked at his job. Every one of us in the office had a healthy respect for him.

A sudden murmur of excitement rippled through the courtroom behind us. Several splashes of light came down the room from the flashbulbs. I didn't have to turn around to know they were coming down the aisle. The sound of whispers plotted that better than radar.

I raised my head and turned toward them just as they were at the railing. Vito had already swung the gate and was standing, his back toward me, allowing his client to precede him. Her eyes caught mine as she looked up to thank him.

Her eyes widened slightly and I began to see inside them. It had been so long. So long ago. Our glance lasted only a moment; then she turned away and hurried to her seat.

I watched her walk. She had that free stride I always remembered, her ankles thin and twinkling in their sheer nylons. She wore a dark, man-tailored suit, and a blue poodle-cloth coat hung from her shoulders. Her hair was a burnished copper-gold, cut short in small ringlets piled high on her head. She sat down circumspectly and adjusted her skirt around her knees. Vito sat down next to her and they began to talk.

Joel's whisper was in my ear. "A real woman."

At the tone of admiration in his voice, I nodded my head without speaking.

"There isn't a guy in this court who would turn down a piece of that." He was still whispering.

I had all I could do to keep my anger from showing. That was the trouble. That had always been the trouble. She was the kind of woman whose sex fit her like a halo. No man could ever miss it.

"It's almost a shame to put a woman on the rack for doing what's she's made for," he kept on, with a little laugh. "And from what I hear, there's nothing she likes better."

This time I couldn't keep my anger from bursting out.

"Can it, Joel," I said coldly. "This is a courtroom, not a poolroom."

He started to speak, then caught a glimpse of my eyes. The words froze on his lips and he turned back to the papers on the table before him. I picked up a pencil and began to doodle on a scratch pad. Alec nudged me and I looked up.

Henry Vito was walking toward our table. I watched him stroll assuredly until he was opposite me. He looked down at me, smiling confidently. "How's the Old Man, Mike?" he asked.

"Coming along, Hank," I said, smiling back at him.

His voice was just low enough to carry to the press rows. "Mighty lucky appendix he suddenly came up with."

I stretched my voice so they could hear my answer. "All the luck coming out of that appendix landed on your side of the court."

He didn't change expression. "If he ever becomes Governor, Mike, he'll owe you a big vote of thanks."

I got to my feet slowly. Vito was a tall man, but I'm taller. I stand six foot two in my stocking feet, and I'm broad-shouldered and with my broken nose look ugly enough to make him seem frail. He looked up into my face and I smiled. "Thanks for them kind words, Hank. I know after the trial you'll agree I deserved them."

The smile was still on his face, but he didn't speak. I blocked him off from his audience, so there wasn't any reason for him to continue. He turned back to his table with a jaunty wave of his hand. I watched him walk across the court before I returned to my seat.

Joel was whispering in my ear. "Don't let him get your goat, Mike."

I smiled coldly. "I won't."

"I thought you were going to slug him when he got up," Alec whispered from the other side.

My smile turned into a grin. "I thought about it."

"I could see that look on your face—" Alec's whisper was interrupted by the tapping of the gavel.

There was a quick rustle of clothing as we got to our feet. The judge was coming into the court. Peter Amelie was a short, stocky man and as he went to the bench he looked like a little kewpie doll with his cherubic face and bald head rising from the black cloth of his official robes. He sat down and with a quick motion tapped the bench before him with a gavel.

The clerk's voice boomed out. "Hear ye, hear ye. The Court of General Sessions, Part Three, is now in session. The Honorable Justice Peter Amelie presiding."

This was it. There was no turning back now. The fight was on, the referee in the ring. Suddenly all the tension left me. From now on nothing would bother me, no memories torture me. I would have no time for them. I had a job to do.

A few moments later, at a nod from the judge, I got to my feet. I walked slowly across the court to the jury box. She didn't look up as I passed the defendant's table, yet I knew she was watching every motion I made in that crazy way she had of seeing out of the corners of her eyes. I stopped in front of the jury and gave them a chance to look me over.

After a few seconds I began to speak. I started slowly. "Ladies and gentlemen of the jury, I feel pretty much like a pinch hitter being sent in to bat for Di Maggio. For who—" I paused a moment to let a ripple of warm laughter die down in the courtroom. "For who can follow Di Maggio?" I continued, and answered my own question: "Nobody."

I let the faint, friendly smile fade from my lips. "But the people of the State of New York are entitled to the representation and protection of their elected officers. And the people of the State of New York through their Grand Jury found grounds to present to this court an indictment against a certain person for violating its laws and its decencies. So I humbly beg your indulgence while I, in my poor fashion and manner, represent the people of the State of New York against the crimes of Maryann Flood."

Vito came in on schedule with his objection. As I expected, the court upheld it. But I had made my point. I turned back to the jury.

"I would like to read from the indictment currently before this court. It is charged in this indictment that the defendant, Maryann Flood, has committed and engaged in the following activities, which we will prove beyond a reasonable doubt.

"Maryann Flood, hiding behind the façade of a respectable model agency, Park Avenue Models, Inc., procured for profit young girls and women for illicit and immoral purposes and led them to lead lives of prostitution.

"Maryann Flood in several instances paid off or bribed certain public officials, in order to protect her illicit activities.

"Maryann Flood, by virtue of her contacts in this nefarious trade, was able to extort varying sums of money from her clients by threatening them with exposure."

I let the indictment drop to my side and looked at the jury. I could sense their interest.

"Procurement for purposes of prostitution.

"Bribery of public officials.

"Extortion and blackmail.

"Not a pretty picture for the people of the State of New

York to contemplate. Each year thousands of young girls come to New York with their eyes on the stars. Broadway, TV, modeling. Each with their connotations of glamour and success.

"And lying in wait for these poor innocents is someone like Maryann Flood. Secure in the knowledge that her bribery and extortion will protect her from harm and molestation by such prosaic and mundane things as the laws of the people of the State of New York."

For the first time I turned to face the defendant's table. She was looking down at the table, a pencil tightly clutched in her fingers. Vito had a thin smile on his lips.

"Maryann Flood!" I called out.

Automatically she raised her head, and her eyes fixed on mine. There was something hurt in them I had never seen before. I let mine go hard and blank as I turned back to the jury and spoke as if I hadn't called to her.

"Maryann Flood," I repeated, "sits before her court of judgment, before a jury of her peers, charged with violating the laws of her society.

"And we, the people of the State of New York, the people for whom she had so much contempt, will prove these charges we make against her so that there will never be in any mind a vestige of doubt as to her guilt. We will follow, step by step, each and every action of her illicit and illegal career. We will establish in detail each action. And when the whole of the story is revealed, you, the jury, will be called upon to render such a verdict as to discourage and restrain any person who feels he has a right to flaunt and evade the responsibilities and laws of the people."

I gave the jury time to chew on what I had said while I went back to my table and exchanged the indictment for some other papers. Then slowly I walked back to the jury box.

"Ladies and gentlemen of the jury, I would like to trace for you the manner in which the State became acquainted with the activities of Maryann Flood." The jurors leaned forward, a look of interest on their faces. "One afternoon last May a young woman was admitted to Roosevelt Hospital. She was hemorrhaging internally. The result of an illegal operation. Despite all efforts, she began to sink rapidly.

"As is usual in matters of this kind, our office was notified. The girl was too weak to answer many questions, but this much we were able to learn from her. She was a model registered with Park Avenue Models, Inc. She also asked that Miss Flood be notified. She seemed sure that Miss Flood would be able to help her.

"A first routine telephone call to Park Avenue Models, Inc., brought forth the reply that they had never heard of a model by that name. About an hour later Miss Flood called our office, saying that there had been a mistake on the part of one of her employees. That this young woman had been registered with her agency. In particular she seemed concerned about what the girl had said, and as an afterthought offered her assistance.

"Both the telephone call and the offer of assistance came too late. The young woman had died shortly before.

"A check of the young woman's acquaintances revealed that she had come to New York approximately a year before. For six months she had been barely able to make ends meet. Suddenly she blossomed forth in a complete new wardrobe and furs. To her friends she explained her newfound prosperity by saying that she had made a connection with Park Avenue Models. She began to go out frequently, and her friends saw less and less of her. She explained this to them by saying she was constantly on call. That her work kept her busy all hours of the day and night.

"Yet when these statements were checked with the employment record maintained by the agency, there was a great discrepancy. The agency had listed only two or three jobs for her during that six-month period. Her total earnings during that period, after commissions were deducted, came to about one hundred and twenty-five dollars."

I shuffled some papers in my hand and pretended to look at them while I rested. After a moment I looked up at the jury. They were ready for me to continue.

"While this routine investigation was taking place, a report came to the Vice Squad of wild parties being held at the East Side apartment of a prominent manufacturer of ladies' undergarments. It was also brought to the attention of the police that the man had made statements in various quarters that he had contacts with a certain model agency that enabled him to have a supply of girls at any hour of the day or night and that his friends just had to call on him for the favor.

"On the last day of May the police interrupted a party going on in his apartment. Four men and six women were found in varying stages of undress and in certain—shall we say for the sake of being delicate?—compromising attitudes.

"Each of the girls gave her occupation as model. One admitted she was registered at Park Avenue Models, Inc. Several of the other girls whispered something to her. Immediately the girl retracted her statement. A check proved that each of the girls was registered there.

"It was at that point that the police and the District Attorney's office realized they had come across a vicious example of organized vice. An investigation of the agency immediately ensued."

I switched papers in my hand and began reading from one of them. "Park Avenue Models, Inc. Incorporated June 1948. Licensed to represent models for art, photography, fashion shows, etc. President, Maryann Flood."

I turned the page. The next sheet was a police report on Marja. I scanned it quickly as I walked silently toward the jury. *Maryann Flood, born November 16, 1919, New York City. Unmarried. Record of first arrest, April 1936. Charge —assault with a deadly weapon against stepfather. Before Magistrate Ross, Juvenile Court. Committed to Rose Geyer Home for Wayward Girls, May 1936. Discharged November 1937 upon reaching age of eighteen. Arrested February 1938. Charge—loitering for the purpose of and committing an act of prostitution. Pleaded guilty. Received thirty days in the workhouse. Arrested April 1943. Charge—grand larceny after committing an act of prostitution. Pleaded not guilty. Case dismissed for lack of evidence. No further record of arrests. Was known as associate of persons with criminal records. Held as material witness in slaying of Ross Drego, prominent gambler and racketeer, in Los Angeles, California, in September 1950.*

I put the papers carefully together in my hand and pointed them at the jury. "From this beginning the State began to assemble a story of vice and corruption that made even its most callous and hardened officers sick to their stomachs. A story of innocent young girls being forced into a life of prostitution and perversion, of extortion, blackmail, and corruption that reached high into the business, social, and official life of our city. And behind all this sorry mess the evidence points to the machinations and planning of just one person."

I turned and pointed the papers dramatically at the defendant's table. "Maryann Flood!"

Without looking back at the jury I crossed the room to my table. I sat down amid the rising murmur of voices in the courtroom behind me. I stared down at the table. My eyes were burning. I blinked them wearily.

"Good boy!" I heard them whisper.

"You sure pasted her!" Alec's voice came from the other side.

I didn't look up. I didn't want to have to see her. It seemed as if a thousand years had passed since I had got up to address the jury.

I heard the sound of the judge's gavel on his desk. Then his heavy voice: "The court will adjourn until two o'clock."

Automatically I got to my feet as he left the court. Then without speaking I made for the private entrance to the District Attorney's offices.

We ducked the reporters by going out to lunch through the Tombs. I went into the Old Mill restaurant and was given a table in the far corner. I sat down with my back to the room, facing Joel and Alec. The waitress came up to us.

"I need a drink," I said and ordered a gin over rocks, with a twist of lemon peel. "How about you fellows?"

They shook their heads and ordered their food. There was a murmur in the room behind us. I didn't have to turn around to know who had come in. I looked questioningly at Joel.

He nodded. "They're here."

I smiled thinly. "It's a free country." Suddenly I couldn't wait for the drink. I wished the damn waitress would hurry back. "Where's my drink?" I growled irritably.

"The waitress stopped to pick up their order on the way back," Alec said quickly.

A moment later she put the drink down in front of me. There was a peculiar expression on her face which I understood the moment I lifted my glass. There was writing on the doily under the glass.

I didn't have to look at the signature to recognize the writing. She still had the same childish scrawl.

"Welcome to the big time, Counselor," it read. "Good luck!" It was signed "Marja."

I crumpled the doily with my fingers so that the others could not see it had been written on, and sipped my drink. That was one thing I had always liked about her. She was afraid of nothing.

She wished me luck knowing full well that if I were lucky she could spend the next ten years of her life in jail. She was like that even when she was a kid.

I remembered once when I tried to stop her from crossing against a light into traffic that was moving wildly. Angrily she shook me off.

"That's the trouble with you, Mike," she had said. "Afraid to take chances. Even on a little thing like this!"

"But, Marja," I had protested, "you could get hurt, or maybe even killed."

She had looked at me, the wild light blazing in her eyes. "So what, Mike?" she said, stepping into the gutter. "It's my body, not yours."

That, in its essence, was the difference between us. That philosophy and a lot of other things. Like the way we had been brought up. She had an amazingly paradoxical capacity for both affection and cruelty.

I sipped again at my drink. The cold sweetish taste of the gin burned its way down my throat. I think my mother put her finger on it one night when I came home dejected from waiting for Marja to return from a date.

I was too big to cry, but the tears hovered beneath my eyes. Mom knew it the moment I came in the door. She moved quickly toward me. I turned away to go to my room, but her hand caught mine and held me.

"She's not for you, Mike," she said softly.

I didn't answer, just stared at her.

"I'm not telling you who to like, son," she added. "It's just that she's not for you. She's been brought up without love and has no understanding of it."

I had pulled my hand away and went to my room, but what she had said stayed in mind. Without love.

Now I could understand at last what Mother had meant. That in all its simplicity was the story of Marja's life. Without love.

Book One

MARJA

Chapter 1

SHE pushed open the door of the candy store and stood there a moment while her eyes adjusted to the dimness. The bright sun behind her framed her face in the shimmering gold of her hair. The violent scarlet slash that was her mouth drew back over white, even teeth in a tentative smile. She walked toward the counter.

There was no one in the store. Impatiently she tapped a coin on the marble top.

There was an immediate answer from the rear of the shop, where Mr. Rannis had his rooms. "Just a minute, just a minute. I'm coming."

"That's all right, Mr. Rannis," she called. "It's only me. I'll wait."

The old man appeared in the doorway of his rear room. His hands were still busy adjusting his clothing. "Marja!" he exclaimed, a pleased tone coming into his voice. He moved stiffly behind the counter toward her. "What can I do for you?"

She smiled at him. "Gimme five Twenty Grands."

Automatically he turned to the shelf behind him, then hesitated. He glanced back at her over his shoulder questioningly.

"It's okay, Mr. Rannis," she said quickly. "I got a nickel."

He picked up an open package and shook five cigarettes out carefully and placed them on the counter before her, his hand covering them.

She pushed a nickel toward him. He lifted his hand from the cigarettes and covered the coin. He slid it back along the counter toward himself and it dropped into the cash drawer just beneath the counter.

The white-papered cigarettes were bright against the dirty gray marble. Slowly she picked one up and stuck it in her mouth. She reached toward the open box of wooden matches on the counter.

Before she could strike a match he had one flaming in front of her. She dipped the cigarette into it and dragged deeply. She could feel the harsh, acrid smoke filter back into her lungs. She exhaled, the smoke rushing from her lips and nostrils. "Man, that's good," she said. She looked at the old man. "I thought I'd never get out of school. I wanted that smoke all day and nobody would even give me a drag."

The old man looked at her, his lips drawing back over his partially toothless gums in a smile. "Where have you been, Marja?" he asked. "I haven't seen you all week."

She stared at him. "I been broke," she answered bluntly. "An' I owe yuh enough."

He rested his elbows on the counter and looked at her in what he thought was a winning way. "Why'd you do that, Marja?" he asked reproachfully. "I never asked you for money, did I?"

She took another puff at the cigarette and didn't answer.

His hand reached across the counter and took her free hand and squeezed it. "You know I'm always glad to see you, Marja."

She looked down at her hand, but made no effort to withdraw it. She flashed her eyes up at him. "You're glad to see any of the girls," she said flatly. "You like all of them."

"None of them like you, Marja," he said earnestly. "I'd rather see you than anybody. You were always my favorite, even when you were a little baby."

"I bet," she said skeptically.

"I mean it," he protested. "You're the only one I give credit to. I wouldn't let nobody else owe three dollars and twenty-five cents and not bother them."

She slipped her hand from his slowly, watching his eyes as she moved. She smiled slightly as she saw a film come over them. "What about Francie Keegan? She said you let her owe yuh."

He ran his tongue over suddenly dry lips. "I made her pay me, though, didn't I?" he demanded. "I never asked you, though."

She stepped back from the counter without speaking and looked around the store questioningly. "Something seems different here."

He smiled proudly. "I had the back rooms painted."

She raised a studied eyebrow. "Oh."

"A nice light green," he added. "I'm thinking of doing the store, too, if I can get the money together."

"Don' gimme that, Mr. Rannis," she laughed. "You got more money than God."

A hurt expression came over his face. "All you kids say that. I don't know why. You see the kind of business I do."

"That's just it," she said. "I do see." She turned suddenly and leaned over the candy counter against the glass.

The old man caught his breath. The full young lines of her body were revealed against the glass. Her strong young breasts pressed against the thin white blouse. "Want some candy?" he asked.

She looked at him over the counter top, her eyes speculative. "I haven't any more money," she said carefully.

"I didn't ask you for any, did I?" he asked, quickly bending down behind the counter and opening the door. He stared up at her through the glass. "What would you like?"

Her eyes were laughing as they met his. "Anything. A Milky Way."

Without taking his eyes from her, he reached for a candy bar. His hands were trembling. The bright light from the street behind her framed her body through the flimsy skirt. He had long ago found this vantage point of observation. It was one of the main reasons he kept the store lights dim. The other was the high cost of electricity.

She looked down at him, wondering how long he would stay there. It was a standing joke among the girls in the neighborhood. She knew what he was looking at. The Rannis display case worked both ways, but she didn't care. He was a horny old goat and it served him right if you could get something out of him. Especially for nothing.

In a few seconds she became bored with her little game and moved back to the other counter. Almost immediately he got to his feet, the candy bar in his hand.

His face was flushed with the exertion of kneeling. He pushed the candy across the counter to her with one hand and grabbed hers with the other as she reached for it. She let her hand remain still as he spoke.

"You're the prettiest girl in the neighborhood, Marja," he said.

She sniffed disdainfully.

"I mean it, Marja," he said, squeezing her hand earnestly. He turned her hand over in his and opened it. "You got pretty hands, too, for a kid."

"I'm no kid," she said quickly. "I'm goin' on sixteen."

"You are?" he asked in a surprised voice. Time went so quickly in this neighborhood. They grew up in a hurry. Before you could turn around, they were married and gone.

"Sure," she said confidently. "In the fall."

"I bet the boys in school are all wild for you," he said.

She shrugged her shoulders noncommittally.

He looked down at her hands. "I bet they're always trying to get you in corners."

She purposely made a puzzled expression. "What do yuh mean, Mr. Rannis?" she asked innocently.

"You know what I mean," he said.

"No, I don't, Mr. Rannis," she insisted, a glimmer of laughter lurking in her eyes. "You tell me."

He withdrew his hand with the candy bar, released hers, and walked down behind the counter to the back of the store. At the end of the counter, where the display concealed him from the front of the store, he called to her. "Come back here, Marja," he said, "and I'll tell you."

Slowly she walked to the back of the store. There was a half-smile on her lips. She stepped partly behind the display stand and looked up into his face.

His face was flushed and there were beads of moisture on his upper lip. His mouth worked tensely, but no words came out.

Her smile grew broader. "What, Mr. Rannis?"

His hand reached toward her. She stood very still. "Don't they ever want to touch you?" he asked in a hoarse voice.

She looked down at his hand a few inches from her and then up at his face. "Where?" she asked.

He brushed his fingertips against the front of her blouse lightly. The firm flesh sent a flame up his fingers. "Here?" he asked tensely, watching her face for signs of fear.

There were none. She didn't even make a move to get away from him. Instead she smiled. "Oh," she answered. "Yes, Mr. Rannis. All the time."

Her answer took him by surprise. He almost forgot that he was holding her. "You let them?"

Her eyes were still frankly fixed on his. "Sometimes I do. Sometimes I don't. It depends on how I feel. If I like it." She turned slightly, moving away from him. "My candy, Mr. Rannis," she said, holding out her hand.

Without thinking, he gave it to her. He stared at her, the memory of her breasts in his fingers still flooding his mind. "You want to see the paint job in the back room?" he asked.

She didn't answer, just looked at him as she unwrapped the bar and bit it slowly.

"If you come in the back," he said anxiously. "Maybe if you're real nice, I'll forget about the three and a quarter you owe me."

She swallowed a piece of the candy and looked at him reflectively. Then, without answering, she turned and started for the door.

"Marja!" he called after her in a pleading voice. "I'll even give you some money!"

She paused at the marble-topped counter and picked up her cigarettes and a few matches, then continued on to the door. She started to open it.

"Marja!" the old man pleaded. "I'll give you anything you want!"

She stood there a moment, her hand on the door before answering. When she did speak, he realized that she had been thinking over her reply.

"No, Mr. Rannis," she said politely in her husky voice. "I ain't ready for yuh. Not just yet."

The door closed behind her and the store seemed dull and empty without the bright, flashing gold of her hair. Wearily, as if he had been in battle, he turned and went into the back room.

Chapter 2

THE EARLY June sun had baked the city streets to a soft spongelike asphalt surface that clung maliciously to the feet and made every step an effort. It bounced wildly off the flat concrete walls of the tenements and beat against the face like the licking flame of an open fire.

She hesitated a moment in the doorway of the store before stepping into the inferno of the street. Slowly she ate the last of the candy bar while her eyes scanned the street for signs of life.

It was almost deserted except for a few children who were playing down near the corner of Second Avenue. One lone woman came out of Hochmeyer's Pork Store carrying a shopping-bag and made her way up the block. A taxi roared down the street, leaving bluish tracks in the pavement.

The candy was finished, and carefully she wiped her fingers on the wrapper and threw the paper into the gutter. She slipped the cigarettes into a small purse and stepped down onto the sidewalk. The heat and the sun hit her face and she blinked her eyes rapidly. She could feel the perspiration spring out like a flood all over her body. For a moment she regretted not having stayed in the candy store and played the old man along for a little while. At least it was almost cool in there.

She headed up the street toward her house reluctantly. The clock in one of the store windows told her it was near three. She hesitated. If it weren't so warm she wouldn't be going home, but only a fool would stay out on the street on a day like this. She wished she had the money to go to the show. The RKO 86th Street Theatre had a cooling-system. Fans blowing over big cakes of ice. For a dime you could stay in there all day and beat the heat.

"Marja!" A girl's voice behind her called.

She turned and looked back. It was her friend Francie Keegan. She waited for the girl to come up to her. "Hi, Francie."

Francie was out of breath from hurrying up the block. She was a big girl, heavy-set, with full, ripe breasts and hips. She was a year older than Marja and had thick black hair and dark-blue eyes. "Where yuh goin', Marj?" she asked, still breathing harshly.

"Home," Marja answered succinctly. "It's too damn hot to stay out."

A look of disappointment crossed Francie's face. "I thought we might go to a show."

"Got money?" Marja asked.

"No."

"Neither have I," Marja said and turned back up the block.

Her friend fell into step with her. "Christ!" she exclaimed. "Everybody in the whole world is broke!"

A half-smile crossed Marja's face. She looked at her friend out of the corners of her eyes. "Now she tells me."

They walked another few steps silently; then Francie put her hand on Marja's arm. "I got an idea."

Marja looked at her.

"Old Man Rannis," Francie explained. "Maybe we can promote some change outta him."

Marja shook her head. "Uh-huh. I just been there."

"An'?" Francie asked curiously.

"Nothin'," Marja said. "I got a candy bar after lettin' him use his X ray on me."

"So?"

"That's all," Marja continued. "Then he wanted me to go in the back with him an' see the new paint job, but no money. I owe him three and a quarter already. I even gave him a feel, but all he wanted was to go in the back."

Francie thought over her friend's statement. At last she spoke. "Akey's on the candy bar."

Marja smiled. "Too late." She rubbed her stomach meaningly. "I already ate it."

"Damn!" Francie swore. "I got no luck today at all." She began to walk again. "I guess we might as well go home." She wiped her face on the short cotton sleeve of her dress. "Damn! It's hot."

Marja didn't speak. They walked silently. They were almost halfway up the block before they exchanged another word.

"Who's home?" Francie asked.

"Everybody, I guess," Marja answered. "My mother doesn't go to work until five o'clock." Her mother was a cleaning woman in an office downtown and worked until two in the morning.

"Your stepfather, too?"

A cold look came into Marja's eyes, making them almost black. "Especially him," she said contemptuously. "He wouldn't leave his three cans of beer for all the money in the world."

"Doesn't he work at all? Ever?" Francie asked.

Marja laughed. "Why should he? He never had it so good. Three squares an' all the beer he can drink. He's no dope. Jus' sits aroun' all day an' burps."

A strange look came into Francie's eyes. "He stopped me in the hall the other day."

Marja turned to her. "What'd he want?"

"He asked some questions about you."

"Like what?"

"Like about what you did outside. With boys. That kind uh thing."

"Oh." Marja thought for a moment. "He's always asking me, too. What'd you tell him?"

"Nothin'," Francie answered. "I'm no dope."

A mild sigh of relief escaped Marja's lips. "He'd just love to get somethin' on me. He hates me."

"I know," Francie said. "Sometimes I can hear him hollerin' upstairs." Francie lived in the apartment over Marja.

"He's always hollerin'," Marja answered.

They were almost at the house now. The tenements were all alike on this block. The same faceless brown stone that once had known better days, black and dirty windows staring blindly into the street.

They stopped at the stoop. There was an uncovered garbage can near the entrance. While they stood there, a gray alley cat jumped up onto it, chasing the swarm of flies, and began to rummage through it. They watched him silently.

Marja wrinkled up her nose. "You'd think the super would have the brains to cover the can in this weather." She sniffed the air. "It stinks."

Francie didn't speak. They started up the steps. A wolf whistle came from across the street. They both turned around.

Three boys had just come from the pool parlor opposite their house and were looking at them. One of them called out: "Hey, Francie, who's yer blond friend?"

The girls exchanged looks quickly and a tight smile came to their lips. "Why'n't yuh come over an' find out?" Francie called back.

The three boys whispered something to each other in the doorway while Marja tried to recognize them. The one who had called to Francie she had seen several times before. He lived down the block. She couldn't remember his name. The other two she had never seen.

The two strangers were both tall. One was fair-haired— brown, almost blond—with an open face and gentle blue eyes; the other, almost the opposite. Dark, good-looking, with handsome Grecian features and a full, sensual mouth. After a moment the blond one walked away from the others with a wave of his hand and the remaining boys sauntered slowly across the street.

"Hullo, Jimmy," Francie said as they drew near.

Jimmy was a thin boy, his eyes slightly protruding, his face covered with the remains of a vanishing acne. He smiled, showing white buck teeth. "Where yuh been keepin' yerself, Francie?" he asked.

"Aroun'," she answered. "You?"

He looked down at the sidewalk a moment before he answered. "Around." He looked at his friend quickly. "What're yuh doin'?"

"Nothin'," Francie answered. "We were jus' goin' up to get outta this heat."

"Ross an' me were jus' goin' fer a swim," Jimmy said quickly. "Wanna come?"

Francie looked at Marja, who had been silent up to now. There was a glimmer of interest in Marja's eyes. "If we go upstairs to get our bathing-suits," she explained, "we couldn't come back."

The other boy laughed. His laugh was surprisingly deep. "We can get suits where we're going," he said.

"Ross's got a car," Jimmy said. "We were goin' out tuh Coney Island."

Marja spoke for the first time. "Then what're we standin' here talkin' for?"

The other boy reached for Marja's arm. His grip was firm and sure, and she came down off the stoop toward him. The laughter was still deep in his throat. "That's it, baby," he said, his eyes challenging her. "I like a girl what knows her mind."

She fell into step beside him and looked up at him, her own eyes meeting his challenge. "It ain't my mind I know," she laughed. "It's my body. And it's hot."

"Can't be too hot for me," he said.

The others fell into step behind them. She looked over her shoulder at Francie. Jimmy was whispering something to her and Francie was smiling and nodding. She looked up at the boy next to her. "Where yuh parked?"

"Just around the corner," he said. "My name's Ross Drego, what's yours?"

"Marja," she answered.

"Your whole name, I mean," he insisted.

She looked into his eyes. "Marja Anna Flood."

"Flood's an English name," he said in a puzzled voice.

"I'm Polish," she said quickly. "It was changed from Fluudjincki."

"I can see why." His smile took the edge off his phrase.

They were around the corner now, and he steered her to a Buick roadster with the top down. He opened the door with a flourish. "Your chariot, girls."

Marja stopped and looked at the car, then at him.

"What are you waiting for?" he asked. "Get in."

She shook her head. "Uh-uh. This looks like the wrong kind uh hot to me."

A puzzled expression came into Ross's eyes. "What do you mean?"

"I ain't goin' for no joy ride in a stolen car," she said. "I can get into enough trouble on my own."

Ross began to laugh. "The car isn't stolen," he said. "It's mine."

She looked at him doubtfully. "Oh, yeah? Where do you come to a job like this? That's probably why your friend didn't want to go with yuh."

Ross grinned. "You mean Mike Keyes? He had to go back to work. He helps his old man around the house. He's the super."

She was still skeptical. "I don't buy it," she insisted stubbornly.

Jimmy's voice came over her shoulder. "Go ahead, get in. It's his car, all right. His old man gave it to him."

She stepped back from the car. "Prove it first," she said.

The laughter had left Ross's eyes. "You don't believe me?" His voice was flat and cold.

"I believe yuh," she said, looking right at him. "But I ain't takin' any chances. I know a girl on the block who also believed a guy and she's up in Bedford now."

A flush of anger surged into his dark face. "Then blow,"

he said tensely. "I can get a thousand cheap chips like you to come with me."

She turned and began to walk back up the street. She was almost to the corner when his voice stopped her. She waited for him to catch up to her.

"Wait a minute, Marja," he said, his hand fishing in his pocket. "It's my car. I'll show you."

He took out a wallet and handed it to her. She looked down at it. There was more green folding money in there than she had ever seen in her life. She looked at him questioningly.

She opened the wallet. On one side was a driver's license, on the other was an owner's registration. Both were made out to Ross Drego, 987 Park Avenue, N.Y.C. She glanced at his age quickly. He was eighteen. Silently she closed it and gave it back to him.

"Now will you come?" he asked.

"Why couldn't you do that in the first place?" she countered.

"I was sore," he said quickly. A smile came to his lips. "I'm sorry. Forgive me?"

She stared at him for a moment. He was a strange guy. She had never met anyone like him. He spoke so well, and yet there was a wildness and meanness in him that she could feel. But it disappeared when he smiled. An answering smile parted her lips.

She reached out and took his arm. "C'mon, hurry," she said. "It's so damn hot, I can't wait to get into the water."

Chapter 3

"WHAT PART of Coney Island is this?" Marja asked as Ross stopped the car at a gate and tooted the horn.

He looked at her, a smile in his eyes. "Sea Gate. We have a house here."

"What d'yuh mean, house? A locker?" she said.

The smile slipped to his lips. "No. A regular house. This is a private section."

A gateman peered through the grating at them.

"Open up, Joe," Ross called.

"Oh, it's you, Mr. Drego," the gateman said. Slowly the big iron gate began to swing open.

"It's a summer house," Ross explained as he drove through the entrance. "We stay here when Dad is too busy to get away from the office."

Marja looked around. On either side of the road were beautiful houses set on rolling lawns and shaded by towering trees. "Christ!" she exclaimed. "It's like livin' in a park."

Ross didn't answer. She turned around to Francie in the back seat. "Ain't it, Francie?" she asked.

Francie and Jimmy were impressed, too. Both of them were goggling at the homes along the road. Francie nodded. "I bet ony millionaires live here," she said.

Marja turned back to Ross. "Did yuh hear that?" she asked.

Ross nodded without speaking, his eyes watching the road.

"Is that true?" she asked.

Ross shook his head. "No."

"Your old man must be rich," she said.

He turned the car into a driveway and stopped. He reached forward and cut the ignition. Then he looked at her, his eyes bleak and cold. "Does it make any difference to you what my father is?" he asked. "*I* brought you here."

Marja stared at him, wondering what she had said to make him angry. After a moment she answered: "No."

Quickly as it had appeared, the coldness left his eyes and he smiled. "Then, come on in and get a suit. The water looks great from here."

She followed his pointing finger past the house. The beach and the rolling ocean were right behind it. He jumped out of the car and held the door for her. She got out and looked at the house.

It was a big house. Two stories. Wood and shingles, painted a cool dark green. She didn't care what Ross said, his old man had to have plenty of cabbage to keep a joint like this.

He led them up the front porch and, taking out a key, opened the door. "Follow me," he said, starting up a flight of stairs.

She caught a glimpse of an elaborately furnished parlor

and dining-room as she went up. She looked down at the steps. Her shoes didn't make a sound on the thick carpeting. She had never known people could live like this except in the movies.

He stopped in front of a door and opened it. "This is my sister's room," he said. "Come inside and we'll find a bathing suit that'll fit you."

Marja followed him into the room. Behind her, she could hear Francie's gasp. Without turning, Marja knew what she meant. Never in her life had she seen a room like this.

It was all pink and blue satin. The drapes, the bedspread, even the long, funny chair near the bed. The carpet was a warm rose color and the furniture a rich cherry-tinted wood.

Ross opened a closet. "The suits are here," he announced. He pointed to another door. "That's the bathroom." He moved back toward the doorway in which Jimmy stood. "We'll give you ten minutes to get ready."

Jimmy snickered. "Maybe the girls can use some help."

Francie giggled.

He came into the room. Ross's voice stopped him. "Come on, Jimmy. We'll get our suits."

Obediently Jimmy went back through the door, and it closed behind them. The two girls looked at each other.

"I don't care what Ross says," Francie whispered. "His old man must be a millionaire."

Marja's voice dropped to a whisper. "Either that or he's a racketeer."

Francie's eyes grew big and round. "What d'yuh think?"

Marja smiled. "I think we better get dressed before they come back." She walked over to the closet. "My God, Francie!" she exclaimed. "Look here."

Francie peered through the open door. "Jeez!" she said in speechless wonder.

There were about twenty bathing-suits hanging there. Gently Francie reached out and touched one. "Marja, feel it. Real wool!" She turned to her friend.

Marja had already slipped out of her blouse and skirt and was busy unfastening her brassiere.

She came racing out of the water, laughing breathlessly, Ross at her heels. "Don't, Ross, don't!" she cried. "I'll get my head full of sand."

"It can be washed," he laughed, trying to grab her ankle. She turned away from him and he stumbled to his knees.

She looked over her shoulder. Ross picked himself up and lunged at her. His hand caught her flying ankle and she tumbled into the sand. He fell down beside her.

They lay there quietly, trying to catch their breath. She could hear the wind whistling deep in his chest. At last her breath came back to her and she rolled over on her back. The sun was warm on her face. She closed her eyes. It was like living in paradise.

She could hear the breath still in him, and now he was lying there quietly. Slowly she opened her eyes.

He was resting on one elbow, looking at her. "Having a good time?" he said, smiling.

She smiled back at him. "I'm havin' a ball," she answered.

"I'm glad," he said. He rolled over and sat up. "Francie and Jimmy are still in the water."

She liked the way he said "water." *Wahter*—quick like. She looked down the beach. "I don't blame them," she answered. "It's real great."

He turned to her. "Then why did you come out?"

"I had enough," she said. "I'm not greedy. Besides, too much of a good thing'll spoil me. An' I can't afford it."

His face came down very close to hers. "I'd like to spoil you," he said in a low voice. "And I can afford it."

Her eyes stared directly into his. After a moment his lids began to feel heavy. No one had ever looked at him like this. So straight and unwinking, as if her eyes looked into the very depths and crevices of his mind.

"How d'yuh know?" she asked huskily. "Maybe I'm too rich for yuh blood."

"I know," he answered, putting his hand on her shoulder. Her lips were parted and waiting for him. Her tongue traced the corners of his mouth, leaving tiny flames in its wake. A pulse began to pound in his temple.

He pressed her head back into the beach, his arm beneath her neck. Her hands pressed lightly against the back of his head. He closed his eyes. No one had ever kissed him like this.

Her eyes were still open, and she watched him. A pleasant warmth was flowing through her. It was funny when they kissed her how they all looked alike. When their faces were so close that their two eyes blurred almost into one before they closed. At least in this he was no different from anyone else.

She felt his searching hand. She liked his touch. It was warm and somehow gentle. Not like others who had hurt her. She let the suit strap slip so that she could feel his hand on her naked skin. His breath began to come hard into her mouth.

She let her fingers drift lightly across his wet bathing-suit from his stomach to his thigh. He was strong, too. All ridged muscles etched sharply on him. She closed her hand gently on him. She took her face from him and pressed his head down to her breast.

She felt his teeth hard behind his lips. He tried to turn his face, but she held him tight. She looked down at him, half smiling to herself. This was what was so wonderful. What they would do for her, what she could make them do. This was what she liked about being a woman. Because, in the end, she was always the stronger.

"Ross," she whispered. She could see the flaming agony in his eyes.

He almost cried aloud. She felt him shudder, then the heat of his body came through his wet bathing-suit. An echoing warmth ran through her and she caught her breath. For a moment she clung to him tightly, then it was gone and they were still.

He rolled away from her and lay face downward on the sand. He was breathing deeply.

She turned toward him and stroked his hair gently. "Ross, baby," she whispered. "You're sweet."

Slowly he turned his face to her. There was a curious shame in his eyes. "Why did you do that, Marja?" he asked harshly.

Her eyes were wide, the smile on her lips held the knowledge of all women. "Because I like you, honey," she replied easily. "And I wanted you to be happy."

The corners of his mouth worked as he tried to keep his lips from trembling. For a moment he felt on the verge of tears. He knew he was older than she, but right now he felt like a child next to her. He tore his eyes from her gaze. "Don't do it again. Ever." His voice was cracked and rough.

"Don't you like it, honey?" she asked softly.

He didn't look at her. He spat out his answer. "No."

"Then I won't, honey," she said.

He felt her move in the sand beside him and turned to look at her. She was sitting up, running her hand through the sparkling gold of her hair. An animal vitality seemed to flow from her.

She looked down at him and smiled. "I told yuh the sand would get in my hair." She got to her feet. "I'm goin' in to wash it out. Come in with me." She held out her hands toward him.

He didn't move from his place in the sand. He looked up at her over his shoulder. "Go ahead in," he said. "I'll be along in a minute."

He watched her run into the water and tumble into a breaker before he got to his feet and ran down the beach after her.

Chapter 4

THE FIRST dusky purple of evening clouded the sky.
In the west the sun still fought back the night, a flaming
red ball reaching back desperately to all its yesterdays.
The warmth began to leave the air.

Marja sat up on the blanket Ross had spread for them.
"I wonder what time it is," she said.

He opened his eyes and squinted at the sky. "About a
quarter after six," he answered.

"How can you tell?"

He grinned at her. "I was a Boy Scout once."

"I never knew a Boy Scout before," she laughed, dropping her hand to his knee.

Instinctively he tensed. She felt his movement and took
her hand away quickly. "I'm sorry, I forgot."

"Don't be sorry," he said.

"But you don't like me to touch you," she said.

He shook his head. "It's not that, really. I'm just not
used to it, I guess."

49

"Then you do like me?" she asked.

"I liked you from the moment I saw you through the dirty windows of the poolroom."

"Honest?" She was smiling now.

"Honest," he answered, his eyes serious. "I saw you walking down the block with Francie and I couldn't keep my eyes off you. You ruined my game. Mike took me to the cleaners."

"Mike?" she said questioningly. "That's the blond boy who didn't want to come with us?"

He nodded. "He didn't even look up from the table when I told him about you."

She was piqued. "What did you say?"

He grinned. " 'Mama,' I said, 'buy me some of that!' "

She punched his side playfully. "Fresh!"

"It's a good thing Jimmy was around. Otherwise, I might never have met you," he said.

"Yeah," she said sarcastically. "Your other friend wouldn't have been no help."

"Mike is all right," he protested. "It's just that he's too serious. He never bothers with girls. Studies all the time. He's going to be a lawyer."

"Is he as old as you?" she asked.

He shook his head. "A year younger. But we're in the same class at school."

Her vanity was hurt. It was a matter of pride that all boys must like her. "I bet he's not as nice as you are."

"Thanks," he said dryly. "You're the first girl I know that thinks so. Usually when they see him, I'm a gone pigeon."

"He must be terribly conceited," she said flatly. "I can't stand conceited fellas."

"He's really very nice," Ross said. "I don't think he even knows that they like him."

She shivered slightly as the cool of twilight hit her shoulders. "I don't care about him, anyway," she said indifferently. She looked down the beach. "Where's Francie?"

"They went up to the house about an hour ago while you were dozing," he answered. "Francie said it was getting too cold for her."

She got to her feet and stretched. "I guess we'd better go, too. I'm beginnin' to feel it."

He stared up at her. Idly he wondered how old she was. About seventeen, he guessed. He had never known a girl to be so much a woman at her age, though. Her clear, fair skin and high cheekbones, the wide, sensual, almost sullen mouth, the firm cast of her chin. She stretched again, holding her arms high over her head. He could see the tiny blond tufts in her armpits trailing down to the curve of her young full breasts, which molded down to a tiny, solid waist and then flared out into generous hips and rounded high flanks. She stood squarely on long, straight, yet feminine legs.

She was aware of his inventory. She smiled down at him. She liked him to look at her.

The question came involuntarily to his lips. "How old are you, Marja?"

"Guess," she answered, still smiling.

"Seventeen," he ventured.

She felt proud that he thought her older. "Almost," she said with just the right degree of hesitation.

He put his arms around her legs and toppled her toward him. She fell, laughing, her face very close to his. He made a fierce scowl. "Ready for a kiss, me fair young beauty?" he said in his best villainous voice.

Her eyes didn't change expression. "Always ready," she said huskily.

He put his mouth to her lips. He was vaguely surprised to find that she was right. Again her lips worked against his mouth, making a place for her tongue. This time he was going to be ready for her. She wasn't going to take him by surprise. He fought the surge of passion in him. He held her close but cautiously. He felt her fingers trailing lightly on his cheek and the flame leaped high inside him and he knew that he had lost.

Desperately, almost angrily, he pulled his mouth from her. "I think we'd better get going," he said sullenly.

"Okay," she said quietly. She got to her feet and waited for him.

Avoiding her gaze, he began to gather up the blanket. When it was folded, he slipped his arm through it and rose to his feet, holding it in front of him. He started back to the house without looking at her.

She fell in step beside him. Her hand reached out and touched the blanket. He looked at her. She was smiling. "Hiding something, honey?" she asked.

His face flamed scarlet. An angry retort was on his lips, but they were already at the house. Instead of speaking, he silently held the door open for her.

They entered the house through the beach entrance. It was the rear section of the cellar, made over into a sort of bath house. She stepped into the room and then stood very still. She reached a hand behind her and gestured a finger to her lips to silence him.

"Look," she whispered, a teasing smile on her lips. "The lovers."

He stared. Francie and Jimmy were fast asleep on the couch in each other's arms. Both were completely nude.

His first impulse was one of shock, but it quickly gave
way to laughter. It was funny. Jimmy was so skinny and
Francie was a big girl. He put his hand over his mouth to
still his laughter.

"Shall we wake them?" he whispered.

She shook her head. "No. They look so tired, the poor
darlings."

Quietly they tiptoed past them and into the hall. She
looked at him. "How do I get back to the bedroom?" she
asked. "I want to get dressed."

He gestured and she followed him up the stairs. He
opened the door of her room. She turned to look at him.
"Can I take a shower?" she asked.

"If you won't mind the cold water," he answered. "The
hot-water heater hasn't been turned on yet."

"I don't mind," she said. She picked up her clothing
from the chair and went into the bathroom. She closed and
locked the bathroom door, then waited, listening. She heard
the bedroom door click behind him as he left. Then, smiling to herself, she stepped into the tub, pulled the shower
curtain around her, and turned on the water.

Even cold, it was wonderful. She loved showers. At
home all they had was a tub, and that was in the kitchen.
The toilet was out in the hall. This was the way to live.
She began to sing in a clear, unmusical voice. She had been
there almost ten minutes when she reluctantly turned off
the water.

She pulled aside the shower curtain and had one foot out
of the tub before she looked up. Her hand flew to her
mouth in surprise. "Oh!"

Ross was standing there smiling, a big bath towel in his
outstretched hands. "I thought you could use this," he
said.

She didn't move. "How did you get in?" she asked.

"My door." He gestured behind him. "It's on the other side." He stared down at her. "Better take this," he said, holding the towel toward her. "I hear real blondes are very susceptible to colds."

She took the towel and wrapped it around her. "Thank you," she said coldly.

"Wait a minute," he said. "You're not angry, are you?"

She shook her head. "I don't like people sneaking up on me, that's all."

He pulled her toward him. "It was just a joke, Marja." He tried to kiss her.

She turned a cheek toward him. "It's not funny," she said. "Now leave me alone. I wanna get dressed."

He could feel the warmth of her through the thick towel. An excitement began to run through him. In his mind he could see the couple downstairs on the couch as they had tiptoed through the room. He held her tightly to him. "You're not going to leave me like this," he said in a strained voice, his heart hammering inside him.

She stared up into his eyes. Her eyes were the coldest he had ever seen. She didn't speak.

Anger ran through him violently. He tried to force his lips to her mouth. Silently she squirmed and twisted away from him. He couldn't hold her still. He leaned his weight against her and pushed her back against the wall. Now she couldn't move away from him.

He stared into her eyes, breathing heavily. She looked back at him without fear. "Cut the teasing, Marja," he said harshly. "What do you think I brought you out here for?"

She didn't answer. Just kept watching him.

He tried to rip the towel from her, but she held it tightly. He felt his temper run away with him. There was a wild joy in his violence. He slapped her across the face with the back of his hand. "Come on, you bitch!" he snapped. "Put out! Francie said you would!"

He felt her freeze and straighten up against the wall. He looked at her. The marks of his fingers were white against her sun-flushed cheek. A half-smile came to her lips, her eyelids drooped. "Ross, baby," she whispered gently.

A confident smile came to his lips. These cheap little tramps were all alike. Sometimes they needed a little handling to show them who was boss. He moved toward her surely.

He didn't see the vicious upward sweep of her knee until the pain exploded in his groin. He stood there unbelieving for a moment, swaying in front of her. "Marja!" he said in a shocked voice, through rapidly whitening lips. "My God! Marja?" Then the second climax of pain tumbled him to the floor in front of her.

He could see her watching him coldly through his pain-blurred eyes as he lay doubled up before her. He writhed as the waves of agony ripped through him.

He felt rather than saw her step over him and pick up her clothing from the chair. He felt a draft on his cheek as she opened the door. He strained, trying to look up at her.

She was in the doorway looking back at him. Her voice fell coldly on his ears. "If that was what you wanted, why didn't you pick Francie?"

The pain was receding now. He could breathe again, but didn't dare move for fear it would return. He forced himself to speak. "Because it was you I wanted, Marja," he mumbled through numb lips.

Her voice was not quite so cold now. "There's some things I do, some things I don't," she said patiently, as if

Chapter 5

WEARILY he opened his eyes. The room was dark, the night outside the windows still. He rolled over, the soft bed giving beneath him; the blanket caught his arms and held them. Vaguely he wondered how he had got here. An ache came back to him and he began to remember. He had stumbled from the bathroom and tumbled into bed. He remembered sinking into its welcoming softness, but that was all. He didn't remember covering himself.

"Feeling better, Ross?"

He turned his head toward Marja's voice. A cigarette glowed from a chair in the corner of the room. He sat up. Now he remembered everything. She had come into the room and covered him while he was dozing. He had been shivering as if with a chill.

"Yes," he answered sullenly.

The cigarette made an upward sweep, glowed bright, and then dimmed. "Want a drag?" she asked.

"Please."

He heard her move in the darkness, then her silhouette crossed the window. He felt the bed sink beneath her weight. The cigarette was in front of him. He took it gratefully and put it between his lips. The acrid smoke filtered deep into his lungs. He began to feel better.

"What time is it?" he asked.

"About nine," she answered.

He puffed again at the cigarette and let the smoke drift slowly out his nostrils. It seemed to help him waken. "Where are the others?" he asked, trying unsuccessfully to see her in the glow of the cigarette. "Still downstairs?"

"No," she answered shortly. "Francie was scared when we came upstairs and found you on the bed. She wanted to go home. Jimmy went with her."

He thought silently, bitterly: Fine friends, run out when you need them. But it was just what he could expect from Jimmy. Mike would never have done that. A thought ran through his mind. "Did you tell them what happened?"

"No," she replied. "Why should I? That was between us."

"Then what did they think?" he asked.

"I tol' 'em you were sick," she answered. The bed shook slightly as if she was laughing, but he couldn't tell. "Yuh sure acted like it. Shiverin' away."

A resentment came up in him. If they thought he was really sick, that made their actions even more cowardly. He might have really needed them. He tried to see her, but it was too dark. He leaned over and turned on a light near the bed. For a moment the light hurt his eyes and he blinked; then he turned toward her. "Why didn't you go with them?" he asked bitterly.

She didn't answer.

"You knew what happened, you didn't have to stay," he added. "I could have managed."

Her eyes were luminous in the light from the lamp. Her hair, almost white in its glow, was pulled straight back across her head and tied behind with a tiny ribbon. Her mouth was scarlet with lipstick, and full and shining. She sat motionlessly opposite him, still not speaking.

"Well?" he asked nastily. "Lost your tongue?"

"I came with you," she said quietly. "I was going back with you."

A perverseness prompted his tongue. "Did you think I was going to take you back after what happened? That I would want to?"

She watched him silently, the pupils of her eyes growing large and black so that the irises almost seemed to disappear. That was the strangest thing about her. Her eyes always seemed to be speaking, yet he could never understand what they were saying.

"Did you?" he asked again.

She took a deep breath and silently got to her feet. She walked back to the chair in the corner, picked up her tiny purse, and started for the door. She didn't look at him.

He waited until she had her hand on the door before he spoke. "Marja!"

She stopped and looked down at him silently.

"Where are you going?" he asked unnecessarily.

"Home," she answered in a flat, expressionless voice. "You're okay now."

"Do you have carfare?"

"I can manage," she said in the same flat voice.

His hand moved swiftly, snatching the tiny purse from her grasp. "Where did you get money?" he asked coldly. "Francie said neither of you had a cent with you."

She didn't answer. The expression on her face didn't change. "I said I could manage," she repeated expressionlessly.

He opened the purse and looked into it. It was empty except for a lipstick, two slightly beaten cigarettes, a comb, and some wooden matches.

"Your wallet is under your pillow," she said quietly. "I put it there."

Instinctively he reached for it and flipped it open. The bills were still there. He began to feel ashamed of his suspicion.

"Now kin I have my bag back?" she asked. "I wanna get goin'. It's late."

He looked up at her, then down at her empty purse. He took a ten-dollar bill from his wallet and stuffed it into her purse. "Take a cab," he said, handing the purse back to her.

The ten-dollar bill fluttered back onto the bed. "No, thanks," she said dryly. "I don't want nothin' from you." The door closed behind her.

He sat there for a moment in surprise, then jumped to his feet. At the last second he realized that they had stripped the wet bathing-suit from him. Pulling the bedspread around him to hide his nakedness, he ran into the hall after her. "Marja!" he called. "Marja! Wait a minute!" He stumbled over the trailing bedspread and grabbed at the railing to keep from falling down the staircase.

She was already at the bottom of the steps when she turned to look back at him. She stared for a moment, then a smile spread across her face and she began to roar with laughter.

Her laughter floated mockingly up to him. He began to

get angry. "What the hell are you laughing at?" he yelled.

She couldn't stop. "Look at yerself, Ross," she gasped, pointing. "You look like a pitcher of a ghost!"

He turned to the full-length mirror on the wall near him. His pale face and wild hair over the white bedspread did make him look like a ghost. He began to smile and then, laughing, turned back to her. "Give me time to get dressed, Marja," he said, "and I'll take you home."

"Better stop the car and let me out here," she said as they came to her corner. "My stepfather might be sittin' at the window."

Silently he pulled the car to the curb. He got out of the car and walked stiffly around it and opened her door. He held her hand as she stepped out.

They stood there awkwardly on the sidewalk for a moment, then she put out her hand. "Thanks for a nice time, Ross," she said politely.

He searched her eyes for a trace of sarcasm, but there was none. He took her hand. "Will I see you again, Marja?" he asked.

Her hand was quiet in his. "If you want," she answered.

He put his foot on the running-board. The movement made him wince. "I want to," he said.

She noticed the flash of pain on his face. "I didn't mean to hurt you so bad, Ross," she said quietly.

He looked into her eyes. "I deserved it," he said simply. "I should have known better."

A few seconds passed and then she withdrew her hand. "I better go," she said. "The ol' man'll be wild."

"What's your number?" he asked quickly. He saw a puzzled expression on her face. "So I can call you," he added.

"Oh," she replied, suddenly understanding. "We haven't got a phone."

"Then how will I get in touch with you?" he asked. It was his turn to be puzzled. He had always thought everyone had a telephone.

She looked up at him. "I'm generally at Rannis's candy store at three o'clock. It's up the block, across the street from the poolroom."

"I'll call you there tomorrow," he said.

"Okay." She hesitated a moment. "Good night, Ross."

He smiled. "Good night, Marja."

He watched her walk up the block, her half-high heels clicking on the pavement. He liked the way she walked, her head high, her step sure, her body swaying slightly as if she owned the earth. There was a natural pride in her.

He waited until he saw her walk up the steps and into her house before he got back into the car. He turned up the block after her. The lights were on in the poolroom as he passed by. On an impulse he stopped the car and got out.

He had been right. Jimmy was in there, leaning over a table cue in hand, in the midst of a group of boys.

He heard Jimmy's voice as he approached. It was low, but with the confidential penetration of lewdness. "—like a mink," he was saying. "Ross was layin' on the bed there like he had his ears screwed off. Stoned. My girl says we better get out before the cops come. Th' blonde says somebody gotta stay wit' him. So we blows an' leaves him there wit' th' blonde—"

A sixth sense made him look up. He forced a smile to his face. "Ross," he said, the tone of his voice changing. "Hi yuh feelin', pal? Man, did we have a ball or didn't we?"

Ross's face was cold, his eyes bleak. His lips scarcely

moved, but the words spilled out like vitriol. "Chicken-livered bastard! What did you run away for?"

"Francie got scared, Ross." The words tumbled from his lips in his eagerness to explain. "Somebody had to take her home. Besides, Marja was stayin' wit' yuh. She said she would."

Ross walked around the pool table toward him deliberately. The boys fell away from him as he came closer to Jimmy. "What if I was really sick, Jimmy?" he asked, his voice suddenly deceptively soft. "If I really needed help? And only a girl there to do it?"

The smile was still on Jimmy's lips, but a terror was growing in his eyes. "And that girl sure could do it, couldn't she, Ross?" he said quickly. "I bet she sure knew how."

Ross's fist caught him on the mouth, and he tumbled backward against a table. He braced himself against it for a moment, then, reversing the cue stick in his hand, lunged at Ross's face.

Ross deflected the stick with his arm and stepped in close to Jimmy. His fists moved so quickly they were a blur in the yellow light. The cue stick fell from Jimmy's fingers. A moment later Ross stepped back.

There was a wild throbbing pain in his temples as he watched Jimmy sink slowly to the floor, bleeding from his nose and mouth. Pain was the only way to get even. Jimmy had to know what it was like.

Jimmy was sitting on his haunches, his eyes glazed and bewildered. His lips moved, but no sound came out. Slowly he rolled over on his side on the floor.

Ross picked up the cue stick from the floor and reversed it in his hand. His eyes were like frosty blue icicles as he stood over the prostrate figure. Deliberately he pressed the blunt edge down against Jimmy's trousers. He twisted it in his hand, leaning his weight against it. "Yellow son of a bitch!" he said.

There was an involuntary scream from Jimmy's lips before the others could pull Ross from him. The cue stick broke sharply in Ross's hands.

"Stop it, Ross!" one of them yelled. "Yuh want tuh kill 'im?"

Ross looked at the sharp jagged edge of the broken cue in his hand. The flames were leaping all around him. As if in the distance, he heard a door slam. "That's an idea!" he yelled, breaking from their grip and lunging at Jimmy's face with the stick.

Before he could reach Jimmy, he felt two arms around him, pinning his arms to his waist. He struggled wildly. "Let me go! Let me go!" he screamed. "I'll kill him!"

But the two arms only grew tighter and dragged him back. "Take it easy, Ross," a familiar voice said in his ear. "We don't want no more trouble."

The deep, gentle voice was like a spray of cool water. Ross felt the wild trembling inside him leave and sanity return. He stood very still, his breath rattling deep inside him. At last his control came back and he could speak. "Okay, Mike," he said, without turning around. "You can let me go. I'm all right now."

The strong arms released him. Ross didn't look up. He turned and walked toward the door. At the cashier's desk he stopped and dropped a bill on the counter. "That will pay for the mess I made," he said.

The white-faced old man sitting there didn't speak. Ross went out the door. He got into his car and sat there waiting.

A few seconds later he heard footsteps coming toward the car. They stopped outside the door. "Drive me home, will you please, Mike?" he asked without looking up. "I'm very tired."

The footsteps went around the car. The door on the opposite side opened and his friend got in. A match flared, and a second later he felt a cigarette shoved into his hand. He dragged on it deeply, leaning his head back against the cushion and closing his eyes.

"Good thing I came by just then," he heard his friend's voice say. "I had a hunch I'd better go lookin' for yuh."

A faint smile traced Ross's lips. "Still running interference for me, Mike?" he asked. When they played football together, Mike did the blocking while he carried the ball.

There was a chuckle in Mike's voice. "Why th' hell not? We're buddies, ain't we?" He leaned forward and started the motor. He raced it a moment. "What happened, anyway? Yuh would've killed him if I didn't grab yuh."

"There was this girl—" Ross started to explain.

"That blonde you were creamin' over this afternoon?" Mike interrupted.

"Yes," Ross answered. "She—"

Again Mike's voice cut in. There was a chiding tone in it. "I gave yuh credit for more sense 'n that, Ross."

Ross turned his head. "What do you mean?"

Mike struck a match and held it to his cigarette. The flame flared golden in his eyes. "I don't understand you at all, Ross. No girl's worth gettin' in trouble over."

Ross stared at his friend. Mike was right about one thing—he didn't understand. He closed his eyes and leaned back against the seat. He felt the car start as Mike put it into gear.

Mike didn't understand. It wasn't Marja at all. A faint

doubt came into him. Or was it? He turned and looked at Mike.

Mike was driving carefully, concentrating on the street ahead. But, then, Mike did everything carefully. He allowed no margin for error. That was the trouble with Mike. That was why he ran interference instead of carrying the ball. He didn't like to take chances. It wasn't that he was afraid, it was just the way he was.

Mike didn't understand. How could he? He didn't know Marja.

Chapter 6

SHE could hear the thin wail of the baby as she entered the downstairs hall and began to climb the stairs. It grew louder as she neared her door. A light came from beneath it. She hesitated a moment before opening it.

She blinked as the ugly white light hit her eyes. The baby's cries tore at her ears. She stepped into the room quickly and closed the door behind her. Footsteps came from the hallway on her left. She turned toward them.

Her stepfather was standing there, his trousers hanging loosely over his wide hips. He wore no shirt; the white tops of his B.V.D.'s hung on the mat of coarse black hair that framed his barrel chest. He didn't speak, but his coal-black eyes stared meanly at her.

"What's he cryin' for?" she asked, gesturing toward the bedroom.

"Where yuh been?" he asked in a heavy voice, ignoring her question.

She began moving toward the bedroom. "Swimmin'," she answered succinctly.

"Till ten thirty at night?" he asked, looking at the kitchen clock.

"It's a long way back from Coney Island," she answered, opening the bedroom door.

His hand caught her arm and spun her around. She stared at him, her eyes cold and bleak. "Why didn't you stop an' tell yer mother?" he shot at her angrily. "She was worried about you. An' you know she ain't feelin' too good."

"She'd be a lot better if you got a job so's she wouldn't have to work nights," she replied nastily.

He raised his hands as if to strike her.

"Go ahead, I dare you!" she taunted, her lips bared over her teeth.

He swore at her in Polish. *"Coorva!* Whore!"

A contempt came into her eyes. "Beer-guzzlin' bum!" she snapped. "Yuh wouldn't dare. Yuh know my mother would throw yuh out if yuh did!"

Slowly his hand fell to his side. "If I wasn't such a good friend of your father's when he was alive, I would have no care for you," he muttered.

"Leave him out of this!" she said quickly. "At least he was a man. He took care of his family. He didn't lay aroun' drinkin' beer all day."

He was on the defensive now. She could sense it, and a triumph rose in her. "Your mother doesn't want me to work the buildings any more," he said uncertainly. "She made me promise when we got married. She said losing one man to them was enough."

"You saw him fall," she said coldly. "Was it your promise or your fear that keeps you home?"

The baby's cries grew louder and more urgent. He stood there a moment breathing heavily, then turned away from her. "Go see what Peter wants," he said.

The bedroom door closed behind her. He lumbered over to the icebox and took out a can of beer. Expertly he punctured the top and tilted it over his lips. Some of the beer ran down his cheeks, spilling onto his undershirt. He drank long and thirstily and threw the empty can into a paper bag on the sink.

He looked at the closed bedroom door. The baby's cries had stopped. He stared at the door. She was a bitch, there was no other word for her. He wiped his mouth with the side of his arm. Nobody could do anything with her. It had been like that since the time her mother told her they were to be married.

He closed his eyes with the effort of remembering. It was only three years ago. A month after her father had stepped from a steel girder twenty-three stories in the skies.

He could still see the look of surprise on Henry's face when he realized the scaffold that should have been there, wasn't. It was a moment of paralysis of action. His lips started to form the word "Peter!" His hand reached anxiously for his friend.

Then he spun suddenly toward the earth. Looking down, Peter could see Henry's cap sailing gently away from him, his friend's blond hair sparkling iridescently in the sun as he tumbled over and over.

The beer came up in him at the remembered nausea. He held his breath a moment, then belched. The nausea went away. He could see his friend every time he looked at Marja. The same white-blond hair, high Polack cheekbones, and sensual mouth. And the way she walked, too, reminded him of her father. They both had the same sure-footed, catlike step.

He had first noticed it the night he came to propose to Katti. A month after Marja's father had died. He had put on his best suit, the one he wore to church on Sundays, and bought a two-dollar box of candy at the drugstore. The druggist had assured him it was the best he had, and fresh, too. He had climbed the stairs to the apartment and stood outside in the hall, sweating from the exertion and nervousness. He hesitated a moment, then knocked cautiously at the door.

A moment later he heard her mother's voice. "Who is it?" Katti asked.

"Me, Peter," he answered.

A mumbled hurrying sound came from behind the closed door, then it opened. Marja stood there, looking up at him. Her eyes were wide. "Hello, Uncle Peter," she said.

He smiled down at her, his eyes searching the room for her mother. She was nowhere in sight. The kitchen table was covered with pins and pieces of white material. "Hello, Marja," he answered foolishly. "Is your mother in?"

Marja nodded. "She's putting on a dress." She stepped back from the door. "Come in, Uncle Peter."

He shuffled into the room clumsily and held the box of candy toward her. "I brought candy."

She took it gravely. "Thank you," she said, putting it on the kitchen table. "Mama says for me to take you into the parlor."

He took his hat off and stood there awkwardly. "You don't have to bother," he said formally. "I can stay in the kitchen."

She shook her head commandingly. "Mama says I should take you into the parlor."

Without looking back, she led him into the long, narrow hallway that led to the front room. She was a white shadow dancing in front of him. He stumbled in the sudden dimness. He felt her hand touch his.

"Take my hand, Uncle Peter," she said quietly. "I know the hall. You'll trip in the dark."

Her hand was warm in his big fist. She stopped suddenly and he stumbled into her. "I'm sorry," he said, aware of his clumsiness.

"It's okay," she said, taking her hand away. "I'll turn on the light."

He heard her walk away in the dark, then a click, and light flooded the room. She was standing in front of the lamp, and the light poured through her white dress. He stared at her. She seemed to have nothing underneath it.

She saw him looking, and a slight smile came to her lips. "Like my new graduation dress, Uncle Peter?" she asked archly. "Mama just finished it before you came."

He nodded, his eyes still on the shadow of her. "Very pretty."

She didn't move away from the lamp. "I'm graduating this term, you know."

"I know," he answered. "Your father told me. He was very proud."

A shadow came into her eyes. For a moment he thought she was about to cry, but it vanished quickly. She came away from the lamp. "Next term I'll be going to high school," she said.

"So soon?" he asked in simulated surprise. "I still think of you as a baby."

She was standing in front of him now. She looked up at him. "I'm going on thirteen," she said. "I'm not a baby any more."

He didn't argue with her. He had seen that much.

"But I'm not too old to kiss you for the nice candy you brought us, Uncle Peter," she said, smiling.

He felt an embarrassed flush creep into his face. He shifted awkwardly, not speaking.

"Bend down, Uncle Peter," she said imperiously. "I can't reach you."

He bent forward, holding his cheek toward her. Her action took him by surprise. She put her arms around his neck and kissed him on the lips. It was not the kiss of a child, but the kiss of a woman who had been born for kissing. He felt her young body pressing against his jacket.

Clumsily he put out his hands to push her away, but accidentally they touched her breasts. He dropped his hands to his sides as if they had been in a flaming oven.

She stepped back and looked up at him, a smile in her eyes. "Thanks for the candy, Uncle Peter."

"You're welcome," he answered.

"Sit down," she said, walking past him to the hallway. She paused in the entrance and looked back at him. "I'm not such a baby any more, am I, Uncle Peter?"

"No, you're not," he admitted.

She smiled at him proudly, then turned and ran down the hall. "Mama!" she called out. "Uncle Peter brought us a box of candy!"

He sank into a chair, remembering what her father had said to him a few days before the accident. "Another year, Peter," he had said, "and the boys will be after her like dogs after a bitch in heat."

He shook his head, his fingers still tingling where they had touched her, a strange excitement in him. Henry must have been blind. Surely the boys were after her already.

He heard Katti's footsteps in the hall and got to his feet.

He was standing there, his face flushed, when she came into the room.

She held out her hand, and they shook hands, man fashion. "Peter," she said, "you're too good to us. You shouldn't have brought the candy. It's so expensive."

He still held her hand. "I want to be good to you, Katti," he said huskily.

She withdrew her hand. "Sit down, Peter," she said, seating herself in a chair opposite him.

He studied her. She was a good-looking woman. Big and generously proportioned. An Old Country woman, not like these American women who dieted themselves into matchsticks. And a wonderful cook, too. He remembered the envy he had felt every time Henry opened his lunchbox. The delicious sandwiches she had made for him. All Peter's landlady ever packed was dried-out *wurst*.

He had always told Henry the reason he never married was that there weren't any more women around like Katti. Henry had laughed at him. Said he was too set in his ways to try to please any woman.

But it wasn't so. It was just that any woman wouldn't please him. Katti was the kind of woman that could make him happy.

"I'm making some fresh coffee for you," she said.

"You shouldn't bother," he said awkwardly. "I don't want you should trouble for me."

"It's no bother," she answered.

They sat there silently for a few minutes, then she slipped into Polish. "You like Marja's new dress?"

He nodded, unconsciously answering her in the same tongue. "She's a big girl now."

Katti agreed. "Yes. She graduates on Friday."

"I know," he said quickly. "Henry had told me."

Tears sprang into her eyes, and she averted her face.

"I'm sorry," he said apologetically. "I didn't mean—"

She waved her hand. "I know." The tears continued to run down her cheeks. "Things get too much for me sometimes, and I can't get used to it. I don't know what to do. Henry always knew."

He was on his feet looking down at her. That was what he meant by an Old Country woman. They knew their place, and that it was a man's place to make decisions. A thought came to him. "Yes," he said solemnly. "He always used to say to me: 'Peter, if anything happens, look after Katti and the baby for me.' "

The tears stopped as quickly as they had come. Katti looked at him with wide eyes. "He did?" she breathed in a voice filled with wonder.

He nodded silently.

"Is that why you come to see us twice a week?" she asked.

"At first it was, Katti," he said, a sudden daring in him. "But not now."

She dropped her eyes to the floor. "Now why do you come?" she asked in a hushed voice.

"To see you, Katti," he said, feeling bolder than he ever had in his life. "I want to make a home for you and Marja."

A long moment passed before she spoke. Then her hand sought his. "Peter, you're so good to us."

Later, when the coffee was ready, they went into the kitchen. The pins and material had been cleared from the table, and Marja, who had changed her dress, was seated there doing her homework. The open box of candy was in front of her, and chocolate was smeared on her mouth.

She smiled at him. "The candy is delicious, Uncle Peter."

"I'm glad you like it, child," he said.

Katti had gone over to the stove. "Marja," she said over her shoulder as she poured the coffee, "how would you like Uncle Peter as a father?"

Peter saw the child's eyes widen. There was an expression there he couldn't fathom. "What do you mean, Mama?" she asked in a suddenly hurt voice.

Katti was smiling as she brought the coffee to the table. "I mean your Uncle Peter and me," she said. "We're going to get married."

"Oh, no!" Marja's voice was an anguished cry.

They both stared at her in surprise. She was standing, and the box of candy spilled to the floor in front of her.

Katti's voice grew stern. "Marja," she snapped, "you don't understand now, but you will when you grow up. It's not good for a woman to be alone without a man to take care of her and the children."

Marja was crying. "But, Mama! We were getting along. The two of us. We don't need nobody." She wiped at her eyes with her hands. "Nobody can take Papa's place."

Katti's voice was still gentle. "Nobody will, my child. It's just that Uncle Peter wants to be good to us. He loves us and wants to take care of us."

Marja turned to him savagely. "I don't believe it!" she screamed. "He's a funny, dirty, little black man, not like Papa at all!"

Katti's voice grew stern. "Marja," she snapped, "you mustn't talk like that to your new father."

"He's not my father!" Marja shouted. "And he never will be!" She turned and ran into her room just off the kitchen and slammed the door.

They stared at each other helplessly after she left. Silently Peter sat down at the table. She's wild, he was thinking. Henry had been right when he said Marja had a temper.

She would need some handling. He would take care of her after they were married. A few red marks on that pretty little behind and she would be all right.

Katti came around the table and put her hand on his shoulder. "Don't feel bad, Peter," she said. "She's all upset. Just yesterday she started bleeding. You know how young girls are at that time."

Chapter 7

THE DULL gray light of morning, filtered through the tiny courtyard, crept through the window as Katti opened the door. She stood a moment in the doorway looking at her daughter.

She wondered at the sight of Marja sleeping. Awake, she was almost a woman; now she was like a child. Her features were relaxed and soft, her breath so gentle it barely moved the light cover across her chest. This was the Marja she knew, her quiet, lovely little baby.

She moved into the room and turned to the crib. Quickly she touched the baby. A miracle. He was still dry. He made a small sound at her touch. She turned quickly to look at her daughter.

Marja's eyes were open. She was looking at her mother, all the sleep gone from her eyes. "Mornin', Mama."

Katti didn't answer. She remembered how she had worried yesterday when Marja didn't come home from school.

Peter had said that she had gone swimming. She hadn't come home until almost eleven o'clock.

Marja sat up in bed, the cover falling to her waist, revealing her nude body. She yawned and stretched, the flesh of her breasts startlingly white against the red flush where the sun had burned her.

"Marja! Cover yourself!" Katti exclaimed in a shocked voice. "How many times have I told you you must not go to sleep without your pajamas? It's not nice."

"But, Mama, it was so hot." Marja reached for the pajama top and slipped into it as she spoke. "Besides, nobody's going to see me."

"I don't care!" Katti insisted. "It's not decent to sleep like that. Only animals do it."

Marja kicked back the covers and got out of bed, the pajama top falling to her thighs. She walked over to her mother and kissed her cheek. "Don't be mad, Mama," she said.

In spite of herself, Katti smiled. She pushed her daughter away. "Don't try to make up to me," she said. "I know all your tricks."

Marja smiled back at her mother. "I went swimming yesterday," she said quickly, anticipating her mother's next question. "See my sunburn?"

"I saw," Katti answered dryly. "How could I miss?"

"Francie's friend has a place in Coney Island," Marja explained. "It's a house in Sea Gate."

Katti was impressed. "Sea Gate?" she breathed. "That's very expensive. Her family must be very rich."

"They are," Marja said. She didn't correct her mother's assumption that Francie's friend was a girl. "They live on Park Avenue."

The baby began to cry suddenly. Katti bent over the crib

and picked him up. The baby stopped crying and gurgled at her. "Still, you should have come home to tell me," Katti said over the baby's head to Marja. "I was worried about you."

"There wasn't time, Mama," Marja answered. "We went right after school."

"But you didn't come home until after ten thirty," Katti said, placing the baby on Marja's bed. Deftly she began to remove his diaper.

Marja took a fresh diaper from the top of the old dresser and handed it to her mother. "She wanted me to eat with her, Mama," she answered, "so I did."

Katti glanced at her quickly out of the corners of her eyes. "Don't do it again," she said quietly. "Your father was worried."

A cold look came into Marja's eyes. "Why?" she queried sarcastically. "He run out of beer?"

"Marja!" Katti spoke sharply. "That's no way to talk about your father."

Marja went to the closet and took out a worn bathrobe, which she slipped into. "He's not my father," she said stubbornly.

Katti sighed. "Why do you keep saying that, Marja?" she asked in a hurt voice. "He loves you and wants you to love him. He can't help it if you don't try to like him."

Marja didn't answer. She picked up her toothbrush from a glass tumbler on the dresser and walked to the door. She stopped there and looked back at her mother. "I'll make Peter's bottle," she said.

In the kitchen, she put the baby's bottle in a pan of water on the stove. She turned on the flame beneath it and went to the sink. Quickly, efficiently, she washed herself, then picked up the bottle and went back into her room.

"Give Peter the bottle," Katti said, getting up from the bed. "I'll go make your breakfast. I don't want you to be late for school."

Marja bent over the baby, holding the bottle in her hand. She laughed at him. "Want yuh breakfast, Peter?"

Peter's dark little eyes smiled at her. His tiny hands reached for the bottle, a smile splitting his toothless mouth.

"Yuh're so pretty," she said, putting the bottle to his mouth.

He gurgled happily, his lips closing over the long rubber nipple. A tiny trickle of milk ran down from the corner of his mouth.

"Slob," Marja laughed, wiping him with the towel she still held in her hand. She looked down at him. "Think you can keep from falling off the bed while Marja gets dressed?" she asked.

Peter sucked happily at the bottle.

She straightened up, the baby's dark eyes following her. "I guess you can manage," she said, smiling. She went over to the dresser and took out some clothing.

She threw off the bathrobe and slipped out of the pajama top. Deftly, in almost the same motion, she stepped into her panties and reached for the brassiere on the dresser. A flash of light caught her eye, and she looked into the mirror over the dresser.

The door behind her was open and she could see into the kitchen. Her stepfather was seated at the table, watching her. A look of contempt came into her face. He dropped his eyes.

Still watching him, she slipped the brassiere straps over her arms and fastened it. Then she turned and walked to the door. He looked up again. She stood there silently a moment, then closed the door quickly and finished dressing.

Peter had finished his bottle. She picked him up gaily and went out into the kitchen. Her stepfather was no longer there.

Katti put a bowl of cereal on the table and held out her arms for the baby. "He finish the bottle?" she asked.

Marja nodded. She handed Peter to her mother and sat down. "Oatmeal again?" she asked, staring into the bowl.

"Oatmeal is good for you," Katti said. "Eat it."

Marja made no move toward the food. She wanted a cigarette. She looked at her mother speculatively, wondering if she dared light one before breakfast. She decided against the idea. "I'm not hungry," she said.

Her stepfather had come back into the kitchen. "Isn't oatmeal good enough for your rich tastes?" he asked clumsily. "Maybe you'd prefer ham and eggs?"

Marja stared up at him coldly. "To tell the truth," she said, "I would."

"Isn't that too bad?" he queried sarcastically. He turned to Katti. "I think she's ashamed because we're too poor to afford it."

Marja's eyes were wide. "We wouldn't be if you could tear yourself away from the beer long enough to go to work," she said blandly.

Peter held out his hands hopelessly toward his wife. "Respect for her parents she ain't got," he said. "Only insults. That what she learns bumming around to all hours of the night?"

"Respect for my parents I have," Marja said swiftly. "Not for you."

"Marja! Stop!" her mother spoke sharply.

"Tell him to stop pickin' on me," she answered sullenly, picking up her spoon. She tasted the oatmeal. It was dull and flat.

"Your father is right," Katti continued. "You should speak to him nicer. He's only thinking of you—"

"Crap!" Marja exploded, throwing down her spoon. "The only one he ever thinks about is himself!" She got to her feet. "If he was half a man, he wouldn't let you be out working all night while he sat around the house in his B.V.D.'s He's nothin' but a leech!"

Katti moved quickly, her hand a blur against the gray-white walls. The slap echoed resoundingly in the suddenly quiet kitchen.

Marja's hand was against her cheek, the red flush spreading quickly around the white fingermarks. There was a strange look of wonder in her eyes. "You hit me," she said to her mother, a tone of horror in her voice.

Katti looked at her. She could feel a lump coming into her throat. She realized that this was the first time she had ever slapped her daughter. "To teach you respect for your parents," she said in a suddenly shaking voice.

Marja's eyes seemed to fill, and for a moment Katti thought that her daughter was about to cry. But no tears fell. Instead, a coldness came into them, an icy, chilling calm that told her Marja had grown up and gone away from her.

"Marja!" she said in an appealing voice and took a step toward her.

Marja stepped back. "I'm sorry, Mother," she said softly. It was almost as if she were apologizing for striking her mother. "I'm terribly sorry."

She turned and went quietly out the kitchen door.

Katti turned to Peter. She could hear Marja's steps hurrying down the stairway. She began to cry. "What have I done, Peter? What have I done to my baby?"

He didn't move toward her. There was a distant echo of triumph in his voice. "What you should have done long ago, Katti. You did right."

She looked at him. "You really think so, Peter?" she asked, lapsing into Polish.

He nodded his head, a satisfaction deep in his eyes. "Yes."

She stared at him. The baby in her arms began to cry. Automatically she began to soothe him. She wanted to believe her husband. She wanted to feel she had been right. But no matter how much she wanted to believe, somewhere deep inside her lurked a preying doubt.

Chapter 8

THE TELEPHONE began to ring just as Marja came in the door. "I'll get it, Mr. Rannis," she called. "It's for me."

She pulled the door of the booth closed and picked up the receiver. "Hello."

"Marja?" Ross's voice was thin through the receiver.

"Yeah," she answered.

"Ross," he said.

"I know," she answered.

"What are you doin'?" he asked.

"Nothin'," she answered. "It's too hot."

"Want to go for a ride?" he asked. "We'll go up River-side Drive. It's cool there."

"Okay," she said.

"I'll pick you right up," he said quickly. "Wait there for me."

"No—" She hesitated. "I gotta go home first an' change. My dress is soakin'. I'll meet yuh someplace."

"At the garage," he said. "Eighty-third between Park an' Lex. Will you be long?"

"Half-hour," she said. "So long."

"So long," he answered.

She heard the click of his phone before she replaced the receiver. She came out of the booth.

Mr. Rannis was standing there. He looked at her suspiciously. "Who was that?"

"A friend," she answered noncommittally. She started toward the door.

He put out a hand and stopped her. "How about a Milky Way?"

She shook her head. "No, thanks." She started to move again, but his hand tightened on her arm.

"I'm not askin' for money," he said.

She smiled. "Wouldn't do you no good. I'm flat." She pulled her arm free. "Besides, I gotta go. My mother is expectin' me."

Reluctantly he watched her go to the door. "Don't forget, Marja," he called. " 'f you want anything, all you gotta do is ask me."

"Thanks, Mr. Rannis," she said as she went out the door. "I'll keep it in mind."

Katti was coming out the door as Marja reached the steps to her house. She stood there watching the sun glint in her daughter's hair. She waited until Marja was halfway up the stoop before she spoke. "Hello, Marja."

Marja's voice was quiet. "Hello, Mama."

"Everything go all right in school today?" Katti asked.

Marja glanced quickly at her mother. "Yeah," she answered. "Why shouldn't it?"

Katti felt herself thrown on the defensive. "I was just asking," she answered. She wanted to say she was sorry for what had happened that morning, but she couldn't make the words come from her lips.

"Where yuh goin'?" Marja asked.

"Shopping," Katti answered. She was lying. But she didn't want her daughter to know she was going to the clinic for an examination. "What are you doing this afternoon?"

"I'm goin' over to a friend's house to study," Marja answered. "I just came home to get out of these things. I'm all sweated up."

"Be quiet," Katti said. "The baby's sleeping. I don't want you to wake him."

"I will," Marja answered.

She went upstairs and opened the door softly. The apartment was still. She went into the kitchen and stood in the center of the room listening. There was no sound. Quietly she walked up the hall to the front room and peeked in.

Her stepfather was fast asleep in a chair near the open window, his head lolling to one side, the newspaper across his knees. She tiptoed carefully back through the hall and kitchen to her room.

The baby was sleeping in his crib. Gently she opened the closet door and took out a clean blouse and skirt. She placed them on the bed and, next to them, fresh underclothes. Quickly she slipped out of her blouse and skirt and went back into the kitchen.

She opened the water faucet to a gentle trickle. She didn't want any noise to disturb her stepfather. She shrugged off her brassiere and hung it over the back of a kitchen chair. It took her only a moment to cover the upper half of her body with soap. Another moment to remove the soap with the aid of a wash rag. She then washed her face. Her eyes shut tightly against the soap, she reached for a towel. The rack nearest her was empty. She groped for the next rack.

She pulled the towel down and rubbed her face vigorously, then under her arms and across her body. She put the towel back on the rack and reached behind her for the brassiere. It wasn't on the chair.

She turned, automatically looking at the floor, thinking it might have fallen. Her stepfather's voice startled her.

"It did fall, Marja," he said, holding it toward her. "But I picked it up for you."

She stared at him for a moment, surprise showing in her eyes. Then she reached out her hand, taking it from him. "Gee, thanks," she said sarcastically, holding it in front of her. "It made so much noise falling that it woke you."

He smiled slowly, ignoring her tone of voice. "Your mother used to look like that back in the Old Country when we were young."

"How would you know?" she asked snidely. "She never even knew you were alive then." She started to walk around him, but he stepped in front of her.

He reached out his hand and caught her arm. "Marja, why do you act so mean to me?"

She stared up into his face, her eyes blank. "I don't mean to, Uncle Peter," she said. "It's just that I can't stand seeing you around the house."

He misunderstood her sarcasm completely. "If I got a job?" he asked almost pleadingly. "Then would you be nice to me?"

A calculating glint came into her eyes. "I might," she said.

"Then we could be friends again?" He pulled her toward him and clumsily tried to kiss her.

She turned her face so that his kiss landed awkwardly on

her cheek, and she slipped out of his grasp. At her door she
turned and looked at him. "Maybe," she said.

The door closed behind her. He could feel the pulses
throbbing in his temples. The little bitch. Someday he would
show her what she could do with her teasing. He turned to
the icebox for another can of beer.

Katti sat on the row of benches between two other wom-
en and stoically waited her turn for examination. It
wouldn't take long now. There was only one other woman
before her.

In the corner of the room the young nurse at the recep-
tion desk stared down at the cards in front of her. After a
while all the strange-sounding names came off your tongue
as easily as Smith and Jones. When that happened, you
knew you were a veteran.

An intern stopped at the desk and whispered to her. She
nodded and picked up the next two cards. "Mrs. Martino,
booth four, please. Mrs. Ritchik, booth five."

Katti and the woman next to her got up at the same time.
They smiled at each other in sudden kinship. Katti followed
her to the desk.

The woman took the card the nurse gave her, went into
a booth, and pulled the curtain closed behind her.

Katti spoke to the nurse. "Mrs. Ritchik," she said.

The nurse looked at her without curiosity and handed
her a card. "First visit?" she asked.

Katti shook her head. "No. I was here before. When my
Peter was born."

The nurse shook her head impatiently. These people
were so dumb. "I mean this time."

Katti hesitated. "Yes."

The nurse reached under the desk and found a short,

wide-lipped bottle. "Make a sample," she said, "and give it to the doctor when he comes in to see you."

Katti took the bottle and walked down the aisle past the crowded benches and went into the booth with the number 5 over the door. She pulled the curtain shut.

Methodically she undressed and prepared herself for the doctor. At last everything was ready and she took the cotton sheet from the hook and draped it around her. She sat down on the little stool in the corner and waited for him to arrive.

A few minutes later there was a light tap on the outside of the booth and a student nurse came in. She was carrying a pad. "Mrs. Peter Ritchik?"

Katti nodded.

Then followed the list of questions without which the clinic couldn't operate. It took the nurse only about five minutes because Katti had all the answers ready for her. She remembered the form from the last time she had been here.

The nurse tore the top sheet from her pad and put it in a clip hung just inside the door. She left the booth and a moment later was back with another sheet of paper, which she affixed to the clip. Then she smiled at Katti. "The doctor will be with you in a minute."

"Thank you," Katti said. She sat down stoically to wait. It generally was at least fifteen minutes before the doctor came.

This time it was closer to a half-hour before the curtain lifted and the doctor came in, followed by his retinue of two interns. He took the chart down from the wall and looked at it briefly, then at her. "Mrs. Ritchik?"

She nodded. "Yes, Doctor."

"I'm Dr. Block," he said. "How long have you been pregnant?"

She shrugged her shoulders. "A month, maybe two."

He repressed an expression of distaste. These people were so careless in their habits. "Get up on the table and we'll see," he said curtly.

Silently she climbed onto the small examination table and put her feet in the stirrups. The small yellow bulb in the ceiling over her head shone into her eyes. She blinked.

His voice seemed to float over her. "Take a deep breath."

She filled her lungs with air and held perfectly still against the searching intrusion of his fingers. His touch was light and efficient and was gone in a moment. She started to sit up, but his hand against her shoulder stopped her. She lay quietly waiting.

He lifted the cotton sheet until it shielded her eyes from the light. His voice came quietly through it. He was talking to the interns.

"Caesarian section on last childbirth. Constricted Fallopian tubes. Will need again."

The sheet dropped and she sat up. She looked at the doctor questioningly.

"Why did you become pregnant, Mrs. Ritchik?" he asked. "According to the chart, you were told to be careful, that you would endanger your life if you had another child."

She shrugged her shoulders. These men never understood. To them everything was simple.

The doctor turned away from her and began to wash his hands in a clean basin of water just left there for him by the student nurse. He spoke to her over his shoulder. The words were routine to him. He knew that they would be ignored.

"Get plenty of sunshine and fresh air and rest. Refrain from cohabitation for at least two months. Eat plenty of nourishing foods, milk, orange juice." He scribbled a prescription and handed it to her. "Take this, and come in next month."

She looked at him. "When will the baby come, Doctor?"

His eyes were bleak. "Your baby won't come," he said cruelly. "We'll have to take it from you."

She kept her face impassive. She had known that before he did. "When, Doctor?" she persisted gently.

"November or December," he answered. "We can't let you carry the full nine months."

"Thank you, Doctor," she said quietly.

The doctor turned and went out, the two interns following him silently. The curtain fell rustling behind them.

Slowly Katti got off the table and reached for her clothes. It wasn't so bad. She would be able to work right up to October. The curtain rustled and she held her dress up in front of her.

It was one of the interns. He smiled at her apologetically. "Excuse me, Mrs. Ritchik," he said, "but I forgot this." He reached up and took the urine sample from the shelf.

"It's okay," she said.

He glanced at her quickly, then smiled again, a shy smile. "Don't worry, Mrs. Ritchik," he said. "Everything will be all right."

She smiled back at him. "Thank you, Doctor."

The curtain fell and he was gone. Quietly she finished dressing and went outside and paid the nurse the fifty-cent clinic fee. Then she went down the hall to the dispensary and gave them the prescription.

While she was waiting for the prescription to be filled, she wondered how she would tell Marja. Marja wouldn't understand. She would only take it as another rebuff and be hurt.

They called her name and she picked up the prescription. Tablets. She had to take them three times a day. She put them in her pocketbook and went out into the street. Down the block she could see the spires of St. Augustine.

She decided to stop there and talk to Father Janowicz. He was a very smart man. He would tell her what to do.

Chapter 9

MARJA sat up in the grass and hugged her knees, looking across the Hudson River. It was dusk, and lights were coming on like fireflies on the Jersey shore. A slight warm breeze rustled her hair. "I gotta get a job for the summer," she said suddenly.

Ross rolled over on his side and looked up at her. "Why?" he asked, smiling.

"We need the dough," she answered simply. "My old man loves the beer too much to go to work. My mother works nights. There ain't enough to go round."

"What can you do?" he asked curiously. "What kind of a job do you want?"

"I dunno," she answered honestly. "I never thought about it before. Maybe clerk in the five-and-ten."

He laughed.

"What's so funny?" she asked.

"You don't get much for that," he said. "Maybe eight bucks a week."

"Eight bucks is eight bucks," she retorted. "It's a lot better'n nothin'."

He looked at her quizzically. His sister often spoke about going to work, but somehow never got around to it. "You mean it?"

She nodded.

He pulled a blade of grass from the ground and chewed it reflectively. In some ways she reminded him of Mike. They were both so serious about money. He had an idea. "Do you dance?" he asked.

She glanced at him curiously. "Sure," she said.

"I mean, good?" he persisted.

She nodded. "Pretty good."

He got to his feet and brushed off his trousers. He reached out a hand toward her and pulled her to her feet. "C'mon," he said, starting toward his car. "We'll see."

The faint discordant bleat of a dance band trickled down the narrow hallway to them. The walls were covered with pictures of girls, all with the same inviting smile on their lips. Under the pictures was a long white painted sign.

COME AND DANCE WITH ME. ONLY 10 CENTS.

The music grew louder as she followed him up the stairway. At the head of the stairs was a small booth. Ross stopped in front of it.

"Two," he said, pushing a dollar bill through the small grill.

Silently the man shoved two tickets at him. Ross picked them up and led her through the door. Another man took the tickets and put them in a chopper.

The ballroom was long and narrow, painted a dingy

blue. The electric lights were dim. The band at the far end had just finished a number. A few couples, left stranded on the floor, started walking toward the sides of the room. Some girls were seated at tables near the door. They had looked up quickly when Ross came in, smiles coming to their lips automatically, and as automatically fading when they saw he wasn't alone.

On their right were a long, narrow bar and several rows of uncovered tables. Ross led her to one and they sat down. A waiter stood over them immediately.

"Beer," Ross said without looking up. He looked at her questioningly.

"Coke," she answered.

The waiter went away and the band began to play again. It was a soft fox trot.

"Ready?" Ross asked.

That strange smile came to her lips. "Always ready," she answered.

"Let's dance," he said.

His face was warm and flushed when he led her back to the table. There was no doubt in his mind about her dancing. She followed him as if she were part of him. Her rhythm was good, and though other girls danced closer and held him tighter, there was none who could make it seem as if the music flowed through them and held them together.

She smiled as he lifted his beer and drank it. "Well?" she asked.

"You can dance," he said grudgingly, lowering his glass. "Where did you learn?"

"I never took a lesson in my life," she said, still smiling.

They were silent a moment. She was waiting for him to speak.

"The girls here make between twenty and fifty bucks a week," he said.

The smile was still on her lips. "Just from dancing?" There was an echo of skepticism in her voice.

He hesitated. "Mostly."

"The dancing averages about twenty," she guessed.

He nodded, watching her carefully.

She lifted her Coke and sipped it. "Yuh don't have to go?" she asked. "Only dance?"

He nodded again without speaking.

"That's a lot of dough," she said.

Suddenly he was disgusted with himself. He threw a bill on the table and rose to his feet. "Come on," he said, "let's go."

She got to her feet silently. A man's voice boomed over her shoulder. "Hey, Ross, long time no see. Where yuh been?"

She turned, startled. A tall man with gray-black hair and dark, shadowed eyes was standing behind her. He was smiling.

The man looked at her and spoke again before Ross had time to answer. "So don't explain," he boomed. "No wonder my girls ain't good enough for yuh."

Marja smiled and looked at Ross. His lips smiled, but his eyes were cold. "Hello, Joker." He hesitated a moment. "Joker Martin, Marja Flood."

"C'mon over the bar," Martin said. "I'll buy yuh a drink."

Ross shook his head. "No, thanks, Joker. We gotta be going."

Martin put his arm on Ross's elbow. "I ain't seen this guy in four months, young lady," he said to Marja in his loud, harsh voice, "an' now he's in a hurry. Tell him it's okay fer us to have a quick one."

Marja smiled. It was flattering to think that this man thought she could tell Ross what to do. It was almost as if he thought she was Ross's girl.

Ross's voice cut into her thoughts. "Okay, Joker. A quick one."

The men had beers and Marja ordered another Coke. Martin turned to Marja. "I oughtta be mad at you, girl," he said. "Ross here was one of our real good customers. Now we never see him, but when I look at you I don't blame him."

"Joker runs this place, Marja," Ross explained. "He's always thinkin' about money."

Marja's eyes looked up at the gray-haired man. "Who isn't?" she asked.

Joker grinned. His hand clapped her shoulder. "Bright girl," he said. "We can't all be rich like our young friend here." For the first time Marja noticed his eyes. They were shrewd and observant. "Lookin' for a job, girl?" he asked.

Before she could answer, Ross spoke up. "No," he said sharply. "She's still in school."

Wisely, Marja kept silent and sipped her Coke. Joker turned back to Ross. "I'm glad yuh dropped in, Ross," he said. "We got some things squared away here."

Ross looked interested. "How come?"

"Made a connection," Joker replied. "Reg'lar thing now. Stud an' dice in the room behind my office. Lots of action."

Ross's voice was guarded, but a yellow light gleamed for a moment in his eyes. "Maybe I'll come by an' take a look some night."

"Do that," Joker boomed. "An' bring the little lady with yuh fer luck." He looked at Marja. "She's always welcome."

"Thank you, Mr. Martin." She smiled up at him.

They finished their drinks and Joker walked them to the door. His voice echoed flatly against the narrow hallway. "Good seein' yuh again, Ross. Don't be a stranger."

The music started again as they walked down the stairs. It followed them out into the street until it was lost in the sounds of traffic.

"Where to now?" Ross asked as he nosed the car out into the street.

"I don't know," she said. "You're drivin'."

He glanced at her quickly out of the corner of his eyes. She was staring straight ahead. He wished he knew what she was thinking.

"How about coming up to my place and getting a bite to eat?" he asked.

"Your folks won't mind?" she asked.

He shook his head. "They went away for the week-end."

"Okay," she said.

"Evening, Mr. Drego," the doorman said.

"Evening, Mr. Drego," the elevator-operator said as he took them up.

They made small talk until the car stopped and they got off. The door closed behind them and Ross fished in his pocket for a key. The apartment door was opposite the elevator.

He held the door for Marja and she stepped into the apartment. He closed the door behind them and reached for a foyer light.

She put out a hand and stopped him. "I been with yuh all afternoon an' yuh haven't kissed me."

He looked down at her in the semi-darkness, trying to read the expression in her face. He didn't speak.

"What're yuh mad about, honey?" she asked. "Did I do somethin' wrong? Say somethin'?"

He shook his head silently. He couldn't tell her that he was angry with himself for having taken her to the Golden Glow Ballroom. She wouldn't stand a chance with a bunch like that. They would make a whore of her in a week. He never should have thought of it, no matter how much she needed the money.

She stood very close to him and brushed her lips against his cheek. "Don't be mad at me, honey," she whispered.

His hand came away from the light switch and caught her shoulder. He leaned back against the door, pulling her toward him. She came willingly, her weight resting against him. He kissed her.

She made sandwiches and a pot of coffee. He carried them into the living-room, and they ate sitting on the couch with the radio going and a small lamp shining from the corner of the room.

When they were finished, she stretched back against the couch cushions and heaved a sigh of contentment. "I was hungry," she said.

He smiled and lit a cigarette.

"Gimme," she said, her hand outstretched.

He handed it to her. She placed it between her lips and took a deep drag, then closed her eyes and let the smoke idle from her lips. "You don't know how lucky you are," she said.

He was surprised. "Why?"

She opened her eyes and looked at him. "You should see my place," she said. "Then you'd know what I mean. Things are so quiet here. No noise comes up from the street—you're too high. No smells from the courtyard. No noise from the neighbors."

He didn't answer, he didn't know what to answer. He picked up the sandwich tray and carried it into the kitchen. When he came back to the living-room she was lying quietly on the couch, her eyes closed again.

"Marja," he whispered.

She didn't answer. Her chest rose and fell with her quiet breathing.

He sat down on the couch beside her. Her eyes flew open. "I was dozing," she said.

"I know." He smiled.

"What time is it?" she asked.

"Almost ten o'clock."

She sat up suddenly. "I better get goin'," she said quickly.

He gripped her shoulders. "Marja," he said, "you know I'm crazy for you."

She met his gaze evenly for a moment, then nodded.

"Do you like me?" he asked.

She got to her feet and looked at him. His face was white and pleading. "You're the sweetest guy I know," she said. "Of course I like you."

He rose angrily. "I don't mean that!" He pulled her toward him violently and kissed her. "I want you," he said harshly. "You know it, you can feel it. Do you want me the same way?"

She stood quietly in his arms for a moment, her eyes looking into his. When she spoke, her voice was gentle. "Even if I do, Ross, there's nothing I can do about it. I'm a girl, an' if I give in, I wind up in trouble. An' that's no good."

"But there are things—"

She interrupted him. "They don't always work." She pressed her cheek to his face and whispered in his ear:

"I'll do anything you want to make you happy, Ross, but I can't do that."

He stared at her. "Anything?"

"Anything," she answered.

He pulled her to him and they sank back on the couch. He closed his eyes. There was the rustle of their clothing in his ears, then her breast, warm and strong, was in his hand. The pain inside him was intense and agonizing. He pressed her head against his chest. "Help me, Marja," he cried. "Please help me."

He looked down at her. Her white-blond hair shimmered against him. Her whisper came softly to his ears. "I'll help you, Ross, baby. Lie still."

Chapter 10

"SNAP into it, Mike! The *Timeses* are comin' up!" Riordan's voice was harsh from years of hawking papers.

Mike jumped off the small bench and moved toward the sidewalk. The *Times* truck was just pulling to the curb. Automatically Mike looked at the clock in the store window opposite. Ten thirty. Just time enough to get the papers made up for the crowd that would spill out of the 86th Street Theatre a little after eleven.

The helper clambered over a pile of papers. " 's a bitch tonight. Twelve sections," he grumbled.

Mike didn't answer. He didn't care. Each week the papers grew larger. He hefted a bundle to his shoulder, carried it behind the stand, and dropped it. It thudded dully on the sidewalk. He went back to the truck.

By the time he came back with the second bundle, Riordan's wife, a thin, scrawny woman, was already cutting the baling-wire around the first bundle with a pair of pliers. "Yuh better hurry, Mike," she said nervously, looking around the newsstand at her husband. "We ain't got much time."

The sweat was starting to come through his shirt, so he took it off and hung it on a nail. The muscles in his frame glistened damply in the yellow electric light. The sections were spread out now. Rapidly he began to flip them together and stack them in a neat pile.

Other newspapers began to come up, and the night began to race by. It was after one o'clock before he was able to grab a few minutes' rest. He clambered up onto a bale of papers and lit a cigarette. He closed his eyes gratefully. He was tired.

He had worked the elevator in the house all afternoon. The day man had been sick, and chances were that he would have to do the same thing tomorrow. He hoped the night would be over quickly.

"Hey, Mike."

He opened his eyes. Ross was standing in front of him, smiling. He grinned slowly. "I thought you went outta town with your folks," he said.

Ross shook his head. "Uh-uh. I had things to do."

"Like what?" Mike asked skeptically.

Ross gestured at his car. "Like that little blonde there."

Mike peered at the car, but the girl's face was in the shadows and he couldn't see her. He looked back at Ross. "I mighta known it was some twist."

Ross's face flushed. "That's no way to talk, Mike," he chided gently. "You don't even know the kid."

Mike looked at him in some surprise. Ross must be hit hard. He had never known him to act like this. He tried again to see the girl, but the light was too dim.

Ross spoke again. "Come over to the car. I'll introduce you."

A curious perverseness came into Mike. He shook his head. "What for?" he asked in an unnecessarily loud voice. "A broad is a broad. Seen one an' you seen 'em all." He flipped his cigarette butt toward the curb. It spattered sparks in front of the car. He climbed off the bale. "Want your papers, Ross?" he asked.

Ross nodded, not speaking.

Mike bent and pulled out a group of them. He held them toward Ross. Ross dropped a few coins into his hand and took the papers.

Riordan's voice came around the newsstand. "Bring up some *Americans*, Mike. We're runnin' short."

Automatically Mike bent to pick up a stack of papers. When he straightened up, Ross was halfway back to his car. He looked after him. Some guys had it soft. They had nothing to worry about. He hefted the papers to his shoulder and started around the stand.

Ross climbed into the car and leaned forward to touch the starter button. The motor whirred and caught, and he turned out into the street.

"Your friend don't like me," Marja's voice said.

He looked at her. "How could that be?" he asked defensively. "He doesn't even know you."

"I heard what he said," she replied.

"He's just tired," Ross explained. "Usually he's not like that."

They rode a block silently. Then Marja spoke again. "Is that Mike? The one who wouldn't come out to the island with us?"

"Yeah," he answered.

She thought about the way Mike had stood there in back of the stand. The sweat had formed an oily sheen on his arms, and the muscles were like wire cords in his back and arms. "Thinks he's pretty great, doesn't he?" she asked sarcastically. "Too good for the rest of us?"

Wisely, Ross didn't answer. He knew better than to get into a foolish argument. Besides, he didn't care what they thought of each other.

Her voice was speculative. "Maybe someday I'll show him a little bit."

He glanced at her in surprise. There was a hurt expression in her eyes. Suddenly he understood. She was still brooding over what Mike had said.

Katti had started for the front pews of the church as usual, but Marja grabbed her arm.

"There's no room down there, Mama," she whispered. "Let's get in here."

Katti turned into the pew that Marja steered her to. She wasn't thinking about anything except what Father Janowicz had said the other day. To tell Marja as soon as she could. That was the only way to stop worrying about it.

There was a young man in the pew. Katti mumbled an apology and she pushed past him. She settled down heavily on the bench and bent her head forward as the Mass began.

She closed her eyes and prayed hard to God to make everything right. For Marja to understand. For Peter to get a job. She prayed for everyone except herself. When the Mass was over, she felt better. She glanced at Marja.

There was a faint flush on the girl's face, a touch of contentment in the echo of a smile in the corners of her mouth. She was glad she had been able to take Marja to Mass with her.

The congregation was filing out, and Katti pushed past

Marja toward the aisle. She glanced at the young man's face as she crossed in front of him. There were beads of sweat on his forehead. It was warm in the church today.

Marja was a few steps behind her, and she turned, waiting for her to catch up. Marja's eyes were laughing as she took her mother's arm.

For a long moment Katti looked at her daughter. It had been long since she had seen Marja look so happy. She was beautiful when she smiled. Katti decided not to say anything about the baby until the evening.

She didn't want to do anything to take the smile of happiness from Marja's face.

Chapter 11

HE PUT the lock on the elevator door and sat down on the small bench in the hall. He picked up his math book and turned to his place. He wasn't as tired this afternoon as he had expected. He had slept from ten o'clock, when he had come home from church, until almost four, when his mother had awakened him.

He turned the page slowly. He didn't mind Sunday afternoons on the elevator. The house was fairly quiet and he could catch up on his studies.

He heard footsteps come down the hall and go past him into the elevator. He didn't look up. He wanted to finish the last part of his problem.

A soft voice came out of the elevator. It was vaguely familiar. "Today, Mike?"

He dropped the book, startled.

She was standing in the elevator, smiling at him. Her white-blond hair was almost gold in the light. "Any time you're ready," she said.

He got to his feet clumsily, aware of a sudden jumping inside him. He stepped into the elevator and sprang the lock. The door began to close. He looked at her. "How do you know my name?" he asked.

She didn't answer. Her eyes looked right into him. Her lips were parted in a kind of smile, showing even white teeth.

Unable to meet the challenge in her glance, he turned away from her. He could feel the flush creeping red into his cheeks. "Floor, please?" he asked sullenly, pressing down the lever and starting the car.

"Twelve," she answered.

Then he understood. He turned to look at her. "You're Ross's girl." It was more a statement than a question.

Her face was expressionless, she didn't speak.

He stopped the car between floors and turned away from the board. "You are Ross's girl?" he repeated.

"Am I?" she asked challengingly. "You ought to know. You're an expert on broads. Seen one an' you seen 'em all."

His face flushed. She had heard him the other night. No wonder she had acted the way she had. It was her only way to get even. He looked down at the floor. "I'm sorry," he said.

She didn't answer.

He looked up at her. "I said, I'm sorry."

Her gaze was still cold and level. "I heard you."

He began to feel angry. "You might at least say something."

She smiled. "Hooray." Her eyes stared into his. "What're you lookin' for—applause?"

He leaned against the wall of the car. He knew how to treat dames like this. He surveyed her carefully from head to toe. This always made them uncomfortable. No babe liked to be stared at as he was doing.

She didn't speak, and when his eyes came back to her face he saw no trace of embarrassment.

"Ross was right," he said cuttingly. "You're built for it."

There was confidence in her eyes. "Thanks," she said dryly. "I needed you to tell me. I was beginning to worry."

A smile came to his lips. He was sure of himself now. She was nothing but a cheap little teasing floosie. He reached out his hand and pulled her toward him.

She smiled and came toward him willingly. He looked down into her face. Her eyes were sparkling. He bent to kiss her.

He felt her hand move behind his back, and suddenly the elevator floor dropped out sickeningly from beneath him. For a bewildered second he stood paralyzed. Then with a muttered curse he turned and grabbed the lever.

He snapped into stop-and-lock and hoped that it would take. She had thrown it into fast drop. He heard the power whine, and the car stopped.

He turned back to her. "You crazy bitch!" he snarled. "We could've been killed!"

There was a wild excitement in her face that he had never seen on anyone. There was no trace of fear in her. "Really?" she asked, politely sarcastic. "That would have been too bad."

He turned back to the lever and started the car upward again. "Okay," he said. The car rose slowly. He stopped at Ross's floor and opened the door.

She stepped out of the car. "Thank you, Mike," she said politely, smiling at him.

"You're welcome," he said in an equally formal tone. He kept the door open as she walked down the corridor.

He watched her in the small mirror in the corner of the elevator. She had a good walk, and she knew it.

He saw her stop in front of Ross's door and press the buzzer. The door opened almost immediately. He could see the smile on Ross's face and hear his voice.

"Come in, Marja, I was waitin' for you."

The door closed behind them. He stood there a moment, then closed the elevator door and dropped the car back to the lobby. He put the lock on the door and sat down on the bench, picking up his math book again.

He stared down at the pages with unseeing eyes. She was standing there in front of him. He snapped the book angrily shut. It was no use. He couldn't stop thinking about her.

He could see her walking down the corridor away from him. He could see Ross's smile and hear his greeting. He got to his feet and went back into the elevator.

It wasn't until he stopped the car on Ross's floor that it came to him. For the first time in his life he was jealous over a girl.

A buzz came from inside the elevator. He got to his feet and looked at the board. The red letters blinked at him: 12. He snapped the door shut and pulled the lever.

He waited until she came into the car before he spoke. "Marja, I'm sorry. I had yuh pegged wrong."

She looked at him skeptically.

"I mean it, Marja," he said earnestly. "I didn't mean to act nasty."

The doubt began to fade from her eyes. For the first time he realized how deep and dark her eyes were. "Things ain't easy for me like they are for Ross," he continued. "Ross is bright and fast. I don't get nothin' unless I sweat it out."

She smiled at him. It was a real smile, warm and genuine.

"I wasn't so nice either," she admitted. "We'll call it square."

He stuck out his hand. "Deal?"

She took it, smiling. "Deal."

He looked down at her hand, small in his palm. "Are yuh really Ross's girl?"

"Ross is nice to me," she said. "Real nice. Not like most fellas, if yuh know what I mean."

He nodded. "Ross is a nice guy." He looked up at her face, still holding her hand. "Yuh think, sometime, maybe, we can take in a show?"

She nodded silently, her eyes on his face. Something was happening to her. It came from his hand to her, something that had never happened before. She knew a lot of boys, and they never bothered her like this. She was always sure of how she felt about them. But this was different. It was another kind of feeling. A kind of weakness inside.

He stepped toward her. She raised her mouth to his lips. Even the kiss was different. It was warm and sweet and gentle and hungry and possessive. She closed her eyes. It was floating in warm, lazy water. She could feel a heat running through her. Instinctively she knew what it was. This wasn't the game that it had been with others. This was her very own. The way she felt. The beginning of desire.

She pushed him away. Her face was flushed. "Take me down," she said in a small, embarrassed voice.

"Marja," Mike said huskily.

She didn't look at him. "Take me down, please," she repeated, wondering what could be wrong with her. She felt warm and happy, and yet she felt like crying.

He turned and started the car. They didn't speak again until the car stopped at the lobby. He opened the door and turned to her.

"I'll see yuh again?" he asked.

She looked at him for a moment. "If you want to." Then she turned and fled from the elevator and out of the house.

She climbed the stairs slowly to her landing. She didn't understand herself. Boys were all alike. They were a game she played. Something impersonal, like the jacks she used to tumble on the stoop, or hopscotch. It was fun to her, a curious sense of power, of strength, of superiority. But this had been different. Mike had been different. And she didn't know why.

A retching sound came from the toilet in the hall. She glanced toward the closed door, wondering who was sick now. That was one of the things she resented. You couldn't be sick in private when the toilets were in the hallway.

The toilet door opened and her stepfather came out. He saw her standing at the kitchen door. "Get a glass of water," he called. "Your mother is sick!"

Quickly she filled a tumbler at the sink and ran back into the hallway. The toilet door was open now. She could see her mother leaning weakly against the wall, her stepfather's arm under her shoulders.

He took the glass from her hand and held it to Katti's lips. Katti rinsed her mouth quickly and spat into the bowl, then drank the rest of the water thirstily.

It was not until then that Marja spoke. "What's the matter, Mama?"

Katti shook her head weakly. "It's nothing. I just felt nauseous."

"But—" Marja was bewildered. Her mother was never sick to her stomach. Only the last time—when Peter was born. A sudden fear came into her. She looked at her

mother questioningly. It couldn't be that again. The doctor
had said she shouldn't. "Mama, are you all right?"

Katti nodded her head. She started to speak, but her husband took the words from her mouth.

"Of course she's all right," he said coarsely. "It's nothing to throw up when you're pregnant."

Marja stared at her mother, unbelieving. "No, Mama,
you can't be," she said in a hurt, protesting voice. "The
doctor said it was too dangerous."

Katti tried to smile. "You can't always believe them.
They're always trying to scare you."

Peter threw out his chest boastfully. "It will be another
boy," he said proudly. "I got it all figured out."

Marja stared at him coldly. "You got everything figured
out, haven't you?"

He nodded, grinning. "Yah."

"While you're at it, figure out how we're gonna eat when
Mama has to stop working," she snapped.

He stared at her in bewilderment.

"And figure out who's gonna keep yuh in beer, 'cause it
ain't gonna be me." She turned and ran down the stairs.

"Marja!" Katti called. But it was too late. Marja was
already out of sight. Katti could hear her footsteps on the
flight below.

She looked at her husband for a moment, then turned
and walked back into the apartment. A pain ran through
her for a moment, and she felt weak. She wanted to lie
down for a while. Maybe she would feel better then. Maybe this depression she felt would disappear. Father Janowicz was right.

She should have had the courage to tell Marja herself. It
was her own fault. Maybe then she could have made Marja
understand.

Chapter 12

"JOKER'S running a game in the back room," Ross said.

Mike looked up. That familiar expression was in his friend's eyes—a yellow glow of excitement. "So what?" Mike asked.

"I'd like to get in on it," Ross said.

Mike got to his feet and looked down at Ross. "Yuh know what your old man said. Get into trouble an' he packs you off to the country for the summer."

"I won't get into trouble," Ross insisted. "Just feel like a little charge, that's all."

Mike shrugged his shoulders. "That's what you said the last time. Your father yelled bloody murder when he had to get you out of the can."

"He'll never know," Ross answered, remembering the time he had been grabbed with a gang shooting craps behind a garage. "Joker says he's got protection."

"Go ahead," Mike said, turning away. "It's your funeral."

"I wanted you to come with me," Ross said.

Mike looked at him. "What for? I got no dough."

"I'm takin' Marja with me," Ross answered, "an' I don't want those wolves makin' passes when my back is turned."

Mike was interested. "Then leave her home."

"No. I got a hunch she's lucky for me." Ross smiled apologetically. He had a real gambler's apologia for his superstitions. "I think I can make it real big with her around."

"Nuts," Mike said.

Ross looked at him. "Got something better to do?"

Mike shook his head. He was thinking about Marja. It had been more than a week since he had met her in the elevator. He still hadn't been able to get up the courage to try to see her.

"Come on, then," Ross urged. "Live a little. What're you going to do? Spend the rest of your life with your nose in those books?"

"Okay," Mike said.

Marja was waiting in the car. Her eyes widened in surprise as she saw Mike approaching. Ross reached the car first and opened the door.

"I been waiting a long time to get the two of you together," he said. "Marja, my friend Mike. Mike, this is my girl."

A flush crept into Marja's face. A smile came to her lips as she held out her hand. "I heard a lot about you," she said almost formally.

Mike was a little embarrassed. He played along with her. "Me, too," he mumbled, taking her hand. It was warm and electric in his grip. He dropped it quickly.

"Shove over," Ross said to her as he climbed into the car. "Mike is coming with us."

Neither Marja nor Mike spoke until they reached the dance hall. Ross kept a steady flow of comment. If he noticed that they weren't speaking, he said nothing about it. They got a table near the floor. It was almost nine o'clock and the floor was fairly crowded.

Ross ordered beer for Mike and himself and a Coke for Marja. He looked out over the floor, his eyes sparkling. "I gotta check Joker an' see what time the game starts."

"It'll start soon enough," Mike grunted. He looked at Marja, and a slight sarcasm came into his voice. "Why don't you dance with your girl first?"

Ross shook his head peremptorily. "No," he answered. "You two go ahead. I'll check up on things."

Marja got to her feet and Mike stared at her in surprise. She smiled. "Well?"

He got out of his chair and led her to the floor. The orchestra was playing a fast fox trot. He felt himself tighten as she came into the circle of his arms. He stumbled almost immediately, stepping on her foot.

"Oh, I'm sorry," he muttered, his face turning red.

She smiled up at him. "Relax," she said. "I won't eat you."

They danced for a moment in silence, then she spoke again. "I thought you were going to see me."

"I've been busy," he answered. He took a few steps. "Besides, you're Ross's girl."

"I didn't say that," she said.

"But he did," Mike countered. "And you didn't stop him."

"I can't keep him from talkin'," she answered. "Besides, you never told him you knew me."

"You didn't say anything either." He looked down into her face. "I kind uh got the idea you didn't want to."

The music stopped and she broke away from him. She started from the floor and he followed her back to the table. She stopped in front of Ross. "I want a beer," she said.

Ross didn't look at her. "Sure, baby, sure," he answered. He was watching a small door across the floor.

Mike stood behind her chair and she sat down. He pushed his glass toward her. "Drink this," he said. "I'll get another."

She picked it up and drank some. He looked at her, wondering what he had said that had made her angry. She didn't speak.

"Well?" Mike asked Ross.

"I'm waiting," Ross answered. "The waiter said he'd check an' let me know."

Marja was bewildered. "Let you know what?" she asked. "I thought we came to dance."

Ross looked at her. It was almost as if she were a stranger. He didn't seem to see her at all. "Explain it, Mike," he said, waving his hand.

Mike felt an anger inside him. Same old Ross. Leave the dirty work for others. "Explain it yourself," he said.

Ross looked at them, his eyes suddenly clearing. "What's the matter with you two?" he asked.

They didn't answer.

He looked at Marja. "I came to get into the game that Joker spoke to me about, that's all."

Marja got to her feet. "Then what the hell did you ask me to go dancing for?" she asked. "Why didn't you say so in the first place?" She turned away.

Ross grabbed her arm. "I wanted you with me for luck," he said with a smile. "I got a hunch you're good for me."

She looked down at him. "What about Mike?" she questioned shrewdly. "Yuh bring him along to watch out for me?"

"Sure," Ross said, still smiling. "Think I'm gonna take any chances with all these wolves around? At least Mike's my friend. I know I can depend on him."

Mike looked at her, then across the table at him. A slow smile came over his lips. "I wouldn't be too sure of that, Ross," he said.

Ross's eyes grew cold. "What d'yuh mean?"

Mike didn't take his eyes from Marja's face. "Like yuh said, Ross. She's terrific."

A slow smile came to Marja's face and she sat down. "Okay, boys," she said, laughter deep in her voice, "fight over me."

They all burst into a raucous, happy laugh.

The slight beads of perspiration stood out clearly on Ross's forehead as he reached for the dice. He turned to Marja and held them toward her. "Blow on 'em for luck, baby."

Marja pursed her lips and blew into his cupped palm. "Get hot," she said, looking down at the shrinking pile of money in front of Ross. He hadn't been doing well. She figured he must have lost almost forty dollars.

"Blow harder," he said in a tight, tense voice, pushing his clenched palms closer to her lips.

She took a deep breath and blew into his hands. She could see his fingers working smoothly over the dice. They opened for a second and her breath caught in her throat. She looked into his face, her eyes wide.

For a fraction of a second his eyes were cold, then he smiled. He knew that she had seen. "Thanks, baby," he said, turning back to the table.

She stood very still, her eyes going around the table. It seemed improbable that nobody else had seen. Then she understood. Ross had been clever. The others had been watching her.

Ross's voice was harsh. "C'mon dice, now!" The cubes spun twinkling over the green cloth and bounced off the backboard. They tumbled over and over and came to a stop. A natural. Ross pulled the money toward him and scooped the dice with his other hand. He began to shake the cubes.

He looked down the table. "I'm hot," he chortled. "Get your dough down before the fever goes."

He began to cover the bets as she stepped back from the table toward Mike, who was leaning against the wall, watching them. He smiled as she came up. "You did good that time."

Her face was expressionless. He hadn't seen Ross switch dice either. "I've had enough. I want to go," she said.

His voice was surprised. "But Ross isn't finished yet."

"I don't care," she insisted. "I want to go."

"I'll tell Ross," he said.

Her hand stopped him. "No," she said. "Leave him be." She looked at the table. Ross had just thrown another seven. There was an excited, happy look on his face. "He got what he came here for."

Mike stared into her face. "What's wrong?"

"Nothin'," she repeated. "I just wanna go."

"Okay." He took her arm. "We're goin', Ross," he called.

Ross waved his hand at them. It was doubtful that he

even understood what Mike had said. He was shaking the dice again.

The orchestra was playing as they walked through the dance hall. "Dance?" Mike asked.

She shook her head and kept walking. A man blocked the exit in front of her. "Hello, baby."

Without looking up, she started around him. He stepped in front of her. "Runnin' out on your boy friend?" he asked.

She looked up into Joker Martin's face. Her eyes were cold. "I'm tired an' I'm leavin'," she said.

The smile disappeared from Martin's lips. He looked at Mike. Mike shrugged his shoulders. Martin stepped out of the doorway. She started past him, but he stuck out a hand and stopped her.

She looked at him.

There was a strange glint in his eyes as he looked down at her. "I don't know what's eatin' yuh, kid," he said. "But when yuh get over it, I got a job waitin' here at the Golden Glow for yuh."

For the first time her expression changed. "Thanks, Mr. Martin," she said. "I might come back an' take you up on it." She turned and started down the stairway.

Chapter 13

SHE stopped in front of her home and turned to Mike. "Thanks for bringin' me home," she said.

Mike smiled. "My pleasure."

"I didn't mean to break up your evening," she said.

He didn't answer.

She started up the stoop. His voice stopped her. "When 'm I going to see you again?"

"I don't know," she said, hesitating.

He came up to the step below her. "Why?" he asked. "Because you're Ross's girl?"

Her eyes met his. "I'm not Ross's girl," she said. "I told you that before."

"Then when will I see you?" he repeated.

She shook her head. "I really don't know. School will be over next week an' I gotta get a job. It's hard to say."

A twinge of jealousy irked him. "But you'll make time to see Ross," he said sarcastically. "He's got a buck to spend."

Her temper flared. "I'm not gonna see him either. He

can take his dough an' shove it. An' you can tell him I said so."

He was surprised. It showed in his voice. "Why me? You can tell him yourself."

Her eyes stared coldly down at him. "You know damn well why. You both took me there, you both knew what Ross was goin' to do."

"You knew it, too," he said angrily. "You knew he was going to shoot craps, not play tiddlywinks. So what're yuh sore about?"

"Yeah," she answered sarcastically. "I knew he was goin' to gamble after he told me, but I didn't think he was goin' to switch dice. I don't go for that."

"Switch dice?" he asked, puzzled.

"Yeah," she answered. "When I blew on 'em. He knew they'd be watchin' me. I don't like bein' made the patsy."

He let out a breath. Now he knew why she had suddenly decided to leave. "Yuh may not believe it, but I didn't know about that either."

She stared at him skeptically.

"I don't play like that," he said.

She was still for a moment. "I don't know," she said, hesitating. "I could understand it if you played like that. You could use the dough. But Ross? He don't need nothin'."

He reached for her hand. "I didn't know about it, Marja," he said earnestly.

She looked down at his hand, then up into his face. "Okay," she answered finally. "I'll buy." She pulled her hand from his grasp. "Good night."

"Good night, Marja." He watched her go inside the house before he turned toward home.

He turned between the house into the alleyway that led to his family's apartment in the basement of the large apartment building.

Ross stepped out of the darkness toward him. "Mike," he called.

Mike stopped. "Yeah?"

"Where the hell did you disappear to?" Ross asked. "I won almost a hundred and twenty dollars."

"Marja wanted to go home," Mike answered.

Ross ignored his statement. He took a roll of money from his pocket. "I wanted to give you your cut," he said, peeling off some bills. "Here's twenty."

Mike looked down at Ross's outstretched hand, but made no motion to take the money.

"What's the matter with you?" Ross demanded. "Take it."

Mike looked at him. "No, thanks. I want no part of it. It's all yours."

Ross peered into his face. "Don't be a jerk. Take the dough. Is it poison or something?"

"Keep it, Ross," Mike said. "It's all yours. You earned it."

A sudden light came into Ross's eyes. "Oh! Marja's been talkin'."

Mike didn't answer.

Ross grinned suddenly. "It was easy. Like takin' candy from a baby. They were so busy watching Marja when she bent forward that it was a cinch."

Mike still didn't speak.

Ross clapped him on the shoulder. "Here, boy," he said patronizingly, "take the money. It'll all look better in the morning."

"I don't want it!" Mike's hand made a flashing motion,

and the money fluttered out of Ross's grip.

Ross stared at him. "What's got into you?"

"Nothin'," Mike answered angrily. "I just don't like it, that's all. You played the kid for a sucker. If you got caught, we'd all have to pay off. Her, too. That wouldn't uh been so pretty, would it?"

"But we didn't get caught," Ross protested. "So why the beef?"

Mike didn't answer.

Ross knelt to pick up the money. "I don't know what the hell got into you," he muttered. He looked up at Mike, his eyes suddenly growing suspicious. "Where did you take her?" he asked, clambering back to his feet.

"Home, I tol' yuh," Mike answered.

"You took long enough," Ross said. "I've been waitin' here over an hour for you."

"We walked," Mike said succinctly. "My old man never gave me a Buick."

"You didn't stop off in the park for a little?" Ross asked. "Maybe you stopped in some dark corner an' she gave you a hand job. The little whore likes that."

Mike could feel the pulse in his temples explode. His arm flashed up and pinned Ross against the brick wall. "Don't talk like that about her," he snarled.

There was a wild excitement in Ross's eyes. "I was right," he said triumphantly. "She did get to you." A grin came to his lips. "She's the greatest action there is, boy, but don't let it fool you. It's there for everybody."

Mike's hand was a blur in the night. Ross's head snapped back and he slowly slid toward the ground, blood coming from a corner of his mouth. Mike stepped back and looked down at him. "Next time you'll keep your mouth shut," he said.

Ross sat dully on the ground for a moment. Then he raised his hand slowly and held it to his mouth. The blood seeped into his fingers. He looked up at Mike, his eyes growing cold behind their mask of pain.

"I'll pay you back for this, Mike," he mumbled through aching lips. "Pay you back double."

"Try it any time you want," Mike taunted.

Ross still sat on the ground, looking up. "The time will come," he said slowly. "Don't worry."

"I ain't worryin'," Mike said. He went on down the alley toward his apartment.

Chapter 14

ROSS bought a fistful of tickets at the door. He stopped a moment as he entered the dance hall to let his eyes get used to the light. He looked around.

She was there. Sitting with the girls in the corner. Even in one of the cheap gowns that Martin supplied to his girls, there was something about her that made her stand out from the others. There was an excitement about her. A man-and-woman kind of excitement that few women ever had.

He walked down the steps and stopped in front of her. "Hello, Marja," he said.

She looked up at him. "Hello, Ross." Her eyes were masked. He couldn't read any expression in them.

"Want to dance?" he asked awkwardly.

"Got tickets?" she replied.

He held out his hand silently.

She got to her feet. "We'll dance," she said, leading him to the floor.

She slipped into his arms, but it was as if he were holding a total stranger. Automatically they picked up the rhythm of the orchestra.

"It's been two weeks since school closed, Marja," he said. "Three weeks since I saw you."

"Time flies, doesn't it?" she said without smiling.

"You've been ducking me," he accused.

"I've been busy," she said politely. "I gotta work for a living."

"You haven't given me a chance to explain," he said.

"You don't owe me no explanation," she retorted swiftly. "You're a big boy. You run your own life."

"Then why don't you want to see me?" he asked.

She looked up into his eyes. There was something about him that reminded her of an animal. Wild and uncontrollable. Completely selfish. "I don't like bein' used," she said.

The music stopped and she started for the tables. His hand stopped her. There was another ticket in it. She took the ticket and stood waiting until the music started again before she came back into his arms.

"I thought you liked me, Marja," he said.

"I did," she answered. "But you didn't level with me."

"I'm sorry." He smiled. "But everything worked out. Nobody got hurt."

A sad look came into her eyes. "I did," she said. "I thought you were goin' to be different."

"But it was for laughs, Marja," he said, trying to pull her closer to him. He could feel the warmth of her through his jacket. All the excitement was still there. "A guy's gotta get some kicks."

She shook her head. "It wasn't like you needed the dough. I could understand that."

"Marja," he said. They were standing in a dark corner now. He tried to kiss her.

She turned her face. "Cut it, Ross," she said sharply. "I need the job here."

"But, Marja," he pleaded. "I'm goin' away the day after tomorrow and I won't be back for five months. I gotta see you before I go."

She shook her head. "Can't."

"Why?" he demanded.

The music stopped again, and she slipped out of his arms and turned toward the tables. His arm spun her back to him violently.

"Here," he said savagely. "Here's all the damn tickets. Don't be runnin' off every time the music stops."

Silently she took the rack of tickets and stuffed them into a small purse. The music started and she came back into his arms.

"Why can't you see me?" he asked.

She met his eyes. "Yuh really want to know?"

He nodded. "Tell me."

She took a deep breath. "One, I don't want to," she said. "Two, I haven't the time. My mother's sick in bed. She lost her job an' I gotta take care of her an' my baby brother during the day. That enough reasons?"

"No," he said roughly. He backed her into the dark corner again and tried to kiss her. She turned her face. He couldn't see her signaling with her purse. In a moment a rough hand spun him around.

The big apelike bouncer was behind him. Joker Martin was standing next to him, smiling. "Listen, bud," the bouncer said, "you behave yourself or you'll get t'run outta here."

Ross could feel the color leaving his face. He glanced

at Marja. Her face was expressionless. He took a deep breath. "Okay, Marja," he said. "If that's the way you want it." He turned and walked off the floor.

Joker Martin fell into step with her as she started back to the tables. "Your friend seemed pretty mad," he said.

"He's no friend," she said.

He assumed a surprised expression. "But you were so chummy the last time you were here."

"Yeah," she said flatly. "It was different then. But I didn't like somethin' he did."

Martin looked down at her. "What'd he do?"

She shrugged her shoulders noncommittally. "I just didn't like it, that's all."

"Was it somethin' like switchin' dice?" Martin asked in a conversational voice.

The surprise was written on her face.

He smiled. "Yuh think we're stupid, kid? We're pro's. We spotted that right off." He lit a cigarette. "I figured that was why you blew so quick. Did yuh know what he was gonna do?"

"No," she said.

"I figured that, too," he said.

"If you knew, why didn't you do somethin'?" she asked.

He smiled gently. "His old man's gotta lot of pull. Some-day he'll come back an' we'll take the dough back with interest. Until then we can wait. We're patient. They always come back."

She hung the evening dress carefully in her locker. After a quick check of her face in the mirror, she darted out the door. It was a few minutes after twelve. The job wasn't so bad during the week—she was on her feet for only six hours. But Fridays and Saturdays were tough. On those days she worked from five o'clock in the evening until two in the morning.

She stepped out into the noisy street and saw him lounging against a car, waiting for her. He had been there every night since she had begun working.

A smile came to her lips. "Hello, Mike."

He grinned at her. "Hi, baby."

They fell in step. "You don't have to wait for me every night, Mike," she said. "I can get home okay."

"I want to," he said.

"But you must be dead. You work that newsstand for twelve hours a day."

He grinned, "Don't take all the fun outta life, baby," he said gently. "How about some coffee?"

She nodded. "Okay, but it's my turn to buy, don't forget."

"Why d'yuh think I asked yuh?" he laughed.

They turned into a drugstore and climbed onto two counter stools. "Two java," Mike ordered. He looked at her. "Split a jelly doughnut with me?"

She nodded.

He called the order to the counter man and turned back to her. "How's your mother feeling?" he asked.

"Better today, thanks," she said. "The bleeding stopped, and the doctor says if it stays like that she can get out of bed tomorrow."

"Good," he said.

She was quiet for a moment while she thought about her mother. Katti had been in bed almost a week. Had come home early from work when she began to bleed. At first the doctor thought it was a miss, but everything had turned out all right. She couldn't go back to work, though. Those heavy pails and mops were too much for her.

Marja remembered how upset her mother had been when she told her about the job. But the twenty a week had been a life-saver. Without it they all would have starved. Peter was no good for anything.

The counter man put the coffee and a jelly doughnut down in front of her. Quickly she divided it and gave Mike the larger piece.

"How'd it go today?" Mike asked.

"Okay." She smiled. "I was pretty busy."

He grinned. "Good dancer, huh?"

She grinned back. "The best." The smile vanished suddenly. "Ross came in to see me tonight."

Mike stared into his coffee. "What'd he want?"

"He said he was going away for a while. He wanted me to go out with him."

Mike still didn't look at her. "What'd you say?"

"I told him no dice. He got fresh and Mr. Martin came over, so he walked out."

Mike was silent for a moment. "His father's sending him to Europe."

She drew in her breath. "Man," she whispered, "it must be great to have dough like that."

Mike looked down into his coffee again. "You still like him, don't yuh?"

She looked over at Mike. "I don't really know," she said honestly. "He's different than all the other boys I know. He speaks different. He acts different."

"He's got money," Mike said bitterly.

"That's not it," she said quickly.

"What is it, then?" Mike asked.

She looked at him. He could see she was thinking carefully. "It's the way he is. He acts all the time like I want to some of the time. Like he's on top of the world and everybody is gonna play up to him. It must be good to be the guy on top."

She put her hand on his arm. "Y'know," she said, lowering her voice to a confidential whisper, "Mr. Martin knew he switched dice on them that time."

Mike was surprised. "Then why didn't he stop him?"

"On accounta Ross's father," she said. "Mr. Martin said the old man's got a lot of pull." Her voice sounded impressed.

He looked at her. "Is that what you like?"

She put a cigarette in her mouth and lit it. She dragged deeply on it. "Maybe," she answered. "I would like a little of the de luxe. Who wouldn't? It's a hell of a lot better'n livin' the way I am now."

Chapter 15

KATTI put down her sewing and looked at the clock. It was nearly eleven. She got out of her chair and went to the window. The August night was heavy and humid. Wearily she wiped the perspiration from her face with a towel that hung around her neck.

There was a sharp twinge of pain in her back, and she swayed dizzily. She reached quickly for a table and held on to it until the dizziness passed. The doctor had warned her about such spells. He had told her to spend most of her time in bed, to do no work. There was something about her pregnancy that placed too great a strain on her heart.

The dizzy spell passed and she went back into the kitchen and put away her sewing. She would lie down for a while and try to rest.

The house was very still, and in the dark of her room she found herself listening for every sound. Often she could not go to sleep until Marja came home, but tonight was even worse than usual. Peter had gone out after supper and had not as yet returned. She knew what that meant.

He would be nasty and irritated and drunk with beer when he came in. She would have to keep him away from Marja or there would be an argument.

After a few minutes she began to feel better, but still she could not sleep. It was too hot in the room, and her bed was warm with the heat of her body. She got out of her bed and went into Marja's room. In the crib, the baby was sleeping restlessly, his tiny body pink with a faint summer rash. As she looked at him, he suddenly awoke and began to cry.

She picked him up and whispered soothingly, but he continued to cry. She carried him into the kitchen and gave him a bottle of cool water. He sucked at it happily and she placed him back in his crib.

There was a sound at the kitchen door and she turned toward it. It must be Peter, it was too early for Marja to come home. One look at his flushed face and she knew where he had been.

He closed the door and looked at her. His eyes were bloodshot and puffed. "Still up?" he asked.

"You see," she said, walking past him toward the bedroom. "Come to bed."

"It's too hot," he said. He crossed the room to the icebox and opened it. "I want a beer."

"Haven't you had enough?" she asked expressionlessly.

He didn't answer as he punctured a can and held it to his lips. Some of it trickled down his chin and slopped onto his shirt. He put the can down and stared at her. "Mind your own business," he snarled.

She stared back at him for a moment, then turned and went into the parlor. She leaned out the window and looked up the street anxiously. It was almost time for Marja to be home.

"What are you doing?" he asked pugnaciously.

She didn't answer. He knew what she was doing. She began to walk past him.

His hand on her arm stopped her. "Looking for your daughter?" he asked nastily.

"Yes," she answered, lapsing into Polish. "Is there anything wrong in it?"

He answered in the same language. "You don't have to worry about her. She's probably making a few extra bucks in some hallway on the way home with that fellow who walks her home every night."

"Go to bed," she said coldly. "You're drunk."

His grip tightened on her arm. "You think I don't know what I'm saying?" he asked shrewdly.

"I know you don't," she said, pulling her arm from his grip and turning back to the window. She looked out. Marja and Mike were walking down the block toward the house.

A moment's pleasure ran through her. This Mike was such a nice boy. They looked so good walking together. Maybe someday—but that was too far off. Sometimes she had to force herself to realize that Marja was still a child. This wasn't the Old Country. She turned away from the window, the trace of her pleasure still in the corners of her mouth.

"I'm going to bed," she said. "You'd better come, too."

He didn't move. "No. It's too hot. I'm going to have another beer."

She went into the bedroom and began to undress. She could hear him stumbling in the kitchen—the icebox door and the sharp sound when the beer can was opened. She threw a light kimona over her nightgown and went into the kitchen to wash.

He was sitting at the table, the half-empty can in his hand, staring at the door.

"What are you waiting for?" she asked. "Come to bed."

He shook his head stubbornly. "I'll show you who knows what they're talking about. Wait'll she comes in."

She tried to smile. "Don't be a fool, Peter," she said. "Leave the girl alone and come to bed."

"A whore she is," he muttered.

Her stinging slap left a white imprint on his face. He stared up at her in surprise.

Katti's face was white with anger. He had never seen her like this. "Shut up!" she said angrily. "The girl has more brains than you. If it weren't for her, we'd be starving!" She walked toward the bedroom. At the hallway she turned and looked back at him. "You forget it was Marja who got a job when we needed money, not you." Her voice was contemptuous. "She's like her father. You're not half the man he was. I only hope your children are like him, not like you. Else, God help them!"

He got to his feet quickly and moved toward the kitchen door. "I'll show you who's a man!" he shouted, opening it. "No girl in my house is going to be a whore!"

She caught his arm and tried to pull him back into the apartment. "Leave her alone, you drunken bum!" she shouted. "She's *my* daughter, not yours!"

He pushed her away roughly and she stumbled back against the kitchen table. A wave of pain ran through her body. She looked at him, her eyes blurring.

He was pulling his belt from around his waist. He shook it at her. "Hold your tongue, woman!" he said hoarsely. "Or you'll get more of this than she will. When I get through with her, you'll see what she is." He went out into the hall.

Katti took a deep breath and ran after him. The man was crazy. Marja had been right all the time. If only she had listened to her! A wave of dizziness grabbed at her temples, but she fought it off. He was at the stairway now. She grabbed both his arms.

"Leave her alone!" she whispered, trying to hold him back. With an almost superhuman strength she forced him around. Her eyes stared wildly into his. "If you touch her, you'll never come into this house again!"

The words spilled into his brain like a spray of cold water. A sudden sanity returned to his eyes. He shook her hands violently from his arms. She grabbed at the banister to hold herself erect.

He walked past her to the kitchen door, where he turned and looked back at her. "It's your daughter," he said coldly. "May her sins be on your own head!"

The dizziness reached up to her temples, and his face blurred before her. She let go of the railing and took a hesitant step toward the apartment, but the pain in her temples spread a mantle of darkness over her mind.

"Marja!" she screamed into the suddenly aching void. Then time came rushing up to meet her in the shape of a flight of stairs.

They heard the sound, and almost before Mike could move, Marja was halfway up the first flight of steps. He ran after her, his heart pounding in fright at the piercing scream. He got to the third landing a step behind her.

"Mama!" Marja's voice in his ears was like a frightened child's. He saw her sink to her knees beside the crumpled woman. He stood there dumbly.

"Mama!" Marja's voice was the sound of tears in the

cradle. Her blond hair shimmered as she pressed her lips
to the still face.

"Katti!"

Mike looked up. The man's face was ashen as he stood
on the stairway above their heads and stared at them.
"Marja, what happened?"

Marja shook her head dumbly. She turned and looked at
Mike. Her eyes were hurt beyond understanding and dull
with shock.

He reached down and touched her shoulder. He could
feel the trembling in her body. "Is there a phone somewhere
in the house?" he asked.

She didn't answer. Somehow he knew she hadn't heard
him. He looked up the steps. The man was coming down
slowly, both hands gripping the railing tightly as if he was
afraid he might fall.

A door beside him opened and a man's face looked out.
"There's been an accident," Mike said quickly. "Have you
a phone I could use?"

The man nodded and came out into the hall. Behind
him Mike could see a woman clutching a wrapper around
her.

Mike stepped into the apartment. The woman pointed
silently to the telephone. Mike picked it up and was about
to speak when the faint whispering sound came to his ears.

It was the only time in his life he was ever to hear Marja
cry.

Chapter 16

IT WAS a week before Marja went back to work at the Golden Glow. Her face was thin and there were deep hollows under her eyes. First had come Katti's funeral.

The Mass at St. Augustine's had been simple. Father Janowicz had been kind and thoughtful. He spoke graciously of her mother's great courage and devotion to Catholic principles, and prayed fervently that her children would guide themselves by her example.

She sat beside Peter in silence as the lone car followed the hearse to the cemetery. The burial was done quickly and inexpensively, and they returned home.

Welfare was waiting for them. Francie's mother, who had been minding the baby while they were out, went upstairs and left them. The young man and older woman who represented Welfare were concerned with their ability to take proper care of the child.

Marja persuaded them that all would be well. She was home during the day and Peter would be home in the eve-

ning while she was at work. They agreed to let things
stand as they were until fall, when Marja would have to return to school.

She stood in the entrance of the dance hall for a moment. It seemed strange to her that while so much had
changed, the dance hall was still the same. The cheap,
tinselly decorations, the dim blue lights, the tired music
with its false rhythms—everything was the same.

The bouncer came toward her. His apelike, dull face was
without expression. "Mr. Martin wants to see yuh," he
said, jerking his thumb in the direction of the office.

Without answering him, she cut across the dance floor.
She knocked at the door.

Martin's voice came through it. "Come in."

She opened the door. He was seated at his desk, some
papers spread out before him. She hesitated until he looked
up. Then she came into the room, closed the door behind
her, and stood in front of his desk.

"You wanted to see me?" she asked in a dull voice.

He nodded. "Sit down. I'll be with yuh soon's I finish
this."

She slipped into a chair beside the desk and watched
him. His face was harsh and lined, and his gray-black hair
gave his blue eyes an even colder look. His chin was firm
and square, but his lips, though thin, had an almost strange
gentility about them.

At last he looked up. "I'm sorry about your mother,
Marja," he said gently.

She looked down at her hands. "Thanks," she said, her
throat tight and constricted. It was still difficult for her to
talk about it.

He was silent for a moment. "An investigator was here

from the Welfare Department. They were checking up on your job."

Her face held a sudden fear. She looked at him questioningly.

He smiled reassuringly. "Don't be frightened. I told him you were a cashier."

She looked down at her hands again. Her voice was perilously close to breaking. "I don't know how to thank you, Mr. Martin."

He looked down at the papers on his desk. "Why didn't you tell me how old you are, Marja?" he asked suddenly.

"Would you have given me a job if I had?" she countered.

He hesitated. "I guess not."

"That's why," she answered. "Besides, you never asked me."

His eyes searched her face. "I never thought about it. You look old enough."

A faint smile came to her lips. "I am old enough."

He got to his feet and came around the desk to her. His hand reached out and touched her shoulder. He nodded thoughtfully. He remembered his own youth. He had come from a neighborhood very much like Marja's. "I guess you are," he said.

She looked up at him questioningly. "It's okay if I go back to work, then, Mr. Martin?"

"Yes," he answered. "But keep your eyes open. If there's any trouble or anything, get out in a hurry. We can't have you caught here or our license is gone."

"I'll be careful, Mr. Martin," she said, getting to her feet. "I promise."

He opened the door for her and she stood there a moment, a grateful smile on her lips. "Thanks very much,

Mr. Martin," she said in a low, husky voice. "I won't forget how nice you've been."

He stood in the doorway watching her make her way to the dressing-room. He shook his head wonderingly. Even now that he knew, it was still hard to believe. Not even sixteen. Still, some of these Polacks came to it early. He grinned to himself as he closed the door and walked back to his desk.

The calendar would never mean very much to her. She had now all the wisdom she would ever need. She had man sense. It was the sixth sense that most women spent all their lives without ever finding.

She opened the door and stepped into the kitchen. Her stepfather was reading a paper spread on the table. He looked up at her.

"How is the baby?" she asked.

"Okay," he answered stiffly. "He was sleeping quiet all night."

She went into her room and glanced into the crib. Peter was sleeping peacefully, his thumb stuck into the corner of his mouth. Gently she removed it. Suddenly she was aware of her stepfather's gaze. She turned swiftly.

He was standing in the doorway of her room, watching her. His face flushed suddenly.

"What do you want?" she asked.

He cleared his throat. "Nothin'," he answered. He went back into the kitchen.

She slipped out of her dress and slip. Throwing on a robe, she went into the kitchen and turned on the water in the sink.

Peter looked up at her from his chair. "That feller Mike," he asked cautiously. "He come home with you?"

"Yeah," she answered, scrubbing her face vigorously with soap and water.

"He like you, eh?"

"I suppose so," she replied, still busy with her face.

"You spend lots of time with him downstairs?" A leering sound had crept into his voice. "Before you come up?"

She turned on him coldly. "What are you trying to find out?"

He couldn't meet her gaze. He looked down at the table. "Nothing."

"Then mind your own business," she said, crossing the room and going out into the hall.

He was waiting at the door when she came back into the kitchen. His hand caught her arm. She stared up into his face, her eyes narrowing slightly. She didn't speak.

"You're very pretty girl, Marja." His voice had a pleading sound in it.

She still didn't speak.

"Sometime, maybe, you be nice to me like you are to him," he said awkwardly. "Then everybody happy, eh?"

She shook his hand from her arm. She was too weary to be very angry. Her voice was dull and flat. "Peter," she said—it was the first time she had ever called him by his given name without the prefix "Uncle"—"don't be a jerk. I'm stayin' here because that's the way Mama would have wanted it. But that's all. No more."

He followed her to the bedroom door. He sucked in his breath and dared another question. "But, Marja, you know how I always feel about you?"

"I know," she said coldly. "But you're not my type. If you need a woman that bad, go out and get yourself one."

She slammed the door swiftly in his face and turned the

key loudly so he could hear it. She waited there a moment until she could hear his footsteps walking away. Then she quickly finished undressing and climbed into her bed.

She stretched her arms behind her head and let the faint breeze from the window drift over her body. There was a dull, lonely ache inside her. She closed her eyes, and her mother's face jumped before her in the darkness.

"Be a good girl, Marja," Katti seemed to be saying.

"I will, Mama," she promised in a half-whisper, turning on her side. She heard the faint click of the icebox door as she drifted off to sleep.

Chapter 17

JOKER MARTIN looked up at her. She was standing in front of his desk. "I got it fixed," he said. "Welfare agreed it was okay for you to take an afternoon session at school and continue workin' here."

Her hands made a simple expressive gesture. "I don't know how to thank you," she said. "It seems like you're always doin' somethin' nice for me."

He smiled, embarrassed. "Maybe it's because I like yuh."

She didn't speak.

"You're steady, Marja," he said. "You show up every night, yuh never give me no trouble like the other girls. Maybe that's why."

"I still don't know how I can ever pay you back," she said.

He started to speak, but the telephone on his desk began to ring. He picked it up. "Martin speaking."

The voice spoke for a few seconds and Joker looked up

at her. She turned and started to leave, but a gesture of his hand bade her stay. "Hold on a minute," he said into the phone.

He covered the mouthpiece with his hand while he spoke to her. "Here is a way you can pay me back," he said. "I got a very important guy on the phone. He's short a dame on a party tonight. There's five bucks in it for yuh if yuh want to go."

She hesitated. "I—I don't think so, Mr. Martin. I'd be outta place there."

He knew what she meant. "Go on," he said. "This guy's okay. There won't be no rough stuff. All yuh gotta do is dance a little with 'em an' have a few laughs. Yuh'll be outta there by three thirty."

She still hesitated. "You sure?"

He nodded. "Sure."

"But I haven't got the kind of clothes to wear." She shook her head. "I'd better not."

"You can take your gown," he said. "You can bring it back tomorrow night. Besides, you'll be doin' me a big favor."

She drew in her breath. She didn't see how she could refuse to go. He had been so good to her. "Okay."

He smiled. "Good girl." He waved his hand at her. "Go get your bag an' come back here. I'll give you the address."

He waited until the door had closed behind her before he spoke into the phone again. Then he spoke quickly, cautiously. "I'm sendin' over a green kid, Jack, so take it easy. I don't want her scared off."

He was silent while the voice on the other end of the telephone crackled in his ear. The sound stopped and he spoke again, a laughing sound in his voice. "Look, it's the most gorgeous thing you ever saw. But don't let that fool yuh. It's under age, and trouble if anything goes wrong. Play it straight an' give it a little time. It'll come around." He put the telephone down as she came back into the office.

She got out of the cab in front of the large apartment building. The doorman held the door for her while she paid the driver and got out of the cab. "Mr. Ostere's apartment."

There was a knowing look in his eyes. "Penthouse D, seventeenth floor."

The elevator-operator had the same look in his eyes as he took her up. "To your left," he said, holding the door for her.

She heard the elevator door close behind her as she pressed the buzzer. The door opened. A man in full evening dress looked out at her.

"Mr. Ostere?" she asked. "I'm Marja Flood."

The man's face was cold. "Come in," he said formally. "I'll tell Mr. Ostere you're here."

She waited in the foyer. The man disappeared and returned in a moment, followed by a shorter man. This man wore a dark business suit.

He came up to her, his hand outstretched. "I'm Jack Ostere," he said, smiling.

"Marja Flood," she answered, taking his hand.

He stepped back and looked at her. "My God!" he exclaimed dramatically. "Joker was right for once in his life. You are beautiful."

A pleased smile crossed her lips. "Thank you, Mr. Ostere," she said.

"Make it Jack," he answered quickly. "Come inside and let me fix you a drink before the others get here."

He took her arm and steered her into the largest living-room she had ever seen.

He paused before a small portable bar on wheels. "What will it be? Manhattan? Martini?"

"Coke?" she questioned hesitantly.

He wrinkled his brow quizzically, then smiled. "As you wish." He turned and pulled a cord near the wall.

The butler appeared almost immediately. "Yes, sir?"

"Jordan, a Coke for Miss Flood," Ostere said.

The butler's face was impassive. "Yes, sir," he said, turning away.

"With lots of ice," Marja said.

The butler looked at her. "With lots of ice, ma'am." He left the room.

Marja turned to her host. "I hope I wasn't too early. Joker told me to come right over."

Ostere had poured some whisky over ice. He held the glass toward her. "No one as pretty as you could ever be too early, Marja."

A chime sounded in the apartment. "Please excuse me," Ostere apologized. "Some of my guests are arriving and I must greet them."

The butler brought Marja her Coke, and she looked around the room quickly. It must have been forty feet long, and at one end were high French windows that opened onto a terrace.

Her host came bustling back into the room with the new arrivals. Marja's eyes widened.

One of the girls was a movie star whom she had seen many times on the screen at the RKO 86th Street Theatre. And one of the men was a newspaper columnist whose column she often read in the morning paper.

Before Ostere had finished the introductions, the chime

rang again and he hurried off to welcome other guests. Marja's eyes were wide. Even though she did not recognize all the names, they had the familiar ring of the daily paper.

She was quiet and shy most of the time, for she did not know what to say to people like these. From the conversation she gathered that Ostere was a rich man who often dabbled in backing plays.

He was a kind host, however, for though he circulated freely throughout the room talking to his guests, every few minutes he would appear at her side to see that she was happy and comfortable. She liked him. He was such a nice, busy little man.

Once the columnist got her in a corner and asked her what she did for a living. At first she didn't know what to say to him. Then it came to her.

"I'm a dancer," she answered. It was near enough to the truth.

Ostere appeared suddenly beside them and smiled approvingly at her reply.

"Where do you work?" the columnist persisted. "I'll give you a plug in the column."

"I'm not ready for that yet," she said, smiling. "But I'll count on you remembering that when I am."

The columnist had already had a few drinks and was slightly loaded. He knew what kind of girls Ostere usually had around him on evenings like this. He wanted to make her uncomfortable. "Let's see you dance," he said nastily. "I don't believe you."

A silence fell around the room at his words. They looked at Marja curiously, waiting for her reaction. Ostere's girls were no secret.

Marja kept her eyes wide as she answered. "I'd love to," she said. "But unfortunately I can't right now. You see, I suffer from a dancer's occupational hazard at the moment."

"What occupational hazard?" the columnist spoke loudly, almost triumphantly. "I never heard of any."

"You don't know very much, do you?" Marja asked sweetly. "Didn't you ever hear of sore feet?"

The gust of laughter that swept the room eased the tension, and Ostere patted her shoulder and whispered: "Good girl."

The guests began to leave about two thirty, and by three o'clock Marja and Ostere were alone again. He sank into a chair and looked up at her. "My God!" he exclaimed. "I'm glad that's over for this week."

She was puzzled. "If you don't like it, why do you do it?"

He smiled. "I must, my dear. It's business. Besides, they would be disappointed if I didn't. It's become a weekly custom."

"You mean this happens every week?" she asked.

He nodded. "New York wouldn't be the same without Tuesday midnight at Jack Ostere's." His voice held a note of pride.

She shook her head. It was beyond her. She didn't see what difference it made whether anybody came or not. "It's time I was going, Mr. Ostere," she said, suddenly reverting to formality.

He looked up with what he thought was an appealing expression. "Must you go?" he asked archly. "I've got lots of room here."

Her eyes were cold. "I have to, Mr. Ostere. My father's waiting up for me."

He jumped to his feet. "Of course," he said. "I should have realized." He reached into his pocket for a bill, which he pressed into her hand.

She didn't look at it. "Thank you very much, Mr. Ostere," she said, holding out her hand. "I had a very good time."

He pressed her hand. "I enjoyed having you here, my dear. I hope you'll come again. Next week, maybe."

She hesitated. "I can't say. I'd have to check with Mr. Martin."

He smiled as he walked her to the door. "Don't worry about Joker. I'll talk to him."

"Good night, Mr. Ostere."

"Good night, Marja."

The elevator door opened and she stepped into the car. She waved at Ostere, still standing in his doorway, and the elevator door closed on his answering smile. It wasn't until then that she peeked at the bill tightly clutched in her left hand.

A gasp of surprise parted her lips. It was twenty dollars —as much as she made in a whole week's work. She slipped it into her purse quickly, wondering whether he had made a mistake.

The doorman's face held an expression of surprise when she came out of the building. "Cab, ma'am?" he asked.

She stared at him for a moment. Then she shrugged her shoulders. Why not? She was loaded.

Chapter 18

IT WAS three thirty when the cab stopped in front of her door. She got out and started up the steps.

"Marja!" A figure stepped from the shadows near the doorway.

"Mike! What are you doing here?"

His voice was unhappy. "I was waiting for yuh. I was worried. Are you all right?"

She lit a cigarette. The match flared, illuminating her face briefly. "I'm okay."

"I waited down at the Golden Glow until half past twelve," he said, his voice growing unhappier. "Then I asked an' they told me you left early. I came here thinking you weren't feeling well, but your father said you hadn't come home yet."

"You didn't have to wait," she said quickly. "I went to a party."

"Where?"

152

"Jack Ostere's," she answered without thinking. "You don't know him," she added.

"How come?" he asked.

"Joker asked me to go."

His voice was low. "I don't like it."

"Why not?" She was annoyed and her voice betrayed it.

"I just don't like you doing it, that's all," he said. "He's got no right sending you out on things like that."

She was angry now. "Nobody asked you what you thought," she flared.

His voice was stubborn. "You shouldn' 've gone."

"If you didn't hang aroun' spyin' on me," she said angrily, "you never would've known."

"I'm not spying on you, Marja," he said in a hurt, low voice. "I was scared something might have happened to you."

Her voice was cold. "Now that you see I'm okay, you can go home. Yuh're beginnin' to bother me!" She ran up the steps into the hall, leaving him standing in the street looking after her.

He stood there a moment. Then, a strange sadness in him, he turned and began to walk home. There were times when he felt that he didn't know her at all.

Peter was sitting at the table, the inevitable can of beer in front of him. He looked at her with bloodshot eyes. "Where you been?" he asked.

"Workin'," she answered briefly.

His eyes took in her dress. "Your boy frien', he says you left early. You didn't come home."

She didn't answer, but started through the kitchen to her room. He was out of his chair quickly, blocking her path. "Where you been in that dress?"

She stared into his eyes levelly. "Workin', I said."

His hands gripped her shoulders. "Like that? With your tits hangin' out?"

"This is my working clothes," she answered. "I was too tired to change, so I came home in them." She tried to shake off his grip. "Lay off. I gotta return it tomorrow. It ain't mine."

His hand fell from her shoulder swiftly. Before she could stop him, he had opened her purse and spilled its contents on the table. The twenty-dollar bill lay on top of the pile. He picked it up and turned it over in his hand. "Where'd you get this?"

She stared at him. "It was a tip."

"They don't give tips like this for just dancing," he said.

She didn't answer.

His hand lashed out. "Slut!"

She spun half around and stumbled against the wall, a white blotch on her face. The snap of her shoulder strap opened and her dress began to fall. She clutched it to her breast.

His voice was harsh. "I told your mother what you were, but she didn't believe me. It's a good thing she's not here to see this."

Her voice was expressionless. "Good for you, you mean."

His hand began to pull the belt from around his waist. He moved toward her menacingly.

She ducked around him and pulled a sharp meat knife from the table drawer. She held it, its gleaming edge pointing viciously at his face. Her teeth drew back over her lips in a snarl. "Come on!" she taunted. "Try somethin'!"

He stared at the knife, then at her. Her eyes were flaming

with hate. He stepped back. "Marja! You don't know what you're doin'!"

She grinned. "Wanna bet?"

He took a deep breath. The girl was mad. Cautiously he backed away from her. "Okay, okay," he said anxiously.

"The money." Her eyes were still on his face.

He tossed the twenty-dollar bill on the table. She shoveled it quickly into her bag along with the other things.

Her face was still and grim. "If yuh ever come near me," she said in a low, deadly voice, "or try to touch me, so help me God, I'll kill yuh."

He didn't answer. He had no doubt that she meant every word she said. Her door closed behind her, and he turned to the icebox with a suddenly trembling hand.

Marja leaned her back against the closed door and shut her eyes. It was as if a thousand years had passed since her mother had died, yet it was only a little more than a month. She opened her eyes and looked down at the knife she held in her hand.

A cold chill ran through her and she shuddered convulsively. She dropped the knife on the bed and began to undress. She didn't notice it again until she was about to get into bed. Then, thoughtfully she slipped it under the corner of her mattress. She never went to bed after that without checking first to see that it was there.

Chapter 19

FROM that time on, she went where Joker sent her. Gradually she came to trust him. She never had trouble with any of the men she met. They were more respectful to her than the boys in school.

The boys were always ganging up on her and grabbing at her. She didn't mind them. She felt superior in many ways to the children in school around her. What did they know of what was going on in the world?

She began to see Mike less and less as the winter wore on. Several times she made dates with him and then had to break them because Joker had a job for her. Since the night he had waited at her house, he had stopped waiting for her at the dance hall. Then one evening she was called to the phone at the dance hall.

"Hello," she said into the speaker.

"Marja?" the familiar voice spoke in her ear. "It's Mike."

A sudden warmth came into her. She hadn't realized until this minute how much she had missed him. She smiled into the phone. "How are yuh, Mike?"

"Fine," he answered. "And you?"

"Okay," she answered.

"I wanted to talk to you," he said, "but I've been busy up at school."

"I'm glad you called, Mike," she said softly. "I missed you."

His voice was suddenly light and happy. "You did?"

"Honest, Mike."

"Meet me when you get through work?" he asked.

"Sure," she answered quickly.

"Downstairs. Same place. First car off the corner," he said quickly.

"Okay."

"Marja?" He hesitated.

"What, Mike?"

"You won't stand me up this time?" he pleaded.

"I'll be there, Mike," she said as she put down the telephone.

He was leaning against a car when she came out. He straightened up as she walked toward him. She looked up into his face. He seemed tired and thin. "Hi," she said.

A crooked smile split his face. "Hi."

They stood there staring at each other for a moment. Marja broke the silence. "Aren't you gonna ask me for a cup of coffee?"

"Sure," he said. "You took the words outta my mouth."

She started toward the drugstore, but he took her arm and steered her to a restaurant near by. They entered and sat down at a table.

She looked down at the white tablecloth. "Boy, we're livin'."

He grinned. "Nothin' but the best."

But she noticed he was careful in ordering. "What you been doin'?" she asked.

"Nothin' much," he answered. "School. Studying. Working."

"You lost weight," she said.

He shrugged his shoulders. "I was getting too heavy, anyway."

The waiter put the coffee and buns in front of them. She took a sip of coffee and waited for him to speak.

"How is little Peter?" he asked.

"Fine." She smiled. "He's walking and beginning to talk. He calls me 'Ja-Ja.'" She noticed he didn't ask about her stepfather.

"How's the job going?" he asked.

"Okay," she answered.

He was silent as he watched her drink the coffee, but he didn't touch the cup in front of him. "You're not drinkin' your coffee," she said.

"I'm not hungry," he answered. He got to his feet abruptly, throwing a bill on the table. "C'mon, let's go."

She followed him out into the street. "What's wrong, Mike?"

He looked into her face. "I got a message for yuh," he said expressionlessly.

She was puzzled. "For me?"

He nodded. "From Ross. He said to tell yuh he'd be home next month."

Her hand fell from his arm. "Is that why you called me? To give me a message?"

He didn't answer. His face was grim.

"What am I supposed to do?" she asked sarcastically. "Do somersaults?"

He was still quiet.

She stopped. He took two steps before he realized she wasn't with him. "What?" he asked in a puzzled tone.

"Okay, so I got the message," she said in a cold voice. "Thanks."

"He still thinks you're his girl," he said.

Her eyes were wide in the night. "What do *you* think?"

He stood there miserably. "I don't know what to think. He seems so sure of himself."

She backed into a dark doorway. "Mike," she said.

"Yes?"

"C'mere, Mike."

He followed her into the doorway. She put her arms around his shoulders and pulled his face down to her. She kissed him. At first he stood frozen, then his arms tightened and pulled her close to him. They stood there for moments while rockets exploded in his brain.

Finally she drew back. All her body was tingling from the tightness of his embrace. "*Now* what do you think, Mike?"

"But you never said anything," he said confusedly. "You didn't act like you wanted to see me. Like the last time you stood me up. I waited over an hour for you to show up, but you didn't."

Her eyes were green in the night and glowed like a cat's. "I gotta work, Mike. I need the dough. You know that."

"There's just so much you can do for money," he said.

She shook her head. "I don't do anything wrong. I just want enough so I don't have to live like my mother did. I saw what happened to her."

"But you never—"

"Shut up," she said softly, pressing her fingers to his lips. "Yuh talk too much. You never tried to kiss me. I was wonderin' if there was somethin' the matter with you."

He smiled. It was as if his whole face lit up. He bent his face to her. "Maybe it's just as well," he said. "I got that much more to make up for."

The street was quiet when they reached her house. The last winds of March were beating faintly at them as they stepped into the vestibule. She closed the door quietly and looked up into his face.

He stared down at her. His eyes were serious, and he spoke in a whisper. "I love yuh, Marja. Yuh know that, don't you?"

She nodded.

"I loved yuh since that day in the elevator, but I never thought you could see me. Ross has so much. I got nothin'."

"I never asked for anything," she said.

"I know," he answered. "But you can get anything you want. Every guy you meet is crazy for yuh."

She smiled slowly. "I know," she said contentedly. "But I don't care about them. They're all jerks. They all think they can get something out of me, but I ain't givin'."

He grinned teasingly. "I'm a jerk, too?"

"You're the biggest of them all," she taunted gently. "Except me. I go for you."

He pulled her toward him. She came willingly into his arms. Her lips and mouth were warm and open. Her tongue flashed fires into his mouth. He caught his breath sharply, then closed his eyes, slipping into the vortex of heat.

She drew back suddenly, a puzzled look in her eyes. "Mike, yuh make me crazy."

"Good," he said.

She shook her head. "I don't understand it. Nobody ever made me feel like that."

He pulled her to him again. "That'll teach yuh not to mess around with me, gal," he laughed. He kissed her throat. "Now you really got a feller."

Chapter 20

PETER sat at the window in the darkness. He looked out into the street. Marja should have been home an hour ago. She wasn't working late tonight. He knew that.

He craned his neck out the window. There were two people walking slowly up the block. They passed a street light. One was Marja.

That boy was with her. Mike. They were walking with their arms around each other's waists. A twinge of jealousy ran through him. Marja was a woman now. The last few months had made many changes in her. She was sure of herself. It was that job.

He had heard many stories about the girls who worked in dance halls. They were a wild lot. He remembered some that he had known before he married. They were no better than whores, most of them.

Erotic thoughts crowded into his mind. He felt warm. It wasn't right. He had seen Marja before any of them. She had no right to treat him the way she did. Walking around the house that way. Half undressed. She knew that got him excited.

He felt the beads of sweat break out on his forehead. He reeled drunkenly into the dark kitchen and opened the icebox. There was no more beer. He stood there cursing silently. Then he remembered the bottle of slivovitz in the closet.

He took the bottle down and pulled out the cork. He held the bottle to his mouth, feeling the fiery liquor burn its way down his throat and hit his stomach. Its heat radiated through him. He felt strong and capable now.

Holding the bottle carefully, he walked back into the parlor and looked out the window. They weren't in sight. He listened carefully for Marja's footsteps on the stairs. There was no sound.

He waited almost ten minutes. He took another drink from the bottle. She wasn't fooling him. He knew what she was doing downstairs. His thoughts infuriated him. The teasing little bitch. Everybody got their share except him. She laughed at him.

He had a brilliant idea. Softly he walked back through the apartment and out the kitchen door. He crept down the stairway silently to the first landing and peered through the banister to the ground floor.

He could see them standing in the corner of the hall. Marja's arms were around the boy's neck, and they were kissing. The boy's back hid Marja from Peter's gaze, but he knew what they were doing. He could tell from the way they were standing.

A sound of muffled laughter came to his ears, and Marja stepped back from the boy. He could see her face now. Her lips seemed puffed and swollen in the dim yellow light. She was smiling.

"Tomorrow?" he heard Mike ask.

Marja laughed happily. "Tomorrow, for sure." She turned toward the stairway.

Peter scrambled quickly up the stairs to the apartment. He waited at the kitchen door until he could hear her footsteps. Then he hurried through the dark apartment to the parlor.

He sat down in the chair in the corner from which he could watch the kitchen in the mirror on the wall. A wild anger was bursting inside him. There was a tightness in his belly. He held the bottle to his lips. Some of the liquor ran down his chin.

The kitchen door opened, and light from the hall showed Marja standing there. He heard her voice.

"Peter?"

He didn't answer.

"Peter, are you asleep?"

Cautiously he held his breath. Let the bitch think he was asleep. He didn't have to tell her what he was doing.

She came into the kitchen and walked through the darkness to the door of her room. A moment later the soft light from the lamp on her dresser came from the room.

He watched carefully. She thought he was asleep, for she didn't close her door. He saw her cross the room and begin to take off her dress. A faint sound of her humming came to his ears. The little whore sounded actually happy for a change.

She was in her underwear now. She looked up. He held his breath, wondering whether she suspected he was watching her. But apparently that wasn't what was on her mind. She came out of the bedroom and crossed the kitchen to the sink, out of his sight. The sound of pans being lifted from the washtub came to his ears, then the noise of water running softly.

She came back into sight, still humming softly. She unfastened her brassiere as she went into her room. He could see her rubbing her back where the red welt from the straps marked her flesh. She went into a corner of the room near her closet and he couldn't see her.

He lifted the bottle to his lips and took another swift, cautious drink, then wiped his mouth on the back of his hand. He could feel the sudden pounding of his heart. At the sound of footsteps, he looked up again.

She was coming through the doorway, a kimona hanging loosely around her. It flashed open as she moved; she was naked beneath it. She crossed to the washtub, and he heard her fiddling with the faucet. Suddenly he understood. She was going to take a bath.

Usually she waited until he had gone out, but she must believe he was asleep. He grinned to himself. She wasn't so smart. He was much smarter than she.

She crossed the room and went out into the hall, leaving the door half open behind her. He got out of his chair swiftly and moved into the kitchen on silent feet. He listened carefully at the door for a moment. He heard the hall toilet noise and looked around swiftly. There wasn't time for him to get back to the parlor. He ducked into her room and hid behind the open door.

She sat back in the wash basin that served for a tub and let the warm water press against her skin. Someday she would have a real bathtub in a real bathroom. She was tired of bathing in the kitchen and going out into the hall to the toilet. But right now the water felt good. Luxuriously she spread the soap lather all over her.

She closed her eyes and thought of Mike. He was wonderful. It was funny how things worked out. The way he made her feel when he kissed her—it was like the way it happened in books. Warm and exciting inside. There was such a new longing that for a moment when they kissed she could hardly stand, her legs felt so weak.

The water began to cool and she opened her eyes. It was late, time she got to bed. She rinsed off the soap and climbed out of the basin. She pulled the towel from the back of the chair and rubbed herself dry. She could feel her skin glowing and warm. She wrapped the towel around her and went back into her room.

She went right to her closet and hung up her kimona. She pulled her nightgown from her hanger and started to cross to the bed, dropping her towel on the back of a chair. She had begun to raise the gown over her head when an instinct made her look up.

Her heart constricted in her bosom and the sudden pain of fear knifed through her body. Peter was standing in the corner. Her arms dropped and she held the gown in front of her.

He took a step toward her, grinning foolishly. "Marja," he said, his hand reaching for her.

She dodged away from him behind the crib. The fear congealed into an icy anger. "Get out!" she snarled.

He stood there weaving slightly. The sweat stood out on his forehead, his eyes were glazed. His tongue ran over his lips.

"Get out!" she yelled. "Yuh no-good drunken bum!"

"Marja," he mumbled, "why are you all the time mad at me? I like you." He stepped around the crib toward her.

She moved away from him cautiously. "Yuh stink," she said. "Get out!"

The baby woke and suddenly began to cry. Instinctively

her eyes turned to the crib. Peter moved swiftly and caught her hand before she was aware of it. He pulled her to him and tried to kiss her.

She twisted in his grasp, turning her face away from him. Her nails slashed at his face. "Lemme go! Yuh son of a bitch!"

His hand was caught in the gown she held before her. Her hands were raking at his face. With a cry of pain he pulled back, the tearing sound of the gown coming to his ears. He still held her by one wildly waving hand. With his other hand, he reached up to his face. It came away sticky with blood. He stared at it stupidly.

She looked up at him, her chest heaving. "Now will yuh get out?" she gasped.

He shook his head to clear it. "You bitch!" he yelled. "You not goin' to tease me no more! I'll show yuh!"

He raised his hand and hit her across the face. She spun away from him, half falling to the floor. He followed her slowly, his eyes fixed on her face.

There was no fear in her eyes, only an all-consuming hatred. She pulled her legs up under her. Suddenly she sprang, diving past him for the bed, her hand reaching for the knife under the mattress.

He caught her by the hair, snapping her head back so that she lay in a half-arc on the edge of the bed. She saw his hand coming toward her face. She tried to twist away from the blow. A sharp light exploded in her brain and she fell forward, trying to keep tears of pain from coming to her eyes.

She felt his hand turn her over. Quick tiny flashes of pain ran all over her body as his hand became a blur in the dim light. Her body felt heavy, as if there was a great weight upon it. Then the last, most exquisite pain of all burst in her groin and she began to slide almost gratefully into the night that was closing fast around her bed. The last thing she knew was the sound of the baby crying in his crib.

She came awake slowly. Sensation returned to her body and, with it, pain. Her body felt as if a thousand tiny needles were sticking into her. She turned her head cautiously.

The light was still on in the room and she was alone. Gradually memory came back to her. She sat up in the bed, a cry of pain escaping her lips.

She saw Peter's clothing lying on the floor near the bed. Nausea swept through her, and she ran into the kitchen. The pain hit her stomach in wave after wave as she retched into the sink. At last it was gone and a cold chill came over her.

Quickly she turned the hot water on in the basin and climbed into it. Desperately she scrubbed at her skin with the soap, but the grime she felt wasn't on the surface. It was deep inside her where she could never get it out.

But the warm water stilled some of the pain, and at last she got out of the basin. She walked dripping into her room and took a towel from the closet. Slowly she dried herself, then carefully began to dress.

In front of the mirror she carefully applied lipstick and combed back her hair. Her face stared back at her, dull and impassive. Only her eyes were still alive. They were green and filled with hate.

She went to her bed and straightened it. The pillowcase was bloodstained; she found a fresh one. She pulled the blanket tight and tucked it in.

A faint sound came from the crib. She looked into it. The baby was wet. Quickly she changed his diaper, and filling a small bottle with water, placed it near his lips. Then she walked back to the bed and took the knife from under the mattress.

Dully she walked through the apartment to Peter's room. She opened the door silently and looked in. He lay in a hulking shadow across his bed. She pulled the light chain over her head. Light flooded into the room. Peter didn't move.

He lay on his back, breathing heavily, the blanket clutched around him.

She placed the knife close to his face. "Peter, wake up," she said quietly.

He lay silent. A snore escaped his mouth.

Her hand swiped viciously across his face. "Wake up!" Her lips drew back over her teeth in a snarl.

His eyes opened almost immediately. For a moment he lay absolutely still. Then he saw the knife, and terror sprang into his eyes. His voice caught in his throat. "What are you doing, Marja?"

"I've come to keep my promise, Peter." Her voice was very tight and very low. "Remember what I said?"

He stared up at her, afraid to move. "You're crazy!" he gasped.

"No crazier than you." She smiled. The knife swiped viciously across his face.

The flesh parted like a ripe melon bursting in the sun. A pool of blood rushed in to fill the wound from his cheek to his jawbone. He screamed agonizedly and leaped from the bed toward the door, the blanket trailing on the floor behind him.

He ran through the apartment into the hallway, still screaming. Through the open door he could see her walking slowly after him. He began to run down the stairs. He tripped in the blanket and fell the few steps to the next landing.

She stood at the head of the stairway, looking down at him. He was still screaming. She closed her eyes. It was not long since her mother had been lying there. She turned and went back into the apartment.

She closed the door behind her and walked over to the sink. She turned on the water and washed the knife carefully. Then she placed it on the table and sat down in a chair facing the door. It was the same chair that her mother had always sat in while waiting for her to come home.

Her eyes were burning. She was tired, very tired. Her eyelids closed.

There was a heavy knock at the door. She opened her eyes. There was a hint of tears in them. "Come in," she said quietly.

That was how she was when the police came into the room.

Chapter 21

"BUT there must have been a reason for you to do such a thing, Marja," the woman insisted.

Marja looked at the Welfare worker. She shook her head stubbornly. She didn't speak.

"You don't want to be sent to a reform school, do you?" the woman persisted.

Marja shrugged her shoulders. "No matter what I say, I won't be let loose. They're gonna put me away, no matter what."

"But there's a big difference between a correctional institution and a state home," the woman explained.

Marja's eyes were wide. "Not to me. One is as bad as the other."

The woman heaved a sigh. "Don't you want to be with your little brother any more?"

Marja looked at her swiftly. "Would they let me stay with him if I talk? I can work and keep him."

The woman shook her head regretfully. "No, they couldn't do that. You're too young. But—"

"Then it doesn't make any difference, does it?" Marja asked.

The woman didn't answer.

Marja got to her feet. "Come on," she said. "Let's get it over with."

The courtroom was almost empty. Only a few spectators sat in the rows near the railing. She glanced idly at them as she passed. They looked up at her curiously but impersonally. She meant nothing to them.

A hand reached out and brushed her arm as she walked by. "Hello, Marja."

She looked up, startled.

It was Mike. There was a friendly, reassuring smile on his lips. "I tried to see yuh," he whispered quickly, "but they wouldn't let me."

Her face settled into a dull, impassive mask. There was no use telling him she had given orders that she didn't want to see anyone. She continued walking.

The Welfare woman was just behind her. "That's a nice looking boy," she said in a friendly voice. "Your boy friend?"

Marja's eyes were blank. "I don't know who he is. I never saw him before in my life."

The judge was a tired, bored-looking old man. He peered down at Marja. "You are charged with attacking your stepfather with a knife, young woman."

She didn't answer.

"Is Mr. Ritchik here?" he asked, turning to the clerk.

The clerk called: "Mr. Ritchik."

Peter came forward from the back of the court. His face

was still covered with a big white bandage. Marja looked at him. It was as if he were a stranger. The five weeks since she had seen him had been a lifetime.

"Mr. Ritchik," the judge asked, "will you tell us what happened?"

Peter cleared his throat nervously. "She's no good, Your Honor. A tramp. She wouldn't listen to nobody. She worked at the dance hall and never came home nights. When she did, it was late. That night I spoke to her about coming in decent hours like other girls. When I went to sleep, she sneaked into my room and cut me."

Marja had to smile. If it weren't for her mother's memory she would tell them what had really happened. But Katti was entitled to that much peace.

It was over in a little while. She stood in front of the desk while the judge looked down over his spectacles at her.

"Marja," he said, "we are sending you to the Rose Geyer Correctional Home for Girls until you are eighteen. It is my hope that you will put your time there to good use and learn a trade and a Christian way of life."

She looked up at him blankly.

"Any questions?" he asked.

She shook her head.

He rapped his gavel on the desk and got to his feet. Everybody in the court stood as he walked pompously from the bench. The door closed behind him, and the Welfare woman turned to her.

"Come with me, Marja," she said.

Dumbly, Marja followed her. Mike was standing behind the rail. He tried to speak, but she looked right through him. A hurt expression came over his face. It wasn't until she was through the door that she realized he was crying.

The Rose Geyer Home was in the far end of the Bronx.

She looked at it curiously as she got out of the car with the policeman and the Welfare matron. It was almost like the country up here. The Home was surrounded by open fields.

An hour later she was escorted to the doctor's office by one of the girls, who looked at her questioningly, but spoke not a word as they walked down the long gray corridor.

She held the door open for Marja. "In here, honey," she said in a not unpleasant voice. She followed Marja into the office. A thin, gray-haired man looked up. "I got a new fish for you, Doc," the girl said.

The doctor shrugged his shoulders wearily. "In there." He pointed to a small room. "Take off all your clothes."

His examination was brief and efficient. Twenty minutes after she had come into his office she was dressed and back in the entrance room.

The doctor handed her a prescription. "Get this filled at the dispensary and take it all during your pregnancy," he said.

Marja was startled. She cast a quick glance behind her. The girl who had brought her was sitting against the wall. She turned back to the doctor. "Who, me?" she asked incredulously.

The girl's voice came from behind her. It was flat but not without humor. "He don't mean me, honey. I been here without a guy for two years now, damn it!"

Marja looked at the doctor, then at the paper in her hand. Suddenly she realized what it meant. She sank into a chair beside the desk and began to laugh.

The doctor stared at her. "What's so funny?" he asked.

She looked up at him, the tears running down her cheeks. That was the hell of it. He would never know. Nobody would.

The State vs. Maryann Flood

I WAITED while the clerk administered the oath to the State's first witness. She was a tall, dark girl with a dramatic part in the middle of her long jet-black hair. She seemed quite calm and uninterested in the people in the court. Her eyes were dark and unreadable.

"Your name, please?" the clerk asked.

"Raye Marnay," she answered. The voice was surprisingly light and thin in such a tall girl.

The clerk nodded to me and I walked forward slowly. I stopped in front of her and looked up. "How old are you, Miss Marnay?" I asked.

The answer came promptly. "Twenty-three."

"Where were you born?"

"Chillicothe, Ohio."

"When did you come to New York?" I asked.

"About two years ago."

I was beginning to get used to the strange, thin sound of her voice. "What did you do in Chillicothe?"

177

"I lived there," she said.

I could hear the faint sound of laughter in the courtroom. I waited for it to subside before I spoke again. "I meant, what did you work at for a living in Chillicothe, Miss Marnay?"

"Oh," she said. "I didn't know that was what you meant. I was a schoolteacher."

I looked at her. The hell of it was that she really had been a schoolteacher. "What grade did you teach?"

"Kindergarten," she answered promptly. "I love children."

I couldn't help smiling at the way she said it. "I don't doubt that, Miss Marnay," I said. I let the smile leave my face. "What made you decide to come to New York?"

"I wanted to be an actress," she said. "Professor Berg, he was the dramatic teacher at the senior school, wrote a play which we put on in the little theater. It was called *Lark in the Valley,* and I played the leading part in it. He said I had so much talent that it was a shame that I had to waste it in a small town like Chillicothe. He said I was another Mary Astor. So I decided to come to New York."

"And what happened after you arrived in New York?" I asked.

"Nothing," she said. "I walked around for weeks and nobody would even see me. Even with the letters that Professor Berg gave me."

"Then why didn't you go back to Chillicothe?"

"I couldn't," she answered in her small voice. There was a note of hurt in it. "Everybody would know then that I was a failure."

"I see," I said. "Then, what did you do for a living?"

"I got a job in a restaurant on Broadway as a waitress. It was a place where a lot of show people came in. I had heard that many girls who worked there found jobs on the stage."

"How long did you work there?" I asked.

"About three weeks," she said.

"What happened then?"

"I was fired," she answered in an even tinier voice, if that was possible. "The manager said he ran a restaurant, not a dramatic school."

Another ripple of laughter ran through the courtroom. I waited for it to pass. "Then what did you do?"

"I looked for another job, but I didn't find any. One day I was talking to another girl in the rooming-house where I lived. She said with my face and figure I ought to become a model. I thought that was a good idea. Many models become actresses, you know. I asked her how I could become a model. She sent me up to Park Avenue Models."

I nodded. "Was this the first time you had ever thought of modeling?"

"Yes," she answered.

"What did you do then?" I asked.

"I went up to Park Avenue Models and applied for work."

"Who did you speak to when you went up there?"

"Mrs. Morris."

"What did she tell you?"

"She said I would have to get some pictures taken and then she would put them in her file. She gave me a card with the names of about four photographers on it. Until I had them, she said, she couldn't do anything for me. I explained to her that I didn't have the money for it. She said she was sorry but she couldn't do anything for me until then. I was just about to leave when Miss Flood came out of her office and saw me."

"You mean the Miss Flood who is here in this court-room?" I asked.

She nodded. "Yes."

"What happened then?"

"When Miss Flood saw me, she snapped her fingers and said I was the girl. She sent me to the 14th Street Fur Shop. That was the first time I ever modeled. I wore one of their fur coats and walked up and down in their windows so people could see it." There was a note of pride in her voice. "I was their favorite model. You see, I'm very tall, and people can see me a long way off. I worked there at least three days a week ever since."

"What other modeling did you do?" I asked.

She hesitated a moment. "That was the only place I ever worked."

I nodded. "How much did they pay you?"

"Ten dollars a day," she answered.

"That came to about thirty dollars a week," I said. "Was that enough for you to live on?"

She shook her head. "No. My dramatic lessons cost more than that each week."

"How did you make extra money?"

"I used to date a lot," she said.

"Date?" I asked.

She nodded. "That's what we called it."

"Who do you mean by 'we'?" I asked.

"The girls I knew," she said.

"How did you go about this—er—dating, as you call it?"

"It began after I had been working a few weeks as a model. I asked Miss Flood for some extra work and she called me into her office. She said that a model's life was often very difficult and sometimes took a long time in paying off. She told me that sometimes clients called her up and asked her to recommend some girls to go out with them. She said these men were very generous and always tipped the girls well for just spending time with them. She asked if I was interested."

"What did you say?" I asked.

"I was interested," she replied.

Another ripple of laughter ran through the courtroom. I didn't blame them. "What did you do then?"

"Miss Flood arranged a date for me that night. He was a nice gentleman. He took me to dinner, then we went up to his apartment for a few drinks. He was very amusing. He gave me ten dollars when I left. He said that was for being so nice and for me to tell Miss Flood that he was very pleased."

"Is that all you did?" I asked. "Have a few drinks?"

Her face changed color slightly. She seemed to be blushing. "We had two parties," she almost whispered.

"Parties?" I questioned, looking at the jury. "What do you mean by parties?"

"Intercourse." She was still speaking in that low, hard-to-hear voice.

"You mean you had intercourse twice with this man?" I asked.

She nodded. "Yes. That's what I mean."

"Weren't you surprised that the man wanted that? That he took it for granted?"

She shook her head. "No. The men were no different back in Chillicothe. They all look for the same thing."

Laughter scaled the courtroom walls. The judge rapped his gavel. The noise subsided.

"What did you do next?" I asked.

"I went home to sleep. I was tired," she said.

The roar almost blew the courtroom apart. Even I had to

work to keep a straight face. Finally I could speak. "I mean when you went back to Park Avenue Models the next time."

"That was the next day. I went back to thank Miss Flood for being so nice to me. She asked me if I had a good time and if I was willing to go on any more dates. I said I would if all the gentlemen were as nice as this one. She assured me that she knew nothing but nice gentlemen, then she asked me how many parties we had. I told her and she took some money out of her desk and gave it to me. I didn't want to take it, I told her that the gentleman had given me ten dollars. She laughed and said that was my tip, and made me take the money."

"How much was it?" I asked.

"Fifty dollars," she said.

"Did you realize what this meant?" I asked. "That you were committing an act of prostitution?"

"I didn't look at it like that," she protested. "If I didn't like the gentleman, I didn't have to do anything. I wouldn't."

"Did you ever meet any gentleman you didn't like?" I asked sarcastically.

She shook her head. "No. Miss Flood was right. She only knew the finest-type gentlemen."

Laughter again echoed through the court. I waited until it had subsided. "Before you knew Miss Flood, did you ever have intercourse for money?"

She shook her head. "No."

"Did you ever have intercourse for money after you met Miss Flood that she did not arrange?"

"No, sir," she said. "I'm not a whore."

"That's all, thank you," I said, walking away from her. I paused in front of Vito's table. Marja looked up at me. Her eyes, wide and dark and proud, stared right into me. I had the strangest feeling that the pride in them was for me. I kept my eyes carefully guarded and turned to Vito.

"Your witness," I said and continued on to my table. I sat down and watched Vito get slowly to his feet.

There was no doubt about it, he was a real pro. Even the way he walked toward the witness indicated his sureness and his ability. His voice was warm and rich.

"Miss Marnay," he called.

She looked up at him. "Yes, sir."

I nodded to myself in reluctant grudging admiration. In just the way he spoke her name he had asserted his dominance over her.

"You mentioned that you appeared in a play in Chillicothe. *Lark in the Valley,* I believe you called it."

She nodded. "Yes, sir."

"It was written by a Professor Berg, you stated, a professor of dramatics in the senior school?"

"Yes, sir."

"You said that you came to New York after that at the suggestion of the professor, who said you had too much talent to waste it in a small town like Chillicothe?"

"Yes, sir."

"I assume he meant dramatic talent. That was what he meant, wasn't it?"

The girl hesitated.

Vito's voice was impatient. "Come, Miss Marnay. That was what he meant, wasn't it?"

Her voice was even smaller than before. "I think so."

"You can be more positive than that, Miss Marnay," he said sarcastically.

"That was what he meant," she said. "Yes, sir."

"What?" he asked.

"Dramatic talent," she said.

"You said that the play was presented at a little theater in Chillicothe. What theater was it?"

Her brows knotted together. She cast a worried glance at me. I tried to look confident, but I didn't know what the hell he was getting at. "It—it wasn't exactly a theater," she stammered.

"If it wasn't a theater, what was it?" Vito asked.

"It was at the Antelope Club," she said. "It was a special show the professor wrote for their annual affair."

"The Antelope Club," Vito said. He looked at the jury. "I see." He turned back to her. "That wouldn't be a stag affair, would it?"

She looked down at her feet. "I believe it was."

"Were you the only female in the cast?" he asked.

She nodded. "I was."

"What part did you play?"

Her voice hardly carried to my table. "I was the farm girl."

"What was theme of the play? Did you have many lines to speak?" His voice was harsh.

"It was about this girl and the three men that worked on the farm. The farmer, his son, and the hired hand, and what they did on that one particular night. I didn't have any lines to speak. It was all in pantomime. The professor was a great believer in the Stanislavsky method of drama."

"Stanislavsky, hmm . . ." Vito scratched his head. "Wasn't that the Russian who believed in action instead of speech?"

"That's right," she said.

"And the professor's play was all action?" he added.

She nodded. "Yes."

His voice turned very heavy and sarcastic. "So much so

that the play was raided by the police and all of you were charged with giving an indecent performance. As a result of that, you and the professor were dismissed from your posts in school. Isn't that true?"

She didn't answer. She bit her lower lip to keep it from trembling.

Vito was shouting now. "Come now, Miss Marnay, answer my question."

Her face had lost all its color; the rouge stood out in dark blotches on her cheeks. She looked down at the floor. Her voice had vanished into a tiny whisper. "Yes."

"That's all, Miss Marnay." Vito looked at the jury as if to say: *How can you believe anything a girl like that might say?* He half shrugged, and turned back to his table.

Joel and Alec leaned toward me as I called the next witness. Their whispers were hoarse in my ear.

"He sure kicked hell out of her," Joel said.

"Yeah," Alec answered, his glance following the girl as she took her seat. "He really ripped her."

I drew in my breath. "One thing you guys are forgetting. He ripped her, not the story she told about Flood. Notice he stayed away from that?"

Joel nodded. "He's no dope. He's trying to destroy her credibility."

"It won't do him any good," I answered. "The payoff will still come on facts pertinent to the case. And he knows it."

"All the same, I'd be careful, Mike," Alec whispered. "He's got a bagful of tricks."

The clerk was administering the oath to another girl, the second witness for the State. I began to get to my feet. "He'll still have to find something better than the truth if he expects to get anywhere with this one," I said as the court clerk nodded to me. I moved around the table and walked toward the witness stand.

The hospital room was dark and quiet as I came in. I could hear the sounds of the Old Man's breathing. It was slow and easy.

A nurse held her finger to her lips. "He's sleeping."

I nodded and started to back out of the room.

"Who's sleeping?" The Old Man's voice was loud and strong in the quiet. "That you, Mike?"

I stepped forward again. "Yes, sir."

"Come over here and speak up," he said irascibly. "I can't hear you."

I walked over to the head of the bed. His bright, dark eyes looked up at me. A half-smile was on his lips. "How did it go today, Counselor?"

"All right," I said. "We got through the first four witnesses. Vito couldn't do very much with their stories. All he did was bang at the people themselves. I think we did pretty good, on the whole."

"I know," the Old Man said. "I heard."

I glanced at the telephone next to the hospital bed. He must have been burning up the wire all day.

"There's one thing that bothers me, though," he said. "I can't figure Vito's strategy at all. Right now it looks like he's feeding the girl to the wolves."

I didn't speak. There was a curious sinking feeling in my heart. I could have put up a much better argument than Vito had that day. "It's almost as if he didn't care what happens with our case," I said. "He's letting me get away with everything in the book."

"Did you see Flood?" the Old Man asked. "How'd she look?" His eyes were watching me very carefully.

"I saw her," I said. "She seems okay."

"Mike," he said, "it's me you're talkin' to."

"She looks fine," I said. "Real fine."

"Still got the same feeling toward her? Even now?"

"I—I don't know, John," I said "I only know that when I look at her I choke up inside."

He nodded slowly. "I know what you mean, Mike. I spoke to her a couple of times. She's got great strength and real courage, son. She might have been a great lady if she had gone in another direction."

"Maybe she never had a chance, sir," I said.

The shrewd look came back into his eyes. "She had her chance, Mike. No matter what you say or what anyone did, she had the final say. She herself threw it away."

I didn't answer. I was remembering a time long ago. That time she left me standing in the road when I went to pick her up. The day she got out of the Geyer Home.

Something had happened to her up there. I knew it the moment I saw her walking down the path. She was different. It wasn't until I could see her eyes that I knew what it was. She was older. Far older then than I would ever be. I could see her getting into the cab and leaving me standing there on the sidewalk.

I went back to my car, the one I had borrowed to bring her home in, and slowly drove downtown. I walked into the apartment.

Mom and Pop were sitting at the kitchen table. Pop was wearing his Sunday suit and a tie. My feet were like lead as I dragged them into the kitchen. I could see them looking at the doorway behind me.

"She didn't come, Ma," I said slowly.

My mother got to her feet, her eyes soft and calm. "Maybe it's for the best, son," she said gently.

I shook my head violently. So hard that I could feel the tears rolling inside my eyes. "No, Ma," I cried. "It's not for the best. She needs me. I know she needs me. But there's something that's holding her back and I don't know what it is."

My father got to his feet. "I'll put your things back in your room, Mike," he said. He walked slowly out of the kitchen.

I looked after him. Poor Pop. He just didn't understand at all. I turned back to my mother. "What should I do now, Ma?" I asked.

She stared at me for a moment, then spoke softly. "Forget her, son. She's not for you."

"That's easy to say, Mom," I said. "But I'm not a kid any more. I'm almost twenty-one. And I still love her."

"Love her?" My mother's voice was filled with scorn. "What do you know about love? You're still a baby yet. All you can do is hurt and cry." Suddenly her voice broke and she turned away from me.

I went to her quickly and caught at her arms. Her eyes were filled with unshed tears. "Stop it, Ma," I said. "Stop it. It's bad enough the way it is."

There was a look in my mother's eyes I had never seen before. "Stop it?" she cried. "I hate her! May the Good Lord forgive me, but I hate her soul to hell for what she's done to my baby."

"Maybe she can't help it, Ma," I said.

My mother looked up at me. "She can help it, son," she said slowly. "Never forget that. She can always decide what she wants to do."

That had been many years ago, and now it was strange to hear the Old Man say almost the same things. I wondered if I would ever understand their point of view. I had long since given up hoping they would understand mine.

"Who are you calling tomorrow?" the Chief asked.

I told him.

He calculated carefully. "At this rate you should be ready for summation in less than two weeks."

I nodded.

"I'll be out of here by then. Maybe I can give you a hand," he said.

"We made a bargain, John," I said. "It's my show. You promised."

"Oh," he said innocently, "I wouldn't tell you what to do. I would just make a little suggestion and try to be of help."

I grinned. I knew his way of helping—he took over. "No, thanks," I said dryly.

"Okay, okay," he said testily.

I went right to bed when I got home. Somehow I was glad I was alone in the apartment. It was better that way. I had persuaded Ma to stay up in the country. I think the only reason she agreed was that she knew I didn't want her around while the trial was on.

I stretched out on the bed and closed my eyes. Marja's face jumped in front of me. The look on her face was the one I had seen in court that day. I still didn't get it.

Why should she be proud of me? I was trying to send her to jail. A guilt began to run through me. Could it be that she expected me to look out for her? Was it that she was counting on how I felt about her? But she didn't know how I felt now. For all she knew, I could have changed. There could be someone else.

But as soon as I thought it, I knew that she knew. We had that between us. A sense of recognition that no one ever shared.

I rolled over, trying to put her from my mind. But it didn't work. No matter what I did, she kept creeping back. I wondered about her. There were so many things I didn't know, so many things had happened to her that I hadn't shared.

I remembered thinking about her up at the hospital. Strange that it should have come to me there because of what the Old Man had said.

But there was one period that I knew nothing about—the four months between the time she left the Home and the time her name first appeared on the police blotter. She must have gone through hell then. I tried to remember what I was doing during that time. My own memories were too vague, my mind kept turning back to her. What did she do? Where did she go? I didn't know.

I could only sense that she had needed me then more than at any other time in her life.

And I could only feel that I had failed her.

Book Two

MARY

Chapter 1

SHE was standing in the open doorway, the sunlight sparkling iridescently in her white-gold hair. She hesitated a moment; then, transferring her small valise from her right hand to her left, she held out her hand to the woman who stood slightly behind her. "Good-by, Mrs. Foster," she said huskily.

The woman took her hand with an almost masculine grip. "Good-by, Mary," she answered. "Take care of yourself."

A half-smile crossed Mary's lips. "I will, Mrs. Foster," she promised. "I learned a lot in the year an' a half I been here."

There was no humor in the woman's voice. "I hope so, Mary. I wouldn't want to see you in trouble again."

The faint smile disappeared from Mary's mouth. "You won't," she said quietly. She dropped the woman's hand and quickly went out the door. The bright sunlight hit her eyes, and she paused at the head of the steps and blinked.

She heard the door swing shut behind her with the heavy clinking sound of metal. A sudden sense of freedom ran through her, as exhilarating as old wine. She turned and looked back at the closed door.

"Yuh won't see me again," she half-whispered to it. "I learned too much. Yuh taught me too good."

The door stared at her, its two small windows like empty eyes of a stranger. She shivered suddenly as a chill chased the sense of freedom from her. She began to walk toward the street.

She was tall and slim in the thin dark coat authorities had given her. The late November wind pressed it close to her body, outlining her deep breasts, narrow waist, and gently flaring hips. She walked easily on strong, straight legs.

The old man who sat in the little house near the gate came out as he saw her approaching. He smiled at her through rheumy eyes. "Goin' home, Marja?"

She smiled at him. "Got no home, Pop," she said. "Changed everything. My name, too. It's Mary now, remember?"

The old man smiled at her with sudden wisdom. "I remember. But it won't do yuh no good. Yuh still look like Marja to me. The hot Polack blood is still runnin' around inside yuh, and yuh can't change that."

She looked at him, the smile still on her lips. "I'll change lots o' things before I'm through."

"But not yourself," he said quickly. He began to turn the crank that opened the gate. "Where yuh goin'?" he asked.

"I don't know," she said. "But first I'm gonna check into a hotel and sit in a bathtub for two hours without anybody draggin' me out. Then I'm goin' to buy me some clothes I feel good in, not these rags. Then I'm gonna treat myself to a big dinner an' go to the movies, maybe Radio City. Then I'm gonna have me two ice-cream sodas an' go to the hotel an' sleep till two tomorrow afternoon."

"After that, what're you goin' to do?" he asked.

"I'm goin' to find me a job an' go to work," she answered.

"Do that first," he said wisely. "You may need your money." The iron gate was open. He gestured toward it. "Your world waits, Marja. I hope it's kind to you."

She took a half-step toward it, then turned back to the old man. Quickly she kissed him on the cheek. "Good-by, Pop."

"Good-by, Marja," he said, an unexpected sadness in his voice.

Caught by the sound, she looked into the old man's eyes. "You're the only thing about this place I'll miss, Pop."

"Yeah," he said, gruffly embarrassed. "I bet you tell that to all the boys."

A mischievous smile came to her lips. "No, Pop. Only to you. Want a quick feel for old times' sake?"

A curious dignity came into the old man. "No, Marja."

"No?" she echoed, a note of surprise in her voice. "Why?"

"It's only for my girls," he said quietly. "Not for me. It makes 'em feel good to know that someone's botherin' 'em. Even an old man like me. It's bad enough in there. All women, an' not feelin' wanted by nobody. Their families. Nobody. So I bother them an' they laugh an' feel good."

Impulsively she kissed his cheek again. "Thank you, Pop." She turned and started through the gate.

"Be good, Marja," he called after her.

She looked back at him. "I'll try, Pop," she laughed. The gate clanged shut behind her and she walked out into the street. She stepped off the sidewalk into the gutter. Looking down at her feet, she kicked her heel into the pavement.

It made no sound beneath her, and there was a curious softness to its feel. Asphalt, not cement. Cement gave off a funny sound beneath your feet and had no give to it. Cement was beneath your feet everywhere back there. In the halls and on the walks outside. You could hear yourself everywhere you went. But this was quiet. Happily she walked along in the gutter. Free. Really free.

A strong hand closed over hers, the one that gripped the valise. A familiar voice spoke in her ear. "Yuh can get killed walkin' in the street like that. Forget about automobiles?"

She knew who it was without looking up. She had been expecting him from the moment she stepped through the gate. She looked up slowly, still holding onto her valise. Her voice was as expressionless as her eyes. "Yuh forget about a lot of things in a year an' a half, Mike."

There was a nervous smile on Mike's face. "I came to take yuh home, Marja."

She didn't speak.

"I been waiting here all morning," he said.

She drew a deep breath and shook her head. "No," she said. "No."

She could see the hurt creep into his eyes. "But, Marja, I—"

She pulled the valise from his grip. "Yuh got the wrong girl, Mike. Everything's changed. Even the name."

"I don't care what's changed, Marja. I don't care what's

happened. I know yuh never answered my letters, but I came to take yuh home."

She stepped up onto the sidewalk and looked into his eyes. "Who sent for you?" she asked coldly.

His eyes stared back into hers. "I love you, Marja. You said you loved me."

"We were kids then," she said quickly. "We didn't know any better."

"Kids!" he said angrily. "How much older are you now? Two years make that much difference?"

"Yes, Mike," she said slowly. "Two years can make a thousand years' difference. I grew up in a hurry."

"I grew up, too," he said almost boyishly, "but I still feel the same about you. I'll always feel the same."

"I don't," she said.

"What have they done to you, Marja?" There was anguish deep in his voice.

She shook her head wearily. "Nothing," she answered. "I did it all myself. It's over, Mike. We can't go back. We'll never be kids again."

She began to turn away from him, but his strong hands on her shoulders spun her back. "Why, Marja? What happened?"

She didn't answer.

His eyes burned into her face. "Yuh owe me that much for what we were. Tell me!"

He would never forget the mask that dropped over her eyes at that moment. It was as if they were suddenly so deep that nothing was reflected in them, not even the sunlight of the morning. "Tell me, Marja!"

"I had a baby, Mike. While I was in there I had a baby, and I don't even know whether it was a boy or a girl. I signed it away before it was born." Her voice was flat and expressionless. "Yuh still want to know what happened, Mike?"

There was a look of disbelief on his face. His grip on her shoulders had slackened. "Whose was it? Ross's?" he asked hoarsely.

She shook her head. "It couldn't be. He was away. Remember?"

His hands slipped from her shoulders. Lines of pain had formed around his mouth. "You mean there were others?"

She didn't answer.

His eyes were a deep, hurt blue, and there were tears in them. "How could you, Marja? You loved me."

Her voice was still cold, still calm. "There were other things too, Mike. There was a girl back in there. She liked me. She taught me games to help pass the time. Yuh want to hear about them, Mike? It was fun."

"I don't want to hear," he said in a shaking voice. "You're telling me that Ross was right all the time. He said you were a cheap—" He couldn't bring himself to say the word.

She said it for him. "Whore."

His hands gripped her shoulders tightly. He stared down into her face. "Were you, Marja? Were you what he said?"

She didn't answer.

"Why did you lie to me, Marja? Why?" he asked fiercely. "I would have done anything for you. Why did you lie to me?"

Her eyes met his gaze without flinching. "Nothing matters now, Mike," she said slowly. "The truth is something you believe, not what someone tells you."

A taxi came down the block. She signaled, and it pulled in to the curb. "Let me go, Mike. The cab's waiting."

His hands dropped from her shoulders. She entered the cab swiftly and shut the door. As it pulled away from the curb, she looked out the window. Mike was standing there, looking after her. She felt a sudden rush of tears to her eyes. Desperately she fought them back until her eyes were burning. Freedom was so many things she had almost forgotten. It was people you loved and people you hurt. "I love you, Mike," she whispered to herself.

"Where to, lady?"

The cab-driver's voice turned her from the window.

"Hotel Astor on Broadway," she said in a shaking voice.

When she turned back to the window, Mike was gone. Suddenly she could hold the tears back no longer. She could never be right for him. Too many things had happened to her. She was tainted with an ugly scar, and she would have it in her all her life.

He deserved something better. Someone clean and new and fresh. Someone who shone like he did. Not someone like her, who would cheat him of what he deserved.

Chapter 2

SHE looked down at the registration pad the desk clerk pushed toward her. She hesitated a moment. Three and a half dollars a day was a lot of money. Even for a de-luxe room with private bath and shower. Her money wouldn't go too far at this rate. She had only a little more than a hundred dollars.

But she had waited too long for that fact to stop her. She had promised herself this treat ever since she had gone up there. Quickly she began to scrawl:

Mary Flood . . . Yorkville, N. Y. . . . Nov. 20, 1937

She pushed the pad back to the clerk. He looked at it, then punched a bell on the desk. He smiled at her. "Just down from school, Miss Flood?"

She nodded. He didn't know how right he was.

A bellboy came up and picked up her valise. The desk

clerk pushed the key to him. "Show Miss Flood to room twelve-oh-four."

She waited until the door closed behind the bellboy and then threw herself on the bed. She felt herself sinking deliciously into it. It was like resting on a cloud. This was a bed, a real bed. Not one of those imitations they had up there. She rolled completely over and off the other side, and opened the door to the bathroom.

Its shining white porcelain and tiles gleamed at her. She gazed admiringly at the tub. It was the new kind, sunk into the floor. Tentatively she touched its sides. Smooth, not scratchy like the old iron tubs. She let her hand rest on it lightly while she looked around the room.

Turkish towels were on the rack. She moved quickly and picked one up. It was light and soft and fluffy. She buried her face in it. It wasn't coarse like the cotton towels. She took a deep breath. This was living.

She looked at her watch. It was almost noon. She had some shopping to do before she would take that lazy bath she had promised herself. Almost reluctantly she put the towel back on the rack and left the bathroom.

She picked up her handbag and opened it. Once again she counted her money. One hundred and eighteen dollars. That was what she had left of the pay they had given her for working in the laundry. She shook her head for a moment as if to clear it of the steam and the acrid smell of harsh soap and sodium-hypochlorite solution that had hung around her for so long. Resolutely she snapped the bag shut and went to the door.

She stood on the steps of the hotel and looked down at Broadway. It was lunch hour and the streets were even

more crowded than usual. Everybody was going somewhere. People had intent, serious faces and never once
stopped to look around. She marveled at them. They took
so much for granted, so much that she would never take
for granted again.

She looked down the street. The Paramount was playing
the new Bing Crosby picture, the one with Kitty Carlisle.
The Rialto had two horror pictures, and the New Yorker
was showing two westerns. The Nedick's on the corner
across the street was busy, the customers standing three
deep around the counter. The Chinese restaurant between
42nd and 43rd still advertised a thirty-five-cent lunch.
Hector's cafeteria opposite the hotel still boasted the biggest selection of pastry in town, and the faint sound of
music from the dance hall on 45th mingled with the discordant blare of traffic.

With a feeling of contentment she started down the steps
to begin her shopping. There were some stores here where
she knew she could buy clothes fairly cheap. Plymouth for
underwear and blouses, Marker's for skirts and dresses,
Kitty Kelly's for shoes. She found herself humming as she
crossed the street. She had been wrong in what she had told
Pop that morning.

She was home.

She leaned back in the tub lazily, a delicious languor
seeping through her. The water was covered with sparkling,
exploding bubbles, and their perfume hung heavily in the
air. Slowly she stirred, running her hands down over her
body. She could feel the sting of the cheap soap they had
used in the Home. Somehow she had never felt clean after
using it. It seemed to leave a coarse layer over her skin.

But this was different. She could feel her flesh soften in the water.

She pulled a towel from the rack beside the tub and wadded it into a small pillow. Carefully she placed it on the edge of the tub and leaned back on it. It would keep her hair from getting wet, and it made it easier for her to rest. She closed her eyes. It was so good. So good. She was warm and comfortable and safe. No one could bother her now. No one could call her. No one could tell her what to do. She began to doze lightly. It wasn't like the time in the Home.

Not at all like the time when the baby was born.

The pains had been intense through most of the morning. At last the nurse had taken her down to the infirmary. The doctor examined her quickly. He nodded to the nurse. "Get her ready. It won't be long now."

She stretched out, gasping, on a hard white bed. The nurse began to prepare for delivery. Between the waves of pain she was conscious of a sense of shock when the nurse shaved her pubis. Finished at last, the nurse covered her with a white sheet and left the room.

She closed her eyes, breathing heavily. She was glad it was almost over. It had seemed so long to carry a sense of shame and violation inside her. There was a rustling sound at the side of the bed and she turned toward it.

The superintendent was standing there, her gray-black hair frosty over her glasses. She held a sheet of paper in her hand. "How are you, Mary?"

She nodded. "Okay, Mrs. Foster."

"You haven't told me yet about the baby, Mary."

She managed a wan smile. There was nothing to tell. In a little while it would be here. She didn't answer.

"The father, Mary," Mrs. Foster insisted. "He should be made to pay for the child's care."

A pain wrenched through her and she closed her eyes against it. A moment later she turned to the woman. "It doesn't matter," she said in a shaking voice. "It never mattered."

Mrs. Foster shrugged her shoulders and looked down at the sheet of paper. "Okay, Mary. According to this, you want the child placed for adoption."

Mary nodded.

"You know what it means," Mrs. Foster said in a cold voice. "You give up all rights to the child. You may never see it or even know who has it. It will be as if it had never been born, as far as you are concerned."

The girl was silent.

"Did you hear me, Mary?" Mrs. Foster asked.

She nodded.

"You won't know anything about the child," the woman said implacably.

Pain turned into anger in Mary's voice. "I heard you!" she screamed. "I heard you the first time! What do you think I could do about it? Could I take care of it here? Would you let me keep it here?"

"If we knew the father," Mrs. Foster said stolidly, "we could make him contribute to its care. Then we could keep it in a home for you until you are in a position to claim it."

"And when will that be?" Mary's voice was trembling.

"When you have proved that you can support it morally and financially," the woman answered.

"Who decides that?"

"The courts," Mrs. Foster replied.

"Then I can't have it until they say okay. It stays in an orphanage. Right?" Mary asked quietly.

Mrs. Foster nodded.

"But this way it gets adopted? It gets a home right away?"

Mrs. Foster's voice was low. "Yes."

Mary took a deep breath. "That's the way I want it." There was a tone of finality in her voice.

"But—" Mrs. Foster's voice was shaking now.

Pain tore through the girl. It forced her into a half-sitting position on the bed. "That's the way I want it!" she screamed. "Don't you see that's the only chance I can give it?"

The woman turned and left the room and Mary didn't see her again until three hours later. It was all over then. Mrs. Foster stood near the bed again and looked down at her.

Mary's face was white and drawn and there were faint beads of perspiration on her upper lip. Her eyes were shut tight.

"Mary," Mrs. Foster whispered.

She didn't move.

"Mary," the woman said again. "Marja."

Mary's eyes opened slowly and the woman could see she hadn't been asleep.

"You're all right, Marja," Mrs. Foster whispered. "And the baby is fine—"

"Don't tell me!" The girl's voice was a fierce, harsh sound. "I don't want to know!"

"But—" The woman hesitated.

Mary's voice was suddenly weary. She turned her face into the pillow. "Let it go," she whispered. "It's bad enough the way it is."

Mrs. Foster didn't speak. The common bondage of their sex brought them together. Her hand sought the girl's hand beneath the thin cover.

Mary turned her face to the woman, her eyes all pupil,

deep and black. A faint sense of shock came to the woman. It was as if she were gazing into the bottomless wells of time. She felt the slight pressure of the girl's fingers as she began to speak.

"It hurt me," Mary whispered, an echo of pain in her voice. "It hurt me coming out."

"I know, child," the woman said gently. "It always hurts."

"Do yuh, Mrs. Foster?" Mary asked in a wondering voice. And with her next words the woman realized that she didn't know at all. "It didn't hurt the way its father hurt me when he tore me apart to put it there, but the way it hurts you to gain something you know you can't keep."

Suddenly the woman understood. The memory of why the girl had come here came into her mind. Her eyes deepened with sympathy behind her glasses. Now she could see all the pain behind the shadows in the girl's eyes.

They looked deep into each other for a moment, then Mary spoke again. Her voice was very gentle. "Let it go."

Almost without realization the woman nodded her acceptance. "Yes, Mary."

Silently the tears sprang full born to the girl's eyes and began to roll down her cheeks. She made no sound of crying. There were only the tears chasing each other inexorably to the pillow beneath.

Chapter 3

THE DETECTIVE was a slim, polite man. He held the chair for her as she sat down opposite his desk. He studied her for a moment before he walked around the desk to his own seat. This one was born for trouble. There was something about her.

It wasn't the way she looked. There was no coarseness in her. Even the white-blond hair, which cheapened so many of them because of its artificiality, became her. Probably because it was her own. But her face, her body, the way she walked—everything told you this was a woman. The kind that was made for man.

He glanced at the card before him. *Mary Flood*. His eyes widened. Now he understood. He looked up at her. "Where are you staying, Miss Flood?"

"Hotel Astor." Her voice was husky. She took out a cigarette.

Quickly he struck a match and held it for her. He thought he saw a glint of a smile in her dark-brown eyes as she looked over the flame at him. But he could have been wrong. No kid could be that sure of herself on the first visit to the police. It was probably the reflection of the light. "Pretty expensive," he said.

She drew deeply on the cigarette. "It's a treat I promised myself," she answered, as if that explained everything.

He looked down at the card. "Got a job?" he asked.

She shook her head. "I've only been out two days. I haven't even looked yet."

"Don't you think you should?" he asked gently. "They're pretty hard to find."

"I will," she said.

"You can't have much money left," he continued. "I see you bought yourself some new clothes."

For the first time a note of challenge crept into her voice. "It's my dough. There's no law against my doin' what I want with it, is there?"

He shook his head. "No, Miss Flood. We just want to be sure you don't get into trouble, that's all. People get into trouble quicker when they're broke."

"I'm not broke yet," she said quickly.

He didn't answer. He sat there quietly studying her while he lit a cigarette. This girl would have no trouble getting money; her trouble would come from finding too many men willing to give it to her. He waited for her to speak. The one thing they couldn't stand was the silent treatment.

This one was different. She just sat there watching him, her eyes fixed on his face. After a while he began to feel uncomfortable. It was as if he were the probationer and she the reporting officer. He cleared his throat.

"You know the regulations, Miss Flood," he said. "They were explained to you up there."

She nodded.

He repeated them anyway. "You're to report here once each month. You're not to consort or associate with anyone with a criminal record. You're to inform me of any change in your address. You're to let me know where you're working when you get a job. You're not to leave the state unless we give you permission. You're not allowed to possess firearms or other dangerous weapons—" He stopped in surprise. She was smiling. "Why the amusement, Miss Flood?" he asked.

She got to her feet, a half-smile on her lips, and let the coat fall from her shoulders back onto the chair. It seemed to him as if she had disrobed. "Do you think I need any?" she asked.

He felt his face flush. The laws were damned foolish sometimes. But there was nothing you could do about the weapons you were born with. "I'm just reiterating them for your benefit, Miss Flood," he said testily.

"Thank you, lieutenant," she said, sitting down again.

"What kind of a job are you looking for, Miss Flood?" he asked. "Maybe we can help you find one."

She stared at him quizzically. "Do you know of any?"

He nodded. "Waitress or clerk in some of the larger chain stores."

"What do they pay?"

"Twelve to fifteen a week."

"No, thanks," she said dryly.

"What's the matter with them?" he asked, his annoyance showing plainly in his voice.

She smiled suddenly. "It won't even pay my rent. I need a job that pays me a lot of money."

"Not everybody has to live at the Astor," he said sarcastically.

"I like it," she said, still smiling. "I spent enough of my life livin' in dumps. No more."

"Where you going to get that kind of money?" he asked. She didn't answer.

"Whoring?" His voice was flat and cold.

Her eyes were wide on his. The smile disappeared from her lips. "Does it pay that well, lieutenant?"

His voice became threatening again. "You'll get into trouble. Real trouble, not kid stuff. Woman's prison is a lot different than the Home. You'll find out."

"Don't be too sure, lieutenant," she said quietly. "I haven't done anything—yet."

He got to his feet. "Just make sure you don't do anything you'll be sorry for." He pushed the card across the desk toward her and handed her his fountain pen. "Sign the card."

She signed it and he picked it up and looked at her signature. "Okay," he said. "You can go now. But remember what I told you."

She got to her feet, slipped into her coat, and went to the door. When she had opened it, she looked back at him. There was a teasing smile on her lips. "Thanks for the encouragement, lieutenant."

He looked at her coldly. "For your information, I'm not a lieutenant. Just keep in touch with us, that's all."

"I will," she said, still smiling. She looked around the small room slowly, then at him. "Maybe some afternoon when things are dull around here, lieutenant, you'll feel like killing a little time. Drop in on me. We can talk it up awhile."

His mouth dropped open, but he couldn't find any words. His face began to flush.

Her smile grew broader. "You know where I live, lieutenant. Room twelve-oh-four. Just ask the desk clerk to send you on up."

The door closed behind her before he could find an answer. He stared at the closed door thoughtfully. After a minute he picked up his pencil and made a few notes on her card, then reached for the telephone.

"Get Joker Martin for me," he said to the answering voice.

A few seconds later the receiver crackled. "Joker?"

The earphone buzzed.

"This is Egan at the 54th Street station. That girl you were lookin' for just checked in. . . . Yeh. . . . She calls herself Mary now, not Marja. . . . Yeah, same girl. . . . Blonde and built. . . . But real poison, she's not afraid of anything on God's earth. . . . Thanks, Joker. . . . Glad to do you the favor."

Chapter 4

JOKER MARTIN leaned back in his chair and held a match to his cigar. There was a quiet satisfaction in him. The breaks had been right. He had been smart. He had known a year and a half ago that syndication had to come someday. There had been too many killings.

He remembered the time Mike Rafferty had come back to the clubhouse fuming. "Who does that punk think he is?" Iron Mike had growled.

"What punk?" Joker asked.

"Kane. Frank Kane. He calls a meeting up in the hotel. We're all there. He says from now on we all got territories and nobody jumps the line."

Martin turned the name over in his mind. He looked up at Mike. "You mean Fenelli's boy? Where does Silk fit in? Top dog?"

Rafferty shook his head. "No. Kane took over. That's when I walked out. No punk is goin' to tell me what to do."

"How about the others?" Joker asked. "They stay?"

"The chicken-livered bastards!" Iron Mike swore. "They stayed."

Joker hesitated. "Maybe you should've stayed too, Mike."

"I'll burn in hell first!" Rafferty swore. "I always run me own business. Nobody's movin' in on me."

"Okay, Mike," Joker answered.

"I'm goin' home fer dinner," Mike said. "I'll see yuh afterwards. We'll figger out what to do next." He turned and stamped out of the room.

Joker waited until the door had closed behind him, then reached for the phone. Just as the operator spoke, he heard what sounded like the muffled explosion of a backfiring automobile. He put the telephone down quickly and ran to the window.

A crowd was gathering in the street in front of the clubhouse. He couldn't see who was lying on the sidewalk because of the people, but he could see the trail of blood running toward the gutter.

Slowly he walked back to the telephone and picked it up. Iron Mike had been right. He would burn in hell first. Joker wondered whether he liked it. He whispered a number to the operator. A voice answered.

"Mr. Kane," he said in a low, unhurried voice, "this is Joker Martin. No, Iron Mike hasn't changed his mind. It's too late. But I just want yuh to know I'm with yuh. A thousand per cent. . . ."

The breaks had been right and he had prospered. It was a long haul from the dance hall and backroom gambling that Iron Mike had first allotted him. And now Kane had given him this territory and no one could move in on him. He was home now, for Kane kept the peace.

But things were going big and he needed help. Not hood

help, but brains help, class help. Along with the new division of territory he had picked up Park Avenue all the way up to 81st Street. That was when he had first thought of Ross Drego.

The kid was young and wild, but he was bright. He had gambling sense. Good thing his father had cut him off after the last piece of trouble he had been in. It was six months now since Ross had come to Joker, but the kid was worth all the dough he got. He knew all the Park Avenue and big business trade by their first names. He had grown up with them.

The one thing Joker had to watch was the kid's ambition. There were times when it ran away with him. He was in too much of a hurry, he wanted a piece of everything. Joker smiled thoughtfully as he drew on his cigar. He could control Ross, especially now with that new deal that Kane had brought up to the syndicate. It would give Ross something to shoot at and would keep him content until it happened.

He picked up the telephone. His secretary answered. "Is Ross here yet?" he asked.

"He's on his way in now, Mr. Martin," she answered.

He put down the phone as the door opened and Ross came in. He looked down for a moment at the sheet of paper on the desk, then back at Ross. "Got the dough?" he asked.

Ross nodded. He threw a package on the desk. "Ten grand, Joker. Everything I got."

Joker opened a desk drawer and dropped the package into it. He took out a stock certificate from the drawer and pushed it back to Ross.

Ross picked it up and looked at it. Angrily he threw it

back on the desk. "What the hell are you pulling, Joker? This is only one share. I thought it was a big deal."

Joker smiled. "It is."

"Crap!" Ross exploded. "What the hell is this Blue Sky Development Corporation? I never heard of it!"

"That's Las Vegas," Joker answered.

"Las Vegas? Where the hell is that?"

"Nevada," Joker answered. "It's goin' to be the biggest money town in the country. Hotels, gambling, night clubs. And everything legit."

"Give me back my dough," Ross snapped. "If you want me to buy somethin', sell me a piece of Miami or Reno or—"

"Don't be a shmuck," Joker said. "Miami's wrapped up by the Chicago mobs and the stink is climbing up to the heavens. How long do you think that'll last? They gotta wrap up. Reno's a heartbreak city. People won't go there for a ball. Dandy Phil and Big Frank have locked up New Orleans and that'll have to close in time. Sun Valley, Palm Springs, n.g. for gambling."

"So what?" Ross asked. "I know what I'm gettin' there. Real dough."

"Yuh're doin' better here," Joker said. "Yuh're in on the ground floor. We're buyin' the town. Real estate an' all. We'll make the laws. There'll be no stink. Everything'll be legal."

Ross's voice was calmer now. "When is all this goin' to happen?"

"It takes time for a deal like this," Joker answered thoughtfully. "Kane says between five and ten years. Depends on the breaks."

"I'll be an old man by then," Ross snapped.

Joker smiled broadly. "You'll be the richest old man of thirty in the country."

"I don't know." Ross hesitated. "I could use the dough now."

Joker leaned across the desk, his voice lowered to a confidential tone. "Who can't? I got ten shares like yours. Think I wouldn't rather keep a hundred G's kickin' aroun' in my pocket any day? Sure, but not when it'll bring back a million. All legal that nobody can rap you for."

"You got a hundred grand in this?" Ross asked incredulously.

Joker nodded.

"How many shares are there out?" Ross continued.

"One thousand shares." Joker's voice was flat.

"Ten million bucks!" There was a note of awe in the boy's voice.

"An' the only reason I'm lettin' you in on it," Joker said quickly, "is because I got big plans for you."

Ross looked at him through suddenly narrowed eyes. "What plans?"

Joker leaned back in his chair. He took another cigar from his pocket and lit it. "This is a legit operation, see? No hood is goin' to be able to go out there. It has to be real clean. I'm buildin' you up to Kane to be the guy to handle the whole operation for us."

"Do you think it will work?" Ross asked.

"It'll work," Joker said confidently.

Ross picked up the stock certificate and looked at it. "You know, it's beginning to look better to me already."

Joker smiled. "It smells like money, you mean."

Ross laughed as he put the certificate in his pocket. "One of the three smells I can't resist. New money, new cars, and new dames."

Joker grinned. "That reminds me. I just got a line on an old girl of yours, if you're interested."

"Old girls don't interest me," Ross said quickly. "I told you, new dames."

"This one might," Joker said smiling. "That blonde Polack kid—"

"Marja?" Ross's voice had a strange tone. It sounded as if it was almost painful to him to speak the name.

"Yeah." Joker spoke carefully. "I was thinkin' of linin' it up for myself, but first I wanted to check if you still had any ideas."

Ross looked down at his fingers. He had stepped into Joker's trap neatly. There was nothing he could do or say now. He looked up at Joker. The older man was looking at him as an indulgent father would at a child. He kept his voice low. "I got no ideas, Joker. She's all yours."

Chapter 5

SHE sat in the room and waited for the telephone to ring. A pile of cigarettes mounted in the tray. It was Friday morning. She had been here four days, and there was just enough money in her pocketbook for the rent. But Evelyn had said that she would call Friday morning. They had worked out everything between them.

It had started in the laundry about six months before she came out. The slim, dark-haired girl who stood at the ironing board opposite hers looked up suddenly.

"What're you gonna do when you get out, Mary?"

Mary finished a pillowcase and began to fold it neatly. She thought for a moment. "I don't know. Get a job, I guess. I never thought about it."

"What kind of job?"

She began to press a sheet. "I don't know. Any kind I can."

Evelyn laughed. "You'll starve. Your ass'll be out before you know it."

Mary looked at her curiously. "What're you doing?"

"I got plans," Evelyn said mysteriously. "Big plans."

"Like what?"

Evelyn started to answer, but saw a matron coming down the aisle toward them. She spoke quickly out of the corner of her mouth. "See me when the lights are out tonight an' I'll tell yuh. I think we can do somethin' together."

It was almost ten o'clock when Mary stood at the side of Evelyn's bed and looked down at her. "Are yuh up?" she whispered.

The dark-haired girl sat upright. "Yeah."

Mary sat down on the edge of the bed. "What're you goin' to do?"

"I'm gonna make me some real money. I'm goin' into show business. My boy friend is fixin' up a place for me when I get out."

"When is that?" Mary asked.

"Three days after you," Evelyn said. "He tol' me to find a partner and start workin' up an act. That's why I spoke to you. I think we'd make a good team, with you blonde and me dark. That's what they like. Contrast."

Mary hesitated, a growing suspicion in her mind. "What kind of act?" she whispered. "I don't know any routines."

Evelyn laughed silently. "I can show you all the routines in one night."

"Oh," Mary said. "That?"

Evelyn shook her head. "It's better'n beatin' your head in for ten bucks a week."

"I don't know," Mary said. "I never thought about it."

"Pipe down!" a voice called from one of the beds. "We're tryin' to get some sleep."

Evelyn threw back the cover. "Get in here with me,"

she said quickly. "We can talk without them longears hearin' us."

"I think I better go back to bed," Mary said.

Evelyn's white teeth gleamed. "Chicken?"

Mary didn't answer. She moved over on the bed and Evelyn pulled the cover over them. They lay there quietly for a moment. Mary could feel the warmth coming from the girl's body. "What's real money?" she asked.

"Twenty to thirty bucks a day, each," Evelyn whispered. "And it's easy."

Mary was still. Money was the only important thing. Without it you were a bum. Besides, there was nothing more for her. No decent guy would have her if he found out what had happened. "What's the routine?" she asked.

The girl didn't answer. Her hands moved swiftly, and Mary caught her breath. She twisted away. "Cut it!" she snapped.

"You asked me what the routine was," the girl said.

"Yeah," Mary whispered fiercely, "but I didn't think you were a dike."

"I'm not," Evelyn whispered. "That's the routine."

Mary didn't answer. The girl's hands were on her again. She stiffened involuntarily.

"Relax, relax," her friend whispered. "I won't hurt yuh. A little sport will do yuh some good. It makes the time pass easier."

The day before Mary left, Evelyn helped her pack her valise. "Remember what I told you," she said. "Wait in your room Friday morning until I call."

"I'll remember," Mary answered. . . .

She looked at her watch again. It was almost noon. She put out her cigarette and placed her valise on the bed. Slowly she began to pack. There would be no call, and she had to get out anyway while she still had enough money to pay the bill.

The phone rang. She picked it up quickly. "Evelyn?"

A man's voice answered. "This is Joe, Evelyn's boy friend. She's outside in the car. You ready?"

"I'm almost packed," she said.

"Good," he said. "I'll come up and get you."

She had finished packing by the time he knocked at the door. She opened it. A big florid man stood there. She smiled at him. "Joe?"

He nodded and came into the room, holding out his hand. She took it. "You're just as pretty as Evelyn said you would be," he said in a false hearty voice.

She dropped his hand quickly. "Thank you," she said. "I'm ready to go now." She moved toward the phone. "I'll call a boy."

He shook his head. "Don't," he said. "I'll take the bag out the side door for you. You go out the front door as if you're stepping out. No bill that way."

She looked at him steadily. "I pay my bills, thanks."

He shrugged his shoulders. "It's your money."

She picked up the phone and called the desk.

Evelyn was sitting in the car. She smiled as they approached it. "I was wondering if you'd still be there, honey."

"I'd about given you up," Mary confessed as she climbed in beside her.

Evelyn grinned. "Joe was anxious, so we stopped off for a minute while he picked up his bags."

Mary looked quickly at her friend. Evelyn's face was faintly flushed. "He picked up his bags?" she questioned.

"Yeah," Joe grunted as he put the car into gear and

they moved out into traffic. "Yuh don't expect a guy to go away without his clothes."

"Go away?" Mary echoed. "Where are we goin'?"

"Florida," Joe said. "Miami. I got a great little apartment out in North Beach. The pickin's will be great there this season."

The tall gray-haired man stepped up to the desk. "Mary Flood, please. Room twelve-oh-four."

The desk clerk looked up at him. "You just missed her, sir. She checked out five minutes ago."

Joker Martin stared at him. "Checked out?" A suspicion leaped into his mind. "Was there anyone with her?"

The desk clerk nodded. "There was a gentleman, sir."

"What did he look like?" Joker demanded.

"He was a big man, sir. About your height. Red face."

"Oh." Joker turned away from the desk.

"Is there anything wrong, sir?" the desk clerk asked.

Joker looked back at him. "No, nothing wrong." He walked through the lobby to the street. At least it wasn't Ross. At first he had thought it might have been, but Ross was dark and not as tall as he.

He pushed through the revolving door into the street. It served him right for waiting. He should have come right over when he heard about her. He might have known that a girl like her wouldn't take long in making a connection. He pushed a cigar into his mouth and chewed on it without lighting it. Maybe it was just as well for the while. He had too many things on his mind. He could wait.

She would turn up again. Sooner or later they all turned up again.

Chapter 6

FOR the third consecutive morning he watched her coming out of the water. She came from the sea like a goddess. She was wearing a white bathing-suit that hung on her figure as if it were her skin. Her high, full breasts, tiny waist, slim yet generous hips seemed carved out of white marble. Slowly she pulled off the white bathing-cap. A mass of sparkling white-gold hair tumbled down around her sun-darkened face.

Slowly she walked up the beach to her blanket. She bent and picked up a towel and rubbed herself vigorously. He could almost feel the animal tingling of the towel against his skin. He had never seen anyone enjoy herself as much as this girl coming out of the water.

He knew what she would do next. She would stretch out on the blanket, loosen the shoulder straps of her suit, and lie in the sun. Not once would she glance up at the crest of the small hill where his house looked over the ocean. After she had been in the sun for an hour she would get up and neatly pack all her things in a small beach bag. Then she would slip a robe over her shoulders, walk down to the edge of the beach, climb into a small convertible, and drive off.

That was the routine she followed every morning. He could almost set his clock by her. He would see her from his bedroom window every morning walking up the beach at eleven o'clock. This had happened regularly since he had come down to Florida toward the end of January, almost three weeks ago. He had first seen her the night after the Senator's party.

He had awakened with a terrible hangover and had yelled for his man to bring him some tomato juice. But Tom was half deaf and either couldn't or wouldn't hear him. Angrily he tumbled out of bed and crossed to the bellpull near the window. He leaned on it heavily, looking out the window.

She was coming out of the water then. At first he shook his head, thinking he was seeing things. In the hazy morning light he thought she was nude. When his head cleared, he could see her white suit. He turned away thinking himself a fool. But the next morning he found himself at the window hoping she would appear.

"Jerk!" he told himself. "You're Gordon Paynter. You're supposed to be the catch of the season. Every mother in Florida has set her daughter's cap for you, and you're mooning after some dame on the beach. You don't even know who she is. She's probably some cracker without a thought in her head except for the sun and the sand."

Suddenly he was aware of his man standing next to him. He turned quickly. Tom was staring down at the beach. "That's a right purty gal, Mr. Gordon," Tom said.

Gordon smiled. "Is that why I can't get you in the mornings? You've been watching her, too?"

Tom looked up at him. He spoke with a familiarity that

came from long association. "I may be old, Mr. Gordon, but I got eyes."

"Do you know who she is?" Gordon asked.

"Uh-uh," the old man answered. "I never see'd her nowhere but here."

"Do you think she would have lunch up here?"

The old man looked at him with suddenly wise eyes. "Y' cain't tell unless you ax her."

Gordon turned and looked down at the beach. Stretched out on her blanket, she almost blended with the sand. He grinned. "Go ahead, Tom. Ask her to lunch with me."

She lay quietly in the sand, her head resting on her arms. The warm sun burned into her back. It was a good, clean heat. It wasn't a dirty heat like the white lights that had shone down on her at last night's show. She thought of the men whose stares hung heavy on her body almost like something you could feel. What were men like that they could find their kicks in second-hand exhibitions?

The worst part of the whole thing was making them understand, after the show was over, that that was all. She had nothing more for them. She and Evelyn would dress and they would wait outside in the car while Joe picked up the other half of their money. Then they would drive off.

Usually Evelyn and Joe would go out somewhere, but she went right home and climbed into the tub. A hot bath cleaned out a lot of the poisons. Then she would go to bed, read awhile, and then fall asleep. Sometimes she would awaken when Joe and Evelyn came home. There would be sounds in the night, and she would be very still until there was silence again.

In the morning she would be up while they were still asleep, put on her bathing-suit, go out to the car, and drive

down to the beach. They would be up when she got back
from the beach, and usually she would make breakfast.
Then Joe and Evelyn would dress and go to the race track.
They would come back in the late afternoon. Occasionally
they blew all their money and had to borrow from her for
the next day. They never repaid her, but she knew better
than to ask them for it.

On the whole, it wasn't too bad. She had managed to
save about five hundred dollars, which she kept in a savings
bank in Miami. Once a week she would go into town and
catch a picture, have lunch, and stop at the bank. The
routines, as Evelyn called them, had long since stopped
bothering her. She was able to regard them impersonally.
After all, they were a kind of performance. You didn't
have to feel anything to put on an act.

It was almost time for her to turn over. Her back was
warm and toasted. As she began to roll over, she became
aware of someone standing near her. She sat up quickly,
her hands holding the bathing-suit straps in front of her.

A wizened, gray-haired colored man was standing there.
He smiled at her. "Ma'am," he said in a gentle, hesitating
voice.

"Yes?" she answered coldly.

"Mistuh Gordon Payntuh's compliments to you, ma'am,"
the old man said formally, "an' would like you to jine him
for lunch up in his house."

Her eyes followed the half-wave of his hand to the house
on the crest. She had noticed the house before. It was a
rich man's place, with an iron fence running all around it
and right down to the beach. She turned back to the
colored man. "Tell Mr. Paynter that I appreciate his in-
vitation, but if he wants to ask me to lunch, he can damn
well come down here and ask me himself."

A smile twinkled deep in the old man's eyes. "Yes, ma'am," he said gravely. "I'll sho' tell him." He bowed slightly and turned back toward the house.

Mary watched him walk away and begin the climb toward the house. Then she stretched out on the sand and closed her eyes. A strange way to pick up a girl—send a servant after her. She wondered what Mr. Paynter was like. Probably some old geezer with one foot in the grave. Probably she had put him in his place. She dozed a few minutes, then prepared to leave.

She had already packed her bag and was starting toward the car when she heard the sound of footsteps in the sand. She turned back.

A young man was running toward her. He was wearing white duck pants and a white knit shirt. His hair was light brown and curly in the ocean wind. "Miss!" he called. "Miss!"

She waited for him to come up. He was tall, and his eyes were light blue. His face was a little heavy and there were slight lines of dissipation around his mouth and eyes.

"I thought you would leave before I got here." His voice rasped heavily after his unaccustomed exercise. "But I had to get some clothes on."

She didn't speak.

He smiled suddenly. "Man, am I out of condition! I can't catch my breath. I'm Gordon Paynter."

He watched her closely. She made no sign of recognizing the name. She still didn't speak.

"I've seen you swimming several times. People generally don't come this far up the beach. It's too lonely here." He was breathing easier now.

Her voice was low. "That's why I like it. I don't want to be bothered by people."

"Oh, I'm sorry," he said. "I didn't mean to intrude. I just thought it would be nice if—"

"Thanks, Mr. Paynter," she said quickly. "It was nice of you. Maybe some other time." She turned away.

"Let me walk to your car with you," he said. "I've seen you somewhere, I'm sure. Was it at the Senator's party?"

She looked at him swiftly. His face was open and free of guile. He didn't look like the type who attended those stags. He was just fishing. She smiled slowly. "I don't think we've met, Mr. Paynter."

"You're sure, Miss, er—Miss—?"

She didn't answer. When they reached the car, she threw her bag into the back seat and climbed in.

"You're from New York," he said, looking at the license plate. "I am, too. Maybe we met up—"

"No, Mr. Paynter." She turned on the ignition. "We've never met, I'm sure."

"Look, Miss—Miss—" He gave up waiting for her to supply her name. "I hope you won't let me drive you away from the beach."

"You won't," she said quickly. "I like it here."

"Maybe you'll come to lunch tomorrow then?" he asked, encouraged.

The motor roared as it caught. "Maybe," she laughed. "Why don't you ask me tomorrow, Mr. Paynter?" The car moved away.

He stood at the edge of the road looking after it. He scratched his head. Strange girl. She didn't sound as if she had ever heard of him. He wondered if she was putting on an act. He shook his head as he turned back to the house. Maybe he would find out tomorrow.

Chapter 7

WHEN she got to the beach the next morning, she blinked her eyes in amazement. A table stood on the sand, an umbrella over it. It was completely set with food, and Gordon Paynter stood next to it.

He grinned. "You're ten minutes late."

"I—uh—" She couldn't speak.

"I wasn't taking any chances. I had Tom set us up down here," he explained.

"It seems to me that you're goin' to a lot of trouble for nothing, Mr. Paynter," she said.

"I don't think so, Miss No-name," he said.

"What'd you call me?" she asked.

"Miss No-name," he answered quickly. "I kind of like it. Makes you very mysterious."

She smiled slowly. "I don't think I'm very mysterious."

"Any girl without a name is mysterious in Miami." He turned to the table. "I hope you like shrimp. Tom makes the meanest shrimp salad."

229

"I love shrimp," she said.

"Good," he said, sitting down. "Let's eat."

She dropped her robe on the beach. "I'd like to swim first."

"Okay," he said. He stood up and took off his shirt. He dropped his trousers into the sand beside her robe. He was wearing a bright yellow pair of shorts. "Let's go."

He followed her down to the water. She dove into a breaker and came up sputtering. "The water's cold," she shouted back to him, her teeth chattering.

He grinned. "I'll speak to Tom about it. I'll see if we can run some hot-water pipes down here for you."

"Crazy man," she laughed, her back to the breakers. A big wave broke behind her and tumbled her to her knees. She felt his hands grab her under the shoulders and lift her to her feet. She stood there staring into his face.

His eyes were serious. "Now that I've saved your life, miss, do you think you can tell me your name?"

She caught her breath. There was something about his eyes that reminded her of Mike. They had the same decency about them, the same gentleness in the way they looked at her. She smiled slowly. "I guess it's only polite," she said.

He nodded, still holding her. "It's only polite."

"Flood," she said, "Mary Flood."

"Pleased to meet you, Miss Flood." he said. He kissed her cheek quickly and let her go. "Very pleased to meet you, Miss Flood."

"I never ate so much in my life, Gordon," she said, pushing her plate away from her.

He smiled. "Tom will be happy. He likes people to enjoy his food."

"You can tell him for me that it's the greatest," she said, grinning.

"More coffee?" he asked.

She shook her head. "No, thanks. I've had it." She looked at her watch. "Golly! It's after one. I've gotta run!"

"What about tonight, Mary?" he asked. "Have we got a date?"

"Uh-uh," she said. "I'd like to, but I can't."

"Why?" he asked.

"I've gotta work," she said.

"Tomorrow night, then?"

She shook her head. "No nights. That's when I work."

"What do you do?" he asked curiously.

"My girl friend and I have a routine," she said carefully. "We work a different club every night."

"Where are you working tonight?" he asked. "I'll come and see you."

"I don't know," she said quickly. "We're a fill-in. We wait at the agent's place until we get a call. When some act doesn't show up, then we rush over and go on."

"Oh," he said. "Maybe some time when you know in advance you'll tell me."

She nodded. "I will, Gordon." She picked up the bag from the sand beside her. "Thanks for the lunch."

"Let me carry it to the car for you," he said, taking the bag from her.

"Okay."

They walked slowly to the car. "I'll see you tomorrow," he said.

She looked down at her feet in the sand. She had already made up her mind. She wasn't coming back to this beach. Ever. She would have to find another place to swim. "Sure," she said.

They were at the car now. He opened the door for her, and she got inside. He put the bag on the seat beside her. "Thanks for everything, Gordon," she said.

"Thank you, Mary."

She held out her hand. He took her by surprise. Instead of shaking it, he held it to his lips. "Until tomorrow," he said.

He let go of her hand and she turned on the ignition. The motor roared. "Good-by, Gordon," she said. "You've been real sweet. Thanks again."

She came into the apartment humming. Joe and Evelyn were sitting at the table having coffee. Joe looked up at her. "What do you feel so good about?"

"I just feel good, that's all," she said. "Some guy bought me lunch."

Joe laughed harshly. "He'd better be good for more than lunch. I just got the word from my contact. We're shut down for a couple of weeks."

Mary looked at him. "What do yuh mean?"

"We gotta lay low. The cops are gettin' hot."

"Oh." Mary sat down at the table. She looked at her fingernails carefully. "What're we gonna do?" she asked.

Joe shot a quick glance at Evelyn. Without speaking, he got up and went into the bedroom.

Mary looked over at her. "What's with him?"

Evelyn shrugged her shoulders. "You know Joe," she said. "He's such a sensitive guy about some things."

Mary laughed. Evelyn's words were even funnier to her because of the seriousness with which they were spoken. "The only thing he's sensitive about," she said, "is his wallet."

Evelyn didn't see the humor. "Yeah, that's it," she

agreed. "He's ashamed to ask you for the dough to pick us up outta here an' go to New Orleans."

Mary's eyes opened wide. "What happened to his dough? He gets half of everything we make."

Evelyn didn't meet her gaze. "It's gone. The track. Other reasons." She smiled at Mary. "I told him not to worry. That if you had any dough you'd be glad to put it up for us."

Mary's face was straight. "I got about twenty-two bucks in my bag. He can have that, if it'll help."

A look of disappointment came into Evelyn's eyes. "That all? What about the rest of the dough? You must have a couple of hundred dollars around. You never blew any of it."

Mary smiled. "I spent it on clothes. It wasn't much when yuh go shoppin'."

Joe's voice came angrily from the bedroom door. "I tol' yuh, Evelyn, she ain't goin' to give us nothin'. We been treatin' her too good. There's only one way to make a broad like that understand who's boss." He came threateningly toward Mary.

Calmly she reached into her pocketbook and took out the switch knife she had bought on her first shopping-trip. She looked up into his eyes steadily as she pressed the button, flipping out the blade. Its sharp, shining edge reflected all the light in the room. "Did Evelyn ever tell yuh how come I got sent up to that school?" she asked in a quiet voice.

Joe stopped short, his face flushed. He looked at his girl questioningly.

Evelyn's face was white. "She cut up her stepfather pretty bad."

He looked down at Mary. Idly she began to clean her nails with the blade. He turned back to Evelyn. "Fine class of friends you pick," he said in a disgusted voice. "I thought you said she was a high-class dame."

Chapter 8

SHE went to her room early and read awhile before going to sleep. The low hum of conversation came to her through the closed door. She smiled to herself. Joe had taken the twenty-two dollars without a murmur. She wondered what they were going to do next. At last she turned off the light and went to sleep. Time enough to worry tomorrow.

Bright sunlight was tumbling through the open window when she awakened. She rolled over on the bed and stretched. It was great going to bed at a decent hour. She had almost forgotten what it was like. She climbed out of bed and picked up her housecoat from the chair. There were no closets in this small room, only in the big room which Joe and Evelyn shared.

Slipping into it, she walked into the other room. Her brows knitted in puzzlement. The bed was empty. It hadn't been slept in. She walked over to the window and looked out. The car was gone too.

She went to the sink and filled the coffeepot, still
thinking. They must have gone out last night and not yet
returned. She turned on the burner under the coffee and
walked to the closet.

It was empty. All the clothing was gone. Quickly she
opened the dresser drawers. Everything was gone. She
swore to herself silently. The only clothing in the whole
apartment was what she had on at the moment. A nightgown, a cheap housecoat, and a pair of mules. They had
taken all her clothes, even the bathing-suit.

The coffee was bubbling. She poured herself a cup and
sat down to think. Idly she reached for the package of
cigarettes that was always on the table. Even that was gone.
She went into the bedroom and took the package from her
purse.

A knock came at the door. She opened it. The landlord
was standing there. "Yes?" she asked.

A short, thick-set man, he looked at her from under
bushy eyebrows. "Your friends are gone," he said.

She stood in the doorway. "Yeah," she said.

He made a move to come into the apartment. She
blocked his way. "They said you'd square the rent," he
said, trying to look over her shoulder and see what was
left in the apartment.

"How much do they owe yuh?" she asked.

"Three weeks," he said, his eyes not meeting her gaze.
"Ninety bucks."

She couldn't tell whether he was lying. If he was telling
the truth, Joe had been pocketing her share of the rent.
"He told me he had paid you up to last week," she said.

His eyes turned shrewd. "Got the receipts?"

"They must be here somewhere," she said.

He knew she didn't have them. When he had heard the

motor start in the middle of the night, he had come out of his room in a hurry. He always slept with one ear tuned in on the tenants. You had to be like that in the furnished-apartment business or you'd soon be without your shirt. Someone was always trying to con you out of your rent money.

The man and the girl were putting their bags in the car. "Hey!" he said, tying his bathrobe around him. "Where're you goin'?"

The man turned to him. "We're checkin' out."

"What about my rent?" he asked.

"Your rent is okay," the man said. "The blonde is still there. She ain't comin' with us."

"How do I know she's got the dough?" he demanded.

The man looked over at his girl friend quickly, then took the landlord's arm and led him behind the car where she couldn't hear them. "She's got dough," he whispered. "You can sock her for a couple of weeks, not only this one."

Unconsciously the landlord lowered his voice. "But you got the receipts."

The man chuckled and took a few slips of paper from his pocket. "Now you got 'em back."

The landlord looked down at his hand. They were the printed rent receipts for the last few weeks.

The man chuckled again. "I gotta get out. You know how dames are. My girl is jealous, an' the blonde won't leave me alone." He looked at the landlord as if he had a sudden idea. "You might even—"

The landlord felt his mouth go dry. He had seen her go down to the car in her bathing-suit. "D'ya think?" he asked.

The man nodded. "Easy," he said.

The landlord stood there indecisively. Actually, the rent

was only two days behind. "How do I know?" he asked.

The man put his hand confidentially on his shoulder. "Y'
can't miss," he said. "The kid's got round heels. A real
nympho, can't do without it. All you gotta do is show it to
her."

The landlord took a deep breath. "Okay," he said,
stepping back. "I'll take a chance."

He watched the car drive off into the night and then
went back into his room. Even if the man were wrong, the
worst that could happen was that he would pick up an
extra few bucks. . . .

He put his foot in the jamb of the door. "Look," he
said positively, "the rent wasn't paid. I want my dough."

Mary looked down at his foot, then up at his face. "Yuh
can't get it," she said. "Not until I go down to the bank and
take it out."

He shook his head. "I've had those gags pulled before.
You'll disappear an' I'll be out in the cold. I want it now."

"I haven't got it here," she said.

"You got it," he said, letting his gaze travel meaningly
down her housecoat. "All you need."

She let a smile come to her lips. Understanding came to
her in a hurry. "Okay," she said. "But I'll need a little time
to get ready. I gotta bathe an'—"

He reached a hand toward her. He felt the firm swell of
her breast under the housecoat, then adroitly she slipped
away from him.

She was still smiling. "Not now," she said.

He looked at her. The guy was right. "Okay," he said
magnanimously. "I'll give you an hour."

"Thanks," she said dryly.

"But don't fool around," he said. "The cops down here
are hell on rent-beaters. Especially when they're tourists."

She closed the door behind him and listened to his footsteps go down the corridor. For a moment she stood there, then went back to the table. She picked up her cup and tasted the coffee. It was cold.

Lighting another cigarette, she carried the coffee back to the stove and stood there, thoughtfully looking down at the pot while it was heating. Deep inside her she had always known what would happen. Sooner or later she would have to make up her mind.

When the coffee was hot, she carried it back to the table and sat down. If only she had some clothes in the place, she could get out. But even if she did, the landlord would call the cops. Joe had said the cops were getting hot. Maybe they would recognize her as part of the act. Then things would be even worse.

She sipped at the coffee and lit one cigarette from the end of the other. She smiled grimly to herself. It wasn't as if she had anything to lose. She was no virgin who had to protect this invisible barrier. Her stepfather had seen to that. And she knew how to take care of herself, too. That business would never happen again. That was another thing she had learned up at the school. There was nothing to worry about. Still, something had always held her back.

She closed her eyes almost wearily. They were always after that. Men were all the same. She knew it. She used to laugh at it. It had been a game to her then to see how far she could go with them and still get away. If only there were something inside her that could match their desires. Then maybe she could feel differently about it. Only when she was near Mike had she felt something stirring.

Strange that she should think of him now. It seemed as if he belonged to a completely different world. She wondered if it was the love she felt for him that had made it different. It must have been. She had never felt like that with anyone else.

She finished her second cup of coffee and looked at the clock. Fifteen minutes to go. She got up and rinsed out the cup and saucer. Slowly she dried them and put them neatly back on the shelf. She sat down again and looked at the clock. Ten minutes.

She lit another cigarette and waited, staring up at the clock. She wished she could feel something inside her. Anything. Even fear. But she didn't even feel that. Only the cold certainty that this had been bound to happen, that it had only been a question of time.

She was still staring up at the clock when the knock came at the door. She got to her feet. "Come in," she called.

The door opened and the landlord stood there. He hesitated a moment, then entered the room and shut the door quickly behind him. His face glistened with excitement. "Well?" he asked.

Her eyes looked at him levelly. Automatically she noted that he had shaved and put on a clean shirt. She half smiled to herself. "Well?" she answered.

"Ready?" he asked, walking toward her.

"Always ready," she answered automatically, her eyes still on his face.

His hands reached out for her and pulled her to him roughly. He kissed her. She could feel his teeth hard behind his lips. She didn't move. His hands moved swiftly and the sound of her clothing tearing came almost distantly to her. It was then that she pushed him away.

Regretfully she looked at the torn housecoat on the floor, then at herself. Now she had no clothes at all. She looked at him.

He was staring at her, his eyes white all around the edges. "My God," he was muttering. "My God!" He moved toward her.

She spun him toward the bedroom. Now it was all clear to her. It had taken a long time, but now she understood. It was for this life that she had been born. Some girls were born to be wives, some secretaries, some clerks, some actresses. But she had been born to be a whore. That was why things had always gone as they had for her. That was what everyone else could see in her.

"In there," she said calmly, gesturing toward the door.

He came toward her again.

She shook her head slightly. "What's your hurry?" she asked. "I'm not runnin' away."

He hesitated, then turned and walked into the bedroom, stripping off his shirt as he went. She picked up her torn housecoat and followed him into the room. She could see the faint matting of hair that covered his chest and shoulders.

She remembered Evelyn's line from the routine. It was always good for a wave of excitement from the audience. If she had been born to be a whore, she was going to be the best there was. The words came to her lips as if she had been saying them all her life.

"How d'yuh want it? Straight or special?"

Chapter 9

SHE walked into the hotel lobby and chose a seat in a discreet out-of-the-way corner. Opening a copy of *Vogue* that she had carried with her, she glanced through it idly. Anyone looking at her would think her an attractive girl, young, sun-tanned, healthy, waiting for her boy friend. Which was just what she was doing—in a way.

A few minutes passed. Then a bellboy stopped in front of her. "Room three-eleven," he said in a low voice.

"Three-eleven," she repeated, a smile on her lips.

He nodded. "Right. He's waiting there now."

"Thank you." She smiled, holding out her hand.

"You're welcome, miss," the bellboy answered, taking the two bills from her. He walked away quickly.

Slowly she closed the magazine, glancing around the lobby as she stood up. It was normal. The house dick was looking the other way, the desk clerks were busy with check-ins, the other people in the lobby were all guests.

Satisfied with her quick check, she sauntered toward the elevators. She had nothing to worry about. Everyone was taken care of. Mac, the landlord of the rooming-house, had put her wise to that.

"Pick a place to operate from," he had said knowingly. "Then before you do anything, make sure that everybody who might be interested is paid off. They'll leave you alone then, even help you."

She nodded. "That makes sense."

He looked at her intently. "Just be careful you don't bring nobody here. I'm runnin' a straight joint. I'm not lookin' for no trouble."

"I'll get out, then, if you want," she said.

He thought for a minute. "No, wait. I got an idea. A friend of mine is bell captain at the Osiris. I'll talk to him. Maybe he can set you in right."

The Osiris was one of the new hotels on the beach. The bell captain had been more than willing to co-operate. There was always a call for new girls. In little more than a month she had made more money than she had ever seen in her life, but by the time she was through paying off she kept only a small part of it.

She averaged four visits a day, as she called them. They were spread out among all the hotels that the bell captain had contacts in, so that she wouldn't become too conspicuous. At ten dollars a visit, it came to forty dollars a day. Thirty dollars went into the payoff.

She pressed the button and waited for the elevator. While she waited she took out another bill. The elevator-operator had to be tipped, too. A hand fell on her shoulder.

Involuntarily she jumped as she turned.

Gordon Paynter grinned at her. "I didn't mean to startle you, Miss Flood."

She held her breath. "Mr. Paynter!"

"I was wondering what had happened to you," he said quickly. "You never came back to the beach."

"The act broke up that day," she said. "I was busy looking for somethin' else."

"Come into the bar and have a drink with me," he said. "We'll bring each other up to date."

The elevator doors opened and the operator stuck his head out. "Up, please."

She looked up at Gordon. "I can't," she said. "I have an appointment."

"It can keep a few minutes," he said. "I've been looking all over town for you."

She smiled to herself. She was easy enough to find if you knew the right people. All he had to do was to check into the hotel and order a young blonde. "No, really," she said, "I got to see this man. It's about a job."

"I'll wait," Gordon said. "Will you be long?"

She thought for a moment. "Not long. Half-hour to an hour."

"I'll be in the bar," he said. "You'll be able to recognize me easy. I'll be draped over a martini."

"All right, Mr. Paynter," she said.

"You had already got around to Gordon," he said, smiling.

"Okay, Gordon," she said, going into the elevator. "I'll try not to be too long."

The door closed and the operator turned toward her. "Friend or customer?" he asked in a curious voice.

"Fourth floor, nosey," she said, holding the dollar out to him.

He took it, grinning. "Don't you give anybody discounts, Mary?"

She smiled at him as the elevator stopped. "Can't afford to. Operating-expenses are too high." The doors opened and she walked out.

"Maybe on your night off," he called after her.

"Save your money, bub," she flung back over her shoulder. "I got no nights off."

She heard the door close as she walked down the corridor. At the door of room 311 she stopped and knocked gently.

A man's voice came muffled through the door. "Who is it?"

She spoke softly but strongly enough to be heard through the door. "Room service."

She looked at her watch as she came into the bar. Three quarters of an hour. She paused, waiting for her eyes to get used to the dimness. He was sitting in a booth at the back. He waved to her and got up as she walked toward him.

"Get the job?" he asked as he made room for her.

"In a way," she answered, sitting down.

A waiter came to the table. "Another martini for me," Gordon said. "What about you?"

She looked at him. "Cassis and soda."

"Vermouth cassis and soda," the waiter repeated.

"No vermouth," she corrected. "Just cassis and soda."

As the waiter walked away, Gordon said: "That's a strange drink."

She met his gaze. "That's the way I like it."

"You're a strange girl," he said, finishing the remainder of the drink before him.

She looked at him sharply. Maybe one of the bellboys had put him wise. She didn't speak.

"You never came back, never called. Nothing," he said. "If I hadn't happened to run into you, I might never have seen you again."

"Maybe you would have been better off," she said solemnly.

His eyes narrowed. "What do you mean?"

She looked straight at him. "I'm no bargain. I'm not the kind of a girl you ordinarily run around with."

His lips parted in a smile. So she had heard about him. "What kind of girls are they?" he asked.

"Society an' stuff," she said. "You know what I mean."

"And because you're a working girl I can't bother with you?" he said.

She didn't answer.

The smile left his lips. "You're the real snob," he said. "It's not my fault I don't have to work. It could have happened to you. Nobody picks his parents."

She smiled suddenly. "It should have," she agreed. "I could think of worse things."

His hand reached for her hand across the table. "So could I." He smiled with her.

The waiter placed their drinks on the table. Gordon picked up his martini and held it toward her. "A toast," he said.

She picked up her drink. "To what?"

"To us," he said. "And to our dinner tonight. Tom's been waiting a long time to roast a duck for you."

She hesitated.

"I won't take any refusal," he said quickly. "I'm taking you right out to the beach after this drink."

She took a deep breath. A feeling of disappointment ran through her. He was no different from the others. He wanted the same thing. "Okay," she said.

He still held his drink toward her. "And to no more mysteries. I want to see a lot of you."

She nodded slowly.

"Tom and I think that you're the prettiest girl in Miami Beach," he said. "I think we're both in love with you."

Slowly she put her glass down on the table. "Don't say that," she said. "Don't say it even if you're joking. You don't have to."

Chapter 10

"COFFEE and brandy out on the terrace, Tom," Gordon said, pushing his chair back from the table.

Tom held Mary's chair while she got up. "It was great, Tom." She smiled. "I never ate so much in my life."

The old man grinned at her. "You sho' got a powerful appetite, miss. You eats like a puhson oughter."

"Thanks to you, Tom. Nobody can resist that food."

"Thank you, ma'am." He bowed, grinning.

Gordon held the door for her. She stepped out into the night. The sky was clear, and a soft, cooling breeze blew in from the ocean.

She took a deep breath. "This is like heaven," she said.

He smiled. "It's not simple, but it's home."

She turned to him quickly. "You invite everybody to your home like this, Gordon?"

He was puzzled. "What do you mean?"

"I mean, without knowing them? Really? For all you

know, I might be on the make for yuh. It could be nothing but trouble." Her face was serious.

He grinned. "That kind of trouble I like. Make me."

"I'm serious, Gordon," she insisted. "You're a rich man and well known. Somebody could take advantage of you."

"I wish they would," he said, still laughing. "It would save me the trouble of trying to take advantage of them."

She walked to the railing. The moonlight sparkled on the water below. "There's no use talking to you," she said.

He put his arms on her shoulders and turned her around. His lips were smiling, but his eyes were serious. "Keep talking, baby. It's nice having someone to worry about me for a change. Usually everybody's after me for something."

She stared into his eyes. "You're a nice guy. I don't want nothin' from you."

"I know you don't," he said. "If you did, you would have been back."

She didn't answer.

"You're the first person in a long time who doesn't give a damn that I'm Gordon Paynter," he said.

"I like you," she said. "You're decent."

His hands dropped to his sides. "Famous last words. Just when I was trying to set you up, you take the wind out of my sails."

She smiled at him. "Don't get discouraged. There's a fresh wind coming in from the ocean."

She put down her coffee cup. "You drink an awful lot," she said. "What for?"

He put down his fourth brandy and looked at her. "I like it," he said. He was beginning to feel the liquor. The words weren't coming just right. "Besides, there's nothing else to do."

"Nothing?" she asked in a wondering voice.

"Nothing," he answered heavily. "I keep away from business because every time I try something I lose money. Finally I gave it up. I get all I need without working."

She didn't speak.

He stared at her. "You think that's wrong, don't you?" he asked accusingly.

She shook her head.

He grabbed her arm. "You do, really, don't you? Everybody else does. They think it's terrible that I don't have to work while half the world is starving."

"I don't give a damn about the rest of the world," she said. "I only worry about me."

He let go of her arm. He felt incredibly sad and lonely. "Well, I do," he said. "I think it's terrible."

Her eyes glowed in the dark. "Then why don't you do something about it?"

"They won't let me," he said. He was near tears. "My lawyers won't let me. I can't even give my money away if I want to. They would stop me."

"Poor Gordon," she said, patting his hand.

"Yes, poor Gordon," he agreed.

"I wish I could feel sorry for you," she said.

His head snapped up. His eyes were suddenly clear. "What do you mean?"

She smiled at him. "Nobody ever had it so good."

He began to laugh. He threw his head back and the laughter rolled up from deep inside him. It roared against the house and down toward the surf.

She looked at him with wide eyes. "What're you laughin' at?"

He managed to control himself for a moment. He looked into her face. "Of all places to find an honest woman!" he gasped. "I'd never have believed it. Miami Beach!"

A puzzled look came into her eyes. "What's wrong with Miami Beach?" she asked. "I like it fine."

"I do, too," he said, still laughing. He went to the railing and looked down at the water, then turned back to her. "I have extra bathing-suits inside. How about a swim?" he asked.

She nodded silently.

They came back to the terrace wrapped in big Turkish towels. "Tom!" he yelled. "Some hot coffee. We're freezing!"

There was no answer.

He walked over to the doors and called: "Hey, Tom! Get us some coffee."

Tom's voice came back faintly. "Git it yo'self, boss. I gone to bed already."

Gordon came back from the door shaking his head. "I can't do a thing with him. He's been with me too long."

She smiled. "I can make coffee."

"Would you?" he asked.

"I insist," she said. "I'm cold, too. The water's great, but you gotta be used to it."

He led her into the kitchen. There was coffee on the stove. She lighted the burner under it. A few minutes later they were sitting on the big chaise sipping the coffee from steaming mugs.

"This is good," he said, putting down his cup.

She nodded.

He stretched out flat. "Did you ever notice how big the stars are down here at night?" he asked.

She glanced up at them for a moment, then back at him. "They look the same to me."

He turned toward her. "Woman, have you no romance in your soul?"

She smiled. "It's late. I better be getting dressed." She started to get up.

His hand caught her arm. "Mary Flood," he said.

She looked down at him. "That's my name."

"Don't go away now that I've found you," he said.

"Yuh don't know what you're sayin'," she said.

He pulled her down on the chaise. She looked into his eyes. He put his hands on her cheeks and drew her face to his. His mouth was warm and soft. It wasn't like all the others. A warmth ran through her. She closed her eyes.

She felt his hands on her breasts. She moved her shoulders and the straps slipped off. She heard his breath catch in his throat and she opened her eyes.

He was staring at her. "You're beautiful," he whispered. "Beautiful."

Her arms went around his neck, pulling his head down to her bosom. She could hardly hear his voice.

"Ever since you came out of the water the first morning I saw you," he was saying, "I knew you'd be like this."

She slipped her hands along his waist. She heard him gasp as her fingers touched him.

"I waited and waited," he whispered. "I waited so long."

"Shut up!" she said huskily, a strange fierceness in her. "You talk too much!"

Two days later he asked her to marry him.

Chapter 11

THE COFFEE was bubbling on the stove when a knock came at the door. "Who is it?" she called without turning around.

"Me," came the heavy, muffled voice. "Mac."

"The door's open," she called. "Come in." She filled two cups with coffee and carried them to the table.

He had the papers in his hands. "Yuh see these?" he asked.

She looked at him. "No," she answered. "I been too busy."

"That's what the paper says," he said quickly. "You're in all of them."

Her brows knitted in puzzlement. "Me?"

He nodded. "It says here you're goin' to marry Gordon Paynter."

She shrugged her shoulders. "What'd they print that for?" She sipped her coffee. "What's such a big deal? People get married all the time."

He stared at her. "You kiddin'? Not Gordon Paynter. He's one of the richest guys in the state."

She didn't answer, just reached for the papers and began to scan them. One of them had printed a picture of her leaving the license bureau with Gordon. She hadn't thought anything about it when the photographer snapped the picture. She remembered what Gordon had said before they went to the license bureau: "They'll make a big fuss. Don't pay any attention to them. Nothing they can do will change the way I feel about you."

She had looked up at him, her eyes somber. A sudden fear had begun to come into her. "Maybe we shouldn't do it, Gordon. Maybe we ought to wait a little. You don't know nothin' about me."

He had smiled reassuringly at her. "I know everything I want to know. I don't care what you did. I only know what you are to me. That's the only thing that matters in the end. . . ."

The landlord sipped his coffee. "Is it true, Mary? Are you really marryin' him?"

She lifted her eyes from the paper and nodded slowly. "Yes."

He whistled. "That's a real break. Does he—?"

She didn't let him finish his question. "He says it doesn't matter. That nothing matters," she said quickly, evading the truth.

"He must be real crazy about you." Mac put down his cup and got to his feet. "I guess this means that I lose a tenant."

She didn't answer, just looked at him. Something in his manner had changed. It was a subtle change, but it was there all the same. She sensed a subservience in him that had not been there before. She shook her head. "Not for a while, Mac," she said. "It's three days before we can marry."

He walked to the door and opened it, then stood there looking back at her. "If there's anything you want, Mary," he said in a low voice, "just yell. I'll come a-runnin'."

"Thanks, Mac," she said.

He hesitated a moment. "I jus' don't want yuh to forget I always been your friend."

"I won't forget, Mac," she said. The door closed behind him, and she picked up the cups and put them in the sink. Name and money changed a lot of things. Her lips tightened into a grim line. Her mind was made up. It had taken Mac to show her the way. She would have them both. Then let anybody try to step on her.

Gordon stepped from the shower, pulled a large towel from the rack, and began to rub himself briskly. He began to hum with satisfaction. Only one more day.

He looked in the mirror as he combed his hair. It was thinning a little in the front, but still seemed heavy and luxuriant enough. He wondered how much heredity had to do with it. His father had been bald before thirty. He grinned into the mirror, pleased with himself.

Slowly he began to dress. His physique was still good. The frame was not spare, but neither was he soft. He remembered what Mary had said. Less drinking. She was right about that. He had always known, but it hadn't mattered. There had been nothing else to do.

He walked into the bedroom and picked up his shirt from the pillow where Tom had placed it. A faint scent came from the pillow—the perfume she wore. A stirring of excitement echoed in him. She was like a tiger in her passion. Wild and clawing and demanding. There had never been anyone like her for him, so perfect they were together.

He could hear her muted voice echoing harshly in his ear: "Fill me, lover, drown me." His flesh tingled as if he could still feel her fingers tearing into his skin. He had never felt so much a man.

"Mr. Gordon." Tom's voice floated up from downstairs.

He tore himself from his memories. "Yes, Tom?"

"They's a gen'mun here to see you."

"Who is it?" Gordon was annoyed. He had told him many times to get names.

"He won' say," Tom answered. "He says it's privut an' confidential. About Miss Flood."

Gordon's brow knitted. He wondered what the man wanted. It was probably a reporter, they always acted mysteriously. "Ask him to wait," he called. "I'll be down in a minute."

A few seconds later he walked into the living-room. A heavyset, florid man got out of a chair and stood up. "Mr. Paynter?" he asked.

Gordon nodded, waiting for the man to introduce himself.

"My name is Joe," the man said nervously. "Last name doesn't matter. I'm only here to do you a favor. What d'yuh know about this girl Mary Flood?"

Gordon felt an instinctive anger begin to rise in him. "Get out!" he snapped, jerking his finger at the door.

The man didn't move. "Yuh should know somethin' about her if yuh're goin' to marry her," he said.

"I know all I need to know," Gordon answered, moving threateningly toward the man. "Get out!"

The man shifted nervously. His hand reached into a pocket and came out with a few pieces of paper. "Before yuh lose your temper," he said quickly, "maybe yuh better look at these." He thrust them into Gordon's hand.

Automatically Gordon glanced at them. They were photographs. Two girls. Nude. He could feel a chill running in his blood. One of them was Mary. He looked up at the man. His voice was shaking. "Where did you get these?"

The man didn't answer his question. "Her real name is Marja Fluudjincki. She was released from a reform school in New York less than a year ago. I know where I can get the negatives of these pictures if yuh want them."

Gordon's lips tightened. Blackmail. He walked across the room and picked up the telephone. "Police headquarters," he said to the operator.

The man stared at him. "That won't do yuh no good," he said. "I'm givin' yuh the pictures as a favor. All it will do is get into the papers an' everybody will have a laugh on yuh."

Slowly Gordon put down the phone and sank into a chair. She should have told him. It wasn't right. He looked up at the man. "How do I know they're not fakes?" he asked, a faint hope inside him.

"I'll show yuh," the man said. He went to the door and opened it. "Evelyn!" he called. "Come in here!"

A moment later he came back into the room with a girl. She had short dark hair. Gordon looked down at the pictures. She was the other girl with Mary.

"Tell him the story," the man said.

The girl looked at him nervously. "But, Joe—"

The man's voice was harsh. "Tell him. We didn't drive all night from New Orleans for nothin'. Tell him!"

The girl looked down at Gordon. "I met Marja in the Geyer Home for Girls. We worked up an act and came down here. We worked stags and private clubs and parties. When the cops got hot, Joe an' me left town. Mary stayed here. We heard that—"

Gordon got out of his chair and crossed the room quickly. Her voice faded out as she looked at him, startled. He opened the rolling bar and took out a bottle of whisky. He poured himself a glass and turned back to them. There was a heavy aching pain inside him. "How about a drink?" he asked.

The man answered first. "Don't mind if we do," he said with a forced laugh. "Do we, Evelyn?"

Chapter 12

THE JITNEY dropped her at the house, and she went up the walk to the door and rang the bell. Gordon opened it.

The whisky on his breath hit her as she entered. She turned toward him. "You've been drinking" she said reproachfully. "And you promised you wouldn't."

He laughed nervously. "Jus' celebratin', honey. It isn't every day that old friends stop in for a visit."

"Old friends?" she questioned.

He nodded and led the way into the living-room. She stopped in the doorway, frozen with shock. Evelyn was sprawled on the couch, clad only in a brassiere and panties. Her clothing was strewn all over the room. She waved drunkenly at Mary.

Joe lumbered toward her. "My ol' girl Mary," he cried. "Got a kiss for ol' Joe?" Abruptly he began to sing. "*Here comes the bride—here comes the bride.*"

"What're you doin' here?" she asked angrily.

Joe laughed. "We came to help our girl celebrate the weddin', that's all, honey."

She turned to Gordon. "When did they get here?"

"Thish—thish afternoon." He tried to concentrate his gaze on her, but there was too much pain in his head. He needed another drink. He picked up the bottle and held it toward her. "Drink?"

She shook her head.

He drank from the bottle. The whisky felt good in his throat. It was warm and reassuring. He lowered the bottle and looked at her. "I needed that," he said. "Sure you won't have one?"

"No, thanks," she said dryly. She took out a cigarette and lit it. The smoke curled slowly from her lips.

Joe stood in front of her. "C'mon, have a drink," he urged. "It'll put yuh in the mood for the show."

Her voice was cold. "What show?"

Evelyn staggered from the couch. "We was tellin' your boy frien' about our act. Joe thought it would be fun to put it on for him."

She turned to Gordon, ignoring the girl. "They told you." It was more statement than question.

He nodded.

Her voice was calm. "You listened without giving me a chance to tell you?" This was more question than statement.

He held the photographs toward her. "The pictures did all the talking. I didn't have to hear anything."

She glanced at them briefly, then silently handed them back to him. He threw them on the table and turned away from her, unable to meet her gaze. "You should have told me," he muttered.

"You wouldn't let me," she answered. "Every time I

wanted to, you said you didn't care what I had been. You said you knew enough about me."

He didn't answer.

She turned to Joe, her voice cutting. "Same old Joe. Anything to grab a buck. Hope you made out real good this time."

"Don't be sore, honey," he said, coming toward her. "The heat's off. We can put on the ol' act again." He tried to take her arm.

Her hand moved so swiftly that his eye couldn't follow. There was just the sharp shock, then the red-and-white stain on his face where her open palm had struck.

"Why, you bitch!" he exclaimed, taking an angry step toward her. "I'll learn yuh!"

A taunting smile came to her lips. "Learn me," she said softly.

He stopped, his eyes focused on her hand. The blade gleamed in the light. He stepped back quickly.

Gordon stared at them. "Mary!" he cried.

She turned to him. There was a hurt, angry sound in her voice. "Yuh're just as bad as they are. Yuh wouldn't listen to me, but yuh'd listen to anyone who came to yuh with a story. Did they tell yuh how they ran out an' stuck me without money an' clothes in an apartment? I bet yuh got a big yak outta that, too!"

He didn't speak, but his eyes stared into hers.

"They didn't tell yuh all of it, they didn't know," she continued angrily. "After they left, I hit the turf. I had to. To pay off the rent an' live. I did real good. Forty bucks a day. That's what I was doin' the day yuh picked me up!"

"No, Mary," he groaned.

"But it wasn't enough that I left yuh alone," she said. "You had to come after me. You had to make it a big thing." Her voice broke suddenly and became very small. "I was the sucker, not you. I thought this was the McCoy, the genuine article. I thought that for once there was somethin' in this world for me. I was wrong." She turned and started for the door.

Gordon caught her arm. There was a curious guilt in him. "Mary."

She looked up into his face, a faint flicker of hope coming into her eyes. "Yuh stopping me, Gordon?" she asked.

He didn't answer. He saw the light fade suddenly from her eyes.

She shook his hand from her arm, and the door closed quickly behind her. He stood there staring at it for a moment, then turned to the others.

Joe forced a laugh to his lips. "Yuh're better off without her, buddy."

Gordon didn't answer for a moment. When he spoke, he didn't recognize his own voice. It was harsh and filled with hatred. "Get out!" he said. "Get out, the two of you, before I kill you both!"

She staggered blindly down the walk. Tears filled her eyes and silently spilled down her cheeks.

A gentle voice spoke next to her. "Kin I git you a jitney, Miss Mary?"

She looked up. The old colored man was standing there, a world of understanding in his eyes. She shook her head. "No, thank you, Tom." Her voice was cracked and husky. "I—I think I'll walk a bit."

"I'll walk a ways with you if you allows me, Miss Mary," he said in his gentle, polite voice. "It's lonely out this way at night."

"I'll be all right," she said. "I'm not afraid."

He nodded slowly. "You sho' ain't, Miss Mary. You the mos' woman I seen in a long time."

She stared at him without speaking. Suddenly she understood. "You knew all the time," she said in a wondering voice.

He nodded.

"Yet you never told him. Why?"

His eyes looked right into hers. "Because what I said. You a real woman. But Mr. Gordon, he's nothin' but a boy. I was hopin' you would be his makin'. Not no more. Not ever."

She took a deep breath. "Thank you, Tom." She began to walk away.

He hurried after her. "I got some money, Miss Mary," he said quickly, "in case you is a little short."

For the first time that evening a real warmth seeped through her. Instinctively she took the old man's hand. "I can manage, Tom."

The old man dropped his eyes. "I'm sorry, pow'ful sorry, Miss Mary."

She looked at him for a moment, and a warm, friendly look came into her face. "I've changed my mind, Tom. There is something you can do for me."

He looked up quickly. "Yes, Miss Mary?"

"I'm goin' to ride home. Get me a jitney," she said.

"Yes, Miss Mary."

She watched him hurry down the street toward the main avenue, where cars would be running. She took out another cigarette and lit it. She dragged deeply on the cigarette and looked up at the sky.

The stars were bright and shining and the moon hung heavy in the sky. The faint roar of the surf came to her ears and a warm, soft breeze came from the ocean. Suddenly she snapped the cigarette out into the gutter. Her mind was made up.

She had enough of Florida. She was going back to New York. The stars were too bright down here.

Chapter 13

MIKE lifted his eyes from the book in front of him and rubbed them wearily. They felt red and raw and burning. He looked out the window. It was still snowing. In the next room the telephone began to ring. He could hear his mother's voice answering it.

Slowly he closed the books. It was almost time for him to go to work. He had the night beat this month. He got out of the chair and went into the bathroom. His shaving-gear was already spread out on the sink.

He was working the lather into his face when his mother came to the door behind him. "I'm gettin' your breakfast ready, son," she said.

"Thanks, Mom," he answered, taking the razor and beginning to shave.

She stood there watching him. After a few moments he became conscious of her gaze. "What is it, Mom?" he asked.

She shook her head and began to turn away, then

turned back to him. "You didn't sleep much," she said. "I heard you up around three o'clock."

"I wasn't tired," he answered. "Besides, I had those books to read. The police examinations come up in a couple of months. You wouldn't want me to be a rookie all my life, would you?"

"No," she answered. "But I would like it better if you were more like other lads. It would do you good to go out once in a while instead of all the time burying your nose in them books. Now there's that Gallagher girl, the druggist's daughter. I see her on the street every day, and every time she asks about you—"

"Ma, I told yuh a dozen times I ain't got no time for girls," he said impatiently. "There'll be time enough for that later. Right now I got too much to do."

She met his eyes steadily in the mirror. "If it was that Marja, you would have time."

He could feel his face flush. "Forget her, Mom. I told yuh that was over."

His mother's eyes were suddenly gentle. "I can forget her, son," she said, turning away. "But can you?"

He listened to her footsteps go down the hall, then looked at his face in the mirror. Absently he took a stroke with the razor. A tingling, burning sensation caught his cheek. "Damn!" he said aloud, lowering the razor. He reached for the styptic pencil to stanch the blood.

Quickly he held the white pencil to the cut in his cheek. Its caustic edge burned deeply. Marja, he thought. Marja. He wondered if his mother was right. He dried his face and walked over to the window. It was still snowing.

He wondered what Marja was doing.

The big clock in the lobby said eight o'clock when

Mary came out of the hotel. The snow had covered the streets with a white blanket and muffled all the traffic noises. She turned up 49th Street toward Sixth Avenue. There would be more action around Rockefeller Center.

Altogether, there was a better class of trade. The tourists and the white-collar workers from that area had more to spend. Broadway and Seventh and Eighth Avenues were nothing but two-dollar tricks. A girl had a chance for a five- or ten-dollar trick on Sixth Avenue.

She looked up at the sky. It was still snowing heavily. There wouldn't be much doing tonight, but she couldn't afford to stay in. She had no money left, and rent was due in a few days. She walked along slowly, her face turned away from the street toward the store windows as if she were interested in what they had to offer.

Actually, she was looking at the windows as if they were mirrors. Each man who came by was carefully scrutinized and, by instinct alone, appraised. She turned left on Sixth and walked to the corner of 50th. Almost no one was out. She went into the cafeteria on the corner and ordered a cup of coffee.

She took it to a seat near the window, where she could watch the entrance to the Music Hall across the street. There would be a show break in about twenty minutes. Crowds would pour out then, and very often there was some action in them. The yokel sports made the early show so they could have the night free.

Her cup was almost empty when the theater began to empty. Quickly she finished the coffee and walked across the street. She stood in a corner of the lobby as if waiting for an appointment.

An usher walked by. She glanced at her watch impatiently as if tired of waiting. People pushed by, but they were nothing but faces. The crowd was thinning now. A few minutes more and she would go out into the snow again. It looked as if there was nothing here tonight.

She was about to leave when an instinct made her look up. A man standing across the lobby was watching her. Quickly she looked at his shoes. They were brown. Automatically that made him safe. Cops wore black shoes. Slowly she looked up into his face again, her eyes carefully blank, then turned and sauntered out into the street.

She waited on the corner for the traffic light. Without turning around, she knew that the man had followed her. When the light changed she crossed the street and entered the RCA building. She went down a small flight of stairs into the arcade and stopped in front of a window.

In its reflection she could see the man pass behind her. He stopped at a window a few doors away. She walked slowly past him, through the revolving door, and up the steps. She went past the post office and stopped in front of a restaurant that had the lower half of its windows painted black so that you could not see into it. Here she opened her pocketbook and took out a cigarette. She was about to light it when a flame sprang up next to her.

The man's hand was trembling slightly as she looked up at him. He had a round, smooth face and dark eyes. He seemed okay. "Thank you," she said, lighting her cigarette.

He smiled. "Can I buy you a drink?" His voice was guttural and heavy.

She raised an inquiring eyebrow. Her voice was friendly and devoid of insult. "Is that all you want?"

The man seemed flustered. "No-no," he stammered. "But—"

"Then why add to the overhead?" she smiled. "You don't have to spend money on me."

He cleared his throat, drawing himself up as if hoping to appear a man of the world. "Er—ah, how much?"

"Ten dollars," she said quickly, watching him carefully, ready to come down in price if he seemed to balk.

"Okay," he said.

She smiled and took his arm. Together they walked up the stairs and out into the street. She led him toward the hotel. "There's nothing like snow in the winter," she said.

"Yeah," he answered.

"But it's no good in the city. Everything gets all slopped up. You can't do anything."

He ventured a joke. "I'm doin' okay."

She laughed and held his arm tighter. He wasn't so dumb. They were near the hotel now. She took her hand from his arm. "I'm goin' in here," she said. "Give me five minutes, then come up to room 209, second floor. Room 209. Got it?"

He nodded. "Two-oh-nine. Five minutes."

She was wearing a kimona when the knock came at the door. Quickly she crossed the room and opened it. The man stood there hesitantly. "Come in," she said.

He entered slowly and stood in the middle of the room as she closed and locked the door. She turned toward him. "Your coat," she said.

"Oh, yes." He shrugged off his coat and handed it to her. She put it on a hanger and hung it on the door. When she turned back, he already had his jacket off and was loosening his tie.

She smiled and sat on the edge of the bed, her legs

swinging. He watched her as he took off his shirt. Muscles rippled in his shoulders. "What's your name?" he asked.

"Mary," she answered.

"How come you're doin' this, Mary?" he asked. "You seem like too nice a girl—"

A bored look crossed her face. They all had the same question. Sometimes she thought they came more for the story than for anything else. She shrugged her shoulders. "A girl's gotta eat," she said.

He started to loosen his belt.

"Haven't you forgot something?" she asked.

He looked startled. Then understanding came to him. "Yeah," he said, putting his hand in his pocket. He held a bill toward her.

She put it in her pocketbook on the dresser. Then she threw off the kimona and went back to the bed. Completely nude, she stretched out and looked at him.

He was standing there, his trousers still on, staring at her.

"Come on," she said. "What're yuh waitin' for?"

He ran his tongue over his lips. Slowly his hand went into his pocket again and came out with a small black leather wallet. He flipped it open. The sparkling silver of a badge gleamed at her. He turned his face away. "Detective Millersen, Vice Squad," he said. "You're under arrest. Get dressed."

She sat up quickly, her heart pounding inside her. It had to happen sometime. She had always known it. But not so soon.

She forced a smile to her lips. "My mistake, officer," she said. "This one'll be on the house."

He shook his head. "Get dressed." He wouldn't meet her eyes.

"You're pretty good-lookin' for a cop," she said, coming near him.

He walked away and planted himself in front of the door. He was already putting on his shirt. "No use tryin', sister," he said stolidly. "Might as well get your clothes on."

Slowly she began to dress. "What's the rap for this?" she asked.

"This the first offense?"

She nodded, trying to fasten the hook in the back of her dress. Her fingers were trembling so that she couldn't make it. "Be a good felluh, will yuh?" she asked. "See if yuh could forget that badge long enough to hook this for me?"

He came around behind her and hooked the dress. "Thirty days," he said.

"Thirty days for what?" she said, for she had already forgotten her question.

"Thirty days for a first offense," he said, going back to the door.

"Oh," she exclaimed. "What day is this?"

"February 27," he answered.

She opened the closet and took out her coat. "There goes the month of March." She turned to him. "Have I got a few minutes to pack my things? You know these flea bags. Thirty days from now I'll never get my clothes back."

He nodded. "Okay, but snap it up."

He watched as she took a valise from the closet. There wasn't very much to pack. It all fitted into the valise. She snapped the lid down and turned to him. "I'm ready now. Thanks."

He opened the door and followed her out of the room. She looked up into his face as she crossed the threshold. "There must be an easier way to make a living," she said.

His eyes widened with a sudden respect. The girl had guts. He nodded somberly. "There must be."

She took his arm as if they were old friends going for a stroll. Her voice was low and husky. "For both of us, I mean."

The State vs. *Maryann Flood*

I WALKED slowly past the jurors. Their eyes followed me with interest as I went up to the judge to answer Vito's motion for dismissal before he presented his case. I hoped they could hear me despite the fact that I spoke in a low voice.

"There are two things to remember in any court of justice. They are moral guilt and legal guilt. We can punish only for that we find legally guilty. But it is seldom in any court of justice that we find both moral and legal guilt so close together.

"We have carefully presented to the court and jury the accusations against the defendant. We have carefully documented them with facts and evidence and witness. We have presented the State's case without dramatics, without flimflam, and with a deep sense of responsibility to all the parties concerned. We have done our duty without fear or favor, and in so doing have created a structure of guilt that encompasses and incriminates the defendant.

"The people of the State of New York look to you for justice. Justice, for now, will be served by denying the motion of the defendant!"

I walked slowly away from the bench and stopped midway across the court. I heard the judge's voice over my shoulder:

"Motion denied."

Instantly pandemonium broke loose. Behind me reporters were running up the aisles to get the news to their papers. The judge banged his gavel. At last he could make himself heard over the uproar.

"The court will adjourn until ten o'clock tomorrow morning."

I was soaking wet when I walked into my office and sank into a chair.

Joel and Alec were right behind me. "You need a drink, man," Joel said, studying me.

I nodded and closed my eyes. I needed more than that. I didn't know how I would get through the next two weeks of the trial while Vito presented his case. I felt as if I had no strength left in me.

"Here," Joel said.

I opened my eyes, took the glass from him, and threw the liquor down my throat. It burned all the way down to my gut. I coughed.

"Hundred-proof bourbon," he said.

I looked up at him. "Thank God that's over," I said fervently.

Alec grinned. "You were good. Real good."

"Thanks," I said, "but you don't have to say it. I know just how bad I was."

"You weren't bad at all," a new voice said.

We turned to the doorway in surprise. I scrambled to my feet. "Chief!"

He was smiling as he came into the room. "Pretty good, I would say."

Alec and Joel exchanged glances. These were the highest words of praise they had ever heard from the Old Man.

"Thank you, sir," I said.

He held up his hand. "Don't thank me," he said. "It isn't over yet. Vito still has his chance. It's never over until the jury comes back."

I pulled a chair out for the Old Man. He sat down carefully. It was the first time he had come to the office since the operation.

"You're looking very well, sir," Joel said. I glanced at him quickly. He was right back in the groove. Politics as usual.

The Old Man took it in his stride. "I feel pretty good," he said. He took out a package of cigarettes and put one in his mouth. Alec almost broke a finger beating Joel with the light.

I smiled to myself. Normalcy had returned in a hurry. I was beginning to feel better. Maybe it was the whisky warming my stomach.

The Old Man turned to me. "What do you think Vito will do?"

I shook my head. "I don't know, sir."

"I don't like the way he looks," the Old Man said. "He's sitting too easy."

"Vito always looks like that, whether he's got something or not," Joel broke in quickly.

The Old Man shot him a withering glance. "I've known Hank Vito for almost twenty years. I can tell when he's acting. He's not acting this time. He's got something up his sleeve." He took a puff on his cigarette. "I'd give another appendix to know what he's sitting on."

We sat around silently for a moment, each trying to think of some possibility that we had overlooked.

At last the Old Man got to his feet. "Well," he said heavily, "I don't think we'll have long to wait. He'll probably hit us with it first thing in the morning."

"What makes you think that, sir?" Joel asked.

The Old Man walked to the door and looked back at us. "He didn't subpoena any witnesses for tomorrow. Not a solitary one."

The rest of us looked at one another in amazement. It was Alec who drew the first breath. The Old Man's statement had caught us flatfooted.

He looked shrewdly at the three of us. "If any of you guys had been on your toes, you would have checked before you left the courtroom." He disappeared into the corridor.

It was Joel who gave voice to our grudging admiration. "Leave it to the old bastard," he said affectionately. "He may be old, but he hasn't lost any of his marbles."

I stayed at the office until after eleven o'clock that night going over the case. I did everything. Checked the data we had on his witnesses. Matched the questions he had asked the State's witnesses. Nowhere in any of the information I had could I find a pattern that indicated his course of action. At last I closed my desk and took my hat and coat from the clothes tree.

I was tired, but I wasn't sleepy. It was raw cold out, but I decided to walk a bit, hoping the fresh air would clear my head. I headed up Broadway.

Down here Broadway was a dark and deserted street. Far uptown I could see the haze of lights that Times Square threw vividly upward. But here the office buildings loomed large and black with night. Only occasional lights where cleaning women were working flickered sporadically.

I turned up my coat collar to stave off the wind and began to walk briskly. I had gone almost four blocks when I noticed an automobile idling slowly along the street beside me. I glanced at it curiously, but couldn't see into it. It was too dark.

I kept walking, busy with my thoughts. When I reached the next corner the car cut in front of me. I jumped back onto the curb, swearing.

A low burst of laughter reached my ears. It was a familiar laugh. I put my hand on the front door of the car and opened it.

She was seated behind the wheel. In the dim light of the dash I could see the white reflection of her teeth. "Hello, Mike," she said in a husky voice.

"Marja!" I couldn't keep the surprise from my voice. I stood frozen to the curb.

"Get in," she said. "I'll give you a lift."

I hesitated a moment, then got into the car. She put it into gear immediately and the car moved off. I kept staring at her.

At the next corner a traffic signal brought the big car to a stop. She turned and looked at me. "You work pretty late," she said. "I've been parked outside your office since six o'clock."

"Why didn't you let me know?" I said sarcastically. "I wouldn't have kept you waiting."

"Uh-oh," she said, starting the car again. "The man is mad."

I took a cigarette and lit it. In the light from the match her hair was almost white. There was a quiet smile on her lips. She drove silently with casual carelessness.

After a while she spoke. "You were very good today, Mike." It was almost as if she were not on trial.

"Thanks," I said.

She turned the car into a side street, pulled over to the curb, and cut the ignition. From somewhere she pulled a cigarette. I held a match for her.

Her eyes searched mine over the flame. "It's been a long time, Mike."

I nodded. "I've heard those words before—I think."

The match flickered out, but not before I saw a strange hurt leap into her eyes. There was a gladness in me. I hadn't believed anyone had the power to hurt her.

She put her hand on mine. "Let's not fight, Mike." Her voice was gentle.

"What do you think we've been doing ever since this trial began?" I asked angrily. "This isn't a game we're playing."

Her eyes stared into mine over the glow of the cigarettes. "That's something else, Mike. It's got nothing to do with us personally."

I could feel the drag in those eyes. I began to swim dizzily in their depths. Things hadn't changed a bit. I leaned forward and kissed her.

Her mouth was soft and warm. I could feel the pressure of her teeth behind her lips. I felt an instant passion surging in me. I pulled my mouth away from her. This was crazy.

Her eyes were still closed. "Mike," she whispered. Her hand sought mine and held it tightly. "Why did this have to happen to us?"

I dragged on my cigarette. "I don't know," I said harshly. "I've wondered many times myself."

Her eyes opened slowly. Never had they seemed so gentle as now. They looked straight into mine. "Thanks, Mike," she said softly. "I was afraid you had changed."

I didn't answer.

After a minute she spoke again. "How're your folks?"

I didn't look at her. "Pa died two years ago. Heart attack."

"I'm sorry, Mike," she whispered. "I didn't know." She dragged on her cigarette. "And your mother?"

I looked at her quickly, wondering if she was aware of how my mother felt about her. I looked away again. Of course not. How could she be? "Ma's okay. She's in the country right now. I expect her home in a couple of weeks."

We fell silent again. Our cigarettes burned down and I tossed mine out the window. We seemed to have run out of conversation. "I hear you have a daughter," I said.

A smile came to her lips. "Yes."

"She must be very pretty," I said. "Any child of yours would have to be."

A strange look came into her eyes. Her voice was very quiet. "She is."

Again silence descended upon us. There were a million things to say to her, a thousand questions I wanted to ask, but my tongue was frozen with time and circumstance. I cleared my throat.

"Yes, Mike?" she asked.

I looked at her. "I didn't say anything," I said awkwardly.

"Oh," she said.

A police car came down the block and flashed its lights

into our car. I fought an impulse to raise my hand and cover my face, but it kept on going.

I turned to her. "This was a crazy thing to do," I said.

She smiled. "I like crazy things."

"I don't," I said. "That was always one of the differences between us."

"Don't preach, Mike," she said quietly. "I've heard enough of that the last few weeks."

I stared at her. "Why, Marja? Why?"

Her eyes met mine levelly. She shrugged her shoulders. "It happened."

"But why couldn't it be two other people, Marja? Why did it have to be us?"

She didn't answer.

I reached forward and turned the ignition key angrily. "Let's go," I said.

Obediently she started the car. We moved out into the street. "Where to?" she asked.

"You can drop me on Broadway and Canal," I said. "I can get a cab there."

"Okay."

A few minutes later we were there and she pulled to the curb. I opened the door and was halfway out of the car before she spoke. I stopped and looked back at her. There was a reflection from the light in the window of the store on the corner. It threw wild highlights on her face—the high cheekbones, wide mouth, and delicately flaring nostrils.

"I wish it had been two other people, Mike," she said.

There was an ache inside me. "It's too late now."

She took a deep breath. "Not for one thing, Mike."

I stared at her. "What?"

She leaned forward swiftly and her lips brushed my cheek. "I love you, Mike," she whispered. "It's always been you. No matter what happened. I just didn't know any better."

Then the car was off in a roar of the motor and I was standing on the corner looking after it. Its taillight vanished around a corner and I began to walk toward the cab stand.

I could still feel the light pressure of her lips, and the perfume she used clung to my nostrils. I didn't understand. I would never understand. The more I knew her, the less I knew her.

That time during the war, for instance. There had been a wonderful week-end. She was for me then—I knew it, I could feel it. But she had gone away with Ross. I rubbed the broken bridge of my nose reflectively. I didn't need a greater reminder. Ross had done that.

I got into a cab and gave the driver my address, then settled back in the seat. So many years. So many things had changed. Ross was dead. Nothing was the same any more.

I took a deep breath. Nothing—except the way I felt about her.

Book Three

MARYANN

Chapter 1

THE shoeshine boy was waiting when Henry Vito got to his office. He came in briskly, threw his coat on the small leather sofa, and sat down behind his desk. He put his foot on the shine box. "Good morning, Tony," he said, reaching for the stack of papers on his desk.

"*Bon giorno,* Signor Vito," the boy replied, already rubbing the shoe with a polishing-cloth.

Vito looked quickly at the newspaper which was on the top of the pile. The front-page headlines were the same as yesterday's. The Germans were falling back in North Africa, or the Germans were advancing—they had been the same all that spring of 1943. He tossed the paper into the wastebasket and began to skim through the morning mail. Nothing important. Restlessly he changed feet on the box at the boy's tap and looked out the window.

Across the street was a park, and beyond it the gray stone of Criminal Courts. He felt like a gladiator looking out at the arena. It had been always like that, ever since he

287

had been a boy in Little Italy downtown. The challenge of the symbol of authority. To flout the law was too easy; to make it ridiculous by its own standards was the fun. It was the profit too. Freeing the guilty conscience of its legal bonds was a lucrative profession.

He felt a tap on his foot signifying that the shine was finished. He spun a quarter toward the boy and turned back to his desk. The telephone buzzed as the boy left. He picked it up.

"There's a Maryann Flood here to see you," the receptionist's voice said in his ear.

The name wasn't familiar. "What does she want?" he asked.

"Client," the girl's reply came laconically. "She says you were recommended to her."

"By who?" he asked.

"She said she would tell you when she saw you. She also said she pays cash in advance."

Vito grinned to himself. Whoever the woman was, she knew her business. "Send her in," he said.

A moment later the door opened and his secretary appeared, followed by a young woman. Vito struggled to his feet. "Mr. Vito, Miss Flood," his secretary introduced.

The young woman came toward him, her hand outstretched. Vito took her hand. Her grip was firm and casual like a man's, yet there was an electric warmth in it that made you know she was a woman. "Thank you for seeing me," she said. Her voice was low and well modulated.

"You're quite welcome." Vito gestured toward the chair opposite his desk. "Please sit down."

His secretary retrieved his coat from the sofa where he had thrown it, and went out. Vito sat down and looked at the young woman.

She wore a light tweed suit and matching topcoat, and a white silk blouse showed beneath the jacket. Her hands were well shaped. She wore no jewelry, and no make-up other than a gentle shading of lipstick. Her eyes, set wide apart, were large, dark brown, almost black. Faint strands of blond hair peered out from beneath her soft cream-colored beret.

Vito prided himself on his ability to appraise a client. This girl had breeding. It was evident from everything about her. She had come to see him about her brother or some relative who had got himself into trouble. This was the sort of case that he liked. It meant money. He smiled at her. "How can I help you, Miss Flood?" he asked.

The young woman didn't answer immediately. She took out a cigarette and waited for him to light it. He did so, even more sure now of his analysis. Only girls of fine background had that imperious manner of waiting to have their cigarettes lighted. He watched her draw the smoke gently into her mouth.

"I hear you're a good lawyer, Mr. Vito," the young woman said softly. "The best in New York."

He preened inwardly. "That's very flattering, Miss Flood," he said modestly "but not quite true. I do my best, that's all."

"I'm sure that's more than anyone else can do," the girl said. There was a hint of a smile in her eyes.

He noticed it and went on the defensive immediately. He wasn't going to have a society broad mocking him. "I try very hard, Miss Flood," he said, his voice chilling.

The girl looked straight into his eyes. "That's why I came to you, Mr. Vito. I need a lawyer, and I want the best." There was no laughter in her eyes now.

"Why?" he asked.

"I received a call this morning from a friend of mine. A warrant has been issued for my arrest and I'm to be picked up this afternoon." Her voice was flat and emotionless.

A sense of shock ran through him. "You're to be arrested? On what charge?"

She still looked into his eyes. "Grand larceny after committing an act of prostitution."

For a moment his voice failed him. "What?" he managed after his voice came back.

She smiled, genuine amusement in her eyes, and repeated the charge. "That's why I'm here," she added.

He had never been so wrong in his judgment of a client. He took out a fresh cigar, bit off the end, and applied a flaming wooden match until its tip glowed a cherry red. Then he put the match down. By this time he had control of himself. "Tell me what happened," he said unemotionally.

"I was in the bar at the Sherry last night about eleven having a nightcap when this man came up. He was drunk, and insisted on buying me a drink. He told me he was very rich, and waved a fat roll of bills to emphasize it. We had a few drinks there. Then he came up to my place and we continued drinking." Her voice was as flat and unexpressive as if she were reciting a story about someone else. "He left about four thirty. He gave me twenty dollars, and I kissed him good night."

"Then what happened?" he asked.

"I went to bed," she said. "This morning my phone rang. A friend was calling me from headquarters. He said this man had appeared this morning and sworn out a warrant for me."

"Did you take his money?" Vito asked.

"No," the young woman answered. "He put the roll back in his pocket after he gave me the twenty."

"Who recommended me?" he asked.

"Detective Lieutenant Millersen, 54th Street station," she answered. "I've known him for about five years now. He knows I would never do such a thing."

He knew Millersen. A good cop. He wouldn't slip him a bad deal. But the cop could be wrong, too. He shot a shrewd glance at the girl. "Sure you didn't take the money?" he asked. "You can tell me. I don't care whether you did or not. I'll handle the case anyway. I just want to know for myself."

The girl looked at him, her eyes wide and unblinking. Slowly she reached up and took off her beret. She shook her head and her hair tumbled down around her face in a sparkling golden shower. "Mr. Vito," she said in a low husky voice, "I'm a whore, not a thief."

Chapter 2

"MR. BELL, how many drinks did you have before you met Miss Flood that evening?" Vito's voice was clear and unemotional.

The heavy-set man in the witness chair looked uncomfortably at the judge. The judge stared straight in front of him. "I don't know," Bell answered, his voice strained. "I been drinkin' quite a lot."

"Ten drinks? Twelve? Twenty?" Vito's voice was curious.

"Maybe ten," the man admitted.

"Maybe ten." Vito turned back to his client. She nodded slowly. He faced the man again. "And how many drinks did you have with her in the bar?"

"Four?" the man replied in a questioning voice.

"I'm sure I don't know, Mr. Bell," Vito said sarcastically. "You were there, not I."

"But I'm not sure," the man said.

"You're not sure," Vito repeated. He walked a few steps away from the witness chair. "You're not sure how many drinks you had before you met my client, you're not sure how many drinks you had at the bar with her. Is it possible you know how many drinks you had in her apartment?"

"I—I don't know," the man said. "I can't be sure. I had a lot to drink that night."

Vito smiled. "That's something we all are sure of, Mr. Bell." He turned to let the ripple of laughter run through the almost empty courtroom. He turned back to the man in the witness chair. "Apparently you're not sure of anything that happened that night, Mr. Bell, are you?"

Bell flushed. "I had fifteen hundred dollars in my pocket when I started that night," he said angrily. "I didn't have it the next morning."

"When did you first miss the money, Mr. Bell?" Vito asked.

"When I woke up," the man said. "I looked on the dresser. When I saw the money wasn't there, I went through my pockets. It was gone."

"Where was that, and what time, Mr. Bell?"

"In my room at the hotel about nine thirty in the morning."

"And you immediately called the police and reported the theft?" Vito continued.

"No," Bell answered. "I got dressed and called downstairs to the desk to find out if anyone had reported finding the money."

"*Then* you called the police?" Vito's voice was gentle.

"No, I called the cab company to find out if any of their drivers had turned in the money."

"Was that all the money you had on you, Mr. Bell?" Vito asked casually.

Mr. Bell nodded. "Yes, I never keep change in my pock-

ets. It's too much bother. I never take any. I always tell 'em
to keep the change."

"That's all, Mr. Bell. Thank you." Vito walked away
abruptly.

The man looked around him embarrassedly, then awkwardly got down from the chair and went back to a seat.
Vito waited a moment, then called out a name. A short,
thin man got to his feet and went to the witness chair. The
clerk administered the oath and the man sat down.

Vito came toward the man. "What is your occupation,
Mr. Russo?"

"I'm a cab-driver, sir," the man said in a guttural voice.

"Who do you work for?" Vito asked.

"The Shaggy Dog Cab Company," the witness answered.
"I woik nights."

"Do you recognize anyone in this court?" Vito asked.

"Yes, sir," Russo answered. He looked around quickly.
"Him," he said, pointing at Bell.

"Did you know him by name before you came into this
court?" Vito asked.

"No," Russo replied. "I recanized him because I rode
him one night."

"When was that?" Vito asked.

Russo took out a sheet of paper. "I got my ride sheet for
that night. It was Tuesday night a week ago."

Vito took the sheet of paper from him. "What is this?"

"That's my ride sheet. It tells where I pick up a fare and
where I left him off an' how much the clock reads. That's
so the boss can tell how much mileage is on the clock an'
how much is cruising. It also tells the time of each call."

Vito looked at it. "Would you have Mr. Bell's ride on
this sheet?"

The hack man nodded. "Yeah, it's there. Four forty a.m."

"Four forty a.m.," Vito read. "72 Street and C.P.W. to the Sherry Hotel." He looked at the witness. "Is that the ride?"

"Yeah," the cab-driver answered.

"Sixty cents," Vito read from the sheet.

"That's what was on the clock," the cab-driver said quickly.

Vito looked at him. "How did he pay you?"

"He pulled a dollar bill off his roll an' tol' me to keep the change," the cab-driver said.

Vito looked up at the judge, his face innocent of expression. "One more question, Mr. Russo. What was the condition of your fare? Was he intoxicated?"

"He was drunk as a lord," the cab-driver said quickly.

"That's all, Mr. Russo. Thank you." Vito still looked up at the judge. He waited until the witness left the chair and then a faint smile came to his lips.

A twinkle of answering amusement sparkled in the judge's eye. He nodded slightly toward Vito.

Vito was smiling broadly now. "I move that the case against my client be dismissed on the grounds that no evidence of any crime on her part is shown."

"Motion granted. Case dismissed," the judge said.

"Thank you, Your Honor." Vito turned toward Maryann as the judge adjourned the court.

She held out her hand, smiling. "Thank you, Hank."

He grinned at her. "You said I was the best. I dared not do less."

She stood up and he helped her on with her coat. From the corners of his eyes he could see a man handing Bell a paper. He chuckled to himself as they started to walk out.

Bell pushed up to him as they passed. "Mr. Vito," he said angrily, waving the paper, "what is the meaning of this?"

Vito answered calmly: "What?"

"This suit for false arrest. Slander—damages to your client's reputation. Two hundred and fifty thousand dollars!" Bell's voice was trembling with rage.

Vito pushed Maryann down the aisle before him as he answered the man. "Next time you accuse a poor innocent, Mr. Bell, we trust you will remember there are also laws for her protection."

Maryann was laughing when they got out of the courtroom. "You had the paper all ready for him. What if we had lost?"

Vito was smiling. "We couldn't lose."

"We couldn't?" she asked doubtfully.

He didn't answer her question. "We have a date for dinner?" he asked instead.

She nodded.

"What time?"

"Pick me up at my place. Seven thirty," she answered.

"Good," he said. "I got to get back to my office. I'll get you a cab." He signaled and a cab pulled to a stop. He opened the door for her.

She stepped in and looked at him. "What do you mean we couldn't lose? If you hadn't found that cab-driver, we'd have had a hard time."

"Who found the cab-driver?" he asked innocently.

"You mean you—?" She broke off, a growing knowledge in her eyes.

He grinned at her. "Who was to say no? Bell was so drunk he didn't remember which driver he had. It was simple enough to get a man from the same company who could remember more than Bell could. Especially a man who works nights and was willing to pick up a few bucks for an easy afternoon's work."

"You are the best," she said, smiling.

He closed the door. "Seven thirty sharp," he said and walked off whistling.

He looked at his wristwatch. It was almost six o'clock. He picked up the telephone, and when his secretary answered, he said: "Call the barber and tell him to wait for me. I'll be down for a shave in a few minutes."

"Right, Mr. Vito," the girl said. He started to put down the receiver, but her voice continued. "I have Mr. Drego on the telephone."

"I didn't call him," Vito said.

"He called just as you picked up the phone," the girl explained.

Vito punched the connecting button. "Yes, Ross?"

"I gotta see you tonight, Hank." Ross's voice was earnest.

"Can't it keep, kid?" Vito said. "I talked the ol' woman into giving me a night off and I got a beautiful babe lined up. Any other time."

"It's got to be tonight, Hank," Ross answered. "They want me to go out west next week. There's some things we have to straighten out first."

"Christ! I got no luck at all," Vito said.

Ross laughed into the phone. "I won't keep you long."

"Yeah," Vito said.

Ross laughed again. "This babe must be somethin'. I never heard you sweat over a dame before."

"I don't think there's another like her in the world," Vito said. "She was born to be a woman."

"This I gotta see," Ross said. "Bring her along if she can keep her mouth shut."

"Okay," Vito said. "We'll be at your place at eight."

"No," Ross answered, "better make it the Shelton Club at eight thirty. I'll bring a dame, too. That way, if anyone sees us we'll be out on a ball."

"Right," Vito agreed. He put down the telephone. Ross was a bright boy. Sometimes too bright. He picked up the telephone again and dialed a number.

A voice answered. "Get Joker to the phone," he said. Joker was right. Many years ago he had said the kid would need a lot of handling.

Chapter 3

THE CAB dropped him at a brownstone house on West 73rd Street. He paid the driver and walked up the steps. The light in the hall was dim, and he had to strike a match to find her name. *Maryann Flood*. He pressed the bell.

Almost immediately there was an answering buzz at the door. He pushed it open and came into an old-fashioned hallway. Her door, marked by a gold letter *C*, was at the top of a flight of stairs. He was about to knock when she opened it.

"Come in," she said, smiling, and stepped back to let him enter.

He came into the room, taking off his hat. At first glance he was surprised. It was neatly and simply furnished, and still there was a sense of the exotic in the apartment. It was in the thick, rich pile of the rug, the bizarre wall fixtures, a sword, an ancient gun, a cat-o'-nine-tails. The light was soft on the deep-maroon paint of the walls and ceiling. Under the windows were bookshelves filled with books and knick-knacks.

"Your coat?" she asked, still smiling.

"Oh—sure." He slipped it off.

She took it from him. "There's ice and whisky on the side table," she said. "I'll be ready in a few minutes."

He walked over to the side table. The ice bucket was sterling silver. The glasses were good Steuben tumblers. The Scotch was Johnnie Walker Black Label, the rye Canadian, the bourbon Old Grand-dad, the gin House of Lords. "You live pretty good," he said.

Her quilted housecoat of green velvet swirled as she turned to look at him. "I should," she said, unsmiling. "That's the only reward of my profession. And there's no guarantee that it will continue, so I make the most of the moment."

He filled a glass and walked over to the bookshelves. They contained current fiction, some good, some bad. "Did you read all these?" he asked curiously.

She nodded. "I generally have the whole day to kill."

He tasted his whisky. "Can I fix you a drink?" he asked.

"No, thanks," she said. "I'll get one." She poured some creme de cassis into a tumbler, added a few ice cubes and then soda. She raised the glass. "To the smartest lawyer in New York."

He grinned. "Thank you." He held up his own glass. "To the most fascinating client an attorney ever had the good fortune to serve."

"Thank you." She put down her drink and walked toward the bedroom. "How shall I dress? Where are we going?"

He followed her to the bedroom door and stood looking

at her. "Dress it up," he said. "We're going to the Shelton Club. I have to meet a client."

She raised her eyebrows. "The Shelton Club—we're really livin'."

"Nothing but the best," he said, grinning.

She slipped out of her housecoat and sat down in front of a vanity table. He caught his breath, she had done it so casually. She wore nothing but a strapless brassiere, panties, and long silk stockings that were secured to a tiny garter belt around her waist. She glanced at him mischievously. "Excuse the working clothes."

He held his hands in front of his eyes. "I'll be all right in a minute," he said. "It's just that I'm not used to women."

She laughed as she began to put on make-up. "You're nice, Hank. I like you."

"Thanks," he said.

She turned to him. "I mean it. There are very few men I do like. They're mostly animals."

His face was suddenly serious. She ought to know better than most. "I hope we can be friends," he said.

Her eyes were wise. "I hope so," she said candidly, "but I doubt it."

He was surprised. "Why?"

She got to her feet and turned toward him. An indefinable change had come over her. He felt a pulse beating in his temple. In the soft light of the room she seemed suddenly to have turned into an erotic statue; her breasts were full and thrusting, the curve of her belly warm and inviting, her legs like long-stemmed flowers. His mouth was suddenly dry. He held his glass to his mouth, but did not drink from it. He just wanted the cold moistness against his lips. "You're beautiful," he whispered.

A half-smile came to her lips. "Am I?" she asked. "Not

really. My legs are too long, my bust too full, my shoulders too broad, my eyes too big, my chin too square, my cheekbones too high, my mouth too wide. Everything's wrong, according to the fashion. Yet you say I'm beautiful."

"You are," he said.

Her eyes stared through him. "You mean something else, not beauty. You mean I'm good for something else, don't you?"

"What else is the measure of beauty?" he asked.

The smile disappeared from her lips. "That's what I mean. That's why I doubt we can be friends. It always comes to that."

He smiled at her. "I know you," he said softly. "You don't want it any other way. It's your only weapon. It's your only way to be equal."

She stared at him a moment, then sat down again at the vanity table. She picked up a powder puff and offered it to him. "Powder my back," she said. "Maybe you'll be different from all the others. You're smarter."

He stared at the powder puff for a moment, then turned away. "If we're goin' to be friends," he said, "powder your own back. I'm only human."

When she came out of the bedroom he got to his feet and whistled. She wore a simple off-the-shoulder dress of gold lamé that clung lightly to her figure and fell to her calf. Sheer silk stockings and gold shoes. In her ears she wore tiny heart-shaped gold earrings, and around her throat a single large topaz-like stone hung on a gold-mesh chain. Her hair was white-blond and shimmering against the yellow gold of her costume.

She smiled at him. "You like?"

He nodded. "Fabulous!"

She brought his coat from the closet and draped a light-colored mink scarf around her shoulders.

"Ready?" he asked, smiling. Ross's eyes would pop out.

"Always ready," she replied.

As they started for the door, the telephone began to ring. He stopped and looked at her. "Don't you want to answer it?" he asked.

Her eyes met his. "My answering-service will get it. It's probably a client who doesn't know I'm taking a night off."

They sat back in the cab and he gave the driver the destination. She put her hand through his arm. The light scent of her perfume came to him.

"What do you want out of life, Maryann?" he asked.

The darkness hid her eyes from him as she spoke. "Everybody asks the same question. Do you want the stock answer or the truth?"

"The truth, if we're to be friends," he said.

"The same thing that everyone else wants," she said. "Love. A home. Family. Security. Marriage. I'm no different from any other girl."

He hesitated. "But—" he started to say.

She interrupted him. "I'm a whore, you were going to say."

It was as if she picked the thought from his mind. He coughed embarrassedly.

"That doesn't make me a second-class citizen," she said quietly. "I feel everything that any other girl feels. I bleed as much when I'm cut, I cry as much when I'm hurt. I work just as hard at my profession as any other girl works at hers. It's more difficult to be a competent whore than it is to be a competent secretary or clerk."

"Then how come you never tried anything else?"

"How do you know what I tried?" she asked quietly. "Why are you a lawyer instead of a doctor? Because this is what you're best at. Well, this is what I'm best at."

"I'm a lawyer also because it's what I want, what I was born for," he said quickly.

"As one professional to another"—she smiled—"all my life I fought it. Ever since I was a kid and the boys were ganging up after me, I fought it. Someone once told me that this was what I was born for. I didn't believe him, but he was right. I know it now."

He took her hand and patted it gently. Suddenly he realized he liked this girl very much. She had a curious form of honesty. "I hope someday you'll get what you want."

At the restaurant she waited while Vito checked his hat and coat. Ross's back was to them as they approached. He was busy talking to a dark-haired girl seated next to him.

Vito stood behind him, his hand on Maryann's arm. "Ross," he said.

Ross turned around quickly and looked up, smiling, his dark eyes bright. "Hank!"

"Ross, I'd like you to meet Maryann Flood," Hank said. "Maryann, this is Ross Dre—" His voice suddenly vanished.

Ross's face had gone white. For a moment Hank thought the man had become ill, there was such agony in his expression. Only Ross's eyes were alive—alive and bright with a hunger in them that Vito had never seen before. Finally Ross spoke. His voice trembled. "Mar—Marja!"

Vito looked at Maryann. Beneath her make-up her face was pale, but she was more composed than Ross. She held out her hand to him.

"Ross!" she said in a husky voice. "It's been a long time."

"Seven years, Marja," Ross said. He struggled to his feet. "Sit down, Hank."

They seated themselves. "We grew up together, Hank," Ross explained, his eyes on Maryann. "Remember what you said over the phone, Hank? This is the only girl in the world I would believe that about!"

Vito looked from one to the other. The same angry vitality was in each. They were so alike in their differences that they might have come from the same mold, with only a different finish to each. He put his hand on the table and leaned forward. "Tell me about it," he said.

Chapter 4

THE DARK-HAIRED girl who had come with Ross was annoyed. For all the attention she had been getting throughout dinner, she might as well not have been there. It made no difference to her what Ross and Maryann had done when they were kids.

But it did to Hank Vito. It explained to him a lot of things about Ross and about Maryann. Things that had puzzled him. Silently he filed away their reminiscences. He was a collector of odd bits of information about people. In his business, such information not infrequently came in handy.

One thing he saw at once: he would have to wait his turn with Maryann. If ever there had been unfinished business between two people, here it was between these two. He looked at the dark-haired girl and smiled. "What do you say we buzz off and leave these two to their old-times reunion, honey?"

The girl returned his smile gratefully. "I'd like nothing better, Mr. Vito. Other people's memories are so dull."

Hank didn't agree with her, but he got to his feet. "Let's go," he said.

Ross looked up at him. "But we haven't got around to our business yet," he protested.

Hank smiled. "Make it at my office first thing in the morning." He held out a hand to Maryann. "Good night, friend."

Her smile was bright and warm. "Good night, counselor."

Ross watched them leave, then turned to Maryann. "Sit next to me."

Silently she moved into the place the other girl had vacated. Ross covered her hand with his own.

"Another drink?" he asked.

She shook her head. "No thanks."

"I'll have one." He gestured and the waiter brought him another Scotch. "How did you meet Hank Vito?" he asked.

She looked into his eyes. "I was in trouble and needed a lawyer. I went to him."

"You went to the best," Ross said. "He's expensive, but there aren't any better."

"Sometimes the most expensive is the cheapest in the long run," she answered.

"He's my lawyer, too," Ross said.

She raised her eyebrows questioningly.

"I work for the syndicate," Ross said. "You know what that is?"

She nodded.

"I'm clean, though," he said quickly. "I handle the legit operations. Right now they want me to move out to L.A. to set up a construction company. That's why I wanted to see Hank tonight."

She didn't speak.

"Remember Joker Martin?" Ross asked.

She nodded.

"He's one of the wheels now. I used to be with him, but now I'm independent. I convinced them that I'm better off working alone." Ross offered her a cigarette and held a light to it. "He was the only one who would give me a job when the old man kicked me out."

She looked into his eyes. "You're doin' pretty good."

He nodded with satisfaction. "There's a lot of dough around, baby, and I'm in line for it."

"If the Army don't get you," she said.

He laughed. "They won't get me."

"You seem sure."

"It's easy to beat the draft if you know the right medics," he said.

"They can't help once you're down at Grand Central," she said. "All the notes in the world don't hold up there."

He tugged his ear lobe. "I've got draft insurance. A twenty-five-hundred dollar hole in my eardrum."

She shook her head. "You haven't changed a bit, Ross. Still got an angle for everything." Suddenly she was tired. Ross reminded her of times long past and of things she didn't want to remember. She reached for her scarf. "It's getting late, Ross. I think I'll go home."

"I'll take you," he said quickly. "My car's outside."

"Got gas?" she asked.

"Sure," he laughed. "This is Ross you're talkin' to, remember, honey?"

She had never got used to the dimout in the city and the way it made everything seem hushed and quiet. She gave him her address and leaned back in the car as it sped through the night. She closed her eyes, feeling far away from the people and places she knew.

It seemed she had been riding a long time when the car stopped. She opened her eyes. She wasn't home. "Ross!" she said sharply.

"Look, baby." He gestured toward the car window. "It's been a long time."

She turned and looked at the river, sparkling in the occasional flickers of light. Riverside Drive—where they had been together so many times.

She felt his arm move along the seat behind her, and turned to him. "Cut it, Ross. It *has* been a long time, an' yuh can't go back. Take me home."

She saw his mouth set in the petulant look she remembered as he started the car again. A few silent minutes later they were at her door.

Ross looked at her. "You could invite me in for a drink," he said. "Just for old times' sake."

"Okay," she said reluctantly. "Just one."

He followed her into the apartment. "There's liquor on the side table," she said.

She put his coat on a chair and went into the bedroom. A few minutes later she returned wearing a green velvet housecoat.

He looked up at her and smiled. "You're still the greatest."

"Thanks," she said dryly.

He wrinkled his brow quizzically. "What's eatin' you, baby? Still mad over what happened between us so long ago?"

She shook her head. "Not any more, Ross. Too much has happened to me. I can't be angry over that."

He reached for her arm, but she stepped out of reach.

"Then what is it? I still got that big yen for you I always had."

She smiled slowly. "I know. The same yen you have for all the girls."

His voice lowered. "It's different with you, baby. It's always been different."

"Yeah, Ross, yeah." Her voice was sarcastic.

He put down his drink and moved quickly. Catching her shoulders in his big hands, he held her still. Her eyes looked at him without fear. "Still the same little tease, ain't you, baby?"

"Still the same rough-action boy, ain't you, Ross?" she replied.

"I'm older now," he said. "You can't get rid of me as easily as you did the first time." He pulled her to him. Her arms went around his neck. He smiled. "That's better, baby." He bent his head to kiss her.

A sudden blinding pain seared through his temples. With a curse, he slipped to the floor and looked up at her. The pain was gone as soon as he let her go, but there was a dull ache in his neck. "You bitch!" he snarled. "What did you do?"

She smiled down at him. "A friend of mine in the service taught me. It's called pressure points. Judo."

He got to his feet and reached for his drink. "You haven't changed a bit, have you?"

Without answering, she turned to the sideboard and mixed herself a drink. He watched her. "What's that?" he asked.

"Cassis and soda," she said.

He made a face. "That's like medicine."

"I like it," she said.

He looked around the apartment. "Nice place you got here."

"Thanks," she said.

"You must be doin' pretty good yourself."

"I make out."

"What line are you in?" he asked curiously.

She stared at him for a moment. Just then the telephone began to ring. She walked over to it and picked it up. Covering the mouthpiece with her hand, she looked right into his eyes. "I'm a whore," she said.

His breath seemed imprisoned in his chest. As if from a distance he heard her speak into the phone. "No, honey, not right now. I'm busy. Try tomorrow, will yuh?"

She put down the telephone and walked across the room and picked up his coat. She held it toward him. "Now, will yuh go, Ross? I'm tired."

He didn't move from where he stood. His eyes were still on her face. His hand went into his pocket and came out with a roll of bills. He snapped his fingers and the bills shot toward her and cascaded down around her. "I just bought the rest of the night," he said.

They lay quietly in the bed. The faint night sounds of the city seeped into the room through the closed windows. He turned toward her. The glow of her cigarette flickered, throwing a soft red glow on her face.

Something inside him ached. He reached toward her. Her hand was soft and cool. He remembered her touch and the wild excitement that it brought to him. "Marja," he whispered.

He felt the soft answering pressure of her fingers. "Marja," he whispered softly, "didn't you feel anything? Anything at all?"

Her voice was low and husky. "Sure, honey. You're quite a man."

"Marja, I don't mean that!" His sound was an agonized whisper. Suddenly something burst inside him and he began to cry. So much had been lost. Deep, racking sobs tore through him.

Her arms went around him, drawing his head down to her breast. "There, baby, there," she whispered soothingly.

Chapter 5

THE ODOR of frying bacon hit him as he came out of the bathroom, still warm from the shower. He finished rubbing himself briskly, then strode into the kitchen, the towel draped around his waist.

Maryann, wearing a simple housedress, was breaking some eggs into a pan on the small stove. She looked up briefly. "Get dressed," she said. "Breakfast'll be ready in a minute."

He stared at her. Her eyes were clear and she showed no trace of the long and angry night. She wore no make-up, and yet her skin glowed with the same healthy animal quality it had always had. "What for?" he asked. "I'm not goin' anywhere."

"Yes, you are," she said, gesturing to a small clock on the stove. "It's almost noon. That's checkout time in this hotel."

His face flushed. It was almost as if he felt the shame she should have felt. "You're checkin' out with me," he said.

"Don't be a fool," she replied quietly. "You can't afford it."

He walked over to her and took her hand. "Marja," he almost pleaded, "is that all I am to you? Just another Joe?"

Her eyes met his steadily. "The name is Maryann. Marja's gone a long time, and all guys are Joe to Maryann."

His gaze fell before hers. "I want to go back, Marja. I want us to do it over. You and me. I'm grown up now. We can have a lot of things together."

"What?" she asked sarcastically. "Marriage?"

He flushed again.

She didn't give him time to answer. "Uh-uh. I'm satisfied the ways things are. I don't have to tie up with anybody." She began to shake the eggs onto a plate. "Better hurry," she said, "or the eggs'll get cold."

He could feel a futile anger rising in him. "If it was Mike, I bet you wouldn't act like that!" She flinched suddenly and he knew that he had scored. "What has that dope got for you, anyway? He'll never be anything but a jerk cop again once he gets out of the Army!"

Her voice was low. "Mike's in the Army?"

"Yeah," he said. "He enlisted the day after Pearl Harbor. Just a week after he got on the regular force, too."

"Oh," she said. "Is he overseas?"

"How the hell should I know?" he snarled. "I have better things to do than to keep tabs on him!" He turned back to the bedroom. "Maybe you would like me to look him up for you," he flung back nastily over his shoulder. "I'll tell him you have special rates for servicemen!"

Joker Martin entered the restaurant and came over to Vito's table. Vito looked up and signaled the waiter as he sat down. "You look worried, Joker," he said.

"I am worried," Joker answered. "I can't get Ross to stay out west. He keeps comin' in every other month. I just had another wire from him. He's on his way in now."

Vito ordered two drinks. "How about another boy?" he asked.

Joker stared down at the table. "I thought about that, too, but who could I use? The crowd out there likes Ross. His family background is a great cover. Besides, there's no one else smart enough, an' if they are, I can't trust 'em."

Vito scratched on the tablecloth idly with a pencil. "This has been goin' on for about five months now?"

Joker nodded.

Vito threw the pencil down. "It's that dame," he said.

Joker looked at him shrewdly. "What dame?"

"Maryann," Vito said. "She told me that Ross was after her to go out west with him, but she doesn't want to."

"Maryann?" Joker was puzzled. "Who is she? Ross want to marry her?"

Vito shook his head. "No, he doesn't want to marry her. At least, she never said he did. He just flipped his lid over her, that's all." He laughed. "I can't blame him for that, though. I almost did myself."

"Ross never mentioned no dame to me," Joker said. What kind of a broad is she?"

Vito looked at him. "She's a special kind of broad. Made for it. A whore with a code of ethics."

"No hustler's got ethics," Joker said. "The only language they understand is dough."

"You don't know Maryann," Vito said. "You can buy her time, but you can't buy her."

"Maryann," Joker said softly. "That's a queer name for a whore."

"Maryann Flood," Vito said.

Joker's face was suddenly red and excited. "A blonde girl with wide brown eyes that stare right through you?"

"Yeah," Vito answered curiously. "You know her?"

Joker didn't answer. He pounded the table softly with his fist. "The son of a bitch!" he swore. "The no-good bastard!"

"What's got into you?" Vito asked. "What're you sore about?"

Joker picked up his drink and swallowed it. "I should've guessed. Marja Flood."

"That's what Ross calls her," Vito said in a surprised voice. "Then you do know her?"

Joker nodded. "I know her, all right. She worked for me at the Golden Glow when she was a kid. I damn near lost my license for givin' her a job. She was under age then."

"Oh," Vito said.

"She was sent up for cuttin' her stepfather with a kitchen knife. I heard about her when she got out, but lost track after that," Joker said. He signaled for another drink. "Ross always had a yen for that dame, but she couldn't see him. There was another guy, Ross's pal. He was her boy."

"What happened?" Vito asked.

"She got sent up, I tol' yuh," Joker said. "After that I don't know what happened. First I hear in five years is from you."

Vito's legal mind didn't like loose ends. "I mean about this friend of Ross's. What happened to him?"

"He became a cop an' then went into the Army. Ross mentioned it once before he went up for his operation." Joker sipped his drink reflectively. "She was quite a broad even when she was a kid. She had man sense even then. She still the same?"

Vito laughed.

Joker held up his hand. "Don't tell me, I know." He lit a cigarette, and Vito noticed that his fingers were trembling. "I had big plans for that kid myself," Joker said.

The muffled sound of the telephone bell penetrated her sleep. She rolled over on the bed and put her face in the pillow. It kept ringing, and reluctantly she woke up. Only in an emergency did the answering-service let the telephone ring. She picked up the phone. "Hello," she said into it.

"Maryann?" a cautious voice asked. "Frank."

She was wide awake now. It was Frank Millersen. Detective Lieutenant Millersen. "Trouble again, Frank?" she asked, looking at the clock. It was almost ten in the morning. He hadn't called since the time she had been charged with that larceny rap.

"No," the cautious voice laughed softly. "You're okay."

An almost inaudible sigh of relief escaped her lips. It had been a long time since Millersen had first picked her up. A green kid she was then. She had spent thirty days in the can, but she had made friends with him. "What is it, then?" she asked, her voice growing husky. "Want to see me?"

The voice laughed again. "No, thanks, Maryann. I can't afford it on a cop's pay."

"You know it ain't the dough with you, Frank," she said. "I like you."

"Don't con me, Maryann," he laughed. "We both know better. I just called to tell you I located that ex-cop you asked me about a few months ago. The one that went into the Army. Mike Keyes, your girl friend's brother."

An excitement ran through her. She had called him as soon as Ross had left that first time, and told him the first story that came to her mind. "Yeah?" she said, controlling her voice carefully. "Where is he?"

"St. Albans Veterans Hospital," he said. "Been there three weeks. He was wounded in North Africa."

Despite herself, a note of concern crept into her voice. "He was wounded?"

"Yeah. But not too bad, from what I hear. He's gettin' out on a week-end pass tomorrow mornin'. If your girl friend wants to catch him, she better get out there before eight o'clock. Otherwise, it'll be too late. You know how soldiers are." Millersen chuckled again. "The last thing they go lookin' for is their sisters."

"Thanks very much, Frank," she said, putting down the telephone. She reached for a cigarette and lit it thoughtfully. She could see Mike's face in the blue smoke before her. The hurt in his eyes the last time she had seen him.

She wondered what he would do on his week-end pass. His father and mother were in California, where the old man had a defense job. That was what she had been told when she called the house where Mike had lived.

She wondered if he had a girl friend he was going to see. Something inside her ached at that thought. He probably never thought about her any more. Slowly she ground out the cigarette in an ash tray. She was sorry she had ever given in to the impulse to ask Frank to locate Mike for her.

Chapter 6

SHE parked the car across the street from the gate to the hospital and waited. The big A.W.V.S. bus was at the corner, waiting to take the soldiers into the city. She looked at her watch. It was seven thirty. She shivered slightly and lit a cigarette. It had been a long time since she had been up so early in the morning.

After a while she began to feel a little silly. It was stupid to get up in the middle of the night and drive all the way out here just to look at him. Not to talk to him, not to touch him. Just to see him walk a few feet and get into a bus. He would never even know she was here.

She was on her third cigarette when the gate opened and the first group of soldiers came out. A sudden fear came into her. They all looked so much alike in their uniforms. She wondered whether she would recognize him. He might have changed.

A small Red Cross Mobile Canteen was set up in front of the gate, and women were busy handing out doughnuts

319

and cups of hot coffee to the boys. Two more buses came
up and pulled in behind the first one.

Eagerly she scanned the soldiers' faces. The first bus was
full now, and its motors caught with a roar. It pulled off,
and the second bus moved up to take its place. The raucous
sounds of the men's laughter came to her.

The second bus drove off and the last bus moved up. She
looked at her watch nervously. It was a quarter past eight.
Millersen had been wrong. Mike wasn't coming out. There
were fewer soldiers now. The rush was over.

She scanned each face quickly. Maybe she had missed
him in the crowd which had got on the earlier buses. Now
there were only a few soldiers coming down the path. The
Mobile Canteen was shutting its flaps. She heard the woman who seemed to be in charge telling the other that it was
time to go. The Canteen drove off.

She ground out her cigarette in the dashboard tray and
turned on the ignition. Either she had missed him in the
crowd or he wasn't coming out. She pressed the starter, and
the motor caught. The last bus started out into the road before her.

She put the car into gear and started to move. A last impulse made her look across the road. He was just turning
through the gate. Her foot hit the brake automatically and
she stared.

He was thin, terribly thin; his cheekbones stuck out, and
his eyes were blue hollows above them. He walked with a
slight limp, as if favoring his right leg. As he saw the bus
disappearing around the corner, he stopped and she saw
him snap his fingers in a familiar gesture of disappointment. She could almost hear the "Damn!" his lips framed.

Slowly he shifted his small canvas bag from his right
hand to his left hand. He struck a match and lit a cigarette,

then flipped the match into the gutter, and began to walk down the street.

She sat as if paralyzed, looking after him. He seemed strange in a uniform, and yet it was as if he had always worn it. Everything about him was wholly familiar. As she stepped from the car, she felt almost as if a magnet were drawing her. She found herself running after him.

Her hand reached out and covered his own on the handle of the bag. There was such a pounding in her ears that she could hardly hear her own voice. "Carry your bag, soldier?"

He turned slowly. Her vision blurred and she couldn't see his face clearly. Was he annoyed? Frightened, she spoke again. "Carry your bag, soldier?"

The cigarette hanging from his lips began to fall. It tumbled crazily across his lapel and dropped to the sidewalk between them. She stood trembling, waiting for him to speak.

His lips moved, but no sound came out. His face began to whiten and he seemed to sway. She put out a hand to steady him. Then it was as if there were a fire between them, for she was in his arms and kissing his mouth and the salt of someone's tears was on their lips.

She turned the key in the lock and pushed open the door, looking up at him in the shadows of the hallway. "We're home, Mike," she said.

He walked into the room and turned to face her. Her explanations had already been made. She had told him about the friend who had found him for her.

She closed the door behind her, and a sudden shyness came over her. "Sit down and rest," she said. "I'll fix you a drink." She walked over to the sideboard. "What'll it be?"

"Gin over rocks," he said, his eyes following her.

Quickly she poured the drink and handed it to him. She took the cap from his head and studied his face. "You've changed, Mike."

He smiled slowly. "I'm a man now, Marja. I couldn't stay a boy forever. You told me that, remember?"

Her eyes were on his. She nodded.

He raised his drink to her. "To the children we were," he said.

"Mike!" There was the echo of pain in her voice. "Let's not remember. Let's pretend we are just meeting, with all our yesterdays forgotten and nothing but bright tomorrows before us."

The corners of his mouth twisted. "It's pretty hard to pretend, Marja. Too many things are happening all around us."

"For just these few days, then, Mike. Please!"

He put his drink down and held out his arms toward her. She came into them quickly and he placed her head against his chest. She could hear his voice rumbling deep inside him. "I don't have to pretend anything, Marja. Being with you is all I ever wanted."

The telephone began to ring, and he released her.

She shook her head. "I don't want to answer it."

"It may be important," he said.

"The only thing important this week-end is us," she answered.

When the phone stopped ringing, she dialed a number. "This is Miss Flood. I'm going away for the week-end. Will you take all the messages, please, and tell everyone who asks for immediate service."

He watched her put down the telephone. "You must have a pretty good job to be able to afford this place."

She smiled. "I've been lucky."

A kind of pride came into his eyes. "Smart, too. Yuh don't get all these things without being smart."

Suddenly cautious, she studied his face for hidden meanings. Then she drew a deep breath. "I don't want to talk shop," she said. "I get enough of that all week. This weekend is for me."

It was near midnight when they came in from dinner, still laughing at something he had said in the cab. But his face, she realized, was drawn and tired. She was immediately contrite.

"I been havin' such a ball," she said, "I forgot you were just out of the hospital."

"I'm fine," he said.

"No, you're not," she insisted, crossing the bedroom. "I'll make the bed and draw your bath. You're goin' right to sleep."

"Marja," he protested. "You make me feel like a baby."

"For this week-end," she said, smiling at him, "that's just what you are. My baby."

Quickly she turned down the covers of the bed and went into the bathroom and turned on the hot water. When she came out into the bedroom, he was standing in the doorway looking at her.

"You don't have to give up your bed for me," he said. "I can sleep on the couch."

She could feel a flame creeping up in her face. She crossed the room and put her arms around his neck. "Mike," she whispered, "you're such a fool." She kissed him.

He stood very still for a moment, then his arms tightened around her until she could hardly breathe. There were lights spinning before her eyes and the room was turning over and over. She could feel his muscles tighten strongly against her. She closed her eyes. It had never been like this. Never. This was for her. This was her feeling, her emotion, her life force. It was her beginning and her ending. The world and the stars were exploding inside her.

"Mike!" she cried. "I love you, Mike!"

Chapter 7

SHE lay quietly in the bed watching him sleep. The gray light of the morning filtered through the drawn blinds. A stray shaft of sunlight fell across his mouth. He seemed to be smiling. She rested her head on the pillow, scarcely daring to breathe for fear it would disturb him. The weekend had so quickly become yesterday. She closed her eyes to better remember.

"We could be married before I check in." His voice was low.

Startled, she opened her eyes. "I thought you were sleeping," she said.

"We have time. I don't have to report until noon." He was looking right into her eyes.

She didn't answer.

His hand sought her fingers. "What's wrong, Marja?"

She shook her head. "Nothing."

"Something is," he said. "I feel it. Ever since I first asked you yesterday. Don't you want to marry me?"

She turned her face to him. "You know better than that."

"Then what is it?" he asked. "From here I go to officer-candidate school. Lieutenants get pretty good pay. We can manage on that. At least we could be together until I go overseas again."

"Mike," she whispered, "please stop. Don't ask me any more."

"But I love you, baby," he said. "I want you with me always. Is it your job? The money you get?"

She shook her head.

"When I get out of service, I'm goin' to law school," he said. "Lawyers make out pretty good."

"No, Mike, no."

He pulled her to him and kissed her. "If there's something you're afraid of, baby, tell me. I don't care what it is. Nothing you can do or have done can keep us apart. I love you too much."

She looked up into his eyes. "Yuh mean that, don't you?" she whispered.

He nodded.

"Someone else said that to me once, but he didn't mean it."

"He didn't love you like I do," he said. "Nobody ever has or will."

She took a deep breath. "I wish I could believe it. Maybe someday—"

"Marry me and see," he said, smiling.

The doorbell rang sharply. He looked at her. "Expecting someone?"

She shook her head as the bell rang again. "It's probably the milkman. He'll go away."

But the bell didn't stop ringing. "Maybe you better go see who it is," he said.

"Oh, all right," she said, reaching for her robe. She slipped into it and went into the other room, closing the bedroom door behind her.

She opened the hall door. "Yes?" she asked.

"I knew you were home," Ross said, "even though you didn't answer the phone all week-end."

She placed her foot behind the door. "You can't come in," she whispered. "I told you never to come unless we spoke first."

He stared at her balefully. "How's anybody goin' to talk to you when you don't answer the phone?"

"Come back this afternoon," she said, starting to close the door on him.

He pushed it back and she fell back with it. He came into the apartment. She could smell liquor on his breath. "I'm not comin' back this afternoon," he said. "I'm goin' to the coast to stay, an' you're comin' with me!"

"Ross, you're nuts!" she said angrily. "I'm not goin' anywhere with you!"

He grabbed her arm. "You're comin'!" he shouted.

The bedroom door opened and Mike stood there. He didn't recognize Ross at first. "Need any help, Marja?" he asked.

Ross knew him at once. "Mike!" he yelled. Then he began to laugh.

Mike was bewildered. "What's the matter with him?"

"He's drunk," she said.

Ross staggered over to Mike. "My ol' buddy," he said. "Will you tell this crazy broad that she's better off comin' to California with me than stayin' on the turf here?"

Mike's voice was cold. "Cut it, Ross. That's no way to talk in front of Marja."

Ross stopped. He looked first at one, then the other. A

look of shrewd understanding crept over his face. He seemed to sober suddenly. "That's why you didn't answer the phone all week-end," he said to her.

She didn't answer.

"You were shacked up with him."

Still she said nothing.

He turned to Mike. "I hope she gave you a better rate than I got. A hundred bucks a night is a lot of dough for a soldier. Even if she does throw in bacon and eggs for breakfast."

Mike stared at her. Her face was white.

Ross saw the question in Mike's eyes. "You mean to say she didn't tell you?" he said sarcastically. He turned to her. "That's not fair, baby. Waitin' till the last minute to hand him the tab. He might not have that much dough." He took a roll from his pocket and peeled several bills from it. "Here, Marja. This one's on me."

She didn't move, but stared at Ross as one might gaze in fascination on the face of death.

Ross turned back to Mike. "Here, soldier, take the dough. I just bought you a week-end with the best whore in New York. I always wanted to do something for the Army, anyway."

Mike was staring at her. "It's not true," he said in a husky voice. "Tell me it's not true."

Marja didn't speak, but Ross's voice cut in. "Don't be a schmuck, Mike. I don't have to lie."

"You said you loved me," Mike said.

Still she was silent.

Ross's voice was heavy and sarcastic. "And when she held you, did she tell you how handsome you were? And when you kissed her, did she ask you to feed on her? And when you were flying, did she put—"

A low animal growl sounded in Mike's throat as he sprang at Ross. Too late he saw something flashing in Ross's hand. There was a sharp pain across his head, and he tumbled to the floor. He tried to push himself to his feet, but another pain exploded behind his ear and he sank into a welcome darkness.

Ross stood over him, panting heavily. His eyes were glazed with hatred, the small billy still swinging in his hand. He slashed Mike viciously across the face. "I've owed you that for a long time," he said. Then a fever took hold of him and he began to swing wildly.

"Stop, Ross, stop!" she screamed, clawing at him. "You'll kill him!"

"That's just what I want to do," he said crazily. "For a long time now!" He raised his arm again.

"I'll go with you if you stop!" she cried.

His hand was suspended in mid-air. He shook his head as if to clear it. "What'd you say?"

"I'll go with you if you stop." Her voice was clearer now.

Slowly his hand came down. He looked at the billy in it as if surprised that it was there. Slowly he dropped it into his pocket. His eyes were clear, and his voice was as calm as if nothing had happened. "Get your things," he said softly.

She didn't move. She was looking down at Mike.

He followed her gaze to the floor. "Christ! He's a mess!" A note of wonder was in his voice. He bent over and slipped his arms under Mike's shoulders. "I'll get him into bed and clean him up a little while you're packing."

It was almost dark when Mike opened his eyes. There

was a dull, throbbing pain across the bridge of his nose. He stifled a groan. "Marja!" he called.

There was no answer.

Reluctantly, memory came to him. Stiffly he got out of the bed. A wave of dizziness rolled over him. He held on to a chair until he fought it off, then made his way to the bathroom. In the dark he turned on the cold water. He put his mouth to the faucet and drank thirstily. At last the dryness in his throat was gone.

He straightened up and turned on the light. A strange face stared at him from the mirror over the sink. The cheekbones were bruised and sore, the nose crushed and flattened, and the lips cut and split. Most of all, the eyes had changed. They were hollow and deep with pain that was not a physical thing. He closed them slowly, then opened them quickly to see if the look would vanish. It didn't. It was still there.

It would always be there. Just as it was now. A look of pain that no amount of tears could ever wash away.

Chapter 8

THE BRIGHT California sunshine was beginning to slide behind the blue-black shadows of the hills as the tall gray-haired man walked up the steps of the house and pressed the doorbell. From deep within the house came the slight echo of chimes. He looked along the side of the house.

The shimmering aqua blue of the swimming-pool threw off sparkling diamonds of light as the spray reached up into the sun. He could hear the faint sound of a child's laughter coming from the water and the gently admonishing tones of the colored nurse who was patrolling the walk around the pool vigilantly. He was nodding with pleased satisfaction as the door opened.

An old colored man looked out at him. A polite smile of recognition appeared on his face. "Come in, Mr. Martin," he said in a deep, rich voice. "I'll tell Miz Drego you're here."

Joker followed the old man into the large living-room

and went over to the big picture window looking out on the pool. He watched the little girl climb out of the water, her white-gold hair shining. Quickly the nurse threw a big Turkish towel around the child and began to dry her.

The child was just like her mother, he thought. There was nothing of Ross in her. Strange that a man as strong as Ross could make no mark on his child. A faint smile came to his lips. But was Michelle really Ross's child? Only Marja could answer that, and he knew better than to ask her. He thought that Ross did too. Joker was sure that if Ross ever asked, Marja would tell him the truth, even if the truth was not to his liking.

The sound of footsteps behind him made Joker turn around. As always when he saw her, he could feel the faint stirrings inside him. Time had not taken anything from her; if anything it had added. There was something about her so rich and basic and vital that you could almost feel it reaching out and touching you. The smile disappeared from his lips. He held out his hand. "Maryann," he said.

She took it. Her hand was warm and strong. Her even white teeth gleamed quickly. "Joker," she said. "It's been a long time."

He nodded. "Four years." He gestured toward the window. "Michelle was only two years old then. She's a big girl now."

Maryann smiled. "Six."

"She's just like her mother. She's going to be a heartbreaker," Joker laughed.

A strange expression flitted across Maryann's face. "Oh, God, I hope not!" she said fervently.

Joker reached for his cigarettes. "You haven't done so bad."

A shadow came into her eyes. "Depends on what you look for, Joker. We all look for different things."

"True," he said.

She pulled the bell cord next to the window. "Can I get you a drink while you're waiting, Joker? Ross won't be home for another hour yet."

"Thanks," he said. "I can use one."

She glanced at him sharply. "Anything wrong?"

His eyes were shrewd. "Depends on what you look for, Maryann." He held a match to his cigarette. "I didn't come to see Ross this time. I came to see you."

Her face was inscrutable. "Yes?" Her voice had just the right amount of polite curiosity.

The old servant came into the room. "Yes, Miz Drego?"

Maryann turned to him. "Bring Mr. Martin some Scotch."

The old man turned and disappeared. Joker looked after him. "Still have the same man, I see."

She nodded. "I don't know how I'd get along without Tom. He's a real friend."

"He worked for that millionaire that got killed in the plane crash, didn't he? What was his name?"

"Gordon Paynter," she answered. "When I read about it, I went and looked Tom up. I was very lucky that he was willing to come to me. Gordon had left him well taken care of."

"You knew Paynter, then?" His voice was polite.

"I knew him," she answered in a flat voice. "We were almost married."

Tom came into the room bringing Scotch, glasses, and ice. "Shall I fix the drinks, ma'am?" he asked.

Maryann nodded. They were silent until Tom had given

Joker his drink and left the room. Then Joker held up his glass. "Your good health."

"Thank you," she said politely. She sat down in a chair opposite the fireplace and looked at him expectantly. There was that about her which reminded him of a cat. Maybe it was the tawny color of her eyes, or the way she sat there, sensitive and alert.

"Have you noticed any changes in Ross lately?" he asked suddenly.

The expression in her eyes changed only slightly. There was a wariness in them that had not been there a moment before. "What do you mean?" she parried.

His voice was harsh. "You know what I mean."

She didn't answer.

"Ross is getting to be a big man," he said. "Some people can't take it."

"He's very nervous," she said. "He works hard."

"So do I," Joker said flatly. "So do a lot of people, but they don't act like Ross."

"You know Ross," she said. "He's a kid in some ways."

"I know Ross," he said. "That's why I'm out here."

Her eyes looked at him levelly. "What do you expect me to do?" she asked.

He turned to the sideboard and made himself another drink before he spoke. He looked out the window. The child and the nurse were coming toward the house. They disappeared around the corner. "Do you love Ross?" he asked.

There was a faintly admonishing tone in her voice. "Joker, isn't that a silly question?"

He turned from the window and looked at her. "I don't know. You tell me. Is it silly?"

She didn't answer.

"You've been livin' with him for seven years now. You must feel somethin' for him or you wouldn't still be here." He sipped his drink. "All I want to know is whether it is love or not."

Her eyes gazed directly into his. "I like Ross, if that's what you want to know."

He shook his head. "That's not what I want to know. I want to know if you love him."

A shadow came into her eyes. "No, I don't love him."

He let a deep breath escape his lips. He had been counting on just this answer. It would make things easier. He sat down in the chair opposite her. "Ross has an incurable disease," he said slowly. "Ambition. It's going to kill him."

He could see her face whiten under the tan. "It is really incurable or do some people just think it is?"

He shook his head. "It's too far gone, there's no way to cure it now. Nobody has faith in the patient."

"Is it that last hotel? The Shan Du?" she asked.

"That and other things. That was the last straw. He should have known better than to use our money for himself."

"But he paid it all back," she said.

"The money, yes," he said. "But he shared nothing else. We didn't put him out here to be an independent operator. We took too many chances."

"If I spoke to him?" she asked.

"It wouldn't help now," he said. "They've already made up their minds."

"You mean you've made up your mind," she snapped.

He shook his head slowly. "No. The only reason I came out was to see that you're all right."

Chapter 9

"YOU'RE getting too well known, Ross," Joker said as he reached for another roll. "You're goin' to have to cut back a little bit. Too many eyes are on you. The columns report every move you make."

Ross shoved another slice of steak into his mouth. "What difference does it make?" he asked surlily. "I'm gettin' things done."

"We can't afford the publicity," Joker repeated.

Ross threw his fork down angrily. "What's eatin' you guys back east anyway? The only way to get things done out here is to make a big noise. Then everybody knows you an' runs to help."

"Along with the cops and Internal Revenue and the F.B.I.," Joker added, smiling.

"Nobody's been able to tie anything on me yet, have they?" Ross asked.

"Depends on who you're talkin' about," Joker answered. "And what."

Ross looked at him quickly. He pushed his plate away

with a decisive gesture. "You didn't fly out here to give me a lecture on behavior," he snapped. "What's eatin' you?"

Maryann chose that moment to get up. "I'm going up to see that the baby's in bed," she said.

Ross didn't look up. He was staring at Joker as she left the room. "Well?" he asked.

"The Shan Du, for one thing," Joker said softly.

"What about it?" Ross demanded. "It's mine."

Joker shook his head. "You don't understand, kid. That's what's wrong. We got enough opposition without it being from inside."

"There's room in Vegas for twenty more hotels," Ross said.

"Right," Joker answered. "That's why we went into this so long ago. We want as many of them as possible to be ours."

Ross got to his feet. "You mean I can't have anything for myself?"

Joker held up his hands. "Don't get me wrong, Ross. You can have anything you want. I just don't think it's wise."

"I made a lot of dough for you guys," Ross said.

Joker got to his feet and stared at him. "You got your share out of it," he said harshly. "More than just a percentage. Your trouble is that you grab too much. You been like that ever since you were a kid. Always tryin' to grab more than you should. This time you tried too hard." He turned to leave the room.

Ross grabbed at his arm. "What do you mean?"

Joker's eyes were cold and gray. "Remember that time you came to the crap game in the back room of the dance hall? The first time you brought Marja?"

Ross nodded. "What's that got to do with it?"

"You thought you were smart, switchin' dice on us. You weren't so smart. I covered for you then because I thought you'd learn. I can't cover any more." He pulled his arm from Ross's grip and walked out of the room.

Maryann was just coming down the stairs. "Going so soon?" she asked.

He looked at her. "Yeah," he said, "I can't wait. I got some people to see."

"There's no other way?" she asked.

He shook his head almost imperceptibly. He hesitated a moment, then spoke in a very low voice. "I'd take the kid and go for a little trip if I were you."

She stood very still. "It's that bad?"

"It's that bad," he said. "You'll go away?"

She shook her head. "No. I can't leave him now. I'll send the baby away in the morning, though."

A look of admiration crossed his face. "Okay, but be careful. Stay away from the open windows." He walked to the door and opened it. He looked back at her. "I'll call yuh some time."

She watched the door close behind him, then walked into the living-room. Ross was pouring himself a drink. "What did Joker want?" she asked.

"Nothing," he answered.

"Nothing?" she asked. "That's not like him. He didn't come all the way out here for nothing."

He drained the glass quickly. "I said nothing, and that's what I mean." He slammed the glass down on the sideboard. "Leave me alone," he said angrily. "I gotta think."

She stared at him for a moment, then turned and left the room.

When she had gone, he went to the telephone and dialed quickly. A voice answered. "Pete," he said, "I want you to get two boys out here right away. Joker just left."

The receiver crackled. Ross laughed tensely. "It had to come some time," he said. "We couldn't pay off to them forever. . . . No—I'm not worried. They won't dare try anything. They know everybody's watchin' me. I'm just being careful."

He put down the telephone and mixed another drink. He sank into a chair and sipped it. How much did Marja know? he wondered. He could never figure her out. You could only get so far with her and then you ran into a stone wall. He remembered the time she had told him she was pregnant. It had been a long time ago. They had been out here only two months.

He had come into the apartment they had rented temporarily while he was looking for a house. It was a lavish apartment in one of the big hotels. He walked into the bedroom, looking for her.

A valise was on the bed and she was folding her clothing into it. He crossed the room quickly. "Where do you think you're goin'?" he asked.

Her eyes met his gaze calmly. "Away." Her voice was flat and emotionless.

"What for?" he asked. "I'm treatin' you good."

She nodded. "I'm not complaining."

"Then why are you goin'?"

Her eyes looked right into him. "I'm goin' to have a baby," she said.

"Oh, that," he said, a curious relief running through him. "We can get it fixed. I know a doc that'll—"

She shook her head. "Uh-uh. I want this baby."

A proud smile came over his face. "Then have it. We'll get married and—"

"I don't want to marry you," she said.

He was puzzled. "But you said you wanted the baby."

She nodded. "I do." She snapped the valise shut, brought another valise from the closet, and put it on the bed.

He watched her begin to pack the second valise. "Then, why not get married?" he asked. "After all, if I'm going to be a father, everything might as well be right."

Again her eyes met his across the bed. "That's just it. It's not your child."

He stood very still. He could feel the blood running from his face, leaving it white and pallid. "Whose is it?" he asked, his throat suddenly harsh and hurting.

She shrugged her shoulders casually. "What difference does it make, as long as it isn't yours?"

His hand grabbed her arm across the bed and pulled her toward him roughly. She fell across the bed and looked up at him. There was pain in her eyes, but no fear. He spat the word out: "Mike's?"

She didn't answer.

His free hand flew up and slashed viciously across her face. He could see the white marks of his fingers, then the sudden rush of blood to fill the marks. There was a pounding in his temple. "It was Mike, wasn't it?" he snarled.

A painful, taunting smile came to her lips. "What difference does it make? There's been a lot of guys."

He hit her again. Her head spun to one side and a soft moan escaped her lips. Blood trickled from the corner of her mouth.

"Whore!"

Slowly she raised her eyes to his face. "I never said you could call me by my first name."

He whipped his hand back across her face. She slid across the bed and off onto the floor, where she lay huddled in a small heap. He walked around the bed and looked down at her. She didn't move.

He reached out with his foot and roughly pushed her over. She sprawled out on the rug, her eyes staring up at him without emotion. That was the worst thing of all to him. No expression at all. Not even hatred.

"You're not goin' anywhere," he said, "until I get damn good and ready to kick you out."

"It's Mike's baby," she said dully.

"I don't care," he said heavily. "I don't care whose it is. You're mine. That's all I care about."

Chapter 10

SHE was having coffee when he came down for break=
fast. His eyes felt heavy and burning. He hadn't slept all
night. Silently he sat down at the table. "Morning," he
growled.

She smiled. "Good morning." She got up and went into
the kitchen. A few seconds later she reappeared with a tray
of toast and a fresh pot of coffee.

He looked up in surprise. "Where's Bunny?" Bunny was
the maid.

"I sent her away with Michelle," she answered. "I
thought it'd be better if they went up to Arrowhead for a
while. The baby looked peaked."

He glanced up at her in surprise. Her face was blank.
She knew. He could tell that. "Good idea," he said. "Tom
go with them, too?"

"No," she said. "He didn't want to."

She poured some coffee into his cup. He sipped it
quickly. He needed something to straighten him out. He

was tired from tossing and turning all night. Slowly he bit into the toast. It had no taste. He chewed anyway.

"Your watchdogs are waiting in a car outside," she said.

Again surprise ran through him. There was very little she missed. A feeling of bravado ran through his veins. "Joker's not going to get away with this," he said.

She didn't speak.

"You heard me," he said almost hysterically. "Joker can't do anything."

"I heard you," she said softly. "But did Joker?"

He stood up angrily. "I've gone too far to let them push me around."

She didn't speak.

He stared at her for a moment, then left the room. A few minutes later he came back with a gun in his hand. It was an automatic. Quickly he checked the clip, and dropped it in his jacket pocket. He sat down at the table again and picked up his coffee cup. His hands were trembling, and the coffee spilled.

"Give me the gun, Ross," she said quietly.

He frowned at her. "What for?"

"You don't know anything about them," she said. "And you're so jumpy, you might hurt somebody who's got nothing to do with you."

The gun slid across the table, and she dropped it into a drawer. "I feel better this way," she said.

"Maybe you ought to go up to Arrowhead, too," he said.

"Not me." She smiled. "It's lousy for my sinuses. I told you that a thousand times."

"You might get hurt," he said.

"I can fall down the stairs, too," she answered.

He didn't speak, nor did he look at her. He would never

understand her. He put down his cup. "Gotta get goin'."

She got to her feet. "I'll be waitin' for you, Ross."

He looked up at her gratefully. "Thanks, Marja," he said almost humbly.

He climbed into the car and sat between the two men. "What's the latest word?" he asked as the car moved out into the street.

"I spoke to Pete a half-hour ago," one of them said. "Martin hasn't budged out of his hotel room since one this morning."

"Good," he said in a satisfied voice. "Let's go get him."

A tall heavy-bearded man came toward the car as Ross got up. "He's still up there," the man whispered. "I been here all night."

"Thanks, Pete."

"Got the pass key and bribed the freight-elevator boy to go get some coffee," the man continued.

Ross looked at him. "You think of everything."

The tall man's face was impassive. "I do what I'm paid for."

Ross nodded to the two men in the car. Silently they got out and went into the building. Ross could feel his heart pounding inside him. This was it. The big one. He couldn't afford to miss this time. If he did, he was finished.

They walked down a long gray-painted cement-block corridor in the basement of the hotel. Before a door they stopped and Pete pressed a button. The door opened, revealing an elevator. Quickly the men stepped into it.

Pete pressed a button and the door closed. The elevator began to rise. Silently they watched the indicator flash the numbers of the floors. At five the car stopped and the door opened.

"You stay here and hold the car," Pete said to one of the men.

The man nodded and the others walked down the hall. Pete studied the doors. At last he nodded. Quickly Ross looked up and down the corridor. It was empty.

Pete slipped a police positive out of his pocket. With his left hand he quickly screwed a silencer on the muzzle. He handed the key to Ross.

Ross looked down at it. It shone brightly in his palm. He took a deep breath. He could feel the sweat trickling down his face and knew that Pete was watching him closely. "Ready?" he whispered hoarsely.

Pete nodded.

Ross put the key in the lock. It seemed to make a loud ratcheting sound as it turned. Quickly he pushed the door open and Pete leaped into the room. Ross followed, half pushed through the door by the man behind him.

Pete cursed softly and ran through to another room. Ross ran after him, only to hear Pete break into a loud string of curses. "What is it?" Ross called as he reached the other door.

He knew the answer as soon as he stepped into the other room. The sweat began to run down his face again. He stared stupidly at Pete. "What the hell went wrong?" he asked.

Pete shook his head. "I dunno."

Ross stared around the room again. It was clean. The room was empty. Joker had gone.

The drone of the engines made Joker drowsy. They always made him drowsy. He could never decide whether it was the sound of the engines or the dramamine he took to keep from being plane-sick that did it, but he usually spent his trips sleeping. He closed his eyes.

Her face jumped in front of his lids, and he stirred uncomfortably. He wasn't like that with dames. He remembered how she had looked at him a long time ago when she was a kid. She had been too young then. Or had he been a fool? She had never been too young!

Then there was the time she got out of the correctional school. He had missed her by only a few minutes. He took a deep breath. It would not be long now. His turn was coming.

Her kid bothered him, though. If it wasn't Ross's kid, that meant there was someone else. He wondered who it could be. She was no dope. Before he got on the plane he had heard that she'd sent the kid up to Arrowhead at five in the morning.

A half-smile came to his lips. That was one of the things he liked about her. She was smart. If Ross had had only half her brains he wouldn't be in the mess he was in.

Chapter 11

ALMOST a month had passed since Joker had gone, and Ross was beginning to feel reassured. He felt he had been right: they couldn't do anything to him, he was too much in the public eye. Sooner or later they would have to call him and agree to go along on his basis.

He came into the house, a whistle on his lips. Maryann, waiting in the foyer, looked surprised. It was so complete a change from his nervousness of the past few weeks. She looked at the open doorway behind him. There was no one there.

"Where are your watchdogs?" she asked.

He smiled at her. "I sent 'em away. I got tired of them hanging around."

Her eyes widened slightly. "Yuh think it's wise?"

He walked into the living-room and poured himself a drink. "Joker knows when he's licked. They don't dare do anything."

She watched him silently.

He threw the drink down his throat. The whisky burned slightly and warmed him. The evenings were getting chilly. "Tomorrow we'll go up to Arrowhead, pick up the baby, and go down to Vegas for a little vacation," he said.

She shook her head. "I think we ought to wait a little longer."

"I'm tired of hangin' around," he said. "I don't have to be afraid. We're going tomorrow."

"I'll go see if Tom's got dinner ready," she said, leaving the room.

He watched her go, then poured himself another drink. He would never understand her. If she was afraid, why did she stay with him? There was nothing to keep her here. They weren't married. He wouldn't have blamed her if she had gone away. He sipped his drink slowly. Maybe some-day he would know. Maybe someday he would cross the barrier of understanding that lay between them.

She came back into the room. "Dinner's ready," she said.

He stood there for a moment. Suddenly he felt an under-standing come into him. He crossed the room and took her hand. "Marja," he said gently, "let's get married tomorrow. We'll make it a real honeymoon."

She looked up into his eyes. For some reason she could feel an ache steal inside her. "Is it what you really want, Ross?"

He nodded. "I know that now. I need you. It's not like it used to be."

She looked down at her hand. His strong brown fingers gripped it tightly. She knew what he meant. Something about him had changed. It was as if the Ross whom she had always known had suddenly grown up. She looked into his eyes, and for the first time she found nakedness and loneliness there. She felt the muscles in her throat tighten. "Okay, Ross," she whispered. "We'll be married to-morrow."

He pulled her close to him and kissed her. "You won't be sorry," he promised.

At dinner he was gay and filled with plans, and told Tom to open a bottle of champagne. His excitement and happiness reached out to her and she began to respond to it.

"We'll build a house," he said.

She laughed. "What's the matter with this one?"

"I want one for ourselves. With our ideas," he said. "Besides, we can't buy this one. The owner won't sell. He'll only rent."

"We can wait a little while," she said.

He shook his head. "Uh-uh. We'll do it now. I got my eye on some property in the hills. An acre and a half. I want everything to be right."

She assumed a demure expression. "You're the boss."

He put down his coffee cup, got to his feet, and came around to where she sat. "I want you to be happy. That's the only thing that is important now."

She took his hand. "I will be, Ross."

The clock chimed ten as they walked into the living-room. He sprawled on the couch and took out a cigarette. "I feel good," he said. "I feel that everything is goin' to be great."

She struck a match and held it for him. "It will be great, Ross. All we gotta do is try and make it so."

"We will," he said. He pulled her down on the couch beside him and kissed her cheek. "I never told you how great I think you are, did I, baby?" he whispered.

She shook her head.

He pulled her head against his chest. "I love you. You know that, don't you? I guess I always loved you, but I never really knew it. I thought it would make me less to admit it."

She didn't answer.

"I remember how I used to feel when I looked at you," he said. "I could almost have bust."

She grinned. "You don't have to be so nice, Ross," she teased. "I already said yes."

He looked down at her, a smile on his lips. "I mean it," he said, his voice serious. "There are so many things I wanted to tell you and never did, it would take me a whole lifetime to remember them all."

A gentle expression came into her eyes. Impulsively she placed her lips against his cheek. "Thank you, Ross," she whispered.

He cleared his throat with embarrassment. He wasn't used to having her say thank you to him. He sat up. "How about some television?" he asked. "We might as well practice up on our marital behavior."

She smiled. "Okay."

He crossed the room, turned on the set, and adjusted the dials. "How's the picture?" he called over his shoulder.

"Pretty good," she said, watching the wavering figures on the screen.

"Can't do any better," he said, coming back to the couch. "It's a kine."

"I'm not complainin'," she said.

He sat down beside her and took her hand. Silently they watched the comedian on the screen. He wasn't very funny, but he worked very hard. Two weeks ago this show had been done live in New York; the coast re-broadcast was on film. On film it lacked spontaneity.

She studied Ross as he looked at the screen. His black hair fell across his forehead. His eyes were no longer the hard, metallic blue of old; they were soft and somehow warmer. She smiled to herself. He had been a long time in growing up.

The telephone began to ring deep within the house. He paid no attention to it. Abruptly it stopped ringing and she heard Tom's soft voice, but couldn't understand his words. She turned her attention back to the screen.

"Miz Drego," Tom's voice came from the foyer entrance.

She looked up. "Yes?"

"They's a call for you, ma'am," the old man said.

She got to her feet. Ross looked up at her. "Hurry back, baby," he said, smiling.

Impulsively she kissed his forehead. "I will, honey."

She crossed the foyer into the small library and picked up the telephone. "Hello," she said into the mouthpiece.

There was no answer. Just a faint hollow sound on the wire.

An icy chill suddenly ran through her. "Hello, hello," she said.

A whisper with an echo of a familiar sound came through the receiver. "Marja?"

"Yes," she said. "Who is this?"

"Marja?" the voice repeated as if she hadn't spoken.

Her fingers turned white under the pressure of her grip on the phone. She knew the voice. She knew why she had been called to the phone.

"Ross!" she screamed suddenly, her voice bursting in her ears. "Ross!"

The sound of a few faint coughs came from the living-room and was lost in a tinkling of glass. The telephone

fell from her nerveless fingers and she ran back to the
living-room.

Ross was still sitting on the couch. He leaned back
against the armrest, his face white and eyes filled with hurt
and surprise, his hands clasped tight across his chest.
"Marja!" he whispered hoarsely.

She could see blood seeping between his fingers. She
glanced at the big picture window opposite the couch. Half
of it had shattered and fallen into the room.

She ran to Ross. "Tom!" she screamed. "Call a doctor!"

Ross began to fall toward her. She caught him and held
his head against her breast.

"Baby, baby, baby," she cried.

She could feel him shudder with pain. Slowly he turned
his face toward her. "I was wrong, Marja," he whispered.

"No, baby," she said.

He spoke slowly, as if each word had to travel a great
distance before it could leave his lips. "I was wrong, Marja,
but I tried so hard."

"I know, Ross." Tears were running down her cheeks.
She kissed his black hair. It was shiny and soaking with
perspiration.

He looked up at her. "Marja."

"Yes, Ross?"

"I'm glad the phone rang, Marja. I love you very much."
His voice was a hollow echo of pain.

"I love you too, Ross," she said, weeping.

A faint note of surprise was in his voice. "You do,
Marja?"

She nodded violently. "Why did you think I stayed?"

He closed his eyes wearily. "You did stay." He was
silent for a moment. When he opened his eyes again, there
was a curious contentment in them. "I'm glad you stayed,

Marja," he whispered. "I would have been afraid if you hadn't."

"I'll always stay, baby," she cried, turning his head to her breasts.

He coughed and a tiny thread of blood sprayed from his lips across her blouse. His head fell forward. She looked down at him. His eyes were blank and unseeing.

She looked down at her white blouse. The small stain of blood was growing wider and wider. The television blasted at her ears with the roar of audience laughter. Gently she lowered his head to the couch.

She got to her feet.

Tom was standing in the doorway, his dark face an ashen gray. "I called the doctor, Miz Maryann."

"Thank you, Tom," she said wearily and crossed the room to turn off the television set.

Chapter 12

MIKE came into the office and took off his hat. He scaled it onto a chair opposite his desk, his forehead glistening with sweat. He went to his desk and sat down heavily.

Joel looked up from the other desk. "Warm," he said.

Mike smiled. "Very warm for May. From the looks of it, it's goin' to be a bitch of a summer."

Joel leaned back in his chair wearily. "I'm beat. I had a hell of a week-end. I can't take this heat any more. You'd think the Old Man would okay air-conditioners for the offices."

Mike grinned. "He has an idea that good lawyers are distilled from their own sweat."

"I don't think he's ever sweat in his life, he hasn't enough blood," Joel complained. He picked up a paper from his desk and held it toward Mike. "This has been waitin' for you."

Mike took it from him and glanced at it. "Damn!" he swore.

Joel grinned. "What's the matter, baby?"

Mike looked at him and got to his feet slowly. He picked up his hat from the chair. "Don't crap me. You read it."

"What're you complaining about?" Joel laughed. "You're goin' for a nice automobile ride uptown an' spend a couple of hours in a nice, cool, clean-smelling hospital. You're lucky not to have to stay in this stuffy old office."

Mike was already at the door. "Balls," he said and went out, followed into the corridor by Joel's raucous laughter. He pressed the elevator button and looked again at the paper in his hand.

Suspected abortion.

The elevator doors opened and he stepped into the car. He continued to read as the car descended.

Florence Reese. Admitted Roosevelt Hospital, 7:10 a.m., May 10, '54. Internal hemorrhages due to abortion. Condition critical.

The doors opened and he walked out. He crossed the corridor and opened a door. As he entered, a few men looked up from their newspapers and then looked down again. He went through the room to another door whose frosted glass bore the name *Captain F. Millersen.* He opened the door and went in.

The dark-haired man at the desk looked up. "Hello, Mike," he said in a deep voice.

Mike smiled. "Hi, Frank. I need a man to go up to Roosevelt Hospital with me. Suspected abortion." He tossed the slip of paper onto the detective's desk.

Captain Millersen looked at it briefly. "One of those, eh?"

Mike nodded.

The detective got to his feet. "I think I'll go with yuh on this one, Mike."

Mike's eyes widened. Millersen never went out on a case unless it was a big one. Upstairs they said that he had an uncanny instinct for the big ones, that he smelled them coming. "You're comin' with me, Frank?" he asked in tones of disbelief.

The detective nodded. "Yeah, I'm gettin' a little tired of sittin' behind this desk keepin' my fanny warm."

Mike watched him pick up his hat. "You know somethin' about this that I don't?" he asked skeptically.

Millersen put a cigar in his mouth. "I don't know nothin'. Only that I'm tired of sittin'. Let's go."

The smell of disinfectant was all around them as they strode down the green-walled corridor. They followed the nurse into a ward. At its far end, curtains had been drawn around one of the beds.

"She's in here," the nurse said, holding aside the curtains.

"Is she in condition to talk?" Mike asked the nurse.

"She's very weak," the nurse answered. "Be careful."

He stepped through the curtains, followed by Millersen, and stood beside the bed. For a moment they looked silently down at the young girl lying there.

She seemed to be sleeping. Her eyes were closed and her face was white, a pallid bluish-white color, as if there were no blood beneath the skin. Her mouth was open and her lips were only slightly darker than her cheeks.

Mike looked at the detective. Millersen nodded. He spoke softly to the girl: "Miss Reese."

The girl didn't move. He spoke her name again. This time she stirred slightly. Slowly she opened her eyes. They were so filled with agony that Mike couldn't tell their color. Her lips moved, but no sound came out.

Mike moved closer to the bed. "Can you hear me, Miss Reese?"

The girl nodded faintly.

"I'm Mike Keyes and this is Captain Millersen. We're from the District Attorney's office."

The beginnings of fear began to fleck the girl's eyes. Mike spoke quickly to reassure her. "You're perfectly all right, Miss Reese. You're in no trouble. We just have some routine questions to ask so that we may be able to help you."

Slowly the fear began to vanish. Mike waited for a moment. His words echoed mockingly in his ear. No trouble. Of course she was in trouble. She was only dying.

He smiled slowly and reassuringly. "Have you any relatives we can notify for you?"

The girl shook her head.

"In the city, or out?"

"No!" The girl's voice was a whisper.

"Where do you live, Miss Reese?"

"Hotel Allingham," she answered.

Mike nodded. It was one of the less expensive women's hotels on the west side. "You have a job, Miss Reese?"

The girl shook her head.

"What do you do?"

The girl's voice was faint. "Model."

He exchanged a knowing look with the detective. Half the unemployed girls in New York were models, the other half were actresses. "Free lance or agency?" he asked.

"Agency," the girl replied.

"Which agency?"

"Park Avenue Models," the girl answered. For the first

time since Mike had spoken to her, her expression changed.
"Let—let Maryann know—"

It seemed to Mike that the girl had an expression of
hope on her face. "We will," he said. "Maryann who—
where?"

The girl seemed to be gathering her strength for an effort
to speak. "Maryann at—at the agency. She knows what to
do. She is—" Her voice trailed away and her head slipped
to one side.

The nurse stepped quickly to the head of the bed. She
felt for the girl's pulse. "She's sleeping," she announced.
"You'll have to finish your questions later."

Mike turned to Millersen. The detective's face was white,
almost as white as the girl's had been. Mike instantly
changed his opinion about the man. He had heard that
Millersen was as hard as nails.

Millersen nodded and stepped outside the curtain. Mike
followed him. "What d'you think, Frank?"

"We're not going to find anything," Millersen said.

Mike was surprised. "What makes you say that?"

Millersen smiled mirthlessly. "I seen too many of these.
They lead to nowheres."

"But the girl is dying!" Mike said. "We got to do something to find out who did it. The butcher is liable to go to
work on another—"

The detective reached out a quieting hand. "Take it
easy, Mike. We'll look. But we won't find. Unless the girl
tells us."

"I'm gettin' on the phone to that agency. Maybe they'll
have some dope for us." Mike started down the aisle
between the beds.

Millersen's hand caught his arm. "I'll get on the phone,

Mike," he said quickly. "You wait here an' talk to her
when she comes to. She's used to you already."

Mike nodded. "Good idea." He watched Millersen walk
out of the ward, then turned back to the curtains.

The nurse was just coming out. She raised an eyebrow
when she saw him.

"I'll wait until she can talk to me again," Mike explained.

The nurse looked up at him. "You can wait at my desk
out in the corridor," she said. "It'll be a little while before
she can speak again—if ever."

Chapter 13

TOM opened the door gently, balancing the tray with his free hand. "You up, Miz Maryann?" he asked softly.

There was no answer from the large double bed.

He stepped quietly into the room and put the tray down on a small table. Without looking at the bed, he went to the window and drew back the drapes. Bright sunlight spilled into the room. He stood there for a moment looking out the window.

Far below he could see the East River as it wound its way toward the Hudson. The flashing green of Gracie Square Park contrasted with the gray of the buildings surrounding it. He watched a long black automobile turn up the driveway to Gracie Mansion. He looked down at his watch. Eight o'clock. The mayor of this town went to work early. He turned back into the room.

She was already awake, her large brown eyes watching him lazily from the pillow. Slowly she stretched, her arms and shoulders brown and strong.

"Good mornin', Miz Maryann," he said, walking back toward the bed.

She smiled. "Good morning, Tom. What time is it?"

"Eight o'clock," he answered, placing the tray across the bed in front of her. "Time to get up."

She grimaced and sat up. He picked up a silk bed jacket from a chair near the bed and held it while she slipped it over her shoulders. "What's for breakfast, Tom?"

"This diet day, Miz Maryann. Juice an' coffee," he answered.

"But I'm hungry," she protested.

"You very pretty today, Miz Maryann," he said. "You want to stay that way?"

She grinned. "Tom, you're an old butter-spreader."

He grinned back at her. "Go on and eat. Mr. Martin say he goin' come by at ten to take you down to the office."

She picked up the glass of orange juice and sipped it slowly. "Before long you're goin' to be running my whole life, Tom."

"Not me," he said, shaking his gray-flecked kinky black hair. "But I would sho' like to see the man who could."

She laughed and finished her juice. "Any mail?"

"I'll go down and see, Miz Maryann." He turned and left the room, closing the door behind him.

Idly she picked up the paper on the tray and glanced at it. The usual news: rape, arson, murder, and war. She turned to the comic strips as she sipped her coffee. She looked up as Tom came back into the room, carrying a letter.

She took it from him and ripped it open quickly. "It's from Michelle," she said happily.

"Yes'm," he said, even though he had already known. He loved to see her happy. To him, she seemed the saddest and most beautiful woman in the world.

"She passed her midterm exams with the second-highest marks in the class," she said excitedly. "And she can't wait until June and we get out there for her vacation."

A strange look crossed Tom's face. "Kin we go for sure?" he asked.

"I'd like to see anyone try to stop us."

"But Mr. Martin say you might be very busy this summer," he said.

"Mr. Martin can go to hell," she said strongly. "He kept me from going last summer, but he won't this time."

He was waiting in the living-room as she came down the steps of the duplex apartment. He smiled at her. "Good morning, Maryann."

"Morning, Joker. Hope I didn't keep you waiting."

His smile turned into a grin. "I've been waiting a long time now, Maryann. A few minutes won't bother me."

Her eyes met his gaze levelly. "We made a deal."

He nodded.

"A deal's a deal," she said.

"Sometimes I think you're cold as ice."

"Not cold, Joker," she said. "Just bored with it. Enough not to bother any more."

"Even for me?" he asked.

"Even for you," she said. "Remember what we agreed?"

He nodded again. He remembered. Too well.

He had come to the house and Tom had shown him into the living-room. The big picture window had new glass, and through it he could see the edge of the pool. Only this time no child was splashing in its water. He turned when he heard her footsteps.

She stood in the entrance, wearing a simple black dress. Her blond hair shimmered in the fading daylight as she walked toward him. Her face was impassive. "Hello, Joker," she said. She did not extend her hand.

"Maryann," he said.

She didn't take her eyes from his face. "Thanks for the telephone call."

"What call?" he asked.

"Don't pretend, Joker," she said calmly. "I recognize your voice even when you whisper."

He walked over to the couch. "What are you goin' to do now?" he asked.

She shrugged her shoulders. "I don't know. Go to work, if I can find a job."

A look of surprise crossed his face. "I thought Ross left you pretty well fixed."

"He left me nothing," she said without bitterness.

"But you're his widow," he said. "You're even wearing black for him."

"I may be his widow, but I was never his wife," she said. "And that's what they pay off on." A faint smile came to her lips. "Besides, I'm not wearing black for him. It happens to be a good color for me."

He smiled. "It certainly is."

As usual, but still to his surprise, she came directly to the point. "You didn't come here just to tell me how good I look. What did you come for?"

"The boys are worried about you," he said.

Her eyes went blank. "What have they got to worry about? I went through the whole inquest and didn't tell anything."

"They're still worried," he said. "They're afraid someday you might be in trouble and just decide to talk a little bit."

"I know better than that," she said.

"Yeah," he said, "but they're not convinced."

"What do I have to do to convince them?" she asked.

"Come back east with me. They've got a job for you," he answered.

"What kind of job?" she asked suspiciously.

"Running a model agency," he said. "They'll feel better if you're where they can keep an eye on you."

"A model agency?" she asked. "What do I know about that business?"

A smile crossed his lips. "Don't be naïve, Marja."

She stared at him. "And what if I don't come back?"

He took a package of cigarettes from his pocket and held them toward her. She shook her head. He lit one, put the package back in his pocket, and brought out a small photograph. He flicked it over to her.

She looked at it. It was a photograph of a small blonde girl playing on a lawn with her nurse. "It's Michelle," she said, a hollow note of fear in her voice.

He nodded. "Don't worry. She's all right. We just thought you might like to have this picture of her. It was taken up at Arrowhead last week."

She stood there quietly for a moment, then turned and walked to the window. Her voice as it came back to him over her shoulder was empty and resigned. "Nothing else would satisfy them?"

"Nothing else."

"If I do that, there'll be no other ties?" she asked.

"What do you mean?" he asked.

She turned and looked at him with knowing eyes. "Now you're being naïve," she said.

He could feel his face flush. "There'll be no other ties," he said. "But you can't keep a guy from hoping."

She drew in her breath. "Okay," she said.

"Then it's a deal?" he asked.

She nodded.

"I'm glad, Maryann," he said. "I was hoping you wouldn't be stubborn."

"Don't call me Maryann," she said. "Call me madame."

Chapter 14

"YOU can drop me at the corner of Park and 38th," she said. "I'll walk from there."

"Okay," he answered, pulling the car over to the curb. He leaned across the seat and opened the door for her. "Dinner tonight?"

She nodded.

"Pick you up at eight at your place," he said.

"Okay," she answered, closing the door.

He watched her walk into the crowd at the corner and cross in front of him. He liked the way she walked. It was the same young stride she had always had. He smiled to himself as he noticed the involuntary second glances that men threw after her. He didn't blame them. A horn honked behind him and he looked up to see that the light had changed. He put the car into gear.

The house was set back in a row of old-fashioned brownstones that had long since become uneconomical to use as dwellings in New York, and had been converted for use as offices. They were filled with small advertising-agencies and con men who labeled themselves *Enterprises,* and anyone else who wanted to pay a little bit more for a little less space but still have a Park Avenue address.

The polished brass plate at the side of the door gleamed at her. 79 Park Avenue. Below it on smaller brass plates were the names of tenants. The plate cost five dollars a month extra. She opened the large outside door and stepped into a long, old-fashioned corridor. A door on her right was labeled *Park Avenue Models, Inc.,* and along the wall beyond it a flight of stairs led up to the other offices.

She walked past the staircase to another door behind it. There was no name on this one. She unlocked it and stepped directly into a comfortable office. She shrugged off her light coat and sat down behind the desk. The shades had been drawn. She switched on a lamp, and the room sprang suddenly into life. On the walls were two very good paintings, and several color photographs of girls. A basket on the desk contained more pictures, and beside it lay a copy of the models' directory.

She pressed a buzzer. A moment later a middle-aged woman came in, obviously excited. "Miss Flood," she said, "I'm so glad you're here. A man called from the police department!"

Maryann looked up sharply. "What?"

"From the police, Miss Flood," the woman repeated.

"About what, Mrs. Morris?"

"Florence Reese. She's in a hospital. An abortion." Mrs. Morris was out of breath. "They wanted to know if she worked for us."

"What did you tell them?"

Mrs. Morris drew herself up. "I told them she didn't work here, of course. That kind of publicity would ruin us.

We have a hard time getting work for legitimate girls as it is."

Maryann looked thoughtful. "You shouldn't have lied, Mrs. Morris. Maybe the poor kid is in real trouble and needs our help."

Mrs. Morris looked down at her indignantly. "You know how I feel about girls like that, Miss Flood. You shouldn't even waste a minute with them. They don't appreciate it, and all they do is disgrace themselves and everybody they come in contact with."

Maryann looked down at her desk. That was what made Mrs. Morris such a wonderful front—her honest indignation at the abuses to the profession. She would bust a gut if she knew what went on over the two private phones on Maryann's desk. But Maryann had no time now for Mrs. Morris's indignation. She would have to call Hank Vito and find out the right thing to do. "Okay, Mrs. Morris, thank you. Were there any other calls?"

"Two, Miss Flood. One from Mr. Gellard. He needs three special girls this afternoon. Some buyers are in town and he wants to run a show for them. I suggested some girls to him, but he insisted that he talk to you first. The other is from the 14th Street Fur Shop. They needed a window girl. I sent them Raye Marnay."

"Good," Maryann said, reaching for the telephone. "I'll call Mr. Gellard back."

She waited until the woman had closed the door behind her before beginning to dial. She stared at the closed door thoughtfully while the phone at the other end of the wire rang.

Poor Flo. She had told her just last week not to try the abortion. That she had waited too long. She was almost three months gone. It would have been much smarter to have the baby and place it for adoption. That way was cleaner all around, and, besides, Hank would have seen that Flo got a few bucks out of it. But the panic must have set in and she had probably wound up in the hands of a butcher. Maryann could feel an anger rise up inside her. What kind of doctor could the man be if he would take a chance like that with a kid's life? She was a whore, but she was a human being, too.

A man's voice answered the telephone.

"Maryann," she said.

"Oh." The man's voice sounded relieved. "I was afraid I wouldn't hear from you before lunch. I got these three Texans in, and they're howling for something out of this world. They're up in the hotel now. I promised it to them at lunchtime."

"It's pretty short notice, John," Maryann said.

"I can't help it, honey," the man said. "I didn't know myself until I got to the office this morning."

"Full treatment?" she said. "Act and party?"

"Yeah," he answered.

"It'll be a lot of dough," she said.

"How much?"

"A grand," she answered.

He whistled. "Take it easy, honey," he said. "An expense account can only go so far."

"I can't help it," she said. "The Jelke trial has made good performers hard to get."

"Okay," he said after a moment's hesitation. "Tell yuh where to send them."

She made a few notes with her pencil and hung up the telephone. She waited a moment, then dialed again. A woman's voice answered this time.

She spoke quickly. "Luncheon date, Cissie. Get Esther and Millie. Full booking. It's a charge account."

The woman's voice spoke rapidly. "I got another date."

"I'll switch it," Maryann said. "Here's where you go." When she had finished, she lit a cigarette and reached for the telephone again. Before she could touch it, it rang. She picked it up. "Yes?"

"Maryann?"

The man's voice was familiar. "Yes," she answered.

"Frank," he said.

"Anything wrong?"

"Girl at Roosevelt Hospital," he said. "Florence Reese. Your office said she didn't work for you. She says she did. Conflicting stories mean trouble. Your woman there is stupid. If she hadn't denied it, I could have stopped it right there, but now too many people are curious."

"What should I do?" she asked.

"I don't know," he said.

"How's Florence?"

"She's dying," he said flatly.

"The poor kid," she said. "I told her not to."

"Stop worrying about her," he said. "It's too late now. You have to think of something."

"Okay, Frank. I'll call Vito. He'll know what to do." She dragged on her cigarette.

"He'd better," Frank said. "I came out on this with one of the D.A.'s white-haired boys. He's boiling over it."

"Who is he?" she asked absently.

"Keyes. Mike Keyes," he answered.

Her throat tightened. "Mike Keyes?" she repeated.

He hesitated. "Yes. I knew there was something about him I was trying to remember. He used to be a cop. Wasn't the guy you were trying to locate for a dame during the war?"

"I—I don't remember," she stammered. "It was so long ago." Slowly she put down the telephone, staring at the door.

It had been so long ago, it might almost have been another world.

Chapter 15

IT WAS near four in the afternoon when the nurse came out of the ward and walked over to his seat near her desk. He looked up at her expectantly.

"You might as well go back to your office, Mr. Keyes. She's gone," she said unemotionally.

Mike got to his feet slowly. "Just like that," he said in a tired voice.

She nodded. "She never had a chance. She was all torn apart." For the first time he heard a sound of feeling in her voice. "The son-of-a-bitch must have used crocheting needles!"

He picked up his hat from the desk. "Hold the body for a p.m. I'll be in touch with the hospital for the results."

His feet felt like lead as he dragged them down the corridor. Florence Reese. He wondered what it had been like for her. It couldn't have been too good. She seemed just a kid. He reached the steps just as Captain Millersen was coming in.

"Learn anything, Mike?" Millersen asked.

He shook his head. "She never spoke again. You?"

Millersen's face settled into an unreadable mask. "I spoke to the bookkeeper at the model agency this morning. She didn't know anything about her. I checked the hotel. The kid got here from some hick town in Pennsylvania about a year ago. She had it pretty tough until about six months ago. Then she seemed to settle down and do all right."

"Her folks alive?" Mike asked as he followed Millersen down to his car.

Millersen nodded. "I spoke to them about an hour ago. They're on their way here now." He laughed. "They thought their daughter had New York by the balls."

"They didn't know how right they were," Mike said grimly.

He came into the office and scaled his hat onto the chair. Joel Rader looked up from his desk. "Had a call for you about an hour ago."

Mike looked at him wearily. "Who was it?"

"Some dame from that agency. Park Avenue Models. The one you had Frank check. It seems the kid had done some work for them, and the dame wanted to know if there was anything she could do."

Mike took his pen and began to fill in the report. "Nothin' nobody could do now. She's dead."

"Too bad," Joel said. "Was she pretty?"

Mike shrugged his shoulders. "Hard to tell when I saw her. Guess so. Anyway, she was young." He finished the report, signed it, and got to his feet. "I guess I'll knock off. I'm beat."

Joel grinned. "Better not let the Old Man see yuh. He's on the warpath. Chewed Alec out somethin' mean."

"Poor Alec," Mike said, smiling. "He always gets it." He tossed the report onto Joel's desk. "Turn that in for me, will yuh?"

"Sure thing."

Joel spun his chair away from his desk and turned to Mike. "Whatever came of that check you ran on that girl? The abortion case last week?"

Mike shrugged his shoulders. "Nothing. The girl died. Why do you ask?"

Joel handed him a sheet of paper. "Look at that."

It was an arrest-and-release report. Several girls had been arrested in a Vice Squad raid on a party. One of them had first said she was a model working for Park Avenue Models, Inc. Later she had changed her story. All the girls had been released the next morning on bail. They had been represented in court by an attorney from Henry Vito's office. The party had been at the apartment of John Gellard, a manufacturer. The raid had been on the basis of complaints against Mr. Gellard by people and parties unspecified. In their complaints they had said that he had openly bragged of his connections with certain unspecified vice rings. A wiretap set that afternoon had revealed that the party to take place that night would be wide open. Mr. Gellard had also been admitted to bail. He had been represented in court by Henry Vito himself.

Joe waited until Mike had finished reading it. "Wasn't Park Avenue Models the same agency that girl mentioned?"

Mike nodded silently. He read the report again.

"What do you think?" Joel asked.

"Too close for coincidence," Mike answered. He got to his feet. "I'm goin' down to see Frank Millersen with this. Maybe he knows something about it."

"Let me know what happens," Joel said, turning back to his desk.

Frank Millersen looked up as Mike walked into his office. "Hello, Mike, what can I do for you?"

"Look at this, Frank." Mike threw the report down on the desk.

Frank picked it up and scanned it quickly. His face was impassive when he looked up again at Mike. "What about it?"

"You know anything about it I don't?" Mike asked.

Millersen put a pipe in his mouth. "Nothing much," he said, lighting it. "Just a routine Vice Squad action." He laughed shortly. "I spoke to one of the boys. It must have been quite a brawl. He told me when they got there the girls were all—"

"I don't mean that," Mike interrupted. "One of the girls mentioned Park Avenue Models. That's the same one that Florence Reese said she had worked for."

"I don't think that means much," Frank said through a cloud of smoke. "A lot of girls would probably know the name."

"Maybe," Mike admitted. "But why would she later deny it? That's what seems strange to me. Another thing that bothers me is how they could afford Vito's office. He doesn't work for buttons. The ordinary floosie can't get anywhere near him."

"Gellard had him, according to the report," Frank said. "He probably paid for the girls, too. A matter of self-defense."

Mike shook his head. "I don't know. It just doesn't hit me right."

Frank smiled at him. "Forget it, Mike. When you're in

the office long enough, you'll see so many of these co-incidences that you'll stop bothering about it."

"I can't," Mike said. "I keep remembering that poor kid in the hospital. The way she looked. That wasn't what she came to this town for."

Frank nodded. "She didn't come for that. But if a kid's straight, she never gets into that kind of trouble. I spoke to her old man when he came for the body. She was always a wild one."

"There's a difference between wild ones and bad ones," Mike said. He picked up the report and scanned it again. "I wish I could forget it."

"What are you goin' to do?" Frank asked.

Mike looked up from the report. There was a strange expression in the detective's eyes. An unaccustomed wariness guided Mike's tongue. "I don't know," he answered. "I'll sleep on it first. If there's anything more, I'll call you in the morning."

Frank got to his feet, smiling. "That's smart. Maybe a good night's rest will make a big difference. I'll still be here tomorrow if you decide to go further."

"Thanks, Frank." Mike left the office, but as he crossed the corridor toward the elevator he noticed that he had picked up another paper in addition to the report. He turned back.

He walked through the outer office and opened Frank's door. "Frank—" he said, before he noticed that the detective was on the telephone.

"Hold on a minute, Mary," Frank said, quickly covering the mouthpiece with his hand.

Mike looked at him curiously. Millersen's face, usually florid, seemed to blanch suddenly. "I'm sorry, Frank," he apologized automatically. "I didn't know you were on the phone. I picked this up by mistake." He put the paper down on the desk.

A strained smile came to Frank's lips. "That's okay, Mike. I was just talkin' to the little woman. Thanks."

Mike nodded and left the office, closing the door carefully behind him. Not until he began to walk away from the door did he hear the hum of Frank's voice on the telephone. He went back to his own office, sat down heavily, and stared at the report.

"Well?" Joel asked.

Mike frowned. "Millersen thinks it's nothing."

"Frank ought to know," Joel said. "He's the expert."

Mike studied the report again. After a moment he turned to Joel. "Do you happen to know the name of Frank's wife?"

Joel grinned. "Sure. Mrs. Millersen."

"Not funny," Mike said. "Do yuh know?"

"Why?" Joel asked.

"Just curious," Mike answered. "He was talkin' on the phone to her when I came in."

"Elizabeth," Joel said. "I had a few drinks with them one night. He calls her Betty."

Mike lit a cigarette. He turned his chair and stared out the window. Down in the street men were already walking about in shirt sleeves. Summer was racing to New York with all the promising fires of hell. Betty. Why would Millersen lie to him?

He turned back to his desk and picked up the report. Park Avenue Models. What kind of outfit was that? He had never heard of it, and now twice within a few weeks its name had come up. He reached for the telephone on his desk.

"Get Alec Temple for me," he said into it. Alec had just been transferred to the Rackets office.

Alec's voice came on the wire. "Yes, Mike?"

"Do me a favor," Mike said. "I want a q.t. check on an outfit, Park Avenue Models, Inc., 79 Park Avenue, City."

"What d'yuh want to know?" Alec asked.

"Everything you can find out about it," Mike answered. "But it's very important that no word goes downstairs about it. I don't want Millersen's office to hear about it. This is one time I think we can show 'em something."

"Okay, Mike," Alec laughed. There was always a void between the attorneys and the police who were assigned to the office. "I understand."

"As quick as you can, Alec," Mike said.

"Tomorrow morning quick enough?" Alec asked.

"That will be fine. Thanks." Mike put down the phone. He ground out his cigarette just as the phone rang.

He picked it up. "Keyes."

"Mike, Frank Millersen here." Millersen's voice was heavy over the wire.

"Yes, Frank," Mike said.

"I was just thinkin' maybe we ought to look into that model agency if you want." Millersen sounded slightly apologetic.

"Forget it, Frank," Mike said. "You're probably right about it. Just coincidence. Sorry to have bothered you."

"Okay, Mike." Millersen's voice was hesitant. "If you're sure."

"I'm sure, Frank. Thanks anyway," Mike said.

"You're quite welcome, Mike." He rang off, leaving Mike wondering whether that had been a note of relief he had heard in the man's voice.

Chapter 16

THE DISTRICT ATTORNEY peered shrewdly at Mike from behind wide horn-rimmed glasses. He gently tapped the papers on the desk before him with a gold pencil. "So you want to resign?" he asked quietly.

Mike nodded. "Yes, sir."

"Why?"

"Personal reasons, sir," Mike answered stiffly.

The Old Man swung away from him and looked out the window. "Unhappy in your work here, Mike?"

"No, sir."

The Old Man fell silent, and for a long time the only sound in the office was his stertorous breathing. At last he spoke. "I never figured you for chicken, Mike."

Mike didn't answer.

"This job you did on Park Avenue Models is a big one. One of the most important ever to come through this office. Yet, just because it reaches into influential places, you want to quit."

Still Mike didn't speak.

The Old Man turned to face him. "How do you think I feel," he asked suddenly, "when I find my own chief detective involved? Don't you think I want to quit?" He didn't wait for Mike to answer. "But I can't. I took an oath. You took the same oath when I hired you. We can't quit."

"That has nothing to do with it, sir," Mike said.

"Balls!" The Old Man exploded. "So what if a dozen stinking politicians and rich businessmen are involved? Afraid they'll wreck your career?"

Mike didn't reply.

"You'll have no career for them to wreck if you run out now. Everybody will know you're yellow," the Old Man said.

Mike took a deep breath. "I'm sorry, sir. Is that all?"

The Old Man leaned forward over the desk, breathing heavily. "You don't understand, Mike. This is the opportunity of your lifetime. Look where Tom Dewey went with one case like this. After this is over, you can call your shots, you can go anywhere you want. Don't throw your life away, boy."

"May I leave now, sir?" Mike answered.

Contempt crept into the Old Man's voice. "It's seldom I guess wrong on a man, but I guessed wrong when I took you on. It proves that there's more to guts than the ability to stand in front of bullets."

Mike's face flushed. He bit his lips to keep from answering.

"It's bad enough to have to swallow what I must about Millersen, but the thing that does it is to find you're a coward." The tone of his voice changed abruptly. "I'm an old man, Mike. I've spent a good part of my life in this office. All I ever wanted was to do a good job, an honest job, to protect the people who placed their faith in me. This is the first time I ever felt I failed them."

"You didn't fail them, sir," Mike said. "All the information is right there on your desk."

"I am responsible for every man in my office," the Old Man said. "I will pay for Millersen, I will pay for you. Being District Attorney is more than just going before a Grand Jury and getting indictments, it's more than getting a conviction in criminal court. It's pride. Pride in doing your job without fear, without favor. When you quit, it's just as if I quit. The whole world will know it."

Mike didn't speak.

"All right," the Old Man said. "Quit if you want to, but at least have the decency to tell me why. I know you're not a coward."

Mike took a deep breath. Suddenly he realized his hands were trembling.

"Tell me, Mike," the Old Man said gently. "You were a good cop and you were a good assistant. Why are you quitting?"

Mike met the Old Man's eyes. "She was my girl, sir." His voice was dull.

"She?" The Old Man's voice was puzzled. "Who?"

"Marja," Mike said. "Maryann Flood, I mean."

"*This* Maryann Flood?"

Mike nodded.

"But how—what?" The Old Man was confused.

"I didn't know she was in it when I called Alec for the check on Park Avenue Models three weeks ago, sir." Mike paused to light a cigarette. "If I had known, I might not have begun."

The District Attorney looked up at him. There was a

new understanding in his eyes. "I was right," he half whispered. "I was right about you."

Mike went on as if he hadn't heard the Old Man. "Then when I got the report, I had to continue. I sent up and got permission to continue. We got a wiretap and began to check. Everything began to fall into place—things we hadn't even thought about. How so many of our raids missed. Lots of things. Especially when we checked back on her first arrest and found that Frank Millersen was the arresting officer. It was even more convincing when we found out that he had banked close to twenty thousand a year. Isn't a cop in the world that can do that on his pay. From there to the businessmen who kept her in business, to the politicians she paid off, to the cops and detectives the girls took care of. Then, as suddenly as it had begun, the investigation was over. Everything was ready to go before the Grand Jury for an indictment. It was then I knew I couldn't do it. I asked Joel Rader to take it for me."

The Old Man looked up at him. "You called in sick."

Mike nodded. "I was sick. Sick inside."

"But you've come up here while Joel is still in the courtroom."

"Yes," Mike answered. "I want to get out before I know how much damage I've done to her."

"You can't run away from that, Mike," the Old Man said gently.

Mike dragged deeply on the cigarette. "I can try, John."

"You're still in love with her." It was more statement than question.

Mike looked down at him. He didn't speak.

The door behind him opened, and Joel Rader came in, an excited expression on his face.

"You've done it, Mike!" he cried. "We've got an indictment against every one of them. Flood, Millersen. It'll be the biggest thing ever to hit this town!" He turned to the District Attorney, still seated behind the desk. "I've got warrants with me for their arrest. We're going downstairs to pick up Millersen now."

The D.A. got to his feet. "I'll go with you." He looked at Mike. "Coming, copper?"

Frank Millersen stuck a pipe in his mouth and lit it carefully. When it was burning easily, he began to skim through the papers on his desk. Nothing special. He could look forward to a relaxing week-end with Betty and the kids. It would be the first in a long while.

There was a knock at the door. "Come in," he called.

The shuffle of several men's footsteps made him look up. The D.A. was standing in front of his desk, and behind him were Keyes and Rader. Beyond the door he could see the blue uniform of a patrolman. He felt an unaccustomed tightness in his chest, but he forced a smile to his lips and got to his feet, holding out his hand. "It's been a long time since you've been down here, Chief," he said.

His hand hung in space between them. The District Attorney made no move to take it. Awkwardly Millersen raised his hand to remove the pipe from between his lips, trying to make it seem one unbroken gesture.

The D.A.'s voice was low. "We have a warrant for your arrest, Frank."

He could feel his face whiten. "What are the charges, sir?" he asked. But he could read them in Mike's face.

"Do I have to tell you, Frank?" the Old Man asked gently.

Millersen's shoulders drooped, and he slumped into his chair. He was suddenly an old man. He looked down at his desk. Aimlessly his hand shuffled the papers on it. He shook his head. "No."

Without looking up, he knew that the District Attorney had turned and walked out of the office. Rader's voice beat down at his head. "You better come with us, Frank."

He looked up, agony in his eyes. "Give me a minute to get myself together," he said heavily. "I'll be right out."

Joel looked at Mike, who nodded. "Okay," Joel said. "We'll wait for you."

They started out the door. Millersen's voice stopped them. "Mike."

Mike turned to face him.

Millersen forced a smile to his lips. "I should have remembered you were a damn good cop before you joined the D.A. I couldn't have done better myself."

Mike's lips were stiff. "I'm sorry, Frank."

"It was your job, Mike," Frank said quietly.

Mike nodded and followed Joel through the door. Millersen watched it close behind them. He picked up the pipe and stuck it in his mouth and drew on it. He could feel the heavy smoke deep in his lungs.

There was no regret for himself when he opened his desk drawer and took out the blue-gray revolver. There was only a vast sorrow in him for Betty and the kids as he substituted the cold metal of the revolver's muzzle for the warm bit of the pipe in his mouth.

Chapter 17

AS HE wearily opened the door, he could hear his mother talking to someone in the kitchen. He walked through the parlor to his room slowly. He could not remember ever having been so tired, so completely exhausted.

His mother's voice called from the kitchen. "That you, Mike?"

It was an effort for him to raise his voice. "Yes, Ma." He went into his room and closed the door. He took off his jacket and sank into the easy chair near the window. He lit a cigarette and stared out with unseeing eyes.

The door opened behind him. He didn't turn. "Are you all right, son?"

"I'm okay, Ma," he answered.

She came around his chair and looked down at him. "You're home early. Is there anything wrong?"

He looked up at her. Concern was written on her face. "There's nothing wrong, Ma."

"You look poorly," she said. "I'll make you some tea."

A note of annoyance crept into his voice. "Leave me alone, Ma," he said sharply. "I'm okay."

He saw the hurt creeping into her eyes, and he reached for her hand. "I'm sorry, Ma," he said. "I didn't mean to be harsh."

"That's all right, son," she said. "I understand."

"No, Ma," he said. No one could really understand. Only he knew how he felt.

His mother stood there hesitantly. "I know the look on your face, son."

"What look, Ma?" he asked absently, looking out the window again.

"That girl," his mother said. "She's back. I can tell by your eyes."

He looked up quickly. He didn't speak.

"It's the same look you had that time you went up to the Bronx to bring her home and she didn't come with you." His mother's voice was tinged with pain for him. "You can't get her out of your mind, can you, son?"

He dropped her hand. "I tried, Ma. I don't know what it is. It's like she's a part of me."

"You saw her?" his mother asked.

He shook his head. "No, Ma."

"What is it, then?"

"The police are on their way to arrest her now. I prepared a case against her that will send her to jail."

His mother didn't speak for a moment. "It's your job, son."

"Don't you tell me that, Ma," he said with a flash of anger. Millersen had said that too. Now Millersen was dead. "You know better!"

"I told you a long time ago that she's no good for you,"

she said, starting for the door. "Maybe you'll believe me now."

"But what do you do when you know there's no one else for you?" he said in an agonized voice.

Maryann looked up from the desk. Tom was standing in front of her. He was smiling. "I got the cab waiting, Miz Maryann," he said. "We got just an hour to get to the airport."

She smiled back at him. "I'll be just a few minutes, Tom."

"I'll wait outside," he said. "I just cain't wait to see my li'l blonde baby."

"I can't wait either," she said.

Tom went out of the office and the door closed behind him. She looked for a moment at the photograph of Michelle on the desk, then picked up a few papers and scanned them quickly: bills that could wait until she returned in two weeks. She put them in a folder and placed it in the basket on the desk. She locked the desk drawer and got to her feet.

Picking up her coat from a chair, she cast a last glance around the room. The telephone began to ring. She hesitated and then, making a face, started toward the door. If it was Joker, let him find out tomorrow that she had gone. To hell with him! She would be back soon enough. This time she was going to keep her promise to Michelle.

As she reached for the doorknob, the door opened and a tall man confronted her. Automatically her eyes dropped to his feet. She felt the hair on the base of her neck begin to rise. Copper!

"Did you ever hear of knocking before you enter a room?" she asked coldly.

He came into the office, and she saw that there were several men behind him. The first man smiled. "Going someplace, baby?" he asked.

"None of your business," she snapped.

A short, dark man pushed his way through the group. "Cut the comedy, George," he said sharply. He turned to her. "Are you Maryann Flood?"

She nodded.

"I'm Joel Rader of the District Attorney's office. These men are police. We would like you to come with us," he said.

She stepped back against her desk. "Is this an arrest?"

"It sure is, baby," the tall man said coarsely.

She ignored him and spoke to the short, dark man. "What am I charged with, Mr. Rader?" she asked.

"This warrant will spell it out, Miss Flood," Rader said, handing her a folded sheet of paper.

She took it from him and scanned it quickly. When she looked up, her face was impassive. "May I call my attorney?" she asked calmly.

Joel nodded. He watched her admiringly as she walked behind the desk and picked up the telephone. She dialed quickly. No wonder the woman could do what she did. She had nerves of ice.

He could hear a man's voice answer the phone. "Hank," she said quietly, "I've just been arrested. . . . No, I'm still at the office. . . . Yes. . . . I'll see you down there."

She put down the telephone and looked at Joel. "I'm ready now," she said.

He stepped aside to let her pass. She walked through the door to the outer office. The old colored man stood there, his face grayish. She stopped to speak to him. "Don't worry, Tom," she said. "Go home and fix dinner. And wire the baby that we were held up on business."

Tom looked across Vito's office at Joker with a worried expression. "Is Miz Maryann in big trouble?"

Joker looked at Hank Vito, then turned back to Tom. "She's in big trouble."

"All on 'count of that there lawyer? That one they mention in the papers who done prepared the case? That Mr. Keyes? That one that gone on a vacation while Miz Maryann is in all that trouble?" Tom's voice was indignant.

"That's the boy." Joker's voice was quiet.

"He's a mean man, Mr. Joker," Tom said seriously, "to do that to Miz Maryann jus' because she won' marry up with him."

"What?" Joker leaned forward. "What do you mean?" A vague, torturing memory began to bother him. That friend of Ross's, the boy who used to pick her up after work at the dance hall. His name had been Mike. He stared at Tom. "What do you mean?" he repeated.

"He Michelle's father," Tom said.

"How do you know?" Vito asked. "Did she tell you?"

Tom shook his head. "She never do that."

"Then how do you know?" Vito asked. "If we could prove that, I could get her off easy. No jury in the world would believe it was anything but a frame-up."

"She keep Michelle's birth certificate in the dresser at home. It says his name next to *Father*. I see it many times when I clean," Tom said.

Vito got to his feet excitedly. "You go right home and get it. Then bring it right down here. Don't give it to anybody but me. Understand?"

Tom was already on his way to the door. He looked

back at them with a happy grin. "Yes suh, Mr. Hank. I understand."

The door closed behind him and Vito turned to Joker. "Well, what do you make of that?" he asked.

"I'll be damned!" Joker said in wonder. "And all the time she never said a thing to us."

"You think she still goes for the guy?" Vito asked.

Joker shrugged. "I've stopped trying to figure her a long time ago."

"I won't spring it until the trial," Vito said. "I wouldn't want the D.A. to bring it out before we do." He paused, interrupted by a thought. "You think Keyes knows?"

Joker shook his head. "Uh-uh. I don't think she ever told anyone. Except maybe Ross. And he can't tell nobody."

Vito walked behind his desk. "I don't understand that woman," he said in a puzzled voice. "I saw her in jail this morning. It's her third day there, and she never said a word to me. I wonder if she knows that this could spring her."

"Even if she does, I doubt she would say anything." Joker smiled. "Remember what you said to me a long time ago, Hank? When you first told me about her?"

Vito shook his head. "No."

"She's a special kind of broad," Joker quoted. "A whore with a code of ethics."

The State vs. Maryann Flood

JOEL looked up from his desk as I walked into the office. There was a worried expression on his face. "The Old Man has been yelling like hell for yuh," he said. "You better jump upstairs on the double."

"What's he want?" I asked, throwing my hat and coat onto a chair.

"I don't know," Joel said. "I heard Vito was with him. I don't like it."

"Vito?" I questioned.

Joel nodded. "You better snap it up."

The Old Man's secretary waved me right into his office. The Old Man was seated behind his desk, his eyes cold. Vito sat in a chair opposite him. He turned around when I came in.

I walked past him to the desk. "You sent for me, sir?"

The Old Man nodded, his eyes still cold. "You didn't tell me everything about yourself and Miss Flood." His voice was as cold as his eyes.

I felt anger creeping up in me. This was one thing I

hadn't bargained for. I had told the Old Man everything that was pertinent. It was he who had asked me to stay on when I wanted to quit. I made my voice as cold as his. "I'm afraid I don't understand you."

"One Frank Millersen is enough for any man in one lifetime!" the Old Man shouted, his fist pounding the desk.

I kept my voice calm, though my temper was going through the roof. I had been through enough hell without having this old bastard yell at me. "I still don't know what you're talking about."

"Maybe you don't know about this?" the Old Man asked sarcastically, pushing a piece of paper at me.

I picked it up and looked at it. It was a birth certificate. *Michelle Keyes*. I read farther, feeling the blood leave my face. *Mother—Maryann Flood. Father—Michael Keyes.* I looked at the date. I could feel my heart pounding. It had to be right. It matched the time we had been together.

Now I understood a lot of things. That strange look she had given me last night when I asked about her daughter. I hadn't suspected that the child was mine.

The Old Man's voice rasped at my ears. "Why didn't you tell me about it?"

I looked up at him and kept my voice as steady as I could. "How could I?" I asked. "This is the first I ever knew of it."

The Old Man snorted. "You don't expect me to believe that, do you?"

My temper finally blew the roof. "I don't give a damn what you believe!" I shouted.

"You know what this will do to our case?" the Old Man asked. "It will kick it into a cocked hat!"

I glared at him. He was the guy who said the only way to win was to go with the truth. "Why should it?" I asked coldly. "Vito hasn't been able to disprove any of the charges."

For the first time since I had come into the room, he spoke. "Why should I bother?" he asked. "What jury is going to believe your charges when they see this? It'll make everything seem like a frame. A personal vendetta."

I looked down at him and sneered. "I heard you were a good lawyer, Vito. One of the best. I didn't know you included blackmail in your arsenal."

Vito started out of his chair toward me. I pushed him back with one hand. He sat there glaring at me.

The intercom on the Old Man's desk buzzed. He flipped the switch. "Yes?" he barked into it.

"Miss Flood is here," his secretary's voice said.

"Send her in," the Old Man said.

The door opened and Marja came in. Her gold hair was brushed loosely. She wore the same blue poodle-cloth coat she had worn all through the trial. She came into the office with the same sure walk that had always distinguished her from other women.

She ignored me and looked down at Vito. "What's up?" Her voice was husky.

His smile was tight under his elegant mustache. "I think the D.A.'s about to make us a deal."

She looked up at me. A glow came into her eyes. "Mike, are you—?"

Vito's voice was sharp. "I said the D.A., not your boy friend."

The glow faded from her eyes as quickly as it had appeared. She looked at him again. "How come?" she asked.

Silently I handed her the birth certificate. She looked at it quickly, then up at me. A naked pain had come into her eyes. "Where did you get this?" she asked, her voice trembling.

I nodded at Vito.

She looked down at him. "How'd you get this, Vito?" Her voice had gone cold as ice.

He smiled up at her. "Tom brought it to me."

"Why didn't you tell me about it?" she asked.

"And have you louse up your own case because you wanted to protect your boy friend?" he retorted. "I'm your lawyer. I'm supposed to defend you. Even against yourself."

She took a deep breath. "Who cares about him? If I wanted him to know, I would have told him a long time ago. It's Michelle I care about. She's happy now. She thinks her father was killed in the war. How do you think she would feel if she found out how she was born?"

"You think she'd like it better to know that her mother is in the can?" Vito asked.

"It's a lot better than finding out she's a bastard!" Marja snapped.

Vito got to his feet. "You'll do as I say," he said. "There's too much at stake for you to back out now." He turned to the D.A. "Well, John, what do you say?"

The Old Man looked at him silently.

"Have we got a deal?" Vito persisted.

The D.A. spoke softly, his eyes on me. "Keyes is trying the case. I make it a point never to interfere with my assistants. Ask him."

Vito looked at me questioningly.

"There'll be no deal," I said.

"You won't like it, Mike," he said. "I'm goin' to put you on the stand, and when I get through with you, you'll have no place to go. You'll be all washed up here."

"I'll take the chance," I said grimly.

Vito turned back to the Old Man. "That ends your crack at the Governor's chair."

The Old Man's eyes were inscrutable. "I'll go with Mike," he said.

Vito turned toward the door, his face red and angry. "Come on, Maryann."

She started after him.

"Marja," I called.

She stopped and looked back at me. I walked over to her and took her hand. "Why didn't you tell me?" I asked gently.

She didn't answer. Her eyes were shining with a strange brilliance. I wondered if there were tears behind those lids.

"Why, Marja?" I persisted.

Her eyes stared into mine, wide and unblinking. "I lost one baby because they didn't think I could take care of it, Mike," she half whispered. "I didn't want to lose this one."

"Coming, Maryann?" Vito's voice sounded harshly from the doorway.

"I'm sorry, Mike," she whispered, pulling her hand from mine and going out the door.

I walked slowly back to the Old Man. "Well, I really snafued that one for you."

He smiled. "I apologize for not trusting you, Mike."

"Forget it, John," I said. "It's not important now."

He got to his feet heavily. "Court will be open in a few minutes. We better get down there."

I felt as the ancient Roman gladiators must have felt as they marched into the arena. *"Morituri te salutamus,"* I said.

He was busy with his own thoughts. "What's that?" he asked sharply.

I grinned at him. He was proud of his knowledge of Latin. It wasn't often one had the chance to rub him, even if it was through inattention on his part. "We who are about to die salute you," I translated, grinning.

There was an atmosphere of repressed excitement in the courtroom. It was as if some mysterious sense had communicated to everyone there that something was about to break. Even the normally blasé court clerks were fidgeting restlessly.

The judge arrived twenty minutes late. We rose as he ascended the bench. A moment later the court was in session.

Vito rose to his feet and walked toward the bench. His voice rang through the courtroom. "The defense would like to call as its first witness Mr. Michael Keyes of the District Attorney's staff!"

Even the judge was visibly startled. He glanced toward us while a roar went up in the courtroom. I could hear the footsteps of several reporters racing up the aisles to the doors. He banged his gavel for order. A moment later it was quiet.

"That's a most extraordinary request, counselor," he said. "I presume you have sufficient reason for your action."

"I have, Your Honor," Vito answered. "I believe it most important in the interest of securing justice for my client that Mr. Keyes be asked to take the stand."

The judge looked at me and I began to stroll across the court. Vito watched me, his face impassive.

She looked up at me as I walked past her table. Her face

was white and drawn. Then she was behind me and the
witness chair in front of me. I climbed the step and turned
to face the court clerk who was about to administer the
oath. A dozen flashbulbs went off, blinding me for a moment.

I heard her voice while I was blinking my eyes. It was
strong and clear. "Your Honor, may I have a moment to
talk to my attorney? I want to change my plea to guilty!"

Another roar broke out in the courtroom, even greater
than the one that had preceded it. More flashbulbs went off,
and by the time I could see, Vito had gone back to her
table.

They argued visibly for a moment, then Vito looked up
at the judge. "May I ask for a ten-minute recess, Your
Honor? I need a moment with my client in private."

The judge's gavel banged. "The court will recess for ten
minutes." He left the bench and I stepped down from the
witness stand and crossed to my table.

Marja and Vito had already vanished into the conference
room. I looked around the court. The people standing in
the back of the court were packed like sardines. I felt a
hand tugging at my sleeve. I looked down.

It was the Chief. "You were right," he whispered in an
admiring voice. "The girl's sheer guts. All the way!"

The conference door opened and Vito came out alone.
He looked at the crowd, seeming to search for someone. I
tried to follow his gaze, but he was too quick for me. He
made a motion with his head that seemed almost like a nod
and went back into the conference room.

I was still watching the crowd. A moment later a man
got to his feet. His steel-white hair shone in the overhead
lamps. He began to walk up the aisle toward the door. I
recognized him immediately: Joker Martin. I wondered

what he had been doing here, but the conference door opened and I forgot all about it.

Marja came into the court first; her face was set and calm. Vito followed her. They went to their table and sat down.

A moment later the court was in session again. Vito got to his feet and faced the judge. His face was white, but his voice was steady. "My client wishes to enter a plea of guilty to all the charges."

The judge looked down at her: "Is that your wish, Miss Flood?"

She got to her feet slowly. "It is, Your Honor."

We fought our way through the crowd to the elevators. My back ached from all the pounding I had taken from well-wishers. At last I was alone in the elevator with the Chief.

"You'll have my resignation on your desk in the morning, sir," I said.

He didn't look at me.

"I'm sorry about all the mess, sir," I said.

He didn't speak.

The elevator stopped at my floor and I got off, leaving him alone in the car. I walked down the hall to my office. Joel and Alec were still downstairs. I sat down at my desk and pulled out a sheet of paper. I wrote the resignation quickly, put it in an envelope, and sent it up to the Chief.

The phone on my desk rang. I picked it up. "Keyes," I said. I wouldn't be doing this for long.

"Mike, this is Marja."

"Yes, Marja," I said wearily.

"I'm in the Boyd Cocktail Lounge over on Broadway. Can you meet me right away?"

They had certainly worked fast. Her bail had been set at fifty thousand dollars, and here she was in a bar almost before I had time to get upstairs. I hesitated.

"Please, Mike," she said. "It's very important."

"Okay," I said. "I'll be right over." I reached for my coat. I'd come back tomorrow to clean out my desk.

It had begun to snow when I pushed my way through the door into the dimly lit interior. She was seated at a table in the corner. I sat down beside her. A waiter came up.

"What'll it be?" I asked her.

"Cassis and soda," she said.

"Gin over rocks for me," I said to him. He went away, and I turned to her. "You're still drinking that crazy stuff."

"I like it," she said.

The waiter came back and put the drinks before us.

I lifted my drink. "Here's to crime."

Her eyes were steady on me. "I won't drink to that."

I made a face.

"Ross always used to say that," she said. "I'm superstitious about it."

"Got something better?" I asked.

She nodded.

"What?" I asked.

Her eyes looked into mine. "Here's to us," she said steadily.

I could feel the warmth of her reaching out to me. "Good enough," I said, sipping my drink. I put the glass down and looked at her. "What was it you wanted to see me about?"

A man came into the restaurant. She glanced at him briefly, then back at me. "About us, Mike," she said. Her hand moved along the table and rested on mine. "I think it's about time."

I could feel the electricity shooting up my arm from her fingers. I tried to keep my voice calm. "Is it?"

She nodded slowly. "Nobody else will do for me."

I took a deep breath. "It took a long time for you to come to that conclusion."

"I'm sorry, Mike," she said. "I couldn't help it. I didn't know any better. I told you that last night. In the car."

I needed time to think. The pulses in my temples were pounding. I changed the subject. "Who went your bail?" I asked.

The door opened and another man came through. Automatically she looked at him briefly, appraisingly, then back at me. "Joker Martin," she said.

So that was what he had been doing in the courtroom. Vito had probably come out to get an okay from him on the plea. I had heard that he had almost all the rackets in town sewed up. I didn't speak.

She leaned toward me. I could smell the warm perfume of her. "It won't be long, Mike," she said. "I'll be out in a couple of years with good behavior. Then we can go off someplace and start clean. Nobody will know anything about us."

Another man came through the door and her eyes flicked over him, then back to me. Her voice was low and husky. "Are we goin' to make it, Mike?"

I took a deep breath. Slowly I began to disengage our fingers. She looked down at my hands, then up at me. Her eyes were suddenly veiled. "What is it, Mike? The jail sentence?"

I shook my head. I still didn't trust myself to speak.

Her voice was a shade sharper now. "What is it, then? I got a right to know, Mike."

"What's my daughter like, Marja?" My voice seemed to be coming from someone else, not from me.

A sudden flash of understanding came into her eyes. "So that's it," she said.

I nodded. "That's it." I looked down at my hands. I could see the veins on the backs of them pulsing slowly. "I could never keep your child from you the way you did mine from me."

"What else could I do, Mike?" she asked. "We were worlds apart then."

"What makes you think we're any closer now?" I said brutally. I looked right into her eyes. "I spent my life waiting for you. I thought there was nothing you could do that I could not condone or find excuses for. But I was wrong. The one thing you never should have done was cheat me of my child."

"She's my child, too, Mike, don't forget that," she said quickly. "She's the only thing in this world that's mine, really mine. She's more mine than yours."

"That's what I mean, Marja," I said, a weariness creeping into me. "She could have been *our* child. But you were only thinking of yourself. Not of her, not of me. Only that you wanted her."

"It's not too late, Mike. We can still do it over."

"No, Marja." I shook my head. "You can't turn back the clock. You told me that once yourself. Remember?"

Her eyes were wide and dark. So much about them was familiar, and yet they seemed almost like the eyes of a stranger. A moment passed. Then her face settled into an inscrutable mask and she slowly got to her feet. Without a word, she walked out into the street.

Through the glass door I could see her standing in the street, the snow falling like velvet around her. A long black limousine stopped in front of her. A man got out. He took off his dark homburg as he held the door for her. I could see his white hair. It matched the falling snow. He was Joker Martin. He followed her into the car and it moved off slowly.

I threw the rest of my drink down my throat and got to my feet. I tossed a few bills on the table and started for the door.

I walked into the court for my last official act. To hear Marja's sentence.

I could see her face as she faced the bench. She was pale, but her eyes were calm and unafraid as the judge's voice rolled down on her.

"On the first count—procurement for the purposes of prostitution—you hereby are sentenced to imprisonment for an indeterminate term of three to five years and fined five thousand dollars.

"On the second count—bribing certain public officials—you hereby are sentenced to imprisonment for one year and fined five thousand dollars.

"On the third count—extortion by oral threats—you hereby are sentenced to imprisonment for one year and fined five hundred dollars."

The rustle and hum of conversation rose behind us as the judge finished pronouncing sentence. He rapped his gavel for order. The courtroom became quiet.

His voice was very low, but it carried to the back of the courtroom. "It has been brought to the attention of this court by the District Attorney that the defendant by her action has indicated a desire to rehabilitate herself in the eyes of society. Therefore, it is the decision of this court to allow the defendant to serve her various terms of imprisonment concurrently."

A louder buzz ran through the courtroom. This was a real break. It meant that she wouldn't have to serve more than two years, with time off for good behavior. I turned to Alec. "Did you know the Old Man was going to do this?" I asked.

He shook his head. I looked at Joel. He, too, looked blank. I looked across the room at Marja. She was watching me, her eyes steady and somehow grateful. I wanted to tell her that it was the Chief, not I, who had arranged it, but there was no way to speak to her.

Joel fell into step beside me as we left the court. "The Old Man is gettin' soft," he said. "How about a drink?"

I shook my head and left him at the elevator. As I reached the door to my office, it opened suddenly and the Old Man stood there. In his hand he held an envelope which he waved at me excitedly. "You don't think I'd accept this, do you?" he yelled.

I saw that it was my resignation. "Yes, sir," I said. "I think it's only right."

"Then you're even more stupid than I thought, Keyes," he shouted. With a flourishing gesture he tore the letter into shreds and threw them on the floor. He stamped off angrily.

For a moment I stared down at the floor. The tiny bits of paper were startlingly white on the dusty gray flooring. Then I took off after him. I caught his arm and he turned around. "Thanks, Chief," I said.

He nodded testily. "It's okay, Mike. You didn't think I would give up a good assistant that easily, did you?"

I smiled slowly. "Not for me, sir. For Marja."

He looked into my eyes and his gaze grew gentle. "Don't

ever forget, Mike," he said softly, "that the scales of justice must always be tempered with mercy."

I stood there silently for a moment. Mercy. It was a big word. The biggest. I wondered if I would ever be man enough to show it.

Before I could speak, he clapped me on the shoulder. "Go back to your office, lad. There's someone waiting there to see you."

He stomped off down the hall and I turned back to my office. I opened the door slowly. There was no one there. The Old Man must be cracking up. I went in and sat down behind my desk. I heard a rustle of clothing from the small couch against the wall behind the door. I looked up.

A small girl was walking toward me. Her hair was the whitest gold I had ever seen. Her eyes were big and round and blue, and looking into them was like looking into a mirror. They were my eyes. I could feel a tightening in my chest. I couldn't breathe.

She stopped in front of my desk and looked at me solemnly. Her eyes were wide and unwinking. "I'm Michelle," she said. Her voice was young and clear.

I nodded, unable to speak.

"Mother said I was to stay with you for a while," she said.

I nodded again. I wanted to speak, but I couldn't.

"She said you would look after me." The faintest hint of tears began to creep into those beautiful blue eyes.

A pain began to echo in me and my eyes blurred. I moved slowly around the desk and knelt beside her. I took both her hands in mine. "I'll look after you, Michelle."

Praise for Frank Peretti *and* Ted Dekker's novels

"Peretti and Dekker's taut, roller-coaster ride of a thriller will have you tearing through the book at a breakneck pace . . ."
—*Parkersburg News* review of *House*

"If you are looking for a book that will keep you up at night and yet offers hope at some point, then *House* is a must-read for you. My words will never suffice how spectacular this book is, so go out and get this book for yourself. But don't forget to lock the windows and doors, and whatever you do . . . stay out of the basement."
—1340mag.com

"Dekker and Peretti hold their cards close to their chests to the very end in this taut mind-blower."
—*Christian Music Planet*

"The story builds constantly, leaving readers in a state of continuous tension . . . *House* is a must-read for anyone who loves a good suspense thriller."
—*Aspiring Retail*

"You will not be disappointed with this collaboration. The writing is flawless. The seamless continuity of this novel is testament to the two creative minds behind it and their commitment to a quality story."
—Novelreviews.blogspot.com regarding *House*

"Its premise and pacing recall some of the down-and-dirty thrillers of Dean Koontz, and predictable it is not, partly because the authors withhold as much information from us for as long as possible, lending the events in the basement a surreal, nightmarish quality."
—Bookgasm.com review of *House*

"... Peretti is a bona fide publishing phenomenon."
—*BookPage* review of *The Visitation*

"Dekker delivers his signature exploration of good and evil in the context of a genuine thriller that could further enlarge his already sizable audience."
—*Publishers Weekly* review of *Showdown*

"In the world of Christian fiction, the hottest novels are those by Frank Peretti."
—*Newsweek* review of *Monster*

"Exciting, well-written, and resonant with meaning, *Black*, *Red*, and now *White* have won over both critics and genre readers ... An epic journey completed with grace."
—Editors, Barnes and Noble

"... plenty of spine-chilling mayhem ..."
—www.Amazon.com regarding *This Present Darkness*

"Ted Dekker is clearly one of the most gripping story-tellers alive today. He creates plots that keep your heart pounding and palms sweating even after you've finished his books."
—Jeremy Reynalds, Syndicated Columnist

"Not only is Peretti the country's top-selling Christian fiction author, but he has become, by any standard, one of current fiction's biggest stars."
—*Chicago Tribune* regarding *The Visitation*

Reading Group Guide Available at
www.thomasnelson.com/readingguides

HOUSE

FRANK
PERETTI

TED
DEKKER

THOMAS NELSON
Since 1798

NASHVILLE DALLAS MEXICO CITY RIO DE JANEIRO BEIJING

OTHER BOOKS BY
TED DEKKER

Skin
Saint
Showdown
The Martyr's Song
Obsessed
Black
Red
White
Three
Blink
When Heaven Weeps
Thunder of Heaven
Heaven's Wager

Coauthored with Bill Bright
Blessed Child
A Man Called Blessed

Published in Nashville, Tennessee, by Thomas Nelson. Thomas Nelson is a trademark of Thomas Nelson, Inc.

Thomas Nelson, Inc. titles may be purchased in bulk for educational, business, fund-raising, or sales promotional use. For information, please e-mail SpecialMarkets@ThomasNelson.com.

Scripture paraphrased from The Holy Bible: New International Version®. © 1973, 1978, 1984 by International Bible Society. Used by permission of Zondervan Publishing House. All rights reserved.

Publisher's Note: This novel is a work of fiction. Names, characters, places, and incidents are either products of the authors' imaginations or used fictitiously. All characters are fictional, and any similarity to people living or dead is purely coincidental.

Library of Congress Cataloging-in-Publication Data

Peretti, Frank E.
   House / Frank Peretti and Ted Dekker.
      p. cm.
   ISBN: 978-1-59554-155-0 (HC)
   ISBN: 978-1-59554-156-7 (TP)
   ISBN: 978-1-59554-342-4 (SE)
   ISBN: 978-1-59554-362-2 (MM)
   I. Dekker, Ted, 1962– II. Title.
PS3566.E691317H68 2006
813'.54—dc22

Printed in the United States of America
07 08 09 10 11 QW 5 4 3 2 1

The light came into the darkness,
and the darkness did not understand it.

—~—

My heart holds all secrets; my heart tells no lies.

PROLOGUE

HE STOOD MOTIONLESS IN THE ENTRYWAY, staring at his own shadow splayed before him like a stain upon the floor. He studied the patina of dust, sampled the stench of mold and rat urine, listened to a beam settling one more fraction of an inch toward the center of the earth.

This room bore so little evidence of the events that had led to the dawn. From this vantage point, it was just one more abandoned house. Interesting.

But the rest of the house told the truth.

Beneath his boots, the floorboards lay shoulder to shoulder like the buried dead, cupped with creeping moisture, edges buckling, obscured by gray dust and fallen flakes of white paint.

Across the foyer, at the base of a wall, the rose-printed wallpaper fluttered. Behind one of the roses, something scratched, pushed, gnawed, and clawed until a black, whiskered nose burst through. With a wad of shredded wallpaper in its jaws, the rat wriggled through the hole, then rested on its haunches and met his eyes.

Neither found the other's presence alarming. The rat skittered along the baseboard and disappeared around a corner.

At the far end of the room, half a tattered curtain rustled and stirred before a broken window. A pitiful attempt at escape. Apart from the broken window, there was no sign that anyone had been here in years.

But when some curious passerby—or the police, should they be so fortunate as to stumble upon this place— wandered farther in, they'd find signs to the contrary in abundance. And those signs would lead them to the mysteries below.

Death lingered in the musty air, even up here. The walls were like shrouds, enfolding every space in exquisite darkness. It had been a perfect arena for a perfect game.

And already Barsidious White was looking forward to the next.

I

5:17 PM

"JACK, YOU'RE GONNA KILL US!"

His mind jerked out of a daydream and back to the lonely Alabama highway in front of the blue Mustang. The speedometer topped eighty. He cleared his mind and relaxed his right foot. "Sorry."

Stephanie went back to her singing, her voice clear if melancholy, her inflection classic country. *"My heart holds all secrets; my heart tells no lies . . ."*

That one again. She wrote it, so he never criticized it, but those awful lyrics, especially today—

"Jack!"

The speedometer was inching toward eighty again.

"Sorry." He forced his foot to relax.

"What's the matter with you?"

"What's the matter—" *Easy now, Jack. No fuel on the fire.* "A little tense, okay?"

She smiled at him. "You should try singing."

His grip tightened on the steering wheel. "Yeah, that's your answer for everything, isn't it?"

"Excuse me?"

3

He sighed. He had to quit taking her bait. "Sorry." Always apologizing. He looked her way and forced a smile, hoping she would believe it.

She smiled back in a way that said she didn't.

She was beautiful, enough to capture the next man just as she'd captured him—blonde, youthful, a real credit to those jeans—everything the guys in the lounges and bars could want in a country singer. No doubt those blue eyes could still sparkle, but not for him anymore. Right now they were hiding behind fashion-statement sunglasses, and she was craning to see out the back. "I think there's a cop behind us."

He checked the rearview mirror. The highway, which had narrowed to two lanes, curved lazily through late-spring forest and farmland, rose and fell over dips and rises, hiding and revealing, hiding and revealing a single car. It was gaining on them, near enough now for Jack to recognize the light bar atop the roof. He checked his speed. Sixty-five. That should be legal.

The police car kept coming.

"Better slow down."

"I'm doing the speed limit."

"You sure?"

"I can read the signs, Steph."

A few seconds more and the cruiser filled Jack's mirror as if he were towing it. He could see the cop's iron-jawed countenance behind the wheel, reflective black sunglasses obscuring the eyes.

Highway patrol.

Jack double-checked the speedometer, then slowed to sixty, hoping the cop wouldn't rear-end them.

The sedan inched closer.

He was going to rear-end them!

Jack smashed the gas pedal to the floor, and the Mustang shot ahead.

"What are you doing?" Stephanie cried.

"He was gonna hit us!"

The car fell back ten yards. Its red and blue lights flashed to life.

"Oh, great," she muttered, turning and flopping back against her seat. He could hear the blame in her voice. Always the blame. *But you're the one who walked away, Steph.*

The cruiser veered into the oncoming lane and pulled up beside them. The uniformed officer turned his face to Jack. Met his eyes. Or so Jack imagined. Black glasses. No expression. Jack forced his eyes back to the road.

The two cars were side by side, locked in formation at sixty miles an hour.

"What are you doing, Jack? Pull over."

He would if he could. Jack strained to see an opportunity. The forest, a thick tangle of maple, oak, and birch draped with kudzu, encroached like an advancing wall. "I can't. There's no shoulder. I can't just . . ."

He slowed. There had to be a turnout somewhere. Forty miles per hour. Thirty. The cruiser matched his speed.

Jack saw a break in the foliage, a sliver of a shoulder, just enough room. He began to veer off.

The cruiser surged and left them behind, lights blazing in silence. Fifteen seconds later it was a dot on the road between the towering trees, and then it was gone.

"What was that about?" Jack asked, checking his mirrors, rubbernecking, and easing back onto the highway. He wiped a sweaty palm on his jeans.

"You were speeding." She fixed her gaze on the highway, fumbled with a map, avoided his eyes.

"He didn't pull us over. Why was he so close? You see how close he was?"

"That's Alabama, Jack. You don't do things their way, they let you know."

"Yeah, but you don't ram someone in the tail for speeding."

She slapped her lap, a release of frustration. "Jack, will you please just get us there, legally, in one piece? Please?"

He chose silence over a comeback and concentrated on the road. *Save it for the counseling session, Jack.* He wondered what she'd been saving up, what new claims she'd unload tonight.

She shook out her shoulders, put on a smile, and started humming.

You really think it will work, don't you, Jack? You really think you can save something you just don't have anymore?

If smiling and singing could bring back those days, he would laugh like a fool and even sing Stephanie's lyrics, but he was fresh out of illusions. All he had were the memories that stole his mind away even as his eyes remained on the road: her arms about his shoulders and the excitement in her eyes; the inner dawn he felt whenever she entered the room; the secrets they shared with a glance, a smile, a wink; all the things he thought life and love should be—

The accident changed everything.

He imagined himself sitting in the counselor's office, being honest about his feelings. *I'm feeling . . . like I've been had all my life. Life is pointless. If there is a God, he's the devil, and . . . What was that? Oh, you mean Stephanie? No, I've lost her too. She's gone. I mean, she's here, but she's checked out . . .*

He couldn't put away the idea that this whole trip was only a formality, another nail in the coffin of their marriage. Steph would sing her way to Montgomery and back and still get the divorce she wanted, go on her merry way.

"Jack, you're lost."

I sure am.

"Jack."

With a start, he returned his attention to driving. The Mustang purred along at sixty-five, gobbling up the highway. The forest was breaking up now, giving way to crude homesteads and stump-filled pastureland.

She was scanning the map, studying all those little red and black lines. Did she say *he* was lost? Right. *She* was holding the map, but *he* was lost.

He caught the sarcasm before it escaped. Hurtful words came so easily these days. "What do you mean?"

"Didn't you see that highway marker? It said 5."

He glanced at the mirror, then twisted to see the back of the receding sign. "5?"

She studied the map, tracing a route with her finger. "We're supposed to be on Highway 82."

He leaned and tried to read the map. The car swerved. He shot his eyes forward again, corrected the wheel.

"We're going to be late," she said.

Not necessarily. "You see Highway 5 on there? Where does it lead?"

She dragged her finger over the map and stopped about three inches out of Montgomery. "Not to Montgomery, unless you have a week to sightsee. How could you possibly have gotten off 82?"

Dare he defend himself? "I was a little distracted by a cop eating up my bumper."

She pulled her cell phone out of a cup holder and checked the display clock. "There's no way we'll make it."

Was that hope in her voice? He checked his watch. If they turned around now, maybe—

"I canceled a gig to go to this appointment with you." Stephanie hunched in the seat, arms folded.

There it is again. My fault. She started humming. *There it is again.*

Red and blue lights flashed up ahead.

"Oh, great," Stephanie said. "We *really* don't need this."

Jack slowed as they approached the patrol car parked just beyond a turnoff. Orange cones and a sign blocked the road ahead. "Repaving Operation. Highway Closed to Through Traffic," Jack read. "Well, we have to turn around anyway." Jack pulled onto the gravel shoulder but had a second thought. "Let's ask. Maybe there's a faster way."

Jack eased the blue Mustang forward, up to the turnoff, and stopped a few feet behind the patrol car. The cruiser's door swung open and an officer—the officer—stepped out, aviator sunglasses still hiding his eyes.

2

THE PATROLMAN ROLLED HIS HEAD TO CRACK his neck, then kept his face pointed at them as he donned a broad-brimmed smoky-colored hat. He wore a short-sleeved gray shirt, and pants with a black stripe running down the outside of the legs. A breast badge flashed in the late-afternoon sun. His large leather holster hung on his right hip, his baton on his left.

The man touched his hat as if by habit and walked toward them, confident. Cocky. The man's pants looked a tad tight.

"Good night," Stephanie said.

Jack rolled the window down. A hot breeze blew into the Mustang, chased by the sound of crickets. The officer's black leather boots were silent on the pavement.

The patrolman stopped by their window, hand on the butt of his gun. He leaned over and gave them a close-up view of his black lenses. Morton Lawdale, the badge said.

"You mind showing me your license and registration?"

"We—"

"License and registration. Now."

Jack leaned over to the glove box, dug out the papers, and handed them through the window.

The cop took them with a gloved hand and straightened, scanning them at his leisure. "You mind stepping out of the car?"

Jack wasn't sure what to make of the request. "Why?"

"Why? Because I want to show you something, how's that for why?"

"Did I do something wrong?"

"Are all you Alabama boys so dense? An officer tells you to step from your vehicle, you argue as if you're the king of the hill. I have something you need to see. Get your butt out of the car."

Jack exchanged a glance with Stephanie, opened the door, and swung his legs out.

"There, was that so hard?"

"We took a wrong turn," Jack said, looking up. He was at least a head shorter than the patrolman. "We were headed to Montgomery on 82."

Lawdale pulled out his billy club and waved Jack to the back. "Come 'ere."

A chill slipped down Jack's back. How'd he end up here, out in the middle of nowhere with this character, a trigger-happy, blow-'em-away-and-ask-questions-later kind?

He hesitated.

"You gonna make me say everything twice?" The cop slapped his palm with the stick.

"No." Jack walked toward the trunk.

He stopped by the fender, facing the cop who stood with feet spread, staring directly at him. As far as Jack could tell.

Lawdale swung his black stick down to indicate the

left rear brake light. "Were you aware of the fact that your brake light is out?"

Jack breathed. "It is? No."

"It is. I nearly crawled up your backside. I oughta know."

"Oh."

"Oh," the patrolman mimicked. Sweat stained the man's shirt around his collar and under his arms. "And I'd suggest you start driving your car the way it was designed to be driven."

The passenger door opened and Stephanie stepped out, smiling like a ray of sunshine. "Is everything okay?"

"My taillight's out," Jack said.

Stephanie tilted her head playfully. "We'll get it fixed in Montgomery. Right, Jack?"

"Of course. As soon as we get there."

The patrolman tipped his hat at Steph and evaluated her low-rise jeans and silky blue tank top. "And who might you be?"

"Stephanie Singleton."

The man's eyes dropped to her ringless hand. Her taking that off last month had cut Jack more than anything else she'd done. "Siblings? Cousins?"

"Husband and wife," Jack said.

The cop looked at Stephanie. "You let this maniac drive?"

"Maniac?" Jack asked.

The cop dipped his head, pulled down his shades, and stared at Jack over the silver frames.

Blue eyes.

"Are you trying to be smart, boy? No, you're not, are you? You're just a bit thick."

It occurred to Jack how much rudeness one must stand and take when the other person is wearing a uniform.

The patrolman removed his sunglasses and gave Jack a stony blue glare. "Not only *like* a maniac, but a maniac who doesn't *know* he's driving like a maniac, which would make you an idiot. But I'm going to pretend I'm wrong. I'm going to pretend you're not an idiot and can understand what a maniac does. How would that suit you?"

Lawdale expected an answer. Jack could think of several but limited himself to "Fine."

"Fine. Then I'll tell you what a maniac does around here." The cop tapped Jack on the head with a pointed finger, hard enough to hurt. "A maniac doesn't watch his speed, and he doesn't use his mirrors. Use your mirrors, Jack. I was following you for five minutes before you saw I was on your tail. A truck could squash you flat and you'd be dead . . ."

The cop snatched his revolver from its holster, fanned the hammer, and fired into the nearby field like a gunslinger. *Blam!* Both Jack and Stephanie jerked.

". . . just like that." Lawdale blew the smoke from the end of the barrel and slipped the gun into its holster with a precise little spin. "Making a point, my friend. These are dangerous roads out here." He jabbed Jack in the temple again. "Watch your speed and use your mirrors."

All things considered, Jack thought it best to answer succinctly. "I will."

"Good." The patrolman returned Jack's license and registration, then pointed down the road. "Now we got a little detour here. Next three miles of highway is all torn up. Where'd you say you were headed?"

Jack's heart sank as he answered, "Montgomery."

"Montgomery." The cop almost smiled, obviously amused. "Can't you read a map?"

"We missed a turn."

The officer snorted, his way of snickering, Jack supposed, then pointed. "I'd take the detour. It's maybe one hour faster than backtracking to 82—if you know where to go. It's not marked too well, and you don't want to get caught out in the dark."

"Could you show us?" Jack asked.

The man walked back. "You do have a map, don't you?"

Stephanie held out their map, which he unfolded on the trunk of the Mustang and studied briefly. "Old map." He refolded it with a grunt. "Okay. You follow me clearly, you hear? You think *I'm* a bit pickled? Trust me, couple city folk like you don't want to be caught waltzing through the backwoods asking directions from the inbreds. You never know who you'll run into. Now you start here—"

"Inbreds?" Stephanie's smile contradicted her tone.

The cop dismissed the word with a wave. "Backwoods rednecks. Idiots like Jack was trying to be a moment ago. No understanding of any law but their own. Evil folk. Type who haven't discovered the toothbrush, much less the law."

He pointed down the turnoff. "Now you go south on this road until it comes to a *T*. Go left, that'll take you past the flats, back into the forest a ways. You'll be on a dirt road for a good forty miles, but don't worry, it'll dump you out on 82. Should take about an hour."

Jack looked at the gravel road headed south. It disappeared into tree-covered hills topped with heavy clouds. "You sure?"

"Do I look unsure?"

Not again. Jack grinned. "No sir."

Lawdale acknowledged with a slight nod. "Now we're beginning to understand. That's the road I take home every morning. If you break down, just stay on the shoulder. One of us will find you."

"You say that like it's happened before," Jack said.

"It has."

Stephanie followed their eyes, her smile faltering. "Jack, maybe we should just get on back home."

"No need for that," Lawdale said. "If you go now, while there's plenty of light, you'll get through without missing another beat. You all be careful now."

The officer touched the rim of his smoky hat and walked back to his cruiser.

Jack climbed behind the Mustang's wheel and slammed his door shut. "You ever wonder what kind of man patrols the backwoods?"

Stephanie dropped in beside him. "Not really."

"Now you know."

"I'm sure he's pulled plenty of your kind from the ditch. I say we turn around."

Jack checked his watch. Quarter till six. They could still make it. He eased the car forward.

Stephanie pressed it. "The appointment can't possibly be worth this much trouble."

Jack turned onto the gravel detour.

"Jack."

He picked up as much speed as he dared. "We've come this far, right? I'd like to try to get there."

3

7:46 PM

"SLOW DOWN, JACK."

Jack wasn't going that fast, not a shade over forty . . . well, sometimes fifty. The washboard road and potholes made it seem a lot faster. He remembered to use his mirrors but never saw more than a billowing trail of dust behind them. "He said it would take us an hour, but we're going on two." He ventured a sideways glance. "How far did he say it was to 82?"

"I think he said forty miles after the *T*."

Jack checked the odometer as he had several times already. "We've gone sixty at least. Are there any towns around here, any landmarks?"

She sat with her arms crossed, looking out the window. The crazy winding road had taken them back into dense forest. With the exception of a tiny roadside sign a half mile back, they hadn't seen so much as a mailbox. "Wayside Inn," the sign read. "Rest for the Weary Soul, 3 Miles." The sign was painted in cheery yellows, pinks, and blues, with a pink arrow pointing in the same direction they'd been headed for so long.

"This road isn't on the map, Jack. We only know what he told us."

He gripped the wheel and leaned into his driving. He was eating crow—and it was going down sideways. "Would you call and tell them we're running late?"

Steph picked up her phone. "No coverage out here. You may as well relax. We've missed the appointment."

He'd already run some time and mileage figures in his head and knew she was right. Figured.

"Well, apparently there's an inn up here somewhere," Jack said. "Maybe we can at least get off the road for the night." He met her eyes and looked for longing there, the meaningful glances she used to give him before their trouble. Nothing. He turned forward and tried to find words—

What was that? His foot went for the brake—

Bam! Something metallic thudded under the tires and screeched against the floorboards. The car lurched, shuddered, and wobbled, sliding on loose gravel.

Stephanie screamed as Jack struggled with the wheel. The car slid broadside, tires roaring over the rocks and raking the powdery surface into a wall of dust. Sounded like they were riding on rims. The wheel edges dug into the surface, and the car tipped to the passenger side. It teetered, then came down on all four wheels with a crunch of metal and shattering glass, the dust swarming over it.

Silence. Stillness. They were alive.

"You all right?" Jack asked.

Stephanie's voice trembled. "What . . . what happened?"

The left side of his head throbbed. Jack touched his hair and brought his hand away bloody. He must have hit the door.

"There was . . . something in the road."

He unbuckled his seat belt and let it slip into its retractor as he opened his door. Dust drifted in, settling on his clothes and coating his nostrils. He stepped out, unsteady on his feet, and noticed the car was lower to the ground.

All four tires were flat. The skid had nearly torn the shredded rubber from the wheels.

He looked back, squinting through the haze of dust and dusk, and saw a vicious contraption lying in the gravel like roadkill, flopped and twisted from the impact. It was a thick rubber mat, long enough to span the road and bristling with steel spikes.

His guts wrenched. He looked up and down the road, probed the thick forest and creeping kudzu on either side with his eyes. No sounds. No movement. "Steph . . ."

She emerged from the car and gasped at the damage. He pointed up the road at the monstrosity lying in the dust. "It was a trap, or a trick, or . . . I don't know."

She scanned the thick woods on either side of the road. "What do we do?"

His eyes were on the trees, both sides, back and forth. It seemed someone would have made a move by now, would have pounced, ambushed, fired a weapon, *something*.

"Well, whoever did this, they're bound to come back and see what they caught. We'd better get out of here."

"What about the car?"

"It's not going anywhere. Grab your purse. We'll head for the inn."

She ducked inside the car and pulled out the handbag,

then plunked her cell phone in it, her eyes darting every-where, afraid. Jack could see she was weighing the same possibilities: Inbreds. Weird, backwoods people. No regard for the law. Lawdale had warned them about being out here after dark.

"Come on." Jack reached for her hand across the hood of the car, urging her around.

She came to him. He clamped his hand on hers. They started out together, hurrying, looking back at their stricken car for as long as it was in sight.

They settled into a walk-run for nearly two miles. The sunlight continued to fade. They rounded a bend and saw a small sign at the top of a long gravel drive.

WAYSIDE INN

Jack let go of Stephanie's hand and turned up the narrow road. "All right. We'll use their telephone."

The house was nothing Stephanie expected, not out here in the remote Alabama backwoods. When she and Jack reached the gated stone wall and looked up the flag-stone walk, her fear of the gathering darkness and threat-ening weather dropped away; her sore feet and the grit in her sandals became bearable; even their wrecked car and meaningless road trip were not the end of the world. She felt so relieved that tears blurred her eyes.

They could have been looking back in time. Some-how, while vast plantations gave way to open fields and shady lanes decayed into potholed strips of red dust and gravel, this grand old lady stubbornly remained in a more genteel era. She was not quite a mansion, but her impos-

ing white walls, dormer windows, and tall, glowing lights
invited thoughts of hoopskirted southern belles and drawl-
ing, frock-coated gentlemen.

"Oh," was all she could say as relief gave way to joy,
and joy gave way to amazement.

"What's a nice house like that doing in a place like
this?" Jack wondered aloud.

He opened the gate and started up the walk, looked
back, and then waited, which surprised her. She hurried
to join him and they walked together, but *not* hand in
hand, entering another world.

Miniature lamps cast a warm glow on the flagstones
every few yards. The hedges on either side of the walkway were neat and precisely cornered; even in the dim
light, the flower beds were hilarious with color. Beyond
the beds, ancient oaks stood at ease on a parade ground
of manicured green.

"Wish I had my suitcase," she said. "I want to stay
here."

"We'll telephone for some help, then maybe go fetch
our stuff," he replied. "Officer Lawdale might be around
somewhere."

She winced at that. He was probably joking, but it
wasn't funny.

They crossed the veranda and found a note on the
door: *Welcome, weary traveler. Sign in at the front desk.*

Jack put his hand on the knob as she spotted her reflection in the door's ornate stained glass. That flushed, dust-
streaked face and windblown hair would never do in a place
like this. "Wait." She groped in her purse for a brush.

He opened the door, swinging her mirror away.
"Steph, we have enough trouble right now."

She followed her moving reflection, pulling the brush through her hair. He never saw things her way. Her own disgusted face looked back at her. "I'm so sweaty."

Jack went inside without her, and it stung. *Sure, just keep walking, buddy.*

She stowed her brush, worked up a sweet smile, and turned into the foyer, closing the door behind her.

Now she felt all the more dusty, dirty, wrinkled, and out of place. The room was open to a high ceiling, and a fancy chandelier hovered over their heads. The spotless hardwood floor reflected a wide, carpeted staircase. Flower-filled vases perched on tables, in wall niches, and small stands in corners. The living room to their left boasted a yawning fireplace with a carved mantel. She should be dressed for a party, but here she was looking like—

"You don't look like *you* own this place," a man's voice boomed from above.

A man and a woman came down the stairs. He was tall and well built, in crisp jeans and a celery-green sport shirt—the neck was open to show off a color-coordinated T-shirt. She was tall, brunette—not beautiful by Stephanie's estimation, but chic in her stylish white slacks and sleeveless red tunic. Silk, probably. Silver drop-shaped earrings. She descended with a professional grace she must have learned somewhere, and one quick, sizing-up glance from those green eyes made Stephanie's face flush.

"We need a phone," Stephanie said.

If Jack was conscious of his own dusty condition, he didn't show it. The novelist in him never put much stock in physical appearances, to her aggravation. Right now he was dressed as always, casual if not sloppy in baggy chinos and an untucked denim button-down, open over a white T-shirt. His reddish hair could use a comb, but other than that, he was a fine-looking man—yes, even finer than Mr. GQ now taking the stairs like a catalog model. Unfortunately, she needed more than *fine* these days. Her career was about to take off, but Jack was so stuck in the past that he would hold her back, no doubt.

"Run into trouble?" the man asked.

Jack answered, "We had some car trouble a couple miles down the road."

The man's eyes narrowed, and he shared a knowing look with the woman. "So did we."

Now he had Stephanie's wide-eyed, unwavering attention. "Our tires were slashed."

The man's right eyebrow arched. "So were ours."

The revelation alarmed her. "You too? How . . . how's that possible?"

"In these backwoods? Anything is possible," the man said with a coy smile.

"But that can't be a coincidence. Both cars?"

"Settle down, honey. Just some hillbillies laughing their guts out in a tree about now. It'll be just fine. Where you come from?"

"We were coming from the north, from Tuscaloosa," Jack said.

"We were coming from the south, from Montgomery."

"Did you turn off 82?"

"That's right."

"We had to walk for miles," Stephanie reminded him out loud.

"So did we," said the woman, not looking one bit like it.

The man jutted out his hand. "Randy Messarue."

Jack gripped his hand. "Jack Singleton. This is Stephanie, my, uh . . . ." He deferred to her.

"I'm his loving wife," she said.

The woman was taller than Stephanie, which helped her look down when she said, "Charmed." She turned away and offered her hand to Jack. Stephanie bristled. "I'm Leslie Taylor. Randy and I are longtime associates."

"Looks like you hit your head," Randy said. "You okay otherwise?"

Jack touched his head again. The blood was mostly dry now. "Tired, but okay. Have you called the police?"

Randy sneered. "Got a cell phone with service?"

Stephanie pulled her cell phone from her purse. She checked once more, but, "No, no service. Isn't there a landline here?"

"Good luck finding it."

Stephanie's subdued fear raised its head.

"We've checked the main floor and some of the rooms upstairs. If they have one, it's locked away."

"We can ask the owners when they get here," said Leslie.

"Yeah, when they get here," said Randy. "Don't know what kind of a business they think they're running, but you don't just leave a note on the door and leave the customers to fend for themselves."

Leslie smiled, cocked her head. "Randy runs a chain of hotels."

Jack's eyebrows went up. "Wow. That's something."

"And a chain of restaurants, but that's beside the point," said Randy.

Stephanie offered, "Jack's a writer. He's got several novels published."

"Oh," said Randy. "Bring any luggage with you?"

"No," Stephanie answered quickly, giving Jack an appropriate eye stab. *My husband doesn't consider such details.*

But he wasn't looking at her. "It's still back in the car. We were pretty nervous. You know, we figured . . ."

"We thought it was a robbery," Stephanie explained, feeling silly about it now. She forced a giggle. "I left my suitcase, and he left his, and we had a garment bag . . ."

Randy shook his head and sniffed. "It's a robbery *now.*"

"I'd sure love to change out of these dirty clothes."

"Don't worry," Jack said. "We'll figure something out." He pointed at a small table in the corner of the foyer with an open registry and a pen on a chain. "I'll get us signed in."

"And you may as well pick out a room," said Randy. "The keys are in that cabinet."

"Randy, we don't own the place," said Leslie.

Randy ignored her. "I'd recommend room 4, across the hall from us. It has a great view of the gardens in back." Leslie shot him a reproving glare.

Stephanie caught Jack's eye and held up two fingers. As at home, she'd take her own room here, thank you very much. Jack sighed and went to the desk.

Leslie turned her nose down toward Stephanie. "And what do you do?"

"I'm a singer," Stephanie replied. She hummed a bar of her favorite song, an upbeat ditty she'd written called "Always All Right."

"Oh. Creative types."

Jack returned, discreetly bringing two keys. He slipped Stephanie the key to room 4, and she concealed it in her purse. He pocketed another key. Leslie raised an eyebrow in Stephanie's direction but then pretended not to notice. The witch.

"Looks like we're the only ones signed in for tonight," Jack said.

"I don't think they're expecting anyone," said Randy.

"Are you sure?" said Leslie. "The house looks ready for visitors. The lights are all on, the sign was on the front door . . ."

"So where are the owners?"

Stephanie turned on one heel to take in the first level. "The dinner table's set for four."

They all looked through an archway into the dining room opposite the living room.

The room was not lavish, but lovely. A fringed brocade cloth and runner covered the table; the four place settings also included bread plates, salad forks, and dessert spoons. A pitcher of iced tea stood at the near end of the table, beaded with condensation.

Randy went to the table and picked up the pitcher of iced tea. "Anybody thirsty?"

Leslie stepped up. "Randy, that isn't for us." He shot her a look, then filled a glass from one of the place settings. "Randy!" He sipped from the glass, keeping his eyes on her. Stephanie raised an eyebrow in Leslie's direction and then pretended not to notice. So there. Apparently these two had issues of their own.

"So . . . they're expecting four people," said Stephanie.

"Right about now," said Randy.

"Well, they aren't expecting us," said Jack.

"Nope," said Randy, enjoying the tea. "But we're going to be their guests tonight, whether they—" The lights flickered. "Oh, now what?"

The house went black.

Stephanie involuntarily reached out for Jack. "Oh, my Lord."

"Now it's getting fun," she heard Randy say.

⊷

Just like this whole trip, one disaster after another, Jack thought. He looked out the window, now a black rectangle framing a world of bottomless shadows and indistinct shapes. "The yard lights are out too."

"Hold still till we get used to the dark," Leslie said.

"Anybody got a lighter?" Randy asked.

"Stephanie," Jack said. He knew she kept a lighter on hand to offer her smoking friends. He always thought it was weird, since she swore cigarettes were death to the vocal cords, but apparently it was her way of schmoozing. He heard her fumble through her purse, then felt her press the cheap plastic gadget into his hand. He flicked it. Light from the small yellow flame dimly lit the room.

"There you go," said Randy. "At least *she's* prepared. Come on." He headed into the foyer then crossed into the living room. Jack went with him, lighting their way. Randy went to the fireplace and took a decorative oil lamp from the mantel.

"Randy, that's not ours," Leslie called.

Randy took a wooden match from a box on the hearth. The match flared with one scratch on the bricks, and the lamp lit easily. "Now. We can take a look around for candles, matches, a flashlight, anything to take care of this situation—since the owners aren't here to take care of things themselves."

Jack heard a sound he couldn't place. Something resonant. A high note. "Wait a minute!" said Jack, pocketing the lighter.

"What?"

"Shh."

They all listened. Jack thought—

"Cool," said Randy, returning to the foyer, taking the oil lamp with him. "Just like a haunted house, right? Nobody here, then the lights go out, then . . . OOOOOO." He wiggled the fingers of his free hand as the oil lamp cast eerie shadows on his face. "Creaks, and groans, and footsteps in the dark."

Leslie wagged her head in good humor.

"Don't do that," said Stephanie, setting her purse down behind the sofa.

There it was again. "I did hear something," Jack said.

From somewhere in the dark expanse of the old house, timbers groaned under their load and then were silent.

"It's just house noise—," Randy started to say, but Leslie shushed him.

Now, somewhere, floorboards creaked.

"Somebody's here," Stephanie whispered.

Jack put up his hand for silence, cocked his head to hear, listened.

A voice. A song. A child.

He met the eyes of the others, but saw no awareness there. "You hear that?" Randy started to smirk as if Jack was playing around. "I'm not kidding. I hear somebody singing. Sounds like a little girl."

They all listened again, and this time awareness, if not a shade of fear, crossed their faces one by one. They heard it too.

"So the owners have a daughter," Randy said.

Leslie gave a little shrug.

Stephanie only looked at Jack, clearly unnerved.

Two more seconds, and then Randy broke the silence with a commanding voice. "Okay, that's enough Halloween. The kitchen's this way. Let's light this place up."

He led, holding the lamp high. They followed. As a tight band of four, they moved into the dining room, then traveled through an archway, down a short hall, and into a large, well-equipped kitchen.

Randy pointed. "Let's check these cupboards, that pantry over there. Jack, look out on that porch. We're looking for a flashlight, a breaker panel or a fuse box, candles, anything." Then he shouted so loudly Jack flinched. "Hello! Anybody here? You've got company!"

Leslie started going through the cupboards, top and bottom, opening, closing, opening, closing.

Jack opened the back door and used his lighter to probe around the enclosed porch. He found an old icebox and some canned goods on shelves, but nothing they needed at the moment.

━ ━

Stephanie was angry with herself for trembling and hoped the others didn't notice. She'd learned to be brave and independent over the past year—she'd had to. But it was so dark in here; they'd already been through a car wreck and an almost, maybe robbery; and now they were wandering through a big, empty house—

She put her hand to her forehead and tried to get a grip. *Be brave, girl. It's only as bad as you make it. Keep smiling. That's how we get through, remember?*

She tried humming a tune, couldn't think of one, hummed aimlessly anyway.

"How about that pantry?" Randy asked.

Boy, he's bossy. Almost as bossy as Jack.

She found the handle to the closet, but it was hard to see anything inside. Randy had the only light and wouldn't set it down. First she could see into the pantry; then she couldn't. It was deep . . . it was dark . . . her fingers found shelves along the walls . . . it was dark . . . that may have been a mop or something . . . it was dark—

The lights came on. A single bulb dangling on a wire from the center of the ceiling. Stephanie grunted, shielded her eyes. For a second she couldn't see.

"What you doin' in my pantry?"

4

JACK HEARD STEPHANIE'S SCREAM AND WAS at the pantry door in an instant—so were Randy and Leslie. The three collided, then stood staring.

"Screaming like that we save for the outdoors," said a broad-faced woman standing in the pantry, covering her ears. When the screaming stopped, she dropped her hands and took a large jar of applesauce from the shelf.

"I'm sorry," Stephanie gasped. "You startled me."

"Well, it works both ways. I almost thought you were *him*."

Stephanie looked at the others. "Who?"

The woman frowned and handed her the jar. "Here. Pour that in a serving bowl and put a spoon in it." Then she walked into the kitchen, bumping through everyone, went straight to the oven, and peeked inside. For the first time, Jack caught the aroma of a roast. He realized how hungry he was. "Meat's almost ready. Better get the food on the table."

She was big-boned and strong-backed, wearing a housedress with a cheerful flowered pattern. Her graying hair was gathered into a comb behind her head. She turned from the oven. "Well? Am I talking to myself, or are you all standing there?"

Jack was first to come out of the stupor. "Uh, we're, uh, your guests for the night, I think. I'm Jack—" He held out his hand.

"Looking for a bowl?" the woman asked Stephanie. Jack lowered his arm.

Stephanie wasn't but said, "Sure."

Randy stepped forward. "Ma'am, are you the owner of this place?"

"I am. And you're the fellow who helped himself to room 3." She looked past him at Leslie. "Or was that you?"

Leslie put on a disarming smile. "It's both of us. I hope you don't mind—"

"Are you paying for it?"

"Of course."

"Then enjoy it, but keep the noise down." She opened a cupboard and brought down a serving bowl, handing it to Stephanie. "Here, sweetie."

Randy put himself between the middle-aged woman and Stephanie. "We had no idea you were here. It caught us off guard."

She looked at him, then at the lamp in his hand. "The lights are back on."

Randy extinguished the oil lamp and set it on a butcher-block island. "Do you have power failures like this very often?"

She shuffled to the other side of the kitchen. "Only when we have guests." The woman turned to Leslie, "Looking for something to do? Check those peas on the stove and put 'em in a dish." She pulled open a drawer and extracted a dish for that purpose. Leslie set to work. Betty looked at Jack, "Now, what's your problem?"

"Well, actually, we had some . . . car trouble."

"Spikes in the road," said Randy.

"Do you have a phone anywhere—"

The woman came in close, inches from Jack's nose. "Car trouble? That's why you got two rooms? *Car* trouble?" The woman turned to Stephanie. "Is he mad at you or something?"

"Um . . ."

"Can he carry chairs?" The lady turned back to Jack. "Can you carry chairs?"

He nodded. He would have to take mental notes. Use this character in a story sometime.

"Then we're gonna need three more."

"Oh," said Leslie, now apologetic. "You *are* expecting someone else."

"Nope." She pulled plates and saucers from the cupboard and asked Randy, "Know how to set a table?"

"Of course I do. And by the way, my name is Randy Messarue. And this is Les—"

She pushed the plates into his stomach. "Three more place settings."

He nodded in Leslie's direction. "That's Leslie. And you are?"

"Betty. Silverware's in that drawer."

Jack's bewilderment gave way to irritation. "We could really use a phone."

"Don't have none."

"So what do you do when the power goes out?" Randy asked.

"Wait for the guests to leave." Betty waved Jack toward

the hallway with the backs of her fingers. "Chairs! I've got three more in the closet."

He went into the hallway between the kitchen and dining room with no idea where the closet was. There were two doors on his right. He tried the first one—

"Not that one!" Jack jerked his hand away from the knob as if it had burned him. "That's the basement! Nobody goes in the basement! Nobody!"

Oh, for crying out loud. He took a calming breath. "Then why don't you tell me where the closet is?"

She wagged her head and rolled her eyes as if she were dealing with an idiot. "The other door. Try the other door." She turned back into the kitchen, waving him off like unwanted trouble.

Jack opened the next door and found a closet. Inside, three folding chairs leaned against one another, but Jack took his time pulling them out. He needed to breathe a moment, just separate himself from that woman long enough to recover his balance. In one short evening he'd gone from disappointment to anger to fear to exhaustion to frustration, and now, to top it all off, his stomach was growling and the cook was crazy. He heard Stephanie begin to hum in the kitchen.

He wagged his head. Why should he be surprised?

Come on, Jack. After all, it was your decision to turn down that dirt road. You do have to take responsibility for your part . . .

He carried the chairs into the dining room and squeezed them in around the small table as Randy laid out the extra place settings.

"Silverware doesn't match," Randy muttered.

Jack couldn't manage pretending to care.

They headed back to the kitchen, passing Leslie on her way out.

~~~

Leslie took the bowl of peas into the dining room, having to nudge a few plates and glasses aside to make room for it. With three more chairs and place settings, a floral centerpiece, a bowl of applesauce, a pickle dish, a pitcher of iced tea, a bowl of potatoes, condiments, and a soon-to-arrive platter of roast beef, the dining table quickly shifted from close and intimate to packed and crowded. And now the glasses didn't match.

"Coming up behind you." It was Randy with a basket of rolls. She turned.

"We're running out of room."

"We're eating, and we've got a place to spend the night. Don't complain."

She kept her voice down. "Doesn't she strike you as odd?"

"You're the shrink and you're asking me?" He handed her the basket then lowered his own voice. "If I had her people skills, I'd probably have to put spikes on the road to bring in business."

He left her to think about it.

Leslie turned back to the table—

She gasped, fumbled the basket. The rolls tumbled onto the table, dancing on the plates, bouncing off the glasses. One landed in a water glass with a splash.

A man sat there, watching her with obvious fascination, a napkin tucked down the front of his brown bib overalls.

She had never felt so embarrassed—in recent times, at least. "I am so sorry. I didn't see you come in."

"You're pretty," he said, not taking his eyes off her. His boldness gave her pause. She guessed him somewhere in his twenties, a gorilla of a man with biceps the size of his neck and short-cropped blond hair. He wore a soiled T-shirt under the overalls. His stubbled face was dirty and shiny with sweat, and she could smell him.

"Um, my name is Leslie."

He eyed her as if she were naked.

"And you are?" she prodded.

"Better clean up your mess before Mama finds out."

Leslie hastened to gather up the fallen rolls, plucking one from the center of the table, another from a dinner plate. She leaned to grab another from the plate next to his.

He looked down her blouse without the slightest shame.

She straightened, incredulous. He smiled as if she'd done him a favor.

Professional detachment. Emotional distance from the subject. Don't let his issues become yours.

She knew she was glowering, but he'd caught her off guard and vulnerable, two things she'd sworn never to be again. She swallowed, willing herself to be professional, clinical. She softened her expression. "Now," she said in a nurse's bedside tone, "we don't do that."

He wouldn't take his eyes off her. They were childish eyes, vacant and unblinking. What was she dealing with? Mild retardation, apparently. Social ineptitude for certain.

His eyes finally went elsewhere—to her hand, still holding a roll. He pointed.

She rotated her hand and saw a small trickle of blood near the knuckle. "Now, how did I do that?" It must have happened when he startled her. She put the roll with the others, then pulled a small hanky from her pocket to cover the wound. She checked the table and basket for any sharp points or edges. Nothing obvious here.

He reached into a glass, pulled out the sodden roll, and held it out to her, heavy and dripping.

She took it from him and their fingers touched.

Leslie tasted bile.

"All right," Betty hollered from the kitchen, "everybody wash up."

Of course, thought Randy. *Perfect. Everybody handle the food and dishes and then wash up.* He gave Jack and Stephanie a once-over. All that road dust.

The others went up to their rooms to wash. Randy spotted a bathroom opposite the closet in the hallway and thought that more efficient.

The bathroom was clean, with white fixtures, pink towels, a pink bath mat, and a soap dish with red soaps in the shape of roses. The faucet provided hot water in an instant.

Randy soaped up. *Such a contrast. How can anyone so inept at hospitality maintain such a lovely facility? And where are the personnel, or do they always put their guests to work?* Right now he'd give the service in this place a one-star rating.

He felt some tension ease out of his spine as the water massaged his hands. He put in the stopper, then cupped his hands and brought a splash to his face. He allowed the sensation to block out the Wayside Inn for a moment.

"You done yet?" The rumbling voice was followed by the smell of sweat and machine oil, the touch of another body crowding him. Randy opened his eyes.

He saw a reflection in the mirror—a big man looming over him looking none too happy.

Randy reached for the towel by the sink. "Well, good evening to you too. I'm washing up for dinner."

The man snatched the towel away and looked about to slap him with it. "Don't you have a bathroom of your own?" The man was built like a bull without an ounce of fat, big brown eyes, and a long filthy face with a hawk nose. Bald head with three long scars above his left ear.

From somewhere long ago, a deep terror flashed through Randy's body. He slapped it down with a cold, controlled temper he'd honed through years of such encounters. He faced the man, his muscles steeling and ready for whatever might come. "Right now it's this one." He held out his hand. "Towel."

Clearly, the man was not expecting that kind of answer. He held on to the towel, then stuck a dirty finger in Randy's face, his eyes red and bulging. "Guess you don't know whose house you're in."

"They're going to hear about you, bud. Count on it." Randy snatched the towel back and dried his face, careful never to cover his eyes. Then, when he was good and ready, he tossed the towel back. "Try making yourself presentable. You have guests."

He walked out, keeping an eye on the brute. The big man bent over the sink and splashed in the water Randy had left in the sink. "You like the water, don't you?" He gave Randy a sly smile, a leering gaze.

The deep terror returned. Randy felt himself tip and reached out to touch the wall.

He hurried past the dining room into the foyer, walked a few slow circles to calm himself, check the rage, force a smile. He went back to the dining room still trying to relax his clenched fists.

5

BETTY WAS JUST A LITTLE FRAZZLED AS SHE herded everyone into the dining room. "Hey! You like your food cold? Come on, come on!"

"If you don't get it, the hogs will." Stephanie giggled.

Betty failed to see the humor in that.

Jack took the chair to Betty's left, which put him next to the big guy in the brown overalls. The fellow didn't seem too talkative. From his gawky expression, Jack surmised he may have had too much lead in his water. Stephanie took the chair to Betty's right.

Randy came in from the foyer, his smile saying one thing, his body saying another. He paused for an awkward moment, sizing up where Jack and Stephanie were seated; then he selected the chair next to Stephanie. "May I?"

"You may," she said with a bright smile.

He sat next to her, and Leslie sat next to him.

That left one empty chair.

"Stoo-wart!" Betty bellowed. "You stuck on that commode, or did you fall in?"

Jack caught the others exchanging careful little looks, sitting quietly, waiting, acting like polite adults.

Now that they were sitting, maybe he could finally get some answers. He turned to Betty. "Anyway, we've all had some car trouble, and if we could get a telephone or you could tell us where we might find one—"

Her eyes were on the archway leading toward the kitchen. "Stewart!"

A toilet flushed. Heavy footfalls came down the hall.

Randy joined ranks with Jack. "Betty, are you listening? We have a problem here and we need—"

A big man came through the archway, a wide leather belt draped over his hand. The buckle jingled like a horse's bridle. He sent a knife-eyed glare Randy's way.

Randy caught it, cooked up a glare of his own, and shot it back.

Apparently these two had already met.

"Siddown, Stewart," Betty said. "We're always waiting on you."

Stewart fed the belt through the first loop on his trousers, then the second, then the third, as if making a show of it, his eyes always on Randy. When the belt made it all the way around, he cinched up the buckle and sat.

"So you're Stewart," Jack said, just to see if this guy talked.

"Who are you?" the man replied, not smiling.

"Jack Singleton. I'm a writer, live up near Tuscaloosa."

"What about your wife?" asked Betty. Jack didn't understand.

"I live in Tuscaloosa too," Stephanie replied. "When I'm not on the road. We're getting a divorce."

Jack focused on the bowl of peas. *Well, let's just tell the world. And for the record, we haven't agreed to that. Yet.*

"Help yourself to the peas and pass 'em on," Betty said. Looking at Stephanie, Betty said, "So he'd just as soon not talk about you, is that it?"

Was she baiting him, trying to stir something up? He didn't bite; he just took a spoonful of peas. Stephanie kept smiling and dished up her potatoes without comment.

Leslie speared a slice of roast beef while Randy held the platter. "It's a lovely place you have here, just like the old South." Jack was grateful for her intervention. He tried to thank her with his eyes.

"Not as lovely as you," said Stewart.

Leslie smiled. Randy didn't. "Randall and I are from Montgomery. I'm a professor of psychology at Alabama State University, and he's CEO of Home Suite Home—you know the hotel chain?"

"Are you married?" he asked, his first words at the table.

"Pete here would like to get himself hitched," Betty said, patting his hand like a mother would.

Leslie kept her eyes on the roast beef as she served Randy. "We thought we'd take a little road trip, spend a few days in the Talladega National Forest. We weren't planning on dropping in on you like this."

"Are you married?" Pete asked again.

She finally looked at him. "No, but we're very close."

"They're shacking up," said Betty. She cackled. "Probably gonna violate each other up in room 3."

Leslie's mouth fell open slightly, but Randy managed a wry smile and said, "Probably."

"You can be my wife," said Pete.

Leslie spoke down to him like a teacher addressing a kindergartner. "Well, thank you. I'm flattered, but I'm afraid I'm spoken for."

"Eh, she'd be quite a catch, now, wouldn't she, Pete?" said Stewart, seeming to contemplate the prospect.

Jack stole a quick, discreet glance at Leslie to understand what Pete and Stewart saw that he didn't. If beauty was the determining factor here, why weren't they all over Stephanie? His eyes went to his wife, checking her out by way of comparison . . .

Her pursed lips sent him a signal that she didn't care for such comparisons.

He tried the potatoes. A little mealy.

"Stewart, don't encourage him," said Betty, a wad of food in her mouth.

Pete pointed at Leslie. "I want her."

Randy cut in, eyeing Stewart. "Speaking of catches, where do you suppose those spikes in the road came from?"

Stewart sniffed.

"Jack," said Betty, "why don't you tell us about your wife? Leslie told us about Randall."

Jack jumped at the chance for a little damage control. "I'd be delighted to talk about her." Stephanie rolled her eyes. "She's a singer and a songwriter. Country, mostly. She has a great band, sings in clubs and lounges around Tuscaloosa, sometimes Birmingham. Got a good job in Atlanta once."

"And aren't you glad?"

About what? "I think she's done very well—"

Betty asked Stephanie, "You having fun, sweetie?"

Stephanie smiled at Betty and at Jack. "Yes, as a matter of fact. I'm having a lot of fun."

"I s'pose you're on the radio."

Jack said no and then wished he hadn't.

Stephanie's eyes turned down toward her napkin. "But someday," she said.

"Have some iced tea." Betty poured her some. "Want more ice?"

"No thanks."

"You sure?"

"Uh-huh."

"I can get you some more."

"No, thanks; I'm fine."

Randy asked, "So you do listen to the radio?"

"Don't have one," Stewart replied.

"No radio. No telephone either?"

Stewart met Randy's eyes as if challenged. "We have what we want. We don't need what we don't want."

Jack said, "Well, we could sure stand to talk to somebody in the outside world. We've both had our cars damaged—"

"—by spikes someone left in the road," said Randy. "You did hear me mention that, didn't you?"

"*He* did it," said Betty.

"Who?"

Betty just chewed.

"Um, maybe you have some neighbors nearby who might have a phone?" asked Jack.

Betty swallowed and stood. "Let me get you some ice, sweetie."

"No, thank you," said Stephanie. "Really, you don't have to; I'm fine."

But Betty headed for the kitchen.

Pete pointed at Leslie again. "I want her to be my wife."

Leslie sighed.

"Yeah," said Stewart, "she probably wouldn't mind too much, considering where she's been."

Leslie paled just a shade. "I'm taken," she said.

"Makes me wonder how many times she's been a 'wife' before."

"She's taken," said Randy a little louder, and Jack could see the veins and muscles in Randy's neck restraining curses.

"Taken once, taken again."

"Stewart." Randy leaned toward Stewart, gesturing with his fork as if it were a dart. "I'd like you to make it clear to your son Pete that Leslie is not interested in being his wife, and we would both appreciate it if you and he would drop this subject—and while you're at it, try looking at something else."

"Randy, it's oka—"

"And just whose table are you sitting at, young man?" Stewart bristled.

Stephanie said, "Pete, I can sing a song for you."

Jack and Pete looked at Stephanie. *Uh-oh.*

"That's a very good question," Randy said, rising now. "Just what kind of innkeepers don't use matching silverware and glasses, aren't even here when their guests arrive, don't have a telephone . . ."

Stephanie started singing. "Hold my hand, walk me through the darkness . . ."

Jack hated that song too.

"Randy." Leslie put her hand over his.

He brushed off her cautionary touch. ". . . and then put the guests to work. What kind of low-overhead excuse for an inn are you running here?"

". . . we can make it, dear, if we make it together . . ."

"As long as your feet are under this table," Stewart growled, "you will watch that mouth of yours or *button* it!"

"And let's talk about the cars!" Randy demanded. "Pretty strange for both our cars to be spiked not far from your establishment, don't you think?"

". . . we can make it through the night . . ."

Oh, Stephanie, just stop.

The tendons on Randy's neck were showing. "And stranger still that you and Betty won't say a word about it."

Leslie winced and touched her left cheek. Jack noticed a spot of blood. She examined the tines of her fork.

Pete looked curiously—then hungrily—at Leslie.

"And you think you can just help yourself to anything in this place anytime you want?" Stewart said, dropping clenched fists on the table. "Take our rooms, take our lamps, drink our tea, use our bathroom . . ."

"Am I a guest here, or aren't I?" Randy shouted. "Who do you think the rooms and lamps and tea are for? And as far as that bathroom goes—"

Jack was in no mood to referee, but he was getting a bad taste in his mouth. He set down his silverware. "Hey, listen, everybody, look at the bright side here—" Stephanie stopped singing. "Stewart and Betty, you have guests, and that's business, and that's what you want. Now, we've all fumbled a bit, we've had a rocky start, sure, but we can make this work—"

"Now there's a line I've heard before," Stephanie muttered under her breath.

Jack heard her but pretended not to. "We have a wonderful place to spend the night, dinner's on, the food's great—"

The bite that just dropped to his stomach wasn't that great.

Randy noticed Leslie's cut. "What happened?"

She was irritated, dabbing her cheek with her napkin. "I stuck myself again."

"I can kiss it and make it better," said Pete.

Betty strode in with a bucket of ice. "Herrrrre we are." One of her fingernails was blackened. Jack hadn't noticed that before.

"I don't need any more ice," Stephanie insisted, taking a bite of roast. She gagged and spit it out, pushed back from the table.

"Problem?" Randy asked, obviously hoping for one.

Jack looked at the meat on his plate.

It was moving.

Leslie squealed, her hand over her mouth, her eyes on her plate.

Stewart stabbed a slab of meat and crammed the whole thing into his mouth. Pete did the same, filling one cheek.

Jack looked closely at the roast beef on his plate and felt sick.

Tiny white worms were squirming, writhing, tunneling through the meat.

"Sweetie," said Betty, "I brought you more ice."

Stephanie watched her drop a cube into the tea.

Jack's peas were sagging; putrid juice puddled under them. "Looks like we took too long to eat," he said. He thought he'd better add a little chuckle to soften things.

Leslie threw down her fork and almost shouted at Pete, "Will you *please* stop staring at me?"

"Can you blame him?" Stewart asked.

"That's it," Randy said, taking hold of Leslie's arm and lifting her to her feet. "If you'll excuse us."

"Sit down," Stewart said.

"Leslie, come on." They stepped around their chairs.

"SIT DOWN!" Stewart yelled, half rising.

Randy swore, but Stewart laughed in his face. "Kid, you're nothin'."

Leslie tugged at Randy's arm until he left with her.

Betty grinned her gap-toothed grin at Stephanie. "Don't tell me you don't like ice, dear." She lifted a cube from the bucket and shoved it under Stephanie's nose. "You think about it all the time, don't you?"

Stephanie shied back. "No. Please, I don't."

Jack leaned across the table. "Whoa, whoa, wait a minute now!"

Betty followed Stephanie with the ice cube, wiggling it in her face. "I don't hear you singing."

What was it with these people? "Betty, she doesn't want any ice, and she doesn't want to sing. Now put that down!"

Stephanie's voice trembled. "*We can make it through the night . . .*"

Enough. More than enough. Jack went to Stephanie's side. "It's been fun."

Betty cackled again. "You can't rescue that one, boy. Nope, she don't want to be rescued."

Stephanie ran from the room.

Jack ran after her and caught up in the foyer.

She smiled through tears. "Isn't this the strangest

place you've ever been? It's just so . . . so . . ." She started a laugh; it became a sob. "I can't stay here."

He held her to keep her from bolting. "Steph, I understand. But we have to think this through."

"Think *what* through?"

"Reality," said Randy. He and Leslie were near the stairs. Leslie steadied herself with one hand on the railing; with the other she held a hanky to her cheek. She was breathing slow, rhythmic breaths with her eyes closed. "Such as where to go in the middle of the night in the Alabama backwoods without wheels."

"What about Lawdale?" Jack wondered aloud. "He said he drives that road every morning. He'll see our wrecked cars."

"Lawdale?" Randy asked.

"Highway patrol," Jack said.

Stephanie peered over Jack's shoulder, and her eyes filled with dismay.

Jack looked.

Betty, Stewart, and Pete were coming their way, walking shoulder to shoulder with Stewart in the middle. Betty looked hurt. "Always running. What are you always running for?"

Stewart was about ready to take that belt to somebody. "The food was fine till you came in here."

Randy stepped out, hand extended in a clear warning. "Keep your distance, please."

Stephanie bolted for the front door, flung it open, and dashed out onto the veranda. Jack ran after her.

She pulled up at the top step, her hands over her mouth.

"Steph, take it easy now. You—"

She was trembling. She took a step backward. Another step. She was peering down the flagstone walkway.

Jack approached and touched the small of her back—and then he saw it too.

Halfway between the house and the gate loomed the immense shape of a man, a shadowy silhouette veiled by a light rain. A duster draped the body to midcalf, and the face was obscured by the shadow of a wide-brimmed, drooping hat. The man held a shotgun, the barrel glinting in the lights lining the path.

Behind them, Betty sucked in a rasping breath and hissed, "Get inside."

They lingered, unsure.

She lunged and took hold of them. "Get inside! It's *him*!"

The figure started walking their way, the duster billowing, the boot heels clacking on the stones. The barrel of the shotgun swung forward.

6

JACK AND STEPHANIE WERE ALREADY BACK-
pedaling toward the door when they tore their eyes away
from the apparition, turned, and dashed inside.

Jack slammed the door shut and locked it. He
snatched a chair from the foyer and wedged it under the
knob, momentarily uncertain if they were any safer inside.
Well, their hosts were crazy, but they didn't sport a
shotgun.

Randy rushed from the stairs, demanding, "What is
it? What's going on?"

"Get away from the door!" Betty hissed, flicking off the
foyer lights.

"What are you doing?" Randy said.

"You don't want him to see you."

They fell silent, motionless, and heard the sharp,
staccato clicks of boot heels on the veranda. A shadow
rose upon the door's stained glass, a hulking shape topped
by a broad-brimmed hat.

The barrel of the shotgun came up against the glass.
Tap, tap, tap.

Jack and Stephanie pressed themselves against the wall to the side of the door, watching.

Tap, tap, tap.

Leslie whispered, "Who is it?"

Stephanie shook her head, then mouthed and pantomimed, *He has a gun.*

Leslie drew herself up and asked in a calm and quiet voice, "Well, maybe he's a law officer. Why don't we ask him who he is and what he wants?"

Stephanie shook her head.

"He's no law officer," Jack whispered. He grabbed a vase off a stand and took the stand for a weapon, holding it high and ready. "Remember the spikes in the road?" He caught Randy's eye and jerked his head toward the door. "I don't think he's from AAA."

Randy stole close to the wall, taking hold of a chair. "He knows we're in here. That was the whole idea."

"What are we gonna do?" Stephanie squeaked. "Oh, dear God, help us."

Where is the loony crew? Jack did a quick check and saw the three peeking through the dining room's archway. *Best not to expect any help from those three.* Betty disappeared from view. *Click.* Dining room lights went out. Stepping out of the prismatic light coming through the stained glass, Jack tightened his grip on the vase stand. He'd never assaulted anyone with a piece of furniture before.

Randy braced himself against the wall near the lock, the chair ready in his hands. He called, "Who are you?"

The lock began to creak and jiggle.

Jack could feel Stephanie's trembling body next to him.

"Not a chance, pal," Jack shouted, making Stephanie flinch. "The door's locked, you're outnumbered, and we're armed."

Leslie ducked behind the registration table and peered over the top of it.

There was a *clank* like a dead bolt sliding home.

Randy raised the chair above his head.

The shadow remained for a moment, then retreated from the glass. The boot heels clicked across the boards, down the steps, dropped to the flagstones, and went away.

There were audible sighs of relief in the room, but Jack felt no safer, not yet, and he did not part with the vase stand. He asked Betty, "Who was that?"

"It was him," Betty said.

"Who's *him*?" Randy demanded.

"The devil himself."

Leslie stood up behind the desk, her voice professionally calm. "Betty, it's all right. Just tell us who he is and what he wants."

"You'd better start prayin' that lawman friend of yours shows up, is all I can say."

Randy checked the lock.

The knob broke off in his hand.

He cursed. "He did something to the door." He stuck his fingers through the resulting hole, jiggled the latch. The door held fast. Randy banged on the door, kicked it, banged it again. It would not open.

Jack set the stand down and tried to find any crack he could pry into with his fingers. No good.

"You have *got* to get us out of here, Jack," Stephanie cried.

Randy and Jack looked at each other, speaking the same thought—"The back door!"—at the same time, the screen door to the enclosed back porch squeaked.

The men ran through the house, through the dark, groping, skidding at the corner, through the dining room, through the hall, into the light of the kitchen, and across to the back door.

The lock was creaking when they got there.

Jack slammed against the door, grabbed the knob, and tried to twist it.

A stronger hand on the other side torqued the knob against him.

Randy's hand wrapped around his, and together they tried to turn the knob, tried to pull the door open.

Through the pane, Jack saw the drooping hat and, just under the brim where a face should be, a plate of steel with ice-cold eyes watching him through two jagged holes.

There was a *clank* like a dead bolt sliding home.

The knob broke off in their hands, throwing them off balance.

They recovered in time to see the figure crossing the back porch and going out the tattered screen door, the shotgun slung over his shoulder.

Randy exploded in a stream of profanity and grabbed up a broom, ready to dash the handle through the glass. Jack stopped him. "Easy now, easy. Don't lose it."

Randy stood down, got a grip, and threw the broom aside.

The lights in the kitchen flickered, dimmed, and went out.

Another stream of expletives.

Jack stood still and remained quiet, trying to think. *What would happen next? What did this creep have in mind?*

Clumsy footsteps clattered and galloped into the kitchen, and he could see the others as dark shapes against the cabinets.

"Jack?" Stephanie cried.

"Over here," he answered.

She made her way toward him, and he took hold of her hand. She pried it loose but stayed close.

Leslie asked, "Did you see who it was?"

"He was wearing a mask," Jack said, "some tin contraption."

Stephanie groaned and slid down a cabinet to the floor.

Randy pushed himself away from the wall and strode up to Betty and Stewart. "Now you are going to tell us exactly what's going on. Who is this guy?"

"I think he's here to kill us," Betty answered.

The stunned silence lasted only a moment.

"Are you in on this?" Randy got in Stewart's face. "Did you rig the locks to break off?"

Stewart's eyes locked on him like a tiger on its prey. Jack touched Randy's arm but spoke to Betty, "How do you know?"

"Is he connected to the spikes in the road?" Randy demanded.

"You think you're better off stumbling around in the dark?" Betty asked.

Stumbling around . . . ? "Better off than what?" Jack asked.

"Help me find that lamp," Randy ordered no one in particular. "Get me some matches."

Jack, Randy, and Leslie groped about the counter in the dim light until Randy found the lamp he had brought in before dinner. Betty produced a box of matches from a drawer. Soon they all stood in the orange glow, the flame casting eerie, dancing shadows across their faces.

Jack looked toward the windows. He saw faint orange reflections from the room, but outside there was only blackness. "We'd better make sure the house is secure. Just make sure we're safe for the time being, and then we can—"

"Secure the house!" Randy said. "Check the doors, check the windows, and let's get some lights back on."

"Do you have a gun in the house?" Jack asked the strange family.

"Got my shotgun," Stewart replied. "And buckshot."

"Then let's get it—"

Something bumped and creaked above their heads.

They froze in the glow of the lamp, eyes turned upward, listening.

A thump. Another creak. A succession of thumps—like footsteps.

"He's on the roof," Betty whispered.

Randy kicked a cupboard door and started pacing in a show of some bravado, but Jack noticed the sheen of sweat on his forehead. "He's trying for an upstairs window."

Betty looked toward the kitchen windows. "What's wrong with these?"

Randy grabbed the lamp. Jack and Stewart followed him as he took off down the hall toward the stairway, leaving the women in the dark.

—◆—

"Jack!" Stephanie shouted. "Jack! Don't you leave us here!" *Gone again. If you make me cope alone one more time, I'll . . . I'll . . .* She covered her face.

"Stephanie, come on now, it's time to be brave," Leslie said. "There's a time for feelings, and there's a time for strength. This is a time for strength. You have to find it."

Stephanie had no more country-girl smiles left in her tonight. "Don't you talk down to me, Dr. Shrink. I am not your patient."

"Stephanie—"

"And I'm no helpless little bimbo either, if that's what you're thinking, and just for the record, Jack and I are still married." Leslie touched her shoulder, but Stephanie jerked away. "Don't touch me!"

They could hear the running, frantic footfalls of the men upstairs going from room to room, apparently checking all the windows.

"The men are still between us and . . . whoever he is," Leslie offered.

"Humph," grunted Betty, only a shadow in the dark kitchen. "If he wanted in, he'd be in."

Stephanie clung to her anger. She called up her mental catalog of Jack's offenses toward her and started thumbing through them. *You are so insensitive to me, always leaving me alone . . .*

"Can't we get the lights back on?" she heard Leslie say. *. . . and you have never understood what I really need.*

"Nope," Betty replied.

Stephanie recalled the anniversary of Melissa's birthday . . .

"There was another oil lamp on the mantel," Leslie said.

. . . *when Jack completely broke down. Abandoned her again. I want to move on, but you just can't, Jack.*

"Come on," Betty said.

You loved Melissa more than you ever loved me. It wasn't my fault.

"Stephanie."

It wasn't my fault.

"Stephanie." Leslie's voice jerked her out of her mental tirade. Leslie and Betty were leaving the kitchen. Stephanie followed, placing her hands on the walls to guide her as she moved into the hall.

"Wait a minute," Leslie said. "Where's Pete?"

Betty kept moving, leading them into the foyer, which now felt like a subterranean cavern—limitless, unknowable, so dark. Stephanie not only felt the wall, she was sure it felt her. Her fingertips tingled.

Leslie asked again, insistent this time, "Betty, where is Pete?"

"He likes to hide," Betty said.

"Hide?" Stephanie saw Leslie look back over her shoulder and stumble.

"Oh, are we having *feelings*, Doctor?" Stephanie said.

"Not at all!"

Stephanie found her ruffled tone quite satisfying. Dr. Shrink had a chink in her armor. *Ha. Dr. Shrink has a chink.* That was something to sing about.

Betty rounded the corner into the living room and threaded her way through the furniture while Leslie and Stephanie followed with the cautiousness of unfamiliarity. Stephanie could barely discern the huge fireplace, but Betty had no trouble finding and grabbing a second oil lamp from the mantel.

The flare of the match was blinding. Stephanie squinted while Betty lit the lamp and placed it on the hearth. The room appeared in the soft yellow light.

Stephanie and Leslie scanned the sofa, the chairs, the coffee table, and the bookshelves, looking for anything out of place. Stephanie didn't see any shapes or shadows that could be Pete, but this room offered an abundance of places to hide.

A dancing, swinging light shone into the foyer from above, casting elongated shadows of the stair railing and three men on the walls and floor. The guys were coming down the stairs.

"We think he's off the roof," Randy reported. "He didn't get in."

"Considering the locks, I'm beginning to wonder if he wants to keep *us* in," Jack said.

Stephanie asked, "Did you find the gun?"

Leslie leaned close and predicted, "Randy will have it."

Randy led the trio into the living room, carrying the shotgun, loading cartridges. Jack carried the lamp. Stewart brought up the rear, as grim as a thundercloud, boots clomping down the stairs. "He may have left, but we can never be sure," Randy barked. "The upstairs is secure for now."

"None of the windows will open," Jack reported grimly.

"There are seven of us and only one of him," Randy said. "Isn't that right, Stewart?"

Stewart didn't answer, maybe just to spite him.

Betty dug through a stack of newspapers in a basket on the hearth and pulled out a section. She crouched, then flattened it open next to the lamp. "So you want to know who he is?"

She tapped a news article on the front page and stepped aside.

COUPLE FOUND DEAD

Stephanie crowded in with the others, skimming the key phrases: ". . . man and wife, found dead in abandoned house . . . possible suicide, but authorities have not ruled out homicide . . . similarities to other deaths . . . dead for almost two weeks before they were found . . ."

Oh, dear God.

"Seems like it's been going on forever," Betty whispered, her eyes glistening in the lamplight. "People going into old houses and never coming out, and when somebody finds 'em, they been dead so long it's hard to tell how. But me and Stewart, we know it's him."

No, it's not him, right? It can't be him. Not here, not now.

"Who is he?" asked Randy.

"The cops are still trying to find out. We call him White, after the first family he took down. He's been busy in these parts. We were wondering when he'd get around to us."

"Well, nobody's going to die in this house," Randy said. "We'll assign guard posts and hold him off until someone finds our cars—"

Right. Nobody's going to die. Everything's going to be all right. Always all right . . .

A distant thumping. Some creaking. All eyes went toward the ceiling.

"He's still up there," Leslie said with a side look at Randy. "He's still on the roof."

Randy pumped the shotgun once.

"Why the roof?" Jack asked. "Why the roof when any window on the main floor would be easy enough to break through? This guy has to be following a plan."

Then came a sound: a weird, tinny rattling like a soda can falling down a narrow well, careening, pinging, and clinking off the sides. It was close, maybe in the room. Stephanie ducked and swiveled, her hands raised to protect her head. Randy swept the room with the shotgun, making Jack and Stewart duck.

"Pete?" Leslie said, her voice tight with alarm.

"No," Betty said.

Poof. Something landed in the fireplace, sending up a little cloud of ash. It bounced onto the hearth, rolled forward with a gritty, metallic sound, and came to rest inches from the edge.

Jack brought his lamp closer. Betty approached it.

"Don't touch it," Stephanie said.

Betty leaned in for a closer look. "You're right, writer boy. He doesn't want in."

Jack reached down and picked it up.

It was an old soup can, the label faded and half-gone, the print now obscured by a bold message scrawled in black marker. Jack sat on the hearth, set down the lamp, and rotated the can as he read aloud:

Welcome to my house.
House rules:
1. God came to my house and I killed him.
2. I will kill anyone who comes to my house
as I killed God.
3. Give me one dead body, and I
might let rule two slide.
Game over at dawn.

He passed the can to Randy, who read the message to himself. Stephanie began to shake. Leslie touched her arm, and this time, Stephanie took her hand.

Above them, the sound of boot heels crossed the roof, descended the back side, and then stepped off.

Silence.

7

10:27 PM

STEPHANIE WAS THE LAST ONE TO HOLD THE can, rotating it back and forth as she read the message several times over. Jack could hear her quick breaths. "Does he mean . . . ?"

"It means he's one sick character," Randy said, scanning the room like a sentry.

"It's psychological," Leslie said. "He's playing a mind game."

"Except for the dead people," Randy replied, nodding toward the newspaper on the hearth.

"But that's impossible." Leslie looked at Randy, then Jack, then Stephanie. "He doesn't actually expect us to kill each other."

"Not each other." Randy snatched the can from Stephanie and read it one more time. "Just one."

Jack favored Leslie's theory. "I think he wants to divide us, get us at each other's throats."

Betty cackled low.

"Something funny?" Randy asked.

"That'll be easy enough," she said.

Randy leaned toward her. "You're speaking for your-self, of course?"

"We'll find out, won't we?"

"What *is* it with you?"

Jack extended his hand, not touching either of them, just enough to slip in a word. "Hey, come on. We don't have to play his game. We can choose."

"Hoooo!" Betty hooted, twisting her neck to look up at him. "Listen to *you.*"

Leslie brought her wristwatch closer to the lamp. "Ten thirty. Dawn's at six. That gives us seven and a half hours."

"Six seventeen, to be precise." Everyone looked at Stewart. He shrugged. "I have an interest in these things."

Randy snorted. "I won't need that long. I'm ending this right now." He grabbed the lamp off the hearth and strode toward the foyer, shotgun in hand.

Betty took a seat on one of the chairs, mildly interested. Stewart sank onto the couch, a comfortable spectator.

Jack went after him. "Randy."

"Stay back. This'll only take a second."

Leslie followed as far as the archway, then turned back to the living room and said, "Take cover. He's really going to do it."

Before Jack could stop him, Randy had reached the front door, set the lamp on the floor, and taken aim.

Jack wasn't concerned about the door, just Randy and all human bystanders. "Randy, be sure you know—"

Boom! The shotgun spit white fire, and the percussion rattled the house. The lead shot shattered the stained glass.

To Jack, the hole looked large enough to squeeze through. "That should do it. Why don't you put the gun down—"

Randy pumped and fired again, peppering the door, the jamb, the bolt. In the living room, Stephanie screamed. The door quivered as chips of wood flew into the room. The foyer filled with blue smoke.

———

Randy grunted as he chambered a third cartridge. He leveled the shotgun at his hip and centered the barrel on the lock. Fire, lead, and smoke exploded from the barrel; the recoil bruised him. The doorjamb shattered. The dead bolt fell free.

He knew even as he pulled the trigger that his crazy display was asinine given their predicament, but he couldn't stop himself. His own fear had taken over. The realization only steeped his anger.

Try to mess with my mind . . .

One more round rattled the windows, and the door's hinges creaked. He pumped the action, ready to go again—

The chamber was empty. He patted his pockets, then hollered over his shoulder at Jack, "Give me more shells."

Jack just stood there, almost hidden behind the lamp-lit smoke. Randy knew he had more rounds in his pockets, but he wasn't digging after them. "Randy," he said, "the door's open. Give it a rest."

"You bet your life the door's open! Give me some shells before that creep crawls in here!"

Jack still didn't move.

Jack knew Randy's point was valid; they were vulnerable now to danger from outside. But that didn't mean things weren't dangerous inside too. *Give me one dead body* . . . "Why don't you let me take the gun for a while?"

Randy put his face within an inch of Jack's. "Gimme those shells! That creep's still out there!"

"Randy. Just take a short break. Let me have the gun."

Randy wrapped both hands around the weapon. "*I've* got the gun!" He shouted toward the women, "Come on! Let's move, let's get out of here! The shells, Jack! Let's have 'em!"

Leslie spoke from the shadows, "Randy, just let Jack hold the gun until—"

"Shut up! I'm in charge here!"

Jack heard an engine rev. Through the open front door he could see headlights playing about the front yard.

"All right," Leslie conceded, her voice controlled. "You're in charge, Randy." She and Stephanie stepped into the foyer. Leslie went to Randy and put an arm around him. "You're in charge." She stroked his shoulders. "You're the one, Randy. Good job." It seemed to settle him, at least make him reasonable.

Stephanie stood alone in the haze, clutching herself in fear. Her eyes were on those headlights sweeping around out front—

With a lurch, a rattle, and the growl of a half-muffled engine, the headlights lumbered over a flower bed, through a hedge, and onto the flagstone walk. From the fenders and the roundish cab stark against the stone wall, Jack realized it was an old pickup truck. It turned toward the house, disappearing behind the blinding headlights, backlighting a curtain of pouring rain. The light beams blasted through the front door, cutting a rectangular tunnel of brilliance through the smoke.

Jack found himself in that rectangle, his shadow extending behind him as he stood mesmerized, wondering, guessing—but only for an instant.

Whoever was driving that old heap opened the throttle. The vehicle lurched forward, accelerating up the flagstone walk.

Right for the front door.

"Look out! Look out!"

They scattered to the left and right, running for cover, knocking things over, tripping in the shadows and smoke.

Jack was close to the dining room and fled in that direction, the headlights burning against his back, his frantic shadow running in front of him.

The engine's roar, the smashing and splintering of lumber, the screech of metal, the shattering of glass, the crunching of wallboard, trim, and fixtures, all melded into one bone-jarring, earsplitting *crash* as the truck climbed the steps, leaped over the veranda, and punched its way through the front wall of the house. Jack heard screams as he dived and hit the table as bits of wallboard, shards of vases, and a spray of rotten food rained down on him from a roiling cloud of plaster dust.

The skewed lights from the truck flickered, then died.

"Stephanie!" he yelled.

He pulled his feet under him and stood, unsteady,

unsure which direction the foyer was. Turning, squinting, searching through the dark and dust, he sighted a
fuzzy center of orange light bouncing and swinging in
the haze. He followed it, stumbling on debris.

"Leslie!" Randy called, the light moving about in the
murk as Randy searched. "Leslie!"

"Over here," came Leslie's voice.

The light zipped across Jack's vision, across the foyer
into the dining room.

"You're bleeding," Randy cried.

"Stephanie!" Jack called. "Are you all right?"

"I'm okay," she answered, and then he saw her
emerge as out of a fog, meeting him in the middle of the
foyer. He held her and, under the circumstances, she let
him.

The oil lamp returned to the foyer, floating in the
cloud, held high in Randy's hand. Randy was helping
Leslie along with his other arm. She held a hanky to her
forehead. A trickle of blood stained her right cheek, a
mirror twin to the cut she'd sustained during dinner.

"I'm all right," she kept insisting, as if trying to convince herself. "I'm all right. It's just a scratch."

Randy turned his lamp toward the damage. The front
doorway was gone—no frame, no door, no lintel. Shards
of glass, splintered molding, broken pottery, and dashed
houseplants lay everywhere; puzzle pieces of wallboard
dangled from shreds of wallpaper. In place of the door
was the battered, crumpled nose of a brown truck, its
windshield cracked like a collage of spiderwebs, the roof
collapsed, the fenders folded back, the headlights broken
and walleyed. Steam hissed from the radiator as water
trickled onto the hardwood.

Randy let go of Leslie. "Where's the shotgun?"

Nobody saw it.

Randy spun, casting the lamplight in all directions. The dust was still thick in the air. "Where's the shotgun?"

He held the lamp high, letting the light penetrate the crack-webbed windshield and the collapsed cab.

No sign of the driver.

For several long seconds they stood in the gritty air with the taste of dust in their mouths and the pricking particles in their eyes—staring, disbelieving, and then realizing that the front wall had sagged and closed around the hulk of the truck, sealing off the exit.

Jack could read in their silence what he was feeling himself: the game had not ended. If anything, it was just beginning. "I think we should try to find that shotgun."

"Find the shotgun," Randy said, starting to search again.

"Looking for this?" came a rumbling voice out of the haze.

The other lamp came their way from the living room, illuminating two ghostly, furrowed faces. Betty was holding the light. Stewart was holding the shotgun, loading cartridges.

"You dropped it," Stewart said, unhappy about it. "Is this how you treat other people's property?"

Randy rolled his eyes and moved forward, shining the lamp in Stewart's face. "We don't have time for complaints, Stewart."

Stewart brushed past him and perused the damage to the house, in no particular hurry. "Now look what you've done." Outside, the rain intensified, pummeling the roof and pinging off the protruding bed of the truck.

A strong gust blew in under the crumpled carriage and extinguished the flame in Randy's lamp. He swore and set it down.

Randy pressed into Stewart's space, reaching for the weapon. "He means business, Stewart. We can't wait around—"

Stewart pumped the action and raised the barrel, pointing it at Randy's chest.

Horrified, Randy bobbed, first down, then sideways. "Hey! What are you doing?"

Stewart kept the barrel aimed at his head. "One dead body, huh? Maybe it should be yours."

Randy ducked again and ended up on the floor crawling, rolling, backing away while Stewart followed his every move, chuckling with wicked amusement.

"Yeah," Stewart rumbled. "Crawl on the floor. *Squirm.* It's right where you belong!"

Jack ticked off his options. Randy was on the floor between him and Stewart, which put Jack—and Stephanie, still clinging to him—only inches from Stewart's line of fire. "Stewart, easy now . . . just take it easy."

Stewart didn't take his eyes or his shotgun off the cowering Randy. "Don't worry. This punk's not bothering me one bit." Stewart turned to Randy, "*Are* you?"

Leslie sidled close to Betty and whispered, "Betty, can you talk to him?"

Betty just held the lamp high, seemingly mesmerized.

"*Are you?*" Stewart growled.

"No, no," Randy said, his voice trembling.

"Betty," Leslie whispered. "Do something."

Betty looked at Leslie, then said to Stewart, "Stewart, don't you make a big mess now."

Leslie fell back, stunned. Jack searched the woman's half-crazy eyes but could not read them.

"Up against the wall, all of you," Stewart growled, swinging the barrel in an arc toward them.

"Wh-what?" Jack felt the same consternation he saw in the others' faces. He raised his hands, not yet believing. "Stewart. What gives?"

"Against the wall!"

Leslie helped Randy off the floor. Jack guided Stephanie to the wall that separated the foyer from the dining room, putting himself between her and Stewart's line of fire. They fell into place like four deserters before a firing squad.

"Stewart, I don't want you ruining the plaster either," Betty protested.

"Shut up!"

She took her place beside him and remained silent.

Stewart eyed them one by one with murder in his eyes. "You are the sorriest bunch of sinners I ever seen. Come in here acting like you own the place, all well-to-do like we can't tell what lies you're hiding. Filthy atheists! But you're guilty! Guilty as sin!"

Leslie turned on her most soothing, professional tone. "Stewart, perhaps we owe you an apology—"

With a blinding flash and a deafening explosion that mingled with Leslie's scream, Stewart ruined the plaster above Leslie's head. She cowered, hands raised in pleading surrender. Randy grabbed her to keep her from falling. Stephanie collapsed against Jack's legs, almost knocking him over.

"Oh, now you've done it," Betty whined.

Stewart pumped the action again. "Stand up."

Jack helped Stephanie to her feet but didn't let go of her. Her hands quivered in his. His heart was pumping so furiously he could hear it in his skull.

Stewart waved the barrel back and forth, the very picture of murdering madness. He jerked his head at the crumpled wreck embedded in the entry. "We know all about this killer, more than you ever will, so we know it's you that's brought us the trouble. You brought it in here like a dog carrying fleas."

"But we're more than happy to leave," said Jack. "Just let us go and—"

"*Go?* You think he's gonna let anyone out of here? You ain't goin' anywhere till Mr. White gets what he wants."

"But don't you see? This *is* what he wants, for us to harm each other."

"So what's wrong with that?"

Randy looked to Betty. "Betty. You understand what's going on, don't you?" He nodded toward Stewart. "Tell him."

She looked at the mangled truck and what was left of the front entry. "Tell him what?"

"Betty. Are you too stupid to—"

That got her attention. Her icy glare clipped his sentence like a pair of scissors. "What do you want me to say, smart boy? That we do what we have to do?" She eyed Jack. "That life's just a big joke?"

"No . . . ," Stephanie cried, her hand over her mouth.

Betty reached out and tucked a stray strand of blonde hair behind Stephanie's ear. "Or maybe we should just sing a song and make the trouble go away." Stephanie let go of Jack, doubled over, and retched.

"Betty," Leslie said, her voice barely audible, "we're all human beings here. We can be reasonable."

"Human beings?" Betty looked injured. "Sweetheart, this is what human beings do."

Stewart grabbed a fistful of Betty's dress and yanked her back. "That's enough talking. We got ourselves to think about."

"As if I could think of anything else," Betty murmured, sidling up to him.

"But you don't all need to worry," Stewart said. "Just one of you."

8

JACK CONCENTRATED ON STEWART'S EYES, trying to detect the slightest hint of a bluff, a ruse, even a joke. The eyes were glassy, the red vessels distended, and behind them lay a darkness that was eerily familiar, like the hellish depths he'd seen through the window of the back door, through eyeholes cut in a metal mask.

This was no bluff.

Stewart wiggled the barrel toward the hall. "Get moving. Into the kitchen."

Betty moved into the hallway, holding the lamp high, showing the dim way while casting long shadows. Jack exchanged a glance with the others, then followed, hands raised to indicate surrender, to prevent a haphazard shooting. They followed Betty in single file, first Jack, then Stephanie, Leslie, and Randy, all with hands raised. Stewart lumbered behind them, shotgun level.

Jack made a conscious effort to walk slowly, hoping the others were searching the hallway, the doorways, anywhere, just as he was, for any ideas on how to escape.

There were plenty of places to flee from this hallway—
the kitchen, the dining room, the stairs, the living room.
Stewart couldn't possibly contain all four of them if they
bolted, and the darkness would hide them.

But Stewart could kill one for certain, two if he
could pump another round in time, maybe three or even
all four if they could find no other way out of the house.

Jack kept walking, looking, hoping, waiting for *the*
moment.

They entered the kitchen, Stewart prodding them
from behind.

"Betty," Stewart rumbled, "open up the meat locker."

Stephanie gasped then started bawling. "No. No . . ."

Stewart jabbed her with the shotgun and kept her
moving.

Betty said nothing. She only scowled at them—and
Stewart—as she went to the far end of the kitchen,
raised the latch on a thick wooden door, and heaved the
door open. Wisps of chilling fog poured into the kitchen
and snaked along the floor.

"Nooo!" Stephanie tried to bolt, but Stewart grabbed
a fistful of her long hair and yanked her back. She
screamed, stumbling. Jack took hold of her, put her in
front of him and out of Stewart's reach, and stepped into
the locker. The others followed, crowding and stumbling
in the dark. Betty stepped in last, closing the door with a
thud as the orange glow from the lamp filled the room.

The meat locker was much larger than Jack would
have expected, made of sawn timber with bins and
shelves for holding produce and slabs of meat. There was
a huge ax hammer leaning against the far corner, the
kind with one blunt end for knocking out cows and one

sharp end for cutting their heads off. A bloodstained workbench featured an assortment of butcher knives and meat cleavers; meat hooks dangled from the ceiling.

Jack could see his breath. He rubbed his hands together for warmth.

We can't run from here. We shouldn't have let them take us this far. We should have tried something.

"Turn around, hands on the wall," Stewart ordered, and the four faced the wall, hands raised and flat against the rough boards. They were frosty and bloodstained.

"What are you going to do?" Randy asked, his voice high and shaking.

"Can't you read?" Stewart said. "What do you *think* we're gonna do?"

Leslie began, "But we don't deserve—" Stewart pressed the gun barrel against her neck, and she went no further.

"Another lie. Ain't found a sinner yet who thought he deserved it, but they get it every time, now don't they? You all deserve it."

Jack peered over the women's heads and met Randy's eyes. They were frantic, vacant, like a trapped animal's. *Randy, come on. I need you to work the problem with me. We're after an idea, any idea.*

"But we can make this fair," Stewart said. "The killer only wants one, so we'll only take one." He paced behind them, down to Randy, back up to Jack. "And we'll even let *you* decide which one it's gonna be."

They glanced at one another. Stephanie was weeping now, her tears dripping onto the floor.

How could we possibly make that kind of decision? But this is life, right? Just one cruel absurdity after another, Jack thought. "You know we can't do that."

Stewart's voice dropped an octave. "You don't fool me. I know what you can and can't do. I know what you are."

Betty piped up, "No sense talking to him. He thinks it's all a bad joke."

"I don't—"

"How about you, country star?" Stewart moved sideways, touching the barrel to the back of Stephanie's neck, making her flinch. Her crying intensified. "You think there's nobody here you wouldn't trade for your own life? Know what I think we oughta do with you? Leave you right here to freeze to death, long and slow."

"Please help me . . ."

"Now wouldn't that be justice?"

"But it wasn't my fault!" she screamed.

And then she looked at Jack.

Jack's very soul froze at Stewart's words, Stephanie's cutting gaze, his own memories: he'd had such thoughts about her. He'd told himself such things over and over. He never said them; he only thought them. *Justice. I don't know. But if the accident wasn't her fault, the breakup of our marriage sure was.*

"That's more like it, boy," Stewart murmured.

Randy spoke up. "Stewart, listen, this whole situation could work out really well for you. You have the advantage; I have money. We can work out an arrangement. You could be a rich man."

"Ohhhh, yeah." Stewart stood behind Randy, the barrel of the shotgun just under Randy's ear. "Just how did you come by all that money, anyway? By making choices just like this one, am I right?"

It took Randy a moment to formulate an answer. "Good businessmen weigh the alternatives."

"Well, here's an alternative for you: pick somebody to die, or I will." He clutched a fistful of Randy's hair and slammed his head against the wall. "And I'm liking you for the part more and more, so you won't get off easy. No going quick. I'm gonna *drown* you, just like an old cat I wanna be rid of. You think about that!"

He poked Leslie, who stood silent, eyes closed, resolutely bearing up. "As for you, little Miss Taken, we'll wait till Pete's through with you, and then we'll decide."

Leslie maintained her stony expression, but her jaw began to quiver.

"I've chosen!" Jack shouted. He had no idea what his next move would be, but he tried to catch Randy's eye.

He caught everyone's eyes. Now what?

"Well, I'll be. Maybe writer boy really does care," Betty said.

"No," Jack said, meeting Betty's eyes with a boldness that surprised even him. "You were right the first time. I don't care. Life *is* a big joke."

Stewart bored into him with those hateful dark eyes. "This boy's got quite a philosophy."

Jack turned and faced Stewart, his hands raised. "If life made any sense at all, we wouldn't be here having to make this ridiculous choice, and that sadistic killer wouldn't be outside waiting for a body." He allowed himself a short chuckle and caught Randy's gaze. Randy was paying attention at least. "Listen, I've tried to understand why things like this happen to people, and I've given up." But Randy didn't appear to be with him yet. Jack engaged Stewart's eyes. "There's no point to life, and if that's the case, you're right, Stewart, what's so wrong about us harming each other? Why not?"

Randy, Leslie, and Stephanie were staring at him, hands still against the wall. Their eyes were full of questions.

The muzzle of the shotgun filled his vision as Stewart said, "All right. Who's it gonna be?"

Jack shot a nervous glance toward Randy. "Uh, who do you think? I mean, it's obvious."

Come on, Randy. Work with me.

Stephanie's voice was weak. "Jack, you can't possibly mean what you're saying!"

Thanks, Steph. Why don't we have another marital spat right here while Stewart's trying to kill us?

"Don't tell me what I mean!" he shouted at her, trying to stay in character as he moved out from the wall a few inches. "Look around you, Steph. Do you see anything good happening in this room? Do you see any point to any of this? And where's God, huh?" He inched sideways, looking down the barrel of the shotgun that never strayed from his face. "If God cared about us at all, he'd do something about this fix we're in, but guess what? No God, no help, no rescue, no point." He looked at Stewart, even leaned toward him just a little, and said, "And no guilt either. There's no guilt because there's no right or wrong, no sin—there's only that shotgun."

Stewart shoved the barrel at him. "So maybe it oughta be your brains all over the wall."

Betty slapped the back of Stewart's head. "Stewart! Do it outside or you clean up the mess."

Stewart's closing in gave Jack an excuse to back up, moving along the wall, away from the others. The gun followed Jack.

"Hey," Jack protested, trying to catch Randy's eye

over Stewart's shoulder. "You said you were going to be fair, you were going to let us choose which one. Well . . ."

Just a few more inches. Jack didn't have to act scared—he really was—as he continued backing away, drawing Stewart's attention. In his worst nightmares he couldn't have dreamed up a story like this. "Okay. I choose me."

"You? You can't choose you."

Stewart turned his back on the other three.

Jack had to keep his attention. "Why not? Betty's right. I've lost the dearest thing in life to me, and my wife just wants to run off and be a country singer. I don't care if I live anymore." Stephanie looked away. There. A light went on in Randy's eyes. His hands came off the wall. "So in the grand scheme of things, I'm not losing anything and you get your body."

Stewart seemed a bit rattled. "You're supposed to pick somebody else."

Jack looked at Betty, who stood against the workbench to his right. "Betty, talk to him. Doesn't it make sense?"

Betty glowered at him, but mostly at Stewart. "Maybe he ain't the right one. He doesn't seem to mind."

"Shut up," Stewart said, his eyes still on Jack, pushing that barrel in Jack's face.

"Or maybe he is. Drowning the other guy'd take too long."

Stewart looked her way. "I said *shut up*."

Now!

Jack brought both arms down and grabbed the barrel, sweeping it aside.

Boom! The gun discharged, blowing a hole in the floorboards. Stephanie screamed.

Randy, where are you?

After an eternity, Randy pounced on Stewart, riding his back, trying to bring him down, arms groping. "Get the gun, get the gun!"

All three men had a death grip on the shotgun as the barrel swept the room. Leslie and Stephanie dropped to the floor. Jack kept his hand locked on the shotgun's pump action to keep Stewart from chambering another round. Stewart spun, smashing Randy's body against the wall. Jack tripped over Stewart's leg and fell, still clinging to the shotgun even as Stewart's boot came down on his rib cage.

"Run!" he screamed to Stephanie and Leslie. "Get out of here!"

"STOOO-WART!" Betty screamed.

❧

Leslie jumped across the room and took hold of Betty's right arm just as Betty's fist closed around the handle of a meat cleaver. The woman possessed surreal strength, bucking, twirling, and pummeling Leslie's head and face with bony knuckles like little hammers. Leslie, with both hands clamped around Betty's right arm, could only duck, wrestle, and use a knee when she got the chance.

"STOOO-WART!"

❧

Stephanie leaped for the door and threw her weight against the latch plate. The plate depressed, releasing the

latch outside. The big door creaked open, and she stumbled into the kitchen, slipping on the fog-dampened floor.
Before any thought arose in her mind, she was crossing
the kitchen for the hallway, running into deepening
shadow. *Get away, girl; get away! Run!* Betty's screams,
Stewart's roar, and the sound of blows and struggle chased
her up the hallway. *Faster!*

———

Stewart kicked Jack in the gut hard enough to separate Jack's will from his hands. His grip on the shotgun fell
away. Stewart gave a mighty backward thrust with the
shotgun butt and sent Randy backward, doubled up in
pain. Jack heard the pump action chamber another round.

———

Leslie clung by sheer force of will to the tireless,
whirling machine that kept screaming and swinging a
meat cleaver. Much more of Betty's bony fist in her face,
or just one more violent body slam against the rough
planks, and Leslie's strength would fail. A blur that was
Randy's body collided with the wall behind her and doubled over. Jack was still on the floor, trying to get his feet
under him while—

Stewart aimed the shotgun at Jack's head.

Leslie couldn't end Betty's violent struggling, but perhaps she could redirect it. She planted a foot, extended
her other leg to trip Betty, and let both of them tumble
headlong into Stewart, slamming him against the wall.

Boom! Splinters of wood flew up from the floor.

A tangle of bodies, kicking legs, groping arms. Leslie lost her grip on Betty's arm. She looked around—

The meat cleaver thudded into the floorboards inches from her shoulder.

Stewart lurched from a kick to his midsection. Jack was still alive.

Betty bent over Leslie, trying to wrest the meat cleaver from the floor. Leslie brought both legs up and kicked Betty's stomach with enough force to throw her against the opposite wall.

—◦—

Stephanie skidded to a halt in the blackness, then turned and realized she was alone. No one had escaped with her.

Worse yet, she was unsure of where she was. *Was she in the hallway?* A flash of lightning painted momentary streaks on the floor and walls, disguising corners, distorting angles, changing features.

"Jack!"

The sound of the struggle had dropped to a distant rumble, as if behind a wall. She set out to find it, arms extended, feeling her way. She contacted a wall and followed it to a corner. She made the turn, followed farther, and came to another corner. Wasn't there a door somewhere? How had she gotten here?

"Jack." She could hardly whisper.

An outside corner led her into a space that seemed larger, but there was no light to show her the smallest patch of surface. She moved along the wall, groping for a piece of furniture, any object she might recognize. As

far as she might reach, she felt nothing. Fear began turning her guts, making her tremble. She felt faint.

She stopped breathing and listened.

Nothing.

No sound. No light.

She was lost.

9

RANDY WAS SURE HE WOULD NEED SURGERY to repair his bowels, stomach, and liver, but first he would put Stewart down. Jack was still wrestling with the man for possession of the shotgun, slamming against the shelves, careening off the walls. Randy maneuvered, waiting for Stewart's head to pop out of a shadow—

Betty blindsided him, bit him on the hand, took hold of the ax hammer. He screamed in pain.

Leslie came up behind Betty and dashed the back of her skull with a sizable chunk of ice. The ice shattered in all directions and the woman's jaws relaxed, allowing Randy to twist free. "Get her out of here."

Betty went limp as Leslie pulled, wrestled, and dragged the heavy woman toward the locker door. It was a vital mission. With Betty out of the picture, Jack and Randy could deal with Stewart two-on-one. If Leslie could remove Betty permanently, she could return to help, making the match three-on-one. Divide and conquer.

— —

Just inside the locker door, Leslie felt Betty's body go from sack-of-potatoes cooperative to wild-tiger deadly. Screaming like a great cat, Betty lurched, spun, and flung Leslie through the door as if she weighed nothing. Leslie floated through space for an instant, no up, no down—

Her body—head, hips, elbows—hit the floor, and she tumbled over the tile. Her head was spinning when she came to rest, dizzy in the dark. She oriented herself to the dim light of the oil lamp that still burned, righted herself. She was in the kitchen.

She heard the big door shut, slamming with a wooden thud and the clank of the latch falling into place.

Darkness.

Breathing.

"Betty?"

The breathing was through a large windpipe. Not Betty. She heard phlegm rattling, then a low, wheezing chuckle. Three slow footsteps shuffled toward her, and then a flash of lightning through the small window over the sink illuminated a face that seemed to float without a body.

Pete.

"You can't hide from me," the man's thick voice yelled.

Leslie pushed herself to her feet. Another flash of lightning illuminated the archway out of the kitchen and into the hall. She dashed that direction as the light vanished, running madly into the dark unknown.

He shuffled after her.

Jack was losing. He could feel his hands slipping from the shotgun. His ribs screamed in pain with every breath. He tried kicking Stewart—again. He missed—again.

Betty had thrown Leslie out, locked her out. She came rushing to Stewart.

Clunk! Stewart's head jerked sideways, struck by the ax hammer in Randy's hands. The man staggered. Jack lost his grip on the shotgun and let him fall—

Just in time for Jack to see a wild-haired, bulb-eyed wraith charging into the lamplight.

"Randy!"

Randy was still holding the ax hammer at shoulder height. Betty's own momentum brought her forehead dead center with the blunt end, and she bounced off it.

Without having to consult, Jack and Randy half ran, half limped to the door. Randy slammed the latch plate with his palm, they shoved with their full weight, and the big door eased open in no hurry at all. Betty and Stewart were on their feet again. Stewart was loading another cartridge.

Jack bellowed as he and Randy tumbled around the door and pushed it shut.

Almost.

The two bodies on the inside collided with the door,

punching it open. Jack and Randy leaned into it, forcing it shut again, but they couldn't hold it forever.

"We've got to jam this latch," Jack said.

Randy checked his hands, only now discovering they were empty. He'd dropped the ax hammer inside.

Ka-thud! The door jerked again, sending a brief flash of orange light into the kitchen, enough to reveal a mop against the wall a few feet away. Randy reached for it.

Boom! Jack could feel the shock of the shotgun blast on the other side of the door. It jerked.

Randy had the mop. "Push!" Jack and Randy gave the door their shoulders and all that remained of their strength. The latch fell into place, and Randy jammed the mop under the latch handle.

The locking mechanism banged and rattled as Stewart and Betty tried to operate it, but the handle was jammed solid.

"Good work," Jack said.

A *boom-boom-boom!* carried right through the door and into Jack's skull.

The ax hammer.

They began to shout. "Leslie! Stephanie!"

There was no answer from either.

Crack!

They noticed the change in the sound of the blows. Namely, ax instead of hammer.

"They'll be through that door soon enough," Randy said. "Let's find the girls and get out of here."

"Pete went after Leslie," Jack said.

Randy didn't respond.

Jack dug in his pocket for Stephanie's lighter and flicked it. The tiny yellow flame was just enough to guide them through the kitchen and toward the hallway. Randy spotted a rack of kitchen knives near the butcher block and helped himself to an eight-incher, tucking it in his belt. "Bring it on," he muttered.

"Steph!"

"Leslie!"

Still no answer.

———

"Jack!" Stephanie called into the darkness, but only silence answered. "Jack, I'm in here! *Jack!*"

He didn't answer.

"Jack!"

She flopped against an unseen wall as little thoughts buzzed in her mind: she didn't need him anyway. Jack had died with their daughter. Why *should* he answer? Maybe he was being quiet because he *did* hear her.

She started humming, trying to make the thoughts go away. *"My heart holds all secrets; my heart tells no lies . . ."* She couldn't remember the next line. She sang the one she remembered twice, then hummed the melody until the fear eased up and she could think. She'd been on her own since Melissa's death. She could manage this. *Get yourself out, girl. Jack isn't going to do it for you.* Everything would work out okay in the end.

She had no idea where she was. There was still no light. She'd gone through a door into what felt and sounded like a hall, but it wasn't *the* hallway she was hoping to find. She'd encountered a table and some chairs, and then a painting on the wall, but these were entirely unfamiliar. When she tried to backtrack and find the door she came through, her hands found nothing but blank wall.

Jack! So help me . . .

Now she heard commotion and voices, some footsteps far away and muffled. She followed the sound.

⚊⚊✦⚊

Crack! Jack and Randy could hear it from the hallway between the kitchen and dining room. Stewart was making quick work of the barricaded locker.

Jack's lighter illuminated a door that stood half-open. The one Betty had scolded him about.

"The basement," Jack said.

They paused at the threshold. Dirty shiplap walls and wooden stairs descended into a black void beyond.

"What do you think?" Randy asked.

Bam! Crack! Not much time for conversation.

"*Somebody* went down there."

"It wasn't the girls. They got out. They had to."

"Got out to where?"

Bam! Bam!

Randy took off toward the dark foyer, his shoes wandering on the hardwood, stumbling on the debris. "Leslie!" Jack heard bodies collide. A woman screamed. Randy screamed then cursed.

Jack leaped back into the hallway and squinted. Stephanie. She was flailing and pounding Randy, who was only trying to help her. "Steph!"

She stilled, swept the hair off her face. "Where have you been? Didn't you hear me calling you?"

"Not so loud," Jack cautioned.

Stephanie marched at Jack, anger in her steps. "Maybe you don't think I'm worth keeping, but I'm still a human being with feelings, and I'm still your wife!"

"Where is Leslie?" Randy asked.

"I don't know. Jack, can we please get out of here?"

"Was Leslie with you?"

"*No!* Can we go now?"

Jack looked down the basement stairs again. The light caught a sparkle on the first step. He bent and picked up a silver drop-shaped earring, held it up for them to see. "She went down there. She's in the basement."

"That doesn't prove anything," Randy said.

Stephanie paced. "I'm not going down there, Jack. We have to get out."

Boom! The shotgun put another spray of lead into the meat-locker door.

Jack raised his lighter high and turned in place, starving for an idea, a lead, a course of action. He spotted the other door, the closet. He ran to it, jerked it open. Without the extra chairs, there was plenty of room. Coats, enough to conceal someone, hung from a rod.

He motioned to Stephanie. "Steph. Inside."

Her feet were planted. "Are you crazy? I'm not going in there!"

He took firm hold of her arm and got her moving. "We can fight about it later. Right now I need you where I can find you."

She stumbled backward into the black cavity under his firm guidance. "What are you going to do?"

"Find Leslie."

"Oh, so *she's* worth looking for, is that it?"

"Not now, Steph." Everything was all about her, wasn't

it? Her selfishness was wearing thin. "Stay put till we come back. I'll make it quick."

"What about—" He put his hand over her mouth. She pried it off and whispered, "What about Stewart and Betty?"

"They'll be chasing me and Randy. Stay put."

"But you can't leave—"

He closed the closet and went to the basement door. The silence, the darkness down there, was hiding something. He could feel it. "Randy?"

Randy started to argue, "We don't know for sure she's down there—"

Crash! Wood splintered in the kitchen.

Jack stepped into the stairwell.

10:55 PM

BARSIDIOUS WHITE STOOD AT THE TOP OF THE brick stairwell that led into the basement, arms crossed, waiting. Waiting . . . waiting. So much of life was waiting. All good things came to those who waited, as the saying went.

He lifted his face to the pouring rain and focused on the pelting of his skin. Lightning flashed. This storm was the kind that brought flash floods. Good thing to know.

He knew a few things none of those inside knew, naturally. More than a few things. The game was being so perfectly executed that he wondered if his luck would run out before he had a chance to introduce the real stakes.

Or show his true power, for that matter.

If all good things came to those who waited, and he was waiting for evil to work its magic, did that make evil good? If he was waiting for the hour of the killing, did that make killing good?

Killing one person makes you a murderer. Killing a million people makes you a king. Killing them all makes you God.

In the end he would be God, because the game being played behind these dirty white walls wasn't unlike the game all people played everywhere, every day, every last dirty one of them.

In the end they all killed; they all died; they all would rot in hell.

But in this house they would play his game, which boasted enough drama and delight to bring a smile to the blackest of souls. Assuming he won. But he would win. He was born to win, born to rip their filthy heads off their scrawny necks in a way that made it all at least interesting.

White took a deep breath. After weeks of waiting, each second now delivered enough reward to justify it all.

He unfolded his arms and walked to the edge of the stairwell. The sounds of an ax or a hammer slamming into a door resounded with each blow. If he was right, if he'd judged correctly, the players would soon be in the basement, and the real game could begin.

Of course, the real game was already in full swing, but they didn't understand this. By dawn he'd bring everything into clear focus.

Driving the truck into the front door had been a nice touch. Put the fear of God into their hearts. And that would be him because, as he'd just established, he was God.

"Welcome to my house, Jack." He let out an amused grunt. "Jack in the box."

White descended. Packed leaves and dirt had long ago covered the concrete, raising the landing several inches so that when the door opened, decaying leaves tended to spill into the basement. But there was more than a little decay waiting to enter this world tonight.

He put his hand on the keyless door latch and pressed it down. Locked. As it should be. He would wait.

White walked back up into the night. The methodic thumping of the ax inside morphed into a muffled sound of splintering wood. A loud crash. Pounding feet.

White's right hand began to quiver. He made no attempt to stop it. Deep in the backwoods of Alabama where no one was watching and the darkness had swallowed all light, he was allowed to enjoy life a little, wasn't he?

— ~ —

Jack's lighter flickered above the old wooden stairs. Jack paused halfway down, straining for a glimpse of something. A repulsive odor—rotten eggs or sulfur—filled his nose. He tried to breathe shallow.

He wasn't sure what he was looking for, other than Leslie. The floor below was gray concrete and the walls were red brick, he could see that much. Nothing more.

He leaned forward and shouted. "Leslie!"

"What are you doing?" Randy whispered from behind. "They'll hear you!"

"I *want* her to hear me; isn't that the point?"

"*Her*, not the whole house. They'll know we went after her."

"They're in the meat locker making themselves deaf— no way they heard me."

Stephanie's muffled voice called from the closet. "Jack!"

He ignored her and continued four steps before realizing that Randy wasn't following. The man still stood at the top of the stairs.

"You coming?"

"You sure this is a good idea?"

What made him think he could waltz into this dungeon of theirs, find Leslie, deliver her from the brute, and skip off into the woods without catching a blast from their guns? Or from White's. That's the likelihood that awaited them outside.

"We don't have a choice." A few more blows and Stewart would be through. Then he added for Randy's sake, "They have to have more guns down here."

Right. Guns. He turned back down the stairs and descended quickly, now eager to follow his own advice. Gun first, Leslie second, because it was clear that without a gun, they were dead men. Whatever this house was, it wasn't a quaint little inn inhabited by ordinary proprietors filled with goodwill toward weary travelers.

The sickness here was palpable. Death hunted them all, and the only way to survive might very well be to kill.

Jack blinked at the boldness of his own thoughts and stepped onto the concrete floor. Randy clumped slowly down the steps behind.

The basement opened up before Jack. One low-wattage bulb hung from the ceiling. He let the lighter die. A wide concrete-and-brick hall with three corroded steel doors on each side ended in a solid redbrick wall. The corridor looked like something out of an old prison movie.

Water trickled down the right wall in a couple of wet trails, then ran along the floor into a grate.

"What's that smell?" Randy asked. "What is this place?"

"The basement."

"Looks more like a . . . sewer."

"Let's go."

"That smell . . ."

Jack tried to ignore the sickly stench. He walked up the hall, now faced with an unexpected dilemma. The thought of opening one of the doors, any of the doors, struck him as foolish. But short of going back upstairs, there was no other option.

Jack hurried to the first one on his right. Put his hand on the rusted handle. He hesitated.

Crack!

The muffled sound of Stewart's progress on the heavy meat-locker door reminded him of the terror close behind. He turned the knob. Pushed the door.

The room that opened up to them was dimly lit by another bare low-wattage bulb. No immediate threat, no gun in the face, no booby trap, no spring-loaded arrow aimed for their hearts. Just a room.

No, not just a room.

Jack and Randy gazed about. Four burgundy sofas, two quite new, two very old with torn upholstery. Lots of throw pillows. A tan-and-black woven rug covered most of the concrete. Paintings. At least a dozen paintings hung on brick walls. Almost homey in an eccentric sort of way. A strange blend of the old and the new, grungy and clean.

Jack walked in. "Look for a gun, a gun cabinet. Hurry."

There was an old potbellied stove at one end of the room, shined clean as if it had never been used. A thick cobweb peppered with mummified bugs stretched from the top of the stovepipe to the adjacent wall. Why would they clean the stove and leave the web?

Other interesting pieces of furniture were set about—a loom, a coatrack, an antique rocker . . . a rusted washing machine?

The room added a whole new dimension to Jack's understanding of Betty and Stewart. The problem was, the dimension wasn't clear.

And then Jack saw something that cleared things up a bit. There was a pentagram painted in red on the wall to his left. A threat scrawled in black ran through it. *The wages of sin is death.*

Stewart's accusations filled his ears: *Guilty as sin.* Below the pentagram sat a sofa table, and on that table stood a ring of black candles. Looked like the hosts were a religious lot.

Somewhere deep in the house a door slammed.

"What was that?" Randy asked.

"Check that closet," Jack said, pointing to a door beside the pentagram. He ran across the room to a second closet door. "Keep looking!"

The closet he tried was filled with junk. Candles. Rags. A broom. Nothing that looked like a gun or anything he could imagine using to incapacitate Pete, which he thought it might come down to.

"Uh, Jack?"

When he turned back, he saw that Randy's door opened into another room.

"What is it?" He hurried across the room.

"Another room."

"I can see that. What . . ."

He poked his head into the room. Gray concrete, all sides. Heavy cobwebs in all the corners and along the walls. A single writing desk in the middle of the room. No other furniture. Looked like a huge study. Sort of.

Jack stepped in. Long red drapes framed a huge mirror on the left wall. Another pentagram with the same words appeared on opposite wall. *The wages of sin is death*. That was it. Just the desk, the mirror, the graffiti.

And three more doors, one of which looked like it led back out to the main hall. The other two stood straight ahead in the opposite wall. They led deeper into the basement, maybe.

"You think that door leads back out to the hall?" Randy asked. "This isn't good. I don't like it. We have to find the storage room, or wherever they'd keep guns."

He hurried toward one of the doors directly ahead. "Tell me what kind of a freaking place this is . . . ?"

He's beginning to melt down, Jack thought.

Weren't they all?

Randy reached for the knob, pulled up short. He was staring at the mirror. Why, Jack wasn't going to spend precious time finding out.

"Okay, we have to split up. Just go, run." Jack ran toward the door that he guessed opened back into the main hall. "Cover every room and meet back in the hall."

Jack threw open the door and bolted into darkness. Dripping water. Smelled musty, sweet next to the rotten-egg odor that permeated the room behind him.

Randy was still blinking at the mirror, waving at it now.

"Snap out of it, Randy! Did you hear me? We have to move!"

"I don't . . . Something's wrong with this mirror."

"Who cares? Let's go!"

"I don't have a reflection."

The ridiculousness of Randy's claim ballooned in Jack's mind. He released the door and crossed to Randy, who was still staring, stupefied.

Jack stood next to him and looked into the mirror. No reflection.

Correction: no reflection of them. The desk behind them was in clear view. So was the far wall.

"We should leave," Randy said.

"It's a trick mirror or something. They make them like this." Maybe Betty and company had once been a part of some gypsy circus. It might explain a few things.

"No, this isn't some trick mirror. We're like vampires down here, man!"

"Don't be an idiot. Come on, we have to be reasonable about this. Cover the—"

"I'm not splitting up."

"Stop it! Leslie's out there!"

"We're going to die down here, Jack. All of us. We're all going to die."

"Yeah, if we don't move. Follow me."

He ran for the door he'd opened, Randy at his heels now.

"Find a switch." He slapped the wall on the right. Wet and cool. No switch. He raised his hands and started waving high.

A string hung low several yards in. He gave it a gentle tug, lighting a bulb mounted to the beams above. Now this was the kind of room Jack expected to find down here. Wet, mildewed walls lined with wooden racks. Two more doors.

"Root cellar," he said.

"Where's the hall?"

"Must be through that door."

The fact was, based on what he'd seen down here so far, the basement wasn't laid out like any he'd ever seen.

Jack crossed the cellar and pulled open the door. As expected, the main hall. He released the handle with a small measure of satisfaction.

Randy hurried past him.

"Try one of the other doors," Jack said.

The sound of running boots pounded over their heads.

Randy jerked his head up and stared at the labyrinth of pipes that crossed the ceiling. "They're coming!"

As if to emphasize the point, a muffled shotgun blast boomed above. Stephanie? No, she was still in the closet, and the sound had come from the kitchen area. Unless she'd given up after five minutes and made a break for the back door. Would they come directly downstairs or search the upper floors first?

The faint sound of humming came again, as it had upstairs. Jack whirled. "You hear that?"

"The singing . . ."

But neither could place it.

Jack wasn't waiting. He tried the door directly opposite the root cellar's. Locked. The footsteps pounded in the other direction. They couldn't risk it. Jack grabbed Randy's arm and tugged him back into the root cellar. Closed the door behind them.

"Where we going?"

"Anywhere but the hall. Keep it down."

They rushed through the cellar, ignoring a door on their left. Back into the study, past the freaky mirror.

"Where we going?" Randy asked again.

Jack pulled up. "Did we leave the door into the first room open?"

Randy stared at him with dawning horror. "They'll see it! They'll know . . ."

The humming again, from their right, very faint. Then silent.

Jack ran toward one of the doors they hadn't tried yet. He could now hear the sound of footsteps on the stairs.

"Don't say we didn't warn you!" Betty's voice echoed. "Not the basement, we said, but no, you wouldn't listen. Don't you dare say we didn't warn you!"

"Hurry!" Jack said.

He slid up against the door. If their hosts followed the trail of open doors . . .

He grabbed the door handle and pulled. The door moved an inch, then pulled free from his hands and slammed, as if sucked by a vacuum.

"Try the other door!"

Randy ran toward the only door they hadn't tried yet.

Jack pulled the door again. This time it opened six inches—wide enough for him to see the blackness beyond. A deep sucking sound filled the room.

"It's locked!" Randy cried.

Pushed by the threat of Stewart blasting into the room, Jack ignored the voice in his head that suggested forcing a door open against such a strong underground air current was not a good idea.

He pulled harder.

The door gaped wider. Where could such a strong draft come from? The study's one light dimmed. Something was very wrong with this room.

It became immediately clear to him that no matter what the threat behind them was, they could not, should not, enter the space beyond the door. Jack released the handle.

The sucking sound ceased. But instead of slamming shut, the door hung free, gaping where he'd released it.

Beyond, silence. No humming.

"Go!" Randy whispered. "Go!"

Wrong. Something was terribly wrong.

Jack reached out his hand. Before his fingers touched the handle, the door flew open of its own accord. Wide open.

For a brief moment Jack faced a doorway of inky darkness. No floor or walls that he could see.

He felt his body being pulled into the doorway before he became aware of any suction, any draft, any force that drew him.

It was quick and it was silent, like a magnetic force. One second he was staring at the blackness, the next he was flying into it.

Smack! With a bone-crunching jar he crashed into a wall no more than five feet in.

Boom! The door slammed shut.

II

RANDY MESSARUE STARED AT THE DOOR that had slammed shut behind Jack, frozen by indecision. He wasn't sure which was worse: following Jack in, or making a run for it alone. Usually he could make choices in a snap. Must be the house. This stupid, stinking house. And its wacko proprietors. His mind had started to fray the minute Stewart had snuck up on him in the bathroom.

And when the man had turned against them, the erosion of Randy's confidence had become a crumbling of his psyche. He could feel himself coming unglued, disjointed. Weak. Not the stuff CEOs are made of.

He hated himself for it. Hated the way his gut was telling him to run. Hated the fact that he would probably save himself at Leslie's expense if it came right down to it. Hated the terror that had him squealing like a schoolgirl in his own mind.

He was sweating profusely despite the basement's cool air. His hands were trembling and his heart was pounding. *Don't be a wimp,* his dad used to say before taking the belt to him. He probably deserved a good whipping, and Stewart seemed all too eager to oblige.

Clack, clack. Shoes on the concrete, walking, not running. An image of Stewart's large leather boots striding across the floor flashed through his mind.

He leaped to the door and cranked the knob. It refused to budge.

"Don't you dare say we didn't warn you, you filthy atheists!"

Stewart was in the next room.

"Just go easy, Stew," Betty was saying, trying to keep the calm when they all knew there wasn't a bone of calm in that inbred husband of hers. "They got nowhere to hide. You just go easy. Nothing rash."

Randy was out of options. Two doors, locked. The root cellar exposed him to the hall. He spun, frantic for a way out. But there was no way out. *Hide. Hide, you pathetic little baby. Hide!*

He tore his feet from the ground and ran past the desk. Too small. To the curtain that framed the mirror. Behind the curtain.

But he could not still the curtain, and his lungs were wheezing like worn-out bellows. He pressed his back against the wall and willed his muscles to relax.

Clack, clack.

The boots stopped. They were in the doorway. Randy held his breath. For a moment the room fell silent.

"Where are you, you little rat?"

Stewart ordered Betty to shut the door.

The door shut. A lock engaged.

"That one too," he said.

The door to the cellar closed. Locked.

"They came this way, didn't they? I can smell the city stink."

"You think they made it to the tunnel?" Betty asked.

"Not unless they can walk through locked doors, they didn't."

"Then where?"

"Probably through the cellar. For all we know they're at the top of the stairs now, trying to figure out how to get back out."

"No way past that lock," Betty said. "The halls down here will drive them nuts. They'll never make it out."

Stewart had trapped them in the basement?

Stewart grunted. "I say we hunt them ourselves. We got them trapped like rats now."

"That wasn't the deal," Betty said. "You want to live through the night, we open that door for him."

"You open the door. He's not gonna let this slide. I swear he's gonna fillet us like fish. He's gonna slaughter everyone in this basement like he's done a hundred times before. You know how it works."

Pause.

"You think they'll find her?" Betty asked.

"Pete'll find—"

"Not her. The other one."

Stewart paused, breathing loudly through his nose. "Not before we do. And if they do, no doubt she'll use 'em. She's a sneaky little piece of trash."

For a while neither spoke. Then Stewart clacked toward the far corner and Betty followed. Keys rattled. A door squealed. The door closed. They were gone.

Or were they? What if they had seen him and faked

their conversation and exit for his benefit? He'd pull back the curtain and face a loaded shotgun.

Randy waited until he couldn't bear not knowing any longer. He inched his head around the curtain, eyes peeled.

The room was empty.

He ran to each door, testing the knobs. Locked. The one to the room with couches, the one to the root cellar, the one Jack had been sucked through. That left the door Stewart and Betty had used, and he had no intention of following them.

Randy put his ear against the door, heard nothing, and tested the handle. Unlocked. His intentions hardly mattered any longer.

He paced for ten seconds, nerves dicey. If he waited here, they might sneak back and shoot him like a rat in a cage. No options, not a single one, other than going through this door.

He put a trembling hand on the knob, twisted it slowly, and cracked the door. Dim light. No sound. He eased the door wider.

The hall on the other side of the door was made of wood beams supported by thick posts. Stone floor. A bulb in a beam scattered light to the far end where some steps met an old wooden door.

No sign of Betty or Stewart. They must have gone through one of three passages cutting into the hall's left wall.

Staring at the passage, Randy was struck by the scope of what he'd seen in the basement thus far. Clearly the house didn't sit on a square foundation, but on a maze of

rooms and halls. Which meant chances were good the
basement had another exit. If he was right, he was staring at one right now. That door at the end of the hall sat
at the top of three steps. The bottom half was visible to
Randy; the top half seemed to be set above ground.

*You want to live through the night, we open that
door for him,* Betty had said.

Meaning what? That door was the door that would
let *him* in.

White in.

Or Randy out.

He stepped into the passage and walked on his toes.
The first of the three passages cut into the left wall
ended at a door five feet in. But Randy wasn't interested
in another door. He only wanted one thing now, and it
lay at the end of the hall.

He could now see that a large padlock had been
opened and the door's latch was sprung free.

His heart knocked in his chest. White could be on
the other side of the door; he knew that; he did. Knew it
and hated it.

If the killer had come in, he'd have locked the door
behind him, right? Sure he would have. Of course he
would have. Randy repeated that a dozen times as he
eased over the stone floor toward the wooden door.

——— ◆ ———

They'd unlocked the door and left, as White had
requested. Demanded. A request and a demand were
one and the same now, because now they were all playing his game.

When you played White's game, either you did it White's way or you did it the dead way. Everyone learned that sooner or later.

Of course that meant he had to follow the rules as well. His rules.

House rules.

The time had now come to enforce those rules. A little discipline to guide them down the crooked lanes.

He descended the stairs evenly. He straightened his trench coat, took a deep breath, and pushed the door open.

Then White, who was really black, stepped into his house.

～⌒～

Randy was adjacent to the second passage when the door swung in and the boots stepped out of pouring rain, over the threshold, and onto the concrete landing.

There wasn't a shred of confusion in Randy's mind about the identity of this person. The shape of those black boots, the length of the trench coat—these were all emblazoned in Randy's memory with enough clarity to test a thousand hours of therapy. This was the killer they'd all seen on the path leading to the house.

Two things saved him in those first few moments. The first was that the killer didn't have a direct line of sight down the hall as he descended the steps on this side of the landing. The ceiling cut off his vision.

The second was that Randy reacted without thought, before he fully realized the danger that he was in. He jumped to his left. Into the passage.

Against a wall.

And there he froze. He could have tried to sneak farther in, through the door, away from the killer, but he froze.

And this, too, may have saved his life. He had no illusions that White was some ordinary lumberjack with a penchant for killing strangers. He struck Randy as a mastermind of sorts. The slightest sound would undoubtedly alert him.

Randy was breathing heavily again.

He clamped his hand over his mouth and strained to keep his lungs in check. His heart he couldn't control, but he doubted the man was that good.

White reengaged the latch and squeezed the padlock shut, making no attempt at stealth.

He stepped down to the stone floor, then stopped. Randy didn't need eyes to see what was happening. White was staring down the hall, thinking he'd heard something out of place. The patter of a heart. The rush of breath. The seeping of sweat.

For a long time, silence. Then White's boots moved, twelve or fifteen paces. They stopped again.

Water was trickling somewhere. In that moment, Randy felt his last reservoirs of strength fall away. He actually began to relax.

And when he did, a strange kind of resignation—no, peace—began to lap at his mind. A silent resolve not to care. No use fighting White. No use running. He didn't have the strength to run. Or resist at all, for that matter. A small corner of his mind wondered if it might be better to step out and cut a deal with White.

For seconds that stretched into an eternity, nothing happened. He couldn't hear White breathing, so maybe White couldn't hear him.

The boots headed toward the study. A door opened and closed.

Randy slid to the cold stone floor. Okay, so maybe he did care a little. He ground his molars and muttered under his breath, "Take that, you sick vampire."

He was shaking. But he was alive.

Leslie had vanished into these halls. At least, he was pretty sure of it. Was *she* alive? The thought surprised him, more because it was the first time he'd given the matter head-space than because he worried for her safety. Amazing how quickly a little stress can reorganize your priorities.

He hated himself. In reality, he always had. If he managed to survive this night, he might work on that.

The exit was now locked. The room he'd come from was locked.

Randy turned down the passage he was in and tried the door at the end. It led to a small utility room. There was a closet door on his right. Every room in the house seemed to have a closet. He scanned the walls. Shovels, buckets, a pitchfork, rakes. Several rakes.

A shotgun.

Randy blinked at the gun leaning in the corner, not sure his eyes were seeing correctly. Yet there it was, a single-barrel job that looked as old as the house. The question was, did it work? He cocked the barrel open at its hinge. Two rounds. He looked around. Rifled through jars of nails and lightbulb boxes on a shelf. Nothing that looked like ammo. Two would have to do.

A door slammed and footsteps sounded in the hall he'd just come from. *Clack, clack*.

Betty's *clack, clack*? Or Stewart's? Or White's?

Randy picked up the gun as quietly as possible and moved cat-like toward the closet. But even as he moved he realized he was no longer panicking.

"Stewart?" Betty called out.

He yanked the closet open, saw the floor inside was a foot or so lower than the one in the utility room, and stepped down.

Was he afraid? Sure. But he'd made it this far. He closed the door, thinking that he might not have entered a closet after all.

Randy turned around in the space. Not a closet. Not even close. He was in a shadowy concrete tunnel of some kind. It ran from the door to both right and left.

You think they made it to the tunnel? Maybe he should reconsider. A thin crack of light marked the utility-room door's outline. Then again, Betty was somewhere on the other side.

He faced the tunnel again. Maybe, just maybe, it had an exit. He'd seen the pouring rain when White came into the basement—if he found rainwater, he just might find a hatch or something.

He looked both ways, and seeing no reason why he should go either direction, he turned to his left and walked, shotgun in hand.

He had a gun; that was the main thing.

It hit him then that what faint light there was had come from the crack below the door. The tunnel was dark ahead. And behind.

He'd taken maybe twenty steps when a loud *clang*

rang down the tunnel. Like a hatch opening. Back, way back. He turned. Too far back to see anything.

Something dropped into the tunnel. Something heavy. And something that could run. *Thump, thump, thump, thump.* Headed right for him. A steady but heavy breathing chased the echoing footfalls.

Randy whirled and ran for his life.

12

THERE WERE TWO WAYS FOR LESLIE TO LOOK
at her predicament: she had escaped the beast, or she had
simply taken a long and terrible dive over the lip of the
frying pan and into the fire.

Or into hell. Honestly, she didn't know which.

In the terror of her escape from Pete, the open door to
the basement had at first struck her as her only escape. The
fact that they'd been told earlier not to enter barely registered. It was the odor that sharpened her recollection of
Betty's warning. The smell of rotten eggs assaulted her the
moment she landed on the concrete floor. But by then, it
was too late. She heard Pete's grunts upstairs and knew that
he was following. With a glance back, Leslie ran forward,
down the hall, and past three doors before veering into
another hall on her left. She tried to regulate her breathing.

She couldn't shake the feeling that she'd entered far
more than any ordinary basement. The rooms, for one
thing—there were far too many, and if these halls were
any indication, the space reached way beyond what she
thought reasonable for the size of house above her.

But at the moment, the compulsion to escape the man crashing down the stairs behind her pushed caution from her mind. It hardly mattered that the concrete passageway she'd entered was dripping with water and lit only by a naked bulb here and there; it hardly computed that there were too many doors. The suggestion that she was already lost whispered through her mind only once.

She sped forward on her tiptoes, around a corner, through a doorway, into a smaller hall, to the end, and confronted by a door on her left and another on her right, Leslie chose the one on the right.

Into the room without taking stock. She closed the door behind her and locked it, quite sure that the lock couldn't be disengaged from the other side. But she was too unnerved to open the door to make sure.

Leslie turned around and stared at the room she'd entered. Her breathing stopped almost immediately.

Not from fright.

Not from shock.

Not because her body was suffering a heart attack.

Then her heart began to race. She'd been here, she could swear it. This wasn't just any room. Déjà vu swarmed her, so strong that she couldn't separate it from reality.

She stood on a thick Turkish rug. Purple and orange were the first colors she saw, but they were quickly joined by a surprising array of improbable colors for a windowless room tucked away in the corner of some basement maze. Bright colors: green, blue, and red.

But it wasn't the colors that pulled her forward. There was a texture in this room that she found reassuring. Almost safe in its limited power to undo her. It was like facing a familiar monster and knowing that no matter what it did, you were better than it, and you would walk away alive. So really, you were safe. In control, even.

This room emboldened her. She'd been here before and walked away from whatever horror it contained to tell the story. This room was why she'd first decided to study psychology. Her fascination with the human mind began with her own need to understand how she could possibly suffer what she had suffered as a young girl and rise above it all, as so many millions of other women had.

A king-size bed with a tattered red-velvet canopy sat against the main wall. Drapes on either side. A thick lavender comforter with no fewer than a dozen holes chewed through by rats.

She walked forward and put her hand on the comforter, a patchwork of velvet and satin. No, this wasn't simply a figment of her imagination. She was here, in a room at the end of a maze of halls, confronted with a terror so great that it was causing her to hallucinate.

Swaths of red and purple and blue material had been hung from the ceiling to hide the mildewed concrete, which still showed in wide gaps. The room was lit by several strings of white Christmas-type lights behind the material—someone's attempt at ambient lighting.

There was a white dresser with a mirror, the kind with pink accents that might have been in a little girl's room once upon a time. Very similar to the dresser she had in her own room when she was nine, in fact.

The walls were cluttered with painted portraits, mirrors, china plates, candle sconces. Lots of sconces. Several dozen candles. A large pentagram was painted on the wall between two of the sconces. Didn't surprise her.

The one other feature that stood out to Leslie in her

first examination of the room was the two pinball machines opposite the dresser. One was a Batman machine; the other was a Barbie machine. Beside them, mounted on the wall, was a huge round dartboard that spun on an axis. The kind that would be used in a knife-throwing act.

The sweet scent of roses mixed with vanilla commanded her attention. Leslie looked for the source, transfixed by the odd blend of terror and desire. Half of her mind screamed for her to run, to escape the house and its bizarre inhabitants.

But another half suggested that she breathe deep and let that aroma calm her frayed nerves. Her grandmother had kept the stuffed pillows in her old house scented with vanilla and potpourri, and the scent had always brought a cleansing calm to Leslie, even in the worst of times.

Like now.

There had to be an explanation for the eerie familiarity of this room. If she slowed down and applied her mind, she'd make sense of it all. She'd always told herself that, and it always worked.

Leslie walked to the dresser and bent for a whiff from a bowl of potpourri. The pungent odor of lavender and vanilla worked deep into her sinuses. No more roses. She closed her eyes and exhaled slowly. Emotion swelled, and for a moment she thought she might cry. She swallowed hard, melancholy. A slight quiver took to her chin, and she bit her lower lip.

Think, Leslie, think! You're letting emotion bend your mind.

She was here for a reason, wasn't she? No four travelers could possibly find their way into such a strange house without some elaborate scheme drawing them. Whoever this stalker-killer was, he wasn't the Jason-with-a-machete-variety. He was a deeper thinker, much deeper.

Another scent mixed with the vanilla, and Leslie opened her eyes. There was a bowl of cream next to a candle. Without thinking, she lit the candle using a book of matches to one side.

The cream beckoned her. She lifted the bowl and sniffed it. Not a chilled cream. Vanilla pudding laced with caramel.

Again without thinking, Leslie dipped one finger into the cream and put it to her lips. The sweet taste of caramel pudding was unmistakable. Impulsively now, she dipped four fingers into the bowl, scooped out some of the pudding, and shoved it into her mouth. A small glob plopped onto the breast of her red blouse. She dabbed it with her finger and ate that too.

For a brief moment the realization of what she'd just done horrified her. It was unforgivably irrational. And of all people, why was she, who had such control, who rode the crests of reason and logic as a way to make sense of her world, now eating from a bowl in a stranger's bedroom?

She should be vomiting and searching for a way out.

Instead, she moaned, fingers stuck in her mouth like a child who snuck a treat from the refrigerator an hour before dinner when she knew good and well that it would be frowned upon by Mother.

Still, the smell of caramel pudding was so strong, and the forbidden taste so sweet, that rules such as these demanded to be compromised, particularly when the rest of your life was hell.

She froze, fingers in her mouth. The clarity of her predicament sliced through her foggy mind. She was a grown woman in her late twenties, not an adolescent sneaking pudding before dinner. Worse, she was a grown woman in a basement that belonged to Pete . . .

The closet door opened behind her. Leslie dropped the bowl on the dresser and spun, gasping.

Pete stood in the doorway, eyes fixed on her. She had pudding on her lips and on her fingers. Pete looked at her mouth, her fingers, the bowl behind her. But he didn't smile. Didn't flash a grin of wicked intent. Didn't approach her with force.

He just looked at her like a deer in the headlights.

Time seemed to stop.

"My room," Pete finally said, voice thick with pride. He released the closet door and stepped in.

Pete's room.

"Do you like my room?" Pete asked the question like an expectant child.

Leslie faced a critical decision. Did she play along or spit in his face?

She took a long look at the locked door to Pete's right. A long look at Pete, who waited for an answer. But she was alive. And her whole life she'd stayed alive by playing smart. By playing their games. Today was just another day in the game, though this particular game seemed to have unusually high stakes.

Mind over matter. Life was won and lost in the mind, end of story. So here she faced off a man who was her opponent more in mind than in body. And of the two, she had the stronger mind.

"Yes," she said. "Yes, Pete, I do like your room."

Pete lit up like the sun, rushed over to the bed and straightened the cover. Picked up a candle that had fallen to the floor and busily reinserted it in its holder, all the while keeping his eyes on her.

When he finished, he clasped his hands behind his back as if to say, *There, now it's perfect.*

"We have to be quiet," he said, eyes flitting to the door. "Mama will hear. She can't come here."

The candle he'd just put in the holder toppled over, rolled off the dresser, and fell to the floor. He didn't seem to notice. His eyes were singularly focused on her.

It occurred to her at that moment that she really didn't feel threatened by him. He was nothing more than an overgrown child.

Then she reminded herself where she was, and her fear returned, a new kind of fear motivated more by what lay outside this room than by Pete.

An image of Stewart slipped through her mind. He seemed bent on giving the killer a dead body. Betty might be their best hope for survival. Were the others even alive? Or bludgeoned in the meat locker?

She envisioned Jack blasting his way through the door with a shotgun. Jack? Yes, of course, Jack. Randy didn't possess enough backbone to save anyone, even he knew that. She used him just like he used her, but at a time like this, Randy was useless. Jack . . . she sensed Jack was a completely different animal.

The thought surprised her. Did she want him to rush in, put a slug in Pete's skull?

Yes, she thought. She did. A slug through that forehead, no matter what kind of victim Pete himself might be, seemed like the right kind of ending to this mind game she'd never wanted to play.

But short of that, she had to play smart. Play along. Millions of years of evolution had turned the human mind into an amazingly resourceful instrument of survival, capable of far more than ordinary life demanded of it. She'd read dozens of cases that demonstrated this fact, and now she would become one of those cases.

She smiled and clasped her hands behind her back to match his stance. "I like your room very, very much."

Pete blushed. He eased into a large stuffed recliner, leaned forward, and watched her as if he wasn't sure what to do with his catch.

Leslie made a show of interest by examining the room more closely—touching the candles, feeling the bedspread, smelling a few of the other potpourri-filled ceramic bowls.

She could feel his eyes on her, worshiping her. But not in a threatening way. She would have expected terror to fill her mind at a time like this, but it didn't. She was beyond that, she told herself. And being the object of such pure, perhaps even innocent, adoration struck her as interesting at least, even now in this black hellhole.

Perhaps particularly now, in this black hellhole, where the slightest reprieve from suffering would show like a bright beacon of hope.

The smell of sulfur seemed to have dissipated some. Maybe it was the potpourri.

"Where did you get the potpourri?" she asked.

An odd first question from a captive, but a smart question. She had to play smart. Distract him so that when the right opportunity presented itself, she would have the upper hand.

"The what?"

"This," she said, holding up the bowl. "It smells good."

His unblinking eyes remained on hers. "It's for you," he said.

Such sincerity, such innocence in his voice.

"Thank you. Where did you find it?"

"From the house," he said.

"You mean upstairs?"

"Sometimes. There's other houses. Do you like the pictures?"

She set the potpourri down and walked to her left, examining the portraits. "Yes. Do you know any of these people?"

"No. But I won't be lonely now."

Meaning he had her. She felt momentarily nauseated, but the feeling passed. She had to control the conversation, keep him on her track.

"I especially like the dresser. It reminds me of . . ." She stopped in front of the mirror.

She couldn't see herself. The mirror reflected the room but not her.

She turned around. "What's wrong with this mirror?"

"It don't work," he said.

"But . . ." She faced the mirror again. "But it shows other things. Why can't I see myself?"

"It's broken," he said.

Leslie shivered. She wrapped her hands around her bare arms. She'd never heard of such a thing. She reached out and touched the glass. Normal, as far as she could see.

Smart, Leslie, be smart. Don't lose your head.

"Can I ask you some questions, Pete?" She faced him.

"Yes, we can talk. I would like that." He stood, unhooked the bib portion of his overalls, and pulled off his T-shirt. He flexed his biceps, grinning from ear to ear.

"Do you think I'm strong?"

She was so taken aback by his display that she didn't answer him.

His smile faded.

She caught herself short of displaying disgust. "Yes. Yes, you are very strong."

"I can throw you," he said, encouraged again.

"Yes, I suppose you—"

"Look!" He ran to the closet, yanked open the door, and pulled out a huge purple bag of Purina Dog Chow. "Cereal. It makes you strong."

"I'm . . . I'm sure it does. How long have you lived here?"

"Do you want to be strong?"

"Maybe. But can we talk first?"

He carried the bag to her, still gazing into her eyes with boyish wonder, took her left hand, and placed it on his chest. Then he flexed.

There was no room for embarrassment. No need. She was playing his game, and that meant doing what he expected. To a point.

Leslie moved her fingers on his flesh, feeling the hard muscle beneath the skin. "Wow," she said, and a small part of her meant it. His chest was cool and smooth. Maybe he'd shaved it. White skin, nearly translucent, but it showed no veins. Soft skin like lily petals, softer than any of hers. But just below the skin, rocklike muscle.

She kneaded it and raised her hand to his shoulder, where the muscles parted like cords. What was she doing? She pulled her hand back, aghast at her momentary fascination.

But she immediately covered her rejection by smiling. "You are so strong."

"Thank you," he said. But he didn't move. His breath was stale.

Leslie averted her eyes, eager to step beyond this moment and redirect him. "So, how long have you lived here?"

"Do you want to be strong like—"

"If you want me to be your wife, then I have to know more about you, don't I?"

Her challenge caught him off guard.

"Please," she said. "I just want to know more about you."

He stepped back, unsure. "A long time."

"Where did you come from?"

He frowned as if trying to remember. "The circus. We were gypsies and did fun things. But then Stewart killed a man and so did Mama. I killed a man too. Have you done that?"

"No. I don't think killing is a good thing."

"You have to be strong."

"How many people have you killed?"

He shrugged, then smiled. "White kills people too. He's strong."

She had to keep him talking.

"Who is White?"

"White?"

"Yes. Who is he?"

"I think he's going to kill us if we don't kill the girl."

"What girl?"

"Susan."

"There's a girl hiding down here?"

The light went out of Pete's eyes. The expression on his face shifted from boyish innocence to irritation.

"You don't like Susan. Why?" Leslie had slipped into the role of psychoanalyst without thinking.

"She's worse than White."

"Worse than the killer? What does she do?"

His eyes darkened. The flesh below his eyes sagged, and he stared at her as if he might be sick. "You can't trust her," he said.

Pete clenched his eyes and screamed. Leslie caught her breath and stepped back. But as quickly as he gave vent to the terrible emotions, he stopped.

Opened his eyes. Stared at her, lost.

Did anyone hear his scream? Please, Jack. Please tell me you heard that.

"Why does White want you to kill her?" she asked.

No answer. Just that blank stare.

"I have to know things if I'm going to be your wife."

Pete refused to respond.

"Why can't you find her? This is your basement, your house."

"I don't want to talk anymore."

Leslie knew she was losing him, but she pressed anyway. "You have to tell me everything. I have to know more about the girl. I have—"

"No!" His face reddened.

She'd pushed him too far.

"I'm sorry. I won't talk about her."

They faced each other in a long silence. Pete still held the bag of dog food. He reached into it and withdrew a jar filled with the stuff, then dropped the bag.

"You like my pudding," he said. "It's vanilla. I'll mix more with water and smash it for you."

He hurried to the closet, picked up a bowlful of water from the floor, and returned, dumping the jar's contents into the bowl.

"It'll make you strong! Like me."

Leslie blinked at the concoction he mixed. She glanced at the bowl of pudding she'd eaten from a few minutes earlier. The same stuff. But its appeal was now gone. Completely.

"Eat it." He shoved the bowl in her face.

Leslie turned her face from a foul smell. It wasn't just dog food, it was rotten dog food. She thought about dipping her fingers in so eagerly and blanched.

"I already ate some," she said.

"But you have to finish. Mama said. It'll make you strong like me," he repeated. "Eat it."

"No . . . No, really, I can't."

"I know you like it! See?" He scooped some out with his fingers and pushed the mush into his mouth. "Sweet. See?" He picked up the bag and showed her the picture of the large juicy steak that evidently tantalized the dogs who ate this particular brand.

"I'm not going to eat dog food," she said. "I don't like dog food."

His face fell and his jaw slackened. She'd crushed him. But she drew the line here. She would throw up all over him if she even smelled that mush again.

"Eat it," he pleaded. "My mama made me eat it. I'm strong."

She just stared at him.

Pete dug his fingers into the mush and approached her with a scoop. "Here, please . . . please." He came right for her, shoved the stuff in her face.

Leslie turned away and pushed his hand. "Stop it! I—"

He grabbed her hair and tried to force the mush into her mouth. "You were eating; I saw you! Eat it!"

Panicked, she flailed. "Stop it!"

The bowl flew free and clattered on concrete, upside down.

Pete stared at the mess in shock. His face darkened. He slowly lifted enraged eyes. It didn't take the psychologist in Leslie to know she had made a terrible mistake.

He lifted his fist like a hammer and slammed it down on her head. She staggered under the blow, dropped to her knees.

Pete screamed long and loud. Then he scraped the mush off the floor and back into the bowl. He set it in front of her. "You are my wife! Eat it!"

13

AT FIRST JACK WASN'T SURE HE WAS STILL alive.

He had to be. His heart was still hammering, his lungs were sucking and pushing—his breath echoed in the dark chamber into which he'd been sucked.

Maybe he was unconscious. He'd hit the wall hard enough to knock him senseless. But his hands and feet were moving under him, groping on the cool, damp concrete surface.

Were his eyes open? They were. It was just too dark to see.

Jack pushed himself to his knees, then turned and sat on his rear end, trying to clear his head. Where was Randy?

Slowly he reconstructed the events that had deposited him here. Betty and Stewart, the killer, the house, the basement. The black closet, assuming he was inside a closet.

No humming. Nothing but his own breathing.

He stood to his feet shakily and felt around. A wall to his back. Concrete. No door that he could feel.

He inched around, arms extended. Nothing. He walked farther, but he could no longer tell which direction he was walking. Not without light.

The lighter. He dug into his pocket, distinguished it from the spare shotgun shells, and withdrew it. That was some bright idea, putting those two in the same pocket. He made a mental note not to do it again and flicked the lighter. It ignited on the second spark.

A long passageway with a rough concrete floor and an arched brick ceiling ran in both directions. The door . . . there.

He turned back and tried the door in the wall, but it was locked tight.

No draft now. Then what had sucked him in? Could an underground draft be strong enough to do that?

Don't say we didn't warn you.

Jack felt a new kind of fear run through his bones. *Welcome to my house.* What if White knew something about this house that none of them had guessed? What if this game was all about the house? Not White, not the hosts, but the house?

He tried to dismiss the thought. Made no sense. A house was a house. White, on the other hand, was a demented psychopath driven by his thirst for killing. The house might be part of his sick plot, but they had to understand the real threat—flesh and blood, not concrete and brick.

They. He had to get back to the others.

Jack breathed deep, focused on calming the tremble in his hands. The silence, the stillness, the not knowing why or what was getting to him. He should be running down this tunnel, desperate to find a way out. Instead, he stood here frozen, contemplating.

Contemplating and suddenly dizzy. It occurred to him that he was breathing too hard. He closed his mouth and breathed through his nose.

The lighter grew hot, and he released the butane trigger. The tunnel went black. He waited a few seconds, then reignited it.

Both directions looked the same to him, so he headed right. The draft had come from somewhere, maybe from an opening beyond the house. If he could find the exit, he could slip past White, head for the highway, and come back with the authorities.

But he knew that Leslie wouldn't survive long enough for that, even though she was a strong woman. Maybe it was why he had decided to come after her.

Randy, he didn't care about. Unfortunate but true. He'd concluded that the man was a self-absorbed pig.

Stephanie . . . also in the self-absorbed category. He wasn't sure how he felt about Stephanie, but right now he honestly didn't care if she stayed in that closet or not. She could make her choice and let it lead to its natural conclusion for once. How much longer could he protect her from herself? He'd stick to her as he always had, but it was getting harder and harder—

Jack stopped. He wasn't a bitter person by nature. Was he? No. Steph could take the heat for bringing that on. He grunted. The sound echoed down the chamber. His light reached out twenty feet or so before blackness overtook it. Why wasn't he running? He had no business taking a Sunday stroll down this tunnel.

He let go of the lighter again. In that moment, in the pitch blackness, the terror he'd felt earlier came roaring back to the surface, now without any distraction from contemplation.

There was something evil in this house.

He had to find a way out before the lighter decided to give out. How long had he been down here? Jack put flame to the lighter and began to jog.

A long scream reached him from somewhere beyond the brick walls. He pulled up and whirled. The scream ran on, a throaty wail that sounded more male than female.

It ended abruptly.

He ran thirty feet and slid to a stop when the tunnel came to a sudden end at a large wooden door. He tried the handle. Locked. Like every other miserable door in this miserable basement.

Jack raced back in the direction he'd come. It took him less time, much less time, to reach the other end of the tunnel.

Same dead end. Same kind of door. Locked.

How was that possible!? Where had the draft come from? He'd gotten in; there had to be a way out!

The lighter wasn't going to hold out forever. How long did these things last, anyway? The idea of being trapped forever in a dark concrete tunnel filled him with a new urgency. Something close to panic.

He searched for the door he'd come through. Maybe he'd get back out to the study.

He traveled the length of the tunnel. Nothing. The door had vanished.

Impossible. He made a return trip to the other end,

sprinting, with one hand holding out the lighter and the other shielding it from being blown out.

But nothing had changed. The wooden door was locked. He kicked it and found it solid. He cranked on the knob to no avail.

One final sprint to the far side sealed his understanding of his predicament.

There was no way out.

The faint sound of singing reached his ears. The same voice he'd heard a half dozen times since entering the house. A sweet song trapped in his head.

The flame was beginning to wane. He had to save the fuel, for what he didn't know, but the thought of running out terrified him.

Jack slid to his seat along the wall, let the tunnel go dark, and tried to slow his racing pulse.

— ◆ —

There were times when being a trained psychologist came in handy, such as the times when deft mental manipulation justified her choices and her past. And there were times when it was as useful as a degree in stone rolling, such as now. Leslie contemplated this fact in the back of her mind where the subconscious did its thing.

Her head hurt. She wanted to satisfy Pete's childish expectations, but she couldn't bring herself to eat the mush. Unlike him, she wasn't a child who had been forced into a pattern of behavior before the mind was fully formed. Her brain had long ago learned that it was not healthy to ingest food that smelled like something sewers washed away. Her mouth and throat were already reacting—she couldn't will the stuff down if her life depended on it.

And it did, she thought.

She knelt on the floor in front of the mush and began to cry.

That seemed to soften Pete. He backed up and watched her for a few seconds. Minutes.

"Please," he said. "I don't want to hurt you, but you have to be a good wife and eat your pudding. It will make you strong. Do you want to die?"

She was crying too hard to respond.

"Don't cry; please don't cry." He sounded frantic.

"I can't eat it," she managed.

"But you're guilty," he said. "If you don't eat your sin, it will eat you; that's what Mama says. You ate the pudding already. I saw you. Everyone likes the pudding when they try it."

What was it with these people and sin? "I'm not guilty!" she cried, angry now. "I don't care what that witch who calls herself your mother has stuffed into your head. It's sickening!"

Even as she yelled, she knew that she had eaten the pudding. Quite eagerly. And she had eaten something like this pudding before, many times. Like a pig wallowing in its sty.

The thought enraged her. "If your mother forced you to eat this crap, she's a pig," she said.

He put his hands over his ears and paced. "No, no, no, no. Guilty, guilty. You have to eat, you have to eat."

"I'll throw up. I can't—"

He crouched in front of her, desperation etched in his face. "Please, please." He bent to one knee and scooped up some mush. "Please, see?" He eagerly shoved it into his mouth. His eyes begged her. Sweat beaded his forehead.

Okay now. Mind over matter. Eating this garbage was a pivotal part of Pete's psyche. It was part of his religion. As real as heaven and hell to him. An extension of society's obsession with faith in the nonexistent powers of God and Satan.

Leslie had never hated religion as much as she did at that moment.

She had to try; she had to show him that she at least wanted to please him.

"Are you innocent?" he asked.

"Yes," she said.

He stood, shocked. Apparently her claim offended him to the core. "You're better than me?"

She didn't know where he was headed. If she continued to defy him, he might find the need to correct her.

"No."

"Then why won't you eat like me?"

"Okay. Okay, I'll try."

His face relaxed.

Leslie looked at the bowl. She put three fingers into the pasty mush and scooped a portion the size of a candy out. She'd just eaten no less and relished it. And she knew it was no different. Yet now, at the sight, the odor forced bile up her throat. Her hand began to tremble.

She tried, she did. She closed her eyes and held her breath, lifted the stuff to her face, opened her mouth, and gagged.

The day without food had left her stomach empty, and she dry-heaved twice. Then she flung the stuff off her fingers, lay on her side, and began to sob.

Pete was pacing, fists gripped tight, muttering, "Bad wife."

With two long strides he crossed the room, stuck one hand into her waistband, clamped the other around her upper arm, and plucked her from the ground as if she were a Barbie doll.

He threw her on the bed and marched toward the round target board. "You have to learn," he said.

He quickly untied straps on the edge of the board.

"What are you doing?"

"You have to learn."

He grabbed her and slammed her against the board. Strapped her wrists tight. Then her ankles, spread-eagle. He was going to whip her?

"Please . . ."

He pulled a fistful of darts from a can on the ground, gave the wheel a turn, and stepped back.

Leslie's world spun.

"Tell me when you've learned," he said. No doubt he was replaying his own mother's treatment of him. But it invoked no sympathy whatsoever.

"Stop! I've learned . . . I'm guilty!"

Pete either wasn't convinced or wanted to play anyway. He threw his first dart.

It struck her thigh.

Leslie screamed.

14

TWO SOUNDS REACHED OUT TO JACK AS HE sat in the black silence. The first was a distant scream. A woman's this time.

The second was the faint humming again. Closer, much closer than the scream.

He flicked the lighter and stood, listening intently.

Could it be pipes?

He stepped away from the wall and stopped.

Hmm, hmm, hmm. No. Not pipes. The sound of a child humming, faint but clear. As if it was in the tunnel!

"Hello?"

His voice echoed, and the humming stopped.

He crept down the tunnel, nerves on edge.

Hmm, hmm, hmm. Ahead and on the right. How was that possible? He'd already been up and down this tunnel.

A small door edged into the circle of light cast by the dwindling flame. How could he possibly have missed it?

Or was it the door he'd been pulled through, reappeared?

Jack lifted the light.

The door was smaller than the one he'd come through, no more than four feet high. He stopped in front of it.

Hmm, hmm, hmmm.

Then silence.

"Hello?" he whispered, but his voice still sounded disruptively loud in the hollow chamber.

He put his hand on the knob, heart pounding.

This is ridiculous, Jack. Just open it.

He twisted the doorknob and pulled.

A small storage space. A girl, seated on the floor, leaning against the back wall. Her face was pale, and her eyes were closed.

Dead.

The flame in Jack's hand went out, throwing him into darkness. He thumbed the lighter, desperate for light, light, any bit of light. *C'mon, c'mon.* Standing in a doorway facing a dead girl wasn't the time for . . .

The flame caught.

The girl's eyes were open, staring at him but not seeing. Dull circles of gray.

He cried out and slammed the door. Stumbled back to the opposite wall.

Hmm, hmm, hmm.

More singing? She was alive? Then why had she appeared dead? And how could she have hummed if she was dead?

You're losing your mind, Jack. Reality is being distorted by your fear. She's alive!

Still, opening the door again seemed like . . .

Like what? She was a victim, trapped and in need of

help, and she'd been calling to them since they first entered the house. But why wasn't she yelling?

Hmm, hmm, hmm.

Jack stepped up to the door, forced his fears down, then flung it open and jumped back.

The storage space was gone. In its place was a small room filled with junk, lit by an oil lamp. The girl stood now, braced with a board in her hands, ready to strike him. Her face was pale and smudged, but not dead, and her eyes were brown and clear, not gray like the grave. Her dark-brown hair was swept up on both sides and tied at the back. Maybe thirteen years old, but she couldn't be an inch over five feet tall.

She blinked, judging him. But she didn't seem frightened. Resolved to hit him if necessary, but not frightened. By the looks of the rumpled blankets and empty soda cans, she'd been hiding in the room for some time.

"Are . . . are you okay?"

The girl mumbled something that he couldn't understand. He wasn't sure she was entirely lucid.

"Are you okay?"

"Do I look okay?" she asked. "What's your name?"

"Jack. I'm . . ." He glanced up the hall. "I'm trapped down here."

She lowered the board and cautiously walked out of the room, glanced in either direction, and looked up at him. She seemed to be okay.

"Who are you?" he asked.

Again she said something softly, then she paused and spoke clearly. "Susan," she said. "Are you alone?"

"No. There are four of us."

She walked up to Jack, dropped the board on the

ground, and wrapped her arms around his waist. She clung to him.

He put his hand on her head, awkward. She was clearly a victim in the same predicament as they were. He let the lighter die and took her in both of his arms.

"Thank God," she breathed. "Thank God."

He wanted to say something that would comfort her, but his nerves were so shot that he was at a loss. All he could do was stroke her hair, forcing back the knot in his own throat.

"It'll be okay," she whispered. "It'll be . . ." He didn't catch the rest.

What a strange thing for her to say. The poor girl was delusional. He hated to think of what events had brought her here. Or kept her here.

"I . . . you looked like you were sleeping or something when I first opened the door," he said. "Then you were standing. Were you singing? Why didn't you yell?"

Susan stepped back. "There's something wrong with this house," she said. "You know that much, don't you?"

"Wrong?"

"It's haunted."

Jack wasn't a big believer in haunted houses. As a matter of simple fact, there was no such thing.

"How long have you been here?" he asked

She looked toward one of the locked wooden doors. "We should hurry. They might find us now."

The poor girl's fear had been replaced by desperation, he thought. Had the killer done this? Brought her here as part of his game? Jack swallowed.

"Do you know how to get out of this tunnel?"

She reached into a pocket sewn on the front of her

white cotton dress, withdrew a key, and held it up. "They don't know about this room."

Jack sighed with relief. "Smart girl. Okay. Do you know where the tunnel leads?"

"Yes. But you have to be fast."

"Do you know the whole house?"

"No."

Jack paused for a fraction of a second. Could he trust her? Of course he could trust her; she was in the same predicament as he was. He couldn't possibly look into her eyes and *not* trust her.

"Do you know where Pete is? Or Leslie?"

"Who's Leslie?"

Of course. "One of us four. I'm pretty sure she's down here somewhere." Jack looked up the tunnel. "What kind of basement is this?"

"A freaky one, that's for sure. Follow me."

"Hold on. Do you know how to get *out* of the house?"

"Don't *you* know how to get out of the house?"

She had expected him to take her to safety. "No, not yet," he said.

She nodded, remarkably composed.

"We have to find Leslie first."

"Follow me," she said.

15

STEPHANIE SAT IN THE CLOSET, TREMBLING
And crying.

Her predicament had become completely . . .

There was no word to describe how bad her situation was. *Death*, maybe. She was actually dying. Or had
died and was now in hell. The hell the priests of her
childhood had warned her about.

She couldn't think straight. It was dark; she only
had to open her eyes to remember that. Except for a
distant hiss that sounded like it might be rain, the
house was quiet. But Betty and Stewart were out
there. She'd heard them thundering around after they
broke free of the meat locker. After a while she could
hear them creeping around, smell them when they
passed. They stopped in front of the closet once but
didn't enter. She didn't know why. None of it could be
real, but she was having a hard time convincing herself
of that.

The house seemed alive, looking for her. Eccentrics

or inbreds or devils, it didn't matter; they were all the same to her. She thought they might be in the dining room, sliding around, waiting for her to make a sound.

She mumbled a silent prayer. "Oh God oh God oh God." But she didn't really mean *oh God*.

She really meant, *I'm going to strangle you, Jack. I hate you, I hate you, I hate you! I hate you for meeting me, for screwing up my life, for dragging me out here, for leaving me in this closet! For blaming our daughter's death on me. For your unforgiving bitterness. For the way you look at Leslie.*

But her nerves were too frayed to consciously process that long thought over and over, so she just compressed it all into a habitual pseudo-prayer. *Oh God.*

She'd whispered a thousand such prayers since stepping foot into this black space. She even tried to dredge up something from the Book of Common Prayer, which contained a few sentiments she'd memorized, oh, so long ago, but those words eluded her. In any case, she didn't have any illusions that some great being would actually swoop down from the sky, reach his long hand through the roof, and pluck her safely from the closet.

She needed something to hold on to, and it wasn't Jack. And it wasn't a song. Within minutes of Jack's abandoning her in this pit, she'd realized that such a childish, foolish means of escape was no match for this particular reality. In fact, reduced to her shriveling self, she found the idea of singing repulsive.

And she found her raw surging emotion at least somewhat comforting. So she held on to this hatred she felt for Jack.

She hated him for his bitterness.

She hated him for not leaving her, knowing good and well she deserved nothing less.

She hated him for going after Leslie. The tramp might actually seduce him.

She hated him for leaving her to rot in this black closet.

She hated him for making her so angry, because anger meant she still cared for that stubborn, pigheaded mule.

Her mind had snapped again; she knew that much. It snapped first a year ago, when she stood staring at cracked ice over the pond where just a moment earlier her daughter had been standing.

It wasn't really her fault, they all said. There was snow on the ice, and she was from the South—no way to know that the ice was too thin.

No way she could be blamed for posing Melissa on what she thought was snow so that she could take a picture of the toddler in her darling little yellow coat.

No way she could know that the camera would run out of juice at that moment, forcing her to remove her attention from Melissa for those thirty seconds as she replaced the batteries.

She'd spent every waking moment since the tragedy breathing denial; she did know that much. Everything was going to be all right. She just had to move on in the flow of life. Slap on a smile and sing. But here, in this suffocating space, all of that nonsense had been jerked from her.

Give me one dead body, and I might let rule two slide. She'd given her dead body—Melissa—but that wouldn't impress this killer.

While that inbred Stewart had been busy calling them all atheists, Stephanie thought more than once that he might be right. She thought she believed in God. At least she used to, when she was a kid. But someone had once said something to her about being a Christian and still being a "practical atheist," that is, someone who believed in God but didn't follow his ways. Heck, even the demons believed in God and shook, didn't the Bible say that?

She was shaking now. Not because she was a demon, but because she was pretty sure something similar to demons was outside the closet.

Her problem was that she wasn't completely sure she did believe in God. The only demon she knew was herself.

And Jack.

"Oh God oh God oh God . . ."

16

WHEN RANDY HIT THE CONCRETE WALL, HE was running at a full clip in pitch darkness, away from the thumping boots.

Fifteen or twenty seconds at a fast run, then *smack!* He bounced back a few feet and dropped to his butt, dazed and barely conscious. The shotgun clattered to the ground, and he ran his hands about quickly, searching for it.

He needed that gun, needed it like he needed air. He had the knife, but with any luck he wouldn't ever be close enough to Stewart for the blade to do any good. And if the gun didn't work, he'd use it like a bat. Old Stew had a thing or two to learn about baseball.

More than a few times he'd been tempted to stop in his tracks, turn around, and wait for the running feet to catch up before blasting away. Or whaling away.

Either/or, the fact that he was thinking again was encouraging. In some ways he felt more alive running down this tunnel than he had for years playing tough guy. Why?

Terror. Cold-blooded fear was pumping him full of life. Not panic. Just plain, unrelenting fear. The kind that propelled him pell-mell down a pitch-black tunnel.

Straight into a wall.

Randy found the gun. He staggered to his feet, aware that something cool was running over his lips. Sweat or snot or blood.

He faced the coming boots, which he'd decided must belong to Stewart. *We got us one, Betty!* Somehow Randy didn't figure White as the kind who would chase his prey down a tunnel. He'd more likely just show up at the other end.

Randy was fumbling for the trigger, bringing the gun up, when he felt the door handle dig into the small of his back.

Randy grabbed at it, twisted, pulled a door open, and stepped through the opening.

Rather, tripped through the opening. The threshold consisted of a foot-high retainer. He splashed headlong into some water.

Gray light filtered into the puddle from a shaft a hundred feet or so to his left. Must be a sewer, or a drain. Water ran from right to left, maybe six inches deep. Soaked his good shoes.

The pounding feet slowed. Randy lunged to his left just as a shotgun blast crashed through the tunnel, spraying the water on his right.

A snarl of frustration chased the sound.

Not a cry, not a shout, not a *take that, you rat.*

A guttural snarl. It was Stewart, had to be Stewart, and the sound reminded Randy why he'd had no desire to face the man earlier. Maybe the shotgun-as-baseball-bat idea needed refinement.

Randy splashed down the passageway toward the shaft of light. There was a room beyond it, and another light source, both of which he had to reach before Stewart rounded the corner and got off a second . . .

Bam!

Several pellets smacked his left shoulder, and he yelled with pain. But he made the room and pulled up behind the wall on his right before a third shot could be fired. Stewart was sloshing through the water behind him. Walking now.

Taking his time.

Another single bulb in the ceiling. Water streamed down the walls. It was at least a foot deep in here and rippled around old oil drums, pickaxes, large-bit drills, a jackhammer. A hard hat with a cracked lamp floated by.

A two-foot-wide round pipe ran into the concrete wall on one side. But there was a door on the opposite wall. A tall wooden hatch with a curved top, the kind that belonged in dungeons.

Randy glanced back around the corner. No mistaking Stewart's oxlike form striding down the passage, pump-action shotgun in both hands. Fifty feet off.

He had two choices: he could take his chances with this ancient, untried shotgun, or he could see what lay behind the door. The only thing that gave him pause was Stewart's slow pace.

What did he know?

Who cared? Randy ran to the door and jerked it open, grateful that it wasn't locked.

But that's where his gratefulness ended. Stewart, walking straight for him over there, walked toward him in this passage too, now only forty feet away. How—? Stewart shifted the gun to one hand and used the other to unbuckle his belt and slide it out of his waistband, which was crazy 'cause the man had a shotgun, why would he need a belt?

Randy was so horrified by the optical illusion that he fired the shotgun without aiming.

Click. The antique would not fire.

Randy slammed the door shut and jumped back. How was that possible? Two Stewarts? Or was that White? He'd imagined it all. No. Stewart was still coming from the other side.

Now Randy began to panic. This was the end. The only other way out was . . .

He jerked his head to the large pipe that ran into the wall. He could fit into that. Without another thought Randy leaped across the room, threw his shotgun through the opening, climbed onto one of the drums, and shoved his head and arms into the hole.

It was a tight fit with his broad shoulders, but he squirmed through like a snake and dropped out five feet later into a concrete room with two feet of standing water. Above and below the open pipe, metal rods embedded in the wall formed steps, possibly for servicing. Two sources of light here: the hole through which he'd just come and a grate directly overhead, facing the stormy night sky.

Bolted into a concrete ceiling.

Water poured into the room through two six-inch pipes. Rainwater? All the walls were concrete. There were no other openings. What was this place? A septic tank of some kind?

Something eclipsed the light from the pipe.

Stewart was coming after him? He spun, searching again for any way out. Nothing. He was in a sealed coffin. With water pouring in, fast.

And Stewart coming through the only exit.

Randy felt for the shotgun. He'd thrown it through, heard it splash. Good for nothing more than a club now, but he could use a club.

The water was rising quickly.

His fingers bumped the shotgun, and he jerked it out of the water before realizing that he held a spade. Just as good.

Randy screamed and jabbed the sharp end into the hole. The thought of striking his father with a shovel made him tremble, but he had no choice, right? This bigger man was going to kill him!

And Stewart wasn't his father. He was losing his marbles.

A blast of hot lead tore at his side. He jumped back and to one side, slapping at his shirt. Small flesh wound. He was lucky. The next one would cut him in half.

Still the man was coming in, gun first, trigger-happy, and all Randy had was a spade. He'd smack the gun from Stewart's hands when it came out.

It occurred to Randy that the water was now at his waist. And that it was aiming to flow *out* the hole that Stewart was now blocking.

The ingrate grunted. He wasn't coming through so fast. Randy waited for the gun barrel to emerge.

Water was still rising.

Still no gun barrel.

Waiting there in waist-high water, Randy began to

anticipate a scenario that frightened him more than the shotgun. Not that he was any expert on death, but of all the ways he'd ever imagined going out, drowning struck him as one of the least favorable.

Stewart snarled with frustration again.

The barrel poked through the hole, and Randy's vision of drowning disappeared. He raised the spade, waited until the bulk of Stewart's weapon was out, and swung down.

Metal clashed against metal. A flash lit the chamber, harmlessly drilling the concrete with lead. Judging by the amount of trouble Stewart was having getting through the pipe, Randy doubted he'd have room to pump the action for a fresh shell.

He grabbed the barrel with both hands and tugged with all his weight. The shotgun came free, and Randy flew back into the rear wall.

He had his gun. A gun that he knew worked. Salvation was in his hands. He pumped the action, chambering a shell.

Stewart's hands were out and clawing at the mouth of the pipe, pulling himself forward. Randy could see his big beady eyes a couple of feet inside, filled with fear.

He lined the barrel up with the man's triple scar and was about to pull the trigger when his good business sense managed to overpower his passion. The last thing he needed was a dead body wedged in that pipe.

"Help me!" Stewart roared.

Help you?

"I'm stuck!"

Randy knew there wasn't an ounce of fat on Stewart's massive torso. It wasn't lack of power that had momentarily stalled his progress. It was lack of leverage. He did indeed need help.

Randy was too stunned to respond. A moment ago he was ready to blast the man's head from his shoulders given the opportunity. Now that same man wanted his help.

"That room's gonna flood! Push me back!"

"Are you nuts?"

"Please . . ." Stewart jerked, trying to move. "You're gonna drown. Push me!"

Randy looked up at the grate. Rain streamed between the bars. There was no way past the bolts. He looked down at the pipe with that bald head bobbing frantically.

Stewart suddenly let out a terrifying roar, an unnatural roar. His head began to tremble, then shake. And then it was over, and he just stared up at Randy.

"Please," he said. "I swear, if you don't get me out of this pipe, you'll drown. Push me."

"You were trying to kill me!" Randy said, as if this were helpful information.

"I'll get you out; I swear I'll show you how to get out. You got no clue how to get outta this basement, you know. None. You're stuck down here till you die. But I know how. Push me. Please, you gotta get me out!"

Maybe Randy could shoot the man once he pushed him through. One thing was certain: Stewart's body would block the water. Unless he backed out, they would both drown.

Randy pushed the barrel into the hole. "Grab this and push yourself. And remember, my finger's on this trigger."

The man grabbed the barrel and pushed. But it was Randy, not Stewart, who moved.

"You have to push me!" the man said.

"How?"

"My head. Put your hands on my head and push."

The idea of pushing his bald head seemed obscene. Water was at his chest, about to spill into the pipe.

Not wanting to get the shotgun wet, Randy balanced it on one of the bars protruding from the wall over the hole. He braced himself on a lower step, reached into the pipe, and placed both hands on the bald head of the man who'd been bent on his killing.

"Remember, I have the gun."

"Push!" Stewart yelled.

Randy pushed. He could bench 400 and was putting about that much pressure on Stewart's head now. Any ordinary neck might have buckled.

The man moved about six inches then stopped with a cry of pain.

"What?"

"My shoulder. I think you dislocated my shoulder!"

"You're stuck," Randy said.

"I know I'm stuck, you sinner!"

"Settle down. I'm trying to get us out of here!"

They were yelling. Water lapped at the pipe.

"What if I pull you?"

"I'll never get out . . ." The man was whimpering now. "Please, you have to help me. Push me."

"I did!"

"Try again."

Randy tried again, but it became immediately apparent that there was no pushing Stewart out as long as his broad shoulders were wedged tight.

Randy considered the knife tucked in his belt, the

one he'd snagged from the kitchen. Maybe he could cut
Stewart out. Shoot him dead and cut him out.

He pondered this. Randy had never killed a man.
Not in defense, not in war, not in rage. And certainly not
one stuck in a pipe crying for help, never mind that he
was the devil himself.

He suddenly wasn't sure he could do it. The idea of
sticking that barrel into that pipe and blowing Stewart
away was horrifying. Absolutely out of the question. He
began to panic.

Easy, boy. Just take a deep breath. *Give me one dead
body.* This would be the one. Self-defense. You do it or
you die, as simple as that.

"Please . . ."

"Shut up!" Randy screamed.

"Please . . ."

Stewart's own words from earlier in the evening
came back to Randy. *You like water, don't you?*

Water. He might not have the strength to kill the
man outright, but he could let him drown.

Dead or alive, the man was stuck. But Randy had a
knife. And a spade.

"Please!" The man's voice was garbled now, with
water splashing around his mouth. "Get me out of here!"

Randy began to shake.

17

"I SWEAR! I'M GUILTY! STOP IT, STOP IT!"

Leslie was sobbing, not so much from the pain of the two darts protruding from her body, but from the dread of any further damage.

He was a demented boy, and she was the puppy he'd chosen to extract allegiance from. If there were such things as demons, Pete was undoubtedly a demon trapped in a person who had the body of a man and the mind of a child.

Pete stopped the rotating wheel when she was upright.

"You promise?" he asked.

"I promise!"

"Say it again."

"I'm guilty."

"As sin."

"As sin."

"Will you show me how bad you are?"

Meaning what? She sniffed and took a deep breath. *What did he mean by that?*

"Will you eat the cereal?"

His mother had made him eat the rotten dog food to remind him that he was no better than it was. By forcing him to embrace the notion that he was evil, he became evil. Or more accurately, he believed he was evil, and therefore was predisposed to exhibit antisocial behavior—the real definition of *evil* to her way of thinking—in a sane world stripped of religion.

Leslie was now absolutely certain that he could not be saved from those false beliefs anytime soon.

"Yes," she said, sniffing. Saying it brought relief. "I will. And I'm sorry for being such a disobedient wife."

He stared at her. A dumb grin formed on his face.

"Okay."

He untied her wrists and legs and set her on the floor. Then he walked toward the bowl of dog food.

"Can you take these darts out first?" Leslie asked, sitting on the bed. Adrenaline had eased the pain in her thigh, but now the dart in her biceps was throbbing. She could have pulled them out, but she wanted him to do it. Anything to stall him.

Pete returned to the bed, leaving the bowl for the moment. She lay down, unsure if she could avoid breaking down again.

He sat beside her and reached for her arm. But he didn't pull the dart out. He touched her bare skin lightly. Traced it gently.

Instead of recoiling at his touch, she welcomed it. Maybe . . . maybe if she endeared him. Disarmed him with a show of tenderness. When was the last time he'd felt any tenderness toward a human being? From a woman, never.

Leslie reached across her body and rested her hand on his hand. "I'll be a good wife. Would you like that?"

His breathing thickened.

"Take it out."

He carefully pulled the dart from her muscle. She was only dimly aware of her ability to ignore the pain. She was beyond caring about anything so trivial as pain. He'd tried to make her eat rotten dog food and he'd thrown darts at her—by themselves not as terrible as the things she'd imagined White had planned for them. But she felt violated. Worse.

Shredded. Now she contemplated loosing the cords that held her psyche intact and relinquishing her resolve to him completely.

Why? So that she didn't have to eat the dog food? No. Because she felt a desperate need to cling to someone. To find herself in anything but her own shattered soul.

The truth made no real sense to her, not yet. Nothing in the textbooks remotely mirrored the emotions running through her now, while lying on his bed.

Pete pulled the dart from her thigh.

It occurred to her that she couldn't smell the odor anymore. She'd grown accustomed to it.

"You are so pretty," he said slowly.

She reached up and ran her fingers over his head, both repulsed and pleased by her strength to do so anyway.

"And you're so strong." Her head spun.

"The cereal makes me strong," he said.

"Love makes me strong," Leslie said.

That stopped him. His eyes searched hers. "Do . . . do you love me?"

"I'm your wife, aren't I?"

Pete lowered his face into her neck. "You are my wife."

He just sat there bent over her, unmoving, clueless. She was nothing but a favorite toy to him. His cheek was pressed against her cheek, and she could smell the sickly sweet sweat on his neck. What was she doing?

Leslie eased her head away from him and dry-heaved.

Pete straightened, frowned. He rose and went to the little-girl's dresser, opened a drawer, and began rifling around in it.

She began to sob quietly. She was in nothing more or less than the same predicament shared by an endless sea of humans who hid in their own prisons of abuse and alcohol and sex and money and whatever other kind of addiction or vice that both tormented and comforted at once. She was no better or worse than any other person who lived behind whitewashed walls to hide the problems in their basement from the neighbors.

Pete returned, holding a rope.

"More pudding, Leslie?"

⌒⌒

Randy did not move, knowing that Stewart was squirming in the shaft now submerged in water. The man's screams had been swallowed by a throat full of rainwater and then silenced.

Father was dead. Dead, dead, had to be dead. And the water was now around Randy's neck. If he didn't get down there and dig out the cork called Stewart, he would drown as well.

He had a spade. Using a spade underwater might take a few minutes, so he really should get started. But the thought of actually going under and digging at Stewart's torso brought with it a strange brew of fear and eagerness that kept him rooted.

The fact was, he wanted to do it. The fact was, he wasn't sure he could. The fact was, the water was now up to his nose, and in a few minutes it would fill the concrete holding tank.

Randy took a deep breath and dived, spade in hand. He opened his eyes, but the water was muddy brown. He'd have to feel for the hole. Feel for the head.

The prospect of lining up a jab with the shovel by touch alone forced Randy back to the surface.

Water poured in.

He gasped, fighting a fresh burst of panic. He had to do this. He had to get down there and hack away Stewart's dead body. He was dead, for goodness' sake!

Randy went down again, felt for the hole, and found nothing but solid wall. Was he on the wrong wall? How—

The water began to swirl around him. He jerked up and found the surface again. It took only a moment for him to realize that the tank was draining, and draining fast.

Water dripped off his head, splashed into a rushing river of muddy water that was being pulled toward the wall ahead. Toward the hole.

He stood, immobilized legs spread, spade firmly in his grasp. The large pipe that Stewart had clogged just a few moments ago was uncorked. Stewart's body had been pushed out! The buildup of water had freed him?

Randy wasn't taking any chances—no way, not now.

He peered cautiously out of the hole and searched for Stewart. For all he knew, the man hadn't really drowned and was waiting outside.

But then he saw the body, lying in the room where it had evidently been washed by the receding water.

Randy watched the body for a full minute before deciding it was most definitely dead. He retrieved the shotgun from overhead and pushed the weapon out with the spade. He climbed the service steps, then squirmed through the pipe.

He'd killed the man, right? *You like water, Stewart, huh? You think that's funny?*

Now what? He had to get out of this place before everything flooded. And what about that other Stewart he'd seen, coming from the other door? His mind was playing tricks, right? Had to be.

Back to square one. Two ways out of the room. He checked the shotgun. One shell left. The fact that no one had appeared to help Stewart from behind or stood waiting for Randy when he spilled through the pipe was a good sign.

Not that he would have minded facing an accomplice right now. He had a gun. Bring a few on.

He stood in the muddy water, thinking things through.

"What are you doing, Randy?" he asked softly. "You're in a lot of hot water down here."

That right?

"Yeah, that's right. You heard the man. There's no way out of here."

That right?

"Listen to yourself. You think you're on to something?"

Whatever. The facts were still unchanged. He had to find the others. He had to find Leslie. Assuming they were still alive, which he doubted. More important, he had to find a way past White. Nothing would be the same after today, that was for sure. Nothing ever.

He walked to the door that he'd first come through, poked his head around the corner. Empty. But he wasn't going back there.

He crossed the room to the other door, which meant he had to pass Stewart. He trained the gun on the body, which lay facedown. Maybe he should put a blast into it just to make sure. Of course, he only had one shot. And the noise might alert whoever else was crawling around down here.

Randy crept forward, trigger finger ready, totally ready. The form did not move. He stuck his foot out and nudged it. Dead for sure. He shoved the body over with his right leg.

The light was dim, but there was no mistaking Stewart's big bald head, gruesome scar, and grungy bib-overalls. A thin tendril of smoke drifted from the corner of Stewart's twisted, parted lips. A dark fog. Black smoke.

Randy took a step back and stared at the odd sight. There was something evil in that fog, but his mind was numb and he couldn't attach any reason to it. Maybe White had sneaked in, shot Stewart at close range. That might be gunpowder smoke.

He looked out the door, up the tunnel. No one there.

Randy wasn't sure if that was good or bad. There was no evidence Stewart had even been shot. He was drowned, not shot!

Randy dug into Stewart's pockets and pulled out a plastic box of cartridges. Good, definitely good. Now he had the shotgun and about what, fifteen or so shells. Bring 'em on, baby.

He reloaded, then headed up the tunnel.

Shotgun in hand, he wasn't as scared as he thought he should be. Killing that pig back there had felt—

A low whisper cut through the tunnel. "Give me one dead body, Randy."

He spun and discharged the shotgun with his right hand. It nearly jerked his arm off. Nothing there.

In fact . . . In fact, there was no body at all! Stewart's body was gone! Could his accomplice have come back? Was that possible?

"That one didn't count." Again, behind him.

He dropped the spade, whirled, and fired again before the garden tool hit the ground. Nothing but black empty space.

"I'm losing my mind," he whispered.

Interesting. He wasn't so upset about losing his mind. Not even sad.

"God help me, I'm losing my mind."

18

THE GIRL NAMED SUSAN LED JACK THROUGH
a short hall that opened up into the first room that Jack
and Randy had entered upon descending into the
basement, the one with all the sofas.

He pulled up, confused by their entry point. He
didn't remember the door they now came through. The
four bright sofas were the same, as were the paintings
that covered the walls. The potbellied stove.

Susan hurried through the room toward the main
door, gliding with confidence, yet tentative at once.
Jack watched her move, unsure how he should feel
about finding such an innocent but knowing girl who
on one hand seemed as though she'd been made for
this place and on the other hand looked the clear
victim.

"Hold on."

She turned around. Now in the full light he saw that
her dress had been scuffed and torn. Brown streaks
dirtied her cheeks. "Yes?"

"I don't remember seeing this hall." He glanced

back at the door they'd passed through. "I could swear that was a closet."

"It's confusing, I know," she said.

Jack walked past her to the main door. "Haunted."

"Haunted," she said.

He pulled the door open and looked at the main hall. The stairs ascended on the left to the main floor.

The girl was saying something, but Jack had his mind on those stairs. He glanced down the hall, saw that the other doors were all closed, then ran up the stairs. The door at the top was closed. He tugged on it, but it was locked. Figured.

"Locked," the girl said. She was at the base of the stairs. "We can't get caught out here."

Jack pounded on the door. "Stephanie!"

If she was still in the nearby closet, she didn't hear or respond. Knowing her, she'd fled and was lying dead on the flagstone walk.

"We have to go," the girl said. "I might know where your friend is."

He descended the stairs two at a time. "Which door?"

She was already gliding to the last one on the left. Opening it, she ran in, down another hall strung with small bulbs on a wire, like a string of Christmas lights. He followed her around three corners.

Susan passed through a low door and ducked into a crawl space. The low-slung ceiling was strung with pipes. She hurried forward, bent over to keep from hitting her head.

"In there," she whispered, pointing to a small door. "It goes into the closet."

Jack stood by the door, catching his breath. "What closet?"

"It's where he hides."

"Who?"

"The slow one."

Pete? "Where are we, Susan?"

"In the basement," she said.

"I know that. I mean this house. There's a killer stalking us, for heaven's sake. We had our tires slashed and just happened to wander into this house conveniently tucked away with inbreds waiting for the next unfortunate soul to walk into their trap. And then there just happens to be you."

She stared at him with those wide eyes. "Getting out of the basement is a problem."

Okay, then. So he'd deal with the big picture later. "You mean we're stuck down here? How did he get you down here?"

"I mean you shouldn't have come down."

"Trust me, it wasn't exactly my first choice." He looked at the door. "We couldn't just leave Leslie. What's through this door?"

"It goes into a closet."

"And?"

"There's something wrong with this house, Jack. You see things. If you just walk in there, he'll kill you."

"Who? Pete? How do you know he's with her?"

Her eyes suggested she knew a thing or two about Pete.

"How did you get down here?" he asked.

She hesitated. "I've been down here for three days. You're not the only one who wandered into their trap."

"So you got away?"

She stared at him without answering. *Dumb question,*

Jack. Of course she hadn't gotten away. Her clear eyes searched his. He detected the weight of her ordeal and now felt as responsible for her rescue as for Leslie's, even though he really had no clue what to do.

Jack looked at the small door that led to the back of Pete's closet. *And a child shall lead them.* He'd heard that lyric before somewhere. Maybe it was in one of Stephanie's songs. In many ways Susan reminded him of a child, grown now, but innocent. Like Melissa . . .

He cut the thought short.

"Okay, I'm going to see what I can see. You're sure I'll be in a closet?"

"It could be open."

He nodded and reached for the wooden latch that held the door closed.

"Maybe I should go with you," she said.

"No. Is there really no way out of this basement?"

"One dead body," she said.

So, she was part of this insane game as well. *Give me one dead body, and I might let rule two slide.*

Susan motioned to the shadows on their left. "There's a shaft over there. The house is wrong, remember that."

"You mean—"

"I mean evil."

Evil. Haunted. He didn't know what to think about that. Sure, *evil*, but what was evil, really? Right now he was more concerned with surviving people who had meat cleavers and shotguns.

"Okay, I'm just going to take a look. I'll be right back." He lifted the latch.

"Jack?"

"What?" he whispered.

Her hand touched his. "Promise you won't leave me."

Jack turned and saw that her eyes were misted with tears.

He drew her head close and kissed her hair. Another image of his own daughter crossed his mind. "I won't leave you. I promise. Just like I won't leave Leslie. Okay?"

"Okay."

"Don't go anywhere."

Jack pulled the door open and stuck his head into the closet. Junk was piled up on both sides. Some stale-smelling jackets and overalls hung directly in front of him.

Jack withdrew his head. "I'm going in so I can see past the clothes."

Susan didn't say anything.

He eased into the closet, parted two old jackets. He could see light from a dozen thin cracks in the door paneling now. Could hear the sound of a man's muffled voice. Pete's.

Which meant Leslie was probably in there.

Jack glanced around again for a weapon—anything that would come in handy. Saw a board with a handle. A cricket bat. He didn't know why a cricket bat would be here, and he didn't care; he only knew it was here if he needed it.

He stepped gingerly past the coats, willfully stifled his breathing, and pressed one eye up to a thin crack.

At first he saw only Pete, sitting on the side of the bed with his back to the closet, mumbling. But then Pete stood and crossed out of Jack's sight, leaving him a direct view of the bed.

Leslie was strapped to the bedposts by her wrists and

ankles. Still in her white slacks and the red blouse. She was shaking with sobs.

Jack stared, momentarily overwhelmed.

"You have to be a good wife and eat," Pete said, passing the door with a bowl in his hands. He scooped some paste out. He'd tied her down and was trying to force her to eat something!

Jack didn't know what had reduced Leslie to the quivering form on the bed, but it occurred to him that he was shaking too. With revulsion.

Not just revulsion. With rage.

19

STEPHANIE HAD FOUGHT BACK THE TEMP-
tation to leave the closet in search of Jack a hundred
times when the loud *thump* sounded in the dining
room. She jumped. Had she dozed off? A muffled call
reached her.

"Stephanie!"

Who was that? She peeled her eyes wide in the
blackness, fully alert. Who was that? That was Jack!

Something creaked. She held her breath. That was
where the wall was, right? The closet door was on her
left, and the wall was on her right.

There was a long creaking that ran on like a finger-
nail being slowly drawn down a chalkboard. It stopped.

She could hear feet running down the stairs. Jack
was leaving?

"Jack!" she screamed. Her voice rang loud in the
closet. "Jack!"

Now Stephanie was faced with a decision. She
could get out of the closet and find the others, or she
could sit here like she had for the last—how long had

she been here? Minutes or hours? Her cell phone was still in her purse in the living room somewhere.

"Jack, don't you dare leave me again!" She swore.

He was gone.

She set her jaw and rage began to overtake her body, one limb at a time. First her hands and face, then her whole body. The anger didn't feel natural, but it brought her a sliver of warmth and courage, the empowering kind that came from taking charge of a bad situation. Her breathing was heavy, but for the moment she didn't care who heard her. She reoriented herself to the space. Coats. Boots. Back of closet. Sides. She brushed something cold and metallic, and it fell over, scraping the wall and landing with a thud. She picked it up. Examined it with her fingers. A crowbar, maybe.

An image of the ax hammer crossed her mind. Only it was in her hands, not Stewart's. She was swinging it. Maybe at Jack's gut. Maybe at his head. Maybe—

She stopped herself. Someone was whispering. Outside the door. Jack?

But she knew it couldn't be Jack because it was more than one voice, and it was coming from more than one direction.

Something tickled her ankle. Slid up her leg. A long, thin reptilian slither.

Oh God oh God oh God! It was a snake, and it was working its way up her leg!

Stephanie couldn't move to yank it out. The closet filled with a terrible, raw scream. Hers.

The floor under her hands moved. Slithered. The closet floor was crawling with snakes; skinny snakes, cold and slippery snakes.

A place deep in Stephanie's psyche rose from the dead. The place where horror and rage collide with the drive to survive. The place were there are no rules, no absolutes, no God, no devil. Only Stephanie. The place where even great risk of death can be braved if it means the chance to save one's self.

Her scream became a snarl. She dropped the crow-bar and she moved.

She slammed into the door. She cranked the handle and leaped out of the closet. Then spun back and looked at the floor, ready to stomp the snakes. But the closet was empty. They'd fled. She yelled at the floor for good measure.

Stephanie became aware that she was in the hall by the dining room, where the whispers had come from. She turned slowly. They too had fled. Or never had been.

The house creaked, the long creaking sound that she'd heard in the closet, only now it came from all four walls.

Stephanie made her decision then by a reasoning too complex for her to understand. But having made her decision, she moved quickly. She walked to the basement door, twisted the knob, and jerked. It was locked. A dead bolt. She disengaged the bolt. Then she threw open the door and marched down the stairs.

Jack was down here, and she was going to tell Jack a thing or two about what was happening. About how she'd had enough. About how it was time to go home, killer or no killer. About how he could take his self-righteous bull—

The door behind her slammed shut. The sound of

the dead bolt snapping into place was what it was. She couldn't pretend it was anything different.

She stopped on the steps and blinked. Her courage fled.

"Oh God oh God oh God . . ."

20

HE WASN'T SURE THAT HE REALLY INTENDED to rush out of the closet wielding a cricket bat, but he needed a weapon in his hands to satisfy his rage, so Jack reached back and grabbed the cricket bat.

But in his exuberance to get the thing in his hands, he pulled too quickly. And when the bat pulled free it dislodged something else.

That thing clunked.

For a moment everything came to a standstill. Pete stopped his mumbling. Leslie stopped her struggling. Jack stopped his breathing.

He could hear his watch ticking faster than it ought.

His plan of action became clear in that moment. He had to go, and he had to go now.

Jack dived at the door, shoulder leading, cricket bat already back, ready to swing. Whatever mechanism held the door closed snapped under his weight. He leaped across the room and swung the bat before reaching his target.

Pete didn't have time to throw up a guard. The thick

board swooshed through the air and smashed against his skull with a loud *crack!*

He grunted and staggered. Fell to his hands and knees.

Jack reached the bed and ripped the frayed rope that bound both of Leslie's ankles to one bedpost. But her wrists were each tied to either post by her head, and Pete was already pushing himself to his feet.

Jack took another swing at the thug.

Smack!

The stalk hit Pete in his gut, hardly the kind of blow that would send him reeling. But it surprised him.

Jack cocked the bat. "Get back!"

"Hit him again!" Leslie screamed. "Kill him!"

Jack flinched. Kill? He'd never lined a bat up on someone's head with that intent. Not that he didn't have every justification.

Leslie was trying to free her wrists.

Pete took a heavy step forward, like an ox.

Jack swung. The bat bounced off the man's arm and swung low into his right knee. Something cracked, and it wasn't the bat.

Pete blinked. He looked down at his knee.

"Move!" Jack snapped. "By the wall."

"Kill him, Jack!"

"Stop shouting!"

He had to think. He couldn't just beat the man to death. But maybe he could disable Pete and leave him strapped to the bed.

"Kill him!" Leslie was still frantic. One of her wrists started to bleed.

"Hold on!" he snapped. Then to Pete again: "Move!"

Pete limped to the large dart board. "She's . . . she's my wife," he said.

"Shut up!" Jack crossed to the bed. "Don't move."

He worked Leslie's tethers with one hand.

"You have to kill him, Jack," Leslie whispered. "You can't just leave him!"

"Shh, shh, it's okay!" One wrist free.

"No, it's not."

He ran to the other side of the bed and worked the rope with his free hand, eyes on Pete. The man was edging closer to the door.

"Don't move!"

From the corner of his eye, he saw movement at the door. Two dead bolts were engaged on this side. Both had flat brass knobs.

Both knobs were silently turning at the same time. Opening. Seemingly on their own.

He froze. How—

Pete grunted and staggered toward the door.

"Jack!" Leslie screamed.

The door swung in. Betty faced the room with a shotgun leveled hip-high. There was something about her face that looked different. Something wicked in her eyes. The look of a woman who was done playing hostess.

"Back," she said softly.

Jack dropped the bat and lifted his hands. "Okay."

It was all happening too quickly. She was going to pull the trigger.

"Stewart's right. You're all sinners," she said.

Pete dived at his mother. He struck the barrel with both hands as it discharged a load of lead that blasted the bedpost on Jack's right to smithereens.

Leslie tugged at her remaining tether. "Jack!"

"Don't kill my wife!" Pete roared.

Betty lifted the shotgun and brought its butt down on Pete's head. *Thunk!* He dropped to his knees just as Jack ripped the rope free from Leslie's wrist.

"They both have to die!" Betty said.

A soft voice from the closet stopped them all. "No, they don't."

Jack swiveled his head. Susan stood in the open door, staring at Betty, whose face had blanched with shock.

"White's the one who should die," Susan said, stepping into the room. She spoke calmly, but her eyes were wide.

Jack held out his hand. "Susan . . ."

Susan addressed Betty. "You know that if you kill me, White won't have any reason to let you live," Susan said. "As soon as I'm dead, he'll kill the rest of them. Isn't that his deal? And once the rest are dead, he's going to kill you too."

Betty stood like ice.

Susan looked at Jack. "But she can't kill me yet, because White still needs me for his game."

Slowly Betty relaxed. Began to scowl.

Susan threw herself forward.

"Susan! Don't!"

She collided with Betty, who staggered back into the hall.

Leslie rolled off the bed toward Jack, landed squarely on the floor, and broke toward the closet.

Jack stood frozen by the odd sight, this frail girl dressed in a tattered summer dress, throwing herself at the much larger woman. Three days in the basement had clearly redefined her need for self-preservation.

The bedroom door slammed shut behind Susan and Betty.

The shotgun discharged in the hall beyond.

"Jack!" Leslie warned.

Pete had pushed himself up and was plodding toward Leslie.

Jack leaped over the corner of the bed, slammed into Pete. The man crashed into the wall.

"Through the closet!" Jack shouted.

Leslie was already in. Through the back. Into the crawl space.

"On the right!" Jack whispered, racing past. "Follow me!"

He grabbed Leslie's hand and ran crouched, fleeing the roars of Pete, who was ignoring his wounds and smashing his way into the closet.

They found a grate that covered a three-foot-wide shaft. Right where Susan had indicated it would be. An air duct or something similar. Jack pulled the grate free.

"Go!" he whispered.

She scrambled past him, stuck her head in the hole, then looked back at him, eyes wide. "Don't leave me." She was breathing heavily, still frenzied.

"I'm right behind you."

She ducked in.

Jack glanced back just as Pete barged into the crawl space. The oaf looked around, failed to see them, then headed in the opposite direction.

Jack entered the shaft, pulling the grate closed after him.

21

3:02 AM

STEPHANIE WALKED THROUGH THE BASE-
ment so utterly terrified that her fear rekindled her rage.

Room to room, hall to hall, not caring about the
paintings or the improbable decor or the pentagrams.
In fact, she had to ignore it all so that she could stay
focused, because she knew that she was only one
snake away from racing back upstairs, and upstairs was
locked.

She realized that she might run into Stewart before
she found the guys, but she accepted the risk. Or Randy
or Jack, though at the moment she thought she would
prefer finding Randy.

Or was she just wrong about that? Jack was as stubborn as any man who lived on the planet. He wouldn't
back down, never did. In all truth, she needed him now,
if for no reason other than to survive.

Randy, on the other hand, was the kind of man who
would do anything to get ahead, which meant that if
Jack failed her, Randy might be her ticket.

Leslie could rot in the grave as far as Stephanie was

concerned. And judging by the look in Pete's eyes at the dinner table, she was probably already doing that.

Listen to her!

She decided in the last few minutes that she liked the new Stephanie, freed of her denial, of her always-all-right philosophy. Never again. She'd quenched her denial with a deep well of rage that now made her feel as alive as she could remember feeling in years. She could write songs about this for eons. She felt enough spunk at this moment to hit any man or woman who got in her way, and she wasn't sure she'd ever felt that way. Good-bye, sunshine.

She entered a long concrete hall and noticed the water leaking down the wall for the first time.

Water. She stopped. The water was pooling along the floor. The house groaned. Her resolve slipped a little. Maybe she shouldn't have come down. But it was a little too late now. She spied a door near the puddle. Open.

She walked to the door, looked into what looked like a root cellar, and stepped in.

The door slammed. She whirled. A draft must have pulled it shut. She wasn't about to consider anything else. The door to her right gaped wide. Someone had passed this way recently.

Stephanie hesitated, then walked though the door into another much narrower hall. The door at the end was open.

She'd taken three steps when a *bang* from behind startled her.

The door had blown shut. Two in a row.

She spun and ran toward the open door.

—◦—

Jack dropped to the floor of the medium-sized boiler room and examined it in silence. Leslie stood to his right, taking in a dozen iron pipes that rose out of two large boilers on either side and disappeared into chases at the ceiling. A single clear bulb burned above, as in most rooms down here. Two doors stood opposite the boilers.

He saw it all without taking note. His mind was on Susan. It had taken every ounce of resolve on his part not to rush back through Pete's room to find out if she'd survived. He couldn't wrap his mind around what she'd done. He held tenaciously to a whisper of hope that her claims might be true. Maybe the inbreds would keep her alive as leverage. Maybe they knew something that he didn't.

Either way, he'd lost her. He'd promised never to leave her, and although he hadn't exactly, she was gone, maybe dead, maybe just locked up.

Maybe escaped again.

For a moment neither he nor Leslie seemed capable of moving. Not on account of the room but because of what had just happened.

Beside him, Leslie put one hand on her hip, buried her face in her other hand, and silently wept. He lifted a hand to comfort her but thought it might be inappropriate. She turned from him, started to walk away, then returned.

Leslie didn't look at him; she only leaned against him

and lowered her forehead into his neck. He swallowed a knot in his throat and held her with one arm.

"I'm sorry," he said. "I'm so sorry."

She put her arms around him and pulled him close, then seemed to cry harder.

"Leslie . . ." His arms were trembling, but she couldn't have noticed because her whole body was shaking.

He was suddenly eager to comfort her. His need came from more than desire, maybe not desire at all. It came from hours of raw nerves. It came from the dark halls and sickness of the basement. It came from the memory of her lying on Pete's bed.

It came from being trapped in the killer's game.

Jack squeezed her tighter. "I'm sorry . . ."

She caught her sob in her throat and kissed his neck. "No, no, don't be." She kissed his neck again, then his cheek, clinging. "Don't be sorry. Thank you, thank you." Her hands grabbed his shirt, and she kissed him on the cheek again.

She lowered her face into his neck and started to cry again.

They were two lost souls who had escaped death together only to believe that they would still probably die before the night was over. Leslie, the intelligent professor of psychology, and Jack, the bitter writer who'd saved her.

Now both lost again. And alone in this boiler room while the house creaked around them.

For the moment he held on to her as if she were life itself. For the first time in many long months, Jack recalled what it was like to love someone besides his daughter. They were both victims—his daughter of Stephanie's carelessness, and Leslie of a sadistic maniac.

Leslie took his face in both hands and kissed him on the lips. She pressed her lips to his until they hurt. Then she kissed him frantically on the cheek and neck again.

"I love you, Jack. I love you."

Jack blinked. He pushed her gently away. "Shh, shh, shh."

"I love you . . ."

She resisted him, and he gently pried her arms from his neck. "No, it's okay; it's okay. You can't mean that."

That settled her.

She dropped her arms, turned away, and lowered her face into her hands.

"I understand," he said. "I know how you feel—"

"You have no clue how I feel!" she said, spinning back. She thrust her arm up at the vent they'd crawled through. "Do you have any idea what I've been through?"

"Which is why you are so distressed right now. I can't use you like that!"

She stared at him hard, searching his eyes. Then her face softened, and she looked away. "I'm sorry."

In that moment the complete failure of his own marriage came into such sharp focus that Jack lost sight of anything he and Stephanie might have once had together. How long had it been since Stephanie had shown such passion, such a backbone? His bitterness toward her was fueled by her own retreat into denial. He wasn't sure why he'd stuck beside her all this time.

"No, it's okay." He put his hand on her back. "I don't—"

"What on earth do you think you're doing?"

They spun. A man, wet from head to foot, holding a shotgun over one shoulder and a spade over the other, glared at them from an open doorway.

"Randy?" Leslie said.

He walked in and kicked the steel door shut with the back of his heel. "Answer me! For crying out loud!"

"You're alive," Jack said. Randy looked like he'd walked through a sewer. His hair was wet and matted, his color-coordinated green shirts were brown, and the rivets on his crisp new jeans had been torn off, leaving jagged holes near the pockets.

"Disappointed?" Randy said. "I knew it." He slogged toward them and stopped in the middle of the room. Threw the spade down. "I'm gone for an hour, scraping for my life, and I come home to this?"

"Randy . . ." Leslie stepped away from Jack.

"It's not what you think," Jack snapped, feeding on his building resentment toward this man.

"You don't say." His eyes were glazed. "I oughta show you what I do think."

"I was violated, Randy," Leslie said.

"Raped?"

She balked at his offhand tone. "Just as bad."

"I've got news for you. The whole world thinks their uncle violated them. It gives us all an excuse to live like victims."

"Randy!" For a moment Jack thought she might fly at the man and slap his face. When she spoke her lips were trembling. "You're sick."

"You never did take down Uncle Robby, now did you, Leslie? No. But guess what? I have. Only it wasn't Uncle Robby, it was Uncle Stewart, and I can guaran-freaken-tee you he's deader than any man deserves to be." Randy grinned.

"Stewart's dead?" Jack asked.

Jack hadn't taken much notice of the doors opposite each boiler. The second swung in abruptly, and Stephanie ran through and pulled up, panting.

The door slammed shut behind her on its own. She looked back with wide eyes, then turned back to face them.

"Did you see that?"

Jack's mind scrambled. Stephanie, here. Stewart, dead. Randy, soaked.

Sweat made Stephanie's lacy blue top cling to her, and her long blonde hair was a stringy mess, but she'd looked the same an hour ago.

"A draft," Leslie said, eyes fixed on the door.

"Not unless a draft has been following me all the way here," Stephanie said. She strode forward, glaring at Jack. "I've been in that closet forever!"

"Settle down—"

"Don't you dare tell me to settle down!" Her face was red and her arms were rigid. "You said you'd be right back! You swore you'd be back. That was an hour ago!"

He blinked, surprised by her forcefulness. Then irritated. "I've been just a tad busy."

Stephanie glanced at Leslie. "I'm sure you have."

"I caught them red-handed," Randy said.

"What do you mean?"

"I mean it seems Jack and Leslie here evidently have more than the big bad wolf on their minds."

"Shut up!" Jack snapped. "Look, Stephanie, things down here are a little complicated, okay? I've only been gone for—" He checked his watch. That couldn't be. He shook it. Still ticked. Must have busted when he got sucked into the black tunnel. "Does anyone know what time it is?"

Leslie looked. "Almost 3:15."

The four let this sink in.

"That's impossible," said Randy. "We've been here thirty, forty minutes tops."

"My watch says 3:15 too."

Stephanie put a palm on her forehead, started pacing. "I was in the closet for *four hours*? I can't believe you'd do that to me, Jack. I can't believe—"

"'I can't believe,'" Randy mimicked, voice pitched high and free palm on his forehead. Then he got in her face. "Listen to you, Barbie. You think you've had it worse than any of us? Huh? Well, believe this: we've got less than three hours to get ourselves out of this pit or we *die*. Have you completely forgotten that?"

Stephanie sagged against the door, scowling.

Jack glared at her, picked up his explanation for Randy. "Pete . . ." He stopped, reticent to justify himself at Leslie's expense.

"Pete what?" Randy asked.

"I'm okay," Leslie said, glancing at Jack.

"Sure you are," Stephanie said. "Who wouldn't be okay with dear Jack to the rescue?"

"Will you please shut your mouth?" Jack said. Both Randy and Stephanie knew what had been on Pete's mind when he eyed Leslie in the dining room. Maybe the truth was slowly seeping past Randy's thick skull. Stephanie, on the other hand, knew and didn't seem to care.

Jack walked over to the door that Stephanie had come through and locked it. "We're all alive," he said, heading for the second door. As far as he could see, this was the only way in or out besides the shaft.

"For the record, Leslie and I were just expressing

common human emotions of survival. If either of you have a problem with that, save it for tomorrow."

He locked the second door and turned back to them.

"Right now we have to figure out how to survive the next three hours."

22

3:43 AM

IT TOOK THEM HALF AN HOUR OF ARGU-
ment and speculation to figure out what *might* have happened in the last several hours. At least they nailed the
critical details—or so Jack hoped, although he doubted
Randy was as forthcoming as he made himself out to be.

Even after grasping what had supposedly happened
to each of them, they still really didn't know *what* was
happening.

What had sucked Jack into the black hall?

What had crawled up Stephanie's leg?

What had happened to Stewart's body?

Who was Susan, and what had happened to her?

The whys were even worse. Why were doors opening and closing on their own? Why couldn't any of them
see their reflections in the mirrors? Why hadn't the
killer come after them in the basement?

"I can tell you that," Randy said. "He has. You just
don't know it."

Leslie frowned. "Okay, so he has some psychological
grip—"

"I'm not talking psychological. I'm talking physical. I saw him come in."

"You what?" Jack said.

Randy sat on a fifty-five-gallon drum with the shotgun across his lap, staring at Jack, who'd stopped his pacing to face him. Leslie and Stephanie each sat on a plate of steel that stuck out from the boilers.

"The back door," Randy said. "I saw him step in out of the rain."

"What back door? Why didn't you tell us about this?"

"He padlocked the door. And it's not as if I could tell you where it is. But he's in here."

"And you just happened to forget this little detail?" Leslie demanded.

Randy sneered at her. "It's not important. We have other problems."

"Like what?"

"Like getting out."

"You mean getting out alive, don't you?" Leslie asked. "Which means we have to know who our enemies are and where they are."

"Then like I said, we have a lot more to worry about than White," Randy said. He grabbed the shotgun by the pump action and chambered a shell with one hand. "White's one guy. We can take one guy. But you have to ask yourself why Stewart disappeared."

"Because you were hallucinating," Leslie said.

He grabbed his wet shirt. "You call this a hallucination?"

"You let Stewart drown," Leslie said. "Have you ever drowned someone before, Randy? I don't think so. Do you know why they put infantry through hell week at boot camp? So that when they get in a bloody battle they

don't start seeing things. The mind is a fragile instrument. It snaps easily. If there's anything you have to ask
yourself, it's why you've become a completely different
person since you entered this house."

Randy stared at her without responding. It was a
good question. Even he had to see what the stress had
done to him.

"She has a point, Randy," Jack said. "Think about it.
You talk about Stewart dying in the most graphic terms
without batting an eye, and none of us care. You get to a
point where everything starts to shut down, right? The
problem is, we can't shut down yet."

"Excuse me," Stephanie said, "but do we really care
about all this psychobabble? Didn't you hear Randy?
The killer's down here *with* us! People are going to die!
What do you think this is all about? Sucking up some
dog food?"

Jack wanted to reach across the room and smack her.
She wasn't lucid.

Then again, it had been a long time since he'd seen
her so full of emotion. The mix of old and new gave him
pause.

To her credit, Leslie ignored the cruel jab. "I'm just
saying that we really need to get a grip and not let the circumstances get into our heads."

"And I suppose the snakes were in my head too,"
Stephanie said.

"For starters, yes."

Stephanie just stared at her. Maybe she really didn't
know.

Jack paced. "Okay, let's take this methodically."

"I think the question of whether what seems to be

happening is really happening is important," Leslie said. "The answer lays out the entire framework for how we deal with it."

"How's that?"

"Take Stephanie's snakes. If they're real snakes, you kill them with a knife or something. If they're in the mind, you shut your eyes and put them out of your mind."

Made sense. Stephanie huffed.

"Okay," Jack said. "I'll go with that. What else has happened that could fall into that category?"

"I can't believe we're sitting here—"

"Please, Stephanie, try to use more than your mouth. Just go with us here."

She clamped her mouth shut and glared at him. He had to hand it to her, though—she'd found some spunk in that closet. At least she wasn't in denial, running away. He had to respect her for that much.

"Randy, is there anything you've seen that could have been a trick of your mind?"

"I'm with Stephanie. I don't see how this helps us."

"What if you think you see a lock on a door and walk away?" Leslie said. "You walk away when you could have walked out."

"I *heard* him lock the back door. I *saw* the padlock before he locked it—"

"What about the shotgun?" Jack said, gesturing to Randy's lap. "We could blow the locks off."

They all looked at him with dawning awareness. Randy slid off the drum, eyes bright. "I knew the gun would be our ticket out of here. We blow the doors. Lock and load."

"Hold up," Jack said, raising a hand. "Let's think this through."

"What's there to think through?" Stephanie said. "Randy's right!"

"For starters, Stephanie, you just came down the main stairs, right? Do you know how to get back? Don't you find it a little strange that you just *happened* to end up here, with us? The halls down here don't make any sense, but you just waltz on in."

She didn't respond.

"I agree, going for the door with the gun may be a good plan," Jack said. "If we can find it. But let's not blow our chances by going off half-cocked. So let's have it: what have we seen that could be in our minds?"

The house creaked above them, and they all looked up.

After a moment Leslie lowered her eyes. "There. The wind's moving the house. We hear a groan, but our minds are already stretched to the breaking point so we all expect more and look up. Stress-induced deception, pure and simple."

"What about the mirrors?" Jack asked.

"They have to be trick mirrors of some kind," she said. "Pete told me they used to travel with a circus. Did anyone specifically notice a reflection from anything as close to the mirror as you were? Randy?"

"You mean in the foreground? Actually, now that you mention it, no. Jack and I couldn't see either of our reflections, but we could see the room behind us."

"Jack?"

"That's right. I never thought of it that way."

"I know for a fact that a mirror can be manufactured in such a way as to reflect no light within a certain distance."

Jack could feel strength entering the room as if it were a force field. They had a gun, they had answers—two things that might have prevented everything that happened tonight. He resolved in that moment never to travel without a weapon again.

"Okay, what about Stewart's body disappearing?"

Randy looked around at them. *He was returning to sanity by the minute,* Jack thought.

"Okay, I was a bit on edge." He closed his eyes, lifted his chin, and took a deep breath. Silence settled. His vulnerability was palpable.

A long, awkward moment passed.

Randy took another deep breath and looked at them. "When Jack got sucked into that door and I ended up in that rising water, something snapped. I was a dead man. You have no idea what it's like, watching someone drown while you think about carving them up."

"I'm sure it was very difficult," Leslie said. She walked over to him and took his hand in a show of support. "You'll be okay."

Seeing her go to him bothered Jack, but not because he cared for Leslie in that way. He simply didn't trust Randy. The thought of anyone extending him trust was unnerving.

"Okay," Jack said, "so some of what we've seen was probably the product of stressed imagination. For all I know, I could have jumped into the tunnel. A strong draft . . ." He frowned. "I suppose it's possible I thought I was being sucked."

Leslie looked at Randy. "Maybe you saw a dead body because you needed Stewart dead—not unheard of."

He frowned. "Maybe."

Jack raised an eyebrow at Leslie. "And the odor—"

"We've grown accustomed to it due to the stress, so we don't smell it anymore. It's a start, anyway."

Jack took a deep breath and paced, rubbing his face to clear the cobwebs. "So let me get this straight. We were all taken off the road by a serial killer named White who has a thing for elaborate games. He's killed who knows how many people over the years and ends up in the backwoods of Alabama where no one goes but the stray traveler. Good so far?"

Leslie picked up, walking across the room. "We're not the first victims in this house. The last was Susan, who managed to escape. Our hosts are working with White, but this latest miss—with Susan, that is—has changed their relationship, putting pressure on Stewart and Betty. But that fits into White's game, because he wants others to do his killing. He intends to force his victims to extract the penalty for sin themselves. How am I doing?"

"Give me one dead body," Randy said.

"Rule number three," Jack said.

"It's also what I thought I heard White say in the tunnels."

Leslie turned on him. "You heard his voice? Another little detail you forgot to mention?"

"I *thought* I did. Either way, you're right. He wants us to kill each other. That's the whole point, isn't it?"

It was. They all had to know that by now, Jack thought. "So his plan all along was to get us into the house and lure us into this basement, which apparently isn't just a basement at all. How do you explain the basement? I can't get a handle on the layout of this place."

"Tunnels, shafts, holding tanks . . . ," Leslie mused. "Maybe it was part of a mining operation."

"What kind of mining operation in the middle of Alabama would resemble anything like this?" Randy asked.

"Catacombs," Stephanie said. "Maybe it was more than a mining operation. Something built for slaves after the war. For all we know, this house is built on a mass grave."

Randy snickered.

"Please, let's try to stay focused," Leslie said. "This isn't *Poltergeist*."

Stephanie shrugged. "I'm just saying."

"The point is, White's been manipulating us from the beginning," Leslie said. "He's got us locked in this place with four other people. Eight people to pit against each other. The last one alive gets to live . . . or something like that. Betty and Stewart and Pete are as much victims as we are at this point."

"But they don't count," Randy said.

"What?"

"Something else the voice said."

They stared at him.

"Why wouldn't they count?" Jack asked.

"They are like him?" Randy said. "On his team?"

"But Susan said White's going to kill them for letting her go. One way or another, he intends to kill everyone tonight. Or having us kill each other."

"One down," Randy said.

"Then we have to kill Betty and Pete," Stephanie said.

"No, we have to get out," Jack said.

"But if they get in our way, we kill them," Randy said. "I guarantee, if either one of those two perverts comes into my sights, they're dead meat."

Leslie looked at him.

"What? You disagree?"

"No. If you come across Pete, put a round in his groin for me."

Given the circumstances, Jack couldn't fault her sentiment.

"So we're going to get out, right?" Stephanie asked.

"With Stewart out of the way, we might have a shot," Leslie said.

"And when we get out, what then?" Randy asked.

"Unless we manage to disable White, he'll come after us."

"We could use that truck."

"It's trashed. We'll have to make a run for the main road on foot."

"You think there's any chance that someone could have seen the cars and called it in?" Stephanie asked. "I mean, it's possible, right? That highway patrol officer knew we were taking this road. It's only a matter of time before he comes. The only question is, can he get here before dawn?"

"We have to find Susan," Jack said.

None of them responded.

"I'm dead serious; we can't leave here without Susan."

"Well, that's a bit of a problem, isn't it?" Randy said. "We don't know where this Susan is. And if you're right, they will expect us to look for her. We'd be playing right into White's hands. He's no idiot. He knows someone's going to want to save the sweet little girl."

"What's your problem?" Leslie snapped. "She's as much a victim here as we are. You can't just *leave* her!"

"According to you, Betty's a victim too. You want to go save *her*?"

"She's also a cold-blooded killer!"

Randy shook his head, exasperated.

"There's no way you can find this girl down here," Stephanie said. "You said she's been hiding out for days?"

"You do what you want," Randy said. "You find her, fine, we take her out with us. But we can't all stay down here looking for one girl. We have to get *out*!"

It sounded right. But to Jack it felt very wrong. He caught Leslie's look. They both knew that Susan had saved their lives.

The sound of a long, drawn-out creaking filled the boiler room. Jack looked for the source, but there was nothing he could see.

It was as if the walls were made of wood and a strong wind was pushing the planks slowly in one direction.

"You see?" Stephanie cried. "That's what I heard. You're saying that's just in my mind?"

The sound finally abated. Even Leslie was breathing hard.

"Something's wrong with this place," Randy said. "We have to get out. Now." He grabbed the shotgun off the fifty-five-gallon barrel and strode for the same closed door he'd come through.

"Hold on, we haven't agreed on a plan," Jack said.

"We go for the doors, that's the plan."

"Which door? Who goes for which door? And what happens if something goes wrong? Just hold up a second!"

Randy turned around. His expression said clearly enough that he hadn't thought that far ahead. Stephanie had started to follow him. Made sense; they thought alike. Get out and get out now; just go.

Like their marriage.

The creaking returned, not quite as loud but just as long. It was the most unnatural sound Jack could imagine. He shivered reflexively.

Before Randy could set off again, Jack put a thought in his mind. "You sure your gun's going to do the trick against whatever's making that noise?"

"Stop it!" Leslie said. "We're not dealing with ghosts here, for heaven's sake. Act like adults!"

"Then what are we dealing with?" Stephanie demanded, and Jack was thankful she'd asked. "Mass hysteria?"

"I don't know! Pipes? The house above us is moving in the wind. It has a web of rusted pipes underneath. How should I—"

"The sound's coming from the walls, not the pipes," Stephanie insisted.

"Sound travels," Leslie said.

"And the puncture marks on your face and hands? You still think those are incidental? Or were they something more like darts?"

Leslie's face lightened a shade. "What do you mean?"

Stephanie stared her down. "I don't know. But neither do you, do you? And yet you insist that there's *zero* chance we're dealing with anything supernatural here. Are you willing to bet all of our lives on that?"

Leslie didn't answer.

"Well . . ."

"Fine. So maybe there's something going on here that we can't explain without ripping down the house. Call it supernatural if you want. By definition, the supernatural is only that which extends beyond our understanding of nature anyway." She glared angrily. "I'm not even sure there *aren't* such things as ghosts. Some kind of natural existence beyond death—who knows. But your running around frantic because you think an evil spirit is hard on your heels will only get us all killed! You have to keep your head!"

"I *intend* to keep my head!" Stephanie shot back. "Which means getting out of *here*!"

"You and Randy were both ready to tear out of here before we'd even settled on a plan. That's the kind of idiocy that comes from emotionally driven nonsense."

Jack thought it time to intervene. "So you're saying you think *maybe* there could be something supernaturally wrong with the house?" Jack asked Leslie. "Because Susan—"

"I know what Susan said!"

"Take it easy!" he said, drilling her with a stare.

She averted her eyes.

"If White knows there's something wrong with this house—"

"Just say it, Jack," Leslie said. "You mean haunted, don't you? Just say it."

"Okay, I will. If White knows this house is haunted because it was once used to house slaves who were slaughtered here, or whatever . . ."

Giving voice to the possibility felt strange.

". . . which you yourself admit is a possibility, even though we don't understand it . . ."

"Granted."

". . . then wouldn't it be in our interest to know how to deal with a haunted house?"

They looked at him.

"I know it sounds stupid, but isn't that what we're

talking about? We understand something about the killer, as much as serial killers can be understood; we know about Betty and Stewart and Pete. We have a plan to blow the doors off the hinges and go for the main road. But what about the house?"

"You're saying the house may be trying to stop us from getting out?" Leslie asked.

"I'm just making sure all of our bases are covered before we try anything."

"I don't believe in haunted houses," Randy said.

"Neither do I," Leslie said, looking at him. "But that doesn't mean this house isn't . . . unusual. We just covered that; weren't you listening?"

He ignored her.

"The question, if I understand Jack right, is how we deal with a haunted house. Right?"

"Right."

No one offered any suggestions. They were all too busy trying to imagine such a thing. Clearly, none of them had a clue how to deal with a haunted anything.

"Anyone have any holy water?" Stephanie asked.

"What does haunted mean?" Randy asked. "That means some ghost or something is haunting it. So we appease the ghost. Or kill it."

The creaking sound came again, louder than before. And longer. They listened, looking at one another without offering any consolation.

"Pipes," Jack said when it quit.

No one commented.

"We go for the back door first," Jack said. "Can you get us there, Randy?"

"I think so."

Jack nodded. "If we get separated and can't get out, we meet back here."

"If one of us gets out?" Randy said.

"Go for the main road."

"What if we can't get out the back?" Leslie asked.

"Then we go for the one at the top of the main stairs and get out that way."

"Shoot on sight?" Randy asked.

Jack nodded, taking up the spade Randy had dropped. "If we run into Betty, Pete, or White, shoot on sight. Below the waist if possible."

Randy nodded. "Okay. Okay. Let's do it."

He led them to the door he'd come through, shotgun on his hip.

23

3:53 AM

THEY WALKED QUICKLY AND QUIETLY IN single file, with Randy leading, followed by Stephanie, then Leslie. Jack brought up the rear with Randy's spade.

The moment they entered the tunnel he had last seen Stewart in, Randy felt the surge of confidence that had fueled his escape from Stewart earlier.

The shotgun was freshly loaded from the supply of shells he'd taken off Stewart. Eleven more in the box. Randy weighed whether he had the guts to do what had to be done if it came right down to it. He'd learned a few things tonight, and one of them was that putting a gun against someone's head and pulling the trigger wasn't an easy thing to do.

Yes, he did have the guts. He wasn't sure he'd be shouting this down Broadway, but he thought he could do it. And now he was the one leading them down the dark tunnels—without too much fear.

By Randy's estimation, it took only about five minutes to make it back to the room where Stewart had drowned. They were trying to move slowly enough to keep quiet, which it was. Very.

The arched wooden door to the room was still open. Randy stopped.

"What?" Stephanie whispered behind him.

"This is where I saw . . ." He blinked at the concrete floor.

"The body?"

"Yeah."

"What is it?" Leslie whispered, coming up in a crouch.

"Still gone," Randy said.

They looked at one another then back up the tunnel. Enough said. So he'd lost his marbles for a bit. Or White had moved the cadaver. Randy stepped quickly over the riser into the room, eager to prove to them all that the drowned man was indeed drowned.

"Slow down," Stephanie whispered.

I'll slow you down if you don't shut up. Inner thought, meant nothing really.

He could see the water now. The large pipe that disappeared into the holding tank. Randy waded out to the center in ankle-deep water. He turned back, aware that he was grinning and not caring.

The others had stopped at the entry and were looking down.

"This is where it happened," he said.

They looked at him without acknowledging or denying. But that was acknowledgment enough.

"Do you want to see—"

"Just get us out of here," Leslie snapped.

Well, fine then. He cut to his left, over another riser,

and into the adjoining passage. Fifty feet and to the right. Through the door he'd run smack into, which was now open, allowing light into what had been a dark space.

But the door that led into the utility room where he'd found the old shotgun was locked.

"Locked," he said. "This leads to the passage with the back door."

"So what do we do?" Stephanie asked.

You put your fist in your mouth and keep it there. Inner thought.

"Blast it," he said.

"They might hear," Jack said.

"Maybe. But we're insulated by a lot of dirt beyond these concrete walls. And there's a utility room on the other side of this door. I think it's okay."

Before anyone could object, he lifted the gun, put the barrel about a foot from the handle, and . . .

"Randy . . ."

. . . pulled the trigger. *Boom!*

Man, was that loud in here!

"There," he said and pushed the door open.

They entered the utility room and stopped to listen. Nothing. 'Course, his ears were ringing pretty good.

"This way."

"I'm not going out," Jack said.

Randy faced the man. "What do you mean, you're not going out? The door's right—"

"Show me the way. I have to at least try to find Susan first."

Randy reached for the door. "Suit yourself."

They were in the passageway with the back exit visible fifty feet to their left when they heard the muffled voice.

Stephanie gasped. Randy put his fingers to her mouth. Down the hall, past the door that led into the large study with the desk and the pentagram and the mirror that didn't work. Betty.

"Hurry!" Randy turned to run toward the exit, but a hand snagged his elbow.

"Give me a minute!" Jack whispered. "Susan has to be with her."

"Are you crazy? We're right here!"

"You have to wait for me."

"Not a chance."

"If you shoot the lock, she'll hear for sure this time, and I won't stand a chance. One minute, just to see."

"And if I wait for you to come screaming down the hall with a girl in your arms, she'll be on your tail with a gun in her hands. We all lose."

"Just give me a minute! She saved Leslie's life!"

He said it like it was supposed to decide matters. Maybe it did, but Randy's mind was foggy again. He had a shotgun, they were well protected in the passage—a minute wouldn't hurt, considering.

"One minute and we go. We'll wait by the door."

"I'm going with him," Leslie whispered.

"Suit yourself."

❦

Randy and Stephanie stood in the passageway that led to the exit. "Fools," Randy whispered, watching them. "They're going to get us killed."

"Do you think?"

"Guaranteed."

"Maybe we should just go," Stephanie said.

Her suggestion half surprised him. "Just leave them and run?"

"Well, we'd get the cops, right?"

He considered the plan. It wasn't really a plan, more of an everyone-for-themselves strategy. Or at least he and Stephanie for themselves.

Jack and Leslie were still creeping up on the door at the other end. If it wasn't for that little waif they'd met, they'd be out of here by now.

"I can't do that," he finally said.

Stephanie hugged herself and looked around nervously. "I don't like it. We should go."

"Just keep quiet. I said we'd give him a minute, no more. Just—"

The door behind them opened. Randy heard Stephanie grunt. He whirled. Pete was there, with one arm wrapped around her neck and the other over her mouth, dragging her back through the door.

Randy jerked the shotgun around, leveled it at them, and came within an inch of putting a full load of buckshot in her gut. That was the first problem—Stephanie was in the way.

The second was that Jack was right; a shot here would alert the whole house to his location.

Pete ducked through the door and was gone.

Randy's pulse drummed through his skull. He glanced up the hall and saw that Jack was almost at the door to the study, clueless to the turn of events.

He couldn't warn Jack and Leslie without possibly alerting Betty, which wasn't in their favor. He had to either let Pete take off with Stephanie, or he had to go after them before they disappeared.

Randy swore under his breath and tore through the door.

He could hear Stephanie scream through Pete's fingers ahead, on his right. She grunted and was silent.

Pete didn't have a gun and Randy did; that was what made the difference.

The sound of a door slamming rippled past him.

Pete was outgunned, and he had a body in his hands. Or over his shoulder. Either way, Randy should be able to take him easier than he had the oaf's father. Shock and awe. He'd blow the guy away before Pete knew he had any competition.

Randy came to the door that had been slammed, threw it open, and poked his head through. Two directions. He couldn't tell where they'd gone. But if he understood Jack and Leslie correctly, he had a pretty good idea which direction Pete's hideout was, and he was sure that's where they were headed.

To the right again. He jogged around the corner and down a hall he hadn't seen before. The leather soles of his ruined shoes slapped on the concrete. Now who was hunting whom?

A left ahead, the only way. He took it without slowing.

But he was running away from the exit. And White was in here somewhere.

The two thoughts entered his mind together, like a twin blast from a double-barreled shotgun, and drilled something through his chest that he hadn't felt since Stewart's pursuit.

Fear.

He slowed to a walk, heart crashing so hard that he couldn't hear himself think. They had been right there! A single shot through that padlock and out into the rain. With a shotgun in hand! He would have made it.

"You stupid, stupid, stupid . . ." No word that came to mind accurately described how he loathed Stephanie in this moment. But he was committed.

Or was he? He stopped. Looked over his shoulder. Actually, he could go back. Leave them all and make for the road armed with the shotgun. Get to the cell phones he and Leslie had left in their car. Call for help and get to the city.

Somewhere ahead, Stephanie screamed. He'd let go of her mouth. Which probably meant Pete had reached his hideout.

Randy crept forward, resolve all but sapped in the face of the fear and disappointment he felt for the missed opportunity. Each step took him farther in, farther away. Jack and Leslie would probably get the girl, get to the door, and be long gone while he was back here trying to rescue Jack's wench.

He picked up his pace, keeping his heels from making contact with the concrete. How Pete had covered this ground so quickly he had no clue, not with a cracked noggin like Jack said he had.

Randy rounded a corner and came face-to-face with a door, brimming with yellow light. The hall disappeared around another corner ahead, but this had to be it.

He approached the door cautiously. Shock and awe, that was the plan, but he didn't have the energy for shock and awe right now.

"Please . . ." He could hear Stephanie's muffled pleading beyond the door. "Please, I'll do anything."

"You can be my wife," Pete said.

She didn't respond.

Randy leaned forward, listening. He didn't know where in the room they were, and the cracks were too narrow to give him any real view. If Stephanie could distract him . . .

"Can you put that down?" she asked.

Randy pulled back. The man had a gun?

"I want you to eat the cereal," Pete said.

Randy looked back down the hall. He could still take off.

"This cereal?" she asked.

If he took off now, he could still get out. Jack and Leslie had probably already gone. He pictured the door wide open with Betty screaming at the rain.

"It will make you strong like me."

She hesitated. Cried softly.

"Are you sure?" she said.

"Yes, yes! Leslie was a bad girl."

"Leslie wouldn't eat your cereal?"

"Leslie was a bad girl."

"But if I eat your cereal, then I'll be a good girl?" Stephanie said, voice cracking.

"You will be my wife."

"And you'll be good to me?"

"If you want to be strong like me, you have to eat the cereal. Because you're guilty."

"Guilty."

Randy blinked. She was an operator; he'd give her that much.

"Okay. See?"

She was eating it? He put his left hand on the door-knob and twisted a fraction of an inch. It wasn't locked. He nudged it. No dead bolts.

Stephanie was now sobbing softly and continuously.

"You'll be strong," Pete said.

Randy went then, because he knew any red-blooded male into rotten dog food would have his complete atten-tion on Stephanie.

Pete stood with a bowl in one hand, staring at Stephanie, who had three fingers in her mouth. Her face was streaked with tears.

Randy pulled the trigger. *Boom!* Buckshot tore into Pete's side, and he dropped the bowl. But he didn't fall.

Pump the action. Another load. *Boom!*

This one put the man on his knees.

"Come on!" he screamed. "Let's go."

She looked momentarily stunned, then sprang off the bed. But she didn't fall all weeping into his arms with gratitude. She stumbled through the door, face white.

She followed him down the halls at a full run. All Randy could think about now was getting to the pad-locked exit.

It occurred to him he hadn't chambered a round after that last blast, so he did it now, aware but uncaring that Stephanie was falling behind.

He turned the corner and cut into the tunnel that led back to the exit.

That's as far as he got. He wasn't alone in the tunnel. The man with the tin mask was there. Facing him. Twenty yards up the passage, with his hands by his sides, trench coat at his ankles, staring through those jagged holes in his faceplate.

Sickness washed through Randy's gut. He wanted to jerk the shotgun up and put a hole in that face, but he couldn't move.

No sign of Stephanie.

"Hello, Randy," White said. "You're like me; that's why you're going to win this contest."

He still couldn't hear Stephanie; where was Stephanie?

"I need a dead body," White said. "I think Jack will try to kill you. You're scum; they all know that."

Randy's vision swam. White's neck twitched.

"One body, Randy. Give me one body before he kills you."

"I . . . I can't just kill—"

"If you don't kill her, then you will die."

Her? He couldn't think straight. "Leslie?"

"Even the innocent are guilty, Randy."

———

Stephanie had lost sight of Randy, but she was too numb to call out for him to slow down. He had come back for her—he wouldn't leave her now.

Her stomach swam in revulsion from eating the paste, but it was a sickly sweet revulsion. Like chewing on the worm at the bottom of a tequila bottle. No. Worse, much worse—more like sucking up a mouthful of someone else's vomit. But that vomit was laced with a hallucinogen that had sent pleasure running along her nerves.

Her revulsion was for herself, really. For her willingness

to do whatever Pete asked of her. Anything. And for her need to be accepted by him.

It hit her then that what she did had come naturally. Her sickness, her sin, preserving herself at the cost of all principle. At the cost of her own worth. The realization made her nauseated.

She'd become a shell of a woman to save herself from pain, and she was powerless to redeem herself.

Some of the paste was still lodged in her throat. Suddenly the sickly sweetness of it all was only sickly. She stopped, bent at the waist, and threw up.

Wiping her mouth, she staggered on.

"Randy?"

When she finally caught up, Randy stood with his back toward her, shotgun in one hand pointed at the ground. He turned toward her. For a moment she thought he looked different.

"You coming?"

She hurried. "Yes." She spit bile from her mouth.

Randy jogged on.

When they reached the hall where Pete had abducted her, the door Jack and Leslie had approached stood gaping open. The exit was still padlocked. No sign of them.

Stephanie could smell her own breath—like sulfur.

"Come on!" Randy said, running to the exit. "When we get outside we run straight for the forest, not for the front of the house," he said. "We get some cover, and then we figure out how to get back to the main road, okay?"

She didn't answer.

Randy lifted the shotgun to his shoulder, aimed at the padlock, and pulled the trigger.

"Let's go!"

He jumped up on the landing and ripped off the twisted lock with a trembling hand. The door swung open easily. They'd made it?

He whirled back, grabbed Stephanie's elbow, and pulled her roughly through the doorway, outside.

Only they weren't quite outside yet.

In fact, they weren't outside at all. Stephanie blinked, but what she saw didn't change. They were in the boiler room! The hot, suffocating boiler room!

The door clicked shut behind her.

"Oh God oh God oh God!"

24

3:59 AM

JACK EASED TO ONE KNEE BY THE DOOR
and felt Leslie bump into him from behind. She drew
close to his face, and by the look in her eyes he knew
immediately that something had happened.

"They're gone!" He followed her look down the hall.
They'd left Randy and Stephanie less than a minute ago
with a promise from Randy to wait. But there was now
no sign of Randy or Stephanie. The back exit was still
closed.

A distant, muffled cry reached him. Stephanie! Someone had taken her? Pete or White.

For a moment he was torn between giving chase and
going after Susan, who he was sure waited behind this
door. Randy was also gone—as much as he hated to trust
the man, Jack chose to believe that he'd gone after
Stephanie.

He would go after Susan.

Jack had thought about the matter while bringing up
the rear on their walk through the tunnels. The more he
thought about Susan, the more he equated her with his

own daughter, Melissa. It was their innocence, not their age, that bound them.

He hadn't been able to save his own daughter from death, but he would do everything in his power to save Susan. He'd always been a stubborn, loyal guy, but his resolve to save this girl now, in the midst of such chaos, surprised even him.

He'd stopped Leslie back at a corner in the tunnels and told her, "I can't leave Susan. I'm going to find out where the exit is then go after her."

She looked him in the eye. "I'll go with you."

"No."

"Yes." She would not be moved. "You're a good man, Jack."

Now they were here, going after Susan, with the surprising fortune of locating Betty quickly. Whether that fortune was good or bad, they would soon know.

Leslie crouched and leaned against the opposite wall, watching Jack.

"It makes no sense," Betty was saying beyond the door. "Not a lick of sense. Why would anyone risk their neck for you? They won't come."

"Jack will," Susan's voice said.

"They still don't have a clue what they're in for; you know that, don't you? They'll all be dead in a couple of hours."

"Then so will you."

Jack heard a slap.

He nearly went then. But he still hadn't formed a plan. He very carefully cracked the door.

The study, as they called it, lay as he remembered it with the lone desk and the large mirror. Betty faced the mirror with her back to Jack. She had a brush in her hand and was working through Susan's long, tangled hair.

No gun. Not that he could see.

Betty jerked Susan around to face her. "You don't think I know a thing or two about killing? The guilty die. That means White isn't beyond being killed if it comes down to it. He may have done what he did to bring the house alive, but let's not forget who was here first."

"You'll be dead by morning," Susan said.

This time Betty didn't bother slapping her. She put the brush in her hair and tugged. "That's long past your dead time, honey. You're right; they're coming for you. But it's not what they think."

Jack knew he should be going in now, but their words gripped him.

"They're stronger than you know," Susan said.

"If they're so strong, they wouldn't be fooled by you, now would they? They don't know if they're coming or going. And they don't know what the real game is."

Susan didn't respond. Could any of Betty's words be true? Was it possible that Susan was actually with White?

"I don't see what anyone would see in this pretty soft face, anyway." Betty was squeezing Susan's cheeks, and both were looking at the mirror. Which was odd. "I don't care what White says, we should have killed you the day you set foot in this place."

Betty squeezed. Tighter and tighter.

Susan whimpered.

Jack pulled back, breathing steady.

"Is . . . is she with us?" Leslie asked. She'd heard.

"Who do you trust: Susan, who risked her neck to save you, or Betty?" Jack whispered.

"But Betty didn't kill her."

He thought a moment. "Betty has reasons to keep her alive. And Susan saved you."

"It could be part of the game."

"No! We can't leave her, even if she is part of their game. I'm going in."

She glanced at the door. "Okay. Be careful."

Jack took a deep breath, gently pushed the door, and spun into the room, spade raised high.

But Betty was already whirling, using Susan as a shield. Instead of a brush, she now held a knife, and it was pressed against Susan's thin neck. Susan saw Jack, and the corner of her mouth lifted ever so slightly.

"It's about time," Betty said, smiling so that her gaping white teeth were bared. "Drop the spade."

"Don't!" Susan cried.

"I said drop it!"

Leslie stepped in past Jack. "Kill her, Jack."

"I'll give you to three to drop that thing, or I'm slicing her neck," Betty said.

"Then what?" Jack demanded, approaching Betty, jaw set. "Huh? Then what, you sick stain of a woman? I'll make sure you never stand up again, that's what."

Betty backed up, dragging Susan.

"You can't let me kill her; you know that," Betty said. But there was a hint of fear in her eyes now. "She's the only thing keeping you alive! She's part of the game. You'll see that; I swear you will."

"Don't listen to her!" Susan said.

Betty flicked her knife, and Susan gasped. Blood seeped from a thin cut on her chin. "What's the matter, you couldn't get out the back door? Shovel won't help you there, sugarplum."

Leslie walked to the far side of the room, on Betty's right.

"I don't know what you think this sick game is about," she said, "but Stewart's dead and White wants us to kill you. Is that what you want? A bloodbath down here? He won't stop till we're all dead. Surely you see that."

Betty smiled. "You think Stewart is dead? Oh, he drowned all right, but he's got strong lungs."

"Drop the knife," Jack said, stepping closer. "You kill her, and I promise you I'll remove your head. Let her go."

"It's White we have to stop!" Leslie said. "We should be working together, not against each other."

Betty's eyes skipped to Leslie. Jack walked closer. The thought of actually taking her out was turning out to be more difficult than he would have guessed. And there was still the chance that Betty would manage to kill Susan.

Leslie kept walking. She was trying to be confident, but she was trembling.

"Leslie?" Jack said.

"What makes you think you can shove your twisted world down a little boy's throat and not pay for it, huh?" she said in a bitter hiss. *On the edge of snapping,* Jack thought. She was talking about Pete.

"Leslie . . ."

"You're guilty, Betty. You're guilty too. And your sins are about to find you out."

Leslie walked behind her, then past her. Betty's face was drawn tight. She watched Leslie like a hawk. It was the first time Jack had seen her stripped of command.

"You believe in hell, Betty? I don't. But looking at you, I sure wish I did, because whatever hell is, it was made for you and your son. You can either join us against White or we can take you out. How's that for a game?"

Jack was only eight feet from Betty now. But her knife was pressed tight to Susan's neck.

Her eyes swiveled from Leslie to Jack, then back. She suddenly released Susan, dropped the knife, and lifted both hands. Susan ducked to her right.

"Listen to me, Jack," Susan said, spinning back. "He who has ears to hear . . . Can you hear me?"

"Okay, you win," Betty said. "I know . . ."

"Kill her, Jack," Leslie said.

Susan was speaking as well, but Jack couldn't make out her words. The voices spun through his mind.

". . . how to kill White," Betty said. "I can show you . . ."

"Kill her!" Leslie cried.

". . . how to kill him."

Susan finished a long run-on. "And if that doesn't make sense, it's not really supposed to."

What? Jack looked at Susan and Leslie. "What?"

"What?" Leslie repeated, clueless.

"What's she saying? Susan."

Leslie glanced at the girl. "Nothing."

Silence fell. Betty's head jerked spastically for the length of a second, and then her smile returned. Jack's nerves were strung tight. Or had he seen more? Now his mind was really playing tricks.

He tried to summarize the present scenario. Leslie on his right, insisting that he swing away and bludgeon her to kingdom come. Susan on his left, staring at him in shock. Betty in the middle, hands raised by her head, smiling nervously.

"Kill her!" Leslie screamed.

Jack swung. He heard a crack. Betty's skull. The blade hit Betty with enough force to send her reeling into the mirror five feet behind her. The glass shattered.

Betty dropped to the floor and landed on her rear end. A trickle of blood ran from her ear.

They all stared, not quite believing. Black fog seeped from the wound.

"Follow me!" Susan said. "Run!" She ran toward the door that led into the room with four sofas.

Jack spied the shotgun, the one Betty had hauled into Pete's room. Leaning against the desk. He let the spade clatter to the floor, snatched up the better weapon.

"Out the back!" Leslie cried. "Susan—"

"No, Susan's right," Jack said. "We're closer to the stairs. Up the stairs. Come on!" This time he'd shoot the locks off.

He ran after Susan, who was just peeling into the main hall with the stairs when Jack spun into the living room.

Leslie sprinted on his heels.

In that hall was a flight of stairs that ran up to the main floor. If Randy was right and White was in the basement, they'd be safe on the main floor. They could exit from there. And with the gun he would have no trouble dealing with any lock.

Jack's heart pounded. They were going to make it.

What about Stephanie and Randy? Hopefully they'd made it out by now. He had Susan and Leslie.

He spilled into the hall and almost ran over Susan, who'd stopped and was staring in the opposite direction of the stairs.

"Let's go, let's—"

Leslie screamed.

Jack spun back and saw that she too was now staring at the far end of the hall, face white. He whirled.

The killer faced them from the shadows, unmoving. Black trench coat hanging open down the middle. Tin plate covering all but his eyes, and a slit for his mouth. Shotgun pointing casually at the floor.

"One dead body," he said, his voice deadened behind the mask. "The hag doesn't count."

White started to walk toward them.

"Follow me!" Susan cried. She flung open the door directly across the hall and ran through.

White's gun boomed. The load hit the door behind Susan, slamming it shut. If history was any judge, it was probably locked.

"Shoot him!" Leslie screamed.

Jack jerked his shotgun up and fired a wild shot into the wall.

His arms were weak. All Jack could think of now was getting out. Up the stairs, past the door. White's shotgun came up.

"Hurry!"

Jack leaped onto the stairs and took them three at a time with Leslie pounding up behind him. They didn't have Susan, he knew that, but he also knew that they would soon both be dead if he didn't get past this door.

Boom! White's shot tore into the shiplap siding beside him.

He pumped a round into the chamber as he ran, aimed at the door latch, and pulled the trigger before his foot was firmly planted on the landing.

The blast knocked him back into Leslie, who gave him a shove toward the door. It had been released from the shattered locking mechanism and swung free.

"Go, go!"

He dived through the door, tripped on the riser, and sprawled onto the floor.

Leslie was hung up behind him, trapped momentarily by the door, which had bounced off the adjacent wall hard enough to swing shut.

"Leslie!"

A beat passed.

Then she plowed in and pulled up. She took in the room in wonder, ignoring him entirely.

"What . . . what is this?"

A door to Jack's right suddenly flew open. Randy and Stephanie ran through, winded, eyes disbelieving.

Then the rest of the room came into clear view. And it wasn't the hallway he expected to see.

They were back in the boiler room.

"Oh God oh God oh God!" Stephanie mumbled.

25

THE BOILER ROOM HAD CHANGED, LESLIE saw. Large red letters had been scrawled on the walls.

The Wages of Sin Is One Dead Body

Randy's nostrils flared with rage. Stephanie's eyes flittered with fear. Whatever had happened to them had changed them, she thought. Her own mind was in a meltdown; she knew it well, but that didn't preclude her from judging others. Of the four of them, only Jack seemed to be himself.

She was somewhat surprised by how little she felt for Randy now. And Jack hadn't reacted to her advances, not that she had anticipated much more. Still, if there was one person who could lead them out of this, it was probably Jack.

"Give me the shotgun," Randy snapped, glaring at Jack.

"This is wrong, so wrong," Leslie said.

"Give me the gun," Randy repeated, holding out a hand.

Leslie walked in a wide circle on numb legs, staring at that writing in red. "How's this possible? I don't understand. Something spiritual is happening, isn't it?"

"I thought you were too intelligent to believe in the supernatural," Stephanie said.

"I am." And she was. But how could she deny the physical impossibility of what had just happened? "I am. But the house seems to know what we're going to do before we do it! And it knows us!"

"Knows us?"

She looked at Stephanie. "Our weaknesses. Our fears. The sin we—"

"I said, give me the gun!" Randy shouted, lifting his shotgun.

Leslie became enraged. "Stop it!"

"I don't trust him," came the snarl.

"Don't you see what's happening here, you idiot? We're back in the boiler room. And we're turning on each other. We're wearing down!" She knew she was babbling, but she pressed on. "It knows what it's doing! Our minds are wearing us down, knowing what haunts us."

"I see that. I still don't trust him."

Stephanie was blinking at Leslie. "You really think that?"

"You have a better explanation? This whole thing is spiritual. Evil. All that, but it's more personal. But spiritual is really mental, right? I mean, we have to deal with this killer on a different level to satisfy his psychosis. Make him think we are responding on some spiritual level or . . ." Or what. She didn't know or what. "This is crap, just plain crap!"

"I'm not going to give you my gun," Jack said, eyeing Randy suspiciously. He checked to see how many rounds remained. Just one. Good thing he checked. He fished the spare shells out of his pants and loaded them.

Leslie walked over and shoved Randy's gun down. "You're losing your mind! You hear me, Randy? Stop this!"

"Are you two nuts?" Stephanie demanded. "We're trapped in this basement and you're squabbling over guns?"

Randy glanced at her, then slowly lowered his weapon, reloaded it.

"So you still think this is just in our minds?" Stephanie snapped. "If there's anyone who should be shot here, it's you."

Leslie ignored the woman. Nothing any of them said now would surprise her. And Stephanie was right about one thing—they were trapped.

Jack drilled Randy with a stare. "What happened back there? How did you get back in here?"

"Through the back exit," Randy said.

"You're sure it was an exit?"

"I saw White step in through that door earlier. Of course I'm sure."

"How did *you* get in?" Stephanie asked.

"Up the stairs. This was supposed to be the main level."

"We're trapped," Leslie said.

"All in our minds?" Jack said.

She ignored him.

The house groaned.

"And that's *not* the pipes," Stephanie said. "This house is alive."

It was such a clear, obvious truth that none of them dared suggest differently.

Leslie walked over to one of the boilers and put her hand on it. She rapped on it with her knuckles as if testing to see that it was real, then faced them, face flushed.

"There's no way out, is there?"

Her eyes settled on Randy, who was staring at the wall.

The Wages of Sin Is One Dead Body

House rule number three: *Give me one dead body, and I might let rule two slide.*

The killer was demanding one dead body as a payment for their sin. Fanatical, religious nonsense, but Leslie couldn't shake the feeling that if they didn't play the game this way, they would die.

So what was she supposed to do? Kill her sin? Blow Pete's head off? Or kiss his face and do whatever he wanted as a form of penitence?

The inbreds didn't count; they all knew that. They also knew that White could have killed them by now if he wanted to.

This was why religion should be banned in civilized countries. She glared at the wall and stifled a scream of fury.

⸻

Jack gripped the shotgun a little tighter. Of the four of them, Randy was the most likely to satisfy White's demand.

And what about him? If it came right down to it, would he kill one of them to save the other three? In spite of the house rules, Jack suspected White probably wouldn't be satisfied with just one dead body. He recalled the newspaper accounts. Whole families, murdered.

On the other hand, Jack wasn't sure he wouldn't

comply, particularly if it was in self-defense. What confused him was the "wages of sin" bit on the wall. Maybe Leslie was right, and the killer was religiously motivated. Whatever was happening to them was as much spiritual or psychosomatic as physical.

The problem was, he didn't have a clue what that meant. How do you defeat a killer—or a house, for that matter—that's rubbing your own sin in your face?

Comply? *One dead body.* Randy's dead body.

"There's only one way out," Stephanie said.

The sound of metal scraping against metal squealed through the room. Jack swiveled his head up just in time to see something drop through the shadows between two large pipes twenty feet above them.

His pulse spiked. It was a body. On a thick rope.

The body fell for ten feet then bounced at the end of the rope, hung by a noose drawn tight around its neck.

Leslie jumped out of the way with a startled cry.

The rope creaked over the swaying weight. Slowly the body turned until they could all see who it was.

At the end of the rope, as dead as a sack of rocks, hung Randy Messarue.

Randy?

They were all too stunned to react immediately. A voice was screaming through Jack's mind, telling him that this body on the end of this rope had serious implications, but he was too shocked to isolate them.

Randy's dead eyes were closed and his mouth was cracked. From the crack seeped a thin tendril of black smoke that streamed down toward the floor. It hit the ground and spread out on the concrete.

The meaning of this dead body hit Jack then, like an

eighteen-wheeler barreling out of the black night. If Randy was dead, who was the Randy next to him?

White?

He reacted on impulse, swinging his shotgun up and around toward Randy, who stared at his dead twin in shock.

"Drop the gun!" Jack shouted.

"What?"

"Drop it!" His arms trembled. Had he chambered another round? He did so now—*ca-chink!* "Now!"

Randy held the shotgun in one hand, barrel pointed at the floor. His eyes turned to Jack, lit by fear. "What's—"

"What are you doing, Jack?" Stephanie asked.

I'm allowing myself to be manipulated by the killer. I'm being pushed slowly to killing for the killer. Putting myself on the same plane as the killer. Forcing myself to show my true colors. I am evil. We are all evil.

The wages of sin . . . is death. One dead body.

The thoughts flashed through his mind and were gone. They weren't of any use to him now.

"That's not Randy," Jack said, nodding at the living Randy. "Randy's dead."

"You . . . you think that's me?" Randy asked, still dazed.

Jack didn't answer. They were all following the same thread of logic that he'd found.

"Drop . . . the . . . gun."

Stephanie took a step back, eyes on Randy.

"*This* is me!" Randy said, jabbing his chest with his free hand. "It's a trick. He's trying to get you to kill me! One dead body. He told me you'd do this! He told me—"

"When did he tell you, Randy? You bring that gun up even an inch, and I'll take your head off. And for the record, I've done it before. I killed Betty a few minutes ago. I'll do it again in a heartbeat."

The man stared, angrily now. "If that's me, who am I? An apparition?" His eyes darted to the others, looking for support. "You think I'm not real? I just rescued Stephanie . . ."

But not even Stephanie jumped to his defense.

"He could be White," Leslie said.

"Yes, he could," Jack said.

"I'm *not* White!"

"And I'm not willing to take that chance," Jack said.

Randy regarded Leslie bitterly. "So now not only the house is haunted, but the killer can magically appear in any form he wants to? This from a staunch atheist?"

"I don't know what I believe anymore. But there's two of you, and one of you isn't real," Leslie said.

"What if that one's the apparition?" Stephanie asked, pointing to the swinging body.

"Check it, Leslie," Jack said.

She looked momentarily unsure, then slowly stepped up to the body. Jack watched from his peripheral vision as she cautiously lifted a hand and nudged it. The body swung and turned in place, rope creaking softly.

"Real," Jack said.

"And so was the body of Stewart that I saw," Randy said. "And it was leaking smoke too. That's the sign. I'm telling you, I'm not White!"

A thought occurred to Jack. He had reason enough to pull the trigger now, didn't he? If Randy was White, Jack would be acting in self-defense. If Randy really was *Randy*, Jack would be acting in *presumed* self-defense. And they would have their one dead body.

The sudden urge to do it brought a tremor to his index finger, despite the weakness of his reasoning.

"Why would I rescue Stephanie after Pete took her?" Randy asked. "Tell me that."

Jack glanced at Stephanie. "What about it? What happened back there?"

"He . . . he rescued me."

"Was he ever out of your sight? Any time when White might have killed him?"

She looked at Randy, eyes wider.

"Actually, yes."

Randy's brow furrowed. "What?"

"When you disappeared around the corner. He could have killed you then and switched places. You were acting a bit strange."

"Good grief! He threatened to kill me."

"Threatened you how?" Jack demanded. "What did he say?"

"That he'd kill me if I didn't kill you. That you'd try to kill me. Which you are. That time is running out. Dawn is coming."

Leslie gasped. "It's gone!"

Jack looked. The body was gone. Rope and all. They'd imagined it? Impossible!

Behind him a door opened, feet pounded in, Jack whirled. The door slammed. What he saw made his knees threaten to buckle.

Randy and Stephanie had just stumbled into the room through one of the doors. The Randy and Stephanie already in the room stared at their twins, aghast. Identical in every way, down to the shotguns held by both Randys.

"Randy?" Leslie's voice was taut.

Jack stepped back and glanced toward Leslie. But it wasn't just Leslie that he saw.

He saw another Leslie standing five feet from her. And another Jack.

26

4:31 AM

JACK'S LEGS BEGAN TO SHAKE.

There were eight of them in the room now; two Leslies, two Stephanies, two Randys—and two Jacks. All of them were wearing stricken looks of horror, including the other Jack, who gripped his shotgun with white knuckles.

Clearly, four of them weren't real. Right?

The Stephanie who'd just come in whimpered.

As if reacting to an unspoken signal, the two Randys and the new Jack snatched their shotguns to their shoulders and paired off into a stalemate. The Randys' guns on the Jacks, and the Jacks' guns on the Randys.

He'd lost whatever advantage he had, Jack realized. He should have finished this when he had the chance, because he couldn't now—not without knowing who was real and who wasn't, a luxury now clearly out of reach.

The two Randys were breathing hard. At any moment a gun would go off.

"Easy," Jack said.

"No one moves," the other Jack said.

"What's going on?" the new Stephanie asked, trembling.

None of them took a stab at answering. For long seconds they stood in a deadlock, silent. The house groaned again, loud and distant above them.

The other Jack broke their silence. "We have a problem," he said. "No one makes any rash moves. Just take it easy."

"Who are you?" the new Leslie asked, looking at Jack. "How did you get in here?"

"Through the door."

"That couldn't be. Jack and I came through the door a few minutes ago, and the room was empty. We were here first."

Impossible. But she obviously didn't think so.

"Four of you aren't real," the new Jack said. He switched his gun from Randy to Jack. "Beginning with you. Put the gun down."

A bead of perspiration broke down Jack's forehead and snaked around his eye. The new Jack was taking command as if he were the real Jack. Jack's mind tipped dangerously. His finger was tight on the trigger, and he forced himself to ease off.

First one Randy, then the other, swiveled their guns to train on Jack. Now all three shotguns were on him.

"Just take it easy," he breathed. "Nothing rash."

Isn't that what the other Jack had said?

"We have to figure this out. Leslie?"

She didn't answer. He cast her a quick glance. "Tell them."

"Tell them what?" Her eyes darted around. "I don't know what."

"That we're real, for heaven's sake!"

"I . . . I don't know which one of you is the real Jack."

"Are you crazy? We were just in here with the dead body . . ."

"What dead body?" the new Leslie asked.

"Shut up!" Randy snapped.

White had told Randy that he should kill Jack.

Would an apparition's shotgun actually work?

"He's going to kill us," Jack said, glancing at the other Jack. "You know that, don't you? And since he doesn't know which is real, he has to take both of us out."

The new Jack thought about his statement, then turned his gun back on Randy.

The new Randy jerked his gun on the new Jack. They were paired off again.

"He's doing this!" Leslie said. Which Leslie, Jack no longer knew. He no longer knew who was who in relationship to how it all began. He only knew he was the real Jack.

The other Jack also seemed to know about himself. What if he was right?

"White's manipulating us," one Leslie said. "Forcing us to kill someone we think might not be real without knowing for certain."

"She's right," the other Leslie said. "He's trying to extract payment for wrongdoing, which in his sick little mind is death."

The hopelessness of the situation was driving Jack mad. He couldn't seem to still the trembling in his hands.

If they could all be reasonable . . .

The notion of reasoning with an apparition struck

him as pointless. And Randy was out for blood. There was no reasoning with either Randy at this point.

"This is what White told me would happen," Randy said with a wicked smirk. "He said Jack would kill me if I didn't kill him. Not a chance, hero boy."

"Don't do it," the new Jack said.

"Do it," the other Randy said. "He's got his gun on the wrong Randy."

It only took a moment for the first Randy to understand the meaning. "You're saying I'm expendable because you think you're real?"

"I'm saying we got us a standoff. Someone's going to die here, and it isn't going to be me."

Each of them truly believed they were real. If either of the Randys knew they were unreal, they would have started the bloodbath already without fear of dying.

"We can tell which of us is real," the new Jack said. "I doubt an apparition's shotgun will actually fire. We can all fire our weapons at the wall."

Assuming the assumption was correct.

"And then what, kill the ones whose guns misfire?" Randy asked, wearing that smirk of his. "Why don't we just go for it now and see who's alive when the dust settles?"

"Because you may end up dead, that's why," Jack said. He lowered his gun a few inches. "I'll agree to Jack's suggestion."

After a few moments of consideration, the Randys each lowered their shotguns. One turned his gun on the wall and pulled the trigger.

Boom! The room echoed with the blast. Followed almost immediately by another blast.

Boom!

The second Randy had discharged his weapon as well. As one they both trained their guns on Jack. Then one of them switched to the other Jack, who brought his up as well.

Jack followed suit.

"Like I said," one Randy murmured. "I say we just go for it."

"Which probably means you're not the real Randy," Leslie said. "You're egging us all on and into a bloodbath!"

"You think? I think I'm looking at White." His eyes were on Jack. "And the only way to find out is to put some lead in his gut."

"There's another way," the other Randy said.

They waited.

"Stewart's dead body leaked black smoke. I'm thinking that maybe it wasn't real, like the hanged body a few moments ago. And I'm thinking that unreal bodies leak black smoke."

"Betty was real enough, and smoke came out of her," Jack said. "I'm thinking the smoke has to do with being dead."

"Or wounded," Leslie said. "The stuff oozes out the wounds, right?"

"You're saying we should each cut ourselves?"

Randy shrugged. "You afraid of a cut?"

"Okay. We cut ourselves on one condition," Jack said. "We give up our weapons when we get cut. If nothing happens, we get it back. Leslie can hold them, one at a time."

"What's to keep Leslie from taking us out?" Randy demanded.

Would the real Randy say that? Maybe he would.

"Agreed?" Jack pressed.

"Agreed," Jack said.

The Randy who had suggested a standoff hesitated, but the other agreed, followed by the Leslies and the Stephanies.

Sweat streamed past both of Jack's temples. He was sure that if they didn't do something soon, one of them would go ballistic. And he was no longer sure it wouldn't be him.

He impulsively handed his gun to Leslie. "Anyone have a knife?"

Both Randys did. Naturally. The real Randy had taken one from the kitchen upstairs. One of them slid it toward Jack without lowering his gun, eyes glinting.

Jack picked up the knife and held his hand out. He placed the blade's edge against his palm and looked at the others.

"We all go. Anyone refuses, they prove themselves to be unreal. Assuming this works. If anyone smokes black, they're incapacitated, not shot outright. Agreed?"

They all nodded.

Because he was sure that no black smoke would pour out of any cut on his hand, Jack had no difficulty with the test. But he wasn't so sure that Randy would be as eager to cut himself.

"Keep the gun on Randy, Leslie."

"That wasn't part of—"

"It is now," Jack interrupted. "Just to even things out. Consider her impartial."

Leslie lifted the gun so that both Randys were covered.

Jack nodded. He pressed the blade against his skin and pressed. But the knife wasn't as sharp as he'd hoped, forcing him to draw it back until it sliced past the epidermis.

Blood seeped from the cut. He held it out. The sight of red blood had never looked quite so comforting.

He showed them. "Satisfied?"

He tossed the knife back toward Randy. It clattered to his feet. "You're next."

"Why me?"

"To keep it even. You nervous? Leslie, get his gun."

The door behind Randy opened. Susan stood in the doorway, eyes wide, breathing hard.

Jack glanced at the others to see their reactions. They all looked similarly amazed. "Are you okay?"

"What do you think you're doing?" she demanded. "You're going to kill . . . the one thing . . ." Her voice wasn't connecting with Jack. It seemed to be hitting dead spots. Skipping like a bad CD.

None of them had lowered their weapons.

"Is she real?" Stephanie asked. "Maybe she's not the real Susan."

"There's only one of her," Leslie said.

"We should cut *her*," Randy said.

Susan looked up at the writing on the wall.

The Wages of Sin Is One Dead Body

"Maybe you all deserve to die tonight. That's what he wants. That's . . . all of us dead. I thought . . . but I think you're just going to get us all killed. You . . ." Her next few words were garbled. "You . . . ba . . . the way out . . . hate . . . blood."

Susan looked at them as if she hadn't noticed her own speech skipping.

"Only those with eyes to see the truth can see it," she said. "I think you're all blind as ba . . . the . . . finish . . . ma . . . Jack's going to ki . . . heart . . . to die."

"She's with White!" a Leslie said.

A shiver touched the skin on Jack's back. What if she was actually White's ally? It would explain how she'd managed to live so long.

He reached for his weapon.

The black smoke began to pour out of the cut in his palm while his hand was extended toward Leslie.

He froze, stunned by the surreal sight. Black fog pouring out, falling vertically, hitting the ground and spreading. Like liquid nitrogen.

How was that possible? He was unreal? The *other* Jack was the real Jack?

His eyes met Leslie's, which were stricken with terror.

"I told you, Jack," Susan said. "You're all guilty . . . You . . ."

But the rest of her sentence was smothered by a loud moan that reverberated around them.

A thick column of black smoke poured out of the large round vent near the ceiling through which Jack and Leslie had first entered the room. Fog just like the fog that came from Jack's hand. An inky black streak over two feet in diameter. It shot out several feet then took a turn straight down and flowed to the floor, where it spread toward them.

Two thoughts collided in Jack's mind. The first was that Randy was going to most certainly kill him now. And then the other Jack, whom he'd believed to be the real Jack.

The second was that his only chance at survival was

to grab the gun still in Leslie's frozen hand as she stared at the black smoke now filling the room from the bottom up.

The fog rushed around his feet and sent a slicing pain up his legs.

The Leslies screamed. The Randys backpedaled in a hopeless attempt to avoid the rapidly rising blanket of fog.

The fog touched the door where Susan stood, slamming it shut in her face. If she was with White, she was leaving them to their own demise.

Jack stepped forward and grabbed Randy's shotgun from Leslie's grip. He pivoted, expecting hot lead to fill his body at any moment, though he wasn't sure he'd be able to distinguish it from the pain that now screamed through his body. The fog was like an acid.

The other Randy saw what he'd done and swung his gun back in line.

Jack lunged to his left and fired at Randy.

The fog swirled over his head before he could see what, if any, damage he'd inflicted. The sound of another shot buffeted his ears. He chambered another round and fired blindly in the direction of the sound.

Then the room filled with a series of booms, like rolling thunder, as shotguns on all sides fired in rapid succession. Screams and grunts.

The sound of bodies falling. Guns clattering on concrete.

Then nothing but the beating of Jack's heart to accompany the ringing in his ears.

A whooshing sound enveloped him. The black fog began rushing back into the ceiling the way it had come. Jack stood still, blinded by the smoke. He hadn't been hit, but he suddenly wasn't sure that was a good thing. What if Leslie had been struck? Or Stephanie?

His body was shaking from head to toe, more from shock than from the pain brought on by the smoke. Randy had gotten his standoff.

The smoke level fell below his head.

Leslie stood on his left, staring. One Leslie.

Randy and Stephanie stood on his right, shocked. One Randy, one Stephanie.

Then the black fog was gone. No Susan, no dead bodies. Jack, Leslie, Randy, and Stephanie stared at one another in silence.

It was Stephanie who broke the quiet. "Oh, God," she mumbled. And by the way she said it, Jack thought it might be a prayer of desperation.

He looked at his palm. No fog, just red blood. But staring up at them all, Jack knew a few other things now.

He knew that Randy intended to kill him.

He knew he had what it took to kill Randy.

He knew he could leak black smoke.

And he knew that he was guilty of a desire to kill Randy, of bitterness toward Stephanie, of a hundred other smudges on his life. And this killer didn't seem the kind to let them slide.

Not without one dead body. House rules.

The object of this game was to survive by killing, but Jack was sure that real survival wasn't simply a matter of killing or being killed. It was really about confronting the wages of sin, whatever that meant. It was about life as much as it was about death. What kind of contest didn't consist of at least two contestants? If this

27

4:48 AM

IT TOOK THEM SEVERAL MINUTES TO SETTLE into the full dread of their predicament. They were truly, hopelessly trapped by a killer who could reach out and tinker with their lives at his whim in a house that seemed to flow at his will.

Something had happened to Stephanie, but she wasn't talking about it. Her breath smelled like sulfur, and she was oddly quiet.

Jack didn't want to appear threatening to Randy, so he gave the shotgun to Leslie and quietly asked her to keep an eye on Randy. He went out of his way to appear gracious to the man, knowing that he would look for any excuse to force a confrontation.

That left Randy to stew and occasionally glance up at the words on the wall.

The Wages of Sin Is One Dead Body

They tried to make sense of the multiple characters and the fog that had swallowed them. They'd all seen the same thing; that much was a comfort, however slight.

And they all agreed that the house was deliberately manipulating them to expose their own base tendencies. Their sins, maybe. Their eventual submission to the killer's demand that they surrender to the murderer in them all.

This they all agreed on, with Leslie's help. But despite her pinpointing the issues at hand, this shared knowledge didn't offer any solutions. Understanding that you were falling down a cliff didn't provide the proverbial branch to break your fall. Leslie could describe her understanding of the cliff, but she couldn't point to any branches.

"We're screwed," Randy said after a lull in their otherwise-intense discussion. "We're out of options. We're in the sticks in a possessed house that's making us see ghosts or whatever these things that keep popping up are." His voice was resigned. "We're all going to die."

No one argued.

Jack walked over to Leslie and casually took the gun back.

"There's only one way out of this," Randy said.

The gun felt surprisingly comfortable in Jack's hands. Knowing what he did about Randy gave him half a mind to end it right here with a little standoff of his own. He was justified. He knew the man fully intended to kill him at some point.

"What's that, Randy?" he asked, pumping the action. Only two shots left—he would have to be careful.

"You know what I'm talking about," Randy said. He looked at the words on the wall.

"Tell me." Jack faced him, suddenly itching for the same confrontation on Randy's mind.

"He wants one of us dead," Randy said, withdrawing the knife from his belt.

"You want to kill me, Randy? Hmm? Is that it?"

"I didn't say that. Do you want me dead?"

"Did I say that?"

They stared off in silence.

"I'm just saying that he's got us trapped down here for as long as it takes for one of us to kill another. Someone has to die. Either one of us, or the girl."

"The girl? Who said anything about the girl?"

"White told me. The others don't count. Betty, Stewart, Pete—they don't mean anything. But Susan does."

"Unless she's working with him," Leslie said. "She's gone again. Why? There's something wrong with her."

"Maybe," Jack said. "I'm not willing to concede that—"

"Well, what are you willing to concede?" Randy demanded. "He wants a dead body, we give—"

"You *really* believe he'll be satisfied with just one of us blowing someone else's head off?" Jack said.

"I think he'll follow his own rules," Leslie said. "He may not let us all live, but as long as we don't give in to his demands, he won't kill us, either. We start killing each other, and the game is over."

"What's our time?" Randy said.

Jack checked his watch. The crystal was cracked. "Four fifty-two."

Randy chuckled ruefully. Sweat beaded his face. "An hour and change. If one of us doesn't kill someone else pretty soon, he's going to kill us—"

The door rattled. Fists beat on it. "You in there? Let us in!"

A man's voice. Not the familiar sound of White's deep voice behind a tin mask.

Stephanie backed away from the door. "Is . . . is that him?"

"Could be him without the mask," Randy said, standing and raising the knife.

He started forward.

Jack grabbed his arm. "Hold on!"

Pounding again. "This is Officer Lawdale. Open this door immediately!"

Leslie looked a question at Jack. *Who?*

"Lawdale! The highway patrolman Steph and I ran into."

Leslie's face brightened. She ran forward, unlocked the door, and pulled it open.

Highway Patrolman Morton Lawdale stood in the doorway dressed in the same tight gray uniform they'd seen him in yesterday.

He had a revolver out, cocked by his ear. He glanced behind him and then entered the room, locking the door behind him.

"Well, well, well," Lawdale said, scanning the room. "What kind of mess have we gotten ourselves into now?"

28

4:53 AM

THE GAME HADN'T CHANGED, BUT THERE was a new feeling in the air. For the first time Jack felt a genuine sense of hope. Lawdale was undoubtedly quirky, but he carried himself with authority and confidence, something they all desperately needed.

Sweat darkened his gray shirt, which was otherwise dry. Apparently the rain had let up. His black leather boots were muddy, but Lawdale was unscathed. His now hatless head was covered in close-cropped blonde hair. He'd armed himself to the teeth before coming in. A gun on each hip, two more behind the belt at his back, blades on each ankle. Lawdale was nothing short of a gunslinger born into the wrong century.

To his knowledge no one had seen him enter the building, which he'd done without waiting for the backup he'd called in.

After grilling Leslie and Randy as to their identities and then assuring himself that each of the four was not mortally hurt, Lawdale demanded they tell him what had happened, all of it, and they fed it to him in long run-on sentences interrupted by his constant insistence for clarification. As the story quickly unfolded, Lawdale began to pace.

The house was still moaning and screeching above them, attracting his periodic glances to the ceiling. He offered no judgment one way or the other.

He told them how he'd come across Jack's car. His headlights had caught the red taillights of a car in the bush as he passed. Ordinarily he would have called it in without stopping, but he recognized Jack's blue Mustang.

"So we can get out of here, right?" Stephanie said. "You got in, so we can get out."

"Hold on to your high notes, honey. Give me a moment." He holstered his gun and slapped his palm with that black baton of his as he paced.

"Backup's on the way, but it might take them an hour or more."

"You can't just take us out?" Stephanie cried.

He glanced at the ceiling in response to a groan. "You're saying a killer is out there. You're saying you've been hunted by three inbreds armed with shotguns. You're saying the house is haunted. You're saying there's no way out." He leveled his eyes at Stephanie. "I'd say rushing out into the halls with guns blazing is a tad impulsive, wouldn't you? Give me a moment!"

Jack liked the man, quirks and all. Not even Randy in his rabid state would easily run over Lawdale.

"I've heard about the man," Lawdale continued. "A serial killer who's been on the wires for a few months now. Known as Tin Man, which corresponds with this mask you described. His trail has been leading southeast. No surprise he's finally here, then."

Lawdale slapped his palm with the stick. "Betty and Stewart are dead, you say?"

"We think so," Randy said.

"But badly wounded at least," Lawdale said.

"Right."

"And this girl named Susan keeps going missing, which you think means she could be with him. I doubt that a young girl would be much use to a killer. I'd buy the argument that if she's more than a figment—"

"We didn't imagine her," Jack said.

"Fine. Then I would give her the benefit of the doubt. The house, on the other hand . . ." His eyes settled on the wall.

The Wages of Sin Is One Dead Body

". . . The house is what concerns me most."

"But you believe us," Leslie said.

"If I didn't believe you, I wouldn't be concerned, now would I?" He cracked his neck.

"A haunted house," Stephanie said.

"Could be. You can deal with a man like White by putting him back with some lead in his gut. But the supernatural is a whole different thing."

"You're a religious man?" Jack asked.

"Can't say that I am; can't say that I'm not. But I know that if what you're telling me about this house is accurate, it won't matter if we have a whole SWAT team outside."

"But you got in," Stephanie said.

"And I've been thinking about that," Lawdale said. "Something you should do a little more of."

He walked to his right without looking at her. "When you try to leave the basement, you end up back in. Doors lock behind you, open in front of you. As if the house knows you, inside and out. Am I right?"

"Something like that," Jack said.

"The house won't let you out. But that doesn't mean it won't let someone in. Like a flytrap."

"White couldn't get in at first," Randy said.

"Based on what you've told me, doesn't sound like he wanted in, not until he came into the basement. Sounds to me like he was trying to drive you into the basement on your own."

The man's reasoning mirrored Jack's, although Lawdale was coming at it from a different angle.

A few seconds of silence slipped by.

"It's possible, just possible, that I may be able to get out," Lawdale said.

"How?" Randy asked. He stood, seeming renewed. "I'm going with you."

"Back up, boy. What I'm saying is that I know Tin Man didn't see me come in. I saw the truck at the front door and avoided the top floor. Same for the basement entrance in the back. I came in through a grate and up a dried-out tunnel. Place used to be a mining operation but was abandoned when they discovered a mass grave on the grounds."

"A grave?" Stephanie said, shooting an I-told-you-so look at Randy. "That would explain some things."

"Tin Man may have turned this house bad somehow— invited in whatever powers to haunt it—but if there's rules, there's rules. House rules. The house will prevent any-one from leaving it, assuming it knows they're inside."

"You're suggesting the house doesn't know you're inside," Jack said.

"Still the dense one, aren't you, Jack? But you're on the right track."

Leslie grunted. She closed her eyes and took a long, deep breath. Shook her head. "I can't believe we're talking like this. What a crock. A house doesn't know stuff! Listen to you!"

Her old training was awakening, Jack thought. "I thought you changed your—"

She held up her hand and stopped him. "I know, I know. Yes, I said it might be haunted." She waved a hand as she continued. "Spirits, demons, supernatural stuff and all that. I know! That doesn't make it real. It's one thing to talk in general supernatural terms." She looked at the words on the wall. "It's another thing to start talking rules and specifics and . . . whatever. Like there's a whole order or something. Like the house is actually thinking, for heaven's sake! Knows things! Don't tell me that doesn't sound just a little bit crazy to you."

Jack nodded. "But we don't have time to sort out the whys of what's happening yet. We've got barely more than an hour."

"And then what, the house starts beating us to death?" Leslie asked.

"Somehow I think it'll be a little more personal."

"Let's not get our undies in a bunch," Lawdale said to Leslie. "I doubt the house knows anything. But the power, the spirits, the demons, the whatever-you-want-to-call-it that inhabits this house do. And they can change the house at will. Yet it let me walk in unchallenged?" He smacked his palm. "The only explanation is that these powers are limited to time and space and they were preoccupied with you. I made it past unnoticed."

"Which would mean if you can get back to an exit unseen, the house won't know to stop you," Leslie said. "That's your point, right? Assuming these things work like you suggest."

"I'm not saying I know how they work. I'm simply dealing with the facts in front of me and drawing as few conclusions as possible. Something you should be very familiar with in your line of work."

"If you go, I'm going with you," Randy said.

"And you"—Lawdale turned to him—"as a business-man, you should be familiar with basic logic, right?"

Randy blinked, insulted.

"Put it together, city boy. They know you—they'll be all over you."

"And why aren't they all over us now?" Randy demanded.

"Maybe they are," Jack said. "The rules are pretty simple. Tin Man's giving us time to kill each other."

"Even if you get out, how do *we* get out?" Stephanie asked.

"We get out when the officer opens a door for us," Leslie said, staring at Lawdale. "Am I right?"

"Assuming I'm right," he said. "Maybe the doors can be opened from the outside. They let you in, but not out."

He looked at the door by the boiler. He'd given them the first real plan of the night, but he no longer possessed the same confidence he'd come in with, Jack thought.

"If I can get out without being detected, I'll find a way into the house and will open the basement door, the one you say is between the kitchen and the dining room. If you can make it to the top of the stairs quickly, while I have the door open, maybe we can get you out."

They stared at him ambivalently.

"Once out of the basement, we should be able to escape. The basement seems to be the problem."

He paced, concern on his face now even more obvious.

"I don't mind pointing out that I may not make it," Lawdale said, glancing at the door again. He pulled out one of his revolvers and checked the clip. "These things respond to bullets?"

"Yes."

He cracked his neck again. "Okay, tell me the best way to get into the house upstairs. Back door, window, ceiling? Tell me."

"Back door to the kitchen," Randy said. "White bolted it from the outside. If that doesn't work . . ." He shrugged.

"I'll find a way in."

"White didn't," Stephanie said.

"White didn't *want* to," Jack said. "Aren't you listening?"

Lawdale looked at his watch. "Five oh-nine. Give me ten minutes. At exactly—"

"That long?" Stephanie demanded.

"With time for unforeseen difficulties, yes. If I make it, I'll open the main door into the basement at exactly 5:19. Be on the stairs. Can you do that?"

Jack and Leslie synced their watches. Jack glanced at the others, avoiding Randy's stare, and nodded.

Lawdale walked to the door, put his ear against it, and listened for several long seconds. He took a very deep breath and dropped to a crouch.

Unlocked the door. Cracked it. One quick glance outside and closed it again.

"Okay."

"You sure you know the way back?" Leslie asked.

He tapped his head. "I left a few markers. Ten minutes."

Morton Lawdale cocked his gun, extended it out with one hand, opened the door, and disappeared into the hall in a silent, crouched run.

29

5:14 AM

THEY SPENT THE FIRST FIVE MINUTES OF the wait trying to convince one another that Lawdale's plan would work, but there were too many questions voiced by all of them to bring any true comfort.

Lawdale's plan was a hope, nothing more. And a thin hope at that. But Jack knew that short of hope, Randy would have tried something rash. Like killing him. If the highway patrolman hadn't shown up when he did, at least one of them would likely be dead now.

"You're sure you know the way?" Randy asked Jack. "How long will it take us?"

"The stairs are through three halls—been down them twice now. Unless they've changed."

"Great," Stephanie said.

"You come up with a better idea. Otherwise, stick to the plan."

Both she and Randy fidgeted nervously. Leslie had her eyes glued to her watch and had grown quiet.

The house continued to groan and creak.

And what about Susan? The more Jack thought

about her, the more he was convinced that she was nothing more or less than another innocent victim. With every passing minute, he became more convinced that she couldn't be tied in with the killer.

"Down to one minute," Leslie said.

Jack walked toward the door. "Follow me."

They exited the room on edge, in single file. Jack, Leslie, Stephanie, and Randy, bringing up the rear with his shotgun locked and loaded, one spastic forefinger away from alerting the whole house of their location.

"I don't think this is going to work," Stephanie said. She spoke quietly, but her voice sounded shockingly loud in the hall. Jack turned back and drew his fingers across his neck forcefully.

It took them thirty seconds to reach a large wooden door that led into the second hall. So far so good. But it was the hall ahead that concerned Jack the most.

Jack turned back and mouthed instructions to them. "Through this door; stairs are on the right."

"What's that?" Stephanie asked. She was pointing at the floor.

Jack saw it immediately, the black fog they'd encountered in the boiler room was seeping past the crack below the door.

"That stuff's in the hall?" Stephanie said. "We can't—"

"Quiet!" Jack whispered. "We go. Ignore the pain; just get on the steps as fast as you can and run."

Jack grabbed the handle. "Ready?"

He jerked the door open.

Stephanie was the first to scream. They were back in the boiler room, flooded with two feet of black fog. A fist seemed to lodge itself in Jack's throat. Four others stood in the black fog.

One Jack, one Randy, one Leslie, and one Stephanie, facing off with shotguns as they had before. The Jack's hand was bleeding black fog, which also poured from the round vent up high, exactly as before.

They were staring at themselves, as if *they*, not the people in the room, were the unreal among them.

The quartet inside the boiler room spun to the sound of Stephanie's scream. For a moment all eight of them froze, four outside the room, four in the knee-high fog.

"Jack!" Susan stood, panting in an abutting hallway. "Hurry! Follow me!"

Without waiting, she ran down the hall, away from them.

Jack decided that he would follow. Whoever she was, he would follow.

He slammed the door shut and sprinted after the girl.

"What if—"

"Shut up! We don't have time!"

They followed him, hard on his heels, as he gained on the girl. Down one hall and to a large door. He recognized it as the same door they'd just assumed was the way into the main hall.

Susan threw the door open. Fog filled the hall to a height of three feet. She hesitated a moment then ran into it. "Hurry!"

The moment Jack entered the fog, he knew that they were in trouble. The acid, for one, but this he could tolerate. What lay ahead was a different matter.

The house had changed again. And this change brought all five of them to an abrupt halt.

They were still in the hall at the bottom of the stairs. Jack knew that because he saw stairs rising to the main floor to their right. But the stairs now ran the full length of the hall, not the mere ten feet he'd expected.

The passage extended just as far to their left. It had doubled in length.

And width.

But not even the matter of an extra hundred feet of hallway had stopped them. The man standing between them and the stairs did.

Stewart. A shotgun readied. Their sudden arrival had startled him, but he recovered quickly, swinging his gun toward them.

Boom! Randy fired. His shot picked the man up off his feet and dropped him into the fog that filled the hall to their knees.

"Run!" Susan yelled. She ran toward the stairs, leaving swirling fog in her wake.

They took off after her.

"Watch for others!" she cried.

Others?

Jack saw the backs of their claw-scarred bald heads first, just breaking the top of the fog. Rising slowly, as if the fog was giving them birth.

The fog's familiar pain pushed Jack faster, and he crowded the others. "Hurry!"

"The door's not open!" Leslie cried.

"Run!"

The new inbreds were positioned abreast, forcing Jack to brush past as he sprinted. Their rising continued, like a choreographed dance. Their heads showed to the tops of their ears now. All of them faced away, toward the stairs. They were all bald, but that's where their similarity to Stewart ended.

Six of them.

So the basement was infested with more than just Stewart, Betty, and Pete. Why they were rising so slowly, Jack didn't know, but he was sure they were part of White's game.

Susan leaped onto the steps, stumbled on the first one, but scrambled up using her hands. Out of the fog. Randy was right behind her. The others followed, equally frantic, motivated by a desire to get away from the inbreds as much as from the fog.

The door was still closed. Randy fired at the latch. The buckshot bounced off the door. Didn't even chip the paint. Jack was the last to mount the steps. He clambered to the top, where Susan was pounding on the door with both hands. The others piled up on the landing and looked back, faces drawn and pale.

Jack whirled back and felt his heart skip a beat. The bald heads had risen from the fog so that the tops of their heads and their eyes cleared the black sea. Still rising.

Their bald heads and scars were similar to Stewart's. Their eyes were not. They glowed a fluorescent green.

Stephanie had joined Susan on the door, pounding. "Let us out! Let us out!"

Thud, thud, thud. Boots walked the hall's concrete floor. Jack jerked his head around and looked at the hall's far end.

White was walking down the passage, through the rising clones, trench coat dipping into the black fog. The tin mask hid his expression. But his stride said he had been expecting them.

The moment the killer passed the inbreds, they rose to their full height.

Jack whipped his gun up. *Boom!* White jerked once as if hit, then walked on, unabated.

Stephanie was screaming bloody murder now. All five of them pressed back against the door.

Jack was aiming to fire again, when the pressure at his back caved. He stumbled back.

The door was open?

The group surged back through the doorway. But Jack's view was of the hall, not the space they were entering.

The moment the man behind the tin mask saw that the door had been opened, he stopped. But instead of raising his shotgun and firing into his escaping prey, he stood still.

Jack was the last through. He scrambled for the door, eyes glued to the Tin Man.

"Lock it!" Randy screamed. He was seeing what Jack saw. A scene from the darkest of horror stories.

At the last moment, just as they were shoving the door closed, White grabbed his tin mask and tilted it up, exposing his full face.

It was a face from the grave, half of it bared to the bone. White's jaws snapped wide, as wide as the mask itself, and he roared at them.

Black fog streamed from his mouth. Blasted toward the door.

The door slammed shut. Randy threw the bolt.

A shock wave hit the other side of the door with

enough force to bend the wood and send both of them flying against the opposite wall. A thin wisp of black smoke drifted past the cracks.

But it held.

They managed to stand, panting, watching the door. But it didn't move.

"Guys?" Stephanie's voice from the dining room was stretched thin, laced with confusion.

Jack turned around. The first thing he noticed was that some of the lights were back on, blazing bright enough for him to see what Stephanie was looking at.

The once-cheerful dining room now looked as if it had been sitting vacant for a hundred years. Dust covered the paintings and walls. Paper peeled from the walls in long swaths. Most of the furniture remained, but it was covered in dust. The cushions on the good chairs were shredded, chewed by rats.

The table was strewn with rotten food, the same food they'd eaten earlier, crawling with worms and maggots. The stench was similar to the sick sulfuric odor from the basement.

With one glance through the arched entry, Jack saw that the dining room wasn't the only part of the house that had changed.

"It's . . . how's this possible?" Stephanie said.

No one answered as they took it all in, stunned. The house was dead. All of it.

Dead, very dead. But a death that was clearly alive.

30

5:20 AM

IT TOOK THEM A FULL MINUTE TO STEP beyond shock and find reason.

"Are we imagining this?" Jack asked. "Or were we imagining earlier?"

"Is that possible?" Stephanie said. "I mean, we ate at this table, right?"

No one was quick with speculation, much less answers.

"This can't be real," Lawdale said. "I've been in this house a hundred times."

"It's real," Susan said angrily. "I told you there's more going on here than you realize. I told you they're wrong." She said something else. Or did she? Her lips kept moving for a few seconds, but no sound came out. Or was that Jack's imagination?

Jack stared at Susan, meeting her eyes. "They? You mean Stewart?"

She eyed him.

"You're saying they were demons or something?"

"Would explain why they don't count," Randy said.

"Don't be ridiculous," Leslie said. "Demons, please. This is about the imagination, not—"

"Shut up, Leslie!" Randy snapped. "Make up your mind! We don't have time for your psychobabble anymore. Call it what you want, we're in a world of hurt here. And we're running out of time."

". . . and he's going to kill you all," Susan said, finishing her point.

Jack headed toward the kitchen then turned back to Lawdale. "How did you get in?"

"Back door."

It was the first good look at the lawman Jack had taken since Lawdale opened the door. He'd removed his outer shirt and used a strip of it as a makeshift bandage on a wound to his upper arm. A bloody bandanna circled his head. His T-shirt was a well-worn Budweiser variety, untucked and hitched over both guns.

"What happened?"

"I had some trouble getting out. Halfway through the grate someone took a potshot at me, and I fell back through. Took me a few minutes to take him out."

"Could explain why they were waiting," Jack said. "But why did they let us go?"

"You call that letting us go?" Randy said.

Stephanie suddenly broke for the kitchen, running. "They let us go because upstairs is no better than the basement," she said.

Jack followed quickly. He burst into the kitchen just as Stephanie took hold of the back door handle. She gave it a twist. Threw her weight into another twist. Fumbled with the dead bolt.

"It's locked!" she cried.

Jack pushed her aside and tried the door. It wouldn't budge.

"It's locked?" Leslie asked behind him.

Jack spun back and faced Lawdale. "You sure this is the way you came in?"

Lawdale didn't bother responding.

"Stand back," Randy snapped. Within seconds, he'd pulled a plastic box of cartridges out of his pants, loaded the gun, and pumped a round.

Jack and Stephanie stepped back.

The blast tore into wood and shattered the lock. Jack tried again.

No luck. He looked at the seal. It felt like the whole door wasn't a door at all. Solid as a wall. Steel bars ran the length of the broken glass. That was new.

"Surely we can blast a hole," Leslie said, not convincingly.

"How many shells do you have left, Randy?" Jack asked.

The man checked the box. "Eight."

"Okay, save them. Where's that ax?"

Randy set down the shotgun, hurried to the meat locker, stepped over the broken door, and hauled out the ax hammer that Stewart had used to break out.

They watched in silence as he approached the back door, lined up the ax, and took a huge, grunting swing at the window. What glass connected with the ax head shattered. But the bars held firm.

Didn't even bend.

Possible, Jack thought. Some kinds of steel might resist such a blow. But in this old house, improbable.

Randy took another swing. Again, not even a good dent.

"It's the same as the basement!" Stephanie cried.

"Hold on, just take it easy," Lawdale ordered, stepping forward. He held out his hand for the ax, and Randy gave it to him. "There has to be a way out. If the doors are reinforced, we'll go through a wall."

"Too many cabinets in here." Lawdale returned to the dining room, saw there were no outer walls, then followed Jack to the main entrance. The wall around the front door bulged slightly under the force of the truck White had driven into the house.

They stared at the damage in wonder. Lack of damage, rather. Jack recalled splintering wood, flying plaster, disintegrating doorjambs. More illusions? Or was this the illusion?

"If a truck can't break a board at thirty miles an hour, that ax doesn't stand a chance." Randy loaded another round. *Ca-chink*.

But Lawdale wasn't convinced. He stared at the wall in a kind of stupor, unbelieving. He suddenly began swinging at the wall in a rage.

Crash . . . crash . . . crash . . . crash!

Each blow bounced off after removing some paint. The wood itself, however, didn't so much as splinter.

Lawdale paused, breathing hard, then raced into the living room, yanked the sofa roughly out of his way, and smashed the window behind it with a cry of anger.

But the bars beyond didn't bend.

He went again, and a third time, before swiveling and taking a huge swipe at the brick on the fireplace.

Mortar sprayed as the ax hammer smashed through the brick. "Ha!"

"That's inside," Randy said, dropping his shotgun and grabbing the ax from the man. "Try the back wall."

He swung the hammer through the opening, against the back of the fireplace.

Jack knew by the solid sound that it was hopeless. Randy stood back and stared into the ashes. The tin can still sat on one side where Jack had tossed it earlier.

Tin Man's tin can.

They could all see the writing curving over the bleached label.

> *Welcome to my house*
> *House rules:*
> *3. Give me one dead body, and I might*
> *let rule two slide.*

Randy grunted, tossed the ax on the floor, and retrieved his shotgun.

"What's this?" Lawdale reached for the can.

"The can we told you about."

Stephanie was pacing with both hands in her hair, brow wrinkled with stress. She whirled to Jack, eyes blazing with fury.

"How's this possible?! How can this be happening to me?"

"Keep your voice down, miss!" Lawdale snapped.

"And what good are you?" she yelled at him. "You could have gotten us out through that grate you found. Instead you come up with this"—she flung her hand out at him—"cockamamy plan that gets us trapped up here!"

"You got any better ideas?" Randy screamed at her.

Officer Lawdale had one of his pistols out of its holster and cocked by his ear almost too fast for Jack to see. He threw the can into the fireplace.

"The next time one of you yells at me, I put a bullet over your head to show you I mean business; the next time it'll be in your leg to bring you under control. If you hadn't noticed, there's five of us now. And over my dead body, all five of us live through the next hour. You got that?"

"Six," a soft voice said.

Susan stood quietly beside Leslie, who flinched.

"There's six of us," she said.

"Then six. My point stands. Now we have about an hour, is that right?"

"Not quite," Leslie said, holding her watch up to the lamp. "Dawn's at 6:17. Least that's what we've been—"

Something began to pound on the wall behind Jack. He jumped and spun. Again, *thump, thump, thump*, and this time he could see the wall vibrate with each hit. The dining room.

Lawdale pulled out his other gun. "Okay, backup will be here any minute. It's time we make whatever's behind this house think twice. We just have to stall till help comes. But that doesn't mean run. Bring your guns." He strode across the foyer.

Thump, thump, thump!

"You sure that's a good idea?" Leslie said.

"You've been running all night. For all we know, this house is just feeding on your fear."

"We're alive, aren't we?"

"I'm not sure you would be alive if I hadn't come in. Wait here."

Jack raised a brow at Leslie's stare and went after Lawdale and Randy.

"What if it's trying to separate us again?" Stephanie demanded.

Thump, thump, thump!

"Wait!" She ran after them.

"You can't leave us alone!" Leslie's objection covered something Susan was trying to say. They both hurried into the hall after Jack and Stephanie.

After a quick jab of his head into the dining room, SWAT-team style, Lawdale stepped into the room and waved them on.

The pounding had stopped.

The room was as they'd left it. Empty.

"You catch my point," Lawdale said. "From this point on—"

"What's that?" Leslie interrupted.

"What's what?"

She lifted a finger to her lips and listened. A sound like a garbled record, backward masked, played far away. Below them. In front of them.

The sound grew louder, unmistakable now, but unintelligible. Soft wailing bubbling behind, ebbing and flowing. Jack stepped into the hall. It was coming from the door to the basement.

They poured into the hall in a rough semicircle, listening intently to the strange sound, for the words, because it was a voice, most certainly a voice. At least one.

The door suddenly bent slightly inward.

Jack caught his breath.

Thump, thump, thump!

They all jumped as the door shook under the pounding.

A deep moan reverberated through the whole house. Fingers of black fog seeped under the door, drifted over the wood floor, and burned words into the door's surface.

ONE DEAD BODY . . .

OR SIX DEAD BODIES

Then the smoke was sucked back into the cracks, the sound ceased, and absolute stillness returned.

For ten seconds no one moved.

"Okay," Lawdale said, stepping back. The light in his eyes revealed a tinge of panic. When he'd found them in the boiler room, he hadn't yet encountered the horrors of the house. Now he had, and it showed.

But it struck Jack that the look on Lawdale's face might not be panic at all. It could be eager determination. Even desire. What if . . . what if Lawdale was actually a part of the game? Not White's part, but a kind of counterpart? Good come to fight evil.

No. Couldn't be. They'd met him on the highway a hundred miles from here. And all of them could see that he was the same man they'd met.

Lawdale faced them, now clearly unnerved. "We have to get out. We tear this house down if we have to, both floors, all the windows, the attic, everything. Find a way out."

"There is no way out," Randy said.

"We *find* a way out!" Lawdale snapped.

31

5:29 AM

THEY MOVED QUICKLY, FOLLOWING THE cop's orders to split up, thereby dividing the house's attention and confusing it, but Randy held out no hope for that plan. Stephanie had found a crowbar in the coat closet, and he'd raced upstairs with her because doing this last-ditch thing felt like it needed to be done, but only to buy himself a little thinking time before doing what really needed to be done.

Amazing how dramatically the place had changed. Aside from the layout, there was hardly any indication that they were in the same house. And this new house seemed to know that the end was coming. It had settled down, a calm before the storm.

With barely more than thirty minutes to go before this game ended, killing was now the only thing that needed to be done.

The question was, who? Jack, yeah, but Jack had his eyes on him and his barrel pointed in his general direction wherever they went. It was almost like White had visited Jack and warned him.

"The attic!" Stephanie said, panting from the run up the steps. "Find the attic."

Randy ran into one of the rooms, ax hammer in hand, and threw open the closet door. Nothing on the ceilings that showed an entrance to any attic.

"Watch out."

He took a swing at the window, knowing it would be useless. And it was. Crashing glass. Bone-jarring jolt against the bars. He tried another swing, at the wall this time.

The full force of the blow ran up his arms and rattled his teeth. He cursed. Now if that was flesh and blood, like someone's head, the ax would slice clean through, not bounce. They were swinging at the wrong things.

Randy had left his shotgun in the kitchen at Lawdale's insistence—this wasn't the time to go around wasting ammo. Use the ax, the crowbar, and a sledgehammer that Jack had found in the pantry. The guns stayed in the kitchen for now.

And Randy wasn't happy about it. Not the least bit.

"Where's the attic?" Stephanie asked.

"Shut up!"

She was too frantic to show any reaction. She ran for another room. Randy lumbered into the upstairs hall. Time was running out.

Maybe he'd just do Stephanie in and call it good. Slam, bam, thank you, ma'am. One dead body . . .

But the businessman in him was suggesting a few things. If he did Stephanie and the rest of them managed to live as White promised, who would be stuck holding the bag for murder? If he killed Stephanie and the FBI got ahold of it—which they would—he'd fry.

Unless he left no witnesses—killed all of them. But he wasn't sure he could do that.

"In here!" Stephanie screamed out. "I found it!"

Crawling into an attic without light was about the stupidest thing he could think of right now. She'd actually found it?

Stupid. A wedge of panic forced itself into his mind. Time was running out. What if Jack snuck up here and blew his brains out first?

Feet pounded on the stairs, and Randy spun to see the cop coming up, two steps at a time.

"Anything?"

"She found the attic," Randy said.

The officer rushed past Randy, carrying a lit lamp. What about him? Take down the gunslinging cop and testify that he mistook Lawdale for Tin Man in the bad light. One dead body.

Could he kill a cop? If it came right down to it, he just might have to. But would Tin Man accept Lawdale? He wasn't one of the original four.

Five. Susan. Betty had made it abundantly clear that White wanted Susan dead. Maybe he should kill Susan.

Randy hurried into the room and found Lawdale on steps he'd pulled down from a hatch that opened into a dark attic. He scrambled up, lamp first.

"Get up here."

Randy was headed up ahead of Stephanie, holding on to the ax, when it occurred to him that the ax was almost as good a weapon as a gun. He wasn't sure he *could*, but it *would* work. He felt for the knife at his waist. A knife might almost be easier.

The attic had a wood floor piled high with junk along

the sides. The sloping ceiling was made of old gray boards. The single square window in the gable was barred.

The man hurried over to Randy, grabbed the ax, and shoved the lamp at him. "Hold this."

Before Randy could protest the man had traded tools—Randy's ax for a useless light. Of course, with control of the light, he could break the lamp and have control of the situation, so maybe that was a good thing.

He knew he was slipping, really slipping this time, but he let himself go. He needed to slip. It was slip or die.

Lawdale hefted the ax and swung at the sloping ceiling. *Bang/bounce*. Naturally.

What was unnatural was the sudden *groan/screech* that split the air after the blow, loud enough for Randy to feel it in his chest, as if the attic was the source of the groans they'd heard all along.

Stephanie screamed, almost as loud, and Randy came within an inch of grabbing something—anything— and slam-bamming her right then and there. Instead, he reached out and slapped her with the light still in his hands. "Shut up!"

She did. The house fell quiet with her. The look in her eyes reminded him of the moment she came out of Pete's lair.

"Gimme your knife." Lawdale tucked the ax under one arm and held out his other hand.

"What for?" Randy pulled the knife out but didn't want to give it up too quickly.

"For heaven's sake, just give it to me!" Lawdale snatched it from him, started digging with it at the seams between rafters and roof. It barely penetrated. The tip broke off with a snap, leaving a notch in the end of the blade. Lawdale swore and hooked the knife into his belt, took up the ax again.

Lawdale began banging at the wall in a rage. *Bang, bang, bang, bang.* Right along the wall, then on the gable with the window. *Crash, crash,* against the glass.

Nothing.

The cop stood facing the clear black sky outside with his back to Randy and Stephanie, breathing hard. He let the ax down slowly till it hung from one of his hands, solid head just above the floor.

The house groaned softly.

Lawdale breathed heavily.

Randy and Stephanie stared, taken aback by this, the second of the cop's furious banging episodes.

"We're all going to die," the cop said, still looking out the window.

He turned around and faced them. "The Tin Man's never left a victim alive, never failed, never left a clue to his identity, even though he's blazed a trail as wide as the Mississippi through the country in house after house. Now we know why, don't we? But there's no way we can tell the rest of the world."

"What do you mean, we know why?" Randy asked.

The cop looked at the ceiling he'd just lambasted and spoke with more urgency. "It starts with knowledge; it always does. You have to know the game before you can beat it. The world has to know what they're dealing with."

"Well, good luck getting the word out."

Lawdale looked him in the eye. "The killer's game is as much spiritual as physical. The FBI—whoever lies in Tin Man's path—has to know that he can be beat only if they understand the power behind him, that's what I mean. They're not looking at this right. They need to shift paradigms, or he'll go right on killing and leaving a path they'll never understand."

Whatever, Randy thought. "Time's running out," he said.

"Are you listening to a thing I'm saying, boy?" The officer paced. "There's no way out! This"—he gestured at the ceiling, studying the boards, searching for the right words—"this thing, this whole killing spree of his, this house . . . it's about good and evil and about what's inside. But the world doesn't know that!"

They did not have time for this philosophical mumbo jumbo. Lawdale should go find Leslie if that's how he wanted to spend their final minutes. He shone the light in Lawdale's eyes. "Well, unless we beat White, they never will. Got any real ideas? Or are you just talk?"

Lawdale hesitated. "Maybe Tin Man's right. Maybe someone has to die."

Randy felt his heart pound harder.

"Someone has to be sacrificed. We need a sacrificial lamb. The Tin Man wants fresh blood. Innocent blood."

"Who?"

The cop blinked, thought a moment, then shook his head. "I don't know. One of us may have to volunteer."

"What?" Stephanie said. "You actually believe someone will volunteer to die for the rest?"

"Not just the rest of us," Lawdale snapped. "The world out there has to know what's going on!"

"It'll never happen," Randy said.

The cop stared at him for a long time, mind spinning behind those sparkling eyes.

"We'll see," he said. "Think about it. We're running out of time. If someone doesn't die, we all do."

Lawdale picked up the ax. "There's no way out," he said.

Randy swallowed. "We *know*."

The cop nodded. He left the attic without another word, taking the ax with him.

32

5:40 AM

JACK AND LESLIE HAD RUN FROM ROOM
to room on the main floor, looking for any structural feature that appeared even remotely weak. A seam in the
walls, an unbarred window, a place where plumbing had
been ripped free to expose the night outside.

The patrolman's plan wasn't much more than a last
gasp, but Jack couldn't think of a better plan, so he
attacked the search with frantic urgency. But the wood,
the rebar, the siding, the plaster—the house and all of its
materials refused to break.

All the while, the third rule kept drumming through
his mind. *Give me a dead body . . .*

They were in the pantry off the kitchen, the last
room to search on this floor, as far as Jack could tell. But
there was nothing here that looked hopeful. He took a
swing at the shelves anyway.

Empty jars and cans crashed. The sledgehammer
bounced off the wall. Nothing. He stopped and stared,
mind numb. Now what? They'd wasted how much time?
Ten minutes, at least.

Leslie stood behind him in the doorway—he could hear her steady breathing. The house moaned again. Louder this time. He looked up. Now what?

"We're going to die," Leslie said.

It was a simple declaration of fact. Jack knew precisely how she felt, because he felt exactly as she did. There were times when bravery only mocked reality.

"It's coming after me," she said. "It's forcing me to do what I hate the most."

What was she talking about?

"I'm a whore, Jack. That's what this is about. I hate myself, and I'm powerless to stop it. It knows that."

"Who's *it*?"

She looked around, eyes wide and watery. "Me."

He didn't contradict her, but he didn't think she was right.

The house shook violently for a moment, then quieted. More jars toppled from the shelves and shattered at their feet. Cans clattered about them. It felt like the house was being shaken by an earthquake.

"Do you believe in God, Jack?" Leslie whispered.

He'd thought about the question a hundred times already that night, but only in passing. He wasn't sure he believed in God.

"I don't know," he said.

"If he exists, where is he tonight?" She swallowed. "There's evil in this house; there's supernatural entities I never believed in until tonight; there's a serial killer with his sick, demented game. But where is God?"

"In a cathedral somewhere," Jack said. "Taking money from the poor."

"There *is* no God," Leslie said.

"Maybe not," he said. "Not one that can help us."

From somewhere in the house, Susan began to yell. Leslie jerked her head around. The girl was shouting something, running down a hall or through the dining room.

Where had she been? She'd started out with Jack and Leslie, making suggestions that weren't particularly helpful in their search. Jack hadn't noticed when she left.

Doors slammed somewhere deeper in the house. Wood thudded and crashed. Susan screamed again.

"She's in trouble!" Jack said. He snatched up the sledgehammer and led Leslie through the kitchen, through the hall, past the basement door, into the dining room.

"Susan!"

Her cries were louder now. She was screaming something at them from the front of the house. Jack ran into the main foyer.

All of the furniture in the adjacent living room looked as though it had been tossed by a tornado, half of it toppled and shattered. Several pieces seemed to defy gravity, stuck to the wall, like the unbroken chair that sat against the wall halfway up by the fireplace.

Susan stood in one corner, pressed against both walls. The large armoire that had once stood across the room was now six feet from her, moving slowly closer. Its doors were opening and banging shut, not rapidly, but in response to her moves, as if to cut her off.

"Jack!" she screamed. "You have to listen to me! You have to stop it!"

The chair on the wall flew across the room toward Jack. He jumped back and swung the sledgehammer at the flying chair. The weighted head crashed into wooden spindles and effectively redirected the chair's flight, but one of the legs struck him in the shoulder, sending him reeling back into Leslie.

"Listen to . . ." Susan's cry was covered by the sound of a dozen doors slamming together. Not just once, but repeatedly. *Bam, bam!* Every closet, every room, every cabinet in the house, it seemed, repeatedly opening and slamming shut in perfect unison.

Bam. Bam. Bam. Bam. Bam.

The armoire that trapped Susan stopped five feet from her. Jack jumped forward, drew his sledgehammer back, and had just started to swing at the armoire when the right-hand door swung open and struck him broadside.

He staggered, fell, dropped his weapon.

Bam. Bam. Bam. Bam. The doors thundered.

"The sledge, Jack!" Leslie cried. "Watch out!"

His sledgehammer had flown into the air and was floating across the room, cocked at a forty-five-degree angle.

He scrambled back. It flew unaided toward the armoire.

Toward Susan.

Bam. Bam. Bam. Bam.

"Jack!" Susan was crying out something behind the armoire, but he couldn't see her now.

The hammer was now over the armoire, over Susan, intention unmistakable.

Bam. Bam. Bam.

Boom!

Gunfire exploded around them. The sledgehammer

was hit broadside by a full load of buckshot. Its handle splintered just below the head, which slammed into the wall and dropped from sight behind the armoire.

Lawdale leaped over Jack, swept up his fallen sledge by the stubbed handle, and was into a full swing before Jack fully knew it was him.

His first blow shattered the armoire's right-hand door.

The second door began to flop, and the lawman took it off with another swing. Raging like a bull, he threw himself at the heavy piece of furniture and toppled it with a loud grunt.

The slamming doors throughout the house stopped in unison with the crash of the toppled armoire.

Bam!

Dust roiled.

Silence settled.

Susan ran.

Past Lawdale, past Jack, down the hall. "You're going to get us all killed, Jack!" she cried and was gone.

What was she talking about? What was he doing that would get them killed? What were any of them doing that would get them killed?

Or was it something they *weren't* doing?

One dead body.

Lawdale faced them, breathing steadily through his nose. "You okay?"

"I'm alive." Jack pushed himself to his feet.

"I heard her screams, but I had to go back for the shotgun you boys left in the kitchen."

"What caused *that*?" Leslie asked.

"What's causing any of this? Evil. The house has a mind of its own. No luck, right?"

"What do you think? What about Randy?"

"Attic's no help." Lawdale tossed the sledge on the floor. He seemed to have lost his fire. "I think we're all going to die."

"Thanks for the encouragement, Officer, but we've already reached our own conclusions."

"Which are?"

Jack hesitated. "There's no way out."

"The wise man built his house upon a rock," Lawdale said. "Preacher used to say that. Unfortunately, whoever built this house built it on a grave. Unless we expose that grave, we're all going to die."

"Uncover the mass grave this place was built on?"

"Grave. As in death. He obviously thinks we're all deserving of death. One of us has to die. It's the only way."

His statement would have left Jack floored seven, even three hours ago. But he knew that basic logic had brought the lawman to his summary of the matter.

"We can't just kill someone," Leslie said.

"We're running out of time. Someone has to give their life so that the rest can live, not only here, but out there, in the world. Put an end to this lunatic's game."

"Suicide?"

"No, I don't think that will work for him; it doesn't fit his profile. He's not looking for cowardice. Whoever kills has to do it like he would, out of malice."

"That's murder."

"We aren't murderers."

"Evidently not. Not yet. But that may change in the next few minutes."

He paused then said, "And if it comes down to it,

I'm willing to be the victim, even though there may be better choices."

They stared at him. The cop was actually offering to die for them all?

"I've already told the others," Lawdale said. He set the shotgun down. "I'm going to try to find Susan. Twenty-five minutes, my friends. Whatever you do, do it quickly."

He handed Jack his gun, walked past them, and turned toward the dining room where Susan had fled.

Jack glanced at Leslie, who was staring after Lawdale. She turned her head to him, eyes wide.

"It makes sense." Then he added so there would be no misunderstanding, "In a textbook way. Logically."

"This isn't a textbook," she said. "It's a classical case of mass hysteria, and he's contributing to it."

He ignored her. "Maybe he's right; there's a better choice than him."

"Who, Randy?"

Jack didn't answer.

Leslie's jaw flexed. "He may be a bit twisted up here"—she pointed to her head—"but not even Randy deserves to die."

"We can't just ignore what's happening," he said. "White told Randy to kill *me*."

She glared at him.

"Come on, Leslie. You know as well as I do that he's capable of killing *both* of us!" Jack leaned the shotgun against the wall. "If Lawdale told them what he just told us, I guarantee you, Randy's already got me in his sights."

Leslie looked back down the hall. "You can't just kill him, for heaven's sake!"

"And if he comes after me, what would you suggest I do?"

Leslie took a shallow breath. "Pete told me that White wanted the girl dead," Leslie said. "I think this whole thing is about her. I think White really let her go so that we would have someone to kill."

Jack just stared at her, daring her to say what she meant.

"I'm not suggesting you kill Susan," she snapped. "But Randy might try. He's too much of a coward to come after you, but he may try the girl."

The house began to groan again. An indistinguishable scream pierced through the walls. Other screams rose, overlapped.

33

5:40 AM

STEPHANIE DIDN'T AGREE TO THE PLAN, but she didn't stop Randy either. If there was any other way, she would have stopped him, but the only way for them to live through the deadline was for someone else to die, as the cop himself had said.

It didn't sound right; she knew that it couldn't be right. But it was the closest thing to right she could come up with.

Her hands had done their share of shaking through the night, but now she couldn't stop them if she tried. She didn't feel good about killing someone any more than she felt good about eating Pete's dog food. But she wasn't exactly a healthy person. She'd learned that in the last few hours.

The thought of dipping her fingers into his nasty food and placing it into her mouth made her stomach swim with nausea.

Deep down, where she'd managed to run away from herself, she was a very sick, twisted little girl. If anyone deserved to die here, it was probably her. Jack could attest to that. She had abandoned him in his time of deepest need and retreated into her world of denials and self-pity.

A tear slipped down her cheek. She followed Randy out of the room toward the stairs. "Are you sure we should do this?"

Randy stopped and turned back. "You could wait here. I have to get the gun and find the girl, but I'm coming back, like we agreed. There's no way I'm getting hung out to dry on my own. I want Lawdale here when I pull that trigger. He'll back us up."

"And if he doesn't?"

Randy hesitated. "Then we'll have to do them all."

"You never said—"

The house screamed. A dozen overlapping screams. "What's that?"

Randy ignored her and moved forward in a crouch.

The scream sounded like it had come from a little girl. Susan, maybe. Stephanie shivered. And in that second, she understood.

It was Susan. Tin Man wanted Susan. He wanted *them* to kill Susan.

And according to Randy, that's what Lawdale had meant when he said the killer wanted fresh blood.

She was a sick, sick person, and she should be stopping Randy rather than sneaking down the stairs behind him.

But she was too sick to stop him.

They hurried to the kitchen for the shotgun. But the guns were gone. Randy stared, face red. "What now?" He stormed around for a few seconds, checking behind the table and the counter. "He took them! He took 'em both!"

"Randy, I'm not sure—"

"You left the crowbar upstairs," he said, pushing past Stephanie. "We'll do her with the crowbar."

———

Five forty-nine. "We have to go," Jack said. "We have to do this now!"

"And what have you decided to do?"

He wavered again. Kill Lawdale? Kill Randy? Kill Susan? Rage flooded his bones. He slammed his fists against the wall. "This is insane!"

"Jack," a soft voice said.

He whirled to the sound of the girl's voice. Susan stood in a doorway at the end of the foyer, near the stairs.

Tin Man's metal mask hung from her right hand.

Jack was too stunned to speak.

She dropped the mask to the floor where it clattered noisily.

"What's . . . ?" He wasn't even sure what to ask.

"Will you listen to me now?" she asked.

Jack took three steps and stood beside Leslie, who gawked at the sight. There was something unnerving about the way Susan appeared, standing there in her tattered white dress with the killer's mask by her feet.

"Of course we'll listen," Leslie said softly.

"You have to listen carefully. I've been trying to tell you, but you aren't listening."

"Of course I—"

"I tried to warn you. The house is keeping you from listening."

"What do you mean?"

"It messes with your hearing. Makes it so that you can't see things right. Or hear things right. I've been trying to tell you all night. Will you listen now?"

He stared at her. "I . . . I can hear you."

"We're running out of time. Will you listen?"

"Who . . . who are you?"

"I'm the one he wants you to kill. But if you kill me, you'll die. You have to believe me. The only way to survive the game is to destroy him."

"How?"

"I can show you."

If she was right, their hope for survival had been with them most of the night, and they'd ignored her. In that moment Susan was a picture of perfect innocence. His own daughter, Melissa, reaching out to save him. A guiding angel of light sent to save him, even though she was just a girl White had abducted. But in that moment she was more.

"He's trying to kill me, Jack."

He wanted to rush up to her and throw his arms around her and tell her that he'd never leave her again, but he couldn't seem to move.

"I know." Jack went to her. "But that's not going—"

"Lawdale is trying to kill me," Susan said.

He stopped. Blinked. "What? Who . . ."

"Lawdale. The Tin Man, the one who leaks black smoke even up here. I told you before, he wants you to kill me. That's the real game."

His mind spun. A new terror flashed down his spine.

"Did you hear me?" she asked.

"Are you sure? Lawdale?"

"You'll see the smoke, Jack."

A hand reached out from beyond the doorframe and yanked Susan by her hair. She cried out.

Randy stepped through, grinning, eyes wild. "Stay back, Jack. This is our only way out, you know that."

"Randy?" Leslie brushed past Jack. "Randy, what are you doing? You're crazy, she's innocent!"

"I think that's the point, doctor," Randy said; then to the girl, "Let's go, sweet pea."

He jerked her back the way they'd come.

Jack reeled. His own shotgun was still back by the armoire. He spun, four long strides, grabbed up the shotgun. He ran to the doorway that Susan had been snatched from, checked beyond with a jab of his head. Clear.

It split at the end—one way led back to the kitchen, around the back of the dining room; one way to the rest of the lower house and the stairs. Which way?

"What are you doing?" Leslie breathed at his shoulder.

Jack held still, gripped by indecision. He couldn't just blast his way through the house while Randy had the advantage.

Something was wrong with his elbow. He rolled up his denim shirtsleeve and stared at his elbow where the armoire door had plastered him. A small gash leaked red blood.

"Black smoke," he said. "When I was in the basement, I was leaking black smoke. Everyone who was evil leaked black smoke. We all would have. But up here it's different. This is where evil can hide."

"The smoke is only in the basement? I don't understand how—"

"I don't know," he snapped. "But up here evil doesn't

just walk around for us to see it, like it does down in the basement. I'm not leaking black smoke up here."

"I can see that! But what does that have to do with Lawdale?"

"She's saying that he's different, that he'll leak black smoke no matter where he goes."

"How?"

"I don't know! All I know is that we have to believe Susan."

Too much time had passed. He ran toward the kitchen, shouting, "Randy, you can't do this! We need her!"

No sound. Jack threw caution to the wind and ran for the kitchen with Leslie hard behind.

Empty.

"Upstairs, hurry!"

They peeled back through the other hall into the dining room, but it was as far as they got.

Officer Morton Lawdale stood in the archway, holding a large, gleaming knife from the kitchen. Randy's knife? His eyes were wide and his face was white.

"We're out of time," Lawdale said. He thrust the knife into the table and looked into Jack's eyes, eyes pleading and scared.

He didn't look like the Tin Man.

"I want you to kill me," Lawdale said.

34

"KILL YOU?"

"We can't put it off any longer." Sweat beaded Lawdale's forehead below the bloody bandanna. "Someone has to die so the rest can live, and I'm willing. Do it now before I change my mind."

Jack had the shotgun; he could easily lift it and put a hole in the man's chest. If Susan was right, he'd be killing White.

If Susan was wrong, he would be killing a cop. And she could easily be wrong, couldn't she? She wasn't exactly a predictable person.

"Are you deaf, boy?" Lawdale snapped. He began to tremble. "Someone has to die here or we all do. Kill me!"

Jack instinctively lifted the gun. But he couldn't pull the trigger. He just couldn't, not without knowing for sure. Lawdale looked like a man who deserved a medal of honor rather than a bullet. How could he possibly be the Tin Man?

"Jaaack!" Susan's voice screamed from the upper level where Randy had evidently taken her.

What if Susan was working with the Tin Man to destroy their only hope of escape, namely, the lawman, who'd managed to rescue them from the basement?

"Jack?" Leslie's voice quavered.

Lawdale marched forward, angry now.

A small, useful bit of information dropped into Jack's mind. He hadn't chambered a round! He moved to his right with Leslie behind, forcing Lawdale around to their left.

"Randy's going to kill Susan," Jack said, voice ragged.

"Not if you kill me first, Jack." Lawdale walked right up to him. "Pull the trigger."

Before Jack could do so, Lawdale grabbed the barrel with both hands and pulled it toward his forehead. It pressed into his skin just below the bandanna. He clamped his eyes shut.

"Do it before he kills her. Save her. Do it like you despise the ground I walk on, with malice and hate. With the evil sickness raging inside, boy. Do it!"

Jack's hands were shaking badly. He pumped the action to chamber a shell.

"Now!" Lawdale shouted, nostrils flaring with panic.

Jack's mind seemed to be folding in on itself. He gripped the shotgun with white knuckles and began to yell. "Ahhhhhh!"

"Do it!"

But he couldn't do it. Instead he jerked the barrel up, dislodging the blood-soaked bandanna. A two-inch gash over Lawdale's right eye glared at them. Red.

No smoke.

Jack's scream caught in his throat. He stared at the cut in shock.

No black smoke. He'd almost taken Susan's assumption at face value and killed an innocent man?

"Please, Jack," Lawdale pleaded, eyes now clenched shut. He didn't seem to have a clue what Jack had just attempted to do. "I'm losing my nerve . . ."

No black smoke.

He'd come within a breath of blowing the cop's head from his shoulders because he'd been led to believe that he was Tin Man, but there was *no black smoke*!

Jack froze.

Lawdale's mouth gaped in a soft cry. Eyes still clenched tight, face wrinkled in agony, flesh quivering. The man was breaking, losing his nerve. And so was Jack. He'd come within an inch of blowing the man's head off!

Black smoke oozed from Lawdale's gash and fell past his right eye, smoking all the way to the floor—black, coal black.

How . . . how was that . . . what was happening?

Black smoke was happening.

Jack jerked the gun away and stepped back.

Lawdale's eyes were still clenched and his face was trembling with fear. A man about to die.

The black stuff began to flow freely now. A thin black fog pooled at Lawdale's feet, swirled around his boots.

"Kill me, Jack," Lawdale pleaded, seemingly oblivious to what Jack now saw.

"Jack?" Leslie said. "He's leaking smoke, Jack."

Clearly. Jack's hands shook.

"Kill him, Jack," Leslie said.

"Kill me, Jack," Lawdale cried.

"I . . . I . . ."

"Pull the trigger," Leslie snapped.

He pulled the trigger.

Click!

Lawdale gasped. Mouth parted, eyes still closed, but no longer clenched. He looked unsure if he'd been shot.

Jack stepped back again. Pumped. Jerked the trigger again.

Click!

For a long moment the air seemed evacuated of oxygen. Someone had emptied his gun of all but one shell before saving Susan from the flying ax just a few minutes ago.

Lawdale. It could only have been Lawdale, so that the gun would be empty after he shot that last round in the foyer.

Empty so that when Jack tried to kill him he would be rewarded with nothing more than a click.

Empty so that Jack couldn't use it to kill Lawdale.

The man's face was still gripped by false surprise, mouth gaping, eyes closed. Lawdale closed his mouth. He swallowed deliberately, eyes still closed. He cocked his head down.

Then his eyes snapped open, and Jack stared into black, pupil-less eyes that sent a chill to his heels. He knew without a shred of doubt that he was looking into the eyes of the Tin Man.

A terrifying sight, this tall, well-muscled man with cropped blonde hair, head tilted down, black fog pouring from a cut in his forehead, eyes black.

Black.

Leslie screamed.

Tin Man's mouth twisted into a thin smile. "Never leave your gun unattended, Jack."

"Run!" Jack shoved the shotgun at the Tin Man and bolted to his right. He grabbed the knife from the table and spun back, swinging the blade as he turned.

From the corner of his eye, he saw the man casually catch the shotgun with only a slight movement. Jack threw the knife, saw it lodge deep in the man's biceps.

Lawdale flinched, but no more. He held fast to the gun he'd caught in his now wounded arm. He was a man of supreme confidence. With good reason. He'd played his game flawlessly.

But he could be wounded, and if he could be wounded, he could be killed, just like Stewart. White reached for the knife with his free hand.

Jack bolted toward the foyer, hard on Leslie's heels.

A low chuckle reached through the wood. "Very good, Jack. Anger is good."

Jack threw himself at the stairs. Susan was right about Lawdale, which meant her claim that White intended to kill all of them also had to be true.

"Randy!" Leslie screamed. "Don't do it! Wait!"

A scream.

It was too late?

Leslie pounded up the stairs as Jack swung around the banister at the top. "Randy!" He tore down the hall and spun into the first room.

He saw it all in a flash. The orange light of a dim overhead bulb. Stephanie standing to one side of the guest room; Randy beating at a locked closet door with a crowbar.

"Lawdale's the Tin Man," Jack said. "The killer is Lawdale!"

Randy kicked at the door. His mind was on only one thing.

"He's going to kill us all if she dies," Jack shouted.

The door splintered and caved in. Dust roiled. Jack dived at Randy, knocking him off balance. The man slammed into the wall, cursing bitterly.

"How do you know that?" Stephanie asked.

There was no sound of White's pursuit, but in this house that meant nothing. He could be on the stairs already.

Susan ran from the closet and sprinted out of Randy's reach, hid behind Stephanie.

"Jack!" Leslie screamed from the doorway, looking back at the stairs in terror.

She slammed the door shut. Spun and pressed back against the door, eyes like saucers.

"He's coming!"

"I don't believe you," Randy said.

"Shut up, Randy!" Jack snapped.

"He's going to kill us!" Stephanie said.

Knuckles rapped on the door, and Leslie jumped away from it. She ran to Jack and whirled around behind him. They had no guns. No axes in here. No weapons of any kind except the crowbar.

The brass handle turned. The door swung in with a long creak.

Tin Man stood in the opening with his tin mask in place as they'd first seen him, only now dressed in the

Budweiser T-shirt and the gray patrolman's pants. Blood soaked a strip of cloth that he'd hastily wrapped tightly around his wounded bicep.

He held Jack's empty shotgun in one hand, Randy's knife in the other.

"Hello," he said.

35

5:59 AM

THE GAME HAD PLAYED OUT BETTER THAN Barsidious White ever dared hope.

The girl was still alive, but that would soon change. He relished the thought of ending it all precisely as he'd foreseen.

The Tin Man stripped off the mask Susan had dropped and tossed it by the door. After taking a moment to study their drawn faces, he addressed them calmly.

"Sit along the wall."

They moved obediently and sat.

Now he had them all in a row. Five of them. The one called Stephanie, the one called Randy, the one called Leslie, the one called Jack. And the one called Susan. Like five pigeons in a cage, staring at their captor.

He looked at Susan. The mysterious girl who'd appeared at the inn without warning three days ago. An apparently easy prey, but then she disappeared into the basement as if that was her intent the whole time. At first he tried to kill her, but then he discovered something quite unnerving about this child.

She was a good person.

Not a person who just *did* good things to show how good they were, but a person who really was good to the bone. Innocent. The rest were always "guilty as sin," as he liked to say.

But he wasn't so sure that Susan was guilty at all. She hadn't once talked maliciously or revealed any character trait less than virtuous. He always killed the guilty, proving to them that they were as guilty as his own murderous self; every single one of them eventually turned to murder to save their necks.

For the first time he'd met a participant who didn't fit the profile and therefore wreaked significant havoc with his game.

So he'd made her part of the game. Now it wasn't just *kill each other, all ye who are as guilty as sin*. Now it was *kill this innocent one, removing from amongst you the last vestiges of goodness, all ye who are as guilty as sin*.

She stared at him, fearless, then opened her mouth to speak. "I know how—"

Tin Man put a round into the wall next to Leslie, who shrieked.

Susan shut her mouth. She understood. *If you speak, I will kill one of them.*

He withdrew the small roll of tape from his pocket, crossed to her, and placed a long strip over her mouth and around her head. Then he tied her hands. He didn't know how well the house could obscure what she said, but he didn't want them listening, especially now. She knew too much.

He picked up the knife and paced the floor deliberately, enjoying the sound of his boots on the wood.

"It's time for you to know your own fate. We still have a few minutes to play."

They stared at him.

"I have a confession," he said. "Officer Lawdale won't be coming by to rescue you. Unless by 'rescue,' you think in terms of being delivered unto death."

They still didn't move. Pigeons. Stupid pigeons.

"You must appreciate the considerable care I've taken in planning your deaths."

Jack and Leslie stared at him stoically. Randy's eyes glared. Stephanie looked confused.

"I went down to the highway patrolman's house two miles down the road, cut his throat, and took his cruiser. This to be sure I had enough players for tonight's game."

"You . . . you're going to kill us?" Stephanie asked.

"If you don't kill each other yourselves," White said. "And if you ask any more stupid questions, you'll be first."

"Why don't you just kill us now?" Jack asked.

Of them all, only Jack was still thinking straight. The man was strong. Resolute. He'd faced his daughter's death and come away bitter but more seasoned. His death would be the most satisfying.

"Patience, Jack. I will kill you. I will because my eyes are black. Aren't you going to ask about my eyes, Jack?"

Jack hesitated. "Why are your eyes black?"

"Because I'm not really White in the house, I'm really Black in the box, and this is my showdown. Good versus evil, only in your case it's evil versus evil. No contest."

He could tell by their expressions that none of them understood. Except for the girl. Which bothered him.

He threw the knife with a flip of his wrist. It twirled twice and sank cleanly into the wall between Jack's and Leslie's heads. *Thunk!*

"Do you know anything about evil, Jack? Hmmm? The black stuff."

Jack didn't respond.

White lifted up his bandanna and let the black fog dribble then pour out of his gash. It pooled on the floor and began to work its way toward them.

"Evil, the stuff in your heart. It's in my head too."

He replaced the bandanna.

"I've decided to give you all one last chance to figure this mess out. Most people are quite dense. They like little white houses with big stained-glassed churches and prefer to do their killing with looks and words behind one another's backs."

He paused.

"Welcome to my house. No secrets allowed. Here we all do our killing with guns and axes and knives. It's more bloody than what most people are accustomed to, yes, but it's far less brutal."

Surely they understood some of this.

"The wages of sin is death, and this time we're going to show the blood, what do you say? No more stained glass or white houses. Now it's White's house, and in White's house we follow White's rules. House rules."

White could hear his breathing thicken, but he easily calmed himself.

"One last chance to rethink rule number three. The girl was right. On two counts: you haven't been listening to her. Well, blame that on the house. And, yes, I do want you to kill her. The game would have gone on until she was dead. But she's also wrong. If you do kill her, I will let whoever's still alive, live."

He let that sink in for just a few beats.

"And if you don't kill her, I'm going to slaughter you like lambs. All five of you. Starting with the girl, just to show you how you should have done it."

Randy's eyes flittered to his left, then back. A good sign.

"Dawn is coming. I never let the game go past dawn."

He withdrew a match, struck it on his belt, and tossed the flame at the pool of black fog that had fallen from his brow. The fog burned with a whoosh as if it were gasoline. Firelight danced on their frozen faces.

"As you can see, the black stuff likes to burn. This place will go up in flames at first light. That's in six minutes. Six minutes to make your choice."

He retreated to the room's entrance and picked the mask up off the floor. Opened the door. Backed out of the room.

"Six minutes."

White slammed the door shut and began to tremble.

36

6:02 AM

THE LINES BEGAN ETCHING THEMSELVES
in Jack's mind as White talked, dividing competing forces
deep at work behind the obvious here in this house
empowered by evil.

Evil versus evil. Jack didn't totally buy White's claim.
If there was evil, there was also good, and those forces
were in some kind of battle here. Up to this point, except
for the face-off in the boiler room, their abduction had
felt little like a battle with two sides. But maybe that was
the point. He'd been looking at it all wrong! He'd only
seen one side, the evil. So where was the good?

And what if the standoff in the boiler room was
only a foreshadowing of a greater contest to come? Jack
against Jack. In some ways this night was nothing more
than a stark playing out of the struggle he faced every
day of his life. His own limited view of that struggle
focused on what he allowed himself to see. But what if
there was more?

What was the guilt that White seemed so preoccupied with? What were their sins?

Leslie seemed to be fighting long-hidden demons that had come to life in this impossible house of White's. Randy . . . Randy was showing his own obsession with power and control. Stephanie had come face-to-face with her own denial and was now terrified and weak without its facade.

And he? His was hiding behind bitterness, no better than any of the rest.

These were the thoughts racing, drumming, screaming as Tin Man talked. Then White was leveling his final challenge and that challenge was to kill someone.

"Six minutes." Tin Man backed out of the room. The door slammed shut as a hundred doors had slammed this night, but now with such finality that for a moment none of them moved.

And then, as if in deliberate response, a hundred doors throughout the house, below them, around them, slammed in one mighty crash. *Bam!* The house shook and shifted.

An echo lingered. Something had changed in the house.

Jack twisted to his right and grabbed the knife handle. He saw Randy diving for the crowbar as he tugged. But the knife was stuck.

"Jack?"

Stephanie stared at him, pleading with desperate eyes.

"Help me," he said.

She blinked then ran to his side. Her hand covered his over the knife handle, and together they pulled. In that single moment of desperation, he felt an overpowering sense of gratitude toward her. And he thought she might feel the same toward him. They were doing little more than reacting to the horrors that had pressed them to the breaking point, but in that moment, with their hands together grasping the one weapon that might save them, the bitterness and denial that had kept them from so much as a touch for over a year became nothing more than a petty distraction.

For the first time in a year, they hoped for the same thing, together. The knife.

But it refused to budge. It was so firmly embedded that it might as well be one of the steel bars that covered the windows.

Jack whirled around, still on his knees. Randy already had the crowbar in his hand, crouched like a tiger, grinning wickedly at Jack.

"Hold on!" Jack stuck his arm out and swept Stephanie behind him. "Just hold on!"

Randy's eyes swiveled to Susan, who was still bound and taped to Jack's left. She was trying to yell through the tape.

Jack shifted closer to the girl. "It's okay, Susan," he said softly.

She quieted.

"He's going to kill us, no matter what we do," Jack said. "Think about it! We've seen his face; we know he's Lawdale; why would he let us live?"

"Listen to him, Randy," Stephanie said.

He removed his eyes from Susan and glanced at Stephanie, perhaps struck by her change. "I'll take my chances," Randy said. "I'm not willing to risk my life based on some stupid theory. If you don't let me kill her, so help me, I'm coming for you." He swung the crowbar once.

"What are you going to do, Randy? Beat her over the head?"

The man held his ground, but he didn't answer. At least he was thinking that through. Jack moved while Randy was at least partly preoccupied. He leaned over and grabbed the tape that covered Susan's mouth.

Yanked it free.

He held up his hands, tape dangling. "Just hear her out."

Randy stared, unmoving.

"Five minutes," Leslie whimpered.

"Tell him, Susan."

"Tin Man's lying to you," Susan said. "He won't let all of you live. Even if you kill me, at least some of you will die."

"That's a lie," Randy said. "If we don't kill her, we all die. She's trying to save herself at our expense."

"I know how to get out," the girl said. "That's one of the reasons he wants you to kill me."

"You see, Randy?" Jack said. "Just calm down."

Randy hesitated then spoke with a set jaw. "If she knew how to get out, she'd have told us already."

"I've tried," the girl said. "You aren't listening."

"How do we get out, Susan?" Jack asked, keeping his eyes on Randy and his hand out to keep him away.

"I can show you how," she said. "But you have to trust me."

"She's going to get us all killed!" Randy said.

"If you look and listen, you can still win," Susan said.

"Think of the mirror," Jack said quickly. "We weren't seeing ourselves. The truth was hidden from us. We weren't really looking. She's making sense. For heaven's sake, listen to her!"

"What truth?" Randy demanded. "The only truth I'm aware of at this particular moment is that White will be stepping back into this room and killing her anyway. You may be willing to throw your life away because she says so, but we're not. Leslie?"

She was starting to waver, looking from Randy to Jack and then back. "What if she's trying to trick us?"

"She saved your life!" Jack snapped. "What's the matter with you?"

Her face wrinkled in confusion, and she stifled a cry. He might have expected this from Stephanie, but not Leslie.

Stephanie put her hand on Jack's elbow.

"Time's going to run out," Susan said. "You have to choose who you're going to believe. If you don't follow me, you'll all die. But we have to go now!"

"That's the stupidest—"

"You're not listening!" Susan cried. "I've been here longer than you have! You have to trust me, or you'll die!"

"White will *kill* us!" Randy screamed.

Jack threw himself at Randy then, like a torpedo. The crowbar swung, but Randy was caught off guard and his swing was weak. The iron glanced off his back as his head struck Randy's hips.

They hit the floor hard, with Jack on top. He wasn't a fighter under normal circumstances, but this was anything but normal. Randy began to thrash. A knee crashed into Jack's side, and he felt himself losing the advantage as quickly as he'd gained it.

Jack did the only thing that came to him at that moment. He screamed at the top of his lungs, a raging cry that flooded his veins with adrenaline.

Another voice joined his. Stephanie's, screaming.

He heard Randy cry out in pain as he rolled to his knees. Stephanie had stomped on the hand clinging to the crowbar.

Jack watched her plant her left foot on the floor like a world-class punter and take a swing at him with her right foot.

She was wearing spring sandals, but the toes were hard and pointed, and Randy was kneeling, presenting a broad target for her. Her sharp shoe slammed into the side of his head.

He rolled to his side, dazed.

Susan was already beside Stephanie. "Get my hands free! Hurry!"

She spun Susan around and attacked the tape.

"Jack?" Leslie was watching, frozen.

Randy was still a threat, but they didn't have time to secure him.

"Follow me!" Susan said.

Randy was already pushing himself up.

Jack held a hand out to Leslie. "Come on!"

She hesitated then took a step.

Jack hurried after Susan and Stephanie, who'd reached the door.

"Ready?" Susan said, hand on the door handle.

"He's coming around," Jack said.

"Whatever happens, follow me. Open your eyes. Don't let the house turn you back."

"Where are we going?"

"Downstairs," she said and pulled the door open.

A rushing sound swallowed Jack. The door opened to blackness, not the hall.

Then he saw the stairs, the black fog, the dim bulbs, and he knew that this door now led into the basement. The house had shifted under them when White had slammed the door.

Fear pinged along Jack's nerves from the top of his head to the soles of his feet.

"Follow me," Susan cried and plunged down the dark stairwell.

37

6:04 AM

RANDY STAGGERED TO HIS FEET, DAZED. Confusion swirled through his mind like a thick black fog, rushing with the sound of a gale-force wind.

Then he realized that the sound wasn't in his head. It was coming from the open door that the others had just run through. The doorway gaped like a black throat that descended into hell.

Into the basement.

He stood, swaying on his feet, fighting the confusion. Follow Susan? Not a chance in hell. The fools were actually listening to a girl who'd been trapped in the house for three days.

He inched forward on shaking legs and peered down. Leslie had stopped halfway down and was staring at the black fog that covered the basement floor at the bottom of the steps. The rest of them, including Susan, were already out of sight.

Leslie didn't move. She'd lost her nerve. Funny how he'd lost interest in her over the last few hours. Funny how he had to fight back an urge to kick her in the head now, while her back faced him. Funny how he hated her as much as he hated himself.

How much time? He still had time, didn't he? The Tin Man didn't say the time would end if they left the room. No way six minutes had passed. He could still get to them. Maybe this way was better, because they wouldn't expect him from behind. If he killed the girl, the Stewarts would vanish or something. He would shake hands with White, and then he would walk away from this place the one free man who'd used his head to escape certain death.

Randy looked around for a weapon and saw the knife stuck in the wall. He scooped up the crowbar and ran to the wall. Grabbed the knife and pulled.

It came out like it was set in butter.

A small grin nudged his lips. See, now White was helping. Or the house was. Either way, he was doing the right thing.

He ran to the stairs and stopped at the top. The black fog was thick on the basement floor. No Stewarts. No White. Just Leslie, a step or two higher than a moment ago.

There was something moving in the fog below. Swimming just under the surface—he could see its wake, sweeping slowly across the fog.

Randy gripped the knife in his left hand, the crowbar in his right hand, and put one foot on the landing. Then the other.

He stood shaking, momentarily stalled. Then he forced himself down the stairs.

Leslie watched the moving fog, glued to the steps. Jack and Stephanie had followed Susan into the fog, but as they disappeared, she realized that she couldn't make it.

Wouldn't make it. Panic had seized her feet. And her mind. Susan's words drummed through her skull, but Leslie couldn't accept them. Running into the basement was suicide. And based on the urging of a girl who couldn't possibly know what she was talking about.

At the same time, Leslie couldn't ignore the evidence. The moving house. The shifting fog. She knew now, staring into the pit of hell, what was happening to her. She was facing her own sin. She'd been abused as a child, but as an adult she'd embraced that abuse by becoming an active participant.

What was abuse, except the bending of something that doesn't want to be bent? Any psychologist could attest to the fact that circumstances are subject to the participant caught within the circumstance. Beauty is in the eye of the beholder.

So is evil.

She'd become promiscuous and inviting, and she thrived on the power that she held over men. More important, she allowed that power to shape her identity.

The horrors of this night were highlighted by the one thin voice that had haunted her for the last two hours: she didn't hate Pete. Or what he'd done to her. In fact, in many ways she *was* Pete.

They shared a terrifying bond. The truth of it made her ill. But she had always been ill.

She briefly wondered if she should go to his room now. See how sick she really was.

Yet she was who she was.

Leslie stood, unmoving, staring at the moving fog.

—◦—

Jack followed at Stephanie's heels, down the stairs, keeping his eyes on the steps in front of him.

Susan dropped into the fog, which hit her at the waist. "Come on!"

Stephanie stopped on the last step before entering the black stuff. "Will it hurt?" she asked.

Susan ran toward the first door that Jack and Randy had entered.

He nudged Stephanie. "Go! Just go."

She stepped into the fog and cried out with pain. But she was committed, and she rushed after Susan.

The moment Jack's foot passed the surface, pain seared his skin through his shoes and socks. He grunted and pushed on.

It was his third time in the fog, and the pain this time was by far the worst. Sharper, deeper.

He staggered out of the fog into the room with four sofas.

Susan threw the door shut. "Do you see it now?"

Jack looked around. "See what?"

"You're not looking!" she snapped angrily.

"What are we looking for?" Stephanie demanded. "Just tell us!"

"I have told you!"

"Told us wh—"

"The paintings!" Jack said.

The paintings on the walls were no longer actually on the walls. They hung in space a foot or two from the walls, moving slowly, facing him. All of them.

And they were all portraits of . . . of him! Odd and distorted, but unmistakably him!

The one directly in front of him showed him without eyes. The image's crooked smile sent a shiver down his back.

Jack dropped to one knee, eyes still on the portraits. Him, all of them—terrifying images that didn't really look like him at all. White's imagination was demented.

"What do you see?" Stephanie asked.

"They're me," he said.

"That's not what I see. They're me. They . . . they're horrible!"

"He's doing this—"

"No," Susan said. "This isn't White."

The door from the study flew open, and Jack barged in, panting.

Jack?

Dressed exactly like him, the same kind of Jack that was in the boiler room, only this time Jack didn't pay them any attention whatsoever. It was as if he didn't see them.

He threw the door closed and quickly scanned the portraits.

"It's . . . that's me!" Stephanie whispered. She was seeing her own version of what Jack saw. They were both seeing themselves.

"Now do you understand?" Susan asked. She sounded urgent, demanding.

But Jack didn't understand. "I . . ." Jack didn't know what to say.

The new Jack focused on something across the room. His face twisted into a furious snarl, and his hands tightened into fists, a terrifying image of raw bitterness and rage.

Then he was moving like a tiger across the room, sweeping up a lamp as he went. Over a couch in a single leap.

Jack saw what he was looking at. Three of the portraits in the far corner were no longer images of him. Two of them were of people he knew from the publishing world—an agent who'd left him out to dry before his first novel was published, and a critic who'd trashed that same novel when it was finally published.

The other portrait was of Stephanie, posing dumbly in a yellow dress.

The new Jack went for the portrait of Stephanie, screaming. He swung the lamp at the canvas, tearing through Stephanie's face. Jack didn't stop there. He proceeded to rip the frame apart, stick from stick, breaking each piece over his knee.

Then he tore down the other two portraits and stomped on them. He finally stood back, assured himself that there were no other offenders in his presence, and strode angrily from the room, slamming the door.

When Jack looked back at the portraits he'd shredded, they were hanging in the air again, displaying his own distorted face.

"Do you understand?" Susan demanded. "We have to get out, but I can't get us out. If it were my house, I could do it, but it's yours, each of you. White made this *your* house. You have to get us out, and it won't be easy, so you have to—"

"I'm trying to think!" Jack said. He looked around. "*My* house? I don't see . . ."

His eyes settled on an old wooden placard that hung on the wall above the portraits. An old familiar saying was burned into the wood.

Home Is Where the Heart Is. And he knew then what Susan was trying to show them.

"This house is mirroring our hearts." He blinked. "It's drawing its power from the evil in us!"

"That's what I've been saying," Susan said.

"It's a haunted house that reflects the hearts of those who enter?" Stephanie said.

"Possessed by a power to mirror our hearts," Jack said. "You see the portraits of yourself, and I see them of me. Each of our experiences is unique. We're caught in a basement that's been empowered by White to reflect the evil in our hearts!"

"We've been fighting our own hearts?"

"No," Susan said. "The evil in your hearts."

"The ultimate haunted house," Jack said, staring at the portraits again. "We've been facing ourselves this whole time." He turned to Stephanie. "Our own sins are haunting us."

"I'm sorry, Jack." Her eyes were misted with both fear and sorrow, but he dismissed the fear and accepted only the sorrow. He felt it wash over his own heart. "I'm so sorry."

"No." Jack went to her, horrified by the image of himself tearing into the portrait of Stephanie with so much hatred. That was the truth of his heart!

"I'm the one who should be sorry. I've been so stubborn." He took her in his arms and held her tight, hoping desperately that he wasn't reconciling for his own gain.

She clung to him and cried in his neck. "I'm sorry, Jack."

He still loved her. Regardless of what happened tonight, he did love her. The realization made him squeeze her tighter.

"We have to hurry," Susan said.

Jack faced her, his new understanding increasing his sense of urgency. The fact that none of the pictures on the walls had changed wasn't lost on him.

"If we defeat the sin, we take away the house's power?"

Susan eyed him for a few moments. "No. That's not the way it works. It's not about the sins. It's about the heart. It's about you."

Stephanie stepped forward. "That doesn't make sense! We are what we do!"

"Follow me." Susan hurried to the door that led into the study. "I'll show you the way." If Jack was right, she was headed for the back exit.

The notion that all the evil he'd confronted in the last seven hours had been mostly his own doing flogged at Jack's mind. He was evil? Or was the evil so strong in him that he couldn't see the good?

Susan? She was one of White's victims, come into the killer's own world, but she was more. She was the light in this darkness, wasn't she?

A dozen meaningless sayings cried out to him. A house divided cannot stand. Love your neighbor as yourself.

Light came into the darkness, but the darkness did not understand it.

Susan pulled the door open, took a deep breath, then stepped back. Jack saw what she saw over her shoulder. Stewart, Betty, and Pete stood abreast, bearing shotguns, standing in black fog, glaring at them with glowing eyes. Behind them, the room was filled with twenty or thirty men wearing Tin Man masks, armed with axes. They were all dressed like Jack.

Were Jacks.

"They're me!" Stephanie whispered.

Not possible, not possible. But real, very real, standing right before him.

For a moment, none of them moved. The house moaned. There was a terrible wail behind the deep, guttural sound.

"Guilty as sin," Betty said. She thrust out her finger. "Kill them!"

The Jacks surged forward.

Susan slammed the door, locked it, and ran past Jack. "Run! After me!"

The room reverberated with the sound of splintering wood.

"Run!"

38

6:05 AM

TIME CAME TO A STANDSTILL FOR RANDY the moment he put his foot on the first step leading into the basement.

Fear stopped him—terrible waves of fear that felt like real waves crashing into his body. *Whump, whump, whump.* His ears rang in their wake.

Leslie began to move again, down the steps toward the fog.

"Leslie?"

His voice was hoarse and soft, so he said it again.

"Leslie?"

She looked back up at him, and he saw that her cheeks were wet. She jerked her head around and stepped down. Into the fog. Up to her knees. And ran, fog swirling in her wake.

Then she was gone.

Randy forced himself down slowly, every step meeting him with a new wave of fear. Which was confusing to him, because he'd been sure that White wanted him to do his business. He'd let him have the knife, hadn't he?

He walked a few steps with more confidence and stopped just above the sea of black fog. Another wave of fear hit him full in the face.

It was Stewart, standing bald and glaring with bulging eyes. Not just Stewart. Six Stewarts, each unique in their own way. All armed with shotguns or axes.

He jumped back up one step and lifted the crowbar.

But they weren't coming at him. Right? They stood still, legs planted in the fog, staring at him without moving.

Maybe they weren't a threat to him anymore. In some ways he was on the same team now, trying like them to kill the girl. He'd killed a Stewart, so they probably had some fear of him. Mutual respect.

"I'm going after Susan," he said. His voice echoed softly in the hall.

They didn't move. Neither did he.

The house began to moan, then wail. For a couple of seconds he thought about running back upstairs.

"Hello, Randy."

He whirled around.

The Tin Man stood at the top of the stairs, framed in a gray light from some supernatural source. He was wearing his mask, and he held a shotgun in both hands.

Randy opened his mouth to tell White what his plans were—that he needed just a few extra minutes to take care of the girl. "I—"

That was as far as he got.

White swung his gun down. "Good-bye, Randy."

Randy waited for the fist of lead to hit him. He felt his bladder go. The knife fell from his hand.

"I'll do anything," he said, dropping the crowbar too. "I swear, I'll do anything."

Still no blast. That was good. That was real good. So he said more of the same.

"Anything, I swear, anything . . . I want to be . . . I'll do anything."

Still no blast. The Tin Man had his shotgun angled down so that the shot from its barrel would strike Randy's chest. But he wasn't pulling the trigger. And Tin Man didn't strike him as the kind to hesitate without good reason.

That was good, right?

"Kill her," Tin Man said.

"I'm going to, I swear. That's what I'm doing."

One of the hall doors busted open behind Randy, and he jerked his head around. Leslie stumbled out, pushed by Stewart and another bald inbred who stepped into the hall behind her. Stewarts. Demons, for all she knew.

"Leslie," Tin Man said. "Use the knife."

"Randy?" Leslie sobbed. "What's happening, Randy?"

Tin Man stared at him past the mask, then stepped back and shut the door on the basement, leaving Randy to carry out his orders. Or be killed, for sure. Kill or be killed. No doubt about that.

"Randy! Answer me!" Leslie was broken to pieces anyway. No way she was going to survive this mess. He'd just be putting her out of her misery.

But Randy's legs wobbled like rubber bands as he crouched, felt for the knife beneath the fog, and lifted the weapon into the clear.

"Randy, you can't possibly be thinking about killing me!" Her face wrinkled with terror. "Randy, sweetie . . . Randy?"

He looked at the knife in his hands. He felt nothing for her. Nothing at all. He was going to do this. That's all there was to it. He was going to kill Leslie because he was really on Team Stewart, and the Stewarts always obeyed White.

Randy walked through the fog, toward the woman who had tried to control him without knowing how much he resented it. This was his house. White's house. Stewart's house. Randy's house. Leslie was no longer welcome.

"Randy, you stop right there!" she screamed, spittle flying. "Stop!"

Randy stopped in front of her. Then he thrust the knife forward, into her chest. Deep into her chest. And let go. The Stewarts let go of her too.

She staggered back one step, eyes wide, and fell backward into the fog. Randy found the look of shock on her face interesting.

He stared at the fog where she'd fallen until it settled completely, rich and oily thick. When he lifted his eyes to the closest Stewart—the same Stewart who'd first chased him, the same Stewart who'd drowned—the thing returned a long, expressionless look. Then Stewart turned and headed through the door, followed by the others.

Randy looked around at the empty hallway, saw that he was alone. Silent. Empty, like himself. An odd numbness settled over him. Hollow and numb and a little dizzy.

He grunted and jogged into the open doorway after the Stewart. The Stewart who was his father.

I'm home. Really home.

39

6:09 AM

THEY RAN SINGLE FILE FROM THE LIVING room into the hall, Susan leading, always leading, then Stephanie, then Jack.

The hall was wide again with the stairs rising to their immediate left.

Jack ran blindly on numb legs, Susan his only guide. Through the door, down the hall, desperate to stay ahead of the pursuit. Madly trying to make sense of what was happening but hardly able to string together the conscious thoughts required to do so.

Susan sprinted down two halls. Each time they turned a corner, the pounding of feet thundered from behind. Where was she taking them? White was going to burn the house down at first light, he said. If the fog burned as well as the sample he'd lit upstairs, the house would go up like a can of gasoline with them trapped inside.

The house had become their own hell. But ahead of them ran a young woman who knew far more than she had any business knowing. The notion that he had ever thought she was somehow complicit with White now struck Jack as ludicrous. Susan was their only hope. If she died, they would die.

Follow me, she said, so he followed her, completely at her mercy.

They entered the boiler room, locked the doors, and were halfway up the ladder to the vent when the sound of axes striking at the door echoed through the room.

"Hurry!" Jack said, breathing hard. "Go, go!"

Stephanie grunted and clambered up. "Where are we going?"

"Just hurry," Susan said.

"They will die, right?" Jack asked. "I killed Betty! Why is she still alive?"

"They can die," Susan said. "But demons don't die easily."

"Demons? Real demons? But how—"

"Hurry. Quietly!"

The crawl space outside Pete's room was knee-deep with the black fog and crowded with Jacks, wandering around, peering past their tin masks into the shadows.

Jack climbed from the vent shaft and stared at the Jacks, who clearly couldn't see them in the deep shadow. Stephanie was trembling beside him. He reached for her hand in the darkness, touched her fingers, held her tightly. She stepped closer.

The sound of Jacks climbing up the ladder behind reverberated through the vent. Susan motioned for silence and crept along the crawl-space wall, deep in darkness, to the exit hatch. Jack raised it gently and could see the hall. Crowded with Jacks. They had come the back way and avoided most of the undead, but by all

appearances all the main sections of the basement were
now flooded with Jacks and Stewarts, prowling, hunting
them. No matter where they went, they would face an
army of evil.

Jack was about to draw Susan's attention to this fact
when she lifted herself out of a second hatch he hadn't
noticed. He helped Stephanie out, then they squeezed
through a narrow passageway that spilled into another hall.

No fog. No Jacks.

Perhaps the house seemed to know that White
planned on burning it down, because with each passing
minute its moans took on more urgency, lower and
higher tones entwined into one terrifying wail that ebbed
and flowed.

"This way!" Susan darted down the hall to a wood
door curved at the top. This was one of the doors into the
dark hall in which he'd found Susan.

The safe place.

But with one match, White could change that. *Would*
change that.

They slipped into the passageway, sealed the door
quietly behind them, and stood panting in the dark.

"What now?" Jack asked.

"We just made a circle around the main part of the
basement," Susan said, winded. "The door that sucked
you in earlier leads into the study."

"That door's locked . . ."

"No, it's not. You just thought it was. But we have a bigger problem."

"What?"

"We have to go *through* the study to get to the exit
tunnel."

Their voices echoed gently off the close walls.

"So if we can get to it, we can get out through the back door?" Stephanie asked.

"That one *is* locked," Susan said.

"And the hall?" Jack asked.

"Is where he's probably waiting for us with more of them than you can count."

"That back door's the only way out?" Jack asked, shocked by her frank admissions.

"It's the only way."

"That's impossible! There's no way we can get past him!"

Silence settled in the dark passage.

"He's going to burn the house down," Stephanie whispered.

"Follow me," Susan said, taking their hands.

She led them quickly forward into the darkness. Running was one thing, Jack thought, but heading straight into them?

He pulled up, panting now as much from fear as from their run. "This is crazy. They'll kill us!"

"They might," Susan said. "And they *will* if you don't start dealing with them on their terms."

"I'm supposed to head into a mob of these with my bare hands?" He knew that's not what she meant, but he felt he should point out the considerable imbalance of power.

"He's right," Stephanie said. "We don't stand a chance."

Susan pulled them forward. "Stop thinking about them. You're giving them more power than they really have."

They were speaking in hushed tones, very quickly moving deeper into the tunnel.

"But they're real," he said. "Their axes are real—"

"Of course they're real. I'm not saying you should walk right into them. But there are greater powers beyond what you can see."

"God? You're saying this is about God? Some huge whatever in the sky set this up?"

"*You* set it up."

"What are you talking about? We were just driving by when White slashed our tires and lured us to this hellish house."

"It's your house."

"That's crazy."

"It draws most of its power from you. We've been over this! Accept it, Jack. You're at the heart of the battle between good and evil."

"I've prayed to God," Stephanie said. It sounded like a question.

"Prayed? But do you even believe? Really believe? And do you know how to love, really love?"

"Love the Lord your God with all your heart," Jack said quietly. "Love your neighbor as yourself. Isn't that a famous teaching? Jesus?" He hesitated, meaning settling in his mind like a falling snow. "So what's love look like in a house of horrors?"

"The same way it's always looked," Susan said. Then added after a pause, "It's not just what you do, it's who you are. You've got to change who you are. That's how you change the house. You'll have to see it; words don't mean much at times like this."

One of the far doors opened without warning, flooding the passage with light. One of the Jacks stood backlit in the opening. He issued a grunt and ran in, followed by others.

Susan flew toward a door along the wall now illuminated by the light. He looked into shadows beyond them, frantic for anything. The closet that he'd found Susan in—he couldn't see it, but he knew it was there, farther from the door that led into the study, for which Susan was now headed.

"The closet!" he whispered.

The Jack yelled something. They'd been spotted.

"We don't have time to hide," Susan snapped. "He's going to torch the house!"

But Jack sprinted for the closet anyway. He had to get his mind straight. Susan hesitated only a brief moment, then followed his lead. They ran into the shadows, into the large closet, closed the door, and stilled their breathing as best they could. With any luck they had entered unseen, covered by the darkness.

"He's going to burn the house," Susan said. "You should have followed me."

"We're powerless out here!" Jack whispered.

She put her hand on the knob. "Watch me. When I go, you go, hard and fast. Just try to get a weapon. Anything. Okay?"

He could hear their feet slapping as they approached. With any luck they hadn't been seen entering the closet in the deep shadow. Without that element of surprise, they would be overwhelmed.

"Jack?"

"Shh . . ."

"Jack, I can't do—"

He put his hand on Stephanie's mouth. "Shh . . . shh . . . shh. Yes, you can. We have to trust her."

"I don't know—"

"Shhhhhhhh . . ."

The feet were slapping closer, closer. And then they were there.

Past them. Susan waited a moment longer.

"Now!" she whispered.

She shoved as hard as she could, grunting loudly. The door crunched into a body. A clang of door against tin mask resounded down the passage.

Susan leaped out and sized up the situation. Jack saw it all as if in a dream. Three copies of himself wearing Tin Man masks. Two of them ten feet to the right. One right in front of Susan, surprised by her bold entrance. The ax he'd been carrying fell to the ground.

For a moment they all stood frozen by indecision. And then Susan moved, quickly, soundlessly.

Jack watched as she snatched up the fallen ax before the Jack had time to react. She swung the blade with all her strength as the Jack recovered and tried to jump back.

The blade connected with the man. Sliced into his chest. Through his body. Into thin air, as if the man had been made of all flesh and no bone.

The man roared with pain. The throaty cry immediately rose to a high-pitched scream that hurt Jack's ears. Then the man was sucked into himself and became a twisting pillar of black fog. The fog, heavier than air, collapsed under the tin mask, which clanged to the concrete floor with the man's ax.

No blood. It occurred to Jack then that these copies of himself must come from the fog. *Were* the fog in this haunted place empowered by his heart. The fog of evil.

Human nature.

The two Jacks who'd passed the closet door started back, roaring with fury, wielding knives. The sound was enough to stop Jack's heart.

One of the Jacks threw his knife. It was a large blade, maybe a foot long, and Jack watched it turn lazily in the air, glance off his shoulder, and tumble to the floor.

Pain flared down his arm. "Hurry!" Susan ran for the door that Jack had first been sucked through. They didn't needed any encouragement.

That moment came two seconds later when Susan pulled open the door into the study.

As far as he could see, there was only one person in the room. But this wasn't a Jack. This was Stewart. And Stewart was armed with a shotgun.

Jack pulled up abruptly, barely aware of Stephanie's collision with him from behind.

"Go!" Stephanie cried. "They're coming!"

Jack went.

40

6:12 AM

SUSAN SLAMMED THE DOOR BEHIND THEM the moment they were through, twisting the lock and for the moment protecting their backs.

But their backs were now the least of Jack's worries.

The first and most immediate was Stewart. And his shotgun. He faced them from the middle of the room, amused more than stunned.

Black fog covered the floor to his ankles.

Jack's second concern was a dread that came from his still-dawning realization that the threat facing him was somehow coming from him. From his own heart.

"I believe," he whispered. "I believe; I swear I believe." But he still wasn't sure what that meant.

Stewart still hadn't brought his gun up. He was clearly as aware as Jack that one ax in the hands of a girl was no match for a shotgun at this distance.

Stephanie's cry of frustration upon seeing Stewart was like a dagger.

Susan stepped forward, ax in both hands. She faced

Stewart, putting herself between him and Jack. Stephanie pressed close behind.

Somewhere in the house a dozen doors began to bang in unison. *Bang, bang, bang, bang!*

But Stewart made no move. Susan faced him, eager neither to attack nor retreat. They'd run into a dead end.

Jack wanted to ask what was happening, what he should do, what she was doing, but his mouth wasn't forming the words.

For an extended stretch, they faced off. The floor shook with each bang of the doors beyond. It was as if the house was sending its own signal to all inhabitants.

We have them; we have them; we have them; we have them!

Then Stewart calmly brought the shotgun up and aimed it at Susan. The doors stopped banging in unison. A soft grin nudged the man's lips.

"There's more, isn't there?" Susan said.

The man's smile flattened slightly before he recovered his confidence.

"This is our house now," he said.

"Is it? Do you know who I am?"

"One of them."

"Are you sure?"

Stewart didn't answer.

The door opened and Betty walked in. And behind her, Pete. Betty's head was bandaged with red rags. Jack was quite sure that she was made of more than mere flesh and blood. Either possessed or the stuff of possession.

Still, these monsters could be killed; Susan had made that clear.

Mother and son walked up to Stewart's side and

stared at Susan. Pete's eyes locked on Stephanie over Jack's right shoulder, consumed with lust.

"There she is, Mama," he said.

This demented oaf knew only one thing. He had the emotional dimensions of a lump of coal.

Betty ignored him. "Remember, he wants these three alive."

"You're going to die today," Stewart said. "All three of you. They always die."

"That's what you told me three days ago," Susan said. "I'm still alive."

"Drop the ax," Betty said.

Jack fought panic. How was he supposed to get out of this? He thought about taking the ax from her and going straight at them.

Susan hesitated then set the ax on the floor.

Fear flashed down Jack's back. Not a single bone in his body agreed with anything similar to a plan that included him rushing an armed Stewart. It would be like leaping off a cliff.

But in that moment, Jack ignored the shaking in his limbs, leaped around Susan, grabbed up the ax, and rushed Stewart.

He was halfway there before Susan's cry cut through his ears. "No, Jack!"

No, Jack? He was already committed! He had to do something! Jack responded by screaming as he threw himself forward, ax swinging down.

Oddly enough, Stewart wasn't shooting. In fact, he wasn't demonstrating any sign of concern at all, unlike the Jacks they'd just killed. Stewart wasn't a reflection of him.

At the last second, after the ax was about to complete its trajectory, Stewart moved, easily sidestepping the falling blade. Jack was pulled off balance by the heavy weapon. The butt of Stewart's shotgun slammed into his head as the ax bit through empty air.

He released the handle to catch his own fall and knew then, before the bone-jarring crunch of his knees smashing into the concrete, that whatever strength Susan was talking about came from neither boldness nor idiocy.

He hit the floor hard and felt Stewart's boot crash into his side.

"Fools," the man spat.

"Don't!" Susan shouted, rushing forward.

The shotgun boomed. "Stay back!

Jack pushed himself to his knees, blinking to clear his head. They were restraining Susan and Stephanie, who was protesting loudly. She was silenced with a loud *smack*.

Susan screamed something, but Jack's mind was yanked back to his own predicament as Stewart grabbed him by his arm and hauled him to his feet. Shoved him to the center of the room.

They'd forced Susan and Stephanie to their knees. Blood dripped from Susan's nose. She stared at Jack with sad eyes. Stephanie's cheek was bright red. But they appeared otherwise unharmed.

Stewart forced Jack to his knees beside them.

"Wait for me," Susan whispered.

"Shut your stinking little pie—"

Susan screamed and shot to her feet while Stewart was still standing over Jack. "Now, Jack!"

He didn't know what he was supposed to do *now*, but he dived at Stewart with as much strength as he could assemble on such short notice.

Susan had her hands on his gun when Jack's head crashed into Stewart's head. His left ear was all that came between their skulls, a piece of flesh that had never been designed to withstand such a hit.

Stewart screamed.

Jack plowed forward, threatening to topple the man. From the corner of his eye he saw Pete rushing to help.

Saw Stephanie throw herself into his path like a woman possessed. She brought her knee up into his groin with enough force to stop an elephant, screaming with Susan to maximize her effort.

Betty was screaming as well, but none of their cries mattered, because now Stewart was falling with Jack, and Susan had the gun.

She flipped it around, crammed the butt against her shoulder, and put a round into the ceiling to make sure there was no mistaking that she knew how to use the thing.

"Against the wall!" she shouted, aiming for Betty's head. Then at Pete. "Against the wall!"

Jack rolled off Stewart and came to his feet, breathing hard.

For several seconds Betty, Pete, and Stewart were too stunned by the reversal to move.

"Move," Susan said.

They moved slowly to the wall, eyes fixed, still unsure they had actually been foiled.

"Make sure the doors are locked," Susan said. "Jack, hurry."

He wasn't sure what she had in mind, but he ran to the main door and secured the dead bolts.

"You'll never make it out," Stewart said, resolve back. "You're outnumbered."

"Shut up," Susan said.

Jack hurried for the door that led to the back exit tunnel, eyes on Pete, who even now was fixated on Stephanie. The dead bolt was already engaged.

"Are you going to kill them?" Stephanie asked. "Maybe we should kill them. They're not real people, right?"

"That won't help us," Susan said. "We need to—"

Rap, rap, rap.

Susan jerked her head to the door behind Jack. Knuckles sounded on the door that led to the exit.

Rap, rap, rap!

"No matter what happens," Susan said. "Remember . . ."

The door shook, then bowed under a tremendous force. Black fog seeped into the study.

". . . that light always pierces the darkness."

The door shook violently and bowed again, this time several feet, straining against whatever held it in place.

Jack rushed for the ax. Snatched it up.

"Check the chamber," he said again.

She did.

The door behind them—the one that led into the living room—began to rattle. It too bent. As did the third door and the fourth door.

"Light came into the darkness, but the darkness didn't understand it," Susan said. "Look to the light. Only the light can save you from yourself."

"What's there?" Stephanie asked, eyes darting from door to door.

"He's come," Susan said.

But it sounded like more than one *he*. Jack couldn't help thinking that all of the undead, however many hundreds of them crowded this house of his making, had come and were pressing in on all sides, leaving no escape.

"Jack." Stephanie was whispering, scared. Her eyes darted from door to door. "I don't know what's happening . . ."

The knuckles on the door that led to the exit tunnel rapped again.

The door to the exit tunnel blew open. Wisps of black fog roiled in, but nothing else. The other three doors stilled.

Then they came, like a pack of jackals, a dozen, two dozen Jacks, surging into the room. Half broke to the right, half to the left, forming two fronts like a forward guard.

Jack backpedaled to where Susan and Stephanie stood in the middle of the room.

Still they came, thirty, forty, crowding by the door now, glaring at him, gripping weapons, but otherwise waiting.

All with tin masks.

Except for a handful of inbreds that Jack now recognized from the hall, they were all Jacks. All him. He was facing himself, and it made his knees tremble. Stewart, Betty, and Pete were now content to look on, wearing smirks.

"Susan?"

She had the gun up, but she wasn't shooting. What good would one gun do against so many?

Stephanie held onto Jack's arm tightly. That was one good thing, he thought. Stephanie. She was here, facing no less than he. They would die together. An appropriate end to the misery that had haunted them for so long.

To a man, the Jacks' eyes were on his. Not a single one averted their stare, and for a moment, not a single one blinked.

Then the Jacks by the door parted, and Jack knew that their waiting was over.

Tin Man stepped into the room.

41

THE ROOM STILLED. TIN MAN WALKED toward them and stopped ten feet away at the edge of the lines formed by the Jacks.

He faced them in stoic silence. In his right hand he held the shotgun. The wounds to his arm and his forehead had soaked the bandages, but they hadn't slowed him down.

For a few seconds he just stared at them through the jagged holes in his tin mask. His breathing was hard and steady.

"The wages of sin is death," Tin Man said. "In the end they always pay up."

Susan made no attempt to aim the shotgun at him. The ax in Jack's hands felt small and flimsy. They didn't stand a chance.

"Drop the shotgun."

Susan released the weapon, and it clattered to the ground.

Tin Man's eyes shifted to her, and he regarded her for a moment.

"I'm sorry, Jack," Stephanie whispered frantically. "This is all my fault. They're all staring at me . . . I'm so sorry."

She was seeing herself, Stephanies, not Jacks, and their stares were telling her that she was guilty.

Jack eased sideways on trembling legs, putting himself between Stephanie and White. His heart was banging in his chest. Like the banging of so many doors in this house of his heart.

"Welcome to your house," Tin Man said. He grunted with satisfaction. "Do you like it?"

He unceremoniously lifted the shotgun. Silence sucked all but the sound of ragged breathing from the room. The Jacks stared.

"Kill her," Tin Man said.

At first Jack didn't know what he was ordering. With the tin mask, it was hard to tell whom the man was addressing.

"Kill Susan," White said. "Or I will kill all three of you."

"What?"

"If you kill her, I will let you and Stephanie go. Like I let Randy go."

"Randy?" He'd hardly thought of Randy since entering the basement. He'd been released? What about Leslie?

"Free as a bird," Tin Man said. "Kill her."

Jack couldn't speak. He couldn't kill Susan. And he couldn't *not* kill her and thereby kill Stephanie.

Both choices were unforgivable.

Tin Man breathed hard and slow behind the mask. Jack's mind spun through the most glaring elements of this mad moment.

Element: This was their last chance. Dawn was here.

Element: Tin Man was lying. He would kill them both anyway.

Element: Tin Man had always wanted them to kill Susan, so he probably *wasn't* lying.

Element: He owed Stephanie his life. He'd badly mistreated her in this last year of mourning. She didn't deserve to die. He had to save her.

Element: He could save her with one swing of the ax in his hands.

Element: He could never swing the ax in his hands at Susan!

The thoughts overlapped one another, tilting his orientation toward no clear conclusion.

"Would thirty pieces of silver help?"

Thirty pieces of silver?

"You know you can do it," Tin Man said between breaths. "They all want you to do it. All of you."

As if on cue, all four doors began to rattle. Then shake violently. Bent inward. More black fog.

None of the Jacks turned to look. Their eyes were on Jack.

The doors crashed open, pushed by a sea of Jacks who flowed into the room like a swarm of insects. An army of rushing Tin Man protégés who were Jack, every last one fixed upon him.

Stephanie screamed.

Jack saw beyond them, beyond the doors, where hundreds, maybe thousands of them crowded the basement hallways and rooms. The fog had given birth to a thousand Jacks.

The Jacks packed every conceivable corner, leaving

a ten-foot circle at the center where Jack, Stephanie, and Susan stood.

Their tin masks and weapons clicked and clanked, and their shoes thudded, but they didn't speak. They only drilled him with their eyes through jagged holes.

"Dear God!" Stephanie whimpered. "Oh, dear God."

Tin Man glared at Jack. Impossible to tell if he was relishing the moment or bitter.

"You know you want to kill her."

He'd addressed Jack, but now all the Jacks answered by shifting eagerly on their feet, some bouncing as if to nod. All still drilling Jack with their stares. Their breathing quickened, and now a few couldn't restrain the odd grunt or whimper. They were desperate for him to kill Susan.

Why Susan? Why such an obsession with this one girl?

"Your heart is dark. You have to look to the light," Susan said.

Her words seemed to agitate the Jacks even more. They swayed and jostled and clicked against one another.

"What light?" Stephanie cried.

Tin Man moved toward Stephanie. "Don't be a complete fool," Tin Man said. "Kill her."

Jack's eyes settled on a Jack standing perfectly still to his left. Only it wasn't a Jack. It wore a tin mask and was roughly the same size as the others, but it was dressed differently.

It was dressed like Randy.

Was Randy.

White saw Jack's shift in attention and glanced over at Randy.

"I killed Leslie," Randy said.

Just that. Just *I killed Leslie*, as if he was at once both proud and ashamed of the fact.

Tin Man swung his shotgun to face the man and pulled the trigger. The lead took Randy in the chest and pushed him into the wall of Jacks behind before dropping him to the ground.

The energy from the sea of Jacks doubled. Their sound grew to a dull roar of banging and bouncing. They were urging Jack. Pleading with him.

He felt compelled. Irresistibly drawn to satisfy the demands of these Jacks.

Tin Man swung his gun back in line with Jack. "Kill her."

Jack hesitated for a long moment. He spoke without fully understanding himself.

"No."

Almost immediately the Jacks stilled, as if stunned. He said it again, to assure himself that he'd really said it.

"No."

Silence. Breathing.

"You're a fool," Tin Man said.

Susan took one step out between him and Stephanie, then turned her back on him and looked at Jack.

Tears wet her cheeks, but there was a softness in her eyes.

"Kill her," Tin Man growled, angry, shaken. It was the first time Jack had seen the man lose any control. "She has to die!"

"You think one dead body will satisfy his lust for death?" Susan asked Jack. "Not unless that person has no guilt. Not unless they are blameless. Only one Son

of Man can do that. Look to the light, and you'll understand. I'll show you the way. Look to the Son of Man."

Son of Man?

Tin Man seemed to become unglued behind Susan.
It made no sense. He could just pull the trigger and end
all of this. Instead, he was shaking.

"Kill her," he roared.

Susan spun to face him. "He said no!"

❦

Barsidious White stared at the girl through the holes
in his mask, feeling the hatred boiling in his gut, knowing he couldn't stop himself now.

Until just a few minutes ago, the game had proceeded perfectly, as it always did, even with this interesting new twist presented by the girl. He'd lost track of
how many houses he'd played this game in. He'd enter
the house, invoke the powers of darkness to fill the house
to personify the evil of all who entered. The house, like
himself, obediently became a crucible of power.

To each house he invited enough demons to make
life hell for the victims. Stewarts and Bettys and Petes
and other inbreds. But more important, there were these
hosts of Jacks and Stephanies who mirrored their own
natures.

Jack and Stephanie were guilty, and so in the end
they would die.

But what about Susan?

His earlier suspicions that she might not be guilty at
all were now screaming to the surface. She was less and
more than anything he'd ever confronted.

His urgency to see Jack kill her forced him into betraying his desperation. Jack had said no, and he'd nearly killed the man then. He would have if Susan hadn't stepped in the way.

And why didn't he just kill her? An hour ago he would have said it was because she was for the others to kill.

Now something deep in his psyche suggested her death might not be such a good thing. But he couldn't connect any reasoning to it.

Stephanie's face was distorted, terrified. This much he relished. But the still, small voice of Susan shredded any delight he could milk out of the unfolding scene. She was too confident, too aware of the reality between dark and light.

But who was she? And where had she come from?

Then Susan turned her back on him and spoke clear, soft words, and the Tin Man knew who she was. Or at the very least, what part she was playing in this contest between light and darkness, life and death.

He began to panic.

"Kill her!" he roared.

The girl spun to face him. "He said no!"

Tin Man pulled the trigger in uncontrollable rage.

———

The shotgun spewed fire with a tremendous boom. Jack couldn't see the impact of the shot because Susan was between him and the Tin Man. But he felt the impact a moment later when her body flew backward and crashed into his chest.

He instinctively grabbed her.

Felt the wetness on her belly.

Saw the room tilt as his mind began to shut down.

Susan groaned once, then slumped forward, dead in his arms.

42

6:16 AM

JACK DROPPED SUSAN IN HORROR AND LET the body fall facedown. Blood snaked out from under her body.

Stephanie began to sob. They'd been in some harrowing situations, but this was the first such innocent death, and Jack was surprised by the sudden pain in his gut. Her frail, dead body there on the ground screamed foul.

He felt his heart begin to break in stages, like a tall building being brought down by demolition charges. But there didn't seem to be any foundation to catch all the rubble. It caved in on itself and fell into a deep void of emptiness.

The Jacks had all broken eye contact with him for the first time and now looked at the girl, mesmerized. The Tin Man chambered another round slowly, as if needing time to contemplate what he'd just done.

Jack heard a faint crackling sound. His eyes went to Susan's blood on the floor. But it wasn't the kind of red blood he expected to see. Red, yes, but laced with a crackling white light, as if it carried a charge.

Look to the light.

The Jacks had seen it too. Several directly in front of Jack stepped back. They began to bob anxiously. A murmur swelled. Clicking and banging gradually filled the room.

White stared at the girl.

In frantic style, the hundreds of Jacks crowded into the room began to bounce in a strange, ritualistic dance.

Like the banging door earlier. *Now, now, now, now . . .*

What now?

Or was it some kind of celebration?

Stephanie rushed past Jack and dropped to her knees beside Susan's prone body. She reached a hand out and began to whisper urgently past streaming tears.

"She's the light! She's the light!"

She was the light? Of course, he'd seen the light, but was she actually the light?

White shifted his eyes to Stephanie. Then up to Jack.

Resigned to whatever fate now awaited them, Jack lowered himself to his knees. His throat knotted with pain, but he saw no remedy, no way to survive, no reason to live, no reason to die. He only felt pain.

Look to the light.

Had he seen the light?

The Jacks' bouncing cries rose to a loud roar. For the first time, Jack could actually hear words in their chant. "Kill." They gripped their axes and knives, chanting, and with each chant their voices came closer to unison.

"Kill, kill, kill, kill."

They seemed to be waiting for permission before tearing in. White stood flat-footed, head tilted down to show the lower whites of his eyes.

Stephanie's whispering rose to a shout; he barely heard it above the din. "You are the light!"

Jack's heart quickened. He said it silently with her the first time, staring at her mouth as his mind reached back to make sense. "You are the light."

Is that what Susan had meant? That he should look to a source of light outside himself? The light came into the darkness.

Stephanie's cry changed again, sobbing and wailing at once. And now her words cut through the din so that they were clear.

"Son of Man, have mercy on me, a sinner!" She drew a long, loud, gasping breath and wailed again. "Son of Man, have mercy on me, a sinner!"

Son of Man.

The truth struck Jack full in the face. Susan had taken their death as the guiltless one. She was the light in the darkness, but the wages of sin really was death. The guilty really had to die, just as White insisted. That was the game.

But Susan was the Christ, who had died instead. And Tin Man seemed to know his mistake.

Jack screamed the words with Stephanie, "Son of Man, have mercy on me, a sinner!"

He gripped Stephanie's hand as if it were his last lifeline, and together they cried out at the top of their lungs. Their words stumbled over one another in a jumble.

For long seconds he yelled, until it occurred to him that the hissing had stopped. And so had Stephanie.

He opened his eyes and lowered his head. The room had come to an absolute standstill. The crowding Jacks had stopped two strides back, axes raised but frozen.

Why?

He heard the crackle of electricity again. The light? He glanced down.

The blood from Susan's body was brimming with light again, arcing with white-hot fingers of power. The electricity gathered and blasted into his face. Into his mouth. Into his eyes.

A thick shaft of mind-numbing energy rushed into his body.

He trembled under its power. Too much; it was too much! He jerked his head up and screamed.

And then the power flowed again, as strong as before, only this time *from* his mouth. From his eyes.

Jack could see through the light as it blasted from him, white-hot. He saw it all at what had to be one-tenth of the actual speed, a surreal display of searing power.

The Jack closest to him went rigid at the approaching shaft of light, then screamed and evaporated into a black fog before the light even touched him.

The blaze cut through the Jacks behind him, twenty-deep, as if they were nothing more than ash. The light spread out on all sides, joined by as much light from Stephanie, who was screaming beside him.

The terrible shrieks of the undead filled the room, crumbling to ash before the low, crackling hum of power that came from him and Stephanie.

The light came into the darkness, and the darkness did not understand it, but that no longer mattered because the light was now obliterating the darkness.

Still they screamed. Still the light flowed.

White's body jerked with the full impact of light

streaming from both Jack and Stephanie. He came off
the ground, folded forward, screaming with pain.

For a few moments he hung in the air as if gut-
punched, shaking under the raw power that ran through
his body. His screaming was swallowed by a roar of light.
He was unceremoniously released and dumped to the
floor where he lay in a pile, unmoving.

Still they screamed. Still the light flowed.

And then Jack collapsed.

＊   ＊

From outside the house, no one would know the
horrors that had ravaged Jack and Stephanie deep in the
basement as the dawn showed its face.

A faraway scream now and then, the faint sound
of milling insects . . . all sounds plausibly from the
nearby forest rather than from inside the large, long-
ago-abandoned house.

All the windows were barred and dark, all the doors
sealed tight. Any soul on a casual stroll through the woods
might see the old brown pickup truck wedged up on the
front porch and think a youthful joyride had gone bad,
but otherwise the house looked like many other similarly
abandoned homes in the backwoods.

But all of that changed at precisely 6:17 in the
morning.

It started with a barely visible flash of light that
momentarily lit the house and then was gone, as if a flash
grenade had been set off in the basement.

Then the light was back, only now brimming from

the space below the doors and through the cracks in closed shutters and in some cases glowing bright from uncovered windows.

The light grew brighter, blinding white. Rays of light broke past thin cracks and streamed into the air.

Windows rattled as if attempting to contain the surge of energy that pressed them to the breaking point. The front door creaked, and for a moment the whole house began to tremble.

The shutters and windows throughout the house loosed from their latches with loud bangs and blew open. Light shot into the sky in thick shafts, riding a hum that lasted seven or eight seconds.

Then, as if someone had pulled the plug, the light disappeared, and the house was once again shrouded in grayness. The windows swung lazily on their hinges for a moment.

Then the house was still.

43

7:00 AM

JACK STOOD BEHIND THE STONE WALL A hundred feet from the door, holding Stephanie close to him, staring at the silent house.

To their right, two police cruisers sat with lights flashing red and blue. Three officers were approaching the house, one still on the radio.

"It looks that way. We found Officer Lawdale's cruiser a half mile up the road, abandoned with the other two cars. We have reports of two survivors here who believe the killer impersonated him."

The radio crackled. "You're saying three dead, two survivors?"

"That's unconfirmed, but we're going in now."

"Copy that."

The cop shut the door to his cruiser and turned toward Jack. "You sure you're okay?"

He nodded. "Fine."

"Stay put. We're going in. You're sure no one's alive inside?"

"I'm sure."

The cop nodded and headed toward the house.

An old rusted washing machine sat to the left of the flagstone path. Tall grass rose to their calves. The house itself stood stoically before them, an old abandoned house now showing its true colors.

They could see the concrete stairwell that descended to the basement on the right side of the house. The door at the bottom was still open as they'd left it, and one of the cops had just disappeared through it.

Birds chirped. Insects sang.

They'd woken inside and found only three dead bodies in the basement. Randy, Leslie, and White. No Stewarts, no Bettys, no Petes, no Jacks.

No Susan.

The first police cruiser arrived as they crawled out of the basement. They'd found Officer Morton Lawdale dead in his house an hour earlier; he'd failed to report for his midnight shift. The abandoned cruiser had led them here, to the only structure within three miles, an abandoned house set back off the road.

Jack took Stephanie's hand in his.

"They're dead," Stephanie said.

She meant Randy and Leslie, Jack thought. It was hard to believe. Staggering.

"What about Susan?" he asked.

"I don't know."

"Who was she?"

"I . . . I don't know."

"But she was real, right?"

"I think so. We saw her blood."

They didn't know. What they did know was that they'd come face-to-face with themselves and with evil and perhaps with Lucifer himself and survived only because of her.

They were quiet for a few seconds, awash in the effects of the reality that had presented itself to them in a dark corner of the world.

A hundred miles from here, Tuscaloosa was waking up to one more day of traffic, and appointments, and soap operas, and a thousand other mundane trivialities that consumed the world. Here the authorities were about to be confounded by unbelievable events. Unless they believed in haunted houses and killers filled with the power of darkness.

"Are we sure this really happened?" Stephanie asked.

Jack blinked. "It happened. Like the game of life, it happened, all in one night."

"Game of life?"

"You live your life, and in the end you either live or die, depending on what choice you make."

She said nothing.

Movement on their left filtered into Jack's vision. He looked over and caught his breath.

A girl had stepped out of the trees and was walking toward them. *Susan . . .*

Jack released Stephanie's hand and stepped forward. "Susan?"

"It's her!"

The girl was still dressed in the same tattered white dress, now stained red with blood. Jack glanced back at the house, where three of the officers had just entered. The fourth was making a sweep behind, weapon drawn.

Susan stopped in front of them. A gentle smile softened her face.

"What happened?" Stephanie asked, dumbfounded.

"I knew you could do it," Susan said. She winked.

Jack was unsure of what his eyes were seeing. He asked the same question. "What happened?"

"Light came into the darkness," Susan said. "That's what happened."

Jack caught a glance from Stephanie's wide eyes.

"You . . . who are you?"

"Susan."

"But you're real, aren't you?"

"Of course I'm real. Just as real as the day he locked me in the basement. Although I will admit that I came willingly."

"So . . . so you're an . . ." Stephanie stopped short of the question.

"What?" she asked.

"An angel?" Jack said.

"An angel? You mean a real angel that walks on the earth and looks like a regular person? Think of me as someone who's shown you the way by shedding a little light on the situation."

Jack looked up at Stephanie. He'd heard of such a thing. Angels walking among humans. But he'd never given them a second thought.

The radio in the closest cruiser hissed to life.

"We only have two bodies in here, Bob. Do you copy? Two bodies. A male dressed in what's left of a green shirt and jeans, and a dark-haired woman. Copy?"

Static. "Can you verify that?" More static. "They said there was a killer in there, dressed in Lawdale's slacks."

"Roger that. No sign of a third body, not in the basement."

"Copy. Proceed with caution."

"How . . . how's that possible?" Stephanie said.

"There's something else you should know," Susan said. "White's not finished."

One of the windows to the attic drifted open.

"I thought we beat him, beat the house!" Stephanie said.

"You beat the evil in your heart." She nodded at the house. "Look closely."

Jack and Stephanie stared.

At first Jack saw nothing. It looked exactly the way it had a moment ago, except now all the windows were sealed shut again.

Then he saw the faint gray shape in the attic window. It was a person, staring down at him without moving.

A bald person. Stewart.

And next to Stewart, Betty. And Pete.

He heard Stephanie gasp; she'd seen it too. The undead stared out the window, faint, so faint but there, really there.

Stewart moved away from the window and disappeared into the house.

"They're still there?" Jack asked.

"For a while," Susan said. "They'll find the place a bit too clean for them now. They'll move on."

"Why let them? We could walk in there and wipe them all out," Jack said. "Couldn't we?"

"Yes, I think we could," Stephanie said.

"They'd probably run out the back the moment they saw us coming," Jack said.

"After what we did? They're afraid just looking at us."

Stephanie took two long steps toward the house and shouted so that her intention was unmistakable.

"Shoo!"

The window emptied.

Amazing.

"What do you think, Susan? Are they gone now?"

She didn't answer.

"Susan?" Jack turned around. "Susan?"

But she was gone. He scanned the clearing. "Susan!"

"She's gone," Stephanie said.

"So she *was* an angel?"

"Maybe."

Stephanie looked around and let the silence stretch.

Jack caught a glimpse of a Stewart in one of the windows. "They're not gone yet."

Stephanie turned around, looked at the Stewart for a few moments, then threw up her hands and lunged forward.

"Shoo!" she cried.

It shooed.

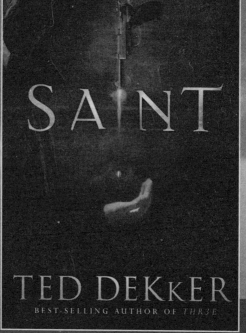

FROM THE MIND OF TED DEKKER

SAINT

TED DEKKER

BEST-SELLING AUTHOR OF *THR3E*

AVAILABLE EVERYWHERE

THOMAS NELSON
Since 1798

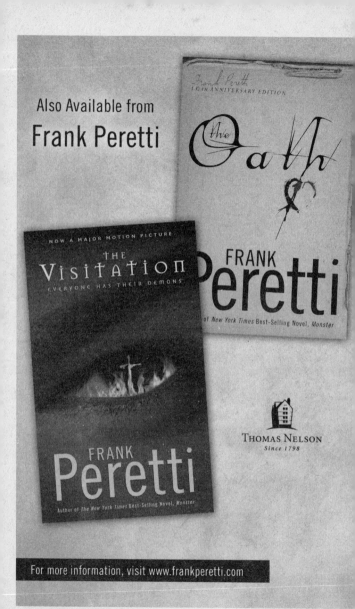